MAN'S BOOK

THE SPRINGERS

Berkely Mather

★

THE BAIT

Dorothy Uhnak

★

THE LONG NIGHT'S WALK

Alan White

ODHAMS BOOKS
LONDON

MADE AND PRINTED IN GREAT BRITAIN
BY ODHAMS (WATFORD) LTD.
S.869.SA.

CONTENTS

THE SPRINGERS

Berkely Mather

'The Springers' is published by
William Collins, Sons & Co. Ltd.

The Author

Berkely Mather began his career as a writer while he was serving in the regular army in 1957. He has written four novels previously to publication of *The Springers*: they are *The Achilles Affair, The Pass Beyond Kashmir, The Road and the Star* and *The Gold of Malabar.* He also writes TV, radio and film scripts. About the only adverse press criticism of him is that he doesn't write enough. He was born in Australia and now lives in Sussex with his wife and two sons.

CHAPTER ONE

CHARLTON WAS TALKING as we walked up the Strand. It's compulsive with him at the start of a job—like some parachutists can't stop yawning before a jump. Smoking helps, but he'd heard somewhere that no gentleman smokes in the street, and he was strong on gentility. There was a fine soaking rain falling, but he would no more have thought of opening his umbrella than of closing his bottom waistcoat button. Outside the Savoy, thank God, we got a taxi and I gave him a cigarette and said unkindly, 'Shut up, Carlovich,' and he lapsed into a hurt silence for a minute and a half, then, near Somerset House, he said, 'They'll confirm in there that it's Charlton. Deed-poll, sure, but is there any need to be bloody offensive?'

I didn't answer, so he went on miffishly: 'Did I ask for the job? Is it a nice thing to be a party to blackmailing one's godfather?' I told him to shut up again, and added something about his godfather, in fractured Shanghai Russian, which held him in a trembling white-faced rage until we got out in Throgmorton Street. I didn't like doing this to him, but I was even more on edge than he was. I'd never worked in England before, whereas he had not been out of the country for fifteen years and was sure of himself, although *my* name is James Wainwright—not by deed-poll.

I let him pay for the taxi, which I knew would please him. He'd charge the office for the whole distance from Edgware now, and add a two bob tip.

The shop was behind Copthall Street, squeezed between a bank and a fifteen-storey cut-down of the United Nations building, all glass and synthetic black marble. It had one of those round blue plaques over the low doorway—the shop, I mean—that said Josiah Wartnaby had lived here in seventeen-eighty, but one felt that that wasn't going to save its mellow brick and exquisite Regency bow windows for much longer, because there were no windows in the adjacent sides of the bank or the black-and-glass monstrosity, and you knew that some developer was going to bridge the gap in the near future. It was double-fronted, two convexes separated by an Adam doorway, like a jewel between breasts. In one window was a Tsientsin rug draped over an ebony Mandarin chair, a large Sung vase and some jade in a small cabinet. In the other were some good scrolls and one pen-painting I'd have given my eye teeth for. Mongolian horses and Wa-hai ducks in flight or anything else you could have bought in the lobby of the Hong Kong Hilton were out. Yes, this chap knew his *objets chinois*. What we were about to do to him seemed a pity.

Through the glass we could see two men moving slowly towards the door, and Charlton jerked at my sleeve.

'Let's move,' he said. 'The other feller's old Chavers. High Court judge. That's the sort of customer he gets. Top class.'

We looked into a clockmaker's window until an old man in a long overcoat and the sort of broad-brimmed black felt hat that judges, top lawyers and Petticoat Lane crockery salesmen wear, had gone down the lane past us, then we went back. Hand on door, Charlton said, 'In Russian to begin with? It sometimes amuses him?'

'Who wants to be amused?' I asked. 'English?'

We heard a buzzer sound softly as we went inside. Everything was soft—the wall-to-wall carpeting, the light from the (real) dragon lamps and the smell which was a mixture of unburned joss-sticks, old leather and the crushed Tonkin beans I could see mixed with camphorwood chips in a big porcelain censer in the middle of the floor. He came out of the shadows at the back of the shop, a tall man with a slight stoop in dark tweeds, old but expensively cut and as mellowed as the bricks outside. He was clean-shaven and his white hair was well barbered, almost cropped, and you had the feeling that it had always been white because, apart from the stoop, he was ageless, his face unlined and his eyes unfaded blue and alive, and his slightly irregular but very white teeth undoubtedly his own. A well-preserved fifty-five, I'd have said, if I hadn't known that Records had him down as born in Leningrad when it was St Petersburg in nineteen hundred. He was either a genuinely kindly man or a good actor, because he seemed really pleased to see his godson, who wasn't everybody's cup of tea. *I* certainly wouldn't have kissed the little jerk on both cheeks as this chap did. But that was the only Russian touch. After that we were all as British as lukewarm bitter.

Charlton said: 'James Wainwright, Uncle Paul—we just happened to be passing. Mr Paul Malcolm—he's not really my uncle, but you remember how it was with us kids in Shanghai? Everybody who didn't have slant eyes and a flat nose was uncle——'

I tried to get a word in as I shook hands with Malcolm, but Charlton was nervous again and wouldn't stop talking. He went on: 'James is still interested in all this bloody Chink stuff. Me, I hate it—sorry, Uncle. How's Auntie, and Sonia and Nicky? I've been trying to get around some Sunday for tea, but you know how it is. Anyhow, we were just passing so I thought——' and in the end I had to do it the rough way. I said: "Shut up, Charlton, for Christ's sake. It isn't necessary. Just vouch for me and beat it, will you.'

Malcolm was still smiling indulgently, but I sensed the change immediately. It was as if a transparent curtain had dropped between us, and surprise tactics, with all their advantage, were out.

'He's from the office,' Charlton mumbled miserably and looked down at the floor. 'I'm sorry, Uncle. The bastards made me do it. I didn't tell them. They knew.' Then the buzzer sounded, the door slammed, and he was gone. Malcolm was still smiling. He said, 'A peculiar boy. He always was. What can I do for you, Mr Wainwright?'

'A spring,' I told him and he looked politely blank.

'A spring? I'm sorry—I'm afraid I'm not with you.'

'Charlton's broken the ice,' I said. 'Shall we start from there, and save some time?'

But he was over the initial shock now, like a boxer who has taken a count of eight and is back on his feet, rested and wary.

'I still don't understand,' he said. 'Suppose you come to the point, Mr Wainwright. I'm a *reasonably* busy man, fortunately.'

'Then we don't save any time,' I answered. 'Very well. From the top. Paul Melkelm, anglicized on naturalization to Malcolm. Father Ukrainian—medical officer in the Czarist forces. He escaped after the nineteen-seventeen Revolution into Mongolia and from there to Shanghai—together with your mother, you and your younger sister. He practised medicine there until his death in nineteen-thirty-five. Correct?

He nodded slowly. 'All on record. But we're still no nearer the point.'

'We'll skip it whenever you wish,' I said. 'I mentioned a spring. Does that refresh your memory now?'

'Not in the slightest.'

'So we go on. From the age of five to your seventeenth year—the time of your family's escape—you were educated at the Imperial Academy for Pages in St Petersburg. You specialized in English and Mandarin, as you were intended for Diplomacy after your military service. Correct?'

Again he nodded.

'Your father sent you to England from Shanghai. Two years' private tuition and then up to Oxford, where you took an honours degree in English. You then returned to Shanghai and taught at St Michael's College for a couple of years.'

'Three, actually. Nineteen-twenty-three to 'twenty-six.'

'Thank you. Then you came back here and taught for a time in the School of Oriental Languages, Bloomsbury. You became a British subject in nineteen-thirty.'

'And as such I have certain acquired, if not inherent, rights,' he said tartly. 'One of which is to refuse to answer questions put to me by unauthorized persons. Who are you, Mr Wainwright, and what the blazes do you want with me?' He was losing his temper. It cheered me a little.

'I told you—a spring.'

'And *I* told *you*—I don't know what the hell you're talking about.'

'Up to you. We recruited you in nineteen-thirty-five.'

'Who is "we" and what are you supposed to have recruited me for?'

'With respect, sir, you know perfectly well what I'm talking about—and where I come from. Your nephew has vouched for me.'

'Godson,' he corrected. 'A doubtful honour I inherited from my father. It's a custom in the Orthodox Church to sponsor the children of servants. *His* father was our gardener. I'm sorry if that sounds horribly snobbish, but I neither like nor trust the little rat.'

'Yet you kissed him upon both cheeks as he crossed the threshold,' I said in Russian.

'As Judas kissed Christ,' he answered in the same language, and added in English, 'So you're another of the bastards, are you?'

'That all depends on which bastards you mean. I'm from the office. The same old firm you belonged to for eleven years—and into which you recruited the little rat you neither like nor trust.'

'Grade Three courier, *under* supervision—and only because we were desperately short of screened personnel who could speak both Russian and Chinese. They seem to have promoted the bloody moujhik if they're sending him round to vouch for people.' Yes, the old boy was a snob. All the real Whites were—but the bloody moujhiks seemed to love them for it.

'A spring,' I said gently. 'Ready to discuss it yet?'

'No,' he snapped. 'Nor anything else. I left all that in 'forty-six—cum laude and a gratuity of two thousand pounds, and a bullet in my arse. The two thousand started this business and my arse aches in wet weather. It's aching now. If you're lucky you might beat a stockbroker to a taxi in Throgmorton Street, but not after five-thirty.' He moved to the door and held it open, the buzzer sounding a sustained note. I sat down on a carved camphorwood chest. He closed the door and came back to me.

'Finished, Mr Wainwright,' he said softly. 'Go back and tell them to read my file again. I saw them draw the red line the day I signed the Official Secrets Act. We split a bottle of inferior champagne and old Farrow gave me an even more inferior cigar. He'd have been before your time, I should imagine. The office was still in Ealing in those days.'

'They've read it,' I told him. 'So have I. Up to the red line and past.'

'There's nothing past the line.'

'A two-page addendum,' I said.

'Routine snooping, no doubt.' He nodded as if recalling something. 'Yes, of course, I'd forgotten that. What does the addendum say, Mr Wainwright? What could it say? That I've been in business here for twenty years——? That I've married?—no, that would be above the line. I married before the war. Two children—a boy of twenty-two, a girl two years older—the former a makee-learn lawyer, as we'd have said in Shanghai, in good chambers in the Middle Temple—no briefs yet, but excellent prospects. Sonia, poor lass, looks after her invalid mother. She did six years at the Royal School of Ballet, but she's never even *looked* reproachful. But they wouldn't have all that, would they?'

'Actually yes. Sonia and Nicholas. Not about their characteristics, of course. Just that Sonia is very beautiful and that Nicholas is well-thought of—and that you're very proud of both of them, and that Mrs Malcolm is an arthritic.'

'Christ! Is there any limit to the impertinence of the Civil Service?' He was really angry now. 'That's all you are, you know. Civil Servants, and as such, with a certain invulnerability. Does it mention my friends? Forgive another display of snobbishness, but I number a round dozen on the Bench, in the Cabinet and in the higher echelons of Fleet Street. I've never used any of them. I hope I'll never be tempted to do so, but just drop the hint back there, Mr Wainwright—in case they think of sending you, or any other—er—other——'

'Moujhik,' I supplied.

'*You* said it—around to talk riddles.'

'I'm afraid they will.'

'Right—then I shall complain. I've done all they ever asked me to do, and more. Now I want to be left in peace.'

'Then suppose we come back to this spring? I'm sorry, I can't go until we've discussed it.' And I was sorry. The Gaffer had warned me that he was likeable, with his mixture of donnish primness and longshoreman's profanity. And I'd seen both his kids and had heard what his poor complaining devil of a wife meant to him, and how he loved this business he had built out of nothing. And his record, above the line, was magnificent—and he had guts and humour. At that moment I would have settled for shovelling ordure in a sewer in preference to this.

He sighed. 'Anything to terminate this distasteful interview. All right—the verb "to spring"—to get somebody out of prison. What about it?'

'Your speciality,' I said, and curiously that eased things. We all have our vanities.

He grinned impishly. 'The best in the business,' he said, and it didn't sound vainglorious because we both knew it was a straight statement of fact. 'Forty-seven agents and a hundred and thirty-eight R.A.F. and American navigators brought out safely. They could train pilots, poor dears, much quicker in those days, so they had to make it on their flat feet or stay where they were. All right—once again, what about it?'

'We'd like you to do another. Just one.'

He smiled sweetly and said sorry.

'Ten thousand pounds—tax free,' I said softly.

'Not for a hundred thousand. I'm getting old and stiff, and I don't do any travelling these days.'

'You do,' I contradicted.

'Oh, Hong Kong? That's not travelling. I commute out there and buy some stuff for the shop from time to time, certainly, but you wouldn't want the services of a highly expensive specialist there, for God's sake. Anyhow, important European prisoners are flown home and do their time in Maidstone. But we're talking nonsense. If you had somebody in Stanley Gaol you'd only have to ask for him.'

'Not Hong Kong,' I said. 'Although that comes into it.'

'A Chinese mainland nick?' he squeaked. 'Don't be silly, my dear chap. Impossible—even for me.'

'European nick,' I said patiently.' But we want the client spirited out to Hong Kong—or somewhere near there.'

'Then I suggest Aladdin and his wonderful lamp.' He yawned. 'I'm sorry for my earlier rudeness,' he said. 'Actually I've enjoyed our little talk, but I'm afraid the answer's still no—*non*—*niet*. You are from Shanghai yourself, aren't you? Not Russian, though. I can spot a China-Rusk a mile off. That godson of mine will never be able to clip those long vowels, spurious O.E. tie, rolled umbrella and bowler hat notwithstanding. Awful little shite, isn't he? What *is* your background, since we're both being rude?'

'My old man was a Chief Inspector in the International Concession police,' I told him.

'And you were educated where?'

'St Michael's—after your time of course—then St Paul's on a Mackinnon Scholarship.'

'Army?'

'National Service. Six months in the ranks, six at Mons OCTU, twelve as a Second Lieutenant with the Parachutes. All post-war.'

'Got you absolutely.' He looked pleased with himself. 'How did you get into this murky racket? Or is that *too* rude?'

'A little,' I said.

'It couldn't be the pay. God, they're mean, aren't they? In my heyday I ranked with a half-colonel but got less than an R.A.S.C. major. And the expenses! Do you know what? I once had a taxi bill in Berlin queried—in *nineteen-forty-three*. I was bringing out two clients—Frenchmen. I had to borrow from them to complete the last stage—tube from Victoria to Baker Street.'

'Still the same,' I told him. 'But they're doing *you* all right. Ten thousand quid—*and* expenses.'

'Ten years ago it might have tempted me,' he said.

'I'm afraid you'll still have to be tempted.'

'I don't have to be anything I don't choose to be,' he flashed. He was getting angry again. 'Good night, Mr Wainwright. I'd like to say drop in again some time for another little talk, but that would be insincere. You wouldn't be a really interesting conversationalist until you had been red-lined for the statutory fourteen years, and you'll probably be found dead in highly discreditable circumstances up a dark lane or in a bawdy house long before then. I had enough sense to get out while the going was good—and I'm not coming back.'

'I'm sorry,' I said, and again I meant it. 'You're obliging *me* to be a shite now. You've been back—as a freelance—two years ago. That's in the addendum too.'

That was my first victory, if you could call it such. His face showed nothing because he was now sitting on another carved chest, with his back to one of the dragon lamps. It was just something one felt. He was silent for a long moment, then he said quietly: 'Prove it.'

'Wally Wharton, the bank robber. Out of the top security wing in Lanchester. You were promised twenty thousand for that, but you only collected five. You should have had a better guarantee. But it was your first experience with real professional crooks, wasn't it?'

He said again: 'Prove it.'

I said: 'I don't have to. Wharton's dead. His pals leaned on him too heavily—trying to get him to tell where the bulk of the loot was stashed. But his wife's alive—under Special Branch protection. She's being paid a pension which is about treble what she'd get under National Assistance. If that was ever stopped she'd go to the Sunday weeklies—naming names. The Yard would act then. They're straining at the leash as it is. You've no idea how vicious regular police can get when they're under political pressure. You could count on seven years.'

'And I'd do them—gladly. And *I'd* talk then—in court.'

'In camera,' I reminded him. 'Interests of the State.'

'Then before the trial.'

'You're talking wildly now. You'd be in custody, and incommunicado from the moment your collar was felt.'

'There are still ways.'

'Name them. Anyhow, why are we talking about *you*? There's Sonia.'

'Leave my family out of it.'

'I wish I could. But Sonia was the plumber's mate on that job, wasn't she? That's going to lose you a lot of sympathy. She wouldn't get more than eighteen months as a first offender, led astray by her father—but Holloway's a hell of a place for a sensitive girl. Then the effect on young Nicholas's career——'

I didn't have time to dodge it. It wasn't a token slap either. He lifted me right off the camphorwood chest on to my backside. I waited until my ears stopped singing, then I got up and tried to shrug.

'Well, that's it, Mr Malcolm,' I said. 'Think it over. I'll be back this time tomorrow.'

The don was entirely subjugated to the longshoreman now. He cursed filthily for a minute and a half.

'All right,' he growled at last. 'Who is it—and where? And how do I get paid?'

'There'll be somebody along,' I told him. 'I only have to take your answer back. I gather that it's yes?'

'You're the bumboy who shovels the filth in the first place, are you?' he said. 'I'll bet you're good at your job. They'll give you a desk at the end of it all—if somebody doesn't break your bloody neck first. Somebody like me.'

'Your answer please?' I insisted.

'What *can* it be?' he asked bitterly. 'You dirty, scabrous, pustulating lot of bastards. Tell 'em yes.'

'Thank you, Mr Malcolm,' I said.

It must have sounded funny, because he chuckled drily and mimicked me as he let me out, and through the glass I could hear him bellowing as I walked away through the rain.

CHAPTER TWO

I GOT A TAXI by St Paul's and told the driver I wanted the Lazy Rabbit. He didn't know it, which wasn't surprising because I didn't either, so he got out his little book and we hemmed and hawed for a couple of minutes and decided it was the Hazy Hare I wanted, in Knightsbridge. I paid him off as we were passing the Savoy, hopped out quickly, went through the lounge and down the stairs to the ballroom, and out through the Embankment entrance and grabbed a solitary cab going west. Officially I wasn't working and I couldn't think of anybody sufficiently interested in me to be tailing me on spec—other than the office. They sometimes put a legman on to us in the early stages of a job to ensure the Opposition wasn't shadowing us—or so they said. Charlton swore it was Finance who did it, to check on pubs, meals and taxis and so discourage expense-sheet padding. He may have been right.

Tonight I was hoping spitefully that I was giving some poor sod sore feet and a run for his, or their, money.

I did the last two hundred yards on foot, down a cul-de-sac off Victoria Street which has the plate-glass windows of a department store on one side and the screamingly ugly façade of a huge Edwardian tenement the other. The tenement contains a hundred and fifty-three dogbox apartments, mostly let to Members of Parliament when the House is in session, and it is the perfect bolthole, because once inside any of its six street entrances you're in a labyrinth of dark staircases, narrow corridors and usually out-of-order elevators, so unless your tail is right on your heels you can shake him flat.

The Gaffer lived on the second floor. To call one's boss Gaffer or Guv'nor is usually to accord him a certain respect, admiration or even a grudging affection. In this case you can forget the middle and last. He opened in answer to the treble-pause-single ring he always insisted on, and let me into the tiny square hall. The sitting-room was on the left, bedroom on the right and facing was a door into a six-foot-square kitchen. There must have been a bathroom somewhere, but thank God I never had occasion to ask for it. The whole place smelt of dust, damp overcoats and cheese and looked like a stage set of Sherlock Holmes's Baker Street apartment. I never saw out of the windows because they were always covered by dusty brown curtains with bobbles along the edges, and looked, but certainly never opened, on to an air shaft. There was no aspidistra but there was a po-shaped thing with pink roses on it that ought to have held one, standing beside a fireplace the size and shape of the southern approach to Tower Bridge which framed the smallest gas fire I have ever seen. There was a huge overmantel above it heavily carved with vineleaves and scrotum-like bunches of some weird fruit, through which tiny flyspecked mirrors coyly peeped. Steel engravings covering battle scenes from Balaclava to Rorke's Drift plastered the gamboge cauliflowered wallpaper. Whatnots, chiffoniers and the sort of bookcases which come with subscription sets of encyclopaedias filled all the rest of the space that wasn't taken up by an enormous dining table, two 'easy' chairs and a sofa. One chair was occupied by a fat and asthmatic cocker bitch with lumps on its belly like the overmantel carvings, the other I knew was master's. In response to his grunted invitation I took the end of the sofa where the springs hadn't gone, after careful inspection, because I'd once got a punctured behind and a bitten ankle through sitting on a chop bone temporarily abandoned by the cocker.

And the Gaffer fitted perfectly into the whole ghastly setting. They say that some people get to resemble their dogs, or maybe it's the other way round. Here was a case in point. He was fat and asthmatic and his hair seemed to have rubbed off in bare patches rather than normally balded, and you guessed that his yellowing teeth were loose and that he was short-sighted. But in the last you'd have guessed wrong. Those little faded blue piggy peepers behind their thick glasses missed nothing. Age? I don't know. Those of us who suffered under him hoped it wasn't far off retirement point, which in our branch was sixty. He was wearing shapeless, shiny, elephant-arsed blue serge trousers, unbuttoned waistcoat and carpet slippers. His collar and tie were over the back of his chair. He looked like a Tooley Street tally-clerk after a hard shift at the docks.

I thought of that beautiful shop and its likeable old owner and compared both with this place and the slag who was my boss, and I wondered afresh why I could never muster the strength of purpose to quit.

The Gaffer said, 'Well?' and relit a cigarette he had economically nipped earlier. He took a lungful right down, and brought it up again fast. It seemed to come out of his ears as well as his nose and mouth. I waited for the spluttering to subside and said, 'He says yes.'

'Of course he says yes,' he wheezed. 'What the hell else did you expect him to say?'

'I almost hoped he'd say it was blackmail, and tell you to stuff it.'

'That'd be the day. Blackmail my foot.'

'Have you got another term for it?'

'Sure. Face-saving.'

'Call it was you like, it still stinks.'

'Don't talk bloody silly,' he said, and spat at the gas fire. 'You call offering a feller ten thousand *blackmail*? My God! I wish someone'd blackmail *me*.'

'A sick wife—'

'A whining old beldame who makes his life a hell,' he said.

'Two kids—'

'One who takes to grafting as naturally as her old man, the other a useless young bleeder who gets corns on his rump in every discothèque along the King's Road.'

I stared at him. 'If that's the truth, why did you give me a totally contradictory briefing before I went there?' I asked.

'Because that's the line I wanted you to follow—that we were acting more in sorrow than in anger—that we hated to do this to him, but we would if he forced our hands. We'd ruin him, bring sorrow to his invalid wife, and Little Nell his chickabiddies out into the cold, cold snow. If you believed that yourself you'd put it over a damned sight more convincingly than if you were huckstering with your tongue in your cheek. You follow?' He looked knowingly at me with his head on one side.

'I don't.'

He sighed. 'I'll draw you a picture. First of all, I know Malcolm —know everything there is to know about him. I can evaluate him to the last hair. I know what he will do and how he will react in any given set of circumstances—like I know it about a hell of a lot of other people—including quite a few gents who roam in this Babylon.'

'In other words you're good.'

He grinned with one side of his mouth and drew smoke with the other. 'Sarcasm bounces off my hide like peas off a tin roof. You bet I'm good. That's why I sit at the top of the pile and send you young punks legging round the globe when I whistle. You know how I started in this business? I'll tell you. I was a chalk-and-water boy for the Sheffield race gangs back in the middle 'twenties, then I went over to Chicago. I was running a beer truck before I was eighteen. Then I did a bit—more than a bit—of strong-arming for the mobs, until I collected a mob of my own. I quit when Prohibition ended and then it was South America, then China—and finally I came back here in the early days of the war to be a gun-knife-and-general-mayhem professor for the

Commandos. Finished up as a full colonel—then came to this crowd——'

'Yes, good,' I said again. 'We agreed on that, but what's it all got to do with Malcolm, and my having my leg pulled?'

'Psychology,' he said profoundly. 'I've never done a day's bird in my life—never even had my collar felt—but boy, do I know how the villains think and act.'

'But Malcolm isn't a villain.'

'Not a fully-paid-up practising villain, maybe, but he's a first class schizo. Two people pulling in opposite directions. Jekyll and Hyde, if you like. He got a lot of the Hyde out of his system when he was working for us, so Jekyll has generally managed to stay on top, but only just. He slipped badly over the Wharton business and it scared him, and he's got enough sense to know that he's too old for those capers now and he's got to stay on the straight and narrow.'

'You mean there have been other jobs—criminal jobs, I mean—besides the Wharton one?' I asked.

'Five that I know of for certain—two that I suspect,' he said calmly, and I felt a surge of anger.

'And you let me go to him like a bloody innocent and——' I began.

'I didn't *let* you. I sent you,' he snapped. 'Shut up and let me finish. I'm not telling you all this just to bum my load. I want you to understand. If you had gone along there and put it straight on him to do this job for ten thousand, he'd have turned you down flat. Jekyll would have been right on top. If you'd mentioned a whole string of jobs he'd have said balls—do your worst—knowing damn well that we wouldn't dare give him away to the police. He's got too much on us. As it is you've mentioned just one job—the only one that we could tip off to the Yard without in any way getting involved ourselves. You've blackmailed him, as you call it, twisted his arm and thereby given him the excuse *he needs himself* to do it. He has to yield to force majeure now.'

'But what if he changes his mind?'

'He won't,' he chuckled. 'I told you—I know him. He wants to do it. He loves it—but he must be able to justify it to himself. If he doesn't do it his wife and kids will suffer. The blame is shifted from him now. Don't you see?'

I thought I did. Anyhow there was no point in going all over it again. I'd been made a monkey of, but I'd completed my part of it. I yawned and stood up.

'Where are you going?' he demanded.

'Sorry,' I answered, 'I thought you'd finished.'

'Finished be damned. I haven't started yet. I'm giving you your full briefing now—then you're completely on your own. I don't want you near the office again until it's all over.'

And I had been hoping that I slipped it to somebody else now and went back to my own sector when my home leave was over in another week! I sat down feeling injured.

'Do you know Winterton?' he asked.

'I know *of* him—and I was once introduced to him in the Hong Kong Club.'

He's not clubbing at the moment, poor bastard. They're clubbing him. He's working on the breakwater in Amoy. They took him off his ship—accused of smuggling refugees out.'

'He'll get four years' rice and the sayings of Chairman Mao if they make it stick,' I said.

'He's got twenty-five,' he answered. 'We've known for a month but we've been trying to do a deal. They found some undeveloped film down in the bilges.'

'How hot?'

'Middling. Harbour installations on the Whangpu—very amateurishly done. Just the sort of stuff an honest China coast skipper would be dealing in, if he wanted to make a few bob from Admiralty Intelligence. We reckoned it would get him ten years, which would be scrubbed if he was willing to talk.'

I began to see light. 'A furbler?' I said.

He smiled sourly. 'Smart feller. Away ahead of me. Yes, a furbler.'

Don't ask me the etymology of the word. A furbler is something an agent sometimes carries as a red herring to disguise his real mission in the event of exposure. If it's to be worth a damn it has to be something genuine—a bishop to save a queen. Once discovered, the agent is at liberty to talk. How much he spills and the degree of resistance he puts up under intensive interrogation is a matter for his histrionic ability and his animal cunning—I don't use the term personal integrity, but all three come into it. To be convincing, he's got to let it go slowly and reluctantly, however hard they may be leaning on him. When he does break he's got to slobber, literally slobber, the lot—almost invariably under lights and in front of a camera. The danger is, of course, that the chap can be pushed to the point sometimes where he is no longer able to distinguish the shadow from the substance, and demarcation lines get blurred, and he babbles on and throws the real thing. The opposition, being fully aware of this work on it—which is why one can never be really certain of tea and sympathy even after one has sobbed all. They tell you on that part of your training—which takes six months—that a very good furbler in the hands of a resolute man can sometimes save his real mission, but never his skin. It's not meant to. They also tell you that it isn't the damnedest bit of use inventing one of your own. They can be blown too easily—and then you're in real grief. For the reasons I have given, and a lot more I haven't, furblers are strictly for the dons, and on very important business only. Winterton was therefore a don, which surprised me. I knew him, and only slightly at that, as an obscure Hong Kong freighter skipper with a red face, a beer belly and a penchant for wenching in Wanchai.

'What was he really on?' I asked.

'Not bloody likely,' the Gaffer said, 'or we'll have to be giving *you* a furbler—and you don't qualify by a long chalk yet. All you need to know is that front office wants him out.'

'Then Malcolm won't play,' I said. 'You told me, and I told him, that the client was in a European gaol and merely had to be shipped out to Hong Kong. He specifically said that mainland nicks were——'

'If you'll specifically belt up, Wainwright, we might get this finished before morning, and I'll be able to bugger off to bed,' he said wearily. 'Where was I? Oh yes—we want him out. He's sprung his furbler—' he looked maliciously pleased—'which involved five of your blokes being blown.'

'What about me?' I asked bleakly.

'He doesn't know about you.'

'But some of my blokes do!'

'Four leggers and a comprador,' he explained, and I breathed again. We used the old-fashioned five-cell system in my sector. A field man knew only his own cell supervisor, or comprador: a comprador knew his own four and one field man in the cell above. Only in the rarefied heights near the top of the pile did we start knowing each other laterally. Of course one penetrated cell could, through the skill and patience of the opposition—

and the bastards had plenty of both—lead to a chain reaction upward, but that took time and we were usually able to regroup before really serious harm was done.

He went on: 'It's at quasi-diplomatic level at the moment. They're willing to do a swap. Winterton for Carter.'

'*Carter?*' I stared at him. 'But he's been with the Russians for years—right up to the time we caught him.'

'Wheels within wheels.' He smiled twistedly. 'No need to wriggle. They didn't know it at the top—Yanks or us. Carter, like your pal Malcolm, is from Shanghai—and ninety-nine point nine per cent of Shanghai-Rusks are white as the driven snow. Carter's the point one. As English as Malcolm on the surface, but as Russian as droshkis underneath—and as dedicatedly red as the seat of Lenin's underpants right through—yes, all that came out at his trial. What *didn't* come out was that Carter built Mao's intelligence service for him—and was serving him faithfully right up to the split between the Russians and Chinese. He was still serving after the split—but not so single-heartedly. He was leaking to the Russians. The Chinese suspected it, but he got the tip and skipped for Vladivostok before the big chop. He was useless in the Far East then, naturally, but Moscow doesn't believe in passengers. They sent him West. He was out of his element, but he's damn good by any standards. He'd set up three new networks centred in London that not even the Russian Embassy knew of—rubber-heeling on their regular agents—and had suborned a senior civil servant in the Ministry of Power—all inside twelve months. Then the poor bastard walked into a Chink restaurant in Ipswich one night, and the boy who served him happened to be an ex-Shanghai Aliens Bureau dick, two-buttoning for our Special Branch. He recognized him. That bowl of egg-fuyong and noodles cost Carter thirty years.'

'And the Chinese want him back?'

'And how.'

'But what use will he be to them now?'

'Makee-talk in the first place. Oh, sure—the bulk of his Russian stuff will be old hat by now, but some of it will be useful. He could still blow some people in Outer Mongolia—probably a few in China itself. But that's not the point. Come on—you're the expert. What's the most important thing to the Chinese? More important even than respect for ancestors?'

'Face,' I said.

'Exactly,' he nodded. 'Here's a guy who pulled the wool over their eyes for years—then sold them out to people they hate worse than us—worse than the Americans. Plenty of face lost there. Think how much they'd regain that face if they got him back and gave him a bloody big public trial in Peking—Red Guards yowling and all. The long arm of Chairman Mao plucking him right from the heartland of the West and bringing him to justice! Boy! What a triumph that would be.'

'What would they do to him afterwards?' I asked.

He looked at me pityingly. 'Either that question was purely rhetorical, or you're drawing your pay under false pretences. Chop his goddamn head off and stick it on a pole outside the Gate of Heaven. What the hell else?'

'I just wanted to be certain,' I said. 'That, of course, rules out an official exchange for Winterton.'

'That's my boy.' He grinned at me like a jackal savouring a bone. 'He's thinking now. That rules out an official exchange, just like you said. So Malk whisks him over the wall and you take him out there and make a trade—softlee-softlee. Everybody happy.'

'Except Carter.'

'Except Carter—but you can't please everybody, can you? You're not the Fairy Queen.'

'You're bloody right,' I said. 'Or the Wicked Magician either. All right—even presuming Malcolm gets him out of a top security gaol here—an unwilling man. How do I get him across the globe in secret?'

'Your problem, sonny boy.' He grinned even wider. 'A damned interesting one. All you'll have against you are the cops, three assorted branches of our alleged intelligence service, the cops of any countries you move through and, I'm pretty darned certain, the Rusks trying like hell to hijack you en route.'

I said, 'Suppose we drop the comedy for just a few moments. There are some questions I'd like to ask.'

'I'll bet there are—but you'll hear me out first. After that you can say yes or no. If it's no, well it's been nice knowing you. You'll be red-lined, you'll sign the O.S. chit, draw what you have coming to you and go back to polishing your tail in the bank. The bank will offer you a job in London, by the way. Hong Kong will be *terre interdite* to you, naturally.'

'We come back to a word we were discussing earlier,' I said.

'Blackmail? Sure. It's a tool of the trade. You don't need me to explain that to you, surely?'

'How dirty can we get?' I asked of nobody in particular.

'You'd be surprised—really surprised—if we're pushed,' he said. 'It's a very dirty business. Didn't they tell you that when you joined?'

I lit a cigarette, and he went on talking.

'I'm assuming that it's yes,' he said, 'but you can stop me at any time you wish, and walk out—with the provisos I've just mentioned. All right—you go back to Malcolm and tell him that he'll get two thousand five hundred in advance—in fivers through the mail tomorrow morning. You'll get his plan and list of requirements. We'll help to the limit—short of involvement—other than yourself, of course. I don't want to say "if you're nicked you're on your own" because I hate melodramatics, and anyhow you know that already——'

He was still talking at three-thirty and I was listening glumly. Then I left.

CHAPTER THREE

THE DRIZZLE had turned into a steady pelting rain and I was soaked and savage by the time I reached Courtfield Gardens because the only taxi I saw was in Brompton Road and that was engaged. God, how I hated London. In my grade—I'm talking about the bank now—one got two months' home leave every two years. 'Home' was a loose term and provided you didn't exceed the cost of an air tourist return ticket between Hong Kong and London, you could go where you liked. I'd spent my previous leave in Australia and the one before that in America. I suppose I'd better explain about the bank at this point. It was my permanent front but at the same time it was a genuine job and, surprisingly, one I liked. The 'office' had placed me there, of course, long before I even knew of its existence—the 'office' I mean. Everybody knew about the existence of the bank. It was a monument to the acumen of our great-grandfathers and was as much part of Hong Kong as the Peak itself.

My mother died when I was twelve, and the old man when I was half-way through my National Service. His job had gone up the spout when the Communists took over in Shanghai in nineteen-forty-nine, and he was living in London. The British Government paid him a reduced and purely ex gratia pension and gave him sporadic work as an interpreter at the Crown Agents for the Colonies in Horseferry Road. I was serving in Aden at the time of his death and they let me fly back for the funeral. Of necessity I hadn't seen much of the old boy since coming home to school, so I was surprised and touched to find that he had left me seven hundred pounds, a five-year, fully paid-up lease of a three-roomed flat in Courtfield Gardens, and a letter. The letter asked me to see a Mr Kempson at the London Office of the Hong Kong and Southern China Bank. And Kempson, the Assistant General Manager, offered me a job in their foreign exchange department when I came out of the army—and for the want of something better I accepted. It was as casual and as haphazard as that. Or so I thought.

I had been a glorified office boy for a year before anybody approached me, and was seriously thinking of slinging it and trying something else, because, gratitude apart, Gloucester Road to Moorgate and return five days a week was beginning to pall, in spite of a half-promise from Kempson that in due course I might be considered for that plum of plums, a posting to the Head Office in Hong Kong.

Again it was casual; a kindly boss invited a rather lonely junior employee to spend Christmas at his Sussex home. I didn't particularly want to go but I couldn't think of an excuse quick enough when he asked me, so I went down for four days, and his son and daughter tried to interest me in golf at Rye, and on Boxing Night I was inveigled into a yum sing contest—a stupid Chinese drinking game with very simple rules. You just swallow half a tumbler of Scotch every time someone points at you and bellows 'Yum sing'—then you point at somebody else and do the same—and the winner is the last on his feet. I have often wondered if it was intended as some sort of test. If it was I didn't pass it, because I crawled under the billiard table and went to sleep while the rest of the guests, hearty taipan types home on Christmas leave for the most part, were still only getting warmed up.

But I must have had other unsuspected potentialities, certainly by myself, or maybe it was a poor vintage year for recruits, because Kempson invited me to his study the following day, ostensibly to talk about my prospects with the bank, and there were two others of the guests there—and when I came out three hours later, feeling prickly and uncomfortable at some of the questions they had fired at me and even more so at the number of answers they seemed to know already, I knew I had two weeks in which to think things over. I didn't need the two weeks, because I was bored stiff with my job and I was already vacillating between trying to sign on as a deck hand for a long trip somewhere or flogging second-hand cars in Great Portland Street. But they insisted on the pause, and, in fact, Kempson was really very fair. He gave me a rundown on my prospects with the bank if I turned this new proposition down, and they weren't at all bad by any standards. I'd get my move out to Hong Kong before long, and thereafter it would be a steady climb up the seniority ladder with an increment in pay every two years as long as I kept on the ball and off the liquor—an ever present hazard for the Far Eastern businessman—until retiring age in the sixty bracket and a comfortable pension. I ventured a question about the prospects of the other job at this stage, and the three of them smiled kindly and went on with the interview. One thing I did learn, though; my father had been in the business ever since he went out East in the 'twenties, his police job providing the perfect front. Perhaps the answer to my question lay right there. He left, as I have said, seven hundred pounds and a five-year lease on a small flat in Courtfield Gardens. So it can't have been the money that swayed my decision. That, for the record, was the exact equivalent of an army captain's pay, plus allowances but minus tax. Who the hell paid the tax I didn't know then or now, because I never saw anything that remotely resembled a payroll in the 'office'. You got what you had coming to you in cash, through the mail once every fourteen days for some reason or other, in envelopes on which the handwriting and postmarks varied from time to time.

I took some figures in for Kempson to see on the due date, and muttered yes please I'd like to try it—and he nodded noncommittally. Three days later I was posted to one of our subsidiaries in Manchester 'for experience', because, although the bulk of our interests lay in China we were also involved in cotton. I actually went to Manchester, too, where I posted wish-you-were-here views of the Ship Canal to two typists in Foreign

Exchange and then caught a bus to Chester and another on from there to a picturesque market town on the Wirral. There's a black-and-white timbered country house which overlooks the wild estuary of the Dee, a mile outside the town, and there, except for brief educational excursions, I stayed for a year.

There were eight of us on the course, of whom three dropped out fairly early. We all had one thing in common, and that wasn't sex either, because two of the remaining five were girls. It was just that none of us had a single tie in the world. We were orphans, unmarried and completely rootless. Our ages ranged, I should have said at a guess, from a very fit forty down to myself at the bottom of the scale, just pushing twenty-two when I arrived. The girls were something under thirty, and one of them was attractive—to look at, anyhow. I never got the opportunity to explore the beauties of her mind. It wasn't that the teaching faculty discouraged things. One just didn't have the time, because the scope and pace of the course was murderous. The staff numbered over a hundred although no more than fifteen were ever in residence at any one time. They always arrived by car at night, and departed the same way, and what the hell they did in the interregnums I just wouldn't be knowing. But by God they were thorough. Half-way through the summer they gave us a merciful break. Each of us was booked on a different fortnight's package tourist trip. I drew fourteen days down to the Canaries. I would have settled for two weeks with my feet up in London, but they were adamant on this point, as on all others. The Canaries, they said, and like it. Come back with a tan and all batteries recharged—nothing like a complete break. They were so solicitous that I thought it was a prelude to being fired.

I met a girl on the ship. She was dark and intense, a little older than I but bloody good-looking. She was just getting over the break-up of an unhappy marriage. We discovered depths of understanding in each other, and I found I could talk to her as to no other woman I had met up until then—not that there had been many—and she had a single cabin to herself, and we got politely drunk in Funchal. We exchanged addresses when we parted in Liverpool and arranged to meet when I was next in London. I was called in on the mat two days later and told, quite kindly, that my Courtfield Gardens flat was a comfortable and secure little pad but if I wanted to remain there I was not to give the address to casual acquaintances, particularly ones I slept with. I met her again a couple of months later when she came down to instruct on ciphers—sorry—I *saw* her again, but she apparently had forgotten me. Yes, they were thorough.

But at least that must have been my only bad break, because I finished the course and went back to the bank for six months, where I had to slog my guts out on legitimate business during the day and receive a final polish on other things—at Kempson's country house in the weekends and at various addresses round the suburbs in the evenings, including the 'office' in Edgware which fronted as a furniture depository. This is where I first met the Gaffer. He dislocated my shoulder and all but ruptured me during that part of my training. He had already graduated to higher things by this time, but he was a vain old bastard in matters pertaining to his original trade and liked to keep his hand in. His assistants were much better at it and rarely hurt the postulants seriously, although one of them nearly perforated my eardrum during pistol practice.

All this part of the training was treated apologetically—almost tongue in cheek. We should never need it, they told us; if we did it would be because we had made a balls of something and had got into what should have been avoidable trouble. But, as in everything else, they were thorough in it. Mons OCTU was not exactly a bed of roses, and parachute training was even tougher, but neither came anywhere near this. I don't know whether the girls were put through it, because by this time the Wirral house-party had split up and I was entirely on my own. As a matter of fact I've never seen any of them since. I once made the mistake of idly inquiring after them from the Gaffer. He turned a fishlike orb on me and said, 'If you ever met anybody else during training, which I doubt, they were probably makee-learn income tax collectors. Forget 'em.'

And then one day Kempson called me in and congratulated me on my progress—in the bank—and told me they were posting me out to Hong Kong a little ahead of schedule to replace a chap in the Exchange Branch who was being invalided home. Since I had not taken my current year's holidays and would get none for the next two, I was given a month's vacation, to take effect forthwith.

But again there was a catch in it. The Gaffer would call me at all hours of the day and night and tell me to go to such widely diverse places as the Eltham Golf Club, Guildford Cathedral or a factory in Stepney by any method I chose, buying three packets of cigarettes and a pair of gym shoes, or some other such damned silly things, en route. The object was to throw unseen and unknown shadowers. If he could tell me afterwards the addresses of the shops I'd called into, he'd won. If he couldn't, I had. At the end of the month I was winning twice in five times, which I've learned since is a pretty good average.

I arrived in Hong Kong by air and was met at Kai Tak by a rowdy but good-natured crowd of my fellow juniors. We were called cadets and we lived in Mess, a relic of the East India Company days which many of the older banks and merchant houses still follow. If I expected any of these to make mystic signs and start slipping passwords to me, I was disappointed. Actually I was allowed to stew in my own juice for three months, just getting hep to my job in the bank, before someone approached me. He was an assistant manager in one of the commercial branches who was keen on sea fishing. He invited me out on his launch one Sunday. Six miles out on the South China sea, and free from bugging, he made himself known and told me as much as I needed to know at that stage. He was purely a Transmitter, he informed me, and as such passed on orders and received reports from me. If I have given the impression of the bank being one big spy network, let me correct it here and now. Actually on the bank payroll I knew of only three, Kempson, this chap, and somebody much higher up in the hierarchy who could post me at the drop of a hat from one branch to another, or send me on a trip to Singapore, the Philippines or India, or indeed any other place where the bank had business. Since they liked the cadets to get around the territory, sadly shrunk since Chiang Kai-shek took off for Formosa in a hurry in nineteen-forty-nine, there was nothing unusual in sending juniors on sometimes quite important bank business at short notice. But none of this came my way until much later. For the nonce I was just to get on with my ordinary job and merge into my social background which, as a cadet, was by no means dull. The Mess paid a blanket subscription for us at the Hong Kong Club, the Yacht Club on Kellet Island and, of course, the Rugby Club at Happy Valley. I was to swim at Big Wave Bay on Sundays, get mildly tight on occasion, dance, play a little golf, lose an unremarkable amount of money at the races and get to know a couple of acceptable girls—this last not easy, because they are thin on the ground in proportion to the stag population, competition is correspondingly keen, and Hong Kong mothers are as Victorian in the management of their daughters' love lives as they are—some of them I mean—broadminded in their own. I enjoyed it all, and I was sorry that I couldn't have landed a job like this without sidelines. But I couldn't—not now. That was made abundantly clear to me at the outset. If I proved a flop in the sideline, the cover job went up the spout and Hong Kong was out as a domicile. Anybody at all can come into England from any part of the Commonwealth, but you try to squat in the Commonwealth if somebody in a Government office doesn't want you there.

And so my first two years went happily by. Wasted time? Maybe, but who was I to argue? I certainly wasn't straining at any leashes to get started. I did improve my Cantonese and Mandarin though, steadily and unostentatiously. The bank ran classes in both these and we were encouraged to attend them. I also kept very fit, not because I was under orders, but because I like being that way. I played a lot of squash and rugby, swam and practised advanced karate. I was a bit doubtful about this last as I thought it might draw attention to myself, but the cult was sweeping the Colony at that time and every young penpusher in Hong Kong was fancying himself as a dan.

Things were different when I came back from leave, though. They started to move me around—sometimes purely on legitimate bank business, more seldom on a real but unimportant 'office job'. Let me clarify here; an 'office job' is a mission. A mission can be anything to delivering somebody's pay to them or, as the Gaffer once put it, somebody's bloody pay-*off*. Can be, I said. My earlier missions lay somewhere in between the two, and for the most part were extremely dull. The only one in the first six months that involved me in any rough stuff was a delivery and pick-up job in Penang when I was jumped by a couple of big Chinese on the waterfront—Northern Province men—and was badly beaten up. But even then I believe it was a straight attempted robbery because they were satisfied with my watch and wallet and I didn't get the expert rolling I'd have got from a real pro looking for papers.

But the tempo was increasing the whole time. The Vietnam escalation kept us busy because the Americans were using Hong Kong like the rest of us were using West Berlin back in Europe

—crossing point, clearing house for information, watch-tower and finance centre—and that brought in the opposition in shoals, Chinese and Europeans, and our job was primarily one of tabulating and tagging. So when I got my next leave—this one—I felt I'd earned it. But now they'd jumped the gun on me and were making me work in my own time.

I slept until ten o'clock and woke with a stinking cold. I phoned Malcolm and told him he'd be getting a parcel in the mail and that I'd call round later. He said with icy dislike that he'd rather I didn't, not two days running, and that *he'd* get in touch with *me*, and asked for a telephone number. I felt so lousy that for a moment I thought of giving him my own at the flat and staying in bed, which would have been a gross breach of security, but caution prevailed, as I injected even more dislike into my voice and told him I'd call him again later. The old sweats loved pulling ones like that on the rookies.

I called him again in the afternoon and it was his turn to be awkward this time. He said he'd pick me up in his car outside the Earl's Court tube at about four—a grey Rover 2000, and gave me the number. The old bastard kept me waiting in the rain until half-past and he looked quietly pleased when I squelched in alongside him. I told him I hadn't asked for this job any more than he had, but since we were lumbered with each other how about behaving like adults?

'Splendid with me, Mr Wainwright,' he said as he eased out into the traffic. 'How about a safe number where I can call you, and so dispense with this exaggerated security nonsense until it's really necessary?'

'I'm on leave,' I told him. 'Or was until they sprung this on me yesterday. No time to arrange things.'

'Who's in charge?' he asked. 'You or me?'

'Me,' I said positively.

He shrugged. 'Fine. All you've got to do is to get a prisoner out of prison then. I'll be happy to help in any way I can—in an advisory capacity.'

I blew my inflamed nose and told him to drop me by the next phone box. He said: 'Tell your boss I've got the parcel of money in the car. You can have it back and he can do what the hell he likes about it. I'm not working under the orders of an amateur, Mr Wainwright. Not until the merchandise is this side of the wall, anyhow.'

He pulled up at the box outside the Victoria and Albert. There's a double yellow line there so he said he'd drive round the block. I knew he'd be watching me in the rear vision mirror so I crossed to the box briskly, fumbling for change, although I had no clear intention at that point of making myself a chopping-block for the Gaffer's ponderous wit. But what the hell else was there to do? The position was impossible. Maybe this was it. This was where I quit and went back to ledger-keeping full time —until somebody decided to pull me back again, like they were pulling Malcolm, I thought bitterly. But then *he* was vulnerable to blackmail. I wasn't—yet. I'd done nothing the wrong side of the law for my own profit. Again—yet. I still hadn't got my intentions formulated when I stabbed viciously at the dial.

But the Gaffer was surprisingly mild when I had said my piece. He did mention something about going to Covent Garden when he wanted to listen to prima donnas, certainly, but even so the shot was directed more at Malcolm than me—or so I chose to think.

'You'll have to take *some* direction, of course,' he went on conversationally. 'Stands to reason, don't it? But the can still remains yours, and there's no bloody refundable deposit on it. Tell him that. Tell him he's in charge until the goods are delivered—and you hope, and *I* hope, that you'll pull together like two good troupers, blah, blah, blah.'

'I can see his face as I'm saying it,' I said glumly.

He chuckled fatly. 'So can I. But it'll probably work. He *is* a prima donna. You say he's got the parcel of dough in the car?'

'Yes.'

'I bet he hasn't. It'd be easier to squeeze toothpaste back into the tube than to prise him loose from it once he's felt it.'

'Shall I call his bluff?'

'You can if you like—but you're out on a limb if he calls yours and gives it to you. No, I'd try it my way if I were you. All sweet reason and logic. If that fails——' He stopped.

'If that fails?' I prompted.

'If that fails,' he said slowly, 'tell him you'll be taken off the job—and Richworth will be put on.'

'Richworth?' I repeated.

'Yes. But I'd rather you didn't. Not unless the velvet glove doesn't work. But if you do mention that name—now or at any time in the future that he gets awkward—you watch *his* face.'

'I'll remember it,' I said.

'Once again, I'd rather you didn't—except as the ultimate sanction. So long.' He hung up.

I got wet again waiting for Malcolm. He tut-tutted solicitously as I got in the car and we did two circuits of the Park after I had eaten crow and he had accepted our altered status with a graciousness that had me prickly with resentment. He suggested going back to his place then.

'I thought you said you'd rather I didn't, two days running?' I said.

'That only applies during normal business hours,' he told me gently. 'I have several simple basic rules in these matters. I'll explain them as we go along.'

He did, like a kindly schoolmaster. I sat hunched in my misery, thinking longingly of hot whisky and lemon and aspirin for myself, and even more longingly of strychnine for this old devil.

CHAPTER FOUR

A LANE ran past the backs of the two bigger buildings which flanked his shop. What had once been a small garden opened on to this, but he'd had it roofed over and a double garage door had been let into the outside wall. He pressed a button on the dashboard and the doors swung back revealing a single car bay with the rest of the space piled with packing cases. I felt him looking sideways at me like a clever schoolboy expecting applause, but lots of taipans are installing remote controlled garage doors in their Peak mansions in Hong Kong, so I wasn't impressed, and even had I been I wouldn't have given him the satisfaction of showing it. Slightly miffed, he closed the doors with the same button when we drove in, and switched on the lights with another. We got out and I followed him through the piled cases to an inside door. There were no gimmicks here, but there was a burglarproof mortice lock which he opened with a key he kept on a chain, and I noticed in passing that although the door was oak and seemingly as old as the building itself, it was backed by a sheet of steel, and once inside he had to move fast to switch off, then reset, a burglar alarm which was just clearing its throat before blasting off. It was quite a moated keep.

We were in a small square lobby. Another door opened off this, I assumed into the shop, and a flight of carpeted stairs led upwards. Half-way up there was a landing with a window that looked into the shop. The glass had the slightly silvered effect which I knew meant it was one-way. A tired-looking old boy in black jacket and striped trousers was sitting on a mandarin throne almost nodding off. Malcolm put his mouth beside a small mike and said quietly: 'Thank you, Mr Brewster, I'm back now. Would you be so good as to lock up. Good night.' The old boy jumped like a startled rabbit, gazed round wildly and said: 'Thank you, Mr Malcolm. Certainly, Mr Malcolm,' his voice a frightened squeak in the return amplifier.

Malcolm chuckled. 'Poor Brewster,' he said. 'He's been with me for twelve years, but he still hasn't got used to my little tricks.'

He led on up the stairs, past another reinforced door, and then we were in his apartment. Through an open door I could see into a small exquisitely furnished dining-room with an opened serving hatch affording a glimpse of a white-tiled kitchen the other side. He opened yet another door which led into a cloakroom, and helped me off with my overcoat, clucking solicitously over its soggy weight, then he showed me through into another room which I guessed was directly over the shop, and was almost the same in area. There was nothing Chinese here; just good, supremely comfortable period stuff, oak, with the soft dull polished gleam of age on it which robbed it of heaviness, and good leather. Books which, despite their tooled leather bindings, didn't look as if they had been bought by the running foot, covered two walls. There were some pictures on the third, flanking an open wood fire in a cut steel grate and each hung at the correct height to be looked at. I recognized at first glance a Canaletto and a Constable, and they certainly weren't reproductions. Ceiling-to-floor tapestry hangings covered the bow window which formed the fourth wall. There was an alcove to one side of the fireplace in which I could see stairs leading up to the floors above. All in all it was the sort of place to make one who had lived most of his life in schools, barracks and commercial messes ache. He waved me to a deep chair by the fire and took Scotch, glasses and a silver cigarette box from a court dresser and put them beside me. In spite of my efforts to maintain ascendancy I found myself relaxing. He poured two stiff drinks without insulting them with soda, sat opposite me and raised his glass. And he grinned—and for the life of me I couldn't help grinning back.

'That's better,' he said. 'And I'm really sorry about all this nonsense this afternoon—but there *was* a reason for it. I found that out last night.'

'Found what out?' I asked.

'That our property is hot. Very hot indeed.'

'I haven't even named the property.'

He didn't actually tap the side of his nose with his forefinger, but he gave the sort of smile which goes with it. 'Oh, come now, Mr Wainwright,' he said archly. 'Who else *could* it be?'

'You tell me,' I snapped, feeling angry again.

'Carter.' And he wasn't fishing. He just knew. All I could do was to shrug and feel a fool.

'Bluffing does become a habit, doesn't it? And so it should. It bespeaks thorough training.' He was being kind to me and I was hating him again, and he knew it and was pressing his resultant advantage.

'All right, Carter,' I said. 'An easy enough guess from what I've told you already. Shall we stop sparring?'

'Any time you like.'

'Why is Carter hot?'

'Because the Russians want him out also.'

'We know that,' I said. 'But wanting and getting are not quite the same thing. My guess is——'

'I'm not guessing at anything,' he interrupted. 'I'm just telling you. I was approached by them ten days ago.'

'What did you say?'

'I told them I'd need a bit of time to think it over—then I passed it on to the Gaffer.'

'The *bastard*!' I spat.

'Why, didn't he tell you?' He chuckled. 'I'm delighted. That means he's puzzled. Passing the tip back to him wasn't meant as an assurance of my loyalty so much as a feeler. I thought perhaps he knew there'd been a Russian offer.'

'I don't give a damn what *you* thought,' I answered. 'He should have told *me*. Anyhow, if the Russians made the offer, why should you assume that the Gaffer would know about it?'

'The Russians didn't—not directly. It was through a middleman, naturally. A fellow called Wates—a real pro—freelance. The sort of man who might quite easily have leaked it to the Gaffer if he thought it worth while. Anyhow, it tidies things up a bit. I'm reasonably certain now who Wates came from.'

'When did you have to give him your answer?'

'I gave it last night—after you left. I accepted, and I have to see him later on tonight to discuss preliminary details and to haggle about my fee—although I must say that they are much more generous than your people.'

'Why don't you work for them then?' I asked.

He waved his hand round the room. 'This. If I did a job for the Russians I'd exchange it for a twelve-by-eight cell. I'm sorry if I shock you, but I'm damned if I'm going to give you a spiel about loyalty. People who pay less than the rate for the job and threaten one with blackmail, haven't the right to expect it. Still, that needn't worry *you*. Loyalty to the faceless ones and loyalty to the man you're working with are two different things.' He looked at his watch. 'I'm afraid we're wasting a lot of time. I'm meetings Wates at nine o'clock. I hope to be back here by ten. I intend to fix a provisional date with him, which will, in turn, fix *our* date.'

'Better later than sooner,' I said. 'There's a hell of a lot to do beforehand.'

'I'll do what I can, without running the risk of rousing his suspicions.'

'Why should he be suspicious?'

'No reason at all, if I don't depart from my usual form. I'm a better sooner-than-later man myself, and he knows it. We've worked together before.'

'Yes, but what I mean——' I began, but he shut me up with another of his schoolmasterly hand-raisings.

'Let me finish, Mr Wainwright. If the Russians have their escape route planned for a certain date, they'll want me to conform to it, within a reasonable margin. If I start finding fault with any suggested date at this early stage, I *wouldn't* be running true to form. No—my cue at the moment is if he says things are laid on for, say, the fifteenth of next month, to accept it and work out something together on that basis—while you and I fix it for a day or two earlier. You follow?'

Again he was wresting the lead from me. I grunted and tried

to think of a brilliant crusher that would re-establish me, but as always in these cases, none came. He rose and pushed the decanter towards me. 'Do make yourself comfortable until I get back.'

I was comfortable but I saw in this a chance to reassert myself. I rose also. 'I think I'll go back to my flat,' I told him.

'Is that wise?' he asked gently. 'I take it you'll want to know what we've arranged—so that will mean either another meeting or a long telephone conversation—both of which I'd rather avoid.' And, of course, he was right. I sat down again.

'What about your family?' I asked.

'My wife is in a nursing home. You'll be quite on your own,' he said. 'You can disregard the telephone. I'll switch it over to the answering service.'

'Sonia? And your son?'

'My son doesn't live here. If Sonia should happen to arrive before I get back, just introduce yourself.'

'As what?'

'As James Wainwright, lately of Hong Kong—seeing me on business, but I was suddenly called out. Tell her I'll be back at ten, and ask her to get us some supper.' He flashed another smile at me and went.

I helped myself to more Scotch, stretched out my feet to the fire and sank back in that wonderfully comfortable chair—and those three things combined must have sent me straight off inside a minute.

I woke in a panic of choking. A girl was standing over me thumping me between the shoulder blades. I struggled to my feet and stared at her through streaming eyes. She was doing her best to look contrite, but the laughter was bursting through. She said, 'I *am* sorry—I really am——'

'What happened?' I gasped.

'Your head was right back—and your mouth was open—and—well, I'm afraid I chucked a salted almond into it. It was so stupid of me.' And then the laughter took over, but at least she poured me another Scotch so I joined in, albeit a bit hollowly, and we introduced ourselves.

Russian beauty, like olives, is the sort that most men either go for in a big way or leave strictly alone. I mean there is no middle course. Personally I'm a leaver-alone. There were so many of them in Shanghai and they all looked the same, just like the Chinese do in a different way. Dark eyes, chalklike colouring, high cheekbones, wide mouths and identical hairstyles—swept back into a Madonna bun at the nape of the neck. Look at an old picture of Pavlova and a current one of Fonteyn, and try and spot the difference. There isn't any. This girl was just another off the same assembly belt. Every movement—the way she poured and handed me my drink, then sank into a chair without looking round at it, feet crossed at the ankles, hands loosely clasped in her lap—looked as if it were the result of long training. Even if I hadn't known her background I would still have been able to pigeonhole her. And the name was just as right—or trite. Sonia. It couldn't have been anything else, except perhaps Natasha. Oh yes—I knew the type so very, very well—like a Hollywood casting director knows blondes—and was as bored by them. And I was angry at her because the first fall was hers and she was still laughing at me behind her eyes.

I said stiffly: 'Your father was called out suddenly. He asked me to wait. He hopes to be back before ten.' I left out the bit about supper because I had no intention of staying, but she asked me if either of us had eaten. I said Malcolm hadn't, but please not to bother on my account as I wouldn't be staying long after he returned. The smile came out from behind her eyes then. She said, 'You're really angry, aren't you?'

'I'm not,' I said shortly.

'Yes you are. I wonder what makes Shanghai Rusks so thin-skinned.'

I took a deep breath and screwed the safety valve down tight. 'I'm not a Shanghai Rusk,' I told her.

'You sound like one. Like one trying to be terribly English. Am I being rude?'

'Yes.' But it didn't suppress her in the slightest. She lit a cigarette and carried on her detached scrutiny of me through the smoke. I had nothing more to say and I didn't know where to put my hands. She was doing it on purpose, of course. It was disconcerting. She looked so stereotyped, but she was acting right out of pattern and making me feel a fool. I was about to do the sensible thing and break it off and go, but then a bell whirred softly somewhere and she said it was her father arriving back, and went through to meet him at the top of the stairs.

Malcolm came into the room alone and closed the door behind him. He nodded curtly, crossed to the fire and sat opposite me.

He said: 'Tricky, I'm afraid,' and rubbed his chin slowly.

'What's tricky?' I asked.

'The whole bloody thing. Listen. As you probably realize, I have a team—three besides myself—completely trustworthy for the simple reason they know that if I am ever nicked through any shortcomings or doublecrossing on their part I can take the lot of them with me upcreek. You follow?'

I nodded.

'But of course that only applies as far as the police are concerned. If the inducement was great enough they could always sell me out to the Opposition—and I might never know who had fingered me. That's if they knew there *was* an Opposition—and who they were. You see what I mean?'

'This is all a bit elementary, isn't it?' I said. 'You take damned good care they don't know.'

'But they do know, unfortunately. Wates has already approached them directly. They thought originally of doing it on their own and cutting me out.'

'What stopped them?' I asked.

'Not loyalty,' he said drily. 'They're all splendid leg and muscle men, but experience and a little'—he tapped himself on the side of the head with his forefinger—'is still very necessary, and fortunately they know their limitations. After some deliberation they told Wates they would rather papa was in at the head of things.'

'But it's still a straight job as far as they're concerned,' I said. 'They don't know *we're* in it.'

'There's more to it than that.' He was still rubbing his chin, and it irritated me. 'The Russians want it done this month—between the twenty-first and twenty-eighth. There will be a Polish ship in the Pool for that week—with a specially built hidey-hole under the bunkers that not even our rummagers could find without taking her apart. First port Gdynia. Just too easy, damn them. Things never work out like that for *me*,' he finished complainingly.

'Where's the problem?' I asked. 'You don't take him to the ship. You take him to wherever I have arranged.'

'Oh, for God's sake, Wainwright,' he said impatiently. 'Don't you realize that before that man comes over the wall every last-minute foreseeable detail has been studied—every step gone over—every yard of the course covered and timed? If I suddenly depart from the plan with no apparent reason, instant suspicion will be aroused. Don't forget that I will be one against three—four, counting the customer. Oh, I could have two or three good convincing reasons ready, but sooner or later they're going to know that I've pulled a swift one on them—and I've got to live here afterwards.'

I could see his point. *I* was rubbing my chin now.

He broke a long silence: 'Since you've mentioned it yourself, what *have* you arranged, by the way?'

'Nothing yet,' I said lamely. 'I thought that was what we were going to discuss tonight.'

He looked at me in shocked unbelief.

'Nothing?' he repeated. 'Listen, my lad, my contract ends when I deliver the man to some prearranged point. The Russians had *their* point arranged before they ever approached me. You and that ape you work for had better start thinking, hadn't you?'

But he'd pushed it just an inch too far, and I had him.

'Your contract is to deliver him to a point near Hong Kong. I made that perfectly clear when I met you,' I said. 'So don't let's waste time and breath, Malcolm.'

'Listen——' he began.

I stood up. 'I've listened all I'm going to tonight,' I said firmly. 'You and your team, as you call it, have made the balls-up—not us. All right, you can get it sorted out, or not, as you like. In the meantime I'm reporting back to the ape. Now let me out of this crazy bloody monkey-puzzle.'

I stalked out to the hall and got my coat from the cupboard. Sonia looked through the kitchen hatch and wailed that she was cooking Russian omelettes and making salad. I didn't mean her to hear my answer—I swear I didn't—but she had good ears, and when I turned back from the cupboard, shrugging myself into my damp overcoat, she was standing behind me. She had the frying pan in her hand. Her eyes should have warned me.

The omelette was the size of a large dinner plate, beautifully souffléd and topped with sour cream and anchovies.

She gave a flick of her wrist and the whole damned thing wrapped itself lovingly round my kisser.

Malcolm gently pried it loose and dabbed my face with olive oil afterwards, clucking his disapproval and tearing strips off her in Russian, but it wasn't doing much good. The bitch was sitting on the top stair, helpless with laughter. Then I noticed that the corners of Malcolm's mouth were twitching, try as he might to control them. And then—well what the hell does one do in a case like that? And after all I'd asked for it. I grinned sheepishly, and the rot set in quickly, and the three of us sat round the fire and belly-laughed for a good fifteen minutes before full sanity returned.

She went out to make more omelettes.

'I'm sorry, Mr Wainwright,' Malcolm said as the door closed. He looked around quickly, leaned forward and lowered his voice, like one about to impart a guilty secret. 'It's her mother's blood coming out in her. Tashkent. You know what those buggers are like, don't you?'

I didn't actually, but I let it go. He pushed the decanter towards me. 'Well, at least it's served to clear the air a little,' he went on.

But I wasn't letting him off as lightly as that. 'It hasn't solved anything, though,' I reminded him.

'Maybe not—but the ghost of an idea was coming to me even as we were talking. First of all I must know what resources the Gaffer is allowing you.'

'Anything within reason provided there is no lead back to him. I mean, I can have what money I want, but no facilities that we can't arrange ourselves.'

'A job for Kjaer then,' he said.

'Who's he?' I asked.

'You know Finnav, surely?'

'The shipping line?'

He nodded. 'They've got four smallish but fast freighters—Baltic ports to the Far East. Kjaer's the part owner and skipper of one of them. They don't carry passengers, but he would sign on a couple of extra crew members and fiddle the list for a thousand pounds a head.'

'There'd be the three of us—you, me and the customer,' I reminded him, and he looked blank.

'But you wouldn't want *me* to travel with you?' he said.

'Carter won't be a willing passenger,' I said, 'and I couldn't watch him night and day for four or five weeks on my own.'

'You wouldn't have to at sea—and Kjaer would know what to do with him at intervening ports, and going through the Suez. Look, I'm not trying to sidestep anything, but my alibi in this country will be for an air trip out to Hong Kong and back again after a week or so. I couldn't explain a ten or twelve week absence.'

'You wouldn't need all that. You can fly home at the end of it.'

'Still too long,' he said doubtfully. 'And then there's the timing of the thing. I have no idea where Kjaer's ship is at the moment. We might have to keep the client under cover for weeks before he comes through Le Havre.'

'Le Havre?'

'Le Havre and Genoa are the only European ports Kjaer touches at after leaving Helsinki.'

'How the hell do we get across there?' The size and complexity of this thing was appearing in its true proportions for the first time. But this one didn't worry him.

'That's easy,' he told me. 'I've got a safe route from the South Coast. It will cost another five hundred. Not per head—just for the trip.'

'The Gaffer will be delighted,' I said. 'All right then—we assume we get across safely. If we have to wait a long time in Le Havre—what then?'

'Easy again,' he assured me. 'A safe house. Board and lodgings a hundred pounds a week per head, and handy for the docks. Well—so much for that. Now as for——'

But Sonia came in then to tell us supper was ready.

CHAPTER FIVE

THE TELEPHONE WAS RINGING when I let myself into the flat next morning. A girl's voice told me that the two books I'd ordered were now in, but if I was calling for them myself would I please remember that they closed at one o'clock today. 'Books' meant the Gaffer's rabbit warren, and one o'clock minus two meant that he wanted to see me there at eleven. It was already a quarter to, and by the time I'd got the District from Gloucester Road to Victoria and walked the three blocks down I was five minutes late, which gave him the opportunity to needle me about the way I spent my nights. I didn't rise to it and that annoyed the dirty-minded old devil, and in the end he had to ask me where the hell I had been, anyhow. I looked virtuous and told him I'd been at Malcolm's place.

'Did you have to stay all night? I've been trying to raise you since six o'clock yesterday evening,' he grunted.

'I didn't think it advisable to walk through the City looking for a taxi at two o'clock in the morning,' I said smugly. 'Particularly in view of what Malcolm told me about the Russians.'

'What did he tell you?'

'Something you overlooked. That they're trying to spring Carter also.'

'I didn't overlook it,' he said. 'I wanted to see how much Malcolm would volunteer—if anything. If you'd known about it you might have prompted him.'

I was about to ask him just what sort of bloody fool he took me for, but I bit it back. Losing one's temper with the Gaffer was tantamount to swinging a Sunday punch at a judo dan. He just turned it back on one.

'All right,' he went on. 'So Malcolm told you the Russians were in the market too— and that he'd passed the word on to me. Quite correct, he did. But he could have been trying to raise the price. Do *you* believe him?'

This was a new Gaffer. He'd never asked my opinion on anything before. I felt a certain importance.

'I do. He told me the middleman's name and gave me the escape route. There'll be a Polish ship in the Pool between——'

'The *Skagadam*—and between the twenty-first and the twenty-eighth—and Wates—that the feller?' he asked. I stopped feeling important. 'Could be, of course,' he went on ruminatively, as I nodded. 'It fits—but then Malcolm could have *made* it fit—and then again he could be playing us off against Wates, couldn't he?'

I nodded glumly. This was getting just a shade too complicated. Over bacon and eggs this morning I had been trusting Malcolm. Now this old bastard was cutting the ground from under my feet again.

'Well, we've got to start from somewhere,' I said. 'We've got something laid on—in broad outline.'

'Let's have it.'

'He's accepted the Russians' proposition—they're offering double ours, by the way. His fellows make the spring—and then he wants us to hijack Carter very authentically before he reaches the London docks.'

The Gaffer suddenly grinned widely. 'Lovely,' he said. 'If there's anything I like, it's having an intelligent surmise substantiated. That's just what I thought he'd do. You see why, don't you?'

'If we jumped the gun the Russians would be pretty certain to find out,' I said. 'Naturally he wants to avoid that.'

'He doesn't give a monkey's for the Russians,' said the Gaffer flatly. 'If it comes to that he doesn't give a monkey's for us either. He pretends to. To be afraid of somebody disarms them. No—don't you see? He'll jack the Russians up to the hilt for something in advance, so he'll be that much up. I wouldn't put it past him to stick it on them for the lot afterwards, on the grounds that he'd carried out his contract in getting the client out, and if the Rusks couldn't look after him from then on it was *their* fault.'

'They wouldn't be mugs enough to fall for it, surely?' I said.

'I don't know. Twenty thousand quid? Petty cash really. If they paid him in full it would keep his mouth closed—and those of his helpers. If, on the other hand, they felt themselves welshed on through a technicality, they might get vocal about it afterwards. The Rusks would hate that.'

'You mean to say that he'd have the nerve to pull something as raw as that?' I asked.

'I prefer to call it gall,' the Gaffer said. 'And you bet he's got enough of it. Don't ever underestimate Malcolm's gall. Oh well, just let it be clearly understood that he doesn't get a blind sausage out of us until the job has been successfully carried out.'

'What about expenses?'

'He won't have to worry about them. You'll be carrying the bag.'

'He's not going to like it,' I said dubiously. 'He was discussing expenses last night. His team will want two hundred and fifty pounds each beforehand. That's in case——'

'They get nicked on the job and their everlovings and God-forbids are left on National Assistance. Yeah, yeah, yeah, we know all that. How many helpers is he using?'

'Three.'

'Good—so he gives you three addresses. It will go to them through the mail the morning after, *if* there've been no slip-ups.'

'What if he won't wear it?'

'Then he can wear a nice blue battledress with yellow high-escape risk patches sewn on to the arse, knees and elbows of it. Tell him that. Tell him it's the one thing he *can* be certain of on this job.' He leaned forward, emphasizing his points with a stubby forefinger. 'Tell him that his trial will be in camera in the interests of State security, so he can involve anybody he wants to, and it won't do him the bloodiest bit of good. Tell him that even if he has any little ideas beforehand about writing it all down and getting it to the papers after he's been nicked, it still won't do him any good—because we'll slap a "D" Notice across every editor in the country. Tell him that the same goes for his helpers —who are three gents by the names of Maudsley, Ansel and Hessiker. Tell him, in short, that we've got him by the tight and curlies, and if he forces us to twist 'em then, by God, it's going to hurt him more than us. But he shouldn't need telling. He knows it already.'

I nodded and got up. I didn't feel like speaking at that moment. In fact I was feeling just a little bit sick. The man we were talking about had worked well and faithfully for us for half a lifetime. What he had done in the war alone would, in any branch of the service other than this Augean stable, have earned him a chestful of gongs. Granted he had put a foot wrong, but for that he should have been dealt with at the time, not kept on ice until we wanted him again, then blackmailed. Something of what I was thinking must have shown in my face. The Gaffer peered up at me from the depths of his busted chair, like a weasel from a burrow.

'You're not doubting any of this, are you?' he asked. I shook my head.

'Good,' he said. 'Just so as we understand. Because all that *would* happen if he tried to play it crafty—with us, I mean. He can put any bloody thing he likes over on the Rusks—as long as it doesn't jeopardize our interests. Oh yes—make no mistake about it. It'd happen all right—*if there was time for it,* and it seemed expedient—and if he was lucky. If there wasn't time for it, and it didn't seem expedient, then he mightn't be so lucky. The rug might have to be pulled from under him a bit quicker then. It has been known.'

He grunted up out of the chair and moved to the door to let me out. The cocker bitch snarled at me as I passed. Yes, by God, they *were* alike. The Gaffer paused with his hand on the latch, and turned and looked at me again.

'I'm glad we've cleared up any lingering doubts,' he said softly. 'If we haven't, just talk it over with Malcolm. You'll find *he's* a believer. My bloody oath he is. Get him to tell you about what happened to Saunders one of these days. Right—call me here at six each evening—or six in the morning if anything stops you. Be seeing you.' He opened the door, checked that the corridor was clear and let me out. I felt my flesh creeping under my sleeve where the obscene old devil had touched me.

I spent the rest of that day on my own—that is bank—business. There was a hell of a lot to do, and this was something I had to fix up myself as, thank God, the Gaffer had no concern with me in my commercial role. Malcolm had found out that Kjaer's ship didn't call at Le Havre until the tenth of next month. That meant that we would have to stay under cover there for a fortnight to three weeks—and add the voyage of five weeks to it. Seven or eight weeks in all—which would put me a whole month over the top of my leave.

But things worked out much easier than I hoped. My original boss was still there and I went in to see him, and within an hour he had fixed a six-week course for me at the Midland works of a company that was experimenting in a new method of computer accountancy. We both trusted that I wouldn't be called upon to lecture on it when I got back to Hong Kong.

The bank was only a matter of a couple of hundred yards from Malcolm's shop, and it seemed a damned nuisance to have to go back up west in order to reach it, but Malcolm was insisting on full security. He was working for the Rusks now, he said when I phoned him, and they would quite likely put his place under at least sporadic surveillance just as a matter of routine. It would be better if I didn't come to the shop again openly. So he left his mini-van on a meter in Bryanston Square and went off for half an hour, and I got in the back and stayed there until he returned and drove off to his garage. It was a simple ruse but one I'd never heard of before, and he guessed it and gave me a scholarly lecture on the art of tail-shaking all the way back to the City. There was a jack-handle on the floor of the van beside me, and he never knew how close he got to having it wrapped round his skull. But in spite of my tetchiness he was impressing me. The old devil was a professional of professionals, and if you've got to stick your neck out there's something very comforting in doing it in expert company.

The apartment was again an oasis of warmth and soft light, and this time I didn't have to rough it, because Sonia had been prepared and she'd got the guest bedroom ready for me, even to pyjamas, razor and toothbrush, and she was cooking something in the kitchen that smelled damned good. I sat and drank some more of his Scotch and heard six o'clock strike and thought to hell with the Gaffer; I'd give myself the pleasure of spoiling his early morning sleep tomorrow.

Malcolm said: 'Did you settle the matter of my advance?'

'I tried to,' I told him. 'But he said not a sausage. You can give me three addresses and he'll mail it to the helpers the morning after, providing there have been no slip-ups.'

He grunted something about untrusting bastards spoiling ships for ha'porths of tar, but didn't appear to be too upset about it, for which I was thankful because the acrimony of the whole affair to date was getting me down. Something else was getting me down too, and that was the uncertainty of how much Sonia knew about it. Malcolm never broke off or covered up if she came into the room when we were discussing details, but she never joined in. Yet the Gaffer had told me that she actually drove the getaway car when Wally Wharton came out over the wall. And the Wharton job wasn't the only one, I had been given to understand. Had she helped in the others also? And what was more to the point, was she going to be in on this one? The idea frightened me stiff. I had never worked with women, other than the few specialist instructresses during the course. I put it to Malcolm squarely while she was out of the room, but she wasn't out long enough for me to get his answer. She came in just at that instant to tell us supper was ready, and this time he did cover up. Apropos of nothing at all he asked me if I liked chrysanthemums and then went off into a learned discourse on their symbolism in Japanese art. The whole bloody thing was getting more Alice in Wonderlandish every hour.

But I slept well that night and woke early enough to phone the Gaffer on time on the bedside telephone. I didn't know whether Malcolm was listening in on another extension, but it wouldn't have availed him of anything if he had because all I said was that I'd be needing an extra two pints tomorrow, which meant I had nothing special to report, and the Gaffer said he'd attend to it, which told me that he had nothing for me either. I hung up, then, purely as a matter of routine, I unscrewed the dial of the thing and there, sure enough, was a scriber underneath it. A scriber is a circular piece of paper-thin copper which fits out of sight under the moving part of the dial which has a tiny sharp point set in it. The pressure of the dialler's finger is sufficient to bring the point down on the copper, but it springs back when the finger is removed. The resultant marks on the copper can tell anybody who wants to know just what numbers have been called. The Gaffer's number was, of course, ex-directory. I removed the copper, defaced the marks on it with a nail-file, scratched a rude word on it and put it back.

Malcolm took me up west again in the mini-van after breakfast and left me in the underground car park at Marble Arch, and I took a cab back to Courtfield Gardens. I packed a bag and went off to the computer people since I'd be needing the alibi for the bank later on, and Birmingham was as good as anywhere to kick my heels until I was wanted. I attended a few instructional sessions and even managed to stay awake at some of them. I called Malcolm and gave him the number of my hotel. Then I just waited—and waited.

Have you ever spent ten winter days in Birmingham with nothing to do except call someone you didn't like on the telephone at six each evening? Don't. I'd almost reached the point of going sick and asking to be taken off it by the tenth call, but as it turned out it wasn't necessary. The Gaffer said he didn't like the way things were dragging and told me to come back to town.

I felt a surge of relief. I hung up, then called Malcolm's number. Sonia answered and she told me the old man was away on business and she didn't expect him back that night, but she'd like to see me right away. I said I couldn't make it before the following day. She said what a pity because it was about Timoy scrolls, and I felt a prickly sensation start at the nape of my neck and run down to my Achilles' tendon. 'Timoy' means 'peach' in Cantonese—and 'peach' in any language at all meant 'Stand by—urgent'. But how the hell did she know that? Or did she? Maybe there were such things as Timoy scrolls and she'd just used it by chance. But I couldn't risk it. I told her I'd call her again when I'd found out about trains and I ducked round to the station. There was one in twenty minutes that would get me back to town just after ten, but when I called her the second time the number was engaged.

I couldn't waste any more time so I went back to the hotel, worried and puzzled, and collected my bag.

It was sheer bloody-mindedness that held me from calling the Gaffer again. What would have been the use, anyhow? He obviously knew nothing about recent developments, or he would have told me when I spoke to him at six.

I got the answering service from Malcolm's number when I called on arriving in town. It was raining like the devil and there was a taxi queue a mile long, so I humped my bag along the Euston Road until I found a prowler, and I was wet through and in a filthy mood. It would have been stupid to go to the shop openly after all his previous precautions, so I did the sensible thing and went home. I paid the cab off and was just letting myself in when I heard light steps behind me and a hand came out of the darkness and touched my elbow. I turned. I could just make out that it was a woman, but no more.

I said, 'You're miles west of your beat, sweetheart. This is a respectable neighbourhood, not Jermyn Street.'

'Save the humour,' she snapped. 'Let's get inside.' It was Sonia.

Raging, I whipped her through the front door grabbing at the automatic switch inside that lighted up the hall and stairs when the inner vestibule door was opened. I led her up through the darkness and into my flat without speaking. I drew the blinds, then switched on the lights and opened up on her.

'What the hell do you mean by coming here?' I blazed. 'How did you know where I lived? Has that old beat been tailing me?'

'Is that meant to be funny?' She loosened her wet raincoat and shook water like a poodle. 'Light that damned gas fire, for God's sake. I'm frozen.'

'Answer my question,' I said.

'I came here because you told me to.'

'*I* told you to?' I stared at her. 'What on earth are you talking about?'

'You said——' She broke off and it was her turn to stare. 'Well, didn't you?'

There are two ways to get answers from a woman. Gentlemen aren't allowed to use the quick one, so I took her hands and pushed her gently into a chair, put a bob in the meter and lit the fire, because she *was* frozen. Then I poured two drinks and gave her one.

'Right—slowly. From the beginning,' I told her.

'Father went off into the blue two days ago,' she said. 'He rang me tonight and gave me your Birmingham number and told me to tell you that he had some Timoy scrolls. I was just going to do so when you came through.' So that explained *that* part of it.

'All right,' I said. 'But this address that I'm supposed to have given you——?'

'Well, not you, but the reception clerk——'

I nearly switched to the quick way. '*What* bloody clerk——?' I began, took a deep breath and a deeper drink, and got hold of myself again.

'The one at the hotel. He said you had just left for London and would I please leave home *immediately* and meet you at this address as soon as you arrived—and to be very careful of the traffic. He rang about twenty minutes after you did. You mean to say you didn't send that message?'

I shook my head and tried to get things into focus. This phone, like the Gaffer's, was ex-directory. The office were the only people who knew the number—or so I fervently hoped. But why would the office uncover my modest hideout to somebody they didn't trust?

Sonia was talking again. 'I took "immediately" to mean just that, and the bit about the traffic as a warning that I might be followed——'

'So what did you do about it?' I shot at her.

'Left immediately, took the Circle round to Euston, bought a ticket to Crewe, went out on the seven-fifteen and slipped off at Willesden and doubled back to Gloucester Road on the Underground—and I've been cooling my heels, literally, in the bloody laurel bushes across the square for nearly an hour and a half watching this place of yours.' She held out her glass. I refilled it for her. She deserved it. I wouldn't have done it as thoroughly if the Gaffer himself had been on my tail. But that still didn't answer my question. Who the hell had leaked my address to her, and why? Then the telephone rang. There was a drill for answering it if you should happen to have somebody else present. You merely let it ring eight times, then you lifted it and said, 'No, I'm sorry, you've got the wrong number.' You then rang the office when things were clear again. But now I was worried, and I answered the first time. It was the Gaffer.

He said, 'Took your time getting back, didn't you? Is that girl with you?' He must have been worried too, because he neither bawled me out for the procedure breach nor made a dirty crack when I told him she had just arrived.

'Were you the reception clerk?' I asked him, and breathed again when he said yes.

'Keep her there, for Christ's sake,' he told me. 'She's not to go back to the shop under any circumstances whatsoever. Do you understand?'

'No,' I said flatly. 'Maybe I would if I knew what the hell was happening.' I waited for the answering blast but it didn't come. I heard him take a deep and gusty breath—the sort of breath a fat saint would take when praying for patience if the bloke operating the thumbscrews was rather stupid.

He said, almost mildly, 'The goods came over the wall an hour ago. No bother apparently, but the maestro rang me just beforehand and said he thought the vodkas were a mite suspicious and would I get the girl shacked up safe with you somewhere just in case anybody called round at the shop. With it so far?'

'Yes,' I said, 'but——'

'*Stay* with it,' he begged softly. 'Maybe we might meet again sometime in the future, though on your present form that seems unlikely. This number and that of the office is dead, as of now, so it's no use calling again. Sorry and all that but you're far too hot.'

'Thanks,' I said bitterly.

'Don't mention it,' he answered. 'Draw what funds you require from your own bank and the best of British luck to you. Further instructions in your own territory out there—if you make it that far.'

I said meekly: 'May I speak?'

'Keep it very short,' he said.

'You're a bastard,' I told him. 'You're hamstringing me before I even start, but I'll get the goods there if it kills me—just for the pleasure of rubbing your bloody nose in it.'

'I'm sorry,' he said. 'But you know the rules. You got out of touch, let him jump the gun on you, failed to keep me informed, disclosed my number to him, and you're breaking security at this very moment. So am I, but I can tear down and build again—you can't. You're on your bloody own. Sleep tight—both of you.'

CHAPTER SIX

SHE SAID as I put the telephone down, 'It would be manners to pretend I hadn't heard anything—but I did, and I'm worried about my father. Can you tell me anything, please?'

I stalled. 'About your father? Not a thing. I was hoping you could tell *me* something. Any idea where he is?'

'If everything went according to plan—' she glanced at her wristwatch—'at least fifty miles away from Lanchester prison, and travelling fast. But I gather from your talk with the Gaffer that everything *hasn't* gone according to plan. Has Father been caught?'

I picked up my empty glass and stepped across to refill it, so that my back was towards her.

'Quick thinking,' she said. 'But not quick enough. Your eyebrows shot up to your hairline before you turned. Yes—I know all about the Gaffer. I know all about you too.'

Naturally I mumbled something about not knowing what the hell she was talking about, and she came back with Oh, God, anything but that, or words to that effect, but I was saved from further floundering by her going to the television and switching it on.

'Shut up,' she said. 'It's coming up to news time.'

The announcer's face swam up out of the grey mush and his lips were moving soundlessly because she hadn't turned the volume control up sufficiently. I pushed her to one side and adjusted it.

'. . . a Home Office spokesman would neither confirm nor deny that the prisoner was, in fact, Robert Carter, the Russian master spy sentenced in 1965 to thirty years' imprisonment . . .' And then his desk telephone rang and he excused himself and listened, nodding ponderously and looking wise. He went on, 'No, I am sorry. There is no further news at the moment, but our reporter, Dominic Sutcliffe, is travelling down to Lanchester with an outside broadcast camera team and we will give you further details and possibly pictures before the end of the news.' Then he went off about the current rail strike.

I turned down the sound a little and looked at her. I'd recovered a bit now, but she had lost ground. She was white and strained. I was thankful.

'How much do you know about this?' I asked.

'The old devil told me that it was only a final run over the course,' she said. 'He wouldn't let me go with him in case you rang.'

'You mean to say that he just went down on spec and sprang this fellow?' I said aghast. 'Without any preliminary plans?'

'Oh, don't ask such damfool questions,' she snapped. 'Of course he didn't. He had it all worked out to the last detail. He's been on it ever since *you* first turned up and started him off again—blast you. He's behaved himself for four years now.'

'He's *behaved* himself?' I said. 'My information is that he hasn't and *you've* been up to the neck in it too.'

'I've done the driving—twice. In each case it was because of a last-minute slip-up with one of his apes—and it was an attempt to keep him out of mischief.'

'But you've known about the other times?'

'What other times? Are you trying to trap me into something?'

'Why should I want to trap you?'

'Don't give me that starry-eyed piffle. Everybody who works for the Gaffer is in some sort of trap. The more any of you can get on another underling the safer you make it for yourselves. Well, I'm *not* one of your underlings—and neither is my father. You forced him into this. Oh, I know he was a pretty willing victim, but that's not the point. It was just like dangling a bottle of whisky in front of an alcoholic—and just as filthy——'

'Oh, come off it,' I said. 'In this particular case he was all set to make a deal with the Russians. At least he's working for his own side now.'

She looked at me scornfully: 'What's the difference? You both stink, and on balance your side is the worse. You're blackmailing one of your own people, and if anything goes wrong you'll stand by and see him sent down for years without lifting a finger to help him.'

I'd had enough by this time. 'Listen, sister,' I said. 'If he goes down I'll probably go down with him, and there won't be any fingers lifted for *me* either. If it comes to that, you aren't such a hell of a good risk yourself. Suppose we stop fighting and do something constructive?'

'Like what? All I'm interested in at the moment is finding out where my father is. When I've done that I'm going to drag him out of it by the ears——'

And then we saw the announcer lift his telephone again, and

I brought up the sound, just as the picture changed to one of a dark and rainy village street with a sheepskin-coated young man holding a mike.

'I'm talking to you from the High Street of this sleepy old Dorset town. The grim, top-security prison of Lanchester lies a mile away through the darkness, but the police are stopping all traffic and pedestrians from approaching it until a thorough survey of the ground has been made. No official statement has been released as yet, but I think we might take it that it *is* Robert Carter who has escaped. Apparently he was missed before eight o'clock, but no alarm was raised until a thorough search had been made inside the prison first, which took about an hour. It would appear that Carter, although an extremely important prisoner, was not regarded as an escape risk and was, in fact, a blue-band, or trusty, with full privileges and a wide measure of freedom inside the actual walls. We are going to move up to the police cordon now, and in the meantime we are returning you to the studio. This is Dominic Sutcliffe speaking to you from Lanchester . . .'

I heard her sigh with relief as I turned the sound down again. It was almost a sob. She started to button her raincoat, moving towards the door.

I said, 'Where do you think you're going?' which probably wasn't the most tactful way of phrasing the question in the face of her present mood. She told me to mind my own bloody business. I got my back to the door, twisted the key behind me and dropped it into my pocket. She stood facing me, perfectly composed now, but I could see a tiny vein throbbing at the angle of her jaw.

'Let me out, Wainwright,' she said. 'Or I'll raise such a huroosh that you'll have the fire brigade round.'

'You'd better hear what I've got to say first,' I answered. 'You're here at your father's express wish. He rang the Gaffer and told him that the Russians were suspicious and he was afraid that they might drop in on you.'

'I don't believe you,' she said. 'If he had any such instructions for me he'd have got in touch with me direct.'

'Believe what the hell you like. That's what the Gaffer just told me. It was he who did the reception clerk act.'

I could see doubt dawning in her face. 'But why didn't Father tell me so himself?' she said uncertainly. 'He'd only been speaking to me shortly before—when he told me to ring you in Birmingham.'

'Maybe he tried but couldn't get through. *I* tried to call you twice again after I'd spoken to you the first time. Once the phone was engaged, the next time I got the answering service. He was no doubt pushed for time and did the only thing he could.'

She nodded slowly, convinced against her will, and I could see her relaxing a little.

'I'd like to know where the devil he got the Gaffer's number, though,' I went on. 'Certainly not from me, although I've just had my ears removed for it.'

'He did get it from you.' She looked spitefully pleased. 'You called the Gaffer on our phone.'

'Yes, but——' I began.

'You scratched it out on the scriber and wrote a filthy word on it. But you didn't look underneath. Ours works on both sides. You're not terribly bright, are you?'

And I must have looked it. 'All right,' I said glumly. 'Don't rub it in.'

A newsflash was interrupting the weather report. I turned up the sound. They were confirming that it was Carter, and there was a photo of him. It was an anonymous sort of face, that of a man anything between thirty and fifty, completely expressionless as all professionals are when they are being officially mugged. It was about as much use for identification purposes as a passport photo. And they still weren't giving any details except that he had floated and a close watch was being kept on sea and airports. Then a picture of the Home Secretary, who wasn't available for comment, was flashed on. As a matter of fact they didn't look unalike. Both could have been anybody.

I said, 'The bedroom and bathroom are through there. I'd advise you to get some rest while you're waiting.'

'Waiting for what?' she asked coldly.

'Daylight,' I answered. 'If there *is* anybody laying for you on your doorstep you'd at least see what hit you. Anyhow, since your father asked——'

'Oh, damn my father—and you,' she blazed.

'If childish rudeness is all you can contribute, we'd both better shut up,' I said.

'All right, Confucius. What can *you* contribute?'

'I was going to say,' I said with icy dignity, 'that since your father asked you to come here it wouldn't be unreasonable to expect that this is where he will try to get in touch with us.'

She considered this for a moment, then nodded and sat down and rummaged in her handbag for a cigarette. I lit it for her.

'Maybe you're right,' she agreed grudgingly. 'But when I do want to leave, don't try to stop me.'

I went over to the door and put the key back. 'You can go whenever you like. I only wanted you to hear what I had to say.' I picked up her glass. 'Another drink?'

She shook her head. 'You wouldn't be able to raise a cup of coffee, would you? I missed my dinner.'

And that reminded me that I'd missed mine too. I went through to the kitchen and looked into the refrigerator. There were bacon and eggs there which looked sound enough after ten days, even if the milk was a bit doubtful, and a wrapped sliced loaf was no more repulsive than when it was allegedly fresh, so I put on the percolator and set about getting a scratch supper. It smelt all right, and she was a healthy girl, so she came through and took over from me. We didn't talk much until we had finished it, but she wasn't sulking. She looked deathly tired and I felt sorry for her. I was just about to suggest that she went and got her head down when the telephone rang again. We looked at each other. I took a deep breath and picked it up. A man's voice said, 'A Mr Tim Moy is calling Mr John Brown from a call-box in Christchurch. Will you pay for the call?' I said I would and nodded reassuringly at Sonia, and then Malcolm was on the line.

He said, 'Who's with you?'

'You-know-who,' I told him. 'She's just cooked an omelette, but hasn't chucked it in my face this time. Nobody else, so you can go ahead.'

I heard him chuckle faintly. 'I understand. Put her on, please.'

But I boggled at that. 'I want a few details first,' I said.

'Don't waste time, for God's sake,' he said crisply. 'Put her on.'

I handed her the phone. She listened and said yes at intervals, frowning in concentration, but I could see that she was gathering her forces ready to let him have it when he had finished speaking, and I got ready to grab the phone back from her. But he must have guessed it and he hung up on her before she had a chance. She swore and slammed the phone back. I swore too.

Well?' I said.

'Have you got a car?' she asked.

'No—I hire one when I want one.'

'That's a hell of a lot of good. We want one now—tonight.'

'Where have we got to go?'

'Dungeness.'

'Where's that exactly?'

'On the South Coast, between Hastings and Folkestone. Near Rye. He's on his way there with the goods now.'

'Sounds just the sort of place they'll be watching,' I said.

'It's as safe as anywhere else,' she answered. 'A couple of coastguards and about four policemen to cover the whole of Romney Marsh.'

'Used it before, have you?' I said, which was stupid of me because it gave her the opportunity to tell me to mind my own business again.

'Train any good?' I asked helpfully.

She shook her head. 'We wouldn't get one before morning, then we'd still need to hire a car in Rye—and that would be asking for trouble.'

'What about your mini-van?'

'He's using that himself. Oh, blast him! We'll have to take mine. He said I wasn't to go back home, but there's nothing else for it.' She was getting into her raincoat. I didn't like the idea of going to the shop either, but, as she said, there seemed nothing else for it.

It was still raining like hell when we went out. I made her stay in the shadow of the portico while I did a quick recce round the square. If anybody was watching the place he had my sympathy, but apparently nobody was because I walked round a corner and waited a full three minutes to draw him without results. I collected her and we padded miserably along to Gloucester Road tube, then separated and travelled in different coaches, and didn't join up until we came out at Moorgate.

I didn't like this part of it at all. You know how deserted the City is even on a fine night. Tonight not a thing moved anywhere, except us. We stuck out like sore thumbs. I suggested that she waited at the station while I went off for her car, but she turned that one down flat. Anyone trying to enter their place without the proper drill could start all sorts of things buzzing and ringing apparently. So I did the best I could think of and made her walk one side of the street while I took the other, a dozen yards to the rear, feeling naked and helpless.

She made it to the shop without my seeing anybody, but that didn't mean a thing. This was different from Courtfield Gardens. There were side turnings, alleys and deeply-recessed shop doorways by the hundred here, and we could have been under observation from any of them. She reached the front door, let herself in and switched things off inside, and I walked across quickly and followed her. She relocked and led me through the dark shop and up to the flat above. She checked the answering service but there were no messages on it. We didn't waste any time, but went straight down to the garage. Her car, a little blue M.G. Midget, was standing where the mini-van usually parked. She switched on and checked the fuel gauge. It showed three-quarter full, so she got a two-gallon can and topped up, then started it and warmed on full choke. I went to open the sliding door, but she said it was all right, and then I saw that she was equipped with the same electric eye business as the old man had, so I climbed in alongside her. We backed out into the lane and the door slid down into position again—and then I saw movement at the top of the lane. Two figures were running quickly towards us through the driving rain. I yelled a warning to her. She completed the backward turn, whipped into first and stepped hard on the gas and drove straight at them. She had to, as they were coming from the direction we wanted to go. One of them managed to jump clear, but we hit the other and knocked him flat back against the wall. I heard his yell above the roar of the engine, and there was a bump on the side of the car, then we were clear of the lane, and she was through the gears into top like a flash and we were on our way down Throgmorton Street.

'It looks as if Pop was right,' she said. I glanced sideways at her. I couldn't see her face in the darkness, but her voice was quite steady. In fact it was bright and perky as if, now started, she was enjoying the picnic.

I said, 'We might have killed him,' and all she said to that was 'Too bad.' I felt rattled.

'That's all bloody well,' I said, 'but they might have been plain-clothes men—in which case we're going to have a shower of squad cars on our tail in a matter of minutes.'

'I doubt it,' she said coolly. 'Tell me when you last saw a British detective in a belted trenchcoat, except on TV. Those two were Ivans.' And I felt sure she was right, but I didn't love her for it. The wretched woman was taking the show over.

She knew her way and she drove well, with the sense not to go too fast and attract attention. We crossed Blackfriars Bridge and headed for the New Kent Road and the A.20, with me tapping the water off the talc rear window and squinting anxiously behind us from time to time.

'There's no need to get jumpy,' she said. 'They'd have caught up long before this if they were police.'

'Who's getting jumpy?' I snarled.

'You. We're quite safe in the suburbs, but the police sometimes make routine checks on the main roads. If we're stopped we use our own names, because they'll want to see my driving licence. You're my fiancé, and we're going down to the Mermaid Inn, Rye, for the weekend.'

'God forbid,' I said fervently, and felt that the shot had gone home because she maintained a miffish silence thereafter.

But she was right. I *was* jumpy. There was more traffic about here and we had overtaken and been overtaken by several cars, but the lights of one were far too steady for my liking. This fellow was a hundred yards or so behind us and was maintaining the distance, and he switched his headlights off once, and ran on sidelights, then went back after a time to dipped headlights, then on to full again—and always when there were a couple of cars between him and us. This is standard practice when car-tailing at night, to confuse the quarry into thinking you are different cars.

I hated doing it, but in the end I said: 'Jumpy or not, there is someone on our tail.'

'I know it,' she said. 'I've been watching him in the mirror. Light-switching.' The bitch was still a jump ahead of me. 'They're not police or they'd have had us by now. This is somebody who wants to know where we're going.'

'What are you going to do about it?' I asked.

'Throw them if I can.' And she did, as neatly as I've ever seen it done. There were three cars between us and the tailer, and a bus in front of us, just pulling away from a stop. She nipped in between it and the kerb and turned down a side street and went like the clappers with her lights switched off. She turned left at the next turning and left again, crossing the main road we had been travelling on and diving into a dark labyrinth the other side. We threw them all right, but then she was a bit too clever and she found herself in a cul-de-sac and had to back out.

Then she got lost, and told me to do the same when I jeered at her.

We stayed off the main road until we found ourselves in Eltham, but then, on the dual carriageway, I became aware of the same guy on our tail again—or someone damned like him. Of course they knew what we looked like and had our number, whereas they were only a pair of lights behind us. I told her about it.

'Have you got a gun?' she asked.

'Don't talk like a fool,' I snapped. 'Of course I haven't. This is Eltham, not Arizona.'

'Well, I have,' she said calmly. 'And I intend getting to where I'm going without these people on our tail. Hang on.'

Her foot went down hard.

CHAPTER SEVEN

GOD! WHAT A DRIVE THAT WAS. Those sports toys are fast, but they're not heavy enough for the really high brackets—certainly not in rain like that which was coming down now. There was too much water on the windshield for the wipers to cope with and the headlights were a drowned blur in the slanting downpour, but that didn't slow her down any. It was more like water-skiing than motoring. She didn't have the panel lights on, so I couldn't see the clock, but she must have been needling over a hundred in places. I was scared rigid.

But they were no chickens either, and their car, I judged from the spacing of their headlights, was heavier and faster and generally more suited for this sort of lunacy than ours. They kept right on our tail and finally crept up abreast of us and tried to force us on to the verge, but an oncoming truck saved us and they had to brake hard and slide in behind us again and we gained quite a bit of ground as a result. I just had time to see that it was a big dark car and the fellow beside the driver was leaning out through the open window making urgent signs to us to pull up. I felt Sonia fumbling for something on the floor between us. I said, 'I'll get it, whatever it is. Keep your hands on that damned wheel.'

'The gun's in my handbag,' she said.

I groped and found the bag, opened it and fished out a silly little nickel-plated ·22 revolver.

'Good,' I said. 'It's in my pocket now, and it's staying there. Of all the silly, stupid——'

'It must be quite obvious, even to you, that we'll never shake them off,' she interrupted. 'But if you hit one of their tyres——'

'With this scent-spray? You don't know guns. It would bounce off like a pea. Anyhow, who do you think I am? Deadeye Dick?'

'Well, their windshield then.'

'Sheer murder? No thank you. The whole damned works are not important enough for that.'

'We've got to do something. My father's out there in the blue relying on us.' There was a catch in her voice.

'Pathetic,' I said. 'But it's the old goat's own fault. He shouldn't have jumped the gun.'

'You rat,' she raved. '*You* forced him into this. He's done his part of it, and now you want to leave him in the lurch.'

'I don't want to do anything of the sort,' I told her. 'But I'm damned if I'm going to start blasting off with a gun on an English road, especially since we still don't know whether or not they are police.'

'Of course they're not police,' she snapped. 'If they were they'd have whistled up road blocks by radio long ago.' And she was no doubt right, but I still wasn't prepared to risk it.

I saw the traffic lights as we screamed round the next bend, and they were red. I yelled a warning and my hand shot forward to find the ignition key but it was too late; we had already overshot them. They were controlling a long one-way stretch of road, one side of which was under repair, cluttered with graders, rollers and heaps of ballast. And the lights of an uncoming vehicle were blinding us.

Don't ask how we made it. I'm still not prepared to credit her with skill and judgment. Not at that particular instant, anyhow. It was sheer blind luck. She wrenched the wheel over and missed the oncomer by the thickness of a cigarette-paper, skittled a barrier and a row of hurricane lamps, threaded between a miniature mountain of tar macadam and a huge yellow bulldozer, and then was back on the single roadway. But it just wasn't the tailers' night. They didn't make it.

Peering back through the talc I saw the following lights swing to the near side and then soar up and over as the car mounted a steep bank. Then they went out suddenly, and I heard the crash even over the scream of our own tortured engine. The other fellow seemed to have got away with it. It was a huge lumbering truck and it had managed to stop in time.

When I was able to control my voice I said: 'Slow down. You're asking for trouble at this speed, and there's no need for it now. They won't be following anybody any more, except maybe a harp band.'

She didn't answer, but I felt the speed slacken as she lifted her foot, and we proceeded thereafter at a sober fifty.

The reaction set in, as far as I was concerned anyhow, after we had got through Maidstone. A police car with its blue light flashing, closely followed by an ambulance, came towards us, and I waited, prickling. But they swept past us with their sirens wailing. The truck driver must have got to a telephone somewhere. I realized how tired I was then though I did at least make a gesture and offered to drive, but she declined it coldly, so I went to sleep.

I woke as I felt her hand shaking my arm. She said, still coldly: 'We're nearly there.'

I rubbed the moisture off the window and peered through, but could see only dark flatness through the rain which was still bucketing down. There weren't even hedges between us and the fields, and we might well have been in the middle of the steppes. Not even a distant light showed anywhere in a three-sixty degree sweep. I didn't know anywhere as desolate as this existed in England any more—certainly not close to London, and I knew we couldn't be that far away because a glance at my watch told me I'd been asleep less than half an hour.

'Where the devil are we?' I asked.

'Romney Marsh,' she said. 'We should be coming up to a turn-off on the left shortly. Keep your eyes open that side. It's easy to miss it on a night like this.'

And almost immediately I saw it. Two white posts marking the entrance to a cart track. She pulled up, skittering in the wet, and switched off the headlights, then she blipped the sidelights twice. Away to our left a pinpoint of light came up in answer. She turned on to the track and squelched at a snail's pace along muddy ruts until dimly in front of us I saw high mounds silhouetted darkly against the sky, and between them the glimmer of water. She ran the car slowly round the first mound and stopped and climbed out stiffly. I followed suit even more stiffly, feeling damp, cold and miserable. Malcolm loomed up out of the gloom and said testily, 'What on earth kept you?' and I could have hit him. He didn't give us time to reply but just took over like a colonel from a couple of rather dim subalterns.

'Right, this car——' He leaned forward and peered at it. 'Tch, tch! It's yours, Sonia? I told you not to go and collect it. You might quite easily have been followed. You *must* take notice of my instructions. Switch off the lights and leave it. Terry will collect it later. This way, both of you.'

He padded off through the mud and we followed. I could hear Sonia swearing horribly in a choked voice, but for myself I was past it. Just speechless. He led us into a gaunt open-sided shed on the bank of what I could now see was a big pond, and I realized that it was a gravel pit. The rain drummed hollowly on the tin roof of the shed and a cold, salt-laden wind blew through it, bringing with it the distant murmur of the sea on a shingly shore. He used his torch. It fell on the mini-van. He got in behind the wheel.

'You'll both have to cram into the front seat,' he said. 'The back's full. Take Sonia on your knees.'

I'd have preferred to take her by the scruff of her neck, but there was nothing for it. I opened the other door and a rich ripe smell assailed us—of fish. The back of the van was piled high with wooden trays. We squeezed inside, and notwithstanding the discomfort of it, it was good to get out of the cold wind, and close up Sonia was warm and smelled nice. He started up and backed out, then went off down the track. I was bursting with questions but the overladen little van was making heavy weather of it in the mud, roaring its head off in low gear, and anyhow my mouth was pressed hard between Sonia's shoulder-blades. We got back on to the road and he went off at a hell of a clip, but the ride only lasted five minutes or so, for which I was thankful, because although Sonia wasn't a heavyweight, my legs were rapidly going to sleep. We stopped again and extricated ourselves, and I saw we were in another shed—a sort of lean-to arrangement, and the stink of fish was even stronger, and there were more wooden trays stacked tidily along two sides of it. A door opened and I saw the bulky figure of a woman outlined against a dim light.

'Look, Malcolm——' I began. His hand shot out and I felt my arm gripped.

'The name's George, you bloody fool,' he hissed. 'Just George. My daughter is Jessie, and if I have to address you at all, it will be as Tom. Please remember that—and talk as little as possible.'

'I want to know what's going on,' I demanded.

'And so you will—at the proper time,' he told me. 'Now will you please shut up and wait here.' He crossed to the woman. Sonia had melted somewhere into the gloom.

Malcolm said, 'Tickety-boo?'

'The boys is down at the boat,' the woman answered complainingly. 'They waited as long as they could—but the *tide* don't bloody wait, you know.'

'Orlright, orlright,' Malcolm said. 'I haven't been picking daisies for the bleeding fun of it. How'm I going to get the stuff down?'

'The 'andcart's there,' the woman told him. 'But be quick about it, for Cri'sake. It'll be light soon and the coastguards will be manning the tower.' She sniffed loudly and closed the door, cutting off what light there was and leaving us in complete darkness.

'Come on,' said Malcolm briskly in his own voice. 'Help me get the van unloaded. Sonia, hold the torch.' He opened the rear doors and started dragging out the fish-trays. They were piled right to the ceiling, but there weren't many of them—just a wall one tray thick in the front and rear.

In the intervening space there were two men—coiled serpentinely heads and tails and squashed in tight—very tight—because you know how small a mini-van is. They were very still, and I couldn't see their faces. But Malcolm could see mine and it evidently was a study.

'Don't stand there goggling, man,' he commanded. 'Help me get 'em out—and be careful with this one. He's still alive.' He leaned into the van and pulled one of the heads round. 'No, my mistake. The other's our man.'

I heard Sonia say in tones of deep reproach, 'Oh, Father—no?' as if she were taking him to task for spilling mustard on the clean tablecloth.

'*I* didn't kill him,' Malcolm said. 'It was that creature Wates. He lost his head and threatened me with a gun. Chaworth jumped at him, and the fool pulled the trigger and got one of his own people. Come on—out with them.'

He got hold of the twisted forms and hauled. I was beyond coherent speech by this. I was almost beyond thought. I was just moving mechanically under his directions. We slid them out. One, a heavily built man in a gaberdine raincoat, had stiffened into the shape of a question mark and was difficult to handle. The other, slighter and dressed in blue battledress trousers and a windcheater, was more supple, and he groaned faintly as we moved him.

'A thiopentone injection, followed by a massive dose of paraldehyde,' Malcolm said conversationally. 'It will hold him for at least another two hours. Excellent stuff. Now where the hell is that handcart?'

We found it outside the shed and we wheeled it in and strained and heaved to get the two of them on to it. There was some tattered tarpaulin in one corner. Malcolm tore off a hunk of it and covered them.

'Right,' he said briskly. 'Outside and straight down the beach path. If we pass anybody, let me do the talking.'

We trundled the cart out. The sky had lightened perceptibly to the east and I could see that the shed was built on to the side of a house formed by a couple of old railway coaches, and that there were other similar houses scattered irregularly over the wide shingle strip that ran down to the shore. Away to our right was a huge concrete building that looked vaguely like the Battersea powerhouse.

'The nuclear power-station,' Malcolm told me. He was still being brisk but his earlier testiness had passed. 'Biggest of its type in the world. It makes one proud to be British.' And it sounded so off-beat under the circumstances that I giggled like a fool, which was a good thing because it helped me throw off the almost cataleptic trance in which I seemed to be moving.

The wheels of the handcart were sinking in the shifting shingle and it was hard work to keep it going. Sonia came up and lent her strength to it and then we were at the top of a steep slope and the tumbling surf was at the bottom, and we could see the bulk of a boat in the shallows. In fact we could see several boats, some already under way puttering out to sea on their noisy diesels, and others, like the one immediately in front of us, still half aground—the nearest a bare fifty yards away. Men with hurricane lanterns were moving about the decks of most of them.

Malcolm said, 'Keep the wretched cart moving or it will bog down,' and ran forward into the loom of the nearest boat, and as we toiled and shoved we heard him talking in a low tone to somebody. We panted to a stop at the water's edge. The boat was a sturdy, bluff-bowed fifty-footer, towering high above us. Somebody let down a rope ladder. Malcolm said, 'Up you go, Jessie,' and without a word she climbed up nimbly and vanished over the bows. A rope came snaking down. 'Give me a hand,' he said, and we got the end secured under the arms of the live one. Malcolm whistled softly and the rope jerked tight, took the strain and bore the chap aloft, then, after a few moments, it came snaking down again.

'They'll probably be a little awkward about this one,' Malcolm said as we made fast. 'It's not in the contract, and they're law-abiding people. You might have to pay anything up to a couple of hundred extra.' He whistled again, and the grotesque bundle swayed aloft, twisting obscenely against the rapidly lightening sky. I felt a little queasy.

'And now,' Malcolm said briskly, 'what money are you carrying?'

'About nine quid,' I told him and he tut-tutted again irritably. 'You can't blame me,' I went on. 'How did I know you were doing it tonight?'

'I had no choice,' he said. 'I'll tell you all about it later. Meantime, what about funds? You've got an awful long way ahead of you, and in this business everybody wants paying on the nail.'

'What the hell can I do about it now?' I demanded angrily.

'It's no good losing your temper,' he said primly. 'How *were* you to be financed?'

'I can draw what I want from a bank in London,' I said. 'I'd better go back, and join you later.'

He shook his head vigorously. 'That would mean leaving Sonia to make the crossing with the goods alone.'

'Aren't you going?' I asked.

'I can't disappear from my business just like that,' he said. 'That would be inviting suspicion. I must be back in town before my usual opening hour. I've got to keep to my ordinary pattern—attend to routine matters—brief my assistant—go down and see my wife—then leave on a normal business trip. All that will take at least three days. I should be able to join you on Wednesday.'

'What the devil do I do in the meantime?'

'Leave it to Sonia. She knows exactly where to go the other side. Can you depute your drawing powers at the bank to me?'

I thought hard for a moment, then nodded: 'I'll get through to somebody by telephone,' I said. 'They'll get in touch with you. But what about these boat people? Won't *they* want paying on the nail?'

'They've had half. They get the rest on completion, though, as I say, they'll probably want a little more on account of our departed friend—but you can leave all that to me.'

A voice from above said hoarsely, 'Hey! What the hell's going on down there? Think we've got all day?'

'Coming,' Malcolm called, then added hurriedly to me, 'You shouldn't have any trouble with Carter when he comes round—*provided he thinks he's going to the Russians.* As far as he's concerned *you* know nothing. You're just an underling. Play it off the cuff, Wainwright—as intelligently as possible.'

'I'll do my damnedest,' I said, and hoped it sounded sufficiently sarcastic. 'You're the one that'll have to do the cuff-playing, though. There *were* two of them watching your place—Russians, we think. They followed us in a car, but Sonia shook them and they crashed near Maidstone.'

Far from worrying him, it seemed to afford him some satisfaction, because I heard him chuckle and murmur something about always being right in these matters. The old devil was certainly playing it cool, I'll say that for him.

He climbed the ladder, and I followed. The oil-skinned figures were waiting for us—one very tall, the other short, stout and choleric. The boat was flush-decked from high bows to blunt transom, broken only by a winch, a square hatchway amidships, a stumpy mast and a cramped wheelhouse aft. Sonia was nowhere in sight.

The short man said furiously, 'What's the bloody caper, George? One of 'em's a stiff.'

'Sorry, mate,' Malcolm said. 'They rung him in on me. What was I to do? Leave him on the road?'

'That's your pigeon. I'm not having him on my boat——'

'Well, I'm not taking him back to the Smoke. What if I was stopped? Blimey!'

'It's not right,' the short man complained, and appealed to me. 'Is it?'

I said, 'Ah' profoundly, and scratched my chin.

'Get 'im orf,' said the short man.

'And leave him on the beach?' Malcolm asked. 'Up to you, of course, but I shouldn't have thought it advisable myself.' And the short man chattered with rage. His mate looked gloomily over the rail, spat, and said, 'The bloody tide'll be 'aving the 'andcart next.' It was only that which settled matters. Malcolm swung down the ladder and rescued it, hauling it up the shingle slope.

'Give us a hand to shove off,' the short man growled. He went aft and opened up the idling diesel in reverse, then we pushed against the shingle with a thing like an overgrown barge-pole, and slid off into deep water. The taller one jerked his thumb at the hatchway.

'Better get below, mate,' he said. 'We only got two of a crew, and you don't look like neither of us.'

I dropped down over the coaming and found myself in a fish-hold which ran from the bows to a bulkhead about two-thirds of the length back. There was a door in the bulkhead and a light the other side. I looked through into a cluttered and smelly cabin which extended the breadth of the boat. It had a couple of rough wooden berths, a table, a form, and an iron stove. A ladder led up into the wheel-house and a door abaft of it gave access to the engine-room. Sonia sat at the table, hunched into her raincoat, looking sulky and resentful.

A man lay on one of the berths. I recognized the blue trousers and windcheater, and crossed to look at him closer. His eyes were still closed but he seemed to be breathing more naturally, and I had the impression that he was beginning the long climb back to consciousness. I looked round the cabin but could not see the other, and I gathered with relief that they had had the delicacy to put him out of sight somewhere in the fish-hold.

The boat had completed its sternward swing and was now headed offshore and was feeling the long ground-swell. I tried to look out through one of the small portholes which were now greying with the dawn, but they were salt-grimed and opaque. For the want of something to break the silence I offered Sonia a cigarette, but she shook her head and turned away from me. I lit one myself and tried once or twice to make something that resembled normal conversation, but it was no good, so I gave it up and stood on the table and looked out of the open skylight.

The wind had dropped a little and it was no longer raining, though there was promise of more to come in the lowering clouds sweeping up from the south-west. The sun was just appearing over the eastern horizon, gilding the Dover cliffs far away on our port beam. This part of the Channel looked as busy as Piccadilly. The other fishing boats were fanning out and there was a round dozen deep-sea freighters and tankers hove to, picking up and dropping their pilots off the Dungeness Trinity House station, with probably twice as many coasters beating up and down the Channel further off-shore. The boat was beginning to dance now in the short, sharp chop and I had to brace myself against the edge of the skylight. From the wheelhouse just in front of my position I heard the bleeps of the seven o'clock BBC time signal, and strained my ears for the news that would follow, but then somebody below banged my leg to attract my attention.

CHAPTER EIGHT

IT WAS THE TALL MAN. He was holding up a battered kettle and an untidy newspaper bundle to me as I looked down at him.

'A drop of tea like,' he said hospitably. 'And some nice cold bacon sandwiches.'

Sonia exited rapidly from the swaying cabin, her hand over her mouth, and I was louse enough to feel malicious satisfaction. You just can't be superior and seasick at the same time. I climbed down and joined him and we sat each side of the table and ate and drank in silence. He saw me straining my ears to catch the newscast from the wheelhouse, so he obligingly went up the ladder and turned the volume up.

'. . . the prisoners watching television until eight-thirty. Carter, who had been doing some clerical work in his unlocked cell on the third floor of J Block, was not missed when prisoners returned to their cells and were locked in for the night, because of a note on his table which stated that he had gone to the catering office to complete some entries in the ration ledger, so it was not until the night duty officer noticed his still-unlocked door at ten o'clock that a check was made. It is still not known how, or from what point, he actually made his escape, and Scotland Yard states that the possibility of his still being inside lying low in some hiding place cannot be ruled out. Meanwhile the search is being stepped up by the Metropolitan Police and all county forces, while sea and air ports are under the closest surveillance. It is expected that the Home Secretary will make a statement when the House reassembles on Tuesday next and will have to face some searching questions from Opposition members. A report that Carter was seen leaving a plane in Warsaw and boarding another for Moscow has been discounted . . .' He went on with the rest of the news and mentioned, without apparent connection with the main item, an accident on the A.20 near Maidstone involving a car and a lorry, in which a man had been killed and another seriously injured and was still unconscious. No names were given.

So, I realized with relief, unless the bland tone of the announcer was masking some really deep skulduggery on the part of the police, we were in the clear—so far. We didn't deserve it. The planning and carrying out of this operation would have disgraced an unpaid-acting lance-corporal on a field exercise.

The tall man finished his doorstep sandwich, swilled it down with tea, belched and pointed over his shoulder with a scarred and spatulate thumb.

'Nothing about 'im,' he said.

'Who?'

' '*Im.* The stiff. Looks like George got away with it again.'

'George didn't kill him,' I said, more to dissociate myself from it than to defend Malcolm.

'Don't matter who done it,' the tall man said. ' 'E's 'ere and we'd rather 'e wasn't. You'll 'ave to put 'im over the side as soon as it's dark.'

'Couldn't you do that?' I asked.

'Not bloody likely. We don't want nothing to do with that side of it, mate. For God's sake see he's got nothing on him that can be checked—just in case he comes up again.'

I shivered slightly. 'Where is he now?'

He pointed with his thumb again, to the fish-hold. I went through reluctantly. Sonia was hunched miserably on an upturned fish-tub under the open hatch. Past her, up in the nose of the boat I could see something under a tarpaulin.

I said, 'I've got an unpleasant job to do. If you'd rather go back to the cabin——'

She rose and pushed past me through the door without a word. I went forward and pulled the tarpaulin aside. It was very difficult to search him because he was now completely rigid, but there's a drill for it, and I went over him as thoroughly as I'd have done a fellow student at the school under the critical eye of an instructor. This fellow had been a professional all right. There wasn't a thing on him as far as I could see that could point to his possible identity, unless one counted the gun tucked tightly into his waistband. That was Belgian but good, a snub barrelled 9 mm, which told me exactly nothing. His pockets yielded seven pounds in a plastic wallet, a fountain pen, a packet of cigarettes, a cheap lighter, four and eightpence in loose change, an unbroken carton of twenty-five rounds for the gun—from which the label had been torn—and a dirty handkerchief. His clothes were the sort you could buy in any one of a thousand chain tailors, but even so the tags had been carefully picked out.

I kept the gun and the ammunition but replaced the rest of the stuff in his pockets. Maybe the money would have been useful later, but somehow I couldn't face sticking to it. Then I covered him up again, quickly, and went back into the cabin. Sonia had taken my place on the table with her head out of the skylight, for which I was thankful because her company was beginning to pall on me as much as mine, no doubt, was on her. Carter was stirring in his berth. I crossed over to him.

His eyes were wide open, the pupils contracted to pin-points, and his mouth was working drily. I got water from a bulkhead beaker, washed out a tea mug and gave him a drink. He was violently sick. Sonia looked down at us from her perch and turned a pale shade of green. Carter went to sleep again.

We stood up and down in mid-Channel all that day. It was too rough for trawling so they codlined with half-mile lengths of rope with hundreds of baited hooks on them. I would willingly have gone up and helped them in order to get out of that ghastly cabin, but the other boats were all round us and the short man wouldn't hear of it, although he relented to the extent of letting Sonia sit on a box in the wheelhouse. Carter awoke again during the afternoon, looked around vaguely and took another drink. He wasn't sick this time but he certainly showed no desire to talk, and eventually went off once more into a deep sleep. The tall man warmed up stew on the stove and made tea from time to time, and I listened to further news bulletins, which had nothing fresh to offer, and somehow we got through that seemingly endless day.

I went up on deck through the fish hatch when darkness had fallen completely, and leaned on the bulwarks enjoying the breeze, which had freshened considerably, although it was doing nothing to dispel a heavy sea mist which was creeping up from the south. The tall man came out and got a rope rove through a block on the stumpy foremast. He nudged me and muttered that I'd find some net weights down below, then left me to it and went and joined the others in the wheelhouse. I took the running end of the rope and dropped down into the hold. It was now knee-deep in still-wriggling fish and as dark as the pit. I slipped and slithered all over the place but finally got the rope fastened around him, then I climbed back on deck and hauled. He jammed hard under the coaming of the hatch once, and I had to drop down again to free him, then once again to grope round among that damned fish until I found some lead things like crude dumb-bells. They weighed about twenty pounds each, I reckoned, and somehow I managed to get four of them fastened to his ankles with some odds and ends of cordage, but then I had the very devil of a job to lift him up on to the top of the bulwarks. I could see the faces of the two men dimly through the wheelhouse window in the reflected light of the compass, but they didn't want to see me. I slipped on the slimy deck twice and came down hard with the poor devil on top of me, but at last it was done and he went over the side and out of sight into the creaming bow wave. Cold as it was now, I couldn't face that cabin again, so I went up into the nose and sat with my back against the winch and wondered dully who he was, what he got paid and why the hell he, I, or any other of the faceless ones did it anyhow.

I went to sleep before I had worked out any of the answers.

It was Sonia who wakened me eventually. I was cold, stiff and wet, though somebody had had the decency to cover me with a piece of canvas. She shook my shoulder and I sat up. She handed me a mug of tea without a word. The fog had closed down solid now and I couldn't see the length of the boat. The wind had died and we were hardly moving. Somewhere in the distance a foghorn moaned at intervals, while nearer, a bell clanged monotonously.

I gulped the tea gratefully. It was laced with rum and it pulled me together.

I said, 'What's the score?'

'They're putting us ashore here.'

'Where's "here"?'

'They say we're just to the west of Dieppe.'

'And we have to get to——?'

'Le Havre. That's about a hundred kilometres further along the coast.'

'Three foreign scarecrows stinking like the Billingsgate fish markets! No passports and damned little money! How far do you think we'd get before we had every cop in Northern France on our tails?' I climbed to my feet and started to grope my way aft. 'I'm going to have it out with them. They either take us closer to Le Havre or they won't collect the balance of their fee.'

'You can try it,' she said tiredly, and followed me.

But I was just butting my head against a brick wall. They wouldn't even listen to me, and looking back I can't say that I really blamed them, because now they had their hands full. Another bell-buoy was clanging on our starboard beam, and high above us where the fog was thinner we could see the reflected flash of a lighthouse beam. The diesel was throttled down to a throaty whisper and we were inching forward at a snail's pace, the short man crouched over the wheel, the other now up in the bows with a lead line.

I gave it up and went down below to thaw out at the stove.

Carter was sitting at the table. There was only a smoky oil lamp, and that was on the bulkhead behind him, so that his face was in shadow.

I said, 'How are you feeling?'

He didn't answer for a moment or so, as if he were sizing me up and searching for words, but when he did speak his voice was clear enough and he had no trace of foreign accent.

'Not too bad,' he said. 'But I'd be happy to know a little of what's going on.'

'We're going ashore,' I told him. 'Then we've got some travelling ahead of us—to a place where you'll be lying low for a bit.'

'And then?'

I shrugged. 'Don't ask *me*, cocker. Somebody else will be taking you over, I expect.'

'Why was I drugged?' he asked.

'Search me,' I said. 'I took you over like that on this boat. I've got to get you to somewhere. That's all I know—that's all I want to know.'

'I'm sorry,' he said, very quietly, 'but that's not good enough. I was told the form in prison, and what to expect, but now something totally different has happened—and I've a right to know why. I remember a fight starting just after we came over the wall. Somebody used a gun—then this needle was shoved into my arm and I passed out——'

'Passed out is right,' I said shortly. 'You passed out of the nick, so what the hell have you got to belly-ache about?'

'I want to know *who* got me out of the nick,' he insisted, 'and where I'm being taken to—and what my ultimate destination is to be. Unless that is made clear, here and now, I'm not prepared to go a step further.'

'Suits me,' I said, and hoped that I sounded like a reasonable man who had done his best under trying circumstances but was now prepared to wash his hands of the whole affair. 'Stay on the boat and go back with them. They'll dump you somewhere on the English coast and then get the hell out of it—and you'll be back inside within a couple of hours.'

'I'd prefer that to——' he began, then broke off.

'To what?' I asked.

'To, shall we say, travelling further with the wrong people—to the wrong place.' And I knew he meant it—and that his suspicions were fully aroused. This fellow was nobody's fool. He knew what to expect if he was, in fact, being shipped back to the Chinese. Nothing we could do to him would be worse than that. He also knew that being shanghaied unconscious aboard a boat was one thing; being made to travel unwillingly in a civilized country was quite another. He had only to sit down now and refuse to budge, to call my bluff. I could have pulled the gun on him and threatened him, but I felt he'd call that bluff too. His worth was alive, on the hoof—and he knew it. I thought of pleading with him, but I knew that would be worse than useless. Then, just as I was about to fall back on the well-worn gambit of sweet reason and a cigarette, Sonia came down the ladder from the wheelhouse. She looked sulky and tired and her face was dirty and her hair was a draggled mess. Anything less like Lola the beautiful spy I've never seen.

She said to me in English, 'Get up on the deck. They want your help to get the boat over the side.' Then she went off into rapid Russian to Carter—so rapid that it left me floundering, though I did catch something to the effect that Carter shouldn't discuss things with sub-human criminal pigs like me. I was only a hired courier, and not a very efficient one at that. And she was doing it perfectly. I grunted and climbed into the wheelhouse. All lights were doused now, but I could feel the short man's sweating nervousness even in the pitch dark.

He said, 'Give me mate a hand to get the inflatable dinghy overside. You can trail a line and we'll haul it back when you've landed——'

But we were saved the trouble. There was a startled yell from the tall man in the bows, and an unprintable blast from the other as the boat struck.

It wasn't a hard strike—just a gentle crunch as her bows ploughed into the shingle beach, but it whipped these two into panic.

'Over the side, you bastards—all of you,' yelled the short man, and Sonia came up the ladder fast, cannoning into us in the darkness, and whatever she had been saying seemed to have been convincing, because Carter followed on her heels. We felt our way forward to where the tall man was pushing off frantically with the barge-pole. Behind us I could hear the diesel being revved up hard in reverse. I didn't waste time looking for the ladder. I just jumped, and yelled to the others to do the same. The drop must have been about twelve feet, and I landed awkwardly, lost my footing and finished on my back in about eighteen inches of exceedingly cold water. And as if that was not sufficient, Sonia, then Carter, landed on me as I tried to get up.

We staggered up on to the beach, spitting salt water and obscenity. Behind us, unseen in the fog, the boat was high-tailing it for deep water. I hoped the bloody thing would hit a rock.

I've never experienced anything quite so bewildering as that fog. It had blanketed us on the boat, but at least one could feel one's way along the bulwarks there. Here there was nothing but the crunch of shingle underfoot and the soft lap of the water behind us that was now covering the receding beat of the diesel. It was only that which gave us direction. We walked away from it until we found ourselves among loose rocks, then hard up against a sheer cliff. Sonia turned left—why, I don't suppose even she knew, because it was anybody's guess now. Anyhow, we followed dumbly and blindly, and after a time I stumbled over a concrete ramp jutting out from the cliff bottom, and it was surmounted by an iron rail. We climbed on to it and found that it was the foot of a path leading upwards, so we toiled onwards until suddenly and dramatically we came out of the fog into the clear. We were about halfway up the cliff, and above us a lighthouse stabbed the darkness four times, waited, then flashed again twice, waited, then repeated. Professional sailors and keen yachtsmen know the flashes of all the Channel lights, I believe. None of us was either, so we were none the wiser until finally we reached the top and found ourselves on a road. There was a signpost here and in the flashes of the lighthouse we read that Veules-les-Roses was six kilometres to our left and St Valéry-en-Caux two the other way. We chose the latter by common consent, mainly, I think, because it was downhill.

It was getting light and the fog below the cliffs was clearing with the dawn, and I was getting increasingly nervous now that I could see the others. Carter and I each had three days' growth of beard. With his windcheater he might have passed as a hippy —but his hair wasn't long enough to sustain the role. I, on the other hand, must have looked just what I was—a gent who had started out in a decent suit and overcoat but had spent a couple of nights in the hold of a dirty little fishing boat and had been dropped in the sea at the end of it. Sonia, also, was looking terrible. The three of us together would have attracted unwelcome attention anywhere. And to make matters worse Carter was beginning to have trouble with his feet and I noticed for the first time that he was wearing flimsy prison hospital slippers and they weren't standing up to the strain. A signpost on the outskirts of the village which told us that Le Havre was seventy-four kilometres off was the last straw. Carter sat down in the ditch and started to vomit, which gave me the opportunity to take matters up with Sonia.

'We'll have to get under cover somewhere before the local law is about,' I said, and for once she didn't give me a sour answer. She just nodded and said we'd better get down to the seafront.

We walked on through the village. It was set in a chine running down to a tiny harbour between towering cliffs and it would no doubt have been picturesque had we been in the mood to appreciate it. We passed an old woman carrying two milk churns on a yoke who twisted her head round like an ancient tortoise and stared at us, but she was the only one astir in the single street, although below us on the quay we could see fishermen moving about. We skirted round the harbour to avoid them, and reached the wide plage which stretched for miles ahead of us to the west, and walked along the hard clean sand—and then had our first break. We saw a cluster of small wooden beach chalets nestling in the curve of the cliff, deserted and heavily shuttered for the winter. We crossed to them and I went from one to the other cursing the French habit of fitting shutters like the doors of bank vaults. But there's an Achilles' heel to most propositions if you take the trouble to look for it. The window frame of one of them had warped sufficiently for me to get my fingers in and wrench the gap wide enough for the slim hand of Sonia to reach the bolt inside. We climbed in and pulled the shutters closed.

It was a single-roomed place, cluttered with the usual beach gear—deckchairs, mattresses and umbrellas, overlaid with a pall of dust that showed that it had not been disturbed for a long time. It matched my mood. There is something unutterably miserable about summer toys laid up for the winter. Carter staggered across to a corner and lowered himself painfully on to a mattress. He looked dreadfully ill and he was shivering like a wet dog. I helped Sonia drag out another mattress to cover him, and I stood looking down at him helplessly. She caught my eye and moved away to the window and climbed back outside. I started to follow her but then realized that she probably wanted a few minutes' decent privacy, so I dumped myself down on another mattress.

I would have to have things out with her when she returned, I decided. This was ridiculous. The whole thing was falling apart. Here we were stuck out in the blue, miles from anywhere, with a sick man who was going to get a damned sight sicker unless we did something for him pretty soon. But what could we do? Three scarecrows who would invite questions from the first rustic gendarme we ran into—no French money, passports—no anything. If I could have seen any way whatsoever out of the mess at that moment, even the base one of quitting cold and leaving them to it, I'd have taken it. We shouldn't have left the boat, I reflected savagely. We should have gone back with them and forced them to hide us up until things could have been arranged properly.

But even in misery there are priorities. Obviously our first was French money. With that I could at least go out after dark and make a call to London. But who to in London? I'd been virtually fired by the Gaffer, so he was out. There was always the bank, of course, though I shuddered at the time lapse that would mean —but money was the first thing. I'd have to change my few pounds to francs. It would be asking for trouble to attempt to do so here in the village. Le Havre—that was it. Spruce up a bit as best I could and thumb a lift in——

But that was as far as I got. I remember thinking that Sonia had been gone a long time, and that was all. Except for uneasy catnaps on the wet deck I had not slept for forty-eight hours. I must have gone out like a light.

I woke stiff and chilled. It was getting dark. I sat up and looked round. Carter was thrashing around on his mattress, muttering deliriously—but there was no sign of Sonia. I peered round the cabin, then climbed out of the window. No sign of her out there either. So the bitch had quit. The thought that I had been ready to do just that myself was no comfort.

Well—that was it. I'd have to extricate myself as best I could. But what about Carter? I couldn't leave the poor devil here to die. An anonymous call to the police once I had put a reasonable bit of distance between myself and this ghastly place——?

I was turning this over when I saw the two figures approaching along the darkening beach.

CHAPTER NINE

One of them was Sonia, and my first thought was that she'd got herself pinched and had brought the law back with her, but the other turned out to be a silent gent in a plastic mac and a beret, carrying a basket.

She said: 'How is he?'

'Not too bright,' I told her. 'Where the hell have you been?' But she didn't think that worth answering. She climbed through the window, and we followed. There was just enough light to see Carter. He was still muttering. She knelt beside him and felt his forehead and his pulse, then she gestured for the basket.

She took a bottle of brandy and a metal cup from it and raised his head and got a little of it between his lips. It was probably the wrong thing since he was in a burning fever, but it did seem to pull him round a little. She passed me the bottle then, and I took a double swallow too quickly and nearly choked. It certainly pulled *me* together. She rose to her feet and said, 'We've got to get him along the beach. We've got a car waiting by the harbour wall.'

'Fine,' I said. 'But who's "we"?' I jerked my head at the silent one.

'Suppose we leave that for the moment,' she said impatiently. 'Help me to get him up.'

We raised Carter to his feet, but his legs buckled under him, and the other man and I had to lift him bodily through the window. Outside she made me put my overcoat round him, then we got one arm over each of our shoulders and half carried him. I was bursting with questions but she didn't volunteer anything and I assumed she didn't want to talk in front of the other man, so we walked the mile down the beach in silence—a weird-looking quartet, although by some feminine miracle Sonia had managed to tidy herself up considerably. It was raining hard again when we got to the harbour, which was all to the good because not a soul seemed to be out. We came up to a battered black Citroën in the shadows, and eased Carter into the back seat. Sonia got in beside him and I rode in the front with the other fellow. We drove soberly up through the village on to the clifftop road, then he put his foot down hard and he had us in the outskirts of Le Havre in something under the hour.

I tried, mainly as an exercise to get my fuddled wits to work again, to keep track of the turns we made after entering the town, but it was hopeless. We finished up down in the dock area, bumping over railway lines and waiting for swing bridges to be lowered for what seemed nearly another hour, until finally he dropped us off in a narrow street running up from the Quai Colbert. Sonia and I took Carter's arms again but I noticed that she made no move until the tail-light of the car had disappeared in the rain, then she led us along the street a hundred yards and took an even narrower turning between two warehouses. There was a group of high-fronted stone houses squeezed into a cramped square at the end, through which I could see the arched gateway of a military barracks. The corner house was a café, the next was a laundry, the others might euphemistically have been called hotels. Two military policemen came out of the café, frog-marching a drunken soldier. They had their hands full, but one of them still managed to pinch Sonia's bottom as they passed. She said something unprintable in French and they laughed and offered to swop drunks as theirs seemed the lighter. Down in this belt we were right in character.

We turned up the steps of the fourth house. There was a light in the basement kitchen but the windows above were dark. I stood holding Carter upright while Sonia fumbled for a bell-push. We waited, the rain trickling down my neck, Carter swaying and threatening to buckle at the knees again and Sonia jabbing angrily at the bell. Then it was opened by somebody I couldn't see in the dark but who smelt of onions and musty clothes. Sonia muttered something I couldn't catch, then we were inside and the door was closed behind us and somebody switched on a light. We were in a narrow and indescribably filthy hallway from which bare wooden stairs with broken banisters ran up beyond the feeble glow of the single bare electric bulb hanging from the ceiling. An old woman in black with a face like a sick and vicious marmoset pointed up the stairs and held up three fingers. We went up, having more difficulty with Carter and stumbling in the darkness until we reached the third and top floor. A door opened letting light out on to the landing and another woman, as old perhaps but not so simian as the first, motioned us to come in.

Surprisingly, there was nothing squalid about this room. It was a plainly but comfortably furnished sitting-room, and a glass-fronted anthracite stove gave out a welcome heat. The woman took us through another door into a bedroom and told us to get Carter undressed. I knew enough French to realize that it wasn't her native tongue either. She stood watching us as we stripped the sodden clothes from him and laid him on the bed, then she came forward with a large bath towel and massaged him with it from head to foot, competently and quickly. She even produced pyjamas and helped us get him into them. Then she got some aspirin between his chattering teeth and we left him to it. Looking back at him as we came out of the room I found myself almost envying him. All he had to do was to lie there and let somebody else do the worrying.

The woman showed us into another room opening off the

landing. It was a bedroom furnished like the first one, with a huge double bed, and there were more pyjamas here and a couple of dressing-gowns, draped frankly on a his'n'hers basis on the turned-down sheets. Sonia asked curtly for yet another room, but the woman shrugged and said this was the limit of her available accommodation—unless m'sieur cared to sleep with the sick man, or perhaps share a room downstairs with an Algerian gentleman. But at least there was a bathroom of sorts with plenty of hot water. Sonia told me to take it first and shook her head impatiently and went out with the woman when I tried to be polite. So I stopped being polite and soaked for a glorious half hour. And there was even a razor and a new toothbrush there.

I came back to the bedroom with a towel round my waist. My wet and stinking clothes had gone, but my possessions had been placed on the dressing-table, even to the gun and ammunition I had taken from the dead man, although her ·22 which I had been carrying had disappeared. I put on the dressing-gown and went back to the sitting-room. There was brandy and a packet of English cigarettes on the table. I helped myself to a stiff snort and went through to look at Carter. He was sleeping peacefully. Somebody had taken his clothes away also. Behind me I heard a chink of crockery. The woman was setting a meal on the table. There was a cassoulet in an earthenware pot that was giving off a rich spicy steam that started the drools running down my chin, cheese, crusty bread and a bottle of wine. Sonia came in behind her. She was pink and flushed from a hot bath and had changed into the other dressing-gown, but she still looked deathly tired. The woman left without a word, closing the door behind her. I poured a brandy and passed it to Sonia, but she shook her head and helped herself sparingly to wine. We were both ravenous and neither of us spoke during the meal, but when we had finished, the silence became uncomfortable.

I said: 'How did this miracle happen?'

'Quite simply,' she answered tonelessly. She lit a cigarette. 'I went out and made a reverse charge call to these people. They sent the car.'

'Who are they?'

She lay back in her chair and closed her eyes. 'Does it matter? People my father has had dealings with before. We are safe here until he gets in touch with us.'

'Why didn't you tell me what you were going to do?'

'Because I was tired of arguing. I'm still tired. You had better take the other bedroom.'

'You take it,' I told her. 'I can shake down on the couch in here.' And for once we *didn't* argue. She went through to the bedroom and came back with a blanket and an eiderdown and dumped them on the couch.

She said: 'I think our friend will sleep through until the morning, but if you should hear him stir, you might look in on him. Good night.'

I got to my feet. 'Good night,' I answered. 'I'm sorry you've been dragged into all this. Sorry—but at the same time very, *very* grateful. I wasn't doing so well on my own.'

She paused with her hand on the door, then turned and looked me straight in the eyes. 'God,' she said quietly. 'If you only knew how I hated you. You and the rest of these jungle animals—on both sides.'

'It's a job that's got to be done,' I mumbled.

'Nonsense,' she said scornfully. 'You choose it. You're all free agents—at the beginning, anyway. You enjoy it. Each miserable little success makes you feel good inside. You get a kick out of being frightened, like children playing dares. But that's not the worst of it. The really sickening part of it is your damned hypocrisy—the way you see yourselves as brave men and patriots. I can understand an honest animal. He's in it for himself alone, but you people use the same methods—lying, cheating, blackmailing—then try and justify it yourselves.'

And she wasn't so far off the beam either, which was why I blew my top.

'Who made you judge and jury?' I shouted. 'What the hell do you know about it, anyhow?'

'You forget. I've been practically brought up in the business,' she said. 'I know. Oh yes—*I* know.'

'And been in on things once or twice,' I spat at her. 'So why put the finger on *me*?'

'I was trapped into it.'

I laughed at her. 'Who's doing the self-justification now?' I asked.

'That's probably what it sounds like,' she said wearily. 'But at least it's true. I saw my father as a Scarlet Pimpernel helping the victims of people like yourself.'

'Sure,' I said. 'Only the Scarlet Pimpernel never got paid for it.'

'And never got blackmailed by his own people either.'

'Don't you believe it,' I said. 'That was only an act. Your father came back into it for exactly the same reasons as you've been ascribing to me—plus the cheque, of course. Anyhow, we're talking in circles. If that's the way you really feel about things why don't you bow out now? As I've already said, I'm grateful for what you've done, but you don't have to stay.'

'I'm staying until my father arrives,' she answered. 'Then I'm taking him home—and I hope I'll never see you again, Mr. Wainwright.'

She went through and closed the door firmly, and I sat on for a time chewing on the cud of my anger and drinking brandy, then I switched off the light and went to sleep.

The grey of a winter's morning was showing round the edge of the blind when I woke. I climbed out of the warmth of the couch with reluctance and went over to the window. A thin, cold sleet was slanting down. Over the roofs of the houses opposite I could see the upper works of ships in the *bassin* on the other side. Down below, on one hand, I could see into the barrack yard where troops in scruffy fatigues were greeting the day like soldiers the world over before breakfast—smoking, gawping, spitting and looking browned off. It made me feel nostalgic for those safe uncomplicated days. The other way pea-jacketed, blue-jeaned dockers were filing in through the dock gates.

I looked at my watch. It was just coming up to seven. I wished I had a transistor to get the news. Sonia's door was still closed, and I hoped it would stay that way for a long time. I'd had enough of that uncomfortable female. I went through to look at Carter. He was still sleeping. I felt his forehead. The fever of the previous night had abated. He looked rather pathetic—thin-faced, pinched round the nostrils and with five days' wispy growth of beard framing a rather weak jaw. I went back to the couch and tried to go to sleep again, but the warmth had gone out of it now, as it had out of the room, because the stove was cold, and anyhow I wanted to pee. I tried the door to the landing but found it was locked.

I felt a surge of blind, insensate fury and started to rattle and kick at it with my bare feet. Sonia's door opened. I turned and glared at her. She pointed to the table and closed the door again. The key was there. She had obvoiusly done what I had neglected to do and locked it during the night. I felt a bloody fool. I crept along the landing to the bathroom.

The woman came up with coffee and croissants and some soup in a teapot for Carter. She laced it with what was left of the brandy and went through to him. Watching her from the door I saw her raise his head gently and feed him through the spout. He hardly woke. She grunted her satisfaction and came away. I asked her about my clothes and she said later, they needed much work, and held her nose, then went.

I saw that there were two cups on the tray and that it must obviously be meant for us both. I didn't know quite what to do, but in the end common courtesy prevailed and I took Sonia's share to the door and knocked. She opened up, looked at the tray, then at me—and then actually smiled her thanks and took it from me. Once again I felt a fool—but also, strangely, a darned sight less gloomy. I almost hoped she'd come out and join me, but she withdrew to her room again.

Our clothes came up at mid-morning, washed, cleaned and pressed. I shaved and bathed, then went into Carter's room and dressed quickly—but Sonia had been quicker, and when I came out again her door was open and she was gone. It didn't matter. I knew what I wanted to do. I was going to find a bureau-de-change, get some French money and make a guarded call to the bank in London. But then I found that my English notes, which I had left on her dressing-table the night before, had gone also. I cursed. Probably she had had the same idea about changing the money and would be back soon, but this was wasting time. Then the woman came up again—and this time she had Charlton with her. I stared at him, pop-eyed.

He waited until the woman had gone down again, then said: 'Man, you're not popular with the Gaffer.'

'All right, Carlovich,' I said. 'I never was. Just give me the message.'

He put a briefcase on the table. 'There's five thousand pounds here. Half in francs, half dollars. You'd better check it.'

'I trust you,' I said sweetly. 'The message.'

'He's to be got aboard the ship——' he began, but then I noticed the open door to Carter's room. He still looked asleep, but I crossed and closed it softly and drew Charlton into Sonia's room.

'Go on,' I said.

'—with less ballsing-up than hitherto—Sorry, his words, not mine—and there'll be orders for you on arrival in Kowloon.' He was enjoying this.

'How does he know I've got him?' I asked.

'My uncle, naturally. He's filled him in on all details.'

'Including the balls-up *he* made in springing the client ahead of the gun?' I asked.

'That couldn't be helped,' Charlton said. 'It was the Rusks who jumped the gun. Wates had everything laid on for that night and they were going to do it on their own. The Gaffer says they've been on to Uncle for weeks, probably—sorry, again his words—through your buggering about. Anyhow, Uncle got wind of it in time and went down and hi-jacked Carter. You know the rest, I believe. Pretty good, I think, considering his age.' He beamed with family pride.

'Pretty good?' I raged. 'Shooting me off cross-Channel without warning—without money—briefing—and loaded with a stiff.'

'But he did send Sonia——'

I said something inexcusable about Sonia and he looked genuinely shocked.

'That's about all, I think,' he said stiffly. 'You know the ship——'

'I don't. That's one of the many things nobody has thought of telling me.'

'The *Nurma*. The captain's a man called Kjaer. She's due in here next Saturday and should be leaving again on Tuesday. You'll have to be careful how you approach him——'

'But surely to God he's already *been* approached?' I said.

Charlton shook his head. 'Unfortunately not. My uncle would have been attending to that here, but now with these new developments——'

'*What* new developments?'

'You haven't given me much opportunity to explain, have you?' he said reprovingly. 'I suggest you listen for a moment. Malcolm is being watched by the Russians very closely. That's only to be expected, of course, and we could take care of it ordinarily, but Special Branch are watching the Russians even more closely, and that could be dangerous——'

And how right he was. We wouldn't give a damn about what the Russians suspected, for the simple reason there was nothing they could do about it officially, but the police were a different proposition. If they smelled a connection between the Russians and Malcolm they'd start digging—and we couldn't stop them.

'—and so you see the Gaffer's point in pulling my uncle right off everything,' Charlton went on. 'He mustn't leave London. He mustn't do a single thing outside his normal round of business. The Russians, of course, know that Sonia is tied up in it somewhere—the Gaffer is *most* upset about your going to the shop to collect her car'—he loved getting that one in—'and *you* must be regarded as compromised as a result, but at least the trail has broken short of this point. The Gaffer thinks that if you stick rigidly to instructions from now on you've still got a chance of bringing things to a successful conclusion——'

I said something inexcusable about the Gaffer also. Since family wasn't concerned he didn't look shocked this time.

'All right,' I said wearily. 'I've got to see this fellow Kjaer when his ship gets in, make a deal with him, get Carter aboard, take him to Hong Kong——'

'Where you'll receive further instructions,' Charlton interrupted. 'I rather gather that those instructions will be to hand over to somebody else, so you have nothing really to worry about.'

'Except explaining my own arrival there out of the blue,' I said. 'Only a minor point, of course, but I'll be expected back by air in the normal way. Friends usually meet one at Kai Tak—there are such things as arrival lists and a social column in the local rag.'

'As you remark,' he said sweetly. 'A minor point. Naturally that will be left to you.' He delved into the briefcase. 'But at least here's your passport.'

'Where the hell did you get it?' I asked, startled.

'From your flat. Where else?' He was pulling flat packs of French and American notes out of the case. 'The Gaffer had it turned over as a matter of routine in case you'd been uncovered and somebody else did it. I don't want a receipt for this money, naturally, but you'll have to account for it sometime. My uncle says a thousand pounds a head for the passages is the correct thing, and don't let Kjaer stick you—and a hundred a week here. The fishing people have been attended to, but I've been asked to clear two points. Did you, in fact, use six lead weights for certain—er—ballasting purposes? They've charged five pounds each, which Accounts think excessive—and meals and drinks on board are down at another thirty.'

'Four weights,' I said spitefully. 'Worth, I should say, five bob each—and meals consisted of three bacon sandwiches, a plate of foul stew and innumerable mugs of tea that tasted of seaboot socks. Call it two pounds, and you're overpaying them.'

'Good,' he said, and rose. 'Now, if I could see Sonia for a moment. I've got her passport and a message from her father.'

'She's out,' I told him, and his eyebrows shot up in pained surprise.

'Do you think that's wise?' he asked.

'Ask her yourself,' I said. 'She certainly didn't ask *me*.'

'She is a little headstrong,' he conceded. 'You'll have to take a strong line with her.'

'Me? Why me? She's all yours, brother, from this point on.' That, in fact, was the only thought that held any sunshine at the moment.

'I'm afraid not,' he said, pursing his lips. 'She goes with you.'

'Not bloody likely,' I said firmly. 'Thanks for the offer, but I can manage on my own.'

'It's not an offer. It's an order.'

'Whose order?'

'The Gaffer's, naturally.'

'I'm not prepared to accept it,' I said, and he looked as if I had blasphemed.

'You are aware of the consequences of that, while you are still serving?'

'Actually I'm not,' I said. 'I'm doubtful whether any consequences could be enforced—particularly since it would appear that I'm being fired after this anyhow. She's not coming with me, that's all.'

He dropped his prissiness. 'Very well, Wainwright,' he said quietly. 'If you really mean that, I take over—and you can find your way back to London. If you've got any doubts about that I'll give you a number you can call for confirmation.'

Call it outraged pride, wounded vanity, pricked conceit—anything you like—but it was that which shot me down. I just couldn't take that. I hadn't shown up too brilliantly so far, admittedly, but that would have been the ultimate humiliation. It must have shown in my face, but I still tried feebly to bluff.

'It's unnecessary—and she'll be another disposal problem in Hong Kong,' I said.

'Just another minor matter,' he said. 'The reason the Gaffer wants her to go with you is because he is afraid the Russians might try a snatch if she shows up in London, or anywhere else in Europe. You know we haven't the facilities for a round-the-clock watch and ward—not without police assistance. On the ship she's out of harm's way until after the swop's made.'

I suppose it made sense. I loathed the idea but, as usual, the bastards weren't giving me any option.

Then Sonia knocked at the door.

CHAPTER TEN

'ALL RIGHT,' I said to Charlton. 'Only you break it to her, and for Christ's sake make it perfectly clear that it isn't *my* idea.' Then I went through to the sitting-room to unlock the door.

'There's a relation of yours in the bedroom,' I said sourly. She pushed past me, looking relieved, expecting no doubt to see her father. I went into Carter's room and closed the door, leaving them to it. He was awake but muzzy. I gave him a drink and he asked peevishly when the hell we would be moving—and where? I soft-talked him and said any minute, but first he had to get his strength back—and in that, at least, I wasn't kidding. He was making progress now, but he was still a very sick man. I don't pretend to any medical knowledge, but I rather guessed that in his weakened condition under that massive anaesthetic and subsequent exposure, he had gone down with pneumonia. It made things simpler for us at the moment, though I wondered how long this would last, as I could sense his unease growing as his wits returned. He said he'd got back all the strength he needed and he wanted a bath. I told him I'd go and get one fixed and made it an excuse to leave.

He said: 'What are the honourable names of your esteemed self and that of your village?'—in perfect Cantonese, but he had timed it badly and I was at the door with my back to him so he missed any reaction that might have shown in my face.

I said: 'Sorry, cocker, I don't speak Russian.'

'The girl does,' he said. 'Where is she?'

'She's around,' I told him casually. 'I'll send her in.' I could feel his eyes fixed on the back of my neck as I went through and closed the door. I hoped it wasn't betraying anything. This fellow, sick as he was, was nobody's goat.

They weren't fighting when I joined them, though Sonia was scowling and Charlton looked as if he'd come through a lively five minutes.

'You've heard this stupid idea, I suppose?' she asked.

'Don't blame me,' I answered. 'Given the choice I'd sooner travel with a lady porcupine. Nothing personal.'

'I'll need to go out and buy some clothes,' she said icily.

'Sonia, you must keep off the streets,' Charlton said earnestly.

'That shouldn't be necessary while that lasts,' I said, nodding at the money on the table.

'Funny man,' she spat. 'My God! Fancy having to put up with that for six weeks.' She went into her bedroom and slammed the door hard.

'That sort of thing doesn't help, if I may say so, Wainwright,' said Charlton severely.

'—— off, Carlovich,' I told him. 'You've said your piece. And tell the Gaffer he can go and ——' and I went into details. Childish, no doubt, but it seemed to help at the moment, particularly since I knew Charlton would report it word for word.

'Neither does gutter filth,' he said with dignity. He gathered up his hat and briefcase and moved to the door. 'One last thing. The Gaffer suggests that it might be a good idea to give our friend the impression that he is being taken the long way round to Vladivostok, as all European routes are dangerous.'

I locked the door behind him and grinned ruefully. He *would* suggest it, and thereby rob me of even that small satisfaction—because I'd already decided to do just that.

What I did then was purely a matter of conditioned reflex. I moved to the window and looked down into the square to watch Charlton leave. One always did that—just in case. And this time, by God, it paid off—or seemed to. He went down the front steps and turned right towards the narrow alley leading to the dock road. I remember reflecting sourly that he was a bright herb to be warning Sonia about going out, because although not conspicuously dressed, he was still too smart for this neighbourhood, and was therefore noticeable. He passed the café at the end of the terrace, walked briskly down the alley and disappeared round the corner. And as he did so a man came out of the café and went off after him. Just a very ordinary man in a very ordinary suit and a beret. Of course he may have been nothing more than that, and this was pure happenstance—but it was something that couldn't be disregarded. It certainly looked as if Charlton was being tailed.

I tapped at Sonia's door. She opened, still angry. I told her, and she stopped looking angry. 'You've been out too,' I reminded her, 'and you came in on Charlton's heels.'

'I wasn't seen,' she said positively. 'Coming or going.'

'How can you be certain of that?' I asked.

'I used the back way. The yard gate opens right by a tram stop. You wait for a tram to halt, open the gate and step on. If nobody gets on with you you're reasonably certain you're not being followed. Coming back you do the same thing in reverse. If anybody gets off with you, or is already hanging about—you go for a walk and lose them. Daddy's been using it for years.' I stared at her. That was one nobody had heard of at the school.

'Why didn't we use it last night, when we arrived?' I asked.

'Cars aren't allowed to. Trams only. In any case it wasn't necessary. The taxi wasn't being followed. I'd made certain of that.'

'So if we've been blown it's that bloody nit who's done it,' I mused. 'I wonder how long *he's* been blown. All right then, let's assume he's been tailed all the way from London—damn, I wish I knew which way he'd travelled.'

'London Airport to Rouen, then he hired a car,' she answered promptly, and added innocently, 'I remembered to ask him. Daddy says one should make that a drill when dealing with low security couriers.'

I didn't hit her. I just swallowed hard—because Daddy was bloody well right, and I'd forgotten to do it.

'Question is, then, was this a single tail or a double?' I asked myself aloud. 'If it's the former the guy will note each place of call and have to whistle up reinforcements to take over. That might take a little time. If it's a double——'

'There's another one holed up somewhere,' she supplied. 'We'll test it if you like.'

'How?'

'I'll go out the front way and you can watch to see if I'm followed.' And she meant it!

I said, 'No, thanks. As it is, they don't know for certain we're here. Your way we'd be giving it to them.'

'Not if I led them a dance and lost them,' she said.

But I turned it down firmly. 'This is a brothel, isn't it?' I asked.

'More or less. The girls are free-lancers who rent rooms here. The clients mostly come from the ships and the barracks.'

'So that means practically anybody can walk in and out?'

'Only if a woman brought him.'

'How would they stop a couple of determined blokes—armed?' I asked.

'There are two Algerian bouncers. If they couldn't cope Madame would have the police round in a matter of minutes. They all pay protection money to the local inspector.'

I looked at her with a new respect. Much as she might inveigh against this business, her father had had an apt pupil in her. She never failed to come up with the answer.

'Could Madame be got at?' I rubbed my forefinger and thumb together.

'Can't everybody, if the price is high enough?' She shrugged. 'But Daddy has always paid well—and he used the place right through the war, with the Gestapo quartered in the barracks practically next door.

'Well, in that case we'd better just play it cool and sit tight,' I said. 'We've got another four days to wait before the ship arrives. It's Carter who worries me. He's getting better, and increasingly more suspicious.'

'Father gave me some stuff in case it should be necessary,' she said. 'But I'd rather not use it if it can be avoided. In his present weakened state it could be very bad for him.' I stared at her, but she was quite serious. It gave me a nasty taste in the back of my throat. It was like a doctor and a hangman discussing the health of a condemned prisoner.

She had brought the English papers in with her. Carter's escape had yielded pride of place to a particularly nasty child murder in the Midlands, but the leader-writers were still screaming, and a retired general was heading a court of inquiry into prison security, while an 'ex-M.I.5 Agent' who naturally preferred to remain anonymous, detailed with meticulous accuracy, and maps, the entire escape route. It was by means, we understood, of a black Jaguar Mark 10 from Lanchester to a disused R.A.F. airfield in Suffolk, thence in a mystery plane flown by an Irishman known as the Mad Squadron Leader, to Warsaw—and Carter was now installed in a dacha outside Moscow waiting to take up translation duties in the Soviet Ministry of Propaganda. The second Russian in the car smash near Maidstone had since died. They, the author was in a position to state, had been a red herring to draw attention away from the real route.

Poor M.I.5. Any bloody liar could claim ex-membership without fear of being disowned, and the more lurid his imagination the greater its feasibility. The writer of this crap, I reflected sourly, would collect more for a couple of hours at a typewriter than I was paid in half a year. Still, more power to his elbow if it threw dust in anybody's eye. But this I doubted. It certainly wouldn't deceive anybody who mattered.

Sonia and I took turns at the window in the forlorn hope of spotting a watcher, but we gave it up after a time by mutual consent. Watchers with turned-down hat brims only read newspapers under the windows of the watched in the movies. This fellow, if there *was* a fellow, would probably be in the café—and if they were doing it properly he'd be relieved from time to time.

Carter started to call querulously at mid-afternoon, so I helped him through to the bathroom and gave him his promised bath and then shaved him. When I got him back to his room Sonia had remade the bed and got him some fresh pyjamas, and he cheered up somewhat. He obviously trusted her more than me. They started to talk in Russian, so I looked bored and went back to the sitting-room, closing the door behind me. He had a light meal later, and then went to sleep again. She came out and joined me.

'Well?' I asked.

'I've told him the truth—with certain variations.'

'Such as?'

'That Wates was working for the Chinese. We got wind of the attempt and snatched him. Wates did the drugging.'

'How did that go down?'

'He appeared to believe it, but one can't tell with a man like that. His real preoccupation is our next move.'

'What did you tell him?'

'That we were awaiting orders.'

'Who does he think we are?'

'He knows perfectly well what *I* am. He picked me as a fellow Mig immediately.'

I jumped at that: 'Shanghai——?' Mig is their own name for expatriate Russians, and Shanghai, after Paris, is where most of them are concentrated. Mig is a contraction of émigré.

'I'm not quite as dumb as that,' she said. 'I've never been to Shanghai, and he could have shot me down within minutes. No, London. Parents dead—brought up by a White grandmother—recruited by Red agents while studying ballet in Paris, now employed on courier and conducting duties—medium security.'

'You mean you volunteered all that?' I jeered. 'He must be laughing his head off. You wouldn't make *low* on that.'

'Nor that dumb either,' she said coldly. 'He wormed it out of me over the course of a couple of hours. I was in and out to him several times during the night while you were sleeping—with the outer door left unlocked.' The bitch had the upper hand again—and she kept it.

'He had no difficulty in placing *you*,' she went on. 'Criminal working purely for the pay cheque. Limited intelligence but good in a rough-house.'

'Yeah. I heard you priming him on the boat,' I said. 'I speak a little Russian myself.'

'So Daddy told me,' she came back. 'Very badly, I understand.' You just couldn't get the last word with her.

The rest of that first day and evening dragged by in much the same way. She'd be quite reasonable, even amiable, for a time then either she or I would say something that the other took umbrage at, and we'd be back at it like a pair of Kilkenny cats. Of course it was nerves, and I think that both of us realized it, but that didn't help.

And, oh God, there was another four days of it ahead before the ship arrived.

I sat up that night, more to rob her of the satisfaction of sneaking back and forth while I was asleep than for reasons of security, because I managed to persuade myself that the man I'd seen leave the café was just one of those things. Madame was mean with the coal, and the stove went out about midnight, so I draped a blanket round my shoulders. Sonia crept through in the darkness once and I said: 'He's all right. I've just looked,' and was childishly pleased when she jumped. I must have dropped off after that.

I awoke as somebody tried to open the door. It was only the softest click but it was unmistakable, and it was followed by a creak from the warped floorboards as whoever it was moved away along the landing. A second door from Carter's room opened on to it, and I'd had the sense to lock that.

I tiptoed through from the sitting-room. Carter was breathing quietly and evenly. I moved to the other door and touched the knob lightly. It turned softly under my hand. The door creaked, as someone evidently tried it with his shoulder then moved away. I went back and collected the gun from the table beside my easy chair, crossed to the landing door, eased the key round and opened it a bare half inch. There was a dim light thrown up the stair-well from the lower landing, and I could see the bulk of a man moving along to the next door—the outer one leading to Sonia's room. He was on his own and his back was towards me. He was small and rattish and was dressed in a pair of dungaree pants and a dirty singlet, and his feet were bare. I motioned him into the sitting-room ahead of me. He started to stammer in bad French that he was looking for the pissoir, but didn't move, so I did, past him and behind him, and I clipped him smartly on the back of the neck with my free hand. He went then, protesting and almost whimpering.

A half-naked tart came up the stairs, saw the gun and started to scream. Sonia came out of her room quickly. She grabbed the tart by the arm and heaved her inside, hissing impolite French. The screams rose in pitch and volume, so Sonia hit her—considerably harder than I'd hit her boy-friend. She stopped screaming and started to snivel. The man was asking in an injured whine whether it was a crime to pee in France? Then Madame came up in a dirty dressing-gown and curl papers. Sonia drew her to one side and they conversed in an undertone and Madame took over, efficiently if somewhat cavalierly. She spat several questions at the girl in French that was too fast for me to follow—shook the answers from her, then backhanded her out on to the landing. She went down the stairs wailing dolorously. Madame told us to wait, and followed her down. The man lapsed into silence—his eyes shifting from me to Sonia and back again, then he delicately brought up the question of the pissoir again. I was about to say something to Sonia, but she signalled me to shut up. I think she was afraid I would speak in English. I prodded the man along to the bathroom. He thanked me with the deepest feeling. He certainly wasn't putting on an act there. His need was of the greatest urgency, and it reassured me a little.

Madame came back with the man's coat and a fistful of papers. They were in Greek and Spanish. She ran a practised eye over them, shrugged and showed them to us. They looked all right to me—but then *my* eye wasn't practised. They were seaman's discharge papers, and pertained to one Yoni Youssakoupolis, engine room greaser, and the photo on them was at least recognizable. His last ship appeared to be the *Santa Sebastiana,* and he'd been paid off in Brest three days previously. Madame spat more questions at him. Brest was a pig of a port, he said plaintively. He'd come up to Le Havre because jobs were easier here. He had quite a good pay-off—a man needed a little relaxation after a long voyage—the lady had picked him up in a bar near the docks—he'd paid fifty francs for the night, plus another ten for the room rent. Where was the crime in this?

Madame drew us into Sonia's room. I stood where I could still see him through the door. She said, 'I *think* he's all right—but it's up to you, mes enfants. His papers are genuine enough—and I know papers. Of course, he *may* be doing a little snooping job for somebody.'

'What about the girl?' I asked.

'Georgette? Been here three years. Hard worker. Her pattern never varies. Four short times and an all-nighter, six days a week,' Madame said with a touch of pride.

'Never on Sundays,' I said like a damned fool, and Sonia looked at me as if I was something that had just crawled from under a flat stone.

'Well, what about it?' Madame said briskly. 'What would you like me to do?'

'What can you do?' I asked.

'I can get him held for riotous behaviour for three days before he appears in court,' she answered. 'Cost you two hundred francs.'

'Can you make that five days?' I asked.

'Cost you another two hundred,' she said promptly.

'He won't be able to get word out to anybody?'

'Completely incommunicado. That's part of the service. Of course another hundred would make it absolutely certain.' The Gaffer would have loved this. He was always moaning about the stolid incorruptibility of our own police.

'Done,' I said.

Madame went off and did some telephoning, and then came back and took the glum Yoni downstairs, and ten minutes later we looked down into the dark square and saw him being hustled off between two gendarmes. I felt sorry for him. He was probably just what he claimed to be, but this was no time to take risks. The door to Carter's room opened. He stood blinking at the light.

'What goes on?' he asked complainingly.

'Nothing to worry about, cocker,' I reassured him. 'Some burk wandering around outside. He's been taken care of. You get back to sleep.'

We got him into bed but he was as restless and petulant as a sick child and kept demanding to know where he was and why he was being held against his will, so in the end Sonia went down and rustled some hot milk from somewhere, but he wouldn't drink it, and when we tried a little mild persuasion it made him vomit. However, he went to sleep then and we tiptoed out and left him. I was feeling a little pleased with myself. I advised Sonia to get back to bed also, and sat down on guard again, feeling and no doubt looking a bit like Horatius on the bridge. It was I who had been on the ball this time, while she slept. She went through to her room looking sour, and slammed the door behind her.

The fag end of that horrible night dragged on and I got colder, stiffer and more miserable every minute. I'd have given my soul for a cup of coffee and I tried to take my mind off it by chain smoking, until my throat and mouth felt like a lime kiln. Then I remembered the hot milk Carter had refused, so I went and got it, and warmed it up a little by burning newspapers in the cold stove. I've eschewed milk since the age of three, but at least this was more palatable than French tap water. It certainly made me sleep. In fact it took a jug of that same tap water plus a series of stinging slaps each side of the kisser to wake me.

Sonia was saying, seemingly from a long way off, 'Couldn't you have just given him your gun and money and let him walk out? Did you *have* to mickey finn yourself as well?'

CHAPTER ELEVEN

SHE SWAM MUZZILY INTO FOCUS. She was standing with her hands on her hips looking down at me, and I've never seen such contempt on a woman's face in my life. Past her I could see Madame moving into range with another jug of water. I got out of my chair hastily and nearly fell flat. It was broad daylight.

'What the hell happened?' I croaked.

'I put something in his milk to quieten him down, and *you* drank it, you bloody fool,' she answered, and Madame murmured something about les Anglais being nice people, but no wonder the General wouldn't let them into the Common Market.

'So he just walked out,' Sonia went on. 'Taking your gun in passing.'

'Clothes——?' I began, but she pointed to the side table where they had been neatly folded after returning from the cleaners, and of course they weren't there.

Please God I'll never go through another five minutes like that again. They spared me nothing—Sonia dealing with me like a vivisectionist working on a live dogfish, and Madame coming in from time to time like a Greek chorus—and when I could take no more and went through to Carter's bedroom to get away from them, there he was in bed, fast asleep. I turned on them, choking and boiling—but they still had me cold.

'That's just what happened,' Sonia said, 'so spare us the righteous indignation. Fortunately he couldn't get the front door unlocked, and the bouncers found him thrashing about in the dark. But he had your gun and he got off two rounds——'

'One of which went through Hassan's foot,' Madame put in. 'That will cost you another two hundred and fifty—plus, of course, yet another two hundred for the police.'

'The shots brought a gendarme,' Sonia explained. 'Our friend demanded to be taken to the Soviet Consulate. We managed to get things straightened out, and he's now under sedation again —but it was touch and go for a time.'

Well, that's the way it was from then on. I sat there like Joe Soap on guard; feeling guilty if I dozed off, although, fair play to her, she let up after a while and urged me to take a proper relief period off from time to time, but I couldn't. I was on edge the whole time. She went out twice, supremely confident, and I found myself almost wishing that she'd run into trouble, or lead a tail back to us, if only to restore my self-respect. But she got away with it each time. She bought some light but serviceable clothes for herself and a list of things I made out for Carter and myself, and on the second day I saw in the shipping columns that the *Nurma* would be berthing at the Didier Dock the next morning.

She inspected me critically before I set out after dark the following evening. The dungarees, jersey and pea-jacket I was wearing were all new, so I'd damped them and rumpled them up a bit, but she thought my face and hands were too pale for a sailor, so she went down and got some permanganate of potash from one of the girls and I washed in a medium solution of it which darkened me down nicely.

'Take the tram at the back gate—the one going downhill,' she told me. 'Get off when you reach the Boulevard François, then walk down towards the outer harbour. The Didier Dock is at the bottom on your right. Coming back, take a No. 8 tram from the Place Vauban, at the top of Boulevard François. This is the eleventh stop. Here's some small change. The fare is fifty centimes.'

I felt like a yobbo being briefed by his mother before going out for an interview for his first job.

'Why don't you give me a cheese sandwich, and wipe my bloody nose for me?' I snarled.

'It's all very necessary,' she said sweetly. 'If I didn't tell you, you'd have to ask directions—and your French, like your Russian, is not terribly good, is it?' Maybe she was right, and I suppose I had asked for it, but, my God, it was galling.

I found my way downstairs and through a filthy kitchen. A dark gentleman sat spitting gloomily on the stove, his foot resting on another chair, bound up like a gouty colonel's. He scowled at me. I assumed him to be Hassan. A fellow who looked like his twin brother loomed up out of the shadows and unlocked the back door, then led me through a cluttered yard to a gate in a high wall. He unbolted it and looked through. Outside was an Arrêt sign, and tramlines ran down a narrow cobbled street. It was again raining and there wasn't a soul in sight. He pointed to a concealed bellpush high under the lintel, then closed the gate again. He waited until we heard the clatter of an approaching tram. He opened the gate and pushed me through. The tram squealed to a halt and I climbed on. It was pretty full, but most of the passengers seemed to be dressed more or less as I was and I felt my nervousness leaving me. It was good to be out again after a week cooped indoors with that hellion.

I got off where she told me and walked downhill to the docks, and found my way to the Didier without difficulty. I saw the *Nurma* in the nearest berth. She was small, clean and streamlined like most post-war Scandinavian freighters, and they were working cargo under decklights. I crossed to her and climbed the gangway. A big blond seaman leaned on the rail at the top. He said 'Yo?' interrogatively and barred my way. I told him that I wanted to see the Capitaine but he shook his head ponderously and told me in French even worse than mine to come back in the morning. I argued that I had an important message for him, and the seaman said fine—give it to him and he'd take it. It wasn't that sort of message, I insisted. I had to deliver it myself—but it got me nowhere. Capitaines didn't see bums out of working hours, apparently. It made me furious. To have got this far and to be balked by a stupid ox like this. I cursed myself for not bringing a letter addressed to the Captain. To have to go back to that damned woman and confess that I couldn't get on board because a sailor wouldn't let me was more than I could face. He had a round, inviting belly and I thought for one desperate moment of bringing my knee up into it and clipping him one as he went down, but there were too many people about. So finally I did what I should have done in the first place, and suborned him with a ten franc note. He pointed over his shoulder to the midship quarters and strolled away aft.

I walked along the deck. A door opened and an officer came out. Past him I saw into a cosy well-furnished saloon where a white-coated Chinese steward was serving food to other officers. I wondered if the captain was one of them, then, as the first man passed me and walked to the rail, I saw he was wearing four gold rings on his cuff. I went up beside him and said, 'Captain Kjaer?' but muffled the pronunciation into 'Kayer' instead of making it rhyme with 'Fire' as it should have done. It seemed to tell him something, because he turned and looked at me sharply, and said, 'Briddish, huh? Naw—we don't have no jobs.' He was a thickset man, built like a Dutch eel barge, with a moon of a face, piggy little blue eyes and almost pure white hair and eyebrows.

I said: 'I don't want a job. I want a passage. I'm willing to pay.'

'You got a passage, mister,' he answered. 'Down the bloddy gangway—for free. We don't have a licence for passengers.'

I turned away from the rail so my back was to the light, and produced a flat wad of American hundred-dollar bills, and riffled the edges with my thumb, like a pack of cards. It must have been the noise that did it, because he certainly didn't turn his head to look. He said: 'Bloddy cold out here. Come and have a drink.'

He led me up a ladder to the bridge deck and into an alleyway that was panelled in polished light wood and smelt cleanly of beeswax. He opened a cabin door and motioned me in with his head. It was panelled like the alleyway, with bright chintz curtains at the ports, and matching covers and cushions on the chairs and settees. A very snug number indeed. He got a bottle of aquavit and glasses from a locker and poured two enormous drinks, then sat down and said, '*Skal*. What that crap you're talking outside? I told you—we don't carry passengers.'

'Then why bring me in here to tell me again?' I asked. '*Skal.*' The stuff tasted like varnish remover but was very warming when it got down.

'Where you want to go—and how much are you thinking of?' he said. 'Not that I'm open for business.'

'Hong Kong—and a thousand a head,' I answered.

'A thousand what?'

'Pounds—what else? The going rate, in other words.'

'Who said it was the going rate?'

'A friend—who you've dealt with before.'

'What friend?'

I had to take a risk here. 'Malcolm,' I said.

He laughed. 'The Meisterspringer? That old bastard still in business?' He pursed his lips and thought for a moment. 'Hm—I don't mind doing the old man a favour but I'd have to have some guarantee that you do come from him.'

'I'm certainly not carrying a letter of introduction,' I said. 'You'll just have to take my word for it.'

'I don't have to take anything, mister, that I don't want to take. How do I know you're not an Amsterdam pirate?' Which showed he'd been around a bit. 'Amsterdam pirate' is the business term for *agent provocateur*.

'Who would I be working for?' I asked. 'An Englishman coming aboard in a French port? What could I be trying to tangle you up in? You'd only have to holler for the cops and I'd be having my arse tickled by the Sûreté inside the hour.'

'All right then—who *are* you working for?'

'I told you. The Meisterspringer. Who *he's* working for I wouldn't be knowing. I don't ask rude questions.'

He grinned slowly and poured more drinks. 'Touché. You tickle *my* arse now, eh? Okay—but you got the going rate wrong. That was in the old days—before the Gyps took to rummaging the hell out of ships going through the Suez—and asking my *crew* rude questions. I got a lot of itchy palms to grease now, mister. A thousand don't leave much for myself.'

'I said a thousand a head. There are three of us.'

'That makes the risk bigger—and the palms itchier. Call it four thousand. I got to cover my overheads.'

I sighed. The tightwads had only allowed me five for the whole operation, and I'd run up a sizeable bill with Madame already. 'All right,' I said wearily. 'Four thousand.'

He beamed and said *skal* again and added as an afterthought, 'Half now—half when you come aboard.'

'Half when we come aboard—half in Kowloon,' I said firmly.

'I can't argue in Kowloon if anything happened on the way—like the rats chewing your wallet or something.'

'No—but you could hand us over as stowaways or something like that, couldn't you?'

'You're a hard case, mister,' he said. 'All right—so we say a thousand now—a thousand when you come aboard and the rest on arrival. That way we can all trust each other.'

So we settled for that. I fought off another drink and he gave me boarding instructions—very, very precisely.

'I run her tight, mister,' he explained. 'She's a small ship so I got a small crew—me, three mates, three engineers, three Swedes on deck—quartermasters. All the rest is Chinks—six topsides, six below, a steward and a cook and a Marconi guy who does supercargo as well. Him I'm a little doubtful about because it's his first trip with me. The others I slip a little something to on top of their pay when I carry anything I don't want talked about, and then I don't worry. You see what I mean?'

I didn't quite, but I realized that in spite of his heartiness he was nervous.

'What's worrying you?' I asked. 'You just slip the Marconi man something too.'

'Sure, sure, sure,' he agreed. 'And maybe it'll all be all right—but I'd still rather he—or the others for that matter—don't know you're aboard until we're at sea. So you'll come aboard the day after tomorrow—dressed like you are now—no luggage—when the stevedores come on for the last bits of cargo. I'll contact you on deck and slip you away somewhere out of sight.'

I nodded slowly. I could see his point, and it made sense, but it also raised a difficulty that I had not foreseen. Carter and I could pass unnoticed among the stevedores—but what about Sonia? I was about to mention this, but then I decided to keep my mouth shut. Kjaer, while more than willing to pick up an easy four thousand pounds, was *not* willing to run too many risks. If he knew in advance that one of the party was to be a woman he might turn the whole thing down, or, at very least, jack the price up beyond the limit. No—let's get her aboard first, and argue afterwards, I thought.

'Anything you say,' I agreed, and started to count American bills on to the table. 'Dollars, two-eighty to the pound. Twenty-eight hundred.'

'Call it three thousand to make it round figures,' he wheedled, but I wouldn't budge. He sighed and gathered it up with stumpy fingers.

'We'll be sailing as soon as they open the dock gates at high water,' he said. 'That'll be at eight in the morning. The stevedores will be changing shift at four. That's when you'll come aboard. All right?'

He opened the cabin door and looked out into the alleyway, then led me through to the open deck and down into the well, and left me without a further word. My friend the Swede was back at his post when I went down the gangway, but he chose to ignore me.

I found my way back through the rainswept docks and up to the Place Vauban feeling pleased with myself. This had been the trickiest bit and so far I thought I'd handled it rather well. Getting Sonia aboard would be only a minor hazard. Men's clothes would take care of that. Four o'clock in the morning, nice and dark, with everybody too sleepy to notice much. Carter? There should be no difficulty with him provided we kept him too muzzy to take interest in things, but still able to walk.

I felt my spirits rising. It was good to be out and about again, with things on the move. I looked at my watch. It was only just after nine. I felt like prolonging things a bit—perhaps dropping into a café for a drink—but then I saw a No. 8 tram coming up through the rain and I decided not to push my luck too much.

Three of us got on the tram; a woman with a laundry basket who had already been waiting at the stop when I arrived, and a man who came up at the last minute—a nondescript-looking guy dressed more or less like myself. It was the woman who held my attention, because she got into a furious argument with the conductor about where she should put the basket. He said it shouldn't go in the aisle where it would obstruct other passengers, and she said for God's sake there were only five other passengers and where should she put it? and he told her, impolitely, and she became even more impolite in turn and appealed to the rest of us for support against this instance of bureaucracy. It was all good Rabelaisian stuff and I found it amusing—so much so that although I was still counting the tram stops subconsciously, I nearly missed getting off at the eleventh and had to jump for it at the last minute. And apparently another passenger was absent-minded also, because I saw him jump off just as the tram disappeared round the next bend. There was an overhead arc-light right at that spot and I saw that it was the man who had got on with me. I went into the ditching drill immediately and ignored the back door to the house.

I continued on up the hill without looking round until I came to a turning off the narrow street. There were no lights here so I was able to peer back down the hill. I saw somebody moving swiftly through the shadows on the dark side, coming up towards me. I went further down the turning and found a deep recessed doorway. The man came into sight again. He stopped and looked round uncertainly. For a moment it seemed as if he was going on, and there would have been no problem, but then the door behind me opened and I found myself bathed in light. A man and an obvious tart looked at me in surprise. The man grunted, pushed past me and went off, but the tart, manifestly, like Georgette, a good worker, fastened on to me as the next client and addressed me loudly and affectionately as *petit chou* and tried to drag me inside. I pulled away and went on down the lane, but the damage had been done. The guy at the corner had seen me.

MAB/72—D*

The lane led into a square which was fairly well lighted, and there were several people about, though the crowd was not thick enough to make tail-shaking easy. I looked round as I crossed a patch of shadow. He was just emerging from the lane. I felt a surge of rage—at myself—because this was sheer bloody inexcusable ineptitude. That back gate had been used by Malcolm for years. The damned girl had used it herself three times in the last couple of days—but I had to go and blow it the very first time I came out. Or had I? Nobody had seen me come out, for the simple reason nobody had got on the tram with me. No—this goon had picked me up outside somewhere—and unless it was somebody who knew me, that could only have been at the docks. That meant the ship was being watched. Somebody had seen me go aboard—probably saw the bit of business with the sailor on the gangway—then my short conversation with the captain on deck—my going off with him to his cabin—then my coming ashore again.

But, with luck, I still hadn't blown the back gate.

Well, there was only one thing for it. He had to be shaken—and there is only one way to do that with any degree of certainty when you're being tailed by somebody who thinks that you know he's tailing you. First of all you've got to rid him of that certainty, and make him think that you *don't* know, because only that way can you hope to get him close enough to deal with him. The interlude in the doorway might have given the game away, but not of necessity. I could have been a man who had mistaken the house—or having seen the wares it had to offer, had thought better of it.

There was a Tabac facing me. I walked in and bought some cigarettes, and then came out and retraced my steps. He wasn't terribly good at it because I caught him unawares and nearly bumped into him. I grunted an apology and went on without a glance at him. I went into a café then and shouldered through the crowd to the loo, hoping I might have a break there, but it was an inside one with no window and a ventilator that wasn't up to its job of admitting air, let alone allowing egress. So I came back and had a drink at the *zinc* and bought a bottle of pastis. There were several brands there and I was choosey, because although I couldn't see him I knew he'd be around somewhere and I didn't want to give anything away by buying the first cheap bottle that came to hand. No, this was something for a man who knew what he wanted and had no other thought than of enjoying it later.

I left the café, stuffing the bottle into the side pocket of my peajacket, and went back up the lane, making up a phrase in my inadequate French that would, I hoped, get quick results. I had to trust to luck now that he was on my heels because I didn't dare look back. I went to the brothel door and knocked. The same tart opened and looked out.

I said quietly: 'You dirty whore. You poxed me last voyage. I'm going to slit your throat,' and stepped forward. She slammed the door in my face. I turned and waited in the darkness. From down the alley he would only have seen the reflected light as the door opened, and would, I hoped, have assumed that I had gone inside.

I heard soft hurrying footsteps and then he was up to the recess, staring in—just a bulk in the dark. I swung the bottle. It didn't break. It would have been better for the poor devil if it had, because that would have proved his skull was the harder of the two, but as it was it sounded like a melon being hit with a sledge hammer.

I dragged him into the recess and left him and then went on to the top of the lane and turned back down the tramlines. I passed the gate and waited in the dark a little further down, just in case there was another of them around, but nothing stirred except a lean cat that rubbed itself against my leg and nearly made me jump out of my skin, so I returned to the gate and pressed the bellpush. It opened after a moment and the Algerian who had let me out admitted me and led me back across the yard and through the kitchen. I gave him the bottle of pastis and he thanked me gravely and the one with the punctured foot said I was *très gentil.*

Sonia let me in. The room was warm and cosy and, surprisingly, I was glad to be back. I think maybe she was too, because she didn't start an argument and even helped me out of my wet peajacket—which was unfortunate, because all the wetness wasn't rain. She looked at her reddened hand, then at me, and I had to tell her.

'You're certain you weren't picked up leaving here?' she asked anxiously.

'There was nobody in sight—and certainly nobody got on the tram with me.'

'And when you got off?'

'As it happened, nobody got off with me either.'

'Then it's a fair assumption that the ship *is* watched,' she said, troubled. 'But why?—why?—why?—before you even approached Kjaer?'

'I don't know,' I said gloomily. 'The whole crazy exercise is bugged.'

I actually was going to say 'buggered', but I clipped it for politeness' sake—then something occurred to me.

'Bugged,' I repeated. 'I *wonder*?'

Then supper arrived.

CHAPTER TWELVE

BUT SHE PULLED that possibility to pieces as we ate, although I still gave the place a thorough going over afterwards. If it was bugged, whoever had done it was a genius, because *I* certainly couldn't find a trace of wiring that couldn't be accounted for.

'It would mean that Madame would have to be in on it,' Sonia said. 'And I'm certain she isn't.'

'You yourself said everybody has their price,' I came back at her.

'Maybe, but my God it would have to be a high one in her case. She's got too much to lose—and she knows it.'

'Then it comes back to the ship,' I said glumly. 'We've just got to accept the fact that it's being watched and that I was picked up and followed back from there.'

'But you *did* break the trail?' She put it in the form of a question and I felt my anger rising again, but I fought it down. This needed clear-headed discussion.

'I broke the trail all right.'

'Did you——'

'Kill him? Quite likely. I didn't mean to, but—well, there you are. Look, let's run over the whole thing. Probabilities first. They know we're here. How? They had a tail on Charlton. Why? He's a known associate of your father's. That sailor the other night. It's pretty clear now that he was one of them—sent in to make a recce. We've stymied them there and they realize that they can't try further strong-arm methods to winkle us out without trouble from the police, but they're watching, waiting for us to make a move—how many of them we don't know, but there's bound to be more than one.'

'We know all that,' she said impatiently. 'But the ship? Why would they be watching that?'

'Pretty obvious, isn't it? China bound—and your father has dealt with Kjaer before.'

She nodded reluctantly, hating to concede too much, but unable to put anything up against it. 'Still, once we're aboard our worries are over until we reach Hong Kong—and then, if your people are on the ball there——'

'I wouldn't be too certain about that,' I said. 'I mean about our worries being over. We've got to go through the Canal, don't forget—and the Russians and Egyptians are friendly at the moment. If they knew for certain we were on board they could hold the ship indefinitely and search us down to the rivets.'

'*If* they knew we were on board. We've got to take damned good care that they don't know.'

'Easier said than done. If they're watching that ship properly they'll know all right.'

'Couldn't we ask Kjaer to——' But I didn't let her finish.

'Kjaer's already told me how we're to come aboard,' I said. 'If I try to vary his very definite instructions he'll know it's because I think we've been blown—and he'll drop the whole thing like a hot potato. No—we've got to get aboard as arranged, but we've got to throw these goons first. Really throw them.'

'Which brings us right back to the beginning. How?'

'Give me a chance,' I begged. 'I need a little time.'

'It's running out. From what you told me, we've got something less than twenty-four hours left.'

'Look—suppose you go to bed,' I suggested, 'and leave me to think.'

'I'd be glad to,' she said waspishly, 'if I thought something might come of it. But on your showing to date you'll have to excuse a certain pessimism on my part.'

And then we were into it again and we wrangled unprofitably until we heard Carter calling sleepily from the other room. She mixed something in a glass and went through to him. He went to sleep again. He must have been as full of dope now as a Flower

Child at a love-in. I almost envied him. At least he didn't have to listen to this bitch.

She came out and went through to her room, and I sat on—and on—and on—until finally I had some sort of a plan. A pretty wobbly one, but at least it was something. I tapped at her door. She must have been awake because she opened immediately.

I said: 'You say as far as you know, Madame can be trusted?'

'As far as I know,' she confirmed.

'What about the help?'

'You mean the girls?'

'Actually I was thinking of the Algerians—but I'll need a girl as well.'

'I'd prefer to put it to Madame herself. What is your idea?'

'A car,' I said. 'We'd go out the front way—me, one of the Algerians and a girl, wearing your clothes. If we picked our time, say at half light, and moved quickly, we ought to be able to get away with it.'

'And what then?'

'Lead them a dance,' I said. 'Not an aimless one. We'd make for another town—either Rouen or Brest—and we'd throw them on the way. Then I'd come back and collect you just before boarding time.'

'I don't think much of that,' she said.

'Neither do I, but it's the best I can do. If you can come up with something better I'd be glad to hear it.'

'What if you don't manage to throw them?'

'I don't come back. If I haven't returned or telephoned by a certain time, you'll have to call your father and tell him what has happened. It will be up to him then.'

'I don't like it.'

'I've told you, neither do I, but——'

'If I came instead of one of the girls——'

'Nothing doing,' I said firmly. 'Both eggs in the same basket if anything goes wrong.'

'All right then—if *I* went, with two Algerians, and you stayed here—' she raised her hand quickly as she saw me take a deep breath and get ready to explode. 'No—please—I'm not being offensive. Carter might require manhandling—even carrying at some stage. I couldn't cope with him on my own.'

It was a shrewd one, but I still wouldn't wear it, so in the end she gave in and went down to knock Madame up. She came up snarling and grumbling, and I knew that this was going to cost somebody plenty. I outlined the idea to her briefly, omitting any reference to the ship.

She chewed over it for a long moment and then said flatly, 'Too dangerous.'

'It needn't be,' I said.

'If you don't manage to lose them, you lead them back here,' she said.

'I don't,' I answered, playing it off the cuff. 'Mademoiselle takes the client away after I have drawn the pursuit off.'

'And suppose you drive fast and crash, or are stopped? Suppose you fight and someone is hurt—killed?' She spread her hands and rolled her eyes.

'Madame's solicitude touches me, but provided anything like that should happen away from here she need not concern herself unduly.'

'With my *porteur*—one without papers—and a lady from this establishment in the car? M'sieur is naive. The police would be round in shoals. With our local inspector things—small things—might be arranged, but not with the headquarters flics.' Of course she was only jacking the price up, but it took a long time, although I must admit that once she had squeezed the last franc out of me she got things moving fast. She routed out Georgette and the Algerian with both sound feet and brought them up, yawning and blinking. The girl ventured a timid question or two but got nowhere with Madame, but the Algerian accepted things with Oriental fatalism, and we got them dressed—in the clothes Sonia and I had been wearing when we arrived. I studied them both doubtfully. In the light neither looked very convincing, but a headscarf over the girl's dark hair and my felt hat pulled down over the Algerian's face helped considerably.

'The car——?' I asked.

'The one that brought you here,' Madame answered. 'Driven by my son—so m'sieur can understand my anxiety. A mother's heart——'

We waited a long time for it to arrive. They garaged it half a mile away, apparently, and Jean sometimes had difficulty in starting it in damp weather, although, Madame assured me earnestly, once going it marched in a manner *très formidable*—and had cost a lot of money.

I waited, fuming and sweating, peering down from behind

the curtains into the square. Sonia wasn't helping either. She was putting into words that which had been bothering me.

'We don't really know if we *are* being watched here, do we?' she said.

'We damned soon will,' I growled.

'Even supposing your hunch is right and they do follow you, does that of necessity mean that they'll withdraw the watch from the ship?'

'We've got to assume *something*. If they're convinced we've gone scooting off in another direction they're hardly likely to waste men watching an abandoned bolt-hole, are they?'

'Who's going to tell them, if the people here go scooting off after *you*?'

'Oh for God's sake stop, will you,' I howled—and then I saw the black Citroën arrive outside. I hustled Georgette and the Algerian downstairs ahead of me, hissing last-minute instructions. Sonia came down too, relenting a little and wishing me luck. I said: 'Give me until midnight. If I haven't shown up by then put a call through to your old man, but don't risk going near the ship.'

I opened the front door and slipped through. It was just getting light and early workers were already moving down towards the docks.

I tried to play it as naturally as possible without overdoing it. I took a fairly searching look around the square and then, as if satisfied, hurried back up the steps and collected the other two. Fair play to them, they did it very well—heads down and coat collars turned up, and wasting no time. I hustled them into the back seat and told them to keep down low, then climbed in beside the driver and told him to get going for Rouen and to step on it, but not to be too rash. This was going to be the tricky part. Too fast, and I might throw them in reality. Too slow and it would be obvious that we were laying a trail. As it was it worked out nicely, because the 'costly' Citroën ran true to form. Not yet properly warmed up, it balked and stalled on starting and in the end Jean had to run downhill slipping his clutch in second gear before the engine took up. That, I reflected with some slight satisfaction, would give them time to get properly organized. I set the rear vision mirror so that I, rather than the driver, could see behind and sat back.

We drove down the alley and out on to the dock road. Parking was permitted on one side of it. If they had a car waiting, this is where it would be. There was plenty of truck traffic moving both ways so we couldn't have speeded even had we wanted to, and twice we were held up by swing bridges before we got clear of the docks. But not a thing had moved out of the parking area, and there was no sign of a car on our tail. I felt, once again, a complete fool. My theorizing had been knocked flat, and all this elaborate nonsense had gone for nothing, not to mention a further five hundred francs of my slender resources being down the drain—because there'd be no refunds from Madame. Now I would have to go back and face that damned girl again and give her best—well, half-best anyhow, because she had been no more nor less certain than I about the place being watched—but she'd had the sneaky feminine foresight to voice her doubts, while I'd been cocksure about it. I was about to tell Jean to take a couple of turns round town to make sure, and then turn back, when I noticed the motor-cyclist.

I don't know where he came from, but I was certain we hadn't overtaken him. He was just there—two trucks behind us—and he made no effort to close the distance when first one, then the other, turned off into the docks. He just kept on at the same speed and allowed other traffic to pass him and fill the gap. I thought for a moment of putting it to the test and telling Jean to make a sudden turn down a side street, but I let it go. That would let him know that we knew he was following us, and that was the last thing I wanted at this juncture.

We came out of the Le Havre suburbs into Harfleur, and here the road forks—left to Fécamp and Dieppe, right to Rouen—and I saw him stop. This was textbook stuff. Unless I was very much mistaken he was acting as contact man for yet another trailer further back, and was waiting to point out the turning we had taken. And I *wasn't* mistaken, because I told Jean to stop for petrol at the next service station and I bought a Michelin Grandes Routes map, and while we were halted a green Peugeot went roaring past—and sure enough some distance along after we had got going again, *it* had stopped for petrol also, and looking out of the corner of my eye as we passed, I saw four men in it.

Thereafter it followed the familiar drill—dropping right back out of sight when we were on a long stretch of road without junctions, but obviously navigating on a map as I was, and closing up when we were coming to a turn-off. Oh, yes—this was the Opposition all right. The question was, what to do with them now?

I started the old routine that sounds so easy at the school, of putting myself in their place. What did they want? Without question, they had fallen for it and they wanted to get hold of Carter. Four of them, undoubtedly armed, should be able to do this without difficulty, given the place and opportunity, and a busy highway in broad daylight was neither. So what would they do? Quite obviously just what they were doing now. They'd keep on our tail until the place and opportunity for a quick snatch *did* present itself. Next question—did they know Carter and/or Sonia by sight? Did they, in fact, know *me*? To be on the safe side one would have to assume that they did. That being the case, if they got a close look at the other two they would know they had been fooled, and would immediately turn round and hightail it to Le Havre and resume their watch, and we'd be right back where we started. So I had to shake this tail without their getting that close look. That in itself shouldn't be too difficult, but we were still within eighty kilometres of Le Havre and if we ditched them too soon it would be a reasonable assumption on their part that the whole thing had been a plant, and that we intended going back, and the heat would be on again.

No—they had to be convinced that we were to hell and gone out of the area. We could do that, no doubt, by continuing on to Paris and really losing them there, then I could get a train back—but that was too dicey. Their was immeasurably the better car of the two, and there was always the chance of their picking a lonely bit of road, overtaking us, forcing us off and blowing the whole thing. There was always the chance, if it came to that, of getting oneself killed. We'd knocked off quite a few of their side so far, and even dedicated Ivans could be expected to show a little exacerbation under the circumstances. Anyhow, I didn't know how the trains ran, and I might be cutting the time factor too fine—and I certainly couldn't risk coming back by a car that was now known to them. And thinking about trains, gave me the ghost of an idea.

As we came through the next town, Yvetot, I called a halt outside the station and sent Jean in, as if *pissoir* bound, to buy a railway timetable. In the mirror I saw the others stop the far side of the Place de la Gare and park unobtrusively among some other cars. Two of them got out and strolled casually in our direction, and for a moment I was almost panicked into sliding into the driving seat and pushing off before they got too close, but I fought it down and muttered to the two in the back to slouch forward, faces buried in collars, as if asleep. Panic now would tell the followers clearly that we knew they were tailing us, and might force their hands. However, Jean came back while they were still a good twenty yards off and we started up and drove away.

They turned and hurried back to their car.

I studied the unfamiliar timetable as we drove fast over the last forty kilometres to Rouen. There was a good train in an hour from now—good insofar that it was fast and only stopped twice before Paris, at Les Andelys and Magny-en-Vexin. With a bit of luck that might do it.

We drove down the hill into Rouen half an hour later, and I dropped off in a traffic jam near the station, telling Jean to keep circling the block until he picked me up again, and I ducked into a café. Looking through the window, I saw them drive past on the tail of the Citroën. They seemed to be arguing and for a moment I thought at least one of them might hop out and follow me, but the flow quickened and they had to move with it after the main quarry. I hurried across to the station and bought three tickets for Paris, ascertaining the platform the train left from, and rejoined the car on its second circuit. I told Jean to drive towards the centre of the town and to time things so that he could be passing the station again in exactly ten minutes, which would give us three minutes to make the train. I was beginning to develop quite an affection for Jean. His conversation was limited to a grunted *oui* or *non* as the situation dictated, but he didn't need a blueprint of a reasonably simple instruction. The other two were, however, becoming a little restless. The Algerian wanted a drink and the lady wanted to pee, and both were complaining that they had missed their breakfast. But I managed to smooth things down with glib promises, and give them precise instructions at the same time.

He timed it exactly, and positioned the car well. We were the inner line of a long flow of taxis and private cars, while the Opposition were well to a flank and our rear with a bus and several cars between us and them. I jumped out, ran round and hauled the Algerian and the girl out, keeping myself between them and the Peugeot and hissing at them to keep their faces down. I hustled them through on to the assembly platform, then raced for the Paris train. They were just closing the barrier and we were the last passengers through—the last legitimate ones, that is. As I pushed the others up into the first coach I glanced round and saw three of the men arguing and scuffling with the ticket-collector who was yelling the place down—and a gendarme was bearing down on them. But one of them made it. He streaked for the train and jumped for the steps and looking back I saw him climb aboard.

I pushed the others ahead of me down the corridor until I found an empty first-class compartment. I bundled them into it and slid the door almost closed and jerked the blinds down.

I peeped through the chink obliquely up the corridor. He came into sight through the door from the next coach, looking into each compartment. He reached ours and I slid the door back and jerked my gun hard into his belly. He grunted and looked surprised.

It was our visitor of a few nights previously—Yoni something-or other. Either Madame or the police were gypping me, because I'd paid for five days in the nick for him.

I pulled him inside and closed the door again and told the Algerian to watch it. I frisked him of an automatic, some money—quite a thick roll of it—and a small but very vicious leather-covered cosh which he carried inside the waistband of his trousers. Georgette seemed pleased to see him, much more than he was to see her. In fact I don't think he even noticed her. He was too busy watching me. I realized it would be a sheer waste of time to question him. These people don't talk when they are caught *in flagrante delicto*—not unless you've got the time and facilities to lean on them really heavily—and I had neither, and he knew it. The Algerian mentioned helpfully that there were tunnels on this line, and glanced at the outer door. Georgette squealed softly, and Yoni's eyes flickered nervously. It would have been a quick solution, no doubt, and one which I might have to take if nothing else offered—but I wanted to avoid it if possible. Beaning a bloke in hot pursuit is one thing—but killing him in cold blood is quite another.

We sat on in a strained silence for a time. Whatever I did would have to be done quickly. This first-class section was empty at the moment, but if a ticket-inspector came along, or other passengers got on at the next stop, I couldn't continue to hold a gun on him, let alone use it, if he chose to make a break.

Georgette started to wriggle, then with a murmured apology got up and made for the corridor. For a moment I thought her womanly heart had been touched at the prospect of an ex-client being done in, and that she had gone to summon help, but she was only going to the loo down the corridor. In the kerfuffle of the last half hour I had forgotten the poor soul's personal needs. But it gave me an idea. I could cosh him and leave him in the lavatory, and we'd get off at the next stop.

But I discarded that one quickly. Coshing, short of the absolute mayhem I had committed with the bottle, is a chancy business at the best of times. He would recover sooner or later, and if it was sooner he might have time to raise an alarm by telephone from Paris. He'd seen the others and he knew they were not Carter and Sonia. No, he had to be kept quiet—really quiet—until after sailing time at least. I found myself looking at the outer door. His eyes followed mine, and again I caught the nervous flicker. He was frightened—which was all to the good—but I still didn't know what the hell to do with him—short of *that*.

The train was slowing down for the first stop, Les Andelys, according to the timetable. We rumbled over a bridge and underneath I could see a muddy canal snaking off to the right where it debouched into a wide river. The Seine, I assumed it to be. It was raining again and the place looked miserable and beautifully deserted. If only I had him down there.

We ground to a halt short of the station. I lowered the window and looked out. Right alongside us on the next line was a stationary goods train. I looked up and down the track. It curved here, so I couldn't see far in either direction and there was nobody in sight. I made up my mind quickly.

I said to Georgette, 'Go on to the next station—Magny-en-Vexin—and stay there until this time tomorrow, then find your own way back.' I gave her her ticket and added a two-hundred-franc *pourboire*. Then I wrenched the door open, hauled Yoni to his feet and spun him round, gestured to the Algerian to follow, and kicked the other in the small of the back. He landed in a heap, six feet below on the tracks, and we were down each side of him before he could yell. I jammed the gun in his ribs and we hustled him underneath the nearest goods truck. Behind us I heard our train jerk forward and run slowly into the station. Peering out between the wheels I saw a line of closed, rain-spattered windows and as far as I could determine, nobody was looking out through any of them. We waited until the last coach had passed and then crawled out the other side. We were just clear of the bridge, and a bank sloped steeply down in front of us to the canal.

I said to Yoni: 'Keep your mouth closed and do as you're told, and you've got a chance.' I think he wanted to believe me. He moistened his lips and nodded.

We slid down the bank. On the towpath under the bridge was, inevitably, a Frenchman sitting on a box fishing with an enormously long bamboo pole. It gave me quite a start, but fishing is more than an avocation in France. It's an all-absorbing way of life, and he didn't spare us a glance.

We walked up the towpath, the Algerian, who knew his job without being told, with Yoni's right arm tucked affectionately and tightly under his left, and me a couple of paces to the rear. I was looking for a lonely shed or, failing that, a good thick clump of bushes, but it just wasn't that sort of country. Here we had the town on the other bank and flat sodden water meadows on this one, with not a hint of cover. But then we passed a string of moored barges—a couple of Dutch ones, a Belgian and three French. I looked at them longingly, but all had the usual living quarters astern and, although nobody was stirring, we couldn't risk sneaking aboard.

But even the longest canal has a turning. We came round the next one and there were more barges—the sort that are towed, without living quarters on them. I went up the gangway of the first one. The hatches were on loosely and I could see grain in bags half-filling the hold. I signalled to the Algerian to bring our friend aboard, and there we struck our first difficulty. He suddenly smelled danger and started to struggle and yell. I went back quickly and beaned him, hard, with his own cosh. He went down like a log and we hefted him aboard and dropped him down on the bags. I took a frightened look round, but there was still nobody in sight, so we jumped down beside him and I tied his wrists behind him with the belt of his raincoat. The Algerian, now thoroughly in the spirit of the thing, and enjoying it, started to gag him with fiendish ingenuity and a mouthful of loose grain kept in place with his own grubby handkerchief, but I stopped that. Grain swells with moisture, and the poor bastard was going to be in a pretty dicey situation as it was if nobody unloaded the barge for a few days.

We walled him in loosely behind some bags, came ashore and walked back towards town. I thought of telling the Algerian to telephone the police the following evening and giving them an anonymous tip about this, but I abandoned that because I knew damned well he wouldn't bother.

We parted after that. I told him, like Georgette, to amuse himself locally until next day and gave him an extra two hundred francs also. With Yoni's unexpected contribution to the kitty, which I found to be just short of two thousand, I felt I could afford it. I went on into town. I didn't risk the train again, but found I could get a bus to Rouen an hour later.

It was dark when I got back to Le Havre. I was crying-weary but I played things safe and went into a long and complicated tail-shaking routine to be on the safe side, finally buying a plastic mac and a peaked cap in place of the knitted one I had been wearing, then I caught a No. 8 tram and came 'home', as I was now thinking of the damned place, and went in the back way.

But Sonia wouldn't leave me alone. She put me through a long catechism about the whole thing while I was having a couple of stiff drinks and a belated supper—then she tried to pick holes in it—but I snarled at her and finally went to sleep in a chair in front of the fire.

She woke me in what I muzzily thought was a bare five minutes later, but when I looked at my watch I saw it was half-past three. I started to rave because that only gave us half an hour before we had to be aboard, and I hadn't even started to think about how we were going to do that, but she told me icily that that had already been arranged, and I noticed her appearance for the first time. She had certainly done it well. She was dressed in slacks, jersey and peajacket and she bulked realistically because she was carrying a lot of spare gear underneath. And she had darkened her face and hands, and her hair was hidden properly under her woollen cap. She looked a typical young longshore yobbo.

Then I saw Madame holding Carter upright. He was able to stand and even take a few steps if he was supported, and his eyes, though glazed, were open. But that was about all. I still didn't see how we were going to take him on a tram, and I said so.

'The trams have stopped running,' Sonia said.

'So we've got to use a car again? From the front?' I shook my head. I was as certain as one could be that I'd drawn them off, but it still seemed an unnecessary risk.

'From the back,' she told me. 'Ordinary traffic often uses that road when the trams are not running and there are no police around.'

And that is how we did it. It was Jean again, but they'd had the savvy to get a different car. But I was still jumpy and I made him drive round a bit until, *this* time, I was certain there was nobody on our tail.

We stopped fifty yards short of the dock gate. It was just four o'clock and the shift was changing. There were no lights except those on the ship itself, so we had no difficulty in mixing with the gang going aboard. Carter revived a little in the cold air and walked without being too conspicuous, but he had started to mumble. I left them both near the winches of number three hold, which wasn't being worked, and went in search of Kjaer. He saw me as I climbed from the well deck and came and met me. He was in high good humour. I was glad somebody was. He led me into the shadow of a lifeboat.

'We fix our little bit of business, eh?' he said, and rubbed his forefinger and thumb under my nose.

I gave him his thousand.

'Count it later,' he chuckled. 'I trust you. Where the others?'

I told him.

'Fine,' he said. 'You'll see an alleyway on the starboard side, leading aft from the well deck. Go down that. I meet you the other end. Pretty small and stinky the place I put you—but that only till we drop the pilot. Maybe two, three hours. Fix you up good then—nice cabin for three.'

'You couldn't make it two cabins?' I asked anxiously.

'Not a chance,' he said, and chuckled again. 'If only one of you had a Marconi ticket you could have Sparks's cabin. The bastard jumped the ship, and I don't see him for two days. Suits me fine—only I got to take the third mate off watches to do his job now. Still, you don't worry about that. This three-berth cabin I give you, bloody nice.'

That was one problem off our shoulders. He had said his crew was reliable, with only this one in doubt. And it had been worrying me vaguely. Malcolm had used this ship before. If the

Opposition knew that—and had planted this fellow—well—even that doubt was removed now.

I went down and collected the others and met Kjaer at the end of the alleyway. He opened a steel door in the bulkhead and ushered us through as if he were showing us into the bridal suite at the Ritz. It was pitch dark and I, leading the way, went arse over head on a paint drum. He clanged the door to and I heard the key turn outside.

We lowered Carter to the deck and found seats for ourselves on other drums and just sat there in silent misery. Time dragged on. We heard clumping and clattering overhead, then the throb of engines—and more clattering—and once I went to sleep and fell off the drum. Carter came round a little and started to shriek, and we had a hell of a job to quieten him down. Then, after what seemed days, but actually was only three hours, we felt the gentle lift of the deck under us that meant we had reached open water. But it was another hour before Kjaer unlocked. We staggered out, and Carter was violently sick, which at least stopped him asking questions. Kjaer hurried back to the bridge.

Overside I could see a small boat making away from us towards the pilot cutter. The coast was astern of us, with the lights paling in the dawn. A fresh breeze was blowing, which was heaven after that hellish paint-locker. I felt my spirits rising. The tough part was over now. There was just a sea voyage ahead of us—a voyage which could, conceivably, be even enjoyable, now that our tautened nerves could relax a little.

Yes—we'd done it—and my little ploy of yesterday had paid off—and had pulled the whole thing off the rocks. Wherever else they thought us, they would be certain we weren't on this ship.

My spirits rose further, and continued to rise. I even turned and grinned amiably at Sonia. Then I stopped grinning.

A man was looking down at us from the deck above. I thought for a moment that he was an Indian wearing a white turban. But *only* for a moment.

His head was heavily bandaged—but there was no mistaking his face.

He was the fellow I had crowned with the bottle in the brothel doorway.

CHAPTER THIRTEEN

HE GAVE NO SIGN of recognition. From where he was we were no doubt just a group of sailors huddled in the half light under the break of the well deck below him, and anyhow he looked a pretty sick man, his face as pale as the bandages. He continued to lean on the rail for a while, then he withdrew out of sight. Sonia happened to turn at that moment, and I must have been looking as sick as the other guy.

She said: 'What's wrong now?'

'Every bloody thing,' I groaned. 'That fellow up there is the one who followed me from the ship.' I felt like a man who has just scaled Everest and come face to face with a Coca-Cola advertisement on the summit. I braced myself for the lash of her scorn, but for once she was at a loss for words. She took a deep breath, like a martyred saint who has been asked to take just that little bit too much, and then Carter, who was being sick in the scuppers, lost his footing as the ship butted into a sharp, steep swell, and rolled on the deck. We helped him up and sat him on the corner of the hatch. We had a job to hold him there, because the breeze was reviving him quickly and I could see panic setting in. I told him to take it easy, but he struggled and tried to break away from us, yelling incoherently. A group of Chinese deckhands came along with brooms and a hose, and when he saw them, the balloon really went up. I think that if he could have made it, he'd have jumped over the rail. Then suddenly the fight went out of him, and he sat hunched with his face in his hands, and he gave a deep, shuddering sob. It was a terrible moment. Up to this point he had been a piece of merchandise on the hoof, but now for the first time I saw him as a human being—a terrified man who was being taken to his death, and who knew it. I may be kidding myself, but I think in looking back that if the pilot cutter had still been within hailing distance I'd have jacked the whole thing in. But she wasn't within hailing distance, so I sought refuge in our carefully planned lie.

I said: 'What the hell's eating you? You're out of gaol and you're on your way back to your own people. All you've got to do now is relax and enjoy the ride.'

'My own people?' he said hopelessly. 'I have no people. Only a wife and two children in Moscow.'

'That would be enough for most blokes,' I said. 'Okay, so you'll be joining them. It will take a bit of time, but at least you're on your way. Why the squawks?' It was apparently too much for Sonia. She moved away to the rail and stood looking out across the sea. From the corner of my eye I saw her drag her woollen cap off and shake her hair free, then turn her face up into the wind and take deep breaths, like someone trying to rid themselves of something that smelt nasty. Carter looked up at me quickly—searching my face—then he shrugged.

'You ask me to believe that?' He gestured towards the Chinese seamen who were now swabbing down the foredeck. 'I know what those people mean. You're taking me back to China.'

'As far as I'm concerned, my orders are to escort you to Vladivostok,' I told him, and again he glanced up at me sharply. I saw a momentary glimmer of hope in his face, but it faded immediately.

'Vladivostock?' he repeated. 'I'm not a child. Why would you transport me right round the globe? I know what my route was to be—Gdynia, Warsaw, Moscow. I was told that weeks ago in prison.'

'I wouldn't be knowing,' I said. 'I get my orders and I carry them out to the best of my ability—and get paid on results at the end of it. I don't ask questions. But things can change,' I went on. 'One door closes, so they open another. The heat was on us the whole time, you know. Pretty fierce. We hadn't a prayer by the European route.'

'Why was I drugged?' he shot at me. 'I was co-operating. I was doing everything I was told to do—while I thought you were working for the Russians.'

'I don't know,' I said. 'You were handed over to us like that. I had nothing to do with your coming over the wall.'

He nodded slowly. 'That I can believe. That is probably the only truth you've spoken so far. I know who brought me out of prison. I knew who to expect. They identified themselves. But then I was hijacked, wasn't I?'

'Not to my knowledge.'

'You're a liar, my friend—and not a very skilled one. You've been renewing the drug at intervals the whole time. You and that girl.' He nodded towards Sonia. 'Why—unless you knew that I might start to ask awkward questions—might, perhaps, make trouble at the wrong time?'

'I told you,' I said. 'I get my orders—and I don't ask questions.'

'Orders from whom? Who are *you*—you personally—working for?'

'Oh, for Christ's sake,' I said wearily. 'You know better than that. Even if I knew, you surely wouldn't expect me to tell you.'

'What harm can it do now?' he asked. 'I can't escape from this ship before you hand me over to somebody else.' He paused, looking at me directly. 'On the other hand we *might* be able to come to some arrangement.'

'Such as?'

'That depends. You mentioned that you were paid at the end of the job—on results?' I was becoming conscious of a change of manner. His initial weakness had been purely the natural reaction of a man surfacing after days of heavy sedation and finding himself in peril. The fear was no doubt still there, but he had had time to collect himself now, and his guard was up again. I felt a certain relief. Nothing is so demoralizing as dealing from a position of strength with a thoroughly defenceless opponent.

He was watching me closely, waiting for my answer. I rubbed my chin slowly, and flicked my eyes towards Sonia warningly. He lowered his voice.

'If we could discuss that fee—and I offered to double it, with a cast iron guarantee—*on results*——' He let the rest trail off. I looked at him shiftily. I didn't have to act it either. I was feeling shifty.

Then Kjaer arrived. He came to the top of the ladder and beckoned peremptorily. He was looking like thunder. I called to Sonia, who still had her back to us, and they both followed me up to the deck above. Kjaer grunted and led us off to the bridge superstructure. He opened a door leading to a smallish cabin on the port side. I could see it had two berths, one above the other, with a third made up on a settee. We started to go in, but he grabbed my elbow and said, 'Not you. I got to talk to you.' He closed the door on the others and half led, half pushed me to his day cabin. He was quivering with rage.

'So you bloddy put it over me, eh?' he roared. 'You think you going to get away with this?'

'What the hell are you beefing about?' I demanded. 'We made a bargain. I'm keeping to my half of it——'

'That goddam woman!' he stormed. 'You don't say nothing about a woman!'

'I said three *people*. You didn't ask our bloody sexes. What difference does it make, anyhow?'

'Difference?' he howled. 'It makes this difference. If I know you had a broad with you I don't carry you—that's all.'

'Well, you know now,' I snapped. 'What are you going to do about it?'

There was nothing he *could* do about it, except curse—and he certainly did plenty of that. He did say, however, that he wanted another couple of thousand, but I said balls to that. He switched then to almost tearful complaint.

'Three men is all right,' he said. 'The crew get used to seeing you around and pretty soon they don't think about it any more. By the time the voyage is over they've forgotten about it. But a woman is different. Those randy buggers in the fo'c'sle they'll talk about nothing else the whole trip—making up stories they'd like to believe. If she hangs up a pair of drawers to dry they'll blow their stacks, like stopped-up billy goats. When they go ashore they'll still be talking—then word gets out—then inquiries start—and I'm in the crap up to my goddam neck.'

'You're making difficulties,' I said. 'When we get to Hong Kong we'll be over the side and away—and even if your crew does talk afterwards nobody could prove anything. Anyhow, you said you could trust them.'

'I said I *know* them,' he grumbled. 'I pay them a few bucks extra to stop their mouths—but to stop them talking about a woman on board I'll have to pay 'em a bloddy sight more——'

'We'll deal with that when we come to it,' I said. 'At the moment I've got something really serious to talk about. You've got a man on board with a bandaged head.'

'Sparks—the Marconi man?' He looked startled. 'What about him?'

I looked startled then. 'But you told me he'd deserted?' I said.

'That's what I thought, but the police put him back on board just as we were coming through the dock gates.'

'Oh my God,' I groaned. 'What happened?'

'He got a smack over the dome in some dive, and he was unconscious for a couple of days. When they found out which ship he was off they put him on again, toute suite. They don't like having to look after foreign bums in a French port. But what do *you* know about it, mister?'

'The night I saw you on board here,' I told him. 'He followed me afterwards. I didn't know he was actually off this ship then, but I took no chances. I led him up an alley and crowned him with a bottle.'

He looked as sick as if I'd crowned *him*. 'I knew it,' he groaned. 'What did I tell you? I got a nose for not-right bastards. I had a feeling——'

'Where did he join you?'

'Helsinki,' he answered. 'Just before sailing. I got a doctor's note to say my regular guy was sick. This fellow came aboard on a pierhead jump. His papers looked all right, so I signed him on.'

'What date was that?'

'The eighteenth. Two days after Carter came out,' he said, and caught my eye. 'Oh, come on, mister—you don't think I didn't know, do you? The Meisterspringer had already sounded me out on it—in Antwerp, on the way up to Helsinki. Only the deal the old sod offered me was for two guys and nothing about a woman.'

'He didn't know then,' I said gloomily. 'Neither did I—or maybe I'd have turned it down myself. Well, that's it, then. They've planted him on us.'

'Looks like it,' he agreed. 'He's not a Rusk, though. German. Hamburg papers—but he could just as easy be East as West.' Then he said, 'Shit!' explosively, and jumped up, fumbling for a bunch of keys on the end of a chain. He opened a small locker on the bulkhead. Inside I could see a large electric switch. He seemed relieved. He relocked it and sat down again. 'Master switch,' he explained. 'When that's out the Sparks can listen all he damn well wants, but can't send. I like to know what goes out from this ship.'

That was certainly a relief, but then a thought struck me. 'In port,' I said. 'Genoa or the Canal? He could get a message ashore——'

'He'll be lucky,' Kjaer said savagely. 'He'll be in a dark hole down below—with you others—when we're in port.' He suddenly beamed like the sun coming from behind clouds. 'Damn lucky that. When he hadn't turned up before sailing I scratched him off articles and had the shipping master stamp it. I haven't had time to put him on again. Officially he ain't aboard, so there'll be no questions if the port doctor called a crew muster.' He rose. 'Well—maybe it could be worse. Bloddy good job you clobbered him. It's put a dhobi mark on him all right—so we know him. But a pity it just wasn't that *liddle* bit harder. You'll all be wanting your breakfast.'

'You can see now why I wanted an extra cabin,' I ventured.

'For the broad? You can shift her in here if you think you're going to be crowded.' He winked lasciviously. 'Briddish? They take a bit of warming up, but it's a wonder what you can do with them in a narrow bunk and the leeboards shipped.'

Unaccountably I was furious. 'Listen, Kjaer, you fat bastard——' I began.

'*Captain* Kjaer on my own ship,' he said with dignity. 'And I ain't fat.' Then he went off into roars of laughter.

We walked along the deck to collect the others. Carter was sitting on a lifebelt rack outside the cabin. He rose as we approached and I introduced him as Mr Jones. Kjaer shook hands and said he was happy to have him aboard, and hoped he would have an enjoyable voyage, and Carter bowed solemnly, and said he was sure he would. He was now in complete control of himself, and it was hard to realize that a short half hour previously he had been sobbing brokenly.

Then Sonia came out of the cabin. She was still dressed in slacks and jersey, but she'd shed the jacket, and with it the bulk she had been carrying beneath it, and by some feminine magic she had stepped back into her own personality. She had got rid of the stain on her face and neck, and the cold, brisk breeze whipped the colour into her really beautiful skin even as she came out on to the deck. She used little make-up—just a slash of lipstick and something very faint round her eyes—that was just exactly *right*. Her hair was tidy when she came out, but the wind played havoc with it—but somehow that was just exactly right also. And her figure certainly did things to the slacks and jersey that would have surprised the young fisher boy they had originally been intended for.

Kjaer's objections to female passengers seemed to disappear like the morning mist before the sun. He engulfed her hand in his huge paw and made porcine sounds of approval and welcome. He really was a most objectionable man. He took us into the comfortably furnished saloon. Two of the mates—the second and third—were having a late breakfast. They must of course have known by this time that there was a woman aboard, so they showed no surprise, but just rose and bowed gravely and murmured greetings in good English—two blond and rather lumpish young men in neat blue uniform. The breakfast the Chinese steward served us was English too—a good one of bacon, eggs, toast, marmalade and wonderful coffee. Kjaer left with his officers then, to go about their business, and shortly afterwards Carter, who had lapsed into a stony, expressionless silence, pushed his untouched plate aside and made a hurried exit, looking once again a bit green about the gills.

I could see that Sonia was bursting with questions, but the steward was within earshot in his small pantry, so I signed to her to come out on deck. We walked to the stern and leaned with our backs to the rail and looked forward along the entire length of the ship. The weather was clearing, but the wind was increasing from the south-west, and from time to time a flurry of spray smacked over her bows. The officers and crew berthed amidships and for'ard respectively, and this part was completely deserted. Behind us the seagulls were wheeling and diving over the wake, and the Normandy coast was receding on our port beam. I realized that this was the first time since that second evening in their London home that we had been alone—really alone. Always we had been conscious of the presence of Carter and the necessity of keeping our voices down—of the possibility of ears at keyholes and watching eyes outside. Now, for a time at least, we were free of all that, and ahead of us was the long run south. True, there were the minor hazards of Genoa and the Canal to be got over, then the immeasurably greater one of the handover in Hong Kong, but for the moment we knew only this blessed relaxation of tension.

I brought her up to date with things, telling her what Kjaer had told me.

She said: 'It's going to be difficult keeping Carter and this other man from getting their heads together. We can't watch them both day and night.'

'We'll just have to do our best, that's all,' I said. 'But even if they do manage it, there's nothing they can do about it.'

'He—the Marconi man I mean—can expose Kjaer afterwards.'

'That's Kjaer's lookout. He knows the risk he's running—and

he's being paid for it. Anyhow, as you say, that will be afterwards. The Russians are realists. They don't waste time, effort and money purely on vengeance—not unless there's some propaganda value attached to it. And there won't be to this—not if they've been done in the eye.'

'I don't know,' she said slowly. 'The ship does go on to Vladivostok, doesn't it? He'll undoubtedly be searched there.'

'They'll find nobody.'

'The Marconi man?'

'If I know Kjaer he'll put him ashore before that. They stop at three or four Chinese ports after Hong Kong.' I was refusing to cross bridges before coming to them.

We strolled back amidships. Kjaer was being the perfect host. He had turfed the third mate out of his cabin and put him in the radio shack. 'Help keep an eye on the bastard,' he said, 'and now the lady gets a cabin to herself.'

We met the rest of the officers at lunch—the mate, an elderly Finn, the three engineers, two Swedes and a Dutchman, and finally the Marconi man, who came in for some heavy ribbing from the others. There is apparently something exquisitely funny among sailors in being beaned in a brothel. He took it well, with just the right mixture of bravado and sheepishness. He was a well-built, quite good-looking type in the middle thirties, and his name was Wetten. He knew his job too. There wasn't a flicker of recognition in his face as he shook hands—first with me, then with Carter. I was watching Carter. There was no recognition in his face either.

The mate, who was old enough to know better, asked Wetten whether he had had his money's worth before being clobbered, and he answered dirtily in English. English, I found, was the *lingua franca* on this polyglot ship. They all spoke it ungrammatically but fluently, plentifully besprinkled with the four-letter words—with o doing duty as u. The chief engineer went into a long and very boring story of a similar experience that had befallen him in Valparaiso many years previously, but which due to his wit, perspicacity and superhuman strength had turned out differently. Then Sonia arrived and the Captain rapped for order.

I had a hell of a shock that night. I took a stroll up and down on deck with Sonia after supper, then I turned in early. Carter was already in the lower berth, his face turned to the wall. I took my money and passport from inside my shirt and put both under my pillow, then started to clear my pockets. And only then did I realize that the gun and packet of ammunition I had been carrying had gone. Both had been there when we came aboard—in the right and left pockets of my peajacket respectively—and I'd left the peajacket hanging behind the door when I'd gone to have a bath in the afternoon. And Carter had been in the cabin. I make no excuses. That's the sort of silly thing a man lulled into a sense of security can sometimes do after a period when the pressure has been on.

I dived for the lower berth and hauled Carter half out and got his neck in the crook of my left arm while I slid my other hand under his pillow.

'Where is it?' I demanded.

'Where's what?' he asked expressionlessly.

'You know damned well what I mean.' I applied a little leverage and he winced. 'My gun.'

'Your gun?' His face twisted into a wry grin. 'The lady took it from your pocket when she was clearing her things out to the other cabin. Didn't she tell you?'

I believed him, but it still might have been a trick to get rid of me while he recovered it, and I was taking no more chances. I hauled him right out and shoved him hard into a corner while I searched thoroughly—under both mattresses, lockers drawers and the small wardrobe.

He stood looking at me contemptuously. I gave it up at last and opened the door.

'Don't try anything, Carter,' I told him as I stepped outside. 'It will get you nothing except a broken neck.'

He said: 'You're leaving your money on your bunk.'

Furiously I stepped back inside and collected it.

'You're not terribly good at all this, are you?' he went on. 'I'd quit if I were you—while you're still alive. With a tidy little competence there are lots of comfortable places in the sun where a man can live without looking over his shoulder all the time. Let's talk about it, shall we?'

I went out and walked along to Sonia's cabin. There was a light behind the curtained port. She opened the door a chink in answer to my knock.

'My gun,' I said.

She passed it out to me without a word.

'Why the bloody hell didn't you tell me you'd taken it?' I snarled.

'Why the bloody hell did you leave it there?' she asked coldly and closed the door in my face. And once again, after this temporary truce, I was hating her guts.

CHAPTER FOURTEEN

We butted our way down through the Bay of Biscay in bad weather, for which I was thankful because it kept Carter in his bunk. He only got over his seasickness on the fifth day, when we were well into the Mediterranean, with another couple of days to go before we reached Genoa—then he took it up with me again on deck.

'How much do you want?' he said without preamble.

'What for?' I asked.

'To deliver me to the Soviet consulate in Genoa.'

'How would I collect?'

'From them—on my vouching for you. Dollars, sterling, Swiss francs—any currency you wish.'

'And how far do you think I'd get with it?'

He shrugged. 'Surely that's your affair. You could just disappear.'

'You can say that again,' I said drily. 'I'd disappear all right if I started to make deals on my own. My orders are to deliver you to Vladivostock—and that girl's here to see that I do just that. Forget it, Carter.'

'We haven't discussed a price yet.'

'And we're not going to. I said forget it.'

'Ten thousand pounds.'

'I'm getting more than that as it is,' I said.

'I don't believe you, but we'll say fifteen, eh?'

'No—nor fifty.' I broke things off and walked away, but I knew he'd keep at me.

And then Wetten started to give trouble. He complained bitterly to Kjaer about not being able to transmit.

'All you got to do is listen, mister,' Kjaer told him. 'When I want to transmit anything, I tell you.'

'But I got to acknowledge, for God's sake, when anything comes up for us.'

'Don't worry. Just keep on listening.'

'I've had two calls from your own damn agents in Genoa, wanting to know our E.T.A. there. What are they going to think when I don't answer?'

Kjaer smiled sweetly. 'They going to think I got a damnfool Sparks who gets clobbered in a joyhouse and can't do his job properly. They'll be damn right too. Just carry on like I say, mister.'

A couple of hours before we got in, Kjaer took him down below in his dual capacity of supercargo, and came up ten minutes later, alone. He winked at me broadly and told me to collect Sonia and Carter, then he led us down through the engine-room and along the propeller tunnel to where a section of the curved bulkhead had been removed. We went up through this and found ourselves in a compartment some eight feet square, and sat and listened while they bolted the bulkhead back into position. We were well below the water-line but it wasn't as bad as perhaps it sounds, because there was a light there, and air came in through a duct. It had obviously been used for the same purpose before. There were mattresses, a tank of water and some canned provisions. There was even an Elsan there, and Kjaer, the perfect host, had had the delicacy to have a canvas screen erected in front of it. It could have been worse—but it was still hell.

They let us out fifteen hours later. It was a cold, clear night and the lights of Genoa were dropping astern. Sonia went off to her cabin without a word, and I leaned on the rail drawing great breaths of clean air down into my lungs. Carter came up beside me and started again.

'There's still Suez,' he said. 'Easier there.'

'You've seen the form,' I told him wearily. 'Even suppose I wanted to do a deal with you, how could I? We'll be down in that damned place and we could yell our heads off without anybody hearing. Drop it, Carter.'

'You've got some money,' he said. 'A lot of money. Lend me a thousand pounds.'

'What good would that do you?'

'Just lend it to me,' he insisted. 'I'll guarantee you twenty in return.'

'Not a chance,' I snapped, but I was intrigued. What the hell had he thought up? I shuffled my feet and mumbled, 'I'd want to know exactly what you were going to do with it—and I'd still reserve the right to turn it down.'

'Piecee-money,' he said. I knew what that meant, but I played it dumb.

'What's that?'

'I'd tear the notes in half and give them to somebody—with a letter.'

'And then?'

'God—you're not really as stupid as all that, are you? The person concerned only has to slip the letter to a port police official, and he collects the other halves of the notes afterwards—and nobody is any the wiser where the tip came from.'

'Sure,' I said. 'So we do that—and some sailor is a thousand pounds up. But what about me? They make a complete search and we are dragged out. *You* may get clean away with it, but *I* get booked for kidnapping and criminal conspiracy.'

'The letter would completely exonerate you in advance—and would contain a guarantee that you were to get your twenty thousand afterwards. You could read it, of course.'

'I don't read Russian.'

'It would be in English.'

'Sorry,' I said. 'But you've overlooked one thing. The most important thing. As far as I know I'm working for the Russians already. Are they going to pay me twenty thousand over the top for disobeying orders that I've already received? Be your age, Carter.'

'You're not working for the Russians. You're working for the Chinese,' he said flatly.

'You're nuts.'

'Would you like some cards on the table, Mr Wainwright?' he asked quietly. 'My cards, I mean.'

I tried to repress the start, but he was conscious of it even in the darkness. I had never told him my name. I was Smith on this ship—as he was Jones. Then I thought he might have heard Sonia let it slip in an unguarded moment, but he disabused me of that in the next second.

'Oh yes,' he went on. 'I know your name. I know quite a lot about you. You're working for Malcolm—the Masterspringer—at the moment, but your real controller is Henry George Gaffney—or the Gaffer as you call him.'

So much for the school—the years of training—the bloody mumbo-jumbo of schoolboy secrecy they put one through, I thought bitterly. Christ, we were only boy scouts at this game.

'You were recruited in London and trained in England initially,' the flat voice went on. 'Then you were infiltrated into Hong Kong—Hong Kong and Southern China Bank. Not so, Mr Wainwright? Or are you going to waste your time and breath in denying it?'

'I don't know what the hell you're talking about,' I said, but it sounded feeble even to me.

'More cards, Mr Wainwright? Very well—here they come—face up—the lot. Your late lamented father—ex-Shanghai policeman. He defected to the Russians in nineteen-twenty-seven——'

I threw the lot then—right into his lap. 'You're a bloody liar,' I said. 'Get back to the cabin before I throw you over the rail, you bastard.'

'Why the indignation, Mr Wainwright? That's what you've done yourself, isn't it?' he said, and that, curiously enough, enabled me to get a grip on myself again. He was clever all right, and what he knew about me had come in the form of a shock that had had me gasping and floundering for some minutes, but this restored the balance. So I had been blown? If he knew my background and cover, then obviously others did too, so I was out of the game—once I had handed him over. But that was *all* he knew. For the rest he was just guessing and probing. He had overplayed his hand in suggesting I had gone over—and the shrewd one he had whipped in about the poor old man was of the same cloth.

I felt my anger subsiding. I yawned elaborately.

'I've listened to enough cock for tonight,' I told him. 'I'm going to turn in. It's no good trying to rat me for a thousand pounds while I'm asleep, Carter. My money's in a safe place. Anyhow, you'd never find a man on the ship who'd dare pull a fast one on the skipper—except Wetten, and he'll be down in a hole somewhere going through the Canal—just as he was this time.'

'You're still not convinced, are you?' he said. 'A few more cards——?'

'Shove 'em. Good night.' I turned away.

'A pity,' he said softly. 'This way we both die. I've got rather longer than you, because there's quite a lot they want out of me first. But you're booked out too, you know. Your own people will do it. They've got to now.'

'Things are getting a bit mixed,' I said. 'Who are my own people? First you say I'm working for the Chinese—then you say my father and I defected to the Russians.'

'You're mistaken. I didn't say *you* defected to the Russians. Your father—yes—but when the big split came in nineteen-fifty-five he plumped for the Chinese. You never had that agonizing choice—and it *was* agonizing for the real, orthodox Marxian—you went Chinese right from the beginning.'

'Well, at least that tidies things up a little,' I said. 'So now the ungrateful sods are going to rub me out, are they? Why?'

'They've hardly any option, have they? You've been blown for the last eighteen months, Mr Wainwright. You're just about the biggest security risk they're carrying at the moment—less perhaps the Gaffer. I had you on the list long before I went inside.'

'You're losing me again,' I said. 'Who was I blown to? The Russians?'

'Curiously enough, no,' he said. 'They'll know by now, of course, since this London interlude, but you got away with it in Hong Kong. Their set-up is not very good there, as you no doubt know yourself. The Chinese breathe too closely down their necks. No—I was referring to the British.'

'Ah!' I said profoundly. 'Now we're getting somewhere. So the British know all about me, do they?'

'Not all. You were on the doubtful list for quite a long time, but when Winterton blew his furbler in Amoy he named you as a *British* agent—under stringent interrogation. Word got back, as Winterton meant it to—and that was it. Through you Kempson in your London office, and Walters and Blackman in Hong Kong, were then uncovered.'

Then cold breezes *did* start to blow around my tail. My God! He'd named the three key people in the whole set-up as far as I was concerned. And he had already brought the Gaffer into it. He had us all in the wrong context, of course, but he *knew* us—and he was being handed over to the Chinese—and he'd probably either try to make a deal—or break under interrogation. They probably knew all this already, but if they didn't this fellow was going to be a pearl of price to them.

But I'd had enough by this time. My head was reeling. I

turned and walked away abruptly, but he caught me up by the ladder to the upper deck.

'Look, Wainwright,' he said urgently. 'I'm not scared for my own hide. What these bastards will do to me will be unpleasant, but that, as we both know, is one of the contingent liabilities of the job. But what *is* burning me up is the thought that this can be avoided. Just let me fix that letter—and we're out of it.'

'How could you guarantee that?' I demanded. Any pitiable scrap of information I could pick up out of this lousy affair might be useful to somebody afterwards.

'The letter will be addressed to a certain consular official in Port Said. Within a matter of minutes it will be relayed to Cairo. We'll be off this damned ship before we get through the Canal——'

'And splurged across every front page in the world,' I said. 'What chance would *I* have?'

'What chance have you got now, you bloody fool?' he came back at me. 'You think you're going to hand me over in Amoy or Shanghai or some other Chinese port, and then just drift back into circulation again? For God's sake, haven't I told you enough? The British *know* you. Your rope's run out. You'll be picked up as soon as you show your face in Hong Kong if you've got any ideas of trying to make a break for it there—and if you get away with less than thirty years you'll be lucky. But personally I don't think you'll reach Hong Kong. The Chinese will bump you off.'

'If the British have known about me all this time, why haven't they picked me up before?' I asked.

He laughed shortly. 'I don't want to be insulting,' he said, 'but you've been quite a useful bloke to them, haven't you? You've blundered around so much that you've uncovered everybody you've had contact with. They've been using you as a stalking-horse, for Christ's sake—but now your usefulness is finished. You'll just be swept up into the dustpan. My way you'll come off this ship with me—and Wetten—and there won't be a word on *any* front page. You have a passport. You can take your own chances—or you can be on a plane with me to Moscow the same day.' He laughed again. 'You wouldn't be lonely. There's quite a colony of us there nowadays.'

'What about the girl?' I asked. 'What happens to her?'

'Does that make any difference?'

'It does to me.'

'In which case I can see no objection to her coming with us. *She* hasn't such a hell of a rosy future anywhere else either.'

I said: 'I'll have to think about it.'

'You haven't got much time,' he said. 'None of us has.'

I went to the saloon. Everybody not on watch was there, including Wetten. He looked up and nodded as I entered, showing no resentment for his sojourn in the bowels of the ship. The others were watching Italian television, entranced. It was something they only saw in port and for a couple of hours thereafter.

Kjaer yelled: 'Old Sparks here bloddy good. He get this damn thing to work after the bloddy third pour beer in it. That little piece there with the nice ass—wouldn't mind having *her* aboard. Have a drink.'

I needed one. I felt as though I'd been put through a wringer.

I thought of going along and knocking Sonia up, but I dropped the idea. She would be tired and edgy after our spell in the tank and wouldn't be much help in this. But I couldn't face another session of cross-talk and double-think in the cabin, and I knew Carter wouldn't let up on me now, so I found a sheltered corner right down at the stern and sat on the deck and smoked. The son of a bitch had certainly shaken me.

They knew so much. True, they had misinterpreted a lot of it —but they still *knew*. They knew the Gaffer. Henry George Gaffney. God damn it, not even I had known his real name until tonight. Did *he* know he was blown? If I got out of this in one piece it would afford me the acutest satisfaction in telling him. But then, I reflected sourly, he would without a doubt blame *me* for it. Kempson, my boss in the bank in London—the man who had recruited me in the first place. He was only on liaison work admittedly, but he was still a pretty big wheel. But it was the thought of Walters, the deep-sea fishing *aficionado*, and Blackman, my immediate controller, being uncovered that really frightened me. They, I had no doubt, would be the ones who would be arranging our reception in Hong Kong. If they were in a fool's paradise we were walking straight into a trap.

What a bloody mess!

I tried to sort things out in my own mind. Three parties, mutually antagonistic—the Russians, the Chinese, ourselves. Carter was a Russian. We held him. We were going to give him to the Chinese in return for Winterton. The Russians were trying to rescue him before the exchange took place. That was the problem reduced to its simplest terms. What were the factors affecting it? First and foremost, for reasons of policy we, the British, had to work secretly—without the knowledge and co-operation of our own orthodox agencies. Factors to our advantage at the moment: A. We were holding Carter. B. Secrecy, insofar as the said orthodox agencies were concerned, had been preserved up to this point. And that was *all* I could find to our advantage. Factors against us: A. The Russians knew we were holding Carter. B. Although we might have broken the trail in Le Havre, it would still be a reasonable assumption that the exchange would be made in or near the only place where the British and Chinese frontiers touched—Hong Kong. Therefore the watches would be on there. C. The Russians knew our people in Hong Kong. D. I had every reason to believe that our people didn't know that the Russians were aware of them. They would therefore, except for normal precautions, be off their guard to that extent. E. Whatever the outcome of this, our Hong Kong set-up was now irretrievably blown. But at least to get another set-up going was somebody else's headache.

Numerically the advantages were overwhelmingly with the Russians.

There was one other factor that remained a wild joker without apparent advantage or disadvantage to either side. The Russians thought that we—that is, the Gaffer, Kempson, Walters, Blackman, myself and others known or unknown—were working for the Chinese. I wondered what the hell gave them that idea? They had been so right—so frighteningly on the beam—about everything else. Was that a deliberate thing on our part? A carefully and diabolically clever smoke-screen laid by our higher-ups?

Then, in spite of the cold breeze, I suddenly found myself breaking into a prickly sweat. *Were* the Russians wrong? What did *I* know about the higher echelons? Just four men. Couldn't I have been a complete catspaw all along? Couldn't those four be working for the Chinese?

I scrabbled round for something concrete to batter at this terrifying new hypothesis. The school? They surely couldn't run as elaborate a thing as that right in the heart of England? Or could they? After all, security had been as tight there as anything I had ever known. The Gaffer? He, of course, could be anybody's meat and I disliked him so much that I would be prepared to believe anything about him. But the three senior bank officials—

comfortable, secure, affluent—the epitomization of English upper middle class—? No, that was too fantastic. But what about a couple of senior diplomats and a round half-dozen scientists who were forming the nucleus of the Moscow colony that Carter had mentioned? What about a man who had been at the top of our orthodox Secret Service itself—now living comfortably in a dacha? A consulate official who had been whisked over the wall just as Carter had been——?

The Meisterspringer? Sonia? Where did they fit into it? Just hirelings who would work for anybody who paid them? That was the impression Malcolm seemed deliberately and cynically to give me. But Sonia? Was she here only for her own safety—or was she rubber-heeling on me to make certain there were no slip-ups? Well, whatever the answer to that last one was, I couldn't trust her again.

Then I thought I saw a chink of light at the end of the dark tunnel through which I was crawling. For God's sake, if they were all working for the Chinese why this complicated exchange business? Why bring Winterton into it at all? Once they had sprung Carter all they would need to do would be to dump him on this ship and hand him over in a Chinese port. Then, pathetically, that one crumbled. I, in my innocence, would still have to be supplied with a valid reason for it all. If I had just been told to hand Carter over to the Chinese I might have started to think—and that would be the last thing they'd want. Perhaps there was no question of an exchange. I handed him over—and then, as Carter had suggested, got quietly knocked off—my usefulness, such as it had been, ended.

But would they have gone to all this trouble, the years of training, just for this? Hardly. No—I was just a gullible starry-eye who thought he was working for his own country. Probably there were many others in the same position. Pawns being moved, without any clear ideas of who was doing the moving. Carefully conditioned not to question or reason why. Taught to regard our own real security services as our worst enemies. This job was a natural for me. It just cropped up—and I was in the right place at the right time. And boy—was I expendable!

So, assuming all this to be right, what the hell was I to do now? Was there a choice in the two evils of turning Carter over to the Russians in preference to the Chinese? I just couldn't answer that one.

How about throwing the whole thing when I got to Hong Kong? Going to the police and making a clean breast of it? Telling them I had been acting in good faith—and naming names? Then I started to sweat afresh. Suppose I wasn't right, and that all this was fantastic theorizing, and I blew the whole thing needlessly?

No—anything but that. I shuddered.

I finally fell into a fitful, bedevilled sleep, and woke shivering and damp as day was breaking.

Carter was awake when I went to the cabin. I avoided his eye and swore at him when he said good morning, but, knew he could see what a lather I was in and was marking it up as a point to himself.

CHAPTER FIFTEEN

I AVOIDED HIM all that day. I avoided Sonia too—by the simple expedient of being just plain damned rude to her when she spoke to me, which distressed Kjaer. He saw me and said: 'What the hell goes on? Sonia bloddy mad at you. She asks me to go in a hole by herself when we go through the Canal.'

'Good idea,' I said. 'You do that.'

He shook his head. 'Can't put a lady in the bilges. Bloddy big rats down there, and it stinks like hell.'

'Well, put her somewhere else.'

'Not so. Only two really safe places on this ship, if the Gyps got nosey.'

'All right—I'll go in the bilges.'

'You're nuts,' he said. 'But please yourself.'

That meant the three others would be together, cooking up God knows what, but they could do that anyhow on a long trip. This way it meant I didn't have to talk to anybody.

But Carter still made it. He corralled me in the cabin two hours before we came up to the outer bar in Port Said.

'What about it?' he said without preamble.

'Not a chance,' I answered.

'You're forcing my hand, Wainwright.' He was looking straight at me, unwaveringly.

'And you're breaking my heart—but the answer's still no. And don't try slipping any of the crew a note without the piecee-money. They know they'd never collect it afterwards. I've warned Kjaer.'

'Wainwright, listen to me,' he begged. 'There's one thing I haven't told you——'

'Save it.'

'—one last thing which I hoped I wouldn't have to tell. But the position is desperate now. I'm working for the British. I always have.'

I laughed. 'I'd have said the Krauts on that. It was Hitler who said the bigger the lie the better its chance of being believed, wasn't it?'

'It's true.'

'All right—so it's true. But what difference does that make? I'm working for the people who pay me. In this case it's the Chinese. You told me that yourself. They're paying me to deliver you somewhere on the hoof. Skip it, Carter. That one wasn't up to your usual standard.'

'Wainwright—*it's the truth,*' he repeated—and by God he was almost convincing me. I've never before or since heard a man put so much conviction into three simple words. Once more I was standing on shifting sands, but I fought back.

'Maybe you were—once—but you went over, didn't you—first to the Chinks, then to the Rusks—and the British caught up with you and you were clobbered with thirty years.'

He stepped forward and took my arm. I could feel his fingers digging into the muscle like steel prongs. His voice and his eyes were steady. This was no frightened man begging for his life.

'Just listen to this. It will give you something to think about in the comparatively short time you've got left, if nothing else. I went over to the Chinese. With my background and antecedents that was easy. White Russian—anti-Red. I was a natural—on the surface. But I was already in a Red cell. I doubled for the Russians right from the beginning—long before the split came. Then I was uncovered in Amoy and had to skip for Russia. My admittance was already bought, paid for and guaranteed by ten years' solid and valuable work for them—but naturally I was useless in the Far East. But I still had a potential in the West. They did what we were banking on—and sent me to London. I did a good job for them there too—but of course I was leaking it back to our own people——'

'"Our own people" being the British?' I interrupted.

'That's right.'

'Then why the bloody hell did "our own people" give you thirty years?'

'If you'll listen a little longer I'll explain,' he said. 'In terms which even you might understand. I was blown by a Chinaman in Ipswich. Blown in a manner that our own people couldn't hush up. The police came into it—and it leaked to the newspapers. I was as bare as a badger's arse, shivering in the cold. Our own people had the choice of clearing me, or letting matters take their course. But it really wasn't a choice. Clearing me would automatically have blown a whole string of other people—a chain reaction through at least fifty cells in Russia—with strings leading back to God knows how many more in China. So matters had to take their course. The prosecution was supplied with just enough to make a watertight case against me—and no more. All good straight stuff—nothing faked—but not a hint of who I really worked for. So I went down for thirty years.'

'Without a squawk?'

'Naturally. Even if I'd wanted to squawk, what good would it have done me? Our people would just have denied it.'

'So?'

'So this. One good point about the Russians is that none of their top people are ever caught and imprisoned by the Opposition without their moving heaven and earth to get them out again. Exchange is the usual thing. They offered two commercial travellers and a journalist for me who they'd arrested in Moscow.'

'Why didn't we settle for that?'

'Because none of them was worth a damn. They knew it, and they knew that we knew it too. To the British I was a very big salmon indeed. They wouldn't be likely to exchange me for three tiddlers. They did offer me in return for an American, but the Russians wouldn't wear it. This guy knew too much and could still be very useful to C.I.A. So we just sat on our asses and waited for what we knew would eventually come. A spring.'

Kjaer came along the deck then and put his head into the cabin. 'Time you boys wasn't here,' he said. 'The breakwater's in sight and we'll be having the pilot alongside before long.'

'Just a moment,' begged Carter, and Kjaer grunted and went away. 'The Russians approached the Meisterspringer, and he was ready to do it, but he got a tip from somewhere that it had leaked, so he dropped it like a hot potato. Then they went to a fellow called Wates, who had done three commercial jobs but no politicals. He was cagey at first, but the price went up and up—until he took it on. But now the Meisterspringer had got word of it—and the old bastard sold the tip to the Gaffer, who was already cooking one up for the Chinese. *You* know more about things from then on——'

'Possibly I do,' I said. 'But how the hell do *you* know so much? You were inside—and you've had no contact with anybody other than the girl and myself since you came out.'

He laughed shortly. 'How naïve can you get, Wainwright?' he asked. 'I was kept abreast of every detail, right from the time I arrived in Lanchester. I was a highly-privileged good-conduct prisoner, making myself useful to the screws, working in the ration office and in the school. I was allowed any books I wanted from outside. I was even allowed a radio in my cell—a beautiful transistor job with one of those earplug things—so damned simple that it was laughable. Hold it the right way up and it received. Turn it upside down and it transmitted over a distance of ten miles—twenty if I hung a tiny coil of fuse wire out of the window—on a wavelength tucked away between the BBC and the police and amateur bands. I was briefed right up to the moment I came down that ladder. Wates and another fellow met me and gave me the word I was expecting, and we went off across a field to a waiting car. Then we were jumped—jumped by *one man*—someone was shot—the others hared away like hell into the darkness—and in the confusion I felt a needle jabbed into me, and that was it.'

And it fitted. It all fitted together so convincingly. This could so easily be the truth—and yet—and yet——. He pulled a letter from his pocket; the envelope was unsealed. He held it out to me.

'This is our last chance, Wainwright,' he said. 'For either of us. There's a quartermaster—a Swede—Olsen. I've sounded him out. He'll do it—but he's got to have the piecee-money. Give it to him—and I'll take you into Russia with me—or you can shag off on your own—and if you ever want to go back to England I can even fix that too—*working for us*—the British—really this time.'

And then Kjaer was back with us, roaring: 'Mister Jones—for Christ's sake—down that bloddy engine-room and along the shaft tunnel. Mister Smith—find the mate and he'll show you where to go. You think we got all bloddy day?'

Carter gave me one last look. Threatening? Beseeching? Questioning? I don't know. Perhaps a mixture of all three. Kjaer hustled him off. I pushed the letter into my pocket and went forward.

I still had time to do it. Olsen, the sailor who had been on the gangway the first time I came aboard, was along the deck preparing a rope ladder for the pilot to come aboard. My pack of money was tucked inside my shirt. I just had to tear some hundred dollar bills in two and give them to him with the letter. If this was the truth I had been listening to I would be instrumental in getting a top British agent back into Russia—quite apart from probably saving my own neck, and incidentally his. If the Gaffer and the others were what he represented them to be, I'd be blowing them sky-high. If——

But then a whistle sounded from the bridge, and Olsen dropped what he was doing and hurried towards the ladder without a glance at me—and simultaneously the mate descended on me in a crimson burst of profanity and hurried me down into the well deck, and through an iron door, and down into the tween decks, and lower and lower still, until he lifted a trap over a dark and stinking hole and flashed his torch downwards. I dropped through wearily. The decision appeared to have been made for me.

'A jar of water and some grub in a canister. Piss where you like—All yours, mister,' said the mate, and dropped the trap into place. And he didn't even leave me the torch.

I was in complete and absolute darkness, with barely headroom when I stood upright. Oily water slopped round my ankles, and from somewhere the other side of a bulkhead came the hellish din of the engines, but suddenly there was a tinkle of a telegraph and the din dropped to a purr. I pushed upwards on the trap to relieve, if only for a moment, the ghastly claustrophobic panic that I felt welling up, but it was securely clamped down the other side. I groped around with my feet and eventually found the two-gallon jar and a big square canister with a screw top. I turned it on its side and used it as a seat and felt about me for some dry spot above the level of the water to put my feet. I found a stringer at just the right height running between the steel ribs of the ship but then something soft and furry ran over my ankles and, squeaked as I yelled and kicked, so I settled for the footbath again.

I tried to read the letter, but the air was so bad that my matches didn't give sufficient light, then, if that wasn't enough, I dropped the damned thing in the water and in scrabbling for it I dropped the matches also, which put paid to it anyhow.

The engines started up again, ran for half an hour or so, then stopped and stayed still, except for the throbbing of a dynamo, for a long time. I preferred them to run because then one couldn't hear the squeaking of the rats. The place was lousy with them. Eventually we got under way again and I guessed we were now in the Canal, because she was rock steady with the engines throttled down.

But why dwell on it? It went on for thirty-six hours all told, and what with the thought of those rats and the agony of mind I was suffering anyhow, I was as near completely nuts when they let me out as made no difference. I followed the mate up the ladders, howling obscenities at him, but he only grinned. The light on deck nearly blinded me at first. We were well south of Suez now, with the barren shores of the Gulf widening out and receding on either side—and the Red Sea was incredibly blue. I went into the saloon and took three fingers of straight aquavit from Kjaer's private bottle, then staggered off to the bathroom and lay in warm water for nearly an hour.

Carter was lying on his back on his bunk when I came into the cabin, with his hands behind his head. He said, slowly and distinctly, without looking at me: 'You yellow-livered bastard.'

'Why yellow?' I asked him wearily. 'Mine might have been the harder decision.'

'You didn't make a decision, Wainwright,' he said. 'You just let things drift. When they let you have it I hope you'll live long enough to think of what might have been. What *would* have been —if you'd had the guts to hand that letter over.'

'Sure,' I said. 'I might have been handing a golden boy back to the Rusks.'

'And you wouldn't do that because you'd be letting your Chink bosses down, eh? Don't give me that line. Your sort would sell your mothers—if it was safe. You did nothing because you couldn't screw up the resolution.'

'You're wrong,' I told him. 'I didn't do it, because I don't believe you, Carter. You're a liar—a really convincing, bloody clever one—but you've overlooked one thing—and that punctures your whole story.'

He looked up at me quickly.

'What's that?' he asked.

'Find out.'

He swung his legs to the deck and sat up slowly, staring at me. 'I think I *know*,' he said. 'Or rather I think I know what *you* think. And if I'm right then this really is a tragedy—or a comedy—according to what sort of sense of humour you're endowed with.'

'Oh, drop it for Christ's sake,' I said, and prepared to go out on deck. He moved quickly, placing himself between me and the door.

'My story is unpuncturable, Wainwright, for the simple reason that every word I've told you is the truth,' he said very quietly. 'And I haven't overlooked anything. *Not even the possibility that you yourself are a British agent.*'

And he won—hands down. I tried desperately to ride the shock, but it was no good. I felt, and no doubt looked, like a boxer caught by a sucker punch—flat-footed and wide open—and he was reading my face like a book.

'So that's it,' he said, and nodded slowly as if confirming it to himself. 'I was pretty certain. You gave yourself away when you blew your top when I mentioned that your father had gone over. A very old interrogator's trick that. Something dropped in quite incidentally—"Your father defected in 'thirty-six"—"Your wife became Robinson's mistress two years ago"—"Your brother had a homosexual relationship with a War Office clerk." It takes a very well trained man indeed to be on his guard against that particular technique—when he's tired, as you were—and when there is a possibility that it could be true. You're *not* very well trained, are you? A crash course at that place up in the Wirral, I should say—and you've been a lone duck ever since.' He grinned suddenly—not sardonically. There was sympathy in it. 'You jumped as if I'd stuck a pin in your arse when I said "Wirral". So that was it, was it? I'm sorry, Wainwright. I'm not riding you for the fun of it. *I had to know*—for the sake of my own neck.'

I had struggled to the surface by this. 'You don't know a

bloody thing, you son of a bitch,' I said. 'But if it's going to pass the long hours in front of you by thinking up wild ones, go ahead. Only get off *my* back. You're boring the pants off me.'

'I'm not boring you. Confusing you, maybe—even scaring you a bit—but not boring you. *You've* got some long hours of thinking ahead of you too.'

'Carter, you flatter yourself,' I said. 'I'll be spending my long hours sleeping in the sun.'

'*And* wondering. Wondering how the hell I could possibly know as much about you as I do—if I weren't what I represented myself to be—a British agent.'

'I've told you—and you don't know anything. You've made some pretty shrewd guesses, and some of them have been a bit close to the mark, and maybe my reactions showed that. But you've read those reactions wrongly. Now suppose you let me pass—or do I have to take a swing at you?'

But he didn't let me pass—and I did take a swing at him—a hard one. His head hit the door jamb behind him and he slid down to the floor, a thin trickle of blood appearing at the corner of his mouth.

I felt a swine. He was still a sick man, and he was booked for the slaughterhouse anyhow. I shouldn't have let it come to this. I hauled him to his feet and lowered him on to the settee and got some water and a towel.

He opened his eyes and shook his head slowly from side to side as if trying to clear it.

He said thickly: 'What does that settle, Wainwright?'

'Not a thing,' I said miserably. 'I'm sorry—but for God's sake stop it, will you. I've got my orders—and I'm going to carry them out. Nothing can alter that.'

'But you've got your doubts too, haven't you?'

'Not a doubt,' I shook my head firmly.

'Yes you have,' he said. 'But you're clinging to one thing. One thing that shoots my entire story down in flames. Shall I tell you what it is?'

'What difference could it make?' I asked. I handed him the wet towel. 'Stay there and I'll get you a drink from the saloon.' I moved to the door again.

'One thing,' he repeated softly. 'How, if we're both on the same side, could your orders be to hand me over to the Opposition?'

'That's it,' I acknowledged. 'The clincher. You've said it yourself. Now, shall we let it drop?'

'One minute more,' he begged. 'Then I will let it drop—because there's nothing more I can say.'

'Go ahead,' I sighed.

'I accused you of working for the Chinese,' he said. 'You didn't deny it.'

'I didn't confirm it either.'

'You didn't need to—then—because I was positive I was right. It suited your book at the moment to let me go on thinking that. There wasn't a reaction from you.'

'I'll get you that drink,' I said, and started to open the door. He wriggled upright and grabbed my sleeve.

'Wait—But when I changed my tack and mentioned the possibility of your working for the British—you *did* react. My God you did. That wasn't faked. It was only a shot in the dark, but it landed right on target.'

'So we're back where we started,' I said. 'Somebody in the higher reaches has made a balls of things and set dog on eating dog. Too bad. But it doesn't alter a thing. I've always been taught to obey the last order.'

'Nobody has made a balls of anything. But *you've* been made the goat. You *are* working for the Chinese, you pitiful bloody fool, *but you don't know it.*' He was gasping and shaking. If he was putting on an act of a man who had been groping in the dark and suddenly found himself in blinding light, he was certainly doing it well. In fact he put it into those exact words: 'Wainwright—I'm beginning to see the whole thing in the light now. Listen to me, for God's sake.' He started to enumerate off his fingers: 'One—those names I've given you—Gaffney, Kempson, Walters, Blackman, and yourself, who I thought right up to this minute was one of them—one of them knowingly, I mean—You'll admit that I've got those right, won't you? You were all blown at the same time. I told you—I had you all on the last list I got before leaving China. But it wasn't positive. You were all working for us—the British—but there was a possibility that one or all of you were leaking stuff to the Chinese. I was told to investigate from the Chinese side. I found out nothing—but Winterton did. It was I who interrogated him in Amoy. The very last job I did before I was blown myself, and had to skip to Russia. He named you all. I told you earlier that I passed the information back to

Hong Kong. I did—but I never got an acknowledgment, and I certainly hadn't time to check whether it arrived. The fact that you're all still at large rather makes me doubt it now.'

'Couldn't you check from Russia?' I asked.

'I couldn't risk it. I was too busy establishing myself there. I was under rigorous screening for the first six months, anyhow. And it was the same when they sent me to London. I was under the closest rubber-heeling and I certainly couldn't afford to interest myself in something that was no longer in my parish.' He paused to take a deep breath. 'Right—Two—Winterton did, in fact, mention the possibility of your being a starry-eye doing low-category courier work without knowing the side you were working for—but that's a normal recruiting procedure. Three—and believe me I'm sorry about this, Wainwright, if it really hurts—but you couldn't be on any regular British intelligence roster, because of your father's defection. That, at least, is true.'

That one went home again—right under my ribs, in a cold, sickening stab—and I didn't even try to cover it this time. He didn't miss it.

'All right then, I'm not asking you to give me any answers, but I do want you to ask yourself these four questions: one—have you ever had an M.I.5 Positive Vetting? Two—have you ever met a departmental Head or Deputy Head of any regular intelligence agency whom you knew without any shadow of doubt to be such? Three—have you ever been controlled by anybody but the four men I have mentioned? Four—have you received your pay and expenses into your banking account by cheque—*and paid income tax on it*—or has it just been slipped to you in cash? If the answers to all those are in the negative, and you still think you're working for the British, you're *really* in cloud cuckoo land, and I'm sorry for you.'

He lay back and closed his eyes tiredly.

'I could do with that drink,' he said.

And he wasn't on his own. I went out and along the deck with my knees nearly buckling under me—and I was sorry for myself.

CHAPTER SIXTEEN

My God—and how sorry for myself. The more I went over things during the next few days, the more I realized how far out on the limb I was. His whole story was incontrovertible. I tested it link by link, but couldn't find a single flaw—except, perhaps, that school in the Wirral. Surely a spy ring couldn't run as elaborate a show as that right in the heart of England, and get away with it? The two main regular agencies—M.I.5 and 6—were being pilloried in the Press at the moment as inefficient and complacent—but could they possibly be as dumb as that? And the students themselves? Damn it all, with the best will in the world I had nearly blown the place twice myself. What were the other students, anyhow? All starry-eyes like myself—or was I the only mug who thought he was working for the British?

No—that school was genuine. I remembered once seeing a discreet police guard put on it when some high-up came down from London to lecture. But couldn't that have been rigged for some devious purpose of their own? Phoney uniforms——?

That was the whole pattern of it. Every time I thought I detected some slight inconsistency I found myself putting up counter theories to refute it. But that one persisted—and in the end I took it up with Carter—springing it on him one morning while he was still only half awake.

'The school, Carter——?' I began, but he didn't even let me finish.

'A kindergarten with a failure rate of eighty per cent—of which I should imagine you were one,' he said without hesitation. 'What about it?'

'You're asking me to believe that a set-up that size could be run in England without—er—our people—getting wind of it?'

'I'm not asking you to believe anything. I've shot the lot to you now. How much you accept, or reject, is up to you.'

'I reject that anyhow. M.I.5 would have been bound to uncover it sooner or later.'

'M.I.5 run it, you bloody fool,' he said drily. 'They took it over from SIS after the war.'

'SIS?'

'God—you don't know an awful lot, do you? Secret Intelligence Services—back in the days when Five, Six, Admiralty, Foreign Office, S.O.E., Special Branch—the lot—were centralized. Any one of those agencies can nominate a promising recruit to it for *ab initio* training. I imagine Gaffney would have put you in there as a possible for M.I.6—Far East—then picked you up later after you failed to make the grade.'

'Nobody ever told me I'd failed to make the grade,' I snapped.

He chuckled. 'They never do. Shake hands, pat on the back—"don't call us—we'll call you." Isn't that what happened?'

And it was, I reflected sadly.

'Was Gaffney M.I.6?' I asked.

'Was? Probably still is—and likely to stay that way after the balls-up you've made of things. M.I.6 ultimately control everything outside the British Isles. You know that office of his in Portman Square?'

'Yes——?'

'You're a liar. He never had an office in Portman Square. Where *does* the old bastard work from nowadays?'

'Get stuffed,' I snarled.

He chuckled again. 'That's better. Actually it used to be from a building near Waterloo Station—but I bet he never called *you* there. That's genuine M.I.6 country.' He climbed out of his bunk and started to shave. 'I'm willing to bet that you always saw him in some hole-in-the-corner bang in the middle of town—always at night—and that the one thing that you were really trained well in was the art of throwing a tail—and that you never called him except at prearranged times—on an ex-directory number. Right?'

I caught his eyes on me in the mirror. Of course he was right—and he knew it.

'Poor bloody Wainwright,' he said. 'You don't know whether you're on your head or your arse, do you? And I'm sorry. Believe me, *I'm sorry*. I'm not trying to take the mick out of you. I'm trying to make things easier for both of us, but what more can I do? I've told you everything now. If you don't trust me, I can't make you.'

'You've given me nothing I could check.'

'You could check on every single thing I've told you—by radio. But who would you check it *with*?' He turned and looked at me. 'You might have a telegraphic code address—but I bet it would only be to one of the four men I've named. What good would that be—if what I've told you is the truth? If they are still in circulation and you asked for fresh orders, you'd merely have your old ones confirmed. To hand me over to the Chinese. Where *am* I to be handed over, by the way?'

'Vladivostock,' I said obstinately. 'To the Russians.'

'Screw that. We both know it's not true—or if those really are your orders, you'll have them changed long before we reach there.' Again he was right. He turned back to the mirror and carried on shaving in silence. I sat chewing my nails for a long time, then I said, 'There's one way out of this, Carter.'

'I know,' he answered. 'Let's see if we're thinking along the same lines.'

'Hong Kong's the next stop,' I said. 'I go to the police there and make a clean breast of everything.'

He shrugged. 'Given the choice, I'd prefer that to being handed over to the Chinese—but have you considered all the implications?' He looked at me sharply, and saw that I hadn't.

'I'll give them to you,' he went on. 'All that will concern the Hong Kong police is the fact that I am an escaped convict—a very important one—and I'll be extradited by air to England and shoved straight back into gaol to finish my thirty years—in a *real* top-security nick this time. That puts paid to my usefulness to our people, because I'm pretty certain the Russians would then abandon any idea of an exchange.'

'You'll have to take your chance on that,' I told him. 'Somehow I can't see "our people" leaving you inside indefinitely.'

'I wouldn't bank on it. People in our line of business are pragmatists—on both sides. If you're unlucky enough to be caught you're expected to take what's coming. We know that when we take the job on.'

'Well, anyhow, that way your head stays on your shoulders—and not on top of one of Chairman Mao's flagpoles,' I said.

'There's not much in it either way really,' he said quietly as he wiped his razor. 'The thought of thirty years in prison makes my flesh crawl. That's something you'll discover for yourself, although I shouldn't imagine you'd get more than five.'

'Why me?' I said, startled.

'You're not deluding yourself that you'd get away with anything are you?' he asked. 'You'd be for it either way. If I'm telling lies and Gaffney and Company *are* on the British side they'd disown you, and your story would be put down as fantastic guff. They'd have to.'

'But if, on the other hand, you're telling the truth my information would unmask them,' I said hopefully. ' "Our people" would owe me something for that, at least.'

'Don't count on it. You're dealing with some pretty experienced men. They would probably involve you up to the neck in it, if only to discredit your evidence in the eyes of the jury—and you'd be made to look like a willing co-operator who had got cold feet and spilt the beans at the last minute to save his hide.'

'Queen's evidence——' I began.

'Doesn't apply in two cases—murder and treason.' He turned and grinned at me. 'Didn't you get any civil law at the Wirral? I did.'

'What was the lecturer's name?' I shot at him.

'Aileen Fernberry,' he said without a moment's pause. 'Middle-aged woman with a gorgeous figure—viewed from astern—but with a face like the back of a bus and a pronounced impediment in her speech which ruled her out for court work. And if you're still trying to test whether I was there—law lectures were held in the small lecture-room upstairs in the stable block—north side.'

I gave in. 'And still are,' I sighed.

'Oh, yes, I was there all right,' he said. 'That's where it all started. Only I made the grade and went on.'

'Where?'

'To use your own words—get stuffed. As I said—the Wirral was a kindergarten. There's a Middle School above that—and then a university. I'm not surprised that you've never heard of either.' He grinned again. 'No offence meant—but I'm not giving away anything that I don't have to. What I'd be likely to say if the Chinese ever did get to work on me seriously is another matter. That's mainly why I'd like to avoid being handed to them.'

'You won't be,' I said. 'Even if I have to throw the whole thing into the lap of the police.'

'Well, thank you for that, at least,' he said quietly. 'May I ask you one final question? Don't answer if you've got any lingering doubts left whatsoever. It's just this. They must have given you *some* reason for handing me over. What was it?'

'In exchange for Winterton,' I said.

He stared at me open-mouthed. 'For God's sake!' he exploded. 'Winterton's *dead*! He died before I left Amoy—and what's more our people know it. I reported it myself—*and got an acknowledgment.*'

'Then why wasn't it announced? That would be news,' I said.

'I know perfectly well why it wasn't announced. The Chinese hushed it up. Since I was one of the very few there at the time who knew Winterton's real identity I'd have been number one suspect if the news had been published, and my position was already pretty rocky. But that doesn't alter the fact that our *Intelligence* knew.'

So this was another clincher. The final one. If this were true then everything else he had told me was stripped of the last vestige of doubt. Even a fool like me would have questioned the reason for a straight handover. There had to be an exchange to make it valid.

He was reading my thoughts. I don't suppose it was a very difficult task. They must have been written plainly in my face.

'So you see,' he said. 'Even if you're still gagging at the thought of Gaffney being a double agent—even if he's as clean as the driven snow—he *knows* Winterton is dead—everybody in M.I.6 Far East knows it—and yet he sends you—does that make sense?'

'It *mightn't* have got back,' I said feebly. 'You said yourself that other reports had missed—the one naming them.'

'This one didn't miss. I told you—I got an acknowledgment. The other was different—I was on the run—and so were my last two couriers. They may have been scuppered before crossing.' He lit a cigarette and gave me one and sat drawing smoke down deep into his lungs, considering.

'Wainwright,' he said at last, 'you're probably still not entirely satisfied that I'm on the level. I don't blame you in the slightest for that. If I could prove to you that Winterton did in fact die on that—wait a minute—yes—the twenty-second of April last year—and that M.I.6 were made aware of it within a matter of days—would that satisfy you?'

'Completely,' I said. 'But how in hell *can* you prove it?'

'Coded radio to M.I.6'

'London?'

'Hong Kong. I'd need the books for London. Hong Kong I can do from memory with a sheet of paper, a pencil and an hour's quietness.'

I thought for a moment. 'All right—and if you did that—and the answer came back confirming it? What then?'

'Isn't that rather up to you? I should imagine that you then should let me report my exact whereabouts and ask for orders. But the main thing is to let them know where I am.'

I tried to pick holes in this, mulling over it for a long time and then asking questions. I asked them aloud, but I was really interrogating myself more than him.

'So they know where you are—and you ask for disposal orders for yourself? What would they be likely to do? What *could* they do?'

'I think we could safely leave that to them,' he answered. 'My guess is that we would be intercepted somewhere at sea, and I'd be taken off.'

I thought again. This was a pretty big order. To pick up one ship in the vast expanse of ocean we had ahead of us before Hong Kong.

Once again he seemed to guess my thoughts.

'They'd undoubtedly call the Navy in,' he said. 'There's nothing difficult about getting a fix on a ship once we've reported our last noon position, course and speed.'

'Maybe not,' I said. 'But an operation as big as that would be bound to leak.'

'You can leave that to them, too. Clamping a security gag on the Navy at sea is a vastly different thing from trying to muzzle the police and Press in a port like Hong Kong.'

That was valid, of course. I nodded. 'All right. But there's just one thing more. The address? I take it you wouldn't be sending it to "M.I.6, Hong Kong"?'

'Naturally not. The telegraphic address is "Lok Sam, Kowloon".'

And there I put my heels in. 'I'm sorry,' I said firmly. 'But I've got to be absolutely certain. As far as I know "Lok Sam" could just as easily be "Ivan Ivanovich"—and the warship that intercepts us, a Russian one.'

'In other words you still don't believe me?' he said.

'I want to—but as I said, this has got to be one hundred per cent.'

'So what do you suggest?'

'You'll have to break procedure and address it *en clair*.'

He shook his head. 'Not a hope in hell. The Wireless and Cable Company would bounce it straight back at us—"Addressee Unknown—please clarify"—or at best it would be sent round to the Hong Kong Police Special Branch, and that's something we have to avoid, isn't it?'

'We'll just have to take the chance.'

'But there *isn't* a chance, Wainwright,' he said patiently. 'Even supposing it did reach them, they wouldn't act on it. And could you blame them? Every bona fide agent has his own telegraphic address. It's part of his identification. A signal to "Lok Sam" could only originate from me. If I sent it to M.I.6 they would assume that somebody had got hold of my code and had broken it—or that I was sending it under duress, and was giving them the tip by not using the code address. See what I mean?'

I did, unfortunately. I tried again: 'Then direct to the Governor. Surely to God *he* knows the M.I.6 people.'

'I'm bloody certain he doesn't. He wouldn't *want* to know. It's not a case of trust, or lack of it—it's just that M.I.6 are not answerable to him, and the less he knows about them the less he is likely to be embarrassed if they act outside the strict letter of the law—as they do most of the time. Do they still tell that story at the Wirral about George the Fifth and Pecksniff?'

I nodded. It was a venerable chestnut told during the security lectures—probably apocryphal, although they swore it was true. George the Fifth is alleged to have asked the titular head of his Secret Service during World War One, 'Who is the *real* head of the Secret Service, Pecksniff?'

'Sir, I cannot tell you,' answered Pecksniff.

'What if I said, "Off with your head," Pecksniff?'

'Then, Sir,' answered Pecksniff, 'my head would roll, but my lips would still be sealed.'

It illustrated Carter's point perfectly. The Governor was out —and that being so, who the hell else was there to go to? But I still tried desperately.

'But surely the Governor would have to be brought into it if the Navy was to participate?' I said.

'Not of necessity,' he answered. 'M.I.6 deals directly with London. The Navy would get their orders from the Admiralty.'

He had stopped every runway. There was no other argument I could put up.

I rose from the settee.

'Make out your signal,' I told him.

'Thanks,' he said quietly. 'You've made the right decision—but

I know what sort of load you're carrying at this moment—and I can sympathize. May I offer one last word of advice?'

'What's that?'

'For her own sake, don't take Miss Malcolm into your confidence about any of this.'

'So you know who she is?'

'The Meisterspringer's daughter?' he said. 'Oh yes—I know her, or rather of her.'

'Why "her own sake"?'

'For the simple reason that she *is* the Meisterspringer's daughter, and as such, unreliable. He works for whoever pays him. At present he's working for the Chinese. His next job could be for the Russians—or conceivably even for us. When this is over you're going to be debriefed by our people. That means anything up to a couple of months' screening an intensive interrogation. The sort of thing I was put through when I went from China to Russia. They'll have everything out of you—*everything*. At the same time they'll be doing it to her. If I succeed in getting back into Russia, and they had reason to believe that she or her father knew I was a British agent I can see it being a very long time indeed before they were back in circulation.'

'That could go for me as well,' I said, startled again.

'It could indeed—but at least you'll have a lot working for you. I can speak for you—I couldn't for them. I believe in your good faith—I tested it by the offer of a heavy bribe and an easy way out, but you stood firm. You only co-operated when I convinced you of my bona fides. All those are points in your favour. But it still isn't going to be easy for you. At the present moment only you and I on this ship know where I really stand. Don't make it harder for either of us by letting it out to anybody else.'

'I see what you mean,' I said. 'But there's a wild joker aboard. Wetten. Where does he stand—and how much does he know?'

'I wish I could answer that,' he said thoughtfully. 'On the face of it I should say that he was planted by the Russians when they realized I had been hijacked. It would have been a routine measure. There are half a dozen skippers who do this sort of thing. They would probably have whipped a man on to every one of them that happened to be in a European port at the time. Their orders would be to report it by radio or to get word ashore at some port as soon as they were certain I was aboard—but Kjaer, the crafty bastard, has stymied this one with his master-switch.'

'If that were so, wouldn't Wetten have made some approach to you?' I asked.

'He hasn't, although I've given him every opportunity of doing so. That makes me wonder. He may either be put on by the Chinese to keep tabs on you—that's just the sort of thing they might very well do—or even be completely in the clear.'

'You can scrub that one,' I told him. 'That bump on his bean was put there by me. He followed me from this ship the night I first came to see Kjaer. I thought I'd got rid of him, but the police put him back aboard at the last minute.'

'That settles it then. He's not in the clear—but we don't know who he's working for. We'll just have to play it by ear—but I'll want to be standing over him when he's transmitting in case he whips a quick one in to somebody else. Better still, I'd prefer to be on the key myself.'

We went along to breakfast then. We were late and only Sonia was there. She looked altogether lovely—fresh, healthy, tanned—and she was wearing a simple blue cotton frock, one of the half dozen she must have brought aboard rolled under her peajacket. She looked up at us and smiled. She and I had made peace again after our last fight and I would have given a lot to have gone out on the deck with her and along to our place at the stern, and to have talked this over with her. She had always been so sane—and her decisions had all along been right. I think I would have done just that had it not been for Carter's warning—but I saw the force of his reasoning and fought the temptation down, knowing that it was going to place a further strain on me. However much we had quarrelled up to now we had at least trusted each other.

Usually after breakfast we walked a statutory twelve complete circuits of the ship for exercise, but this morning I was glad when she said she had some washing to do, and went off and left us. Carter took a sheaf of stationery from the saloon rack, nodded curtly to me and went back to the cabin. I sat out on deck for the next couple of hours until he came and collected me, and I went back with him. He handed me a sheet of paper.

'Lok Sam, Kowloon, HK:' I read. 'Following cotton staple quotations received ex Manchester exchange. Advise earliest how compare local prices.' Then followed blocks of letters and figures. It was obviously a code, but just the type of thing that trading companies work out between themselves. I had seen a lot of this work myself at the bank, and I knew that in the ordinary way it would excite no suspicion. I looked at him and nodded. He handed me a second sheet: it was the translation.

> 'G 327 aboard *Nurma.* Co-operation escort Wainwright secured provident upon answer one question, namely present condition with significant dates Winterton. Further signal upon receipt. Axiom.'

He said, 'I'll take you through it if you wish,' and pointed to a pile of other sheets which had been ruled out into squared grids, with letters along the horizontals and figures down the verticals. 'It's a bit complicated, but try and bear with me. Right—ten sheets, each ruled into four verticals and ten horizontals—forty squares per sheet. Four hundred basic words plus two proper names, yours and the ship's, which have been anagramized—I'll show you that later. Now, if we take the sheet numbers——'

But what the hell was the use? I tried to follow, and fair play to him he was very patient, but he lost me. It had been the same at the school. I was just no good at ciphers. He realized it and his temper frayed in the end.

'Wainwright, for Christ's sake try and concentrate, will you? It's no good just looking intelligent and nodding. It's only a simple slidex after all,' he said.

'I'll take your word for it,' I mumbled ruefully.

'Up to you,' he shrugged. 'You're not cut out for this work, are you? Are you still wondering why you were dropped at the Wirral?'

'No, and I don't bloody well care either,' I snapped. 'It's not the work that gets me down. It's the bastards one has to mix with. Give me the message. I'll go and fix it with Kjaer.'

'I've got to be there when it goes out,' he insisted.

'You don't need to be,' I told him. 'I'll be standing over Wetten and I'll karate the son of a bitch if he departs from that by one letter. There's nothing wrong with my Morse even if my ciphering is lousy.'

'Well, just remember that it's your neck as well as mine if things go wrong,' he answered, and gave me the coded sheet.

I went up to the bridge. Kjaer was having a pre-lunch nap in a deck-chair. I shook him gently and handed him the sheet. He cocked an irritable eye at it.

'What's this?' he asked.

'A message. I'd like it sent out—just like that,' I said.

'Just like that, eh?' He passed the sheet back to me. 'Fok off, Mr Smith,' he said, and closed his eyes again.

CHAPTER SEVENTEEN

I BEGAN SOFTLY and reasonably, but he wouldn't budge. Then I went over to money—raising my own bids to the limit of what I was carrying and even above that. But he just wasn't having any. Then I started to rave.

'You bloody, stupid, square-headed bastard,' I swore. 'What possible difference could it make to you? It's purely to let our people in Hong Kong know we're aboard—so they can make arrangements to get us off.'

'Arrangements should have been made already, mister,' he said mildly. 'If they haven't been, then I make my own—bloddy quick—but I ain't telling anybody beforehand that you're aboard. No goddam fear. No messages, Mr Smith.'

'Look——'

'I looked plenty. I tell you *no*. You think this the first bloddy time I run blackbirds?'

I made the mistake then of grabbing a handful of his shirt and hauling him to his feet out of the deck-chair. His belly looked round and flabby but when he butted me with it I thought I'd been hit with a bag of concrete. I skittered backwards across the deck and finished hard up against the rail.

'You do that again, Mr Smith,' he said very quietly, 'and I'll have you in irons and down the bloddy bilges quicker than a Hamburg whore can get her drawers off on payday.'

And I knew he meant exactly that. Sadly I went back to Carter. It was a measure of the man that he neither blew his top nor looked dismayed. He just sat thinking for some minutes, rubbing his chin and gazing into the distance.

'I can't altogether blame him,' he said at last. 'If the news leaked and he were caught running illegal passengers he could be barred the port, have a thumping fine smacked across him and be damned lucky not to have the ship seized into the bargain.'

'How the hell could the news leak, if the signal is to who you say it is?' I demanded.

'It wouldn't leak, but he's not to know that. The bloke's only taking sensible precautions. I wonder what his own arrangements for getting people ashore are—if he doesn't like what's been laid on?'

'Ask the son of a bitch,' I suggested.

'I don't suppose for one moment he'd tell me. Pity. No—we'll have to try it another way. That signal's got to go out.'

'All right—you tell me another way. He's got a master-switch in his cabin.'

'Where?' he asked quickly.

'Forget it. It's in a locker with a heavy steel door—in fact I think it's also the ship's safe—and he carries the key on him.'

'So that rules out an attempt while he's in at dinner or up on the bridge. Oh, well—only one thing for it.'

'What?'

'We'll have to get into his cabin when he's asleep—slug him—engage the switch and go along to the radio shack and send it ourselves.'

I stared at him. 'You must be joking,' I said.

'Can you think of anything better?'

'I can't think of anything at all—but I know that's out. A. His cabin is up on the bridge and there's always an officer on watch and a quartermaster at the wheel. B. The radio shack is just abaft the wheelhouse and they could hear the key going. Damn it all, you can hear it down here when Wetten is sending.'

'Yes, Wetten does send from time to time,' he said thoughtfully.

'You can forget that, too,' I told him. 'The skipper or the third mate is always with him when he does.'

But he still reconnoitred the position—for days—and only gave up when he was convinced of the complete hopelessness of it, by which time we were across the Indian Ocean, through the Malacca Straits and standing up towards the China coast—with only two days to go before reaching Hong Kong. Then he asked me for my gun.

I said, 'Not bloody likely. What do you want it for?'

'When we get in,' he said. 'He's bound to put us down below until after the port police, medical and customs have been aboard and given him clearance. Right?'

'I should imagine so.'

'After that I should think it would be a foregone conclusion that we would be going ashore at night. You agree?'

I nodded.

'All right,' he went on. 'Well, try and picture it. We will either be anchored out in the stream, waiting for a berth—or we'll be alongside. In the first instance whoever is coming for us would be in a launch—two or three men. They wouldn't risk a big party because it would be conspicuous. It would be unnecessary, anyhow, as you're on their side. Agreed?'

'The probable circumstances, yes,' I said. 'But what do you think you could do about it? Start a gun battle in the middle of the harbour?'

'No, but I'd certainly make a run for it when we got near the shore—and a gun would give me a better chance.'

'Nothing doing,' I said flatly. 'I'll keep the gun—*and* the responsibility of using it, or not, as I think.'

He said, 'Sorry, Wainwright—but I don't think you'd have the resolution.'

'Go on being sorry,' I told him. 'That's the way it's going to be.'

'So after all, you really do intend handing me over tamely if all else fails?' He shook his head slowly. 'You're a funny bloke, Wainwright. I once called you yellow. I don't think you are really, but you're incapable of making up your mind—of setting yourself a course and following it. You let circumstances take control and just drift with the stream—hoping to God something will turn up to get you out of the mulligatawny.'

And he wasn't so far wrong at that. But this time I *had* got some sort of idea.

'I don't intend handing you over,' I said. 'I told you that. If the worst comes to the worst, I'll call the police in.'

'You may not have the chance. You'll be in the same boat—literally.'

'Sure—but as you said yourself, unsuspected. Anyhow we may not be in a boat. We may go down the gangway on to the wharf. Whichever way it is there'll be police all over the place—patrol launches on the harbour—armed police on the docks. There always are. They won't be able to get too rough in the early stages. You've been drawing pictures—lots of them. Let me draw just one. Wherever they take us, it has to be by car. Right? Very well—that's the limit. We don't get into any cars. If you haven't had a chance to make a break for it I'll start shooting if necessary. *But that decision has to be mine.* I've got more than your hide to think of.'

'The girl?' he said. 'That's what I'm afraid of.'

'I haven't gone soft on her, if that's what you mean.'

'It wouldn't pay you to. She's tougher than her old man, and he's nobody's tenderhearted chicken, the bastard.' He shook his head. 'No, that wasn't what I was thinking of. The thing that worries me is that you are still instinctively thinking of her as an ally. She's *not*. She's on *that* side.'

'How do you know? She may be a starry-eye, like me.'

'Starry-eye my rump,' he snorted. 'What's *she* got to be starry-eyed about—except the cheque at the end of it? Listen, Wainwright—if she saw that cheque walking away from her she'd pull a gun—*and* use it—on you or anybody else who got in the way. She's got a gun, you know. I saw the shape of it in the hip pocket of her slacks when she was getting her stuff out of here. I wish I'd jumped her for it. It'd be about the only thing I *would* jump her for. I like mine a bit exclusive.'

'Cut that out, you dirty-mouthed bastard,' I said.

'You do give yourself away, don't you?' he said calmly. 'I don't make cracks like that normally. But it proves my point. I'm not accusing you of going soft on her, as you put it, but I *am* afraid that in an emergency you might act the gentleman at the wrong moment and get both our blocks knocked off.'

'You *wouldn't* act the gentleman under any circumstances I take it?'

'Not likely. I was cured of that for all time in 'fifty-five. I went to the assistance of a lovely young White Russian nun on the Bund in Shanghai. She was being roughed up by a bunch of the younger Comrades. She was very grateful—until I got her back to the convent door.'

'What happened then?' I asked, interested in spite of myself.

'She side-swiped me and then nearly debollicked me with a bloody great cleaver she was carrying under her robes—and got away with my despatch case. The bitch had been working for Chiang Kai-shek for years.' He grinned impishly, and for a moment I almost stopped disliking him.

'Don't worry about Sonia,' I assured him. 'Actually she was only sent along because her father thought there was a chance of her being snatched in London.'

'By whom?' he asked.

'The Russians.'

He shook his head over that. 'That's not the impression I had,' he said. 'That girl works for Poppa.'

'Unwillingly. I told you—don't worry. She'll do as I say—so long as she doesn't think her father is being put in any danger.' But I could see that he was more uneasy over the girl than over any other aspect of the business. He kept coming back to it all through that last day. He wanted me to persuade Kjaer to put her down below and take her on to Amoy, but I turned that down flatly.

And then the whole thing was taken out of our hands.

We sat over dinner very late that last night—all of us jumpy, even Kjaer. Carter caught my eye several times and signalled me to come out on deck, but in the saloon I was safe from further argument so I acted dumb and pretended not to understand. But then the mate, whose watch it was, blew down the bridge speaking-tube urgently. Kjaer listened, and I saw dawning panic in his face. He reached the door in two bounds and shot up the bridge ladder. We followed him out.

It was a perfect night. There was no moon, but the stars gave a lot of light and the sea was like a mill pond. We saw the flashing light immediately. It was ahead and slightly to port of us. Carter and I started to read aloud, confusing each other, so I moved to one side out of earshot. They were giving the 'I say again' flash, which meant that they had completed their first transmission and were going to repeat.

'Query name and registration,' I read. Overhead on the wing of the bridge I could hear Kjaer and the mate jabbering excitedly in Finnish. Carter raced past me and yelled up to them, 'Ask who they are. Stall! For Christ's stake, stall!' and Kjaer took time out from arguing to tell him to mind his own goddam business, but told the third mate to do that nevertheless. The bridge Morse lamp flickered the 'Declare identity' signal but before we had finished they were flashing us to heave to. I strained my eyes into the darkness, but it was impossible to make out the other ship. She was just a blacker bulk against the loom of the coast. Carter went up the bridge ladder two at a time, and I followed close behind him.

'Don't heave to,' he shouted, and that seemed to accord with Kjaer's own view, although he told us both profanely to get the hell off his bridge. He blew down the engine-room tube and bellowed in the ship's patois to 'Hurry up like bloddy hell—*Schnell! Schnell! Schnell!*' and I felt the steady throb of the engines increasing. Then the other ship stopped flashing and there was a stab of flame that lit the water between us for a split second. I started to count instinctively, but only got to three before the boom reached us, and there was a hell of a splash dead ahead of us. And that decided Kjaer. I don't suppose one could blame him. After all, he was part owner of his ship. I heard the telegraph sound faintly down below, and the engines ceased abruptly and then went astern in a crash stop that had us all nearly off our feet.

I felt my sleeve being tugged. 'Listen, mister,' he implored tearfully. 'I give you your money back—the lot—only you got to say you're stowaways. You say you sneaked aboard in the Canal, eh?'

'If you'd let me send that signal this mightn't have happened,' I told him with malice aforethought. 'Who do you think these people are?'

'Who the hell could they be, but the Navy or maybe the police?' he asked dolefully. 'What about it, mister? It don't make any difference to you now. You say that—all of you. I'm in plenty of trouble already.'

'Maybe it's only a routine check,' I said hopefully. 'In that case they won't search you. If we're down below——'

But he shook his head. 'No good. They flash our name first and tell us to confirm. They know who we are.'

Carter said, 'How could they know unless you'd reported your position to them first? It's your own fault, Kjaer. Better do as we say. Put us down below and try and bluff it out.'

'I don't report to nobody,' Kjaer raved. 'That's why I don't let you send anything out. I was going to say our radio had packed in because we don't have a proper Sparks aboard. My way *nobody* would have known until we arrived there. I was going to put you ashore nice and quiet at night and there wouldn't have been no trouble. Mister—you've got to help me—you've got to. I played straight with you.'

'Fifty-fifty,' Carter said. 'You put us down below. If it's only a routine check and you don't get searched, fine—nothing's altered. If they do know we're aboard and we get hauled out, we'll say we're stowaways. How's that?'

'Lousy,' Kjaer snapped. 'They'd know bloddy well that four

people couldn't stow away from the Canal to Hong Kong without me knowing they're aboard. They'll want to know why I don't report it to the officer as soon as he comes up the bloddy gangway. No—no good—I got to report you as illegal passengers right away—and no hiding.'

'In that case I'll sell you downriver, you bastard,' Carter said, and Kjaer moaned sorrowfully. We could hear the engines of the other ship as they closed the distance between us.

'What about it, Kjaer?' I asked. 'You've got a chance our way—and you get paid—in full.'

I was beginning to feel sorry for him. A fat man in dire trouble is always pitiful. He said, 'God forgive you. If I lose my ship and my ticket, *I* don't. I'll bloddy kill you. The lot.' And he told the third mate to get us below—all four of us, because Wetten was just as slimy a son of a bitch as the rest. I grabbed a few things from the cabin and chucked a few others over the side and ran along to collect Sonia, but there was no need, because she had heard everything and was waiting for us at the bottom of the bridge ladder—once more bulky under her peajacket—and probably the calmest of any of us. The girl was a wonder, and I found myself warming to her afresh.

The three of us scurried down into the engine-room and along the shaft tunnel into the hole, but there was some delay about putting the steel plate back in place because they couldn't find Wetten at first—but eventually the mate brought him down, and his right eye was swelling badly and there was a trickle of blood coming from his nose. The mate said murderously: 'Beat the damn hell out of the bastard. We catch him trying to signal with a torch from the stern.'

They slammed the plate back in position. Carter looked at Wetten. The German, though battered, was not nervous. He didn't need to be. He shrugged and sat down on the deck with his back to the bulkhead. Carter kicked him heavily in the ribs. I saw no use in this and disliked it intensely on Sonia's behalf. I said, 'Cut it out, Carter. What good will that do?' He didn't appear to hear me.

He said to Wetten: 'Do you want to live?'

Wetten was gasping and retching, but he managed to spit in the general direction of Carter. I got in between them, and stopped the second kick with my own leg. It made me angry and I swung at Carter, but he saw it coming and dodged.

Sonia said coolly: 'If you really want to find out anything from this man, I suggest you stop crowding each other. What are you trying to establish, Mr Carter?'

'Just who these people are,' he answered.

'Is that going to make any difference at this moment?' she asked.

'It could—a little,' said Carter. 'Ask sonny-boy here to stop interfering, will you?'

'Sit down, Carter,' I told him. 'We'll know soon enough. If it's just a routine check by the Navy or police, we'll be under way again before long. If it's not, we're going to be hauled out of here. What's the use of kicking the daylights out of this bloody rat in the meantime?'

'Thank you, Mr Smith,' said Wetten. His English was fluent but accented. 'If it makes you happier, Carter, it's a Russian destroyer—down from Vladivostok.'

'You're a liar,' said Carter.

'All right—I'm a liar,' he answered. 'Is kicking my ribs going to make me truthful?'

'How did they know where to pick us up?' Carter asked quickly, and Wetten looked tired.

'Oh, for God's sake, I've been in touch with them for the last three days.'

'How?' I demanded.

'I bypassed that damn switch when I fixed the television aerial,' he said with a certain expert's pride. 'But I had to cut it a bit fine. I couldn't transmit direct to anybody that mattered until we came into range.'

'They'd have heard you from the bridge,' I challenged, but he shook his head and smiled.

'Remote key from down astern, Mr Smith,' he said. 'Now suppose we all relax? Mr Carter goes where he wants to go—so do I. Mr Smith and the lady stay on board. What trouble you're in with your own people is your own affair.' He sighed. 'Bloody awful life, isn't it?'

Carter spoke to him in rapid Russian—far too rapid for me. Wetten answered him in the same language. I looked a question at Sonia, but she was too interested in what the others were saying. I felt out in the cold. I butted in with an inconsequential question in English. 'If you were in radio touch with them over the last three days, why were you signalling with a torch just now?'

He smiled at me again. 'Just to save a little time,' he said. 'I told them where we'd be. I could only rig the bypass when the third mate was out of the cabin.'

No joy. I had been vaguely hoping that he was still lying and that the Navy was here, but this fitted. It even seemed to satisfy Carter. He took a deep breath and looked relieved. So now I was back in my old familiar role of Joe Soap. The experts had taken over again. I tried to avoid Sonia's eye, but I needn't have bothered. Once more the three of them were talking in Russian. All Migs together—Old Home Week—working for different bosses maybe, but still brothers and sisters under the skin.

Then we heard the bolts being unscrewed the other side. I tried, pathetically, to make a last gesture. I said, 'Whatever the outcome of this may be, gentlemen, I trust that Miss Malcolm will be kept out of it. She's not here of her own free will.'

The plate was being lowered. Carter and Wetten were standing watching it, their backs to us. Sonia reached out and took my hand and squeezed it. I thought for a moment that it was a friendly little gesture, just a small acknowledgment of the fact that I *had* tried. She leaned towards me and I, like a fool, thought she was going to kiss me, but her lips went to my ear rather than my cheek, and she whispered, 'Watch it. Both these bastards are lying like hell.'

Then the plate came down with a crash, and Carter planted a haymaker under Wetten's jaw that dropped him like a sack of wet sand.

CHAPTER EIGHTEEN

TWO OF THEM pushed in—short, chunky Cantonese in sloppy olive green uniforms festooned with bandoliers, and carrying burp guns. Outside I could see the shaft tunnel was crowded with others, and all were yelling. Whoever says the Chinese are a silent, inscrutable race has never been farther east than Southend Pier. They hauled Carter, then me, through the hole into the shaft. I turning, trying to make way for Sonia so that they would have no reason to start manhandling her, but all I got for my pains was a smack across the back with a gun that knocked the wind out of me. They raced us along the shaft into the engine-room and up the steel ladders to the gratings, then up again and out on to the deck. Alongside I could see a big motor junk, the low waist crowded with more Chinese troops. Kjaer was standing by the rail looking sick and miserable. I thought at first that it was out of sympathy for us, but his first words disabused me of that.

He said: 'I done my part of it, Mr Smith. I suppose you couldn't see your way clear to slip me what you owe me?'

'Ask your pals to loose my arms,' I said unfairly, 'and I might be able to do something about it.'

They swung me over the rail. It was a good twelve-foot drop to her deck and I landed in a heap, with Carter on top of me, then, as we were trying to sort ourselves out, Wetten was added to the pile. At least we made a carpet which broke Sonia's fall. The junk's powerful diesel was chugging in neutral. It roared on a louder note and they cast off, and we headed away into the darkness. I watched the deck lights of the *Nurma* receding, and felt very lonely indeed. Then we were pulled to our feet and hustled along towards the junk's high poop.

There was a large cabin under it, furnished with a table, a chair and an oleograph of Mao Tse Tung, and nothing else. A man sat at the table. He looked up as we were shoved in front of him. They don't wear anything so undemocratic as badges of rank in their army, and he was dressed like the others, even to the burp gun lying on the table in front of him, but he was obviously an officer. He grunted something to our escort and they dived on us each in turn and searched us—first me, then Carter, then Wetten, who had now come round. They got my gun, of course, and the pack of money and my passport. Carter and Wetten didn't yield much except cigarettes and matches. The officer studied the passport intently, but he was bluffing, because he opened it at the back page and solemnly read forward to the beginning, but of course the photograph pinned it on to me. He flicked through the money, but plainly that was beyond him and he told one of the escort, in Cantonese, to fetch Hung Tai, who turned out to be an unpleasant youth with Red Guard patches on the sleeves of his tunic and a lot of food stains down the front of it. He counted the money by the numerals but clearly had no idea of the actual value, because he told the officer that it amounted to over a million Hong Kong dollars.

Then he grinned and spat right in my face and called me a capitalist-imperialist something in excellent Hong Kong pidgin. The officer looked at us each in turn and said inquiringly, 'Kahtah?' The youth identified me from the passport as 'Win-li', which shifted things to the other two. He kicked first Carter and then Wetten hard and repeated, 'Kahtah? Which piecee-one Kahtah? Hully—chop-chop—dirty bastahd.'

Wetten pointed to himself and said: 'Ganz', and mimed tapping a morse key. 'Buzz—buzz-buzz—buzz-buzz-buzz.' That made him buddies with the youth immediately, because he pointed to himself and went into the buzzing routine and then shook hands with him. Wetten pointed to Carter and identified him and then shook hands with the officer, and everybody seemed delighted—except Carter and myself who promptly got another salivation from the youth. I was relieved though, because in the general exchange of pleasantries they forgot to frisk Sonia who, as a mere woman, was standing well to the rear of us. The officer then told the escort to put us down below—Carter, myself and the one he named as the shameless-concubine-who-battened-upon-the-blood-of-the-people. It's all one word in Cantonese. They rushed us out and along the cluttered deck and down into a hold which smelt even worse than the bilges of the *Nurma,* and slid the hatch over us.

We sat in silent misery for quite a long time, then Carter said bitterly, 'If you two hadn't butted in I'd have kicked the truth out of Mister Bloody Wetten before they boarded us.'

'Satisfying, no doubt,' Sonia said icily. 'But what would it have achieved? They'd have got us out in the end.'

'Sir Bloody Lancelot here had a gun and a packet of spare rounds. They could only come in one at time, and they couldn't fire round corners. We could have held out for quite a while. If it comes to that, you have a gun yourself, Miss Malcolm.'

'And I intend keeping it,' Sonia said.

'To save yourself from a fate worse than death?' sneered Carter. 'Don't flatter yourself. Sex is bourgeois decadence to these types. Give it to me and I can at least put it to some use.'

'Such as?' I asked, just for something to say.

'Drop a couple when they came for us,' he said. 'With luck we might get their sub-machine-guns. Better than just waiting for it without doing anything. Or do you feel more comfortable letting things drift?'

And the best I could put up against that was swearing—and even that wasn't as fluent as it might have been, because Sonia's presence cramped my style.

We each drew into ourselves after that. I tried desperately to sleep, but it was no use. This was the worst yet. Almost there, and shot down by that lousy little East German rat. Why the hell hadn't I thought of that possibility? Why hadn't Carter, for that matter? He'd been shooting his superior mouth off about his two-way radio in prison, hadn't he? I saved this one in case he started on me again.

The diesel chugged on interminably. I tried to speculate on the course we were taking. As far as I knew we had been about seventy or eighty miles to the south-west of Hong Kong when we were intercepted. The China coast would have been roughly twenty miles on our port beam in that case. This thing probably made about ten knots so, if we had been heading for the nearest point on the coast, we should have been close inshore long ago. Then the edges of the hatch started to lighten with the dawn—much stronger on the starboard side and to the front of it than the others. That would appear to indicate that we were heading north and east still—on much the same course as the *Nurma* had been on already. I tried to recall the maps of this part of the coast. There was little of importance along here—just an occasional fishing village as far as I could remember. Canton was the nearest port of any size. Yes—quite obviously that was where we were making for. Canton, ninety miles up the Pearl River. It didn't cheer me in the slightest to think that to make the mouth of it we would, if they were disposed to take any short cuts, be in British territorial waters for a short period between Macao and Hong Kong. We never interfered with Chinese shipping unless it was behaving suspiciously.

More light came down into the hold as the day wore on. I was tortured with thirst and guessed that the others must be also. They say that misery loves company, but it didn't seem to apply in our case. We each sat as withdrawn from the others as the confines of the hold would allow. I stood up to ease my cramped limbs. The deckhead was quite low—in fact even on the keel itself I couldn't stand completely upright. To let a little more air into the place I risked lifting the hatch an inch or so. I looked out on to the deck. As so often happens after a very clear night in these latitudes, a heavy sea mist had clamped down and I could barely see the length of the junk. I could see, however, a twenty-millimetre Czech Oerlikon gun under a tarpaulin. That was evidently what they had fired the warning shot from. Christ—it wouldn't have made a dent on the plates of the *Nurma*. If only the windy old devil had clapped on speed earlier and made a run for it.

I looked aft towards the poop. A group of them were clustered round the helm. I could see the officer arguing with the youth Hung Tai. They seemed jittery and nervous. Looking forward I could see why. The fog was a solid wall in front of us and we were belting straight into it at speed. The youth, in the manner of his kind, East or West, seemed to know it all. The others, including the officer, obviously wanted to throttle down a bit. I couldn't hear exactly what they were saying for the simple reason that they were saying it all at once, but then the youth's voice rose above the others. 'Leave it to me. I *know*, you windy lot of bastards,' would be a reasonable paraphrase. Then he went on to say that he was guided by the sayings of Chairman Mao, and produced a little red book to prove it. That held the officer and most of the others for a time, but not the old boy at the helm. He looked like a Hakka to me. They are fishermen, and nobody's fools.

He said: 'My arse to Chairman Mao, and you, you snotty-nosed little Wanchai brothel bastard,' or words to that effect, and put the helm over and tugged at a rusty lever protruding from the deck. The throb of the diesel dropped, and her bows paid off to port. There was a hell of a row then. The youth hauled a pistol out and shoved it in the old man's ribs. The old man clipped him hard, skittering him into the scuppers. I thought I detected veiled approval among the others. It certainly cheered me quite considerably. Then, as in the manner of those bewildering fogs, it lifted suddenly and dead ahead of us I saw the long, lean grey shape of a frigate. I even saw the white ensign fluttering in the stern. She was about a quarter of a mile off and moving very slowly at a tangent to us. Her signalling searchlight started to blink immediately. I made out dot-dot-dot-dot—dot—dot-dash—H-E-A- before the blasted fog clamped down again, blotting her out. Clearly it was the beginning of an order to heave-to.

The officer leapt for the lever and shoved it forward, and the beat of the diesel rose. My affection for the helmsman dimmed a little. If we'd kept on the original course at that speed we'd almost have collided with her.

But as I have said, the Hakka fishermen are no fools. When

they are not fishing they are smuggling, pirating, and running prohibited immigrants from the mainland to Hong Kong, and they are quick thinkers. He knew that the frigate had seen us swing to the west so he held the helm over until he had completed the full turn and were running due east. Unless the Navy realized what we were doing, we would now be heading away from each other.

I felt movement beside me. Carter had come up and was looking towards the stern. He said: 'If only I had had the gun I might have been able to do something when they were all preoccupied then. Speak to this bloody woman, will you?'

'Why you?' I asked sourly. 'You haven't shown up so brilliantly so far.'

Behind us through the fog we heard the dull boom of a gun. There was no following whine so I guessed it was a blank. The helmsman looked astern and made a rude gesture with two fingers, which means the same in China as in Chelsea. The old rip seemed to be enjoying it—but he was a little too previous, because we hit something at that moment—and damned hard. It pulled us up dead and threw Carter and me into a heap at the bottom of the hold. The gang on the poop were raising merry hell, each trying to out-shriek the others. We pulled ourselves up to the look-out again. The helmsman had shoved the lever into reverse and the screw was churning like mad but we seemed to be held fast—then, looking ahead, I saw why. We had run hard aground and right in front of us was a sheer cliff—so close that I could see outcrops of scrub on its rocky face. Between us and it there didn't seem to be any water at all—just hard white sand. The gang on the poop were looking at each other in comical dismay. From behind us came another boom.

The officer was the first to regain his wits. He yelled to the others and leapt the poop rail, running towards us. We dropped down into the bottom of the hold quickly. They threw the hatch back and half a dozen flat yellow faces were looking down at us. One of them dropped a bamboo ladder down. I looked at Carter. Was this a chance? But it wasn't. The officer fired a burst. It splintered the keel right alongside my feet. I stepped aside and gallantly indicated the ladder to Sonia. She went up, looking very angry indeed. I followed her—then came Carter. The officer stuck the gun in my belly and harangued me urgently. The youth translated into pidgin. He didn't need to. I understood perfectly.

We were going over the side chop-chop and we were going to run like bloody hell with guns at our arses—and if we stopped running before we were told, the guns would go off.

We dropped on to the sand. Half the junk was out of the water but she didn't seem to have sustained much damage, and the bar was obviously tidal, and eventually they might be able to float her off without difficulty, but they were taking no chances with us in the meantime—and looking at it strictly from their point of view one could hardly blame them, because the fog was lifting rapidly now—not just clearing in patches—really lifting.

They hustled us across the sand—six of them and, to my sorrow, the youth was one of them—until we came right to the foot of the cliff. Close up it wasn't as sheer as it had appeared from farther out, but sloped at a steep angle. They prodded and shoved at us until we had climbed about a hundred feet and the fog was a flat-topped blanket below us. We could see the frigate clearly. She was about half a mile offshore and halted, and they were swinging a boat out. Immediately below us the junk seemed almost afloat again as the tide was rising rapidly. I heard the officer grunting and gasping that if only that stupid old bastard would get her off and make his way up-coast he would lead the chase away—and come back for us when the thrice-accursed capitalist-imperialist running-dogs had departed. I wondered what he was worrying about, because our people would never dream of making a landing on Chinese territory. Orders are rigid on the subject. This certainly wasn't Hong Kong island, nor any part of the British leased mainland that I recognized—and I knew most of it by sight.

They halted us in a clump of she-oak, and the officer unslung his binoculars and studied the frigate for some minutes. The boat they had put out was still hidden by the dispersing fog, but I caught a brief glimpse of it in a rift. It was proceeding cautiously towards the beach and the junk. The latter was now partially afloat again, its propeller churning sand and water into a porridge, and as we watched it slid a few feet seaward and backed off—but it was too late. The frigate's boat loomed up behind it and I saw a white-clad officer and half a dozen armed ratings swarm aboard. I was sweating and praying inwardly that they would guess someone had landed and would venture ashore after us, but it was a forlorn hope. The swiftly rising tide would have obliterated our footprints. I was on the point of risking everything and yelling, but that bloody Oriental Flower Child was watching me, and hoping, I think, that I would do just that, because he was toying lovingly with the pistol he had frisked from me.

The officer lowered his binoculars and grunted again and they prodded us onward up the hill to the flat ground at the top. Above us, a few hundred yards away, another line of hills rose, covered with scrubby pines. We crossed the flat ground and started to climb again, and then suddenly, without warning, found ourselves in cultivated land. It was just a knife-slash running round the contour of the hill which had been terraced by rough stone walls into rice paddies, and across the other side there was a huddle of thatched mud huts. A man was ploughing through the knee-deep mud with a wood and bamboo contraption pulled by a pair of water buffaloes, and a line of women straggled behind him planting rice shoots in the sloughy trench it made. They wore, both sexes, muddy black tussah trousers and smocks, topped with cartwheel straw hats, which told me exactly nothing because that is the coastwise peasant dress from one end of China to the other. They stopped work and watched us dumbly as we came out of the trees and walked along the top of a bund between the paddies towards them. The officer started to jabber rapidly, in a language I didn't know but which had the odd Hakka word in it. The man with the plough called to an old woman. She climbed out of the mud and beckoned to us and led us through the tiny village and farther up the hill until we came to a goat track which crossed our line of march at right angles. We turned on to this and kept going until we came to another huddle of huts in a valley which cut back into the range. I looked over my shoulder towards the sea, but only for a moment. I would have liked to have looked longer because the view was breath-taking, but the youth clobbered me hard with the butt of the pistol, then screwed the muzzle of it into the back of my neck. I had noticed earlier that the safety catch was off and the damned thing was cocked, so I took the hint without arguing and kept my eyes to the front thereafter. But I had seen in that short time that the frigate was still in sight, steaming very slowly close inshore parallel with the coast.

They separated us here, shoving me into the first hut and taking the others on farther. My hut was a granary, half-filled with rice in matting sacks, and the last thing I saw before they slammed the heavy wooden door was a huge snake coiled up just inside, and the hair on the nape of my neck stood upright. The youth giggled and hissed realistically. I remembered then that this was common practice with the rice farmers and fish-driers of the coast. The snakes they use are a variety of rock python, non-venomous, and even friendly in that they are said to curl up beside sleeping people for warmth—that is sleeping people less jumpy than I. They keep down granary rats far more efficiently than cats, and don't pee on the rice or eat fish.

There were no windows in this place, but the door was made of rough planks which had warped into inch wide cracks. I spent the first hour with one eye glued to a crack and the other swivelling round behind me in the general direction of the snake. Unfortunately I couldn't see seawards here, so I had no idea of whether the frigate was still beating up and down or had made off. I could see the officer and the youth though, and occasionally one or other of the soldiers as they patrolled along the edge of the clearing. They were all certainly on their toes, and the watch they kept was alert and thorough—even nervous.

The day dragged on. In the evening a couple of women came up from the other village with food. The off-watch troops sat in a circle and produced chow-bowls and chopsticks and fed in full view of me. I wished they wouldn't. I wasn't conscious of hunger, but thirst was by now just about driving me mad. But finally they brought me some rice and dried fish and a big bowl of the Chinese peasant's staple drink—hot water—and dumped it down inside the door. I cheered up considerably, because I had heard somewhere that the Chinese, to whom food is sacred, would never dream of feeding anybody they intended to bump off within the next twenty-four hours.

The food was a twofold blessing, because it loosened the tongues of the others, and soon the officer and the youth were arguing like hell. The youth, I gathered, was all for going down to the shore as soon as it was dark, grabbing a boat and pressing on. The officer, on the other hand, wanted to wait for the junk to return. The youth asked what the hell was the good of that? The old bastard wouldn't come back while the frigate was hanging around, and although it was out of sight now, how did they know that it wasn't tucked away round a corner in some bay or other? The officer said they didn't know—but they'd still wait. The youth asked why, since they were inspired and upheld by the Thoughts of Mao, couldn't they spread out and walk round the island until they either saw the frigate's lights or were certain that she had gone? One of the soldiers asked wearily why he didn't do something anatomically uncomfortable with the Thoughts of Mao and then belt up? That enraged the youth, who pulled his gun and threatened the soldier. The soldier knocked him arse over head and took the gun from him, thereby endearing himself to me, and the officer told them *all* to belt up and set a sentry on each of the three huts, with one at the end of the valley to watch seaward. That left three off watch who he told to get some sleep. The youth was on the first watch, outside my hut. He sulkily asked for his gun back and the officer gave it to him, first, I was delighted to see, unloading it and keeping the rounds.

Then Wetten came up. I'd been wondering about him. If the Navy had got him I hoped they might have made him talk. But those hopes were quickly dashed. The officer brought him across while the youth translated from pidgin English to Cantonese.

No, the Navy hadn't got him. He'd reached the shore before the boat came up to the junk and had hidden in the scrub. What were his orders now? The officer asked him if he could get through by radio to Canton to report the position. Wetten said sourly that he couldn't. The youth, apparently, hadn't kept his batteries topped up, and the charging motor was kaput. The youth didn't translate this bit truthfully. The officer then said that they would wait here until the frigate had definitely departed. The junk could anchor offshore. Wetten said he was going to sleep on board in that case because the junk stank less than the village. Then he went off.

I sat on a sack of rice and considered. So we were on an island, and, since the frigate was here, that island was inside British Territorial waters.

You'll have to bear with me a little here, while I give you a brief rundown on the Territory. Hong Kong is itself an island—nine miles by six—lying a mile off the mainland. The city, properly called Victoria, is on the north side of the island. The nearest part of the mainland is the site of another city—Kowloon—bigger in area but not as impressive as Victoria. The main docks are on the Kowloon side and the stretch of water in between is perhaps the finest deep water harbour in the world. If you put the point of a compass on Victoria and extended the other arm twenty miles and drew a circle, you would roughly enclose

British Territory—half of it land, half sea. The land, except for the city of Kowloon itself, which was permanently ceded to Britain with the island, is known as the New Territories and we hold it on lease from the Chinese. The lease is up in 1977. In the seaward half are a number of islands, nearly a hundred, ranging in size from one, Lan Tao, bigger in area than Hong Kong itself but only sparsely populated by peasants, to tiny uninhabited bits of rock. Where the devil the seaward line runs exactly, nobody, not even the Navy, knows, and consequently we and whatever government happens to be in power in Peking are always arguing about the ownership of some of the smaller islands on the outer fringe. In the days of gunboat diplomacy it didn't matter a damn, but nowadays things are different, and we don't push our claims too hard, but the Chinese *do* push theirs.

So we were on an island. The question was, which? At the present moment I could have been sitting on my rump anywhere from two to twenty miles from that holy of holies, the Hong Kong Club. The thing was to find out. And to find out I had to get out.

By the time I had reached this momentous conclusion darkness had fallen and I could hear some full-bodied snoring coming from somewhere—and that bloody youth was sitting on his backside leaning against the door. But I knew that his fangs had been drawn, and that his gun was like those of the Guards outside Buckingham Palace—for moral effect only. But he could still yell.

Skirting the last known position of the snake, I climbed up on top of the rice sacks and explored the possibilities of the thatched roof. It wasn't a formidable obstacle in itself, but the rushes were dry and they crackled loudly as I started to make a hole by the eaves on the side furthest away from the door. But I persevered and eased handfuls out as gently as a beautician working on a wealthy client's eyebrows until I had a space I thought wide enough to wriggle through. It sounded to me that I made a noise like a steeplechaser crashing through a brush jump, but it didn't reach the snorers who kept on with a steady *basso-profundo* throughout.

But junior was more on the job than I gave him credit for. I was just picking myself up from the drop when he came gumshoeing round the corner on tiptoes, the gun at the ready. I reached him before he had time to cut loose with the yell that must have been forming in his throat. I didn't like doing it—not to a kid—even a horror like this—but one can't judge the weight of a palm-edge chop across the Adam's apple—not to a nicety, and certainly not when time is of the essence. I don't suppose the poor little sod ever knew what hit him. His gun rattled on the stones at my feet. I grabbed it, useless as it was, and started in towards the other huts—but then I saw movement by the nearest of them, so I had to nip round the other side smartly.

My first thought had been to loose the others, but I let that go quickly. I hadn't a hope. The sensible thing would be to get help—any sort of help—so I settled for that. I made for the path towards the first village, but then I saw the pinpoint of a cigarette and heard a cough. That way was out. And then the snoring stopped and I realized that the second watch was being called. If they went round to relieve sentries now I'd had it. I took about three seconds to worry things out. They would, I hoped, assume that I'd made for the seashore, and that's the way they would start the chase. I therefore did the opposite and went up the valley, fast.

And for once I wasn't wrong. I hadn't gone a hundred yards before I heard all hell break out behind me. They'd obviously found junior.

CHAPTER NINETEEN

I LET CAUTION go to the winds and really pelted up the slope until I thought my lungs would burst, but for once it seemed that I was getting a break and nobody was on my heels, although I could hear excited voices and see torches flashing far below me. I reached the top of the hill and stopped dead.

They say it's the most beautiful night sight in the world. Try and picture it.

Broadway, Piccadilly and Coney Island rolled into one huge neon cluster and planted in the black velvet of the China Sea and sky—riven through the centre by the darkness of the harbour and repeated on the other shore—Hong Kong to the south and Kowloon to the north—with a jewelled necklace of arc lights surmounting the former, outlining the road up the Peak, and the grim hills of China itself surrounding the latter.

I saw immediately where I was—on Lan Tao, seven miles across the Lamma Channel from the Colony itself. I could place myself by an isolated patch of lights in the shape of a dumb-bell which I knew to be Cheung Chau right in the centre of the channel. Yes, I was on British territory all right—but that didn't help much at the moment. There was a police post here, I knew—but where exactly in its ten miles by ten miles area I hadn't a clue, because this was one of the few bigger islands I had not visited. There was also one on Cheung Chau, but that didn't help either, because I *had* been there and I knew that the post was manned by a Chinese sergeant and a handful of constables—splendid blokes no doubt, but not, I should say, strong on imagination. I'd probably find myself shoved inside until morning if I applied there. No—it was Hong Kong, and the fountainhead that I wanted now, because I knew for the first time what I was going to do.

Far below me I could see a cluster of dim lights on the shore, with brighter ones moving out to sea. It was, I guessed, a fishing village, with boats lit by acetylene flares operating from it. I plunged downhill, falling into gulleys and ravines and getting snarled up in the scrub, but making the village more or less in one piece in about half an hour.

It was just a tiny place—half a dozen huts and a rickety pier jutting out from the beach and, except for a few dim lamps in the windows, it seemed deserted. But as I stood looking round trying to take stock, a harsh glaring light sputtered into being at the end of the pier as somebody lighted an acetylene lamp in a boat. I raced along towards it.

There were two Hakkas aboard coaxing a balky petrol engine into life. I jumped into the boat and gabbled that I wanted to get across to Hong Kong chop-chop, but they just stared at me blankly—even when I promised them more than they'd make in half a year fishing—so in the end there was nothing for it but to pull the gun on them. They understood that all right, poor devils, and shrugged resignedly, and after a few abortive coughs the engine started wheezily and we got under way. I made them dowse the lamp and I sat right up in the nose where I could watch them both.

It took us an hour and a bit to make it, with me prickling with frustration the whole time, but eventually they landed me by the Sulphur Channel, under the shadow of Mount Davis. I told them I'd keep my word and the dough would be sent across to them at their village—then I hopped out and made my way up to the motor road that circles the whole island a few feet above the sea. I was about four miles due west from the centre of Victoria here, so I started to pad east as fast as my leaden limbs would carry me, but then I managed to flag a prowling taxi. The driver looked at me dubiously and didn't want to take me at first and I had to wave that wretched gun again. I could hardly blame him either, because I must have been looking a hell of a sight—three days' growth of beard—a filthy shirt and jeans and bloody scratches all over my dirty face and arms. But, like the fishermen, he was Chinese and philosophical, and took me along the Praya, round the Cricket Ground and up past Murray Barracks towards Magazine Gap.

We stopped where I told him—three-quarters of the way up the Peak. I got out and looked down. The view of the city from here is, if anything, more bewilderingly beautiful than from across the water. But I had no time to admire it now. I told the driver to wait if he wanted his money and walked up a path which led to a large white villa set on a shelf in the hillside in an ordered riot of huge azaleas. Far below I heard three o'clock strike on the cathedral chimes, and somewhere a dog was barking.

I knew his room. It was the one over the porticoed front door. For a moment I thought of climbing the porch and really surprising him, but I discarded the idea. This place was wired. So I rang the front door bell prosaically, and got no joy for a long time until a light appeared in a downstairs room, and then the door was opened cautiously on its chain. It was old Fut Su, his number one boy, and for a time he blinked at me muzzily and didn't know me, but when he did he flew into a flutter and opened up. He said he'd go and call Mastah, but I told him not to bother and took the stairs three at a time.

But 'Mastah' had heard the noise and was already waiting for me at the top, in pyjamas and dressing-gown—and he wasn't even surprised. He just said: 'Where the hell have you been?' and led me to his study without waiting for an answer. He locked the door and went straight to the drinks cabinet and poured me a stiff one, then turned. And now he did look surprised, although not unduly so, because I had the gun on him.

He said: 'A little melodramatic, Wainwright, isn't it? What about this drink? Do you want it?'

'I could do with it,' I told him, 'but it had better wait, Mr

Walters. Right now I'd like you to take me to the Colonial Secretary.'

'Might I ask why?' He moved to his chair by the desk but I motioned him away with the gun and then did what I should have done in the first place and went round behind him and frisked him. He wasn't carrying a gun, but I kept him in the middle of the floor just in case he had one stashed away in a drawer. The moral effect of this one was working perfectly, but I still felt horribly vulnerable.

'Because I knew very well that I'd never get in to see him looking as I do now,' I said, taking up his question. 'You're by way of being my passport, Mr Walters. My guarantor in other words.'

'And what do I guarantee, Wainwright?'

'Just my name and identity,' I told him. 'I'll do the talking after that.'

'And what are you going to talk about?'

'You're asking too many questions,' I said. 'Get moving.'

'May I put my trousers on?' he asked plaintively.

'You can do that,' I agreed. 'Walk ahead of me, and be sensible or I'll blow your head off.'

We went along to his room. I took a pair of slacks and a jacket from a dumb-valet, I looked through the pockets and threw them on the bed. He said severely: 'You're going to allow me a little privacy to change, surely, aren't you?'

'Not bloody likely,' I said. 'Get bouncing—we're both big boys.'

He stripped off his pyjama pants, looking as outraged as a spinster, and pulled on the others, then put the jacket on. I had a brainwave and moved to his bedside cabinet—and it paid off. There was a Browning .38 there. I took it and left the empty one without his noticing it. I motioned him to the door. He gestured towards the telephone.

'I'd better ring him first,' he said. 'I don't think he'd see even me at three in the morning without some sort of explanation.'

'No telephones,' I said. 'We'll risk it. I'd be obliged if you'd bring a little money. There's a taxi to pay.'

'Why not my own car?' he asked.

'Just do as I say,' I said sharply. 'Time's getting short.'

He sighed. 'I hope you know what you're doing, Wainwright,' he said. 'Or that you can persuade an understanding doctor to certify you, if you don't. I'm afraid it will go hard with you otherwise. Very hard.'

'I'll have to risk that too,' I said. 'Get moving, Mr Walters.'

We went down the stairs and out into the darkness.

The taxi was still waiting, the driver curled up asleep in his seat. The Colonial Secretary's house is only a short drive up the Peak Road. There was a police guard at the gate, and there we struck trouble. The Chinese sergeant flatly refused to ring the house until he had first called the European sub-inspector from the Magazine Gap station. So there was another wait, and another argument—but eventually we got in.

The C.S. received us, frostily, in his drawing-room. He looked inquiringly at Walters and distastefully at me. Walters didn't help. He just gestured towards me and said: 'I'm sorry I can't enlighten you, John. This young man brought me here at gun-point.

The C.S. pressed a bell hastily.

And then I felt a complete and utter bloody fool. The whole thing seemed so absurd in this last citadel of British colonialism, with two elderly gentlemen looking at me disapprovingly and curiously.

So I plunged. I said: 'I have been doing certain highly confidential government work, sir—both here and in England. Here I have received my orders from Mr Walters—but I have recently had reason to believe that he is not what he represents himself to be—and that I have unknowingly been working for—well, the other side.'

There was a knock at the door and the European police officer looked in. The C.S. told him to wait outside and then said to me: 'What you're saying is that Mr Walters is your Controller but you think he is doubling—and you've been furbled in reverse, is that it?'

It took me a good half minute to find words—because here was this completely unquestionable senior official using the common jargon of the trade. Actually I *didn't* find words. I just gulped and nodded. The C.S. went on: 'All right—spit it out, boy. What are your reasons for doubting him?'

'I'll have to ask you a question first, sir,' I said, and my voice sounded squeaky—like that of a schoolboy accusing his house-master of something nasty to the Head.

'What?'

'Where is Winterton?'

The C.S. looked at Walters. Walters said promptly: 'He was in Canton Central Gaol on Monday, but we think they moved him downriver on a junk that evening—to await our half of the bargain.'

'I was told that he died in Amoy some months ago,' I said, 'and that the fact was reported back here.'

'It was,' Walters said. 'By Carter. We didn't acknowledge it because lines were cut and Carter was already on the run. It was fortunate we didn't—because we found later that *Carter* was being furbled. They let him think that Winterton was dead as a test to see whether their suspicions were correct and he was leaking back to us. Where did you hear all this?'

'From Carter himself,' I said miserably. 'During the voyage.'

'And you accepted it without corroboration and came in here waving a gun like the sheriff of Deadman's Gulch?' Walters said mildly. 'Amazing. What else did he tell you?'

'Everything—or at least I think everything.'

'Including his doubling for us with the Russians?'

Again I nodded.

'In which case he's told you the truth—although I can't think why,' the C.S. said. 'What was it? Moonlight on the boatdeck or something? Girlish confidences?'

'Carter isn't like that,' said Walters primly. 'And neither is Wainwright. They've both been screened and cleared.'

Well, that at least was something, I thought wryly.

'Aren't we all rather wasting time?' the C.S. said. 'Unless, of course, this young man would like the bloody Governor to vouch for *me*. Incidentally, why did you ask for me, specifically, to vouch or otherwise for Walters?'

'You were the most senior official I knew personally, sir,' I said.

'*Do* you know me?' he asked, raising his eyebrows.

'I was introduced to you when you presented the rugby cup last year at Happy Valley,' I said and felt like a charwoman claiming the acquaintance of a duchess on the strength of a prizegiving at the Women's Institute.

'Ah—you play rugby,' he said, as if that explained a lot. 'I thought some fool had blown me. Four people in this damned Cheltenham-with-chop-suey can do that now. You're the fourth. Watch it, young man—unless you want your next posting to be on Immigrant Control in Wolverhampton. Still—that's not the point. Where the hell is Carter?'

'On Lan Tao,' I said.

'What did you leave him there for?' he asked. 'Malcolm wanted him taken off the ship in the Lamma Channel.'

'There's been a slight box-up,' Walters said nervously. 'He wasn't on board the *Nurma* when Wilson got out to her in the launch—and the captain denied all knowledge of the party, naturally. I had hoped that Wainwright would have explained by now—but things have been rather confused, as I think you'll agree.'

'Actually we were taken off by a party of Chinese,' I said helpfully. 'I managed to escape and get across here——'

I rather admired the C.S.'s self-control. He merely belched as if he had been punched in the belly. Walters I thought was rather unfair.

'You goddam bloody idiot!' he screamed. 'You've wasted half an hour before telling us *that*? I thought you had him holed up in a place of your own contriving—just to show how clever you were! When did you leave him? Who's actually holding him?'

'About five hours ago—a party of six—no five,' I stammered. 'The junk was chased by a frigate and ran ashore——'

'Probably to hell and gone now,' the C.S. said sadly. 'So they've got them both. Lucky Chinese. When are you due for retirement, Walters?'

'Be funny later, John, will you?' snapped Walters. 'At the moment I need help if there's the remotest chance of snatching even half a chestnut——'

'Navy?' asked the C.S.

'Take too long scratching their arses and asking for Admiralty sanction,' said Walters. 'No—I'll need your weight to deal with Malcolm. He's in the Hilton now, refusing to do anything more until he knows where his daughter is. Where is she, anyhow?' he demanded of me.

'On Lan Tao with Carter,' I said.

'Well, that's something,' he said and made for the door. 'Come on, Wainwright. John—call him before we get there and tell him we want full co-operation and no bargaining—or else.'

'Will do,' said the C.S. 'Wainwright, you've earned yourself a commendation: "Tries hard—means well".'

We jumped into the taxi and hared off down the Peak to the

Hilton. I wondered vaguely what sort of impression a furious old gentleman in a scratch collection of garments and a battered sailor would make on the night reception clerk, but Malcolm was waiting for us on the kerb outside. He got in and said tersely: 'All right—John's told me. We want a fast launch. We're probably too late to do anything—but Wainwright—if anything has happened to that girl of mine, I'll cut your bloody throat with my own hands.'

It just wasn't my night.

CHAPTER TWENTY

IT *was* a fast launch, and we made the crossing back in something over a quarter of an hour from Murray Steps—the three of us with a party of ten Chinese plainclothes men under a Yorkshire detective-superintendent. I thought at first that security had now gone by the board, but I realized after a time from the directions Walters was giving them that these were no ordinary police. We landed at the fishing village and I led the way up the slope, hoping to God, but by no means certain, that it was the way I had come down. Fortunately it was, more or less. I offered to do a recce at the top, but Malcolm said not bloody likely, I'd ballsed things up enough already. He just wanted me to show him.

I led them down into the valley. It was now getting light and I could see the huts plainly long before we crept up on them. I knew, of course, that the birds had flown even before we saw the doors standing open and the stamped-out fire they'd had going in the shelter of the rocks.

I looked miserably at Malcolm. His rage seemed to have left him. He was just blankly white-faced and expressionless. I felt the ashes of the fire, feeling silly and boy-scoutish. They were quite cold. Then the superintendent, who had been looking down towards the sea, pointed. A motor junk was standing inshore to the beach. The frigate was nowhere in sight.

The superintendent said: 'That anything like the hooker you arrived in, sir?'

'It might well be it,' I answered. 'The bloody things all look alike to me.'

'Don't take any chances,' said Walters. 'Let's get back to the launch and move round this side—fast. We can cut her off before she gets outside territorial waters. Come on—*move*.'

Malcolm said, 'I'm going down this way on foot. You can pick me up on the beach when you arrive.'

'Do you think that's wise?' Walters asked a little nervously.

'Just leave me alone, Walters,' Malcolm answered flatly.

'I'll leave a few men with you, sir,' the superintendent said.

'I don't want anybody with me,' Malcolm answered—then added. 'Yes, you, Wainwright. You told us you came through another village. You can show me the way there.'

Walters gave in and led off back up the hill. I went along the path ahead of Malcolm, feeling prickly at the back of the neck. Was this just to get me on my own? I wondered.

But I was still on my feet when we reached the edge of the paddy, which was perhaps fortunate for all of us, because the old boy was a bit myopic, and I saw them before he did. I signalled behind me for him to drop and flung myself flat behind a bund.

They were just coming out of the village—the officer and one of the troops—then Sonia and Carter walking in single file—then two more troops bringing up the rear. At the far side of the paddy the remaining soldier was waving a white cloth down to the junk.

We lay there until they had disappeared down the slope into the scrub, then rose and followed. An old man came out of the nearest hut and stared at us. Malcolm addressed him as Honoured Grandfather and told him we were following the *maskee daimen* who had just left, and hoped that none of the villagers would be unkind enough to shout a warning down to them, as there were other soldiers coming shortly and he would prefer not to be put to the necessity of having the whole village decapitated. The old man kowtowed politely and said he hoped so too, but not to worry—this was where the three monkeys originally came from, or words to that effect—in beautifully articulated Cantonese.

We went off after them, sweating now, because the junk had hove to a few yards out and the party in front only had a couple of hundred yards to go, and there was no sign of the launch. I could hear Malcolm alternately swearing and praying in Russian in a strangled undertone.

He said: 'If the worst comes to the worst we'll have to start shooting before they get on board—but intelligently. Drop the officer first. The others won't know quite what to do without orders.'

I thought what a hell of a hope. Two pistols against five burp guns, but I didn't argue.

He went on: 'There's always the chance that they'll shoot the prisoners if they're cornered—in which case I'm afraid I will still have to hold you responsible, Wainwright.' And again I didn't argue.

We were close up behind them now, but still with plenty of cover. They dropped down on to the sands and started to cross to the water's edge. Malcolm doubled forward like a stag and gained the brink of the last drop—and then, thank God, the launch came roaring round the next headland, half her length out of water and a bloody great bow wave creaming up each side of her. The troops stopped and gawped at it, but the officer turned and came running back, roaring at them to hurry. Sonia, the quickest-witted of them all, promptly sat down and refused to move. The officer levelled his gun at her. It was the last thing he ever did, because Malcolm shot him straight through the head.

At thirty paces! I'd never have believed it if I hadn't seen it. One is taught to aim for the thickest part of the body and even then one is lucky if one raises the dust within five yards of the target's feet. Ten paces, yes—but not *thirty*, and while running.

The remaining four reacted more or less to expected form. Two of them started to spray the air in our general direction with their burp guns. The inevitable weak sister one gets in cases like this, broke and ran towards the junk—but the remaining one, sustained no doubt by the Thoughts of the Chairman, remained steadfast to his duty. He came back to the prisoners with his gun cocked—and Malcolm missed this time—and so did I. But fortunately Sonia didn't. She got him in the guts with her chromium toy before he could squeeze the trigger—and twice again before he hit the ground. The weak sister was easy meat. His own outraged comrades got him from the junk, and he finished as a messy splurge in a foot of water.

But then they were pretty well preoccupied with the launch, which had closed right in and was brewing them up with a spigot-mounted Bren. The two sprayers had to stop eventually to change magazines—and even I couldn't miss then.

Carter said: 'If you expect me to say "bloody good show" you can forget it. None of this would have happened if you'd done the proper thing in the first place.'

I said something filthy and turned and looked at Malcolm and Sonia. He had her in his arms and was crying. Sonia was looking rather bored.

The men on the launch had secured the junk by her cable and had boarded her. Some diehard started shooting again. There was a final blast from the Bren, and then everything was quiet. I felt sorry for the old helmsman—and maybe even for Wetten.

Walters came up and said: 'We'll have to get attention for Malcolm. He's bleeding like a pig,' and only then did I realize the true cause of his emotion. It was rage. He'd been hit in the arse again—by an absolute wild one. A soldier's disgrace—twice in a lifetime. I sat on the sand and laughed until I was sick.

But Walters was a hogger for business. He drew Carter and myself to one side and said, 'We haven't got much time left. As far as I know the exchange is still on and it's arranged for two o'clock this afternoon—at Bias Bay—and that's the other side of the wretched Colony.'

'What exchange?' asked Carter.

'You for Winterton,' Walters told him. 'What else?'

'Winterton's dead,' Carter said flatly, and it was nice to hear Walters telling him he was talking cock, and giving him the real facts.

Carter's jaw dropped. 'I'm not doing it,' he said. 'Damn it all —it's asking too much. Russia's one thing—these bastards are a different proposition altogether. They'll have my hide on the barn door—and you know it.'

'With safeguards, naturally,' Walters wheedled.

'What safeguards?'

'It's all laid on. You know the Tai Tun sandbank, a couple of miles off the Bias shoreline? They will put Winterton there, just before high tide. One boat—three men only. We're allowed the same. You pass half-way—you to their boat—Winterton to ours. If there's anything else in sight, the deal's off.'

'It's off already,' Carter said. 'What the hell are you thinking of, Walters? Anyhow, why wasn't I told all this beforehand? Why did you allow a nit like this to break it to me? Why, if it comes to that, wasn't I told the truth about Winterton at the time? Why——?'

'Carter, will you let me finish?' Walters begged. And it was also nice to hear him taking it instead of dishing it out.

'Nothing doing,' said Carter. 'I undertook to go back to Russia—and that's a big enough risk to take, God knows—but not this. You're mad even to think of it. If you can't play straight with your own people——'

'Play straight?' Walters's voice was trembling with indignation. 'What about all these absurd stories you told this wretched fellow about us, eh? Bloody unethical—and it came perilously near to wrecking everything.'

'Necessary at the time,' Carter said shortly. 'I tried him with everything else, but that was the only one the clot would swallow. But that's beside the point. I'm not playing—so what are you going to do about it? Send me back to finish my time?'

'Until we can infiltrate you back to Russia,' sighed Walters. 'You're making it very difficult for us.'

'Difficult for *you*?' exploded Carter. 'Have you ever seen one of these public trials in Peking? Have you ever seen what a man looks like when he's really been under intensive interrogation—the Chinese way? Have you ever seen——?'

'Damn it, Carter,' Walters interrupted. 'You won't *be* on trial. 'You won't ever be in their hands——'

'What do you mean by that?'

'I'm trying to tell you. We've got the place plastered——'

'With what?' Carter demanded. 'More M.I.6 bullshit?'

'With naval frogmen. Twenty of them, working in relays from a submarine resting on the bottom a couple of miles offshore. They've been there for three days.'

I saw the change come over Carter's face, and I shuddered inwardly. He was hooked. What is it that motivates these people? I'm damned certain it's not bravery. Not bravery as I understand it, anyway. Just the terrible fascination of thin ice, maybe. 'Go on,' he said.

'The bank is about eight hundred yards along at half-tide,' Walters explained. 'The two boats meet half-way out to it—for mutual recognition purposes. We'll be even-stevens as I said—three men in each—that is, two besides the principals. When both are satisfied, the boats proceed to opposite ends of the bank. The principals get out and start walking towards each other—you with a certain reluctance until you're threatened with a gun. You'll pass half way—and then you'll yell to Winterton to drop flat—and you'll do the same—because at the first sign of treachery they'll undoubtedly open up with rifle fire. They'll try to shoot both of you.'

'What's to prevent them doing that anyhow?' Carter asked. 'As soon as they've got us both in their sights.'

'They'll only do that as a last resort. They want you alive if possible,' Walters said.

'You can say that again,' Carter said with feeling. 'Go on.'

'As you both drop—the frogmen come up behind their boat. Need I say more?'

'*Bloody* good!' Carter said with even deeper feeling.

And that is what happened—almost. Malcolm and I were supposed to be the ones in the boat—but Malcolm was now out of it, although fair play to him he did volunteer, provided we could find him an air-ring to sit on, but Walters was adamant—and came himself. Carter voiced certain objections to my coming—and I had reservations about Walters—he was pretty doddery—but I *didn't* voice them.

The launch took us round to Bias Bay, picking up a sampan with an outboard motor at Aberdeen, and then casting us loose a couple of miles short of the bank and making off.

We saw the other sampan coming out from the shore. Bias Bay, incidentally, is Tom Tiddler's ground. We have a loose suzerainty up to high-water mark, and they're supposed to own the foreshore—but it's a barren place, and nobody lives there.

We closed up to within about twenty yards. There was a soldier and a man in black peasant clothes in the other boat—both patently Chinese—and we began to think we were being short changed, but then a scarecrow looked over the gunwale and waved feebly—and I heard Carter catch his breath.

'Holy Christ!' he said. 'Yes—that's Winterton. You see what I mean, Walters?'

Carter stood up, wobbling with the motion of the boat. The man in black clothes studied him keenly, then nodded, and without a word we put our helms over and headed for the opposite ends of the long whalebacked bank.

Carter did it very well, arguing and pleading realistically, and we were conscious of two pairs of binoculars on us from the other boat, but they wouldn't let Winterton move a step until our man was on his way. I climbed out and stuck a gun in Carter's back, and he started to move then, slowly, with his shoulders slouched—a picture of a man who has come up to the brink of hopelessness, and then gone over. And I still say the bastard was enjoying it—like a fellow I knew in the Parachute Regiment who used to crawl and gibber before a drop, but who tried to cut his throat when he was transferred to a line battalion.

They got to the crossing point and we heard Carter yell and saw him drop, but Winterton's reactions were blurred and he hesitated a fraction of a second, and when he did drop it was with a bullet in his back. We could see their shots kicking the sand up all round them, but the hump of the bank gave them just that tiny bit of dead ground that hid most of their shapes from the other boat.

Walters had the outboard going by this time. I thought he was leaving them to it, and I got my gun out, but he swung the sampan into the smooth water on the shoreward side of the bank and roared towards the other boat. He was mouthing something I couldn't hear over the noise of the engine, and pointing with his foot to a khaki haversack on the floorboards. I opened it. There were six Mills bombs in it. I saw what he meant then.

The Chinese had stopped firing at the others and were now concentrating on us, but Walters was jinking the sampan violently from side to side, and as we came round the end of the bank I managed to get the pin out and lob the first bomb. It missed badly, but put them off their firing for a moment. The second one did all right. It landed smack between them.

It was a pity that I had drawn the pin from the third one because it wasn't necessary, and the blast from the second made me lose my footing on the slippery bottom boards of the sampan, and I dropped it. They say you've got three and a half seconds with this type. I scrabbled frantically for the damned thing, but lost my footing a second time. I probably got it and threw it clear in three seconds, but it wasn't enough and I've got half an ear and a silver plate in the side of my head to prove it. Walters was never able to prove anything again. He had no head at all.

Yes, that's how it happened. Just as the old gentleman had said. Except that there were no frogmen.

In spite of the chunk out of my dome I wasn't out to it—not then. That came later. I managed to turn the sampan and get back alongside the bank. Carter came down a little way to meet me—and then fell flat and stayed there. I crawled out and up towards him. He'd been hit twice—in the leg and the shoulder—

but was quite conscious. I went on to Winterton. He'd got his smack between the shoulder-blades—but wasn't quite dead as far as I could make out. I dragged them both down to the sampan, and somehow managed to get them into it, with Carter bitching at me the whole time. Then I started for home, but we didn't get far before I passed out, and Carter had to take over with his sound arm. I came to after a time and managed to bandage both him and myself roughly with our combined shirts. Winterton didn't need bandaging, because he wasn't bleeding out of either of the two neat holes in his back or his chest and I thought he had handed in his chips, but he was still breathing when a naval launch picked us up outside the harbour boom. I remember a young sailor being sick as they lifted what was left of Walters out of the sampan.

Unfortunately they shoved us all into the police hospital and somebody recognized Carter before it could be hushed up, but the C.S. had Winterton and myself spirited out of it the same night and I was flown back to London in an R.A.F. plane.

They took me by ambulance to a small and very discreet nursing home in the country, and the Gaffer came down the following day. He stood at the foot of the bed and sucked his horrible teeth, grinning nastily.

'True to form to the very end,' he said. 'One gigantic balls-up.'

'I got them both out,' I said with dignity. 'And if we're on the subject of balls-ups, what about the bloody frogmen we were promised?'

'Frogmen my arse,' he said. 'That was just to put Carter's mind at rest. He was supposed to go over—and you brought him back, you goddamned idiot.'

I nearly vomited. 'You filthy lot of bastards,' I spat at him, but it didn't wipe the grin from his face.

'A bit devious at times,' he admitted. 'But the Chinks wouldn't have knocked him off. They wanted to swap him for one of their own that the Russians are holding. Another Mig—fellow by the name of Kowalski. It would have suited us lovely if it had come off. Winterton out of hock—Carter into Russia—and Kowalski back in circulation. He's been doubling for us for years.'

It was too much for me, I just stared at him, my mouth opening and shutting, but nothing coming out of it. But he still didn't spare me.

'Can't even lob a bomb decent,' he went on accusingly. 'Carter says you let that one off right alongside poor old Walters's ear'ole—and then bloody well brought *him* back as well. Why the hell didn't you put him over the side? Caused us more trouble than anything, that did.'

'How did you explain it?' I asked hollowly.

'They put out a yarn that he'd met with an accident dynamiting fish—but it didn't go down well at the Hong Kong Club, I can tell you. He'd got the Deepsea Sportman's Cup last year, or something.'

'Gaffney,' I begged. 'Do me a favour. Go away. *Please go away.* I'm tired.'

'Is that all the thanks I get for coming down to cheer you up?' he asked, injured. 'All right—I'll be back tomorrow to debrief you. But you're not to see that girl of yours in the meantime. Understand?'

I sat upright. 'I take it you mean Miss Malcolm,' I said. 'Where is she?'

'In town, screaming her head off to know where you are.' He winked lasciviously. 'Carter reckons you were laying her on the ship. She must like it.'

'I'll get into Lanchester and kill the lying bastard when they send him back!' I screamed.

'You won't, you know,' the Gaffer said calmly. 'They're not sending him back. The Meisterspringer is getting him over the wall of Hong Kong Gaol as soon as his leg's out of plaster—and shipping him on to Vladivostok. Must be costing the Rusks a bloody fortune.'

THE BAIT

Dorothy Uhnak

'The Bait' is published by
Hodder & Stoughton Ltd.

The Author

Dorothy Uhnak was born and brought up in New York. She studied sociology at City College and worked with slum children in a Lower East Side settlement house after school hours and full-time during summers. She was a member of the New York City Transit Police Department for fourteen years, was promoted three times and received two commendations including the Outstanding Police Duty bar—the highest award given for heroism. She is married with one daughter and has been writing for as long as she can remember, although *The Bait* is her first novel. Her second is almost completed and is a sequel to *The Bait* with the same running main characters. In addition to writing and keeping house, she is taking a bachelor's degree in Police Science at the City University in New York.

This book is for my daughter, Tracy
—just as I promised

CHAPTER ONE

Christie Opara sat in the small seat outside the empty motorman's cab of the nearly deserted, post-rush hour, downtown IRT local. Her shoulder was pressed against the warm steel wall and her long slim legs, bound by faded green dungarees, tensed against the pitch and sway of the train. Her bare feet felt moist and itchy in the ragged black sneakers as they pressed against the floor. Her hands rested lightly on her schoolbooks and she felt herself becoming part of the motion and monotony of the all-encasing speed which, unmeasured by landscape or anything else framed by the small dirty window facing her, gave no feeling of speed.

The train jerked to an unanticipated stop and Christie's left hand shot out to catch the shoulder bag which slid off her left arm. She caught it before it hit the floor, then, biting her lower lip in annoyance, she leaned forward and collected the books and papers which had fallen between her feet. Although the shoulder bag hadn't opened and there was not the slightest possibility that anything had fallen from it, Christie's fingers automatically slid into the bag and identified each item: the small makeup case, the wad of tissues, sunglasses, ball-point pen, the rough textured butt of her .32 service revolver, the collection of keys on her rabbit's foot chain, the small spiral notebook, then, finally, beneath everything else, the small leather case that held her detective shield.

She snapped the case open within the depths of the bag and, through habit, her fingers traced the embossed lettering: New York City Police Department, then sliding over the word 'Detective', she lightly touched the four numbers '4754' which were cut into the small rectangle at the lower edge of the shield.

Christie dropped the leather case and pulled her hand free. Absently, she pushed the long, dark blond bangs from her forehead and her fingers wandered through the thick, short hair. It was a fruitless attempt to look a little less disheveled and, actually, she looked exactly the way she was supposed to look for this assignment.

At twenty-six, Christie Opara, with her slight, flat-chested, long-legged and almost hipless body and still freckled face, devoid of any makeup except for an excessive amount of white eye-shadow and black eyeliner, appeared to be the bored, desultory twenty-year-old college student she was impersonating. It hadn't been too difficult for her to edge her way into the group at City College. Christie had a talent for picking up not only patterns of speech and gesture, but the more subtle attitudes and postures which could make her an almost faceless, yet vaguely accepted and unsuspected member of any particular gathering. Her presence at City College was for the purpose of identifying and arresting the source of LSD-saturated sugar cubes. This morning, in a particular corner of the school cafeteria, Christie and certain other students with whom she had established a casual and easy rapport, were prepared to purchase these cubes at five dollars each.

It had been a long investigation, requiring over four weeks of careful, tedious work and she was glad it was coming to a climax. It had been even more tiresome and routine for the four other members of the squad working with her, for as Christie supplied them with names of the students involved, they had to check each suspect's background from the exact moment of birth up to and including the present day.

Ordinarily, this would have been a routine case for Narcotics, so the mere fact that it was being handled by the D.A.'s Special Investigations Squad meant that one of the students was 'somebody's' son or daughter and *that* meant things were to be handled tactfully. The arrest this morning was to be effected so discreetly that the prospective purchasers would not even be aware of what had happened to their supplier.

Christie adjusted her body against the hard wicker seat and tried to figure out which student was 'somebody's' offspring. She gave up the attempt in irritation. Although she was instrumental in this investigation and was to be credited with the arrest, Supervising Assistant District Attorney Casey Reardon did not see fit to tell her exactly which student's presence in the group had caused the case to be bucked to the D.A.'s Squad. After nearly a year of working for Reardon, Christie knew she should be able to accept the way he ran things: he asked the questions, his people supplied the answers. Period. She knew Reardon considered his selection of her as the only female detective in his squad of sixteen men a very great compliment. It was the only compliment he had extended to date. No matter how competently she accomplished any of her assignments his reaction was always the same: she did only what was expected of her.

Christie hadn't noticed the sound of the door between the connecting cars slide open or even felt the rush of air, but the door was slammed shut with a loud metallic clanging at the same instant that a shrill, piercing voice streaked through the car.

'In-the-midst-of-Life-we-are-in-Death! I-am-the-Resurrection-and-the-Light! I-am-God-and-you-shall-know-me-or-you-shall-perish!'

Startled by the sound and then by the presence before her, Christie looked up directly into the angry, somewhat glazed eyes of the small man. He was dark and the bones shone through the tightly stretched skin of his face. His body was covered by a huge, dirty white sandwich board which was emblazoned in jagged red and blue lettering: 'Repent! His Day is at Hand! I am Life! I am Death!' He whirled around sharply and before her eyes was a terrible Christ-head, badly drawn and colored in furious streaks of poster paint and yet, incredibly, the face was his: the thin bony cheeks and dark glaring eyes.

The man spun about again, his words now a spate of hissing Spanish. A thin brown hand, roped with blue veins, was thrust from beneath the sandwich board as though to conduct the cadence of his words. Christie sought his eyes but they were focused on some far-off vision of his own. The train lurched to a stop. The doors slid open. A few passengers boarded the car, warily eyeing the now silent and motionless little man and his sandwich board. They carefully found seats at the far end of the car and bent over their morning newspapers.

When the doors closed, the man, as though a switch had clicked inside of him, issued forth with a terrible wailing sound. His hand rose up again and his eyes, burning with frenzy, saw no one. As though he did not exist, no one seemed to see him. He stopped speaking as abruptly as he had begun. A smile pulled his tan lips and his eyes narrowed over some secret which seemed to give him great pleasure. His right hand disappeared beneath his board, then emerged waving a small American flag with a golden tassel.

He clicked his heels together smartly, nodded his head twice and marched down the length of the car.

After a moment of silence, his voice ripped through the car again in his steady, high chant, 'In-the-midst-of-Life-we-are-in-Death! I-am-the-Resurrection-and-the-Light! I-am-God-and-you-shall-know-me-or-you-shall-perish!'

Christie Opara's fingers tightened along the edge of her textbooks and she tried to force the insistent words from her brain. She didn't need anyone to tell her about death. Not today. Not on Friday, May 6: Mike's birthday. Thirty years old. He would have been thirty years old if he hadn't been killed when he was twenty-five years old.

She forced her teeth together and raised her chin so that her face was tilted toward the dim light overhead. She breathed the words into her lungs: in the midst of life. Mike was not in the midst of life: he had *been* life and now he did not exist. Christie closed her eyes tightly but that did not ease the reopened wound any more than her resolution not to notice his birth date each May. She strained against the darkness of her eyelids forcing all images away, trying not to try, just to let it come to her: the fullness of him. But only a flat photographic likeness, unreal and untrue, engraved into her memory by hours of staring at black and white snapshots, appeared. Not the essence of him, not the feel, touch, sense, life of him. She felt a wave of panic. She could not remember what her dead husband looked like.

At twenty-six, Christie was older than Mike had ever been or ever would be. She had become a member of the Police Department because of him. Together, Mike had said, they might become the Department's first husband and wife team. They could make a real contribution in the area of preventive work among juvenile delinquents. Now, nearly five years after his death at the hands of a juvenile narcotics addict, she was a second-grade detective on her way to an assignment involving addicts. Christie shook her head; no. They're not addicts. Reardon had explained that LSD users were not addicts in the true sense of the word.

Christie inhaled sharply and opened her eyes. She was being studied by a middle-aged woman seated diagonally across from her. She was a heavy woman, obviously encased in bulky corsets beneath her two-piece navy-blue crepe dress. The woman regarded the torn black sneakers, the long slender legs covered by taut faded green denims, the black cotton turtleneck and finally the face of the young woman, with that particular expression middle-aged people reserve for the new and terrible generation. The woman's eyes, when they met Christie's, encountered an expression of such cold and unanticipated hostility that her lips twitched compulsively and her head ducked back into her *Reader's Digest.*

Christie stood up abruptly and walked into the vestibule of the train, leaning her narrow body hard against the steel panel. She stared, unseeing, through the smudged window as the tunnel wall raced past and by a conscious, deliberate and fierce act of will, forced herself into the reality of the moment. She glanced at her wristwatch and tried to remember whether it was running four minutes slow or four minutes fast. Not that it really mattered; she had plenty of time. Nine-fifteen, more or less.

Nine-fifteen. That meant Nora and Mickey would be on their way to Mr. Stone's house for their guitar lesson. Christie's eyes traced the image of her small, round mother-in-law against the flat green panel in front of her. Nora Opara, white-haired and pink-faced and filled with as much vitality as her tireless little grandson. Christie smiled at the thought of her son, Mickey, biting his lip in concentration as Nora guided his small, inexperienced hands over the chords.

Again, she looked at her watch. She was getting a little tense, which was good, because that meant she was getting involved and that was essential. She pushed her feet out along the scarred floor, the base of her spine supporting most of her weight. She lowered her head and stared, expressionless, into the car. She began to feel the character, build the mood, go along with it, so that by the time the subway train would arrive at 23rd Street, she would emerge completely transformed into the particular identity required of her. She would be ready to play it.

CHAPTER TWO

MURRAY ROGOFF stood on the subway platform and pressed his shoulder hard against the lumpy steel rivets which protruded every six inches down the length of the black-green pillar, trying to concentrate with every fiber of his body and mind on just that one sensation: that one uncomfortable physical contact, because concentrating on just one particular sensation, he could slow down the steadily building panic which must not be allowed to control him. He visualized the impressions that were being dug into his shoulder and down the hard muscles of his long arm; they would be concave and white at first, the blood forced from the area and then, later, if he pressed hard enough, there would be small reddish-blue bruises at the center of each point of contact. He forced his shoulder cruelly against the pillar but the pain did not stop the questions: how had he come to be here on this station? How long had he been standing here? *Why was he here?*

Why was he here? That, of course, was the question he must destroy with the strength of his body. His strength was so great, his body so powerful and so responsive to the demands he made on it, that Murray considered for a moment what would happen if the steel pillar could no longer resist his efforts. Shifting his body, Rogoff pressed his hip and thigh and calf and foot against the pillar and a small grunt escaped his lips. He could feel within himself a low growling sound, a steady rumbling sound which started at the soles of his feet and vibrated upwards through his body. He slowly realized that the sound was not coming from himself. A subway train was echoing far down the black tunnel and the sound changed: it grew and swelled and the long shining tracks reflected the light which preceded the entrance of the train into the station.

Rogoff backed around the pillar and stood behind it, easily flattening his body so that he was part of the steel which held the station together. He pulled the plaid peaked cap down firmly over his forehead, feeling the leather band constrict the steady beating pulse at his temples. Hearing the subway car so close to him, emitting strange noises like some huge animal, breathing and gasping, Rogoff impulsively came from his hiding place and bent forward and through his thick glasses he saw a face staring blankly out of a window. It was a sleepy, vacant, dazed subway-face, but the eyes, confronting him, suddenly blinked rapidly and were alerted by a strange and urgent alarm. The doors of the train slid closed and the face inside the train gaping at him—it was an old man's face—triggered within Rogoff an anger and he lurched toward the window and pressed his face against the sticky warm glass and the old man recoiled in terror, as though some missile had been hurled at him. The train, moving from the station, flung Rogoff back against the pillar and he stood, hunched now, breathing shallowly, trying to fill his lungs, to hold down the pounding anger within his chest.

He yanked the cap off his head, jamming it under his armpit, and rubbed a calloused palm over his thick-skinned naked skull. His eyes ached and burned beneath the safety of his glasses. He took them off and, knowing he would only make the pain worse, he dug his fingers into his unprotected eyes anyway. With the edge of his dirty tan cotton-knit shirt, he scrubbed at the lenses, then at the special plastic sides which fitted firmly to the contours of his temples, like a welder's eyeshields, helping to build essential moisture inside his lashless and tearless eyes.

There was a clattering of running feet and the excited laughing voices of a young couple. Murray watched them, concealed behind the pillar. They were holding hands and gasping and pressing and bumping their bodies against each other. He wondered what the boy was whispering into the girl's ear. Or was he merely nuzzling her, tasting her, getting the smell and feel and breath of her? She was fat and cinched in at the waist by a narrow belt and her hips were lumpy, but the boy, skinny and sharp-boned, dug his hands into her flesh eagerly.

Murray locked his eyes within the enclosure of his glasses but he could not close out their sounds: heavy, thick obvious sounds. He jammed his cap over his ears, then pressed his hands against the fabric, listening only to the hollow roar within his head.

All he had to do now was to let himself fill completely with the craving he had tried to hold down. Let it rise upwards through him from his loins with the sharp tentacles of need wrapping around his stomach and clenching like tight fists over his heart and lungs so that his breath came painfully hard and his heart throbbed in sharp stabbing bursts. His mind dissolved fully into his body as it had so many times before, bringing him into the night-quiet streets where the shadows would conceal him; into parks, where he could hunch his body behind shrubs in some lonely spot and watch and wait.

And sometimes, like now, when the bright sun cleared the streets of hiding places, the terrible need would send him into the still-cool damp closeness of a deserted subway station where he would watch the stairways and the passageways and the passing trains. For something.

The lust sharpened his brain with its demands, destroying all other thought. It raced through his blood, touching all parts of his body, but crystallizing into a shrewd awareness which he recognized and was willing to accept. It would not be *satisfied* now. That would come later, the complete and wonderful and joyous emptying of himself. But it *could* be sated and relieved.

Murray Rogoff watched the flashing lights of the train approaching the station and he moved to the edge of the platform because he knew that he had to get on the train. And, without thought, he knew *why*.

CHAPTER THREE

CHRISTIE STARED VACANTLY into the darkness that slid past the window of the vestibule, leaning her body into the steel corner. She didn't realize that she had been aware of the large figure approaching her until the man entered the vestibule, hesitated at the door leading to the next car, then, looking at her, dropped his hand from the brass handle and moved into the corner of the vestibule diagonally across from her. She had seen him in an automatic, encompassing glance down the length of the car, her mind not particularly registering the tall, lumbering figure: neither wary nor curious. But now, the man hovering in the semi-darkness, pressing himself into a corner, came sharply into focus.

Christie felt herself tensing, the old familiar readiness, that peculiar sense of warning which started at the back of her throat and ran downwards into her stomach. She breathed easily and steadily trying to slow down the quickening senses of her body. She shifted her books to her left hand: her right hand was free now and rested lightly on the flap of her shoulder bag. Not looking at the man, her face averted from him, she could see his body reflected in the window of the car door directly to her right. The small vestibule was filled with his presence: by the heavy, deep-breathing, living sound of him and the pervasive, acid odor of him. Christie's eyes scanned the length of the car, darting along both sides of the nearly empty, past-rush hour, down-town local. There were five, maybe six passengers, each carefully avoiding contact with anyone else: faces vacantly regarding the colorful advertisements or heads bent over morning newspapers.

Even without directly observing him, Christie knew the man

was a degenerate. It was the kind of knowledge that she had absorbed day after day in the movie houses, the parks, along the side streets near schools, an awareness as intangible but as definite as a radar flash. There was a small, sharp, breathy sound from the corner where he stood: the man was exposing himself. With certain, harsh clarity, Christie acknowledged two facts: the man was a degenerate performing a degenerate act; she was on her way to an assignment where four Squad members awaited her arrival and she could take no official action.

Without a sound, without another glance toward him, without any indication that she had been even slightly aware of him, Christie moved casually from the vestibule and entered the car, sitting halfway down the length of wicker seats, on the left side of the train so that she faced the empty portion of the vestibule. She felt a helpless anger. None of the passengers in the car was aware of the man in the vestibule; nor, for that matter, would they have acted any differently had they been aware of him. Christie sat stiffly, eyes averted from the end of the car, regretting her inability to act. The train pulled into the station and she glanced toward the vestibule. He had not exited.

Two small girls entered the car by the center door. Dressed in crisply identical uniforms of navy-blue school jumpers, white blouses, little blue bow ties and berets, emblazoned in gold with school emblems, the children were chattering excitedly and clutching their schoolbooks to them.

Sit down, sit down; oh, come on, little girls, sit down. Christie pleaded with them silently but their skinny legs couldn't stand still. Radiantly alive in the deadness of the yellow-lit subway car, their bright faces overly animated compared to the sleepy dullness of the older passengers, the children seemed unable to settle down. Looking up and down the subway car, trying to decide in which direction they should go, they turned and headed toward the vestibule.

Christie moved rapidly toward the subway map at the end of the car. The man had switched sides: he was leaning into the corner, facing into the car now, waiting. The two young schoolgirls, trying to get their footing as the car lurched into a turn, moved toward him.

Acting swiftly now, as the small girls approached the vestibule, Christie turned from the map, confronting them, blocking their way and their view into the vestibule. Confused, the two children tried to walk past her, but Christie, with the graceful force of her body, spun them about so casually that no one but the children was aware of her actions. 'Stay out of there,' she commanded in so low and harsh a whisper that the children, startled, didn't look back at her, but took seats midway down the car.

In a determined motion, Christie, her hand extracting her detective shield from the small pocket inside the shoulder bag, pushed the schoolbooks under her arm, transferred the shield to her left hand, right hand free. She moved swiftly into the vestibule, confronting the man directly.

'Police officer,' she said quietly, the flash of shield confirming her words. 'You're under arrest.' Her right hand grasped the man's belt, her fingers twisted into the leather. Her eyes searched for his face, hidden somewhere beneath the plaid cap and strange goggles. 'Close your trousers. We're getting off at the next station.' Standing close to the man, she was sickeningly aware of his size. Her voice wavered and she spoke lower. 'I have a gun in my pocket-book. I don't want to use it, but that will be up to you.'

The man's hands moved and he zipped his trousers. Wordlessly, he seemed to be regarding her but Christie could not see his features. She was only conscious of the massiveness of his body and she swallowed dryly as the station slid into place outside the door. Still grasping his belt, she tugged at him and he exited with her through the opened door.

'Nice and easy,' she intoned. It was more of a prayer than a command, but the man, stooping forward slightly obeyed her. No one else got off the train and the station seemed deserted. Christie, with a sinking sensation, heard the doors close behind her, felt the rumble as the train pulled away from the station. She looked about with an empty feeling and stepped away from the edge of the platform and the very real possibility of being tossed against the rapidly moving train. With her still holding his belt and him still obeying every tug and direction, they moved against the wall. Down the far end of the station was a tall, easy-moving figure in a blue uniform. A Transit Patrolman. The patrolman stiffened curiously, approaching them now, his chin raised in question. Christie directed her prisoner to place his hands against the tile wall, high over his head, feet apart and well back, his weight balanced on his fingertips. She slid her left foot sideways against his left toe, feeling her schoolbooks edging from beneath her arm.

The policeman, as tall, but lighter than the prisoner, was beside them.

'What's this all about?' he asked warily. Christie could sense the sharpening of the policeman. She unclenched her left hand, the shield pressed against the flesh of her palm, aware that the officer was making a curious appraisal of her levis and sweater and sneakers.

'I'm Detective Opara, District Attorney's Squad. I just took this man off the train—indecent exposure.'

The policeman was very young; his face was as pink and smooth as those of the two small schoolgirls. He whistled softly in admiration and surprise. 'He's a big one.' He measured himself against the height and bulk of the prisoner, then quickly, expertly, the Transit Patrolman ran his hands down the length of Murray Rogoff, shaking his head. 'He's clean. Turn around, fella, let's see what you look like.'

Rogoff obediently turned and faced the two police officers, his hands dangling at his sides. His face was still obscured by the cap which rested on the edge of his glasses. The young policeman squinted, peering for a better look, then asked Christie, 'He give you any trouble?'

Christie glanced at her watch and moved back a few steps. She signaled the cop nearer to her and spoke quickly and quietly. The policeman's eyes remained riveted on the prisoner. 'He hasn't caused me any trouble yet, but he's going to. Look, officer, I'm on an assignment. I'm supposed to be down at City College in about fifteen minutes. I'm on a set-up.' Watching the clean, intense young profile, Christie clenched her teeth, then said, 'Officer, this fellow is an 1140; have you ever had an 1140?'

'No, ma'am,' he answered, his eyes not leaving Rogoff. 'In fact, this is my first collar. I mean, I'll get an assist, won't I?'

Christie took a deep breath and the words came out without pause. 'Look, how'd you like the collar? Your first pinch, as a gift? He's yours.'

The policeman's eyes left the prisoner for just an instant; his face stiffened. 'How's that?'

Trying to read his profile again, Christie said, 'I'm on an assignment. Something very important, for the D.A. We have four men staked out, waiting for me to make a connection, in just about fifteen minutes. We've been on this case for nearly a month and today's *the* day.' She realized her voice was getting a little shaky. There was an intelligent awareness about the young patrolman that unnerved her. Not stopping to measure his reaction, she continued, 'When he got off the train he was exposed—you saw that when you approached us, right?'

The cop's bright face was a frozen mask; the eyes, like two points of ice, stayed on hers now. 'I didn't see him exposed. I can't make the collar. *You're* the arresting officer. *I* have no complainant and *I* can't take him on observation because I *didn't* see him exposed: you did. *He's your prisoner. I'm assisting.*'

Christie's breath exploded into an irritated whistle between her teeth. She could hear a train approaching from the tunnel. All she wanted was to get on that train and ride one more stop to where she was supposed to be: to where the Squad men were waiting for her.

'All right, officer, my mistake. I thought you had observed him. So you didn't. Look, I'll tell you what. He's been a nice, quiet fellow. He isn't going to give me any trouble. You go on with your patrol. There might be a mugger or something down the south end of the station. Why don't you just go about your job and I'll take care of this, okay?'

'No good,' he said in a voice so familiar to her: the voice of every cop who knew he was being conned. 'He's a prisoner. You placed him under arrest. His next stop is the precinct, which you know better than I do, officer. If he was to dump you or something, that would be my responsibility.'

With a feeling close to despair, Christie watched a train pull into the station, saw the doors slide open and then shut; watched it leave the station heading toward 23rd Street . . . without her.

The Transit Patrolman had a firm grasp on Rogoff's arm now, then his face broke into a grin. 'Hey, Sarge,' he called, waving to a stocky blue-clad figure who had just gotten off the train. His voice lower, he said to Christie, 'This guy's a corker; he gives us a look every hour on the hour.' Then, to the sergeant, who came toward them, 'Look what we got here!'

The Transit Sergeant, a compact man of about fifty, with the springy bounce of a light heavyweight, professionally narrowed his eyes which raced from Rogoff to Christie, trying to size up the situation. 'What's this?' he asked sharply, his chin pushing in her direction. 'Couple of beatniks acting up?'

The patrolman grinned. 'She's a detective, Sarge. D.A.'s Squad. Took this guy off the train all by herself. An 1140,' he added.

'Yeah?' the sergeant growled, unconvinced.

Christie held up her shield; then, regarding the shrewd, weary, wise face hopefully, she moved away, motioning him toward her. 'Sergeant, can I talk to you for a minute?' She looked at her watch, groaning. 'Oh, God, I'm going to get murdered.' The sergeant regarded her without expression. 'Sergeant, I'm supposed to be down at City College right now. We're on a big case. Confidential, involving some students and LSD; some big people are pushing this investigation and today is wrap-it-up day. My squad is down there, waiting for me. Casey Reardon is my boss and . . .'

The sergeant's face collapsed now into a different face altogether: the human, warm, pleasant face of someone who has just recognized a friend. 'Casey Reardon?' The smiled recalled some private memories. 'Hey, he still a regular hell-shooter? Geez, I could tell you stories about him.'

Clutching at a sudden, unexpected, possible hope, Christie's voice became conspiratorial: the sergeant knew Reardon. 'Well I'm the one who is going to get shot right straight to the devil if I don't get myself to where I'm supposed to be. It's not just a case, Sarge, you understand that.' He nodded sympathetically and she began to feel a little better. 'Someone "very high up" is waiting on this, Sarge, and putting real pressure on all of us.'

The sergeant's face had its professional look again. 'Why this then?' His thumb jerked over his shoulder, toward Rogoff and the young officer.

Christie explained about the schoolgirls, watching the sergeant's face relax again. 'I wouldn't have touched him with a ten-foot pole otherwise. Believe me, Sarge, I don't want him. I would have called your headquarters and I'm sure your teams would have picked him up in the act another day. I was just afraid he'd expose himself to the kids—or maybe worse—after I detrained at 23rd Street.' Then, not hiding her bitterness, 'I didn't expect to run into your bright, efficient and very helpful young patrolman. Sergeant, I'm in a jam.'

The sergeant thoughtfully rubbed the back of his neck. His face was sympathetic. 'I understand the situation. Casey Reardon!' His soft whistle did not help Christie. 'You see'—his eyes flashed over to the young cop—'we just turned these kids out. Two weeks on the line; bright-eyed, bushy-tailed young turks, most of them. This one is a good kid; going to make a real good cop out of him. Book smart and head smart.'

Christie felt the subway platform being pulled from under her and it was a long, long way down.

'If it was *me* had been on the station, well, I *might* have seen him exposed, you know? But these new kids—it's a big deal. First collar. And these are *good* kids, know what I mean?'

Christie nodded with heavy resignation. 'I know what you mean, Sarge. And thanks for the ear, anyway.' More to herself, she said, 'Reardon might bounce me all the way back to the Woman's Bureau.'

Without conviction, the sergeant tried to comfort her. 'Aw, maybe it won't be that bad, kid. Under the circumstances, what the hell could you do?'

The agent in the change booth, a wiry man with a thin leather face, pushed the telephone on the little steel revolving platform from his booth so that the Transit Patrolman could call his Headquarters. The agent continued counting his tokens, his fingers automatically pushing them two at a time from one part of the smooth wooden board to the other, not missing count but also not missing a word being said into the telephone.

'That's right, Lieutenant, 1140, Indecent Exposure. On southbound IRT local en route between 33rd and 28th Street. Arresting Officer, Detective Christie Opara (he spelled it phonetically into the phone 'O-per-uh' and Christie didn't correct him, because then he would call her, as everyone did, O'Para); shield number 4754, D.A.'s Squad—Investigations.' The patrolman listened for a moment, then, 'Oh, all right, I didn't know you wanted the prisoner's pedigree now, just a minute.' Carefully cradling the telephone against his shoulder, he turned the pages of his notebook. 'Here we go: Murray Rogoff—two f's—male—white—36 years—born U.S.; height, 6′ 1″, weight, approximately 185.' Then turning to Rogoff, 'Hey, fella, what color are your eyes?'

The sergeant peered at Rogoff. 'Take off your cap, mister.'

Rogoff reached up and removed his cap. The sergeant whistled in blunt surprise at the stony skull. 'You wouldn't miss this guy a mile away. Those special glasses, buddy? What have you got, trouble with your eyes?'

Rogoff removed his glasses without being told and his lashless eyes blinked rapidly, unprotected now. His face was browless and as smooth as his head with no stubble or indication of any beard growth. The sergeant called out, 'Eyes, light brown. Go ahead, buddy, put the glasses back on if it hurts your eyes.' Then, to

Christie, who at the moment couldn't care less, 'Those are special moisture glasses; I've seen them before. Guy I know got burned in a forest fire once—pal of mine, used to be a ranger. Holds the moisture in, right, Rogoff?' The sergeant wasn't annoyed by the unanswered question. He whispered to Christie, 'This guy's in a fog; acts like a robot; gotta watch them when they're like that.'

Christie looked around the station again: no telephone. The sergeant, catching her distress, hurried the patrolman off the phone. 'Come on, come on, you can give them more details from the precinct; hell, you can tell them what color shorts he's wearing if you want to.'

Christie took a deep breath, inserted her index finger in the dial, spinning it completely for an outside line. She heard the steady buzzing of the dial tone, then dialed her office number.

The first ring was interrupted by the slurred words: 'District-Attorney's-Squad-Detective Martin.'

'Stoney? This is Christie.'

There was a silence lasting approximately two seconds. 'Is it now?'

'Yes. Stoney, listen . . .'

'Christie, where the hell are you? It's after ten. Marty called twice; Ferranti called once; O'Hanlon's been ringing steady and Mr. Reardon is getting what you might call a little tense, only that's not what you really might call it.'

'Well, Stoney, a funny thing happened to me on my way to City College.' Her voice fell as she realized he wasn't responding. 'I'm at the 28th Street station of the IRT subway.'

Another voice blared into her ear, harsh, cold and deliberate. 'And exactly what the hell are you doing at the 28th Street station of the IRT subway?' Casey Reardon demanded.

Christie caught her breath. The sergeant, standing next to her, was pointing at himself. Would it help if he spoke? She shook her head. 'Well, sir, it's a long story.'

Irritably, she was ordered to tell it fast. 'Well, I got this 1140.' She hoped the sergeant hadn't heard the words that were blasted into her ear. He probably had, for he was strolling discreetly toward the prisoner. Christie's mind went blank and she felt the words struggling inside her mouth, not forming first carefully inside her brain. She wondered if Mr. Reardon even heard her: it seemed as though his steady, furious cursing continued as she spoke, trying to tell him the facts. 'And this Transit cop gave me an assist, and . . .' This triggered another barrage of words and then the voice receded and Stoney's voice spoke to her again.

'Christie,' he said carefully, 'Mr. Reardon says as soon as you get your prisoner arraigned you get yourself into the office. Hold it a minute.' She heard an angry consultation, then Stoney again. 'When you get to court, see Tommy Kalman, you know him, the blond court attendant. Have him get you in and out fast—tell him Mr. Reardon's orders, then you come in, right?'

'Right. What about the other fellas?'

'Yeah, how 'bout them?' Stoney asked her. 'I'll probably be hearing from them in the immediate future and I'll call them in.' She heard Reardon's voice moving further away, then cut off completely by the explosive sound of a slamming door. Stoney sighed and his voice was softer now. 'Christie, you better wear a suit of armour; Mr. Reardon is what you might say "unhappy".'

'Thanks a lot.' Christie hung up the phone and pushed it back into the booth. Mr. Reardon's unhappy.

Regretfully, Christie waved to the sergeant as he stood looking out the window of the subway train which was picking up speed, hurtling toward 23rd Street.

'Good God,' the desk lieutenant at the precinct said, 'Look what Transit is sending us now: a twelve-year-old cop and a beatnik female detective. What's your prisoner, a circus strong man? Look at the build on this guy!'

The uniformed clerical man lifted his head from the large sheet of paper he was charting, nodded without comment, and continued his work.

Christie held up her shield. 'I'm P.D., Lieutenant. D.A.'s Squad. Prisoner is an 1140. I took him off a train and this officer from Transit is assisting me.'

'An 1140? Off a subway train? And you're D.A.'s Squad?' The lieutenant's voice was loud in contrast to her own.

'Yes sir,' Christie said shortly. 'I was heading for an assignment and came across this man. Can we bring him up to Detectives now?'

The lieutenant waved in the direction of the iron staircase and Christie signaled for the young officer to follow her with the prisoner.

Transit Patrolman Alexander looked a little upset. He was seeing for the first time the translation of the crisp, cold official words of police procedure into reality and he was groping. 'He gets printed, doesn't he?' he asked Christie.

She nodded, then stopped in the dampish, musty hallway. Ptl. Alexander was trying very hard. 'Look,' she explained, 'remember Section 552 of the Code of Criminal Procedure?'

Ptl. Alexander tried to remember. 'Code of Criminal Procedure . . . 552 covers certain misdemeanours and offenses.'

'Section 552 of the Code of Criminal Procedure is probably one of the most important sections you're going to deal with.' She tried to keep the impatience from her voice. 'It covers various misdemeanours and offenses that require the fingerprinting and photographing of a prisoner, remember?'

Ptl. Alexander brightened. 'Yes. Included are jostling, certain forms of disorderly conduct, possession of certain drugs not covered by narcotics laws, indecent exposure and . . .'

'I *know* what's included,' Christie said. 'The main point for you to remember is that although 1140 of the Penal Law is an offense, the prisoner is processed exactly as though it were a felony. He is printed, photoed and arraigned in Felony Court.'

The young officer nodded. He remembered now.

The detective from the squad neatly and expertly rolled Rogoff's fingers on the ink pad, then carefully transferred them to the official Criminal Identification form. 'You know how to back them up, don't you, Transit?'

The patrolman nodded uncertainly and Christie took the sheets of fingerprints to the typewriter, while the detective led Rogoff to the men's room, to wash his hands. Filling in the required information; name, description, address, scars, characteristics. Christie was unaware of the sensation Rogoff was creating among a newly arrived group of detectives from the precinct. Unrolling the pedigree sheet from the machine, she looked up curiously, getting a good look at her prisoner for the first time. He was rubbing his wet fingers along the seams of his trousers.

His face was large and expressionless, the broad bony structure clearly outlined beneath the taut stretch of yellow skin. His eyes blinked incessantly beneath the unusual glasses, appearing to see no further than the smudged limits of the lenses themselves. Though he responded to the orders and requests of the detectives who were studying him, he did not speak or seem to be aware of his surroundings. As he turned toward her, she noticed a bulge of heavy bone at the top of his forehead, then as his head moved toward the sound of his name, Christie observed that the mass of bone flattened out at the base of his skull. His head was like a piece of sculpture roughly shaped by an artist who had abandoned his work without polishing it into a finished symmetry.

'Jesus, not a hair on him,' one detective said. 'Any hair on your body, mister?'

The naked head swung back and forth. Rogoff removed his glasses, letting them examine his lashless eyes, then, wiping the lenses against his dirty shirt, he wedged them on again and jammed his cap over his skull. His ears were bent by the pressure.

'You're entitled to a phone call, buddy. Who do you want to call? You just tell me, and I'll make the call for you.'

Rogoff shrugged, his long, powerful arms falling on either side of the wooden chair where he sat, slumped to one side. The detective pulled up a chair beside him, his voice patient, and he began moving his hands, as though speaking to one who didn't understand English. 'Here's a piece of paper and a pencil. You write down who you want to be notified and the phone number. That's right.' Then, examining the words on the paper, the detective asked, 'David Rogoff, huh? That your father? No? Your brother, huh? Okay, Murray, I'll give him a call and tell him you'll be arraigned in Felony Court.'

The detective stopped beside Christie. 'He's a real beaut. He give you any trouble?'

'Not a sound out of him. As you see him, that's how he's been.'

The detective turned and regarded Rogoff across the room. 'You're pretty lucky, kid. That's some powerful guy.' Then, pulling at his mouth, 'You were crazy to take him alone.'

'Crazier than you know,' Christie said. Rogoff's arms, hanging limply, were long and hard and tautly muscled, the fingers long and thick, the wrists powerful. It was the complete hairlessness that made his body look so dangerous: like some indestructible living stone. If there was anything to be grateful for in all of this, it was that Rogoff had been so submissive. For an instant, it flashed through Christie that it might have been better if he *had* resisted. At least, if she had a bloody nose or a black eye, she might get some sympathy from Reardon and the men in the Squad. But looking again at those powerful hands and arms and wide shoulders and strange, hoodlike head, Christie dismissed the thought.

They waited at the precinct for over an hour before a patrol wagon picked them up. 'You ride in the back with him, Patrolman Alexander. I'll be up front with the driver. First stop is the Photo Gallery. One of the squad detectives dropped the prints at the B.C.I., so if Rogoff has a yellow sheet, it will be in the complaint room at Felony Court by the time we get there—I hope.'

Transit Patrolman George Alexander nodded solemnly. There was a marked change in him now: *he* was responsible for Rogoff.

Gripping his prisoner firmly, Ptl. Alexander emerged from the rear of the patrol wagon, his eyes searching for the entrance to the Photo Gallery, located in the basement of Police Headquarters. Following Christie, he escorted Rogoff into the confusion of the room where prisoners from all over the city were milling about, each one individually guarded and watched in varying degrees of intensity by the particular arresting officer. The photographer waved Alexander away from Rogoff, who had been placed, face-front small name-board and identification number strung around his neck.

'C'mon, Transit, move it,' the detective-photographer yelled. 'You want to be mugged too?'

'Gee-zuz, look at the light bounce off that guy's skull. He's a weird one, ain't he, with those glasses?' A runty little prisoner with tiny rat's eyes nudged the lanky detective who had arrested him for attempted robbery. 'How'd you like to meet *him* in the dark?'

Christie checked her watch against the wall clock. It was nearly 11:30. Someone grabbed her wrist, holding her hand over her head.

'Hey, who belong to this? Who you with, sister?'

Wrenching her hand free, Christie glared at the detective. 'I'm with *my* prisoner, brother, do you mind?'

The detective grinned good-naturedly. 'Can't tell the good guys from the bad guys anymore.'

They waited another twenty minutes for the patrol wagon to fill with prisoners heading for Criminal Courts Building. Seeing the fleeting panic on his face as Alexander emerged once again from the patrol wagon, Christie impatiently explained, 'Follow the parade to the Detention section. You sign him in and then Correction has him. Then ask somebody, or just follow the cops up to the Complaint Room. I'll be up there getting the complaint drawn up.'

The young officer moved resolutely into the crowd. There was a long line in the Complaint Room and Christie looked around rapidly, spotting a familiar form on line amidst the many uniformed and plainclothes police officers, and the bewilderment of frightened complainant victims. Crashing through the milling confusion, Christie came alongside her target.

'Excuse me, mister, could you help out a poor girl who's lost?'

The large head turned, a suspicious scowl pulling all the blunt features. 'What?' The eyes, narowed, recognized her and all the features of his face, everything—mouth, brows, cheeks—turned upward. 'Well, I'll be damned! Christie Opara. My God,' he said, looking her up and down, 'things that tough in the D.A.'s Squad?'

'Guess I wouldn't pass muster back home at BOSSI, huh?'

'Well, we never had you down that low, kid. The Squad Commander wouldn't let you past the door in that get-up.' The warm brown eyes rested on hers, and the heavy neck leaned to Christie's face. 'What you got, Chris—something special?'

Making a face, Christie muttered, '1140.'

Jack Maxwell raised all his features in surprise. 'You're kidding—1140? D.A.'s Squad? They send you out on that stuff?'

'No, just something I ran into. Look, Jack, I'm in a jam; very long story, very short on time. Can I crowd you out, Jack, old friend, old former teammate. Please?'

Detective Maxwell stepped back, forcing the line in back of him to stagger a little more. He ignored the hard glares he was getting from two officers directly behind him and he called out to no one in particular, 'You guys don't mind, do you? We'll help the little lady out.' Then leaning forward again, 'How's things over there, Christie? I heard Reardon's still going full-steam ahead. What kind of boss is he?'

Christie forced a smile. 'Okay. He's okay. But I do get a little homesick. Say, Jack, keep an eye out for a young Transit cop, will you? He gave me an assist and I'm trying to show him the ropes. First time out for him.'

'Transit? You training Transit cops now? That what they got you doing?' Jack spotted the tall, clean-cut young officer. 'Holy mackerel, he looks twelve years old.'

'He's thirteen,' Christie said. 'Hey, George, over here.'

Relieved of his prisoner, Patrolman Alexander looked around the room with interest, 'Wow, lot of action, huh? This go on every day?'

'Every day and every night, Saturdays, Sundays and holidays included. Patrolman Alexander, meet Detective Maxwell, Bureau of Special Services.'

The policeman, boyishly unguarded, shook hands with Jack. 'Special Services? BOSSI? Wow!'

Jack shook his head wearily. ' "Wow",' he repeated softly, then to Christie, 'It's a sign of advancing age when you look at a kid like this and he's in a policeman's uniform. How old are you, son?'

Patrolman Alexander's chin raised slightly and his lips tightened. He pulled his hand from Maxwell's grasp. 'Old enough.'

Maxwell studied the smooth young face with something close to sympathy. His expression was thoughtful, remembering some other time, some other young cop. 'Relax, officer, you're among friends,' he said, not unkindly.

'Come on, George, watch how it's done.' She leaned over the high counter, recited her information to the bored clerk who punched the keys of the typewriter, handed Christie the affidavit and the yellow sheet which one of the detectives had dropped off for her. 'No previous,' she said. 'Just our arrest. Jack, see you around, and thanks again.'

'Take care, Christie; you too, Junior.'

'Now,' Christie told Patrolman Alexander, 'go back to Detention, show the affidavit to the Corrections man, get Rogoff and meet me up in Felony Court. Follow the signs or ask someone; I'll meet you right by the detention pen in the front of the court.'

Christie went into the ladies' room, ran cold water over her wrists, splashed her face and swallowed a mouthful of water from her cupped hands. Patting her face with tissues, she wrinkled her nose at her reflection in the mirror. She pulled a comb through her thick hair, trying to soften the straight disheveled bangs. With a tissue, she wiped the pale eye-shadow from her lids, then dug again into the shoulder bag, finding a turquoise shadow stick. Christie rubbed her finger on the makeup, then slid some color on to each lid. That looked a little better. The only lipstick she could find was a medium pink: at least, it was a little deeper than her colorless lips. Tugging at the jersey turtleneck, she craned her neck, then decided she had to make the best of things. Christie looped the shoulder bag over her arm and absently reached for her textbooks, which weren't there. She stood motionless for a moment: damn. She had lost two textbooks and one spiral notebook somewhere along the way.

She walked down the wide, high-ceilinged marble-walled corridor, pulled the heavy oak door and entered the cathedral-like courtroom where felony cases and certain misdemeanor cases were arraigned. Walking silently on the sneakers, Christie felt the familiar sensation that always overtook her when she entered this place. It was like being in a church or in a museum or in some sacred, ancient tomb. The ceiling was two stories high; the windows began midway up the side of one wall and extended almost to the ceiling, letting in long narrow slashes of dust-filled light. The chandeliers, massive and systematically ranged across the ceiling, glowed with a dim tanness which did not penetrate the semi-darkness. The benches filling the room were of a smooth, polished wood. Over all the whispered, worried, earnest conversations taking place throughout the room, a heavy layer of silence seemed to press downward like a lid over the bowed heads and cupped mouths.

Avoiding the center aisle, Christie walked close to the right wall, feeling invisible. No one noticed her or was interested in her; everyone here had his own concerns. Court Attendant Tommy Kalman spotted Christie at the same moment she saw him, raising her hand to attract his attention. He motioned her forward inside the gate which separated the long rows of benches from the area reserved for officers of the court, police officers, attorneys and prisoners. Immediately behind this section was the high, long desk where the Magistrate, robed in black, was presiding.

'Hey, Christie, come on. I got your docket number moved up.' Noting her surprise, he added, 'Stoner Martin called me. Seems like Reardon wants you out fast.'

'Thanks, Tommy. My prisoner is with a young Transit cop. Has he come up yet?' Then, seeing Alexander resolutely hanging on to Rogoff's arm, she nodded toward the detention cage. 'There he is.'

Kalman ushered the Transit officer and Rogoff into the courtroom, clanging the cage door behind him. Alexander glanced back at the meshed-steel cage which protruded into the courtroom, set over a stairway leading to the detention cells. The prisoners, lining the stairway, awaiting their appearance in court, were craning their necks in hope of spotting someone—wife, friend, attorney—anyone, within the courtroom.

'Take your cap off, mister. Judge sees that and he'll flip.' Kalman regarded Rogoff's odd skull without expression of any kind. There was nothing that Tommy Kalman hadn't seen before. There was nothing, no person, no deed, no crime, no event, no deformity, no beauty, nothing that would ever register on Kalman's placid features.

Christie kept her eyes on Kalman, watching him move easily among the people milling before the Magistrate's bench: speaking quickly with the court clerk, indicating her, handing him the affidavits, crossing to the Assistant District Attorney, standing on his toes, speaking up to the Magistrate, then signaling for Christie to approach.

'Let's go,' she said softly to the Transit Patrolman who moved forward with Rogoff. 'Stand to his left and slightly behind him,' she instructed.

The young A.D.A. raised his face from the affidavit. 'You the arresting officer?' She nodded and he lifted his face questioningly toward Alexander. 'He assisted,' she explained.

The court clerk rapidly read the complaint in a monotone of mumbling and Christie, holding up her right hand, answered, 'I do' when asked to swear to the truth of the words. So indistinguishable had his reading been—it always was—she could be swearing to the fact that she was a spy from another planet.

Rogoff, head down, seemed unaware that any words had been directed to him. The D.A. repeated, 'Mister, the judge wants to know if you want Legal Aide assigned.' Rogoff regarded him blankly. 'Can you afford an attorney? If you can't, the court will appoint Legal Aide.' Rogoff blinked rapidly but remained silent. The D.A. turned impatiently to Christie. 'What's the story here—he psycho or what?'

'He hasn't opened his mouth since we arrested him.'

The magistrate leaned forward, his horn-rimmed glasses resting on his forehead. 'Did he have any identification on him, officer? And has anyone been notified of his arrest?'

'Yes, sir, he had identification. A call was made to his brother, your Honor.'

The magistrate slid his glasses over his eyes, addressing the D.A. 'What is your pleasure, Mr. Martinelli?'

The D.A. consulted his calendar pad. 'One thousand dollars bail, your Honor—adjourn to May tenth—that okay with you, officer?'

Christie nodded. 'Wait a minute,' she whispered to Patrolman Alexander. 'Stand over there, I'll get the commitment papers.' She took the papers, which the magistrate had signed, from Tommy Kalman and thanked him for saving her a few hours' waiting time. 'Here, George, bring him back down to Detention, give these to the Correction officer, sign him in and you're on your way.'

Alexander seemed a little nervous again. 'Look,' she said, glancing at the large round clock embedded high in the wall at the back of the courtroom, 'that's all there is to it. You won't be called on the case. It's adjourned back to this court for the twelfth. Then he'll probably waive to Special Sessions for a plea. He'll probably get bailed out later in the day when his brother, or whoever, shows. When the case is disposed of, I'll call your command with the details, okay?'

'Okay.' Then, his youthful excitement overcame his strenuous attempts at professionalism. He leaned forward, whispering to Christie, 'Hey, Detective Opara, you know who they have down there? You know that guy all over the *Daily News* this morning—murdered his wife and drowned his four kids? *He's* down there,' Patrolman Alexander said, as though the detention pen in the Criminal Courts Building was the last place in the world he'd expect to find a murderer. 'I guess that's why all the photographers were hanging around out back.' He shook his head in wonder. 'Boy, you know something—he's just a medium-sized guy. I mean, he looks just like *anybody* else, you know. Stabbed his wife twenty-two times, then drowned his four kids, then made himself some scrambled eggs! The detectives were telling me, down there. He looks just like anybody else,' he repeated.

'Yes, I'm sure he does,' Christie said. '*Everyone* looks just like *anybody* else. Well, I better get to my office. Thanks for all your help, officer.' He looked so earnest; it didn't seem possible that he was only five years younger than she. But then, she had five years more on the job than he had. 'Good luck in your career,' she said, 'I'm sure you're going to be just fine.'

He grinned, holding his prisoner with his left hand, so that his right hand was free to grasp hers. 'Thanks a lot, Detective Opara, this has all been very interesting. Oh, and good luck with your boss.'

Transit Patrolman George Alexander, age twenty-one, disappeared with his prisoner into the detention cage. Detective

Christie Opara looked at the clock on the wall, and wished she could disappear too.

CHAPTER FOUR

IT WAS 1:00 P.M. when Detective Christie Opara turned the cold brass doorknob to the drab, green-walled office identified by the neatly stenciled legend in the smoked-glass upper half of the door: 'District Attorney's Squad—Investigations.' She was prepared for the reaction of the members of her Squad. She had worked too long with men not to anticipate exactly what her reception would be.

Detective Marty Ginsburg was leaning over the battered old wooden desk in the far corner of the Squad room. It was a relic handed down from generations of municipal offices and, out of respect for the uniform gray metal and black-rubber-topped newer standard desks, it had been placed in the least conspicuous area of the room. Invariably, Marty, when in the office, claimed it for his own. Each of the four scarred drawers contained a nondescript collection of things held in value by Marty Ginsburg. At the moment, half of the desk top was covered with coins: nickels, dimes, quarters. The other half was covered with large grains of salt and pretzel crumbs. A large cardboard carton bulged with thick, doughy pretzels. Peering from beneath a heavy, lank strand of dark hair, Marty rasped, 'Yeah, kid, what do you want? You the delivery boy for the 'Quik-Lunch'? Where's the coffee and how come it took you so long?'

Christie held up her large leather shoulder bag. 'Mailman, mister. Say, are you selling those pretzels?'

Marty dug his arm into the box. 'These are *bagels*—not pretzels. Italians sell pretzels. Jews sell *bagels.* Two-fer-a-quarter, three-fer-fifty cents.' Marty winked. 'That's how we make all our money. You want the bargain deal or what?'

'I don't think I could swallow anything right now, but thanks anyway.'

Pat O'Hanlon, a tall man with a light voice and a bland pale face, pointed a long index finger at Christie and asked no one in particular, '*What-is-that?*'

Stoner Martin, first-grade and senior detective in the Squad, finished the sentence he had been pounding out on the five-year-old Royal, the best typewriter in the Squad and his by claim of seniority.

He stood up and walked over beside O'Hanlon. '*That*, Patrick, is a second-grade detective. A *female* second-grade detective. Opara, I believe. Am I correct, officer?'

Stoner's black eyes glinted in his dark face. He was a handsome, dark-skinned Negro, a powerful man, his lean hard torso outlined by a narrow custom-made white shirt. He was the only man in the Squad who could successfully wear close-fitting, beltless slacks: he was absolutely hipless and stomachless.

The three men regarded Christie as though she were an inanimate curiosity. She hoisted herself easily on to the long table against one wall, her sneakers dangling a good six inches from the floor. She leaned the palms of her hands on either side of her body, hunching her shoulders against their words, which were good-natured, but sharp.

'We had a second-grade female detective in this Squad, once, remember, Stoney?'

Stoner scratched his chin thoughtfully, then snapped his fingers. 'Oh, yes, that's right. She was a real ace, wasn't she?' Stoner's musical voice played over his mockingly admiring words. 'I remember now. A regular one-girl crime-buster. "Lock'em-up-Susie"—that's what we used to call her.'

O'Hanlon nodded earnestly. 'She sure made the Squad look good. Lifted the Squad's activity record way up, carried the rest of us non-productive foot soldiers.'

'Yeah, and us bagel vendors,' Marty chimed in.

Stoner fixed his eye on Ginsburg, who was eating another pretzel. 'Marty, if you think you are going to fill your already adequate stomach with enough of that poisoned dough to get you on sick leave, forget it. Mr. Reardon is not in a particularly sympathetic mood as of this moment and if you begin to feel a little queasy, you better not get a little queasy on these immediate premises.'

Marty gasped, 'I don't feel so good. When I don't feel so good, I eat. I can't help it. I'm a compulsive eater.'

'I've heard of compulsive eaters,' O'Hanlon said. 'Stoney, have you ever heard of compulsive lock-'em-up second-grade female detectives?'

Christie sighed. 'Okay, fellas. Anyone want to hear what happened?'

O'Hanlon looked at Ginsburg. 'Marty, do you want to hear what happened?'

Marty shook his head. 'Not me. I don't want to hear what happened. Do you want to hear what happened, Paddy?'

'Hell, no, I don't want to hear what happened. Stoney, do you want to hear what happened?'

Motioning Christie toward his typewriter, Stoner Martin said, 'No, I don't want to hear what happened. But Mr. Reardon in there, *he* wants to hear what happened. But first he wants us to *read* what happened, Detective Opara, so will you just put your typing fingers on this keyboard and type up a "complete-the-Man-said" report of what happened, so that the Man will know completely what happened?'

Christie set up the papers: one original and two onionskin copies, and found some small consolation in the fact that Stoney had relinquished the Royal and now muttered over the inadequacies of the ancient Underwood. She typed: 'From: Detective Christie Opara, Shield No. 4754; To: Mr. Casey Reardon, Supervising Assistant District Attorney, Investigations.' Turning the paper down four spaces for the body of the report, Christie looked up and flexed her fingers. 'Fellas—Stoney, Pat, Marty—I'm sorry that you got hung up because of my arrest. Really.'

Stoney stared up for a moment, then unlocked two keys which had stuck together. O'Hanlon, without stopping his search for some address in the Manhattan directory, began singing in his soft tenor, 'Who's sorry now? Who's sorry now?'

Marty, a piece of pretzel in one hand, a clutch of coins in the other, came over to her desk. 'For myself, Christie, I don't really mind.' He opened his large hand, revealing a palm filled with money. 'See, I figure I'm about a buck-twenty ahead. And I got breakfast and lunch out of my box.' He leaned toward her and whispered loudly. 'But Bill Ferranti is the guy you're going to have trouble with.'

'Ferranti? Why?' She pictured the mild, clean-cut partner of Marty Ginsburg.

'Well, Bill *looks* like a very nice guy. I mean, gee, no matter where you go with Bill everybody figures—salesman, librarian, IBM technician. He's got that nice manner that makes everybody else look like a bum. But boy, is that a cover-up.' Marty looked around, whispering even louder. 'You see, I've worked with him for five years now, so I know better. What happened was, see, Ferranti with that white hair of his, well, he couldn't be taken for one of the college kids, and it seems somebody got a little nervous, with this dapper white-haired guy hanging around the school cafeteria. Like, if he was a professor or something, he'd be in the teachers' lounge, not in the students' cafeteria.'

Christie frowned. 'What happened?'

'Well, I guess I better tell you. Someone got nervous, like I said, and called the security guard and they gave Ferranti a fast toss and Ferranti blew a fuse. I mean, how would a guy feel, them acting like he was some kind of a nut—hanging around the young college girls, you know?'

'You're kidding?' Christie asked hopefully. Then, seeing Marty's mournful face, 'You're not kidding?'

'I'm telling you what happened is all. So listen, kid, you just stay away from Bill, see, that's the best way. Don't say nothing to him, not even a word. He cools off in complete silence. Mr. Reardon sent him uptown for some information on something, but he'll be back soon, so you just ignore him, okay?' Marty patted her reassuringly on her shoulder and returned to tally up his profits.

Christie called to O'Hanlon. 'Pat? Is that true? What Marty said about Bill?'

O'Hanlon's eyes scanned the ceiling, his mouth stretched. 'Just give him a wide berth, Christie. He always simmers down.' Then, softly to himself, 'After a while, that is.'

The sharp voice cut through the room over the clattering of typewriters. 'Hey, Stoney, is what's her-name here yet?'

Christie's fingers leaped from the keys. Stoner quickly crossed the room and depressed the key of the call box on his desk. 'Yes, sir, she's just typing up the report you wanted.'

'Well, tell her to make it snappy!'

'Yes, sir.' Releasing the key, he turned to Christie. 'The Man said to make it snappy.'

'Yes, I heard him. They probably heard him in Canarsie. What's-her-name is typing as fast as she can.'

Christie typed steadily, then rolled up the paper to read her report. Her fingers found an eraser in the top drawer, her eyes fixed on an error. Carefully, she placed scraps of paper against the carbon and scrubbed away a letter, then, lining the paper up, hit the proper key sharply. 'Damn.' She had placed the letter in the wrong spot, causing a strike-over. Slowing herself down, she neatly erased the strike-over, then repaired the damage as best she could. She pulled the report from the machine, signed her name. 'Okay, Stoney, here it is.'

Stoner took the report and held the first copy up toward the light. His voice was sad. 'Nearly made a hole in the paper. Mr. Reardon doesn't like near-holes in his reports. Oh, well, I better get it in to him anyway.'

She watched Stoner walk down the connecting corridor, rap once on the smoked-glass door and enter Casey Reardon's private office.

Christie walked to Marty's desk, absently pressing a few salt crumbs on her finger tips and licking them with her tongue. 'Marty, what do you think?' she asked, trying to sound casual.

'Well, I think I must have eaten about twenty-two bagels so far and I think I don't feel so good.'

'Come on, Marty, no more jokes.' She hadn't intended to sound quite so urgent.

Marty pressed his hands against his large stomach, then, peering at her through his thick hair, his voice changed, becoming serious. 'Okay, kid. Let's say that you're not officially a member of the Squad until you've been through the fire initiation. We have—one and all, at one time or another—been through it. Now, it's your turn.' He stood up, his heavy hand on her shoulder. 'He's rough, but he's a good boss. Fair. Just don't try to fool him. Tell him what happened straight out, no excuses.'

'Thanks, Marty. I will.'

Stoner rolled into the office with the easy, rhythmic step of an athlete. 'Okay, little one,' he said softly to Christie, 'the Man says *now*.'

Christie swallowed, looking around the room. The men were all very busy; too busy to glance at her.

Christie knocked twice on the door. She didn't realize how loud the second tap was until the voice bellowed out, 'For God's sake, don't break the door down—just come in!'

She entered the large square room, which was a strong contrast to the dinginess of the Squad office. It was flooded by light from windows on two sides. The walls, a light beige, were filled with framed photographs, shiny metal plaques presented to Casey Reardon from an assortment of fraternal, civic and ethnic organizations, certificates, documents, law degrees, diplomas, citations. His desk, a large, modern oiled walnut, was cluttered with an assortment of papers, folders, case files, a haphazard stack of books, two pen sets, and a small, double-framed picture, probably of his family. There was a dark green leather couch against one wall and two straight-backed, wooden-armed chairs, upholstered in the same green leather, directly before the desk.

Reardon was leaning back in his tilt chair, his feet crossed on the top of a desk drawer that had been opened just for that purpose. He was scanning Christie's report through horn-rimmed glasses. He looked up, motioned her toward a chair, then, pushing his glasses up into his dark red hair, he said, 'Wait a minute. Hold it right there.' He stood up, hands on his hips. 'My God. Walk across the room.'

Christie uneasily followed his hand, which waved her from one side of the room to the other.

'Turn around. Go ahead, just turn around. Now, back here.'

Christie's fingers nervously settled on the heavy side seam of her levis. Self-consciously, she hooked her thumbs into her side pockets. Reardon ran his hands roughly over his face, then dug at his eyes for a moment. 'Turn off the radio, will you?'

Christie walked to the cabinet and turned the knob the wrong way. The music blasted into the room. She snapped it off immediately, and muttered, 'sorry.'

'Sit down. Go ahead, relax.' Reardon leaned back again, silently rereading her report.

Christie lifted her eyes from the edge of his desk and studied his face. It was the kind of face which had probably improved with age. The paleness of the typical redhead had deepened. There were still clusters of reddish freckles across the bridge of his short, pugnacious nose, but they too were dark. His eyes, an almost transparent amber, could range from honey to fire-red and they dominated his face. Light darted from them in sharp flickers through the thick, short red lashes. His hair was as dark as bottled iodine and thick and unruly. His face was strong, revealing much of the character of the man: there were some small lines along the edges of his eyes and the start of some heavy expression lines across the forehead. The chin was square and firm with just an indication of light red stubble. It was still a boyish face, yet at forty years of age, there was also a touch of maturity beginning to dominate.

If time had mellowed the visage of the man, it did nothing to blunt the imprint of the West Side longshoreman's son. He still spoke in the flat, tough slangy voice of the street, flavored by four years in the Marine Corps. During Reardon's courtroom years, many a magistrate and judge had demanded in anger or requested in despair that he modify—if not his manner—at least his vocabulary.

Reardon pushed the glasses back into his hair again, and tapped her report on the edge of his desk. 'Very explicit, concise. You write a good report, Opara.'

Christie breathed evenly. 'Thank you Mr. Reardon.'

He regarded her for a moment, then glanced back at the report. 'He was a big guy, this Rogoff. Let's see: six foot one; 185 pounds. Big solid guy, huh?'

His voice betrayed none of the anger she anticipated from their telephone conversation. Possibly he had reconsidered the situation, a condition for which Christie felt grateful. 'Yes sir, he was a big man.'

'Mm-h'mm. Well, I'd like you to give me a different kind of rundown now. In your report—and very efficient too—you describe what happened and what action you took. Now, I'd like you to tell me a couple of things not included in your report. *Rightfully* not included,' he amended quickly. 'Just a few things to satisfy my curiosity, right?'

That seemed reasonable; he just wanted some more details.

'Now, you started from your home with enough time to get to your assigned location, right?' He accepted her nod. 'Judging from your attire, you were fully prepared to report to your scheduled assignment. I assume you're dressed the way you are in anticipation of a "trip party"? Your contacts advised that everyone wear casual clothing?'

'Yes, sir,' Christie said agreeably. 'I wouldn't be dressed like this otherwise.'

'And of course, you hadn't anticipated going into court today under circumstances other than those connected with the pinch we expected at City College?'

'No, sir. The last thing in the world I expected to be doing today was arraigning an 1140.'

His voice was edged with sympathy for her predicament. 'I imagine you must have felt pretty embarrassed, dressed like that. Christ, you look like a little boy.'

There was nothing in his voice to indicate his words had been meant unkindly. 'Yes, sir. They sure gave me the business—in the precinct and at the Photo Gallery and all.

'I guess they did. And I guess they were especially surprised when you told them you were from the *D.A.'s Squad*. Dressed like that. Collaring an 1140. On the subway.'

The pacing of his words had changed. Each phrase was a little more precise. The pause between each statement was just a little longer. Christie felt her fingers tightening around the arms of the chair.

Reardon stood up, loosened his tie, opened the top button of his shirt. He walked to the window, gazed out for a moment, then, rubbing the frame of his glasses along his chin, he turned his attention back to her. 'At what point—*exactly*—did you decide that collaring this 1140 was more important than continuing on to your assignment.'

The unfair question had to be weighed carefully. 'Mr. Reardon, if those two little girls hadn't been on the train, I wouldn't have touched him.'

'Yeah, but the two little girls *were* on the train, weren't they?' His eyes were motionless on her face. His voice switched to an interested, inquiring tone. 'Tell me about those two little girls. Describe them.'

Christie felt her voice going hollow, the way it did when she was testifying on the witness stand. She was being baited; she wasn't sure, yet, where his questions were leading. Carefully, she said, 'They were about eight or nine years old. Two little girls.' She lifted her hand, palm down: 'About this tall. One blond girl; one little brunette. And—well—carrying their schoolbooks—and—' she faltered under his continuing stare.

'Describe what they were wearing. In detail.'

If he were testing her accuracy of observation, she could meet him easily. 'They had on school uniforms. Parochial school. Navy blue jumpers, white blouses with navy bow-ties and navy berets.'

'Any school emblem or insignia?'

She nodded, recalling; her hand touched her head, then her chest. 'Yes, on the jumpers and the berets; gold insignia.'

'What school was it?'

Closing her eyes tightly, straining for the bit of information he was demanding, knowing it had registered somewhere in her brain, she blinked, then said, 'Holy Sepulcher Academy.'

'Uh-huh. Where is the Holy Sepulcher Academy located? On what street?'

Responding to her blank expression, Reardon tapped the walnut cabinet against which he was leaning. 'Get out the Manhattan directory and look it up.'

Christie knelt down, pulling the telephone book from under a pile of books and magazines; still kneeling, she could sense his eyes on the back of her head. She flipped the pages, then her finger ran down a row of tiny print, stopping at a pencil line, which underscored the words: Holy Sepulcher Academy, followed by a Lexington Avenue address and a telephone number. 'Do you want me to write it down?' she asked stupidly; it was obvious he already had the information.

Reardon shook his head slowly, walked to his desk, held up a small scrap of paper. 'No, thank you. I have it here. Come on, put the book away and sit down.' She jammed the phone book into the cabinet, shutting the door firmly so that it wouldn't topple out after her. 'Do you know what street that's on? Let me tell you. Holy Sepulcher Acadamy is located on Lexington Avenue between 22nd and 21st Street.' She sat tensely in the chair. 'What's the matter, Opara? You look a little confused, like you can't figure out what I'm talking about. Think about it for a minute. I have every confidence that you'll come up with something.'

Christie covered her forehead with her hand for a moment, and he prodded, 'Well, how about it? Come up with anything? Any conclusions?'

Resigned, she stated the obvious fact flatly.

'That means the children would have gotten off the train at 23rd Street.'

His voice was falsely pleased. 'Hey, good. *Very good.*' Then he cut back into anger. 'And if you had ridden one more stop, instead of taking this bum off at 28th Street, *if you had ridden just one more stop*, instead of rising to the challenge of protecting the public well-being—you would have seen that these vulnerable little children, whose welfare caused you so much concern, were getting off at 23rd Street—which is where *you* were supposed to get off. And this, this *Rogoff* could have gone on his way. *Right?*'

'I . . . guess so.'

'You guess so?'

Quickly, she amended her reply, but it seemed to Reardon that there was something oddly harsh in her clipped words. 'Right. Yes, sir, that's *right!*'

Leaning back, he rolled her report into a cylinder and rested it against his chin. 'And you wouldn't have had to bother to write this up. And I wouldn't have had to bother reading it.'

Christie breathed slowly; a small cough caught in her throat and she swallowed hard. When she raised her face, Reardon caught the change. Her chin was tilted to one side, the head slightly back; there was a steady pulling at her jaw line and her eyes had darkened. 'And those men out there wouldn't be left hanging,' he continued, 'and the whole investigation wouldn't be exactly *nowhere,* which is exactly where it is, as of right now.'

He sensed the careful weighing of her words, the effort at control. 'Mr. Reardon, the facts are that I *did* run into this degenerate and there *were* two young girls involved and I *did* act in what I felt to be a proper manner as a police officer.'

Reardon smiled without amusement. 'You acted in what you felt was a proper manner at the time. Re-evaluate your action now, in the light of all the circumstances involved.'

'I acted in a proper manner,' she insisted.

'Technically?'

'Yes, sir.'

'All right. Now considering the fact that four other Squad members besides yourself have conducted an investigation for nearly a month, building up to this particular day, and aware of the fact this was a "pressure assignment" directly from "upstairs", what's your evaluation of your action?'

'I had no way of knowing those children were getting off at 23rd Street and in light of the situation in which I found myself, I acted properly. *Considering all the circumstances.*'

Reardon let the report uncurl on his desk. He stretched his arms, then locked his fingers behind his head. He began a different line of questioning. 'When you placed Rogoff under arrest, he was standing against the door that was to open, right?' She nodded. 'Okay. Now, when the train stopped at 28th Street and the door slid open, did it ever occur to you to wait until just before the door was about to close and shove him off the train? Dump him out and continue on your way?'

His words were so reasonably stated: the considered offering of one possible solution to a dilemma. Unguarded, Christie answered quickly, confidingly, 'Mr. Reardon, I wasn't going to take this Rogoff. I just wanted to get him off the train. I nearly died when I saw the Transit cop.'

He said softly, 'I bet you did.'

Encouraged by his renewed sympathy, relinquishing her own anger, she crossed her ankle to her knee, her hands moving over the denim unselfconsciously. 'I was going to let him run. That's what I expected him to do anyway. He was tremendous. I couldn't have taken him alone. I was amazed that he even got off the train when I told him to.'

'Yes,' Casey said, 'that is amazing.'

'I think he would have run as soon as the train pulled out and he got his bearings. If it hadn't been for the Transit cop. Then, I would have gotten on the next train and would have made it in plenty of time to my assignment.'

'If only the Transit cop hadn't been there,' Casey said, almost to himself.

'Yes, sir,' Christie agreed easily.

Casey placed his hands deliberately on the desk before him, his weight on his palms, and leaned toward her. 'Then, in effect, the whole situation was the fault of the Transit cop?'

He recognized the sudden wariness, the realization that she had been led to say too much, to reveal what she should not have revealed.

She bit her lip, not answering him.

'And further,' he accused her, 'you're telling me that your intention, after having placed a man *under arrest,* was to let him escape. Is *that* what you consider *proper police action*?'

Christie felt a cold disgust: she had given him his weapon. She had set herself up; but he had given her a weapon too, and without hesitation, meeting him head-on, she said, 'A minute ago you asked me why I didn't just dump him off the train. Would *that* have been proper police action?' she demanded.

Reardon shook his head slowly. 'That isn't what I asked you. I just asked you if it hadn't *occurred* to you to do that. I didn't even *suggest* that would have been a proper course to take.'

He wondered if she were counting: five seconds, six seconds, or if it was an instinctively timed hesitation. He had seen her do it in court: the gathering of a protective cloak of calmness when she had spoken too hastily, rising to the questions calculated to destroy the validity of her testimony. Her face was red but her eyes met his steadily and without excuse.

'Mr. Reardon, are we playing that old game: heads-you-win, tails-I-lose?'

'I don't consider this a game, Detective Opara. Do you?'

'Well, it seems that no matter what I would have done, I would have acted improperly.'

'And it seems to me that there has been a drastic change in your attitude from the moment you entered this office up to this minute. It seems to me that you came in here seeming to feel that you owed me and the members of this Squad an explanation of why you failed to follow through on your assignment. And that now, you seem to feel that no explanation of any kind is in order.'

Her voice no longer able to conceal the anger which had been glaring from her eyes, she said, 'You're accurate on that score, Mr. Reardon. I walked in here this morning feeling like some kind of a culprit. Well, I'm *not* a culprit and I'm *not* a defendant in a courtroom!'

'Jesus, I'm glad of that. You've made several incriminating admissions relative to highly improper police action which you intended to take and I hope to God you never make those admissions on a witness stand in a courtroom.'

Disregarding some small sense of discretion still warning her, she said, 'In a courtroom, I would hope to have someone on my side. Like the *District Attorney*, so that when counsel for the plaintiff is trying to make *me* the culprit, I would have legal counsel to protect me!'

Reardon stood up. 'It's a little difficult to protect a witness who doesn't know when to shut up!' He walked to the window, his eyes fixed on two yellow taxicabs fighting for position along Foley Square, inching so close they seemed to touch, then bounce apart. He turned, switched the radio on, tuned the music low, listened for a moment, then recognized the melody. He looked back at Christie Opara and noted with astonishment, anger and some amusement: *the little bastard is furious.* She had slid down in the chair, resting almost on the base of her spine, and one long slender leg, outlined by the pale green denim, was crossed on the other, which was stretched out, the foot hidden under the desk. Her hands were gripped around her raised knee and she was completely absorbed in her own thoughts.

Reardon walked behind his desk and she looked up at him, not raising her face, just her eyes. She released her knee, pushed some hair from her forehead, rested her chin against her thumb the index finger pushing into her cheek. She nibbled absently on her pinky. Her eyes, which had seemed gray, now, in the clearer light of the sun which had shifted to touch her face, were a clear, cold green.

'For Christ's sakes, sit up and take your finger out of your mouth!'

It was like speaking to one of his sixteen-year-old twin daughters, and her reaction was what he had come to expect from them. Deliberately, she shifted her position in the chair, placed her feet flat on the floor, slid her hands along the armrests and lifted her body so that her spine hit the back of the chair and she was rigidly straight. Her face had a familiar expression, too: a kind of pleased awareness that she had been able to irritate him. He reached for a scrap of paper.

'When does this guy go to court again?'

'May 10,' she answered, 'Tuesday.'

'You expect him to cop out?' he asked coldly.

'That's up to him, isn't it?'

Casey Reardon looked up. 'Look, Opara, don't get *too* fresh with me, okay?' She focused her eyes on the edge of the desk. At least she knew enough not to engage him again. She'd better not. Not now. 'Wednesday, okay.' He consulted his calendar. 'You can pick the investigation up on Monday and—' He was stopped by the complete change of her expression: the complete absence of any mask. 'Well, what's the matter *now*?'

She shook her head. 'Nothing. Nothing.'

Her eyes were shining and her face, he noticed, had been steadily getting paler. He walked around the desk, standing in front of her. 'Opara, did you think I was going to *dump* you? Jesus, look up at me.' She was trying hard to keep her face expressionless and he was curiously touched by her rapid blinking and the quick licking of her lips. 'Did you really think I was going to dump you for what happened today?'

She shook her head, shrugged, then whispered, 'I don't know. I guess the thought did occur to me.'

He smiled at her bowed head: that was why she had fought him, then. Because she felt it didn't matter. Realizing her struggle to keep the tears back, his voice changed sharply. 'Oh, boy. Hey, Opara, I think I owe you an apology.' Her chin lifted, her eyes narrowed warily. 'You know what the trouble has been here?' He slapped the top of his desk, walking across the front of the room, berating himself. 'Damn it, I'm so used to talking to the *guys*, you know, the other Squad members, as just guys—detectives. When I talk to you as a detective, as a detective second-grade, I talk to you as if you were—just another member of the Squad.' He could see the green eyes hardening. 'You see, I forgot, I think we *all* forget that you're a girl. A female. Hell, dressed like that, you can't blame us. You look like one of the guys!' Sitting down, leaning forward, his voice apologetic, 'You'll just have to give us all a second chance to get used to you. You know, to give you the special considerations a girl is entitled to. We just tended to think a cop is a cop.'

Her voice was low but furious. 'I'm a second-grade detective, Mr. Reardon, and I got second grade on the basis of my *ability* as a cop.'

Reardon's face relaxed and Christie was startled by the sudden sound of his deep, hard laugh. 'Opara, don't ever play poker. You can't hide a thing. I can hear you loud and clear: "You bastard, Reardon!"' He pointed a warning finger at her. 'Don't say it, honey, but when you're thinking it, don't let it show so clearly.' He looked at his watch. 'Look at the time. I have to get going.' He waved her toward him. 'C'mere a minute. Put out your arms.'

Watching him closely, Christie extended her arms as he roughly pushed up the sleeves of her black jersey, his fingers pressing her wrists. 'You ever have a busted wrist? Wait a minute—the *left* wrist?'

She nodded, trying to withdraw her arms, but he held her, his fingers pressing hard on the left wrist. 'Okay. You're going to break it again. Hey, put the chin down. *I'm* not going to break it. Hell, I wouldn't tangle with you, you're probably a karate expert." Releasing her wrists, looking her up and down, he told her, "You ought to take vitamins or something, Opara.' Then, to himself, 'Or something.'

'How am I going to break my wrist, Mr. Reardon? And why?'

'I was afraid you'd never ask,' he said, buttoning his shirt, tightening his tie. 'You're going back to City College Monday morning with your arm in a cast. That's why you couldn't show today: it would have to be something drastic to keep you from It Day. Ginsburg has a cousin who's a veterinarian or something. Marty will take you over there Sunday night you get you into a cast.' He grinned. 'It'll be a nice heavy cast—we want it to look authentic, right?' He slipped on his jacket. 'Then, you get back into your little group of pals and we'll play it by ear from then on.'

'Yes, sir. May I leave now?'

Reardon adjusted the jacket, smoothing it across his shoulders, then he nodded, waiting until her hand was on the doorknob. 'Oh, Detective Opara, just a moment.' He held the report which she had typed, carefully removed the first page, held it up toward the light and squinted at it. 'Here'—he extended the papers to her—'the original copy almost has a hole in it. I don't like reports that almost have holes in them; retype it.' Still holding the report as she tried to take it, he said, 'Relax, tiger, you're getting off easy. And watch the expression, kid, I can read you like radar.'

'Yes, sir. Is that all?'

'For now. Tell Stoney to get his . . . tell Stoney to come in. In a hurry.'

Stoney tapped and entered Reardon's office, offering him some paper. 'Here's the info re the gambling matter on the East Side.'

Reardon stuffed Stoner's information into his battered attaché case, along with a collection of papers from his desk top, then pushed his hat low on his forehead. 'What a fresh little bastard. I mean, *really* fresh.' Then, looking up, 'What's your opinion?'

Stoney grinned. 'I would say—she took you on.'

'Like a tiger cub.' He pressed his lips together thoughtfully. 'No, more like a flyweight who sneaked into the heavyweight class.' He laughed, remembering the angry face. 'Wow, what guts! She's pretty cute. How'd she take the guys? They give her the business?'

Stoney considered for a moment. 'Well, I would say we were up to our usual form. She's played boys' rules before, Casey. She can handle herself.'

'No feminine wiles?'

'Well, she's got a way with her, boss, but I wouldn't say feminine wiles, exactly. Pretty good-natured. You know—one of the guys.'

Reardon nodded, concentrating now on jamming his overstuffed case shut. 'I think she'll be okay. Make sure Ginsburg gets her to his doctor cousin or whatever the hell he is. This damn thing doesn't hold enough.'

'You put too much in it is the problem.'

'Nope. I am never at fault.' Reardon said, accepting Stoney's casual salute. 'Let's move.'

Stoner Martin followed Reardon into the main office where the Squad was expecting him: there was no sudden ducking of heads over suddenly important work, no changing of attitude, yet everyone was aware that Casey was striding through the room, his eyes taking in everyone present, fully cognizant of what was happening in every corner. He nodded at O'Hanlon, who glanced up from the pad on which he was sketching circles and squares while listening to the voice on the telephone. He knew that Christie, staring blankly at the paper in her machine, had hit a wrong key and would correct it as soon as he left. He took the scrap of paper Ferranti, who had just arrived, handed him, scowled, then nodded at the information he wanted. Shoving the paper into his pocket, he waved at Ginsburg, who waved a pretzel back at his boss.

'Hey, Mr. Reardon, you want to buy some bagels?'

'What do you get for them, Marty?'

'Two-fer-a-quarter, three-fer-a-half, but seeing as how you're the boss, a special price: fifteen cents each, flat rate.'

'You crook,' Casey called out, 'you'd swindle your own mother.' Then, 'Stoney, you're top man here. This is a very motley looking group of people. See if you can't clean them up a little, huh?' His eyes swept the room. 'Get Ginsburg out of that apron, he looks like a cook in a greasy-spoon joint.' He looked at Ferranti, then back at Stoney. 'No ties, no jackets, what is this? And try to get Opara into a dress: it might help a little.' His eyes stayed on Christie, but she refused to look up from her steady typing. 'And if Ginsburg makes any sales, you know, for cash, right here on the premises, have Opara write up a summons, or make an arrest, if she feels it's warranted.' Christie stopped typing and glared up at him. 'We want to build up the Squad arrest record. She might make us all look good one day.' Reardon walked out without looking back.

Christie stared at her report, reached over and pulled the papers from her machine, squashing them into a ball which she tossed at the wastebasket. It bounced against the wall and on to the floor. Whispering to herself, she bent down and dropped the papers into the basket, pulled open the drawer and prepared another set of papers and carbons.

Stoney's voice, beside her, was musical and pleasant but something made her stop and listen closely to him. 'You type up a nice report for that man, Christie. Oh, I know you're steaming a little from the pressure cooking he gave you, but I want to tell you something. Casey Reardon spent about forty-five pretty hot minutes himself, upstairs.' Stoney's thumb jerked toward the ceiling, indicating the 'top floor' where the District Attorney of New York County held domain. Stoney's black eyes caught her surprise at his next words. '*Defending you*. Yeah, that's right, defending Detective Christie Opara, who is a member of this here Squad. You see, the Great Master of Us All up there on that top floor, he wasn't too interested in anything except that the case didn't come off today. And he wanted to know *who?* and *why?* but mostly *who* and then why the *who* wasn't removed from the Squad—forthwith.' Stoney flexed his shoulders, straightening his spine, and sighed. 'Now Mr. Reardon *never* tells *who* to the fella up there, and as to the *why*'—he smiled—'well, Mr. Reardon has a pretty good backlog of convenient *whys* that he can draw on, so we still have the investigation and the wind-up has just been put off, temporarily. So if he was a little rough on you, you might feel, under the circumstances, that the Man was entitled, no?'

Christie took a long, deep, grateful breath, nodded wordlessly at Stoney, who winked and moved back to his own desk. Taking her papers with her, she crossed the room, to stand alongside of him. 'Stoney, can I use your typewriter? I'll make it fast. The Royal does a better job'—she grinned—'and I want to give Mr. Reardon a mistake-free, hole-free report, no?'

Stoner Martin groaned wearily. 'Ah, my words always can be turned against my own best interests. Make it quick, Christie, I don't want to spend the rest of my days and nights here, lend-leasing my typewriter.'

She was nearly finished with her report when Bill Ferranti approached her. She turned quickly, catching some wild hand signals from Marty Ginsburg.

Detective Ferranti was a slender, neatly dressed man who wore dark horn-rimmed glasses. His face had a mild, pink-skinned, owlish appearance, and he had thinning, pure white hair. He was always immaculately groomed. 'Christie, did you have your first go-round with Mr. Reardon today?' His voice was friendly and concerned.

'Yes, but it wasn't too bad. Bill, I'm sorry about this morning. I hope . . .'

Ferranti waved his hand in the air. 'So we waited a while; the cafeteria was nice and cool and the coffee is very good. No damage, as long as you got off the hook with Mr. Reardon. He can be very rough, but he's fair.'

Christie grinned and in a loud voice said, 'Well, your partner back there'—turning, she discovered Marty had disappeared from sight—'I think he's hiding under the desk. Bill, you better have a long talk with him. He's been spreading some pretty awful stories about you!'

Ginsburg made groaning sounds, and his hand emerged from under the desk, grasped at a pretzel, then disappeared. The wise-cracks began to crisscross the room, from O'Hanlon, who held his hand over the mouthpiece of the telephone, from Christie, between Bill and Marty. Finally, Stoney called for order. 'Let's hold it down in here! Let's try to act like professional law enforcement officers, gentlemen. And you too, Christie. Let's have a little decorum *if* it isn't too much to ask. After all, we *are* a rather select little group, though we do, some of us anyway, appear a little motley today, like the Man said.'

Christie finished her report without a mistake: the margins neatly lined up, the paragraphs properly indented. Handing the report to Stoner Martin she felt, for the first time since she had been assigned to the District Attorney's Squad, that she was, in fact, a member.

CHAPTER FIVE

DAVID ROGOFF, a pale man of forty, pressed his forehead into his hands, which clung to the steering wheel of his 1965 coffee-color Dodge Dart. He could feel the streams of sweat running under his arms, along the sides of his body, down his chest, making the Dacron shirt cling to his body like a thin layer of clammy paste.

It was totally silent in the cavernous parking lot, two levels below the street. The trip in from Manhasset had been unreal: a mechanical maneuvering of the car along the Expressway, the sudden realization that he was hitting nearly seventy, the jamming on of the brakes, the anger of some indignant housewife, her hair flapping wildly in her convertible behind him as she simultaneously braked and honked to keep herself from racking up on him and to let him know what she thought of him. The sudden maze of lower Manhattan traffic, which hadn't been sudden at all; actually, a slow, steady, continuous building up of traffic and side streets, but David had noticed all of it at once, as though he had been miraculously transported from the cool, dark, understated, elegant showroom of 'Tastefully Yours' in the shopping center to the inexplicable commotion and heavy heat of Canal Street. Consciously fighting traffic, consciously forcing his way through the narrow, congested streets, he had found this municipal garage, had accepted the small pink ticket from the uniformed man in the little glass booth, had followed the endless series of arrows that kept pointing: around, around, lower and lower, to this final depth of white-marked rectangles. Somehow, not scraping either the large gray cement pillar to his right nor the carelessly parked Cadillac to his left, he had brought the Dart to a halt, turned off the motor and sat now in the silent deadness of his car, trying to pull himself together.

David Rogoff rubbed his forehead, trying to erase the panic that had been building from the instant of that fantastic phone call: that hard unfamiliar, unsurprised, unconcerned voice telling him that *Murray had been arrested.*

He took a long and steadying breath, recalling hard-won conclusions, certainties, drawing on them after so many years, trying to form them into a shield around himself.

Murray is not my fault. What happened to Murray is not my fault. Murray is what he is because of what he is: what he had been before the accident and because he could not cope with the thing that happened to him. And there wasn't even real medical proof that the accident initiated Murray's strange, progressively rapid, complete hairlessness. None of the experts could pinpoint it; none of them had pointed a definite finger at the cause. There was no proof. *Was there?* Murray is Murray's own fault. The irony was that he, David, had undertaken long years of therapy when it was Murray who should have learned to accept himself: not David. It wasn't David who needed the help: it was Murray.

David Rogoff bit down on his index finger, trying to let the pressure of his teeth biting into the bone keep him here, now, in the moment, but the scene was before him, before his eyes, which he kept locked tightly behind his horn-rimmed glasses. It *had* been an accident, for who in this world could possibly have imagined that David Rogoff could have caused irreparable physical damage to his young giant of a brother? It came back to him again, as it had come back to him time and again through the last seventeen years, as it would come back to him periodically through all the years of his life.

Murray, sixteen years old, tall, his great height absorbed by the power of his body. His shoulders like carved stone yet flexible as wire, his chest, broad and massive, outlined by the narrow shirt which fitted into his tight pants without a break in the smooth line of his body. Standing outside the Loew's Delancey movie house that hot July night, surrounded by his usual crowd of adolescent worshipers. Murray, running his large hand through his thick mop of yellow hair; the golden boy. That's what Mama always called him: my great golden boy, and Murray's golden glow protected him from all the responsibilities, all the requirements which he, David, small and narrow in the mold of his father, had to meet, but Murray's splendor, stared at and admired by family and neighbors and even by total strangers, passing him on the street, glancing at him, then turning to gaze at him openly, as though he were some natural wonder. Murray didn't have to worry about how he could finish N.Y.U. at night, working as an accountant during the day; about how to pass that lousy C.P.A. exam; about how to plan and scrounge and get the money together so that one day he could have a business of his own. Murray worried about nothing but Murray.

He didn't have to worry about Edna and her tricks. If only Edna hadn't led him on that night. David Rogoff let his body relax, loosened the grip on the steering wheel, let it run through him, let it play itself out.

That August night, Edna had been up to form with her usual teasing and light touching. It was her idea of innocence, to express shock and anger when one careless, unguarded slip of her hand, one playful quick darting of her tongue against his teeth, aroused him. They had quarreled and he had left her in tears and professed confusion and he had sat swaying in the dirty heat of the 'D' train all the way from the Bronx with all those needs and hungers tensing up inside of him. He had gotten off two stations before Delancey Street, needing to run a little, to walk it off, because he knew, as she did, that if it killed him, she wouldn't let him have her until after the wedding in September.

But the jogging walk through the August streets of the lower East Side hadn't helped. The stoops were lined with Puerto Ricans, twining arms and legs around each other, easily, rubbing, touching, nuzzling. The sidewalks were filled with Italians, the men patting their women, the women warning that the children would see but smiling when the men shrugged: so what? Then, coming upon Murray and his cronies; the kid all flushed and smug, running his fingers inside his opened shirt, playing lightly over the golden strong curls of his chest, sliding his fingers along the fly of his trousers and then, telling—*telling* and all his pals, their eyes narrowed and excited, picturing what Murray was saying: that he had laid those little spic sisters, Maria and Delores Gonzalez, twice each in the period of two hours and mockingly had asked *them* to pay *him* and they, seriously, said they would be glad to because Murray was a great, golden god, a gift to them on a hot, languid, uneasy July night. David had tried to shake free of his brother's grasp. He didn't want to hear about Murray's filth. He had pulled away from Murray, warning him, but Murray was too caught up in his story and all his pimply, snotty friends, gleaming their lewd interest, prodded him on.

Then, Murray, the small golden hairs along his cheeks and chin glittering in the flashing lights of the movie marquee, had reached down, grabbing at David playfully, disregarding David's anger, David's warning, and Murray, in surprise, had let out an obscene howl of delight, had made some stupid, lewd, taunting, crude accusation about David's condition and then about Edna. And David had pushed him.

That was all he had done, his 140 pounds of anger (but had it been deeper than anger? had it been some cumulative force of unknown rage?) had shoved at the massive chest and Murray slid on the slippery smoothness of the pseudo-marble floor under the marquee of the Loew's Delancey and he went into a coma caused by an unanticipated, uncalculated, unimagined crashing of the back of his skull on the curbstone and Murray had remained in a coma, still and lifeless on the flat white bed at Bellevue Hospital for three days and three nights.

David Rogoff stared through the windshield of his car, not seeing the concrete wall directly before him: seeing the image of his brother, Murray, flatly huge beneath the white sheet, breathing fitfully, the bottles arranged about his bed, sending fluids into his body through transparent tubes.

David had talked and talked and talked with Dr. Aronowitz: for four and a half years, digging up all the hidden thoughts, all the unknown resentments of the eleven-year-old boy with white skin and sharp elbows and bony legs who was told over and over again, 'Like a little god he is, David, your baby brother! Like Uncle Moishe in the old country, a wonderful great giant!' While he, David, having heard the wondrous stories of the great, unbelievable Uncle Moishe, whose legends ruled his mother's heart, stared at the rapidly growing, powerful child who at seven could easily knock him down.

He had denied the unsuspected words: he hadn't hated Murray. *He hadn't.* That was what Aronowitz had wanted him to say. God, hadn't he taken the kid everywhere with him? Hadn't he lied for him, time and again, when he got into wild scrapes with the neighborhood hooligans? Stealing, pinching things from the candy store, even lifting coins from the register in Papa's fish store, and David, covering it up, making good the coins so that Mama would never know the reincarnation of the legendary Uncle Moishe was just a common little crook. (But Mama would have said she told Murray he could have some loose change: that's what she would have said.) And he had said, 'Stealing from your own parents, Murray—*from your own parents.*' But the light tan eyes regarded him in that special way, the golden lashes, blinking up and down, the mouth, ready with a quick, pleading smile, the face so innocently sorry.

Of course I loved Murray. Everyone loved Murray.

But not now. No more. David eased his body from beneath the steering wheel, struggling into his lightweight suit jacket, the sleeves sticking against the dampness of his shirt. Murray was Murray's fault. He wasn't blind or crippled or disabled. He had refused to wear the dark blond hairpiece which David had bought for him years ago: for three hundred and twenty dollars. He ruined every decent suit David had bought him; walked off every job David had schemed and begged to get him; had antagonized every doctor David had taken him to with the same reaction: bullshit. Now, Murray was on his own. I will go bail for him and get him out of this and then I am finished with him. *This time: finished.*

David carefully checked the front door to make sure he had locked the car, then tested the rear doors. He glanced at his watch. It was three P.M. Murray had been arrested, the policeman's voice had said, at about nine fifteen. Well, he couldn't have gotten into the city any earlier. He had had to sit and think, after the call, what to do: whom to contact. How he had remembered Frankie Santino was still a mystery to him. How he had even vaguely recalled that Frankie Santino, that skinny, sleazy little Italian kid who worked part-time in his parents pizza joint on Sheriff Street, was now a lawyer, was one of those peculiar little bits of information he had absorbed somehow. When the secretary had said, in a cool, unsurprised way, 'I'll see if *Mr. Santino* is in, just a moment please,' he had sat there in his office, watching through the lush artificial rubber plant so that his partner, Jerry, wouldn't see him. He could not picture Frankie Santino, a lawyer now.

He couldn't have called their attorney, Sam Gerstein. My God, what could he have said to Sam: what would he know about a brother who got arrested on a subway train for being a degenerate?

Frankie had said he would meet him outside of Felony Court, like that was under the Statue of Liberty: anyone would know where.

David stood immobilized in the center of the square lobby of the Criminal Courts Building, his eyes seeking some direction, some sign. People were moving, quickly, slowly, lingeringly, hurriedly, like ants from one side of the lobby to the other, arms around shoulders, voices urgent. Breathing with a slight wheezing sound (that's all I need an asthma attack), feeling the beginning light-headedness of nausea, David emitted a startled gasp at the unexpected clutching of a hand at his shoulder. Turning around, he regarded the man before him without recognition.

He was a short, stocky man with a thick neck emerging from a tightly buttoned white-on-white shirt worn beneath a shiny black Italian silk suit. An inch of pure white emerged at each sleeve and the hand, which reached for David's, had a large, grayish-blue star sapphire ring turned outward on the pinky. David squinted, trying to see Frankie Santino somewhere in the face which was nearly strangled by the silvery white silk tie at the neck. It was a broad, blunt, dark face with black eyes which danced all over David, and the thick, curly black hair was now a heavy fringed semi-circle accenting the swarthy skull.

'Davey Rogoff! You haven't changed, you haven't changed,' the unfamiliar voice informed him loudly. The skinny, blotchy kid with the greasy curls had had a shrill, tough little voice. 'A little filled out maybe, but then aren't we all?' The laugh was unpleasant.

'Mr. Santino?' he asked uncertainly.

'Hell, what is this "Mr. Santino" crap?' the lawyer bellowed at him, seeming delighted to see David. 'I'm still Frankie, *Frankie*,' he said expansively. 'My God, Davey, you look great.' Stepping back, he surveyed David shrewdly, noting that David's dark gray suit fitted a small but compact body which had not succumbed to the years. The dark tie was neatly correct against the expensive shirt. The horn-rimmed glasses added a certain polish and refinement to David's face. The dark brown hair, Santino noted, had been razor cut: the sonuvabitch took good care of himself. Probably went to a health club and took sauna baths.

'Davey-boy, you look real Long Island suburbs. Manhasset? You said the furniture business? You got your own place?'

Carefully, David said, 'Not really my own—I have a partner. We have a small showroom in Manhasset. My home is in Great Neck.'

Santino shook one hand lightly—the hand with the ring—letting it dangle from his wrist. 'Hey! The million-dollar mile—Manhasset!'

David spoke rapidly, putting things in their proper place. 'Well, not exactly. We're sort of on the fringes of the million-dollar mile. Showroom is in Manhasset and we have a small plant in Jersey. It helps with the tax structure to have the factory in Jersey.' He could see the small dark eyes calculating what his business was worth. 'We do small stuff—an occasional office, but mostly dens and playrooms.'

'Sure, sure.' Santino nodded. Then he took David's shoulder, leading him to the large, flat, wide stairway, his voice dropping now, his face pulling into a look of urgent concern. 'Hey, tough shit about Murray, huh? The kid never really pulled out of it, huh? Jee-zus I remember old Murray-the-Norseman: that's what we used to call him. I haven't seen old Murray for years. Never got over the accident, huh?'

David, walking close to the wall, tried to ease himself from Santino's grasp. Just let me get through all of this, he pleaded, just let me get through this minute, this hour, this day, and let me get back home, back into my own life.

He followed where Santino, obviously at home and comfortable and familiar with the workings of the vast building, led him by a series of pressures on his elbow and arm. He sat in a small room with benches where Santino had placed him, handed him the crisp, freshly withdrawn fifty-dollar bills, while Santino set about getting a bail bondsman.

Thirty-five minutes later Santino slid himself next to David, exhaled his minty breath into David's face and told him, in that same, loud, whispering, confidential way which David observed all around him, 'The kid'll be out in about twenty minutes.'

Santino winked, holding his right eye closed for several seconds and jabbed David's ribs with a well-padded elbow. 'Old Frankie's got the right connections, kid. We got the bond and the kid comes up for pleading next Tuesday, May 10th.' David stared blankly at the lawyer. 'Don't worry, don't worry. This is all a formality, all in a day's work, nothing unusual, nothing spectacular. Now, I saw Murray.' His expression was somewhere between pity and disgust. 'Wow, he is some helluva mess: dirty. He still living with mama and papa?'

David winced. 'Yes.'

'Helluva thing for them, but you don't have to tell them nothing—say he got a ticket for jay-walking or something and didn't have the price of the fine, you know? And Dave, clean him up for court on the 10th: get him showered and into a suit and shirt and tie. He sure is a mess, but man, he still got the built!'

'What happens then, Frank, on May 10th?'

'Formal arraignment—we waive to Sessions.' His voice softened, apologetically acknowledging David's puzzled expression. 'He was set bail this morning, but he wasn't represented by an attorney so what happens is, they put the formal arraignment over to the tenth. Then, we show up with him and what we do is we waive him to Special Sessions, Part One. Then, in about another week, he comes before the magistrate and makes his plea.'

David felt his stomach beginning to rumble and his chest felt heavy. Next week. And then another week. And then another.

Hurriedly, confidently, his hand covering the lower half of his face, Frankie told him, 'I know the cop who locked him up. A sharp little cookie, this kid—a girl cop. She bagged him off the train; I've tangled with this kid a few times in court, on cases like this.'

The phrase was repeated over and over inside David's head: cases like this; cases like this. Murray was a case, like other cases like this.

'Some of these cops are no good, hell in my book, they'd all frame their own fathers for a pinch. But this kid is straight—strictly on the level. There's no doubt that Murray waved his jewels at her so I think we better cop him out.' He smiled and patiently explained, 'Plead him guilty and take our chances. He doesn't have any previous, thank God, so he'll probably get an S.S.—suspended sentence. In fact'—he looked around, his eyes darting in circles, his voice falling a pitch or two—'I'm *sure*

I can get him an S.S. I got a few contacts.' The hooded slow wink of the right eye: '*You know.*'

David could feel the heat pressing around him, inside his clothing. His mouth felt yellow and sticky. He nodded: anything, anything, okay, Frank, okay. He walked a few steps to the water fountain, leaning his face low into the small, hollow alcove. Depressing the shining steel handle, he sucked at the small, inch-high stream of warmish water, holding the water in his mouth, around his teeth, then swallowing. He watched Frank Santino: he was hanging on to the shoulder of some fat man with a spiral of wavy yellow hair, winking and nodding and smirking.

'Okay, Davey, let's go. Murray will be out soon. We go around to the side of the building; the bondsman will point him in the right direction. I told Murray we'd be waiting.'

David shielded his eyes with his forearm against the glare of late afternoon sun, avoiding the glances of the other people who were standing uneasily at the gate where prisoners were being released on bail. A skinny Puerto Rican girl, her thin hand clutching the collar of a bright-eyed little boy, her other arm holding a sleeping infant against her body, let out a high sound: some word, some name, and a pale, emaciated, boy-sized man rushed through the gate, breaking into a toothless grin, jabbered at her in a rush of incomprehensible words and embraced her so tightly that the infant was crushed and shrieked itself awake with an angry scream. They both laughed, the man took the infant, ruffled the head of the little boy, and the girl placed her thin arm around his narrow waist. The family walked off, directly into the sunlight.

'Hey, here we go, Davey,' Frankie said, his eyes darting from the prison gate to his watch. He had other things to do this afternoon. 'Hey, Murray, over here, boy.'

David Rogoff steeled himself against the sight of his younger brother, raised his eyes slowly, swallowed hard.

Murray, directed by Frank Santino, who half-embraced him, shuffled, blinking in the strong light, toward David. He looked down blankly at David, who had drawn back but then with effort stepped toward him and reached for Murray's hand, which was cold and limp.

David hadn't seen his brother for more than a year. The sun, shining directly onto his glasses, sparked out Murray's eyes; all David could see was the large head and the yellowness of Murray's face and the broad expanse of thickened bone extending backward like a hood into his filthy shirt. His eyes ran over the soiled and stale clothing and he looked away nervously, nodding and muttering at the final directions Santino was giving him. He shook hands with Santino, accepted his rough slap on the shoulder and tight squeeze on his upper arm, then didn't look after him as he hurried off.

David, his voice unfamiliar in his own ears, not looking at Murray, said, 'I have my car around the corner in the Municipal Parking Garage. I'll drop you off at home.'

Murray followed wordlessly. David, staring straight ahead, was aware of the stooped, forward shuffle, the sliding of the large heavy feet along the pavement, the lurching movement slightly to the right and slightly behind him. He could hear the deep intake of stifling air as they thudded down the iron-caged stairway that led, prison-like, to the lowest level of the parking lot.

Opening the door on the driver's side, David stretched himself across the front seat, pulled up the door lock and motioned Murray around the car. Sitting now behind the wheel of his car, David forced his mind to hardness: to steel. He would drive Murray home; let him off on the street, not see his parents. He couldn't face that. He would do only what he was capable of doing: no more, no less. He could feel Murray settling his large body into the seat beside him; shuddered at the explosive sound of the door being slammed.

And then, for the first time, he heard his brother's voice. Unwillingly, he turned toward the words and looked directly at Murray.

'Gee, Davey, I got a terrible headache,' Murray said, the large hand brutally rubbing the top of his skull, the fingers pulling the glasses from his face, digging at the closed eyes, trying to rub the pain away. The voice was from some long dead, long buried time and Murray's face, twisted now into a look of utter, complete bewilderment, asked him, 'Davey, what was that place? I can't figure it out. I just got this terrible headache, like pounding the top of my head off.'

David said nothing, fighting back the flood of words. He forced his lips tight against each other, kept his hands rigidly on the steering wheel. Murray's hands swept upwards over his face, then down his head and pressed hard on the back of his neck, then suddenly, he opened his eyes and his expression changed, his entire face changed. He smiled a delighted, purely happy smile. 'Hey, Davey, you know what? I got this *feeling*: you know, like something *really* good is going to happen to me today.'

It all collapsed. Somewhere inside of David, it all fell apart. All the years of all the Wednesday nights with Dr. Aronowitz; all of his resolve, firmness, decision. It all collapsed.

The face before him, large and yellowish, the nose too prominent now, the eyes frantically blinking, the mouth, smiling like a child's guileless and mystified, the powerful hand extended by the long and still strong arm to the back of his bare neck, the strong legs, bent at the knees sideways so that his body could settle into the smallness of the car: it all rushed at him and David pulled his own glasses from his face, pressed his hand into his eyes, not trying to stop the tears, just spreading them over his face.

'Hey, Davey,' the voice, concerned, frightened, called to him. 'Don't do that, Davey, don't do that.'

David's right hand reached out blindly, touching the cheek, the neck, the powerful shoulder of his kid brother, and over and over again, he sobbed, 'Murray—Murray—Murray. Oh God! Murray—why? Murray—why?'

CHAPTER SIX

Christie Opara stood facing her body in the full-length mirror set into the door of her bedroom closet, ignoring the small puddles of water forming around her feet. The towel wrapped around her was practically dry: she was usually in too much of a hurry to dry herself after a shower, though now she wasn't in a hurry. She had a date to meet Dan Biers at eight; Nora wouldn't be back with Mickey from their dental appointment until 5:30.

A date with Dan was always a relaxing experience; the conversation, over good food, interesting, informative. Being a corporation attorney, Dan never baited her, never provoked her into those touchy arguments about the role of the police officer in a changing society. Nor did Dan ever suggest they should end their evening, after the theater, in his apartment. (Just that first time, and he accepted her refusal good-naturedly, filing it away for future reference.) She considered Dan, who was legally separated from his wife and son, as an attractive, pleasant, intelligent, good friend. If he were to telephone ten minutes before she left the house, begging off on their date for some reason or other, she would experience no stabbing resentment, no bitter wound, just mild disappointment. In five years of widowhood, she had suffered a few such wounds and had learned how to avoid them.

When she was with Dan, thirty-two years old, darkly good looking rather than classically handsome, Christie was aware of her femininity in a way that did not relate to any of the more basic female needs: his consistent courtesy, his unassuming natural awareness of her intelligence, his planning for an evening that she would find entertaining, made her feel attractive. And yet, at the same time, did not make her feel particularly desirable. This was exactly the way she wanted it.

Standing alone in her room, the house silent except for the soft music of the radio, Christie ignored the fact that she was soaking wet, that her short hair, clinging to her head, was drippng, and she critically studied herself, drawing the towel tightly around her waist so that there was a sharp, bony curving out at the hips. Finally, she let the towel fall to her feet.

Regarding her naked body, she stretched her arms over her head with an athlete's sense of well-being, aware of her own easy flexibility, pleased with the trim firmness of her stomach and thighs. Christie let her head fall back, enjoying the pull along her throat and the pressure at the back of her neck. Leaning forward, she placed the palms of her hands on the floor in front of her, then slowly uncoiled her spine: not just standing up, but unwinding herself in specific sequence. Turning sideways, stretching her arms over her head, she frowned. The slight contours of her body flattened: like a boy's. She leaned forward from the waist, placing her hands on her knees. There. Now she had breasts. But she couldn't very well walk around bent over like that. Straightening up, she rotated her shoulders backwards. That was supposed to help. But she had tried that before: all she had gotten out of that particular exercise was aching shoulders.

Christie picked up the towel with her toes, flipping it through the air, so that it landed on her head. She rubbed her short hair vigorously until it was damp, then brushed it. Well, it might be short, but it could still be sexy. She set a series of rollers across her forehead so that the bangs would be soft, then four rollers at the crown. She pulled a few hairs forward on her cheeks, setting them in place with Scotch tape.

She opened her lingerie drawer sniffing at the clean, fresh fragrance of Tweed. She pulled out the flame-red Vanity Fair bra and matching pantie girdle, sprinkled herself freely with the toilet water, drying her fingers on her underwear. I *feel* sexy and I *smell* sexy. I can't help it if I don't *look* sexy.

Absently, she fingered her left wrist, feeling the slight indentation where the bone had been fractured when she was twelve. She had run the football right through the line, right through her older brothers, right through all of them, to score the point, even though she had felt her wrist snap. She had gotten up and wouldn't stop and wouldn't let go of the ball until she had passed the playground goalpost. To make the point.

Christie stepped into the half-slip, pulling it up over her hips. 'Now that,' she said into the mirror, 'looks sexy.'

By the time Nora and Mickey returned, Christie had her hair brushed and placed just the way she wanted: soft and casual. She slipped on a jersey shift: bright orange-red. It fitted her easily, outlining her small breasts, resting lightly on each sharp hipbone, her waist suggestively ignored by the fabric. Not bad.

'For heaven's sakes,' Nora Opara said as she sank into the rocking chair by the window of Christie's room, 'I thought you were going out with Dan Biers tonight.'

'I am. Why?'

Nora surveyed her daughter-in-law carefully. 'I don't know, it just looks like you had someone else in mind besides "ole buddy Dan". You're wasting that dress on a *pal*.'

Ignoring Nora's familiar taunt, she asked, 'Any cavities?'

'Me, no. As for our little hero: nobody knows. He began screaming the minute Dr. Endleman said, "Well, now, young man, let's have a look at you." That's all the poor man said. Mickey yelled like he'd been stuck full of darts. Frankly, I think we ought to just let his teeth rot or make him brush with all the magic anti-cavity toothpastes and chew Dentyne gum.'

'Oh, Nora. *I* should have taken him.'

Nora shrugged easily. 'Don't worry about it. I just shoved him back into the waiting room and glared around at everyone there and asked if anybody knew this terrible child. Of course, everyone immediately denied responsibility for him, so I told him to sit and read a magazine until the child authorities showed up for him. Then I had my teeth cleaned and collected Mickey from a coloring book he was sharing with a little curly-headed girl. Very cute, too. He has good taste. We'll go back and try again next month. What a little character.'

The clear, watercolor-blue eyes narrowed with amusement, recalling her grandson's rebellion. Nora Opara, at nearly fifty (her exact age was Nora's secret), had bright pink skin over a face unlined except for laugh crinkles at the sides of her mouth and eyes. Her face was constantly in motion, registering the expression of every fairytale character she created for her grandson or in perfect imitation of every sales clerk, deliveryman or neighbor with whom she had dealings. In every incident she related, she pointed up the comical aspect of the human condition, with kindness and understanding. There was no trace, no slight hint that the clear bright face had ever experienced tragedy or discomfort of any kind. There were no visible scars of the sudden, violent widowhood she had suffered nearly sixteen years ago; no mark of the grief and torment of having endured a second inspector's funeral some five years ago when she saw her only son, Mickey's father, buried 'in the best traditions of the New York City Police Department—killed while performing his duty', with the added distinction of following the tradition of his father before him.

Yet, sometimes, in the late evening, when she seemed engrossed in the latest lending-library novel, her face, in repose and unaware, revealed a great and heavy sadness. This childishly slender woman, with her female awareness of the continuity of life, had been Christie's strength during those unbelievable days when Mike had been killed and had to be buried and the whole situation had to be borne.

Nora kicked off her shoes, stretched her toes, then regarded Christie thoughtfully. 'Well, your mind isn't on your son's rotting teeth. What's the matter, Chris?'

'Nora, I want to ask you something. Oh, something silly, I guess.'

'I'll probably have a silly answer for you, so go ahead.'

Christie seemed fidgety, her fingers poking at her hair. 'Nora, when—when Mike first told you about me, you know, that we were serious, what did he say?'

It was one of the strong bonds between them: their resolution, through the years since Mike's death at twenty-five, that they would speak of him easily, naturally. It had been Nora, cutting through the shock and pain, with the sharpened experience of her own widowhood, who had told Christie that they *could* speak of him.

Nora studied Christie's face intently: it wasn't the 'Mike blues'; not this time. There was something else bothering her daughter-in-law.

'Well, he came home one night, all flustered and talking his fool head off about "this girl, Christie Choriopolous", and of course, I said, "Christie What-ee-opolous?" and then I shut up because I saw he was really saying something. *Something important.*'

Impatiently, Christie shook her head. 'No, that's not what I meant. Nora, did Mike ever say—well—I guess a man doesn't say that to his mother.' She made an annoyed clicking sound against her teeth, then blurted out, 'Did he ever describe me as "sexy"?'

Nora's spontaneous laugh was clear and honest. 'My God, no! He said, "Mom, this kid is so damn cute: a regular little tomboy!"' Nora bit down on her lower lip. 'Oh-oh. I think I said exactly the wrong thing, didn't I?'

'No,' Christie said shortly, 'you just told the truth, dammit, like you usually do. Nora, do I still look like a "regular little tomboy"?'

Christie jutted out one hip, shifting her weight, her hands resting on the back of her hips. She lowered her head, striking a pose, peering at Nora, who studied her.

'Not exactly. But honey, let's face it. There's not a damn thing you can do about your bustline or that flat fanny, so make the best of what you have.' She stood up, turning Christie around. 'At least, you won't get all saggy and sloppy. You're built to last. You're the slim type. You'll never have to worry about the calories, like some people do.' She thumped her own round rear. 'And I'll tell you a secret: I think I would have hated you if you had been a real sex-pot, one of those sweatery, curvy gals.'

'Oh, swell. I was good for *your* morale.'

'Honey, it wasn't easy facing mother-in-law-hood and possible grandmotherhood in my early forties. Christie, I know what your problem is. You don't get around enough.' She held her hand playfully over Christie's mouth, stifling her protests. 'Oh, I know, good old Dan takes you out regularly. But you know as well as I do that Dan is *safe*: all tied up and unavailable. And such a perfect gentleman that he would never say, the hell with what you *say,* kiddo, I'm male, you're female.'

'Nora, you're beginning to sound like my-mother-the-matchmaker. I remember your friend Mrs. O'Donnell's son, Jeffrey with the curly blond hair. And the opinions.' Her mouth pulled back. 'Jeffrey O'Donnell had more opinions than there are subjects to have opinions on. Particularly about the New York City Police Department and all members of that "authoritarian, perverted" city agency. He and I sure had something in common: a natural antagonism for each other.' She put her arm affectionately around her mother-in-law, giving her a sharp pinch. 'Stop playing the nervous mother with me, okay?'

'Okay, okay. But you tell me then: when are you going to meet some men? And don't tell me that you're around men all day. They're either married cops or loony criminals. And what about Mickey? You know as well as I do . . .'

'Nora, don't preach what you didn't practice. You were a widow when Mike was fourteen years old; you were still young, but you didn't remarry.'

Nora brushed that away. 'I was afraid Mike would have a resurgence of his Oedipus complex; after all, he was in the throes of adolescence.' Then, flippantly, 'You know, I think I read too much in those days. But anyway, even if I didn't remarry, I had *fun*. Remind me, sometime, to tell you a few things.'

Christie grinned. 'Nora O'Malley Opara, you are an Irish phony.'

Nora winked. 'That's what you think.' Then, she stopped at the doorway and turned, her voice serious. 'Listen, you just keep on being *Christie,* you hear? That was good enough for Mike, and he was a pretty discerning fellow. I know—I raised him. There'll be another man—a perfectly *available* man—who is looking for *exactly* the same Christie who knocked Mike Opara silly. Don't change yourself: you just be you. That's what makes you the very special girl you are.'

Christie blotted her lips on a Kleenex, thinking of Nora. Whoever invented all the nasty mother-in-law stories hadn't met the likes of Nora. She started down the stairs, but was halted midway by Mickey, his face steamy with dirt, his baseball cap tilted over one eye.

'Ah, gee whiz, Ma. Gee whiz, why are you all dressed up like that? Gee whiz,' he muttered disgustedly.

'Well, ah gee whiz, I thought maybe you'd say your mother looked just a little nice.'

Wrapped up in his own problem, Mickey said, 'Mr. Silverman was supposed to pitch for us in the driveway and he had to go somewhere for his wife and I told the kids my mother would pitch.' Mickey banged his glove against the banister, his face pulled down. 'Gee, Ma, it's the *big* guys—eight and nine years old—and the only reason they're going to let me play is if you pitch. Can't you change into pants or something?'

'Sorry, my boy. You scout up somebody else's father. I'm somebody's mother, remember?'

The small face crumpled. Mickey rubbed the large glove across his forehead, leaving long dark streak marks. He let Christie steer him to the door, then wriggled free of her hand, darting to the kitchen. 'Hey, Nora? Gran? Can't you get Mom to come out and play ball with the guys?'

Nora, her hand on Mickey's neck, called, 'Hey, Mom, can't you go out and play ball with the guys? They need a good pitcher?'

Christie looked at the two of them, Nora's face warm with amusement, Mickey's heat-flushed and hopeful. She glanced at her watch. 'For one half of one hour—not a minute more. Not one single minute more. I *do* have a date in Manhattan. Remember, now, Mickey, at *exactly* six-thirty, I have to drop out and shower *again* and get dressed *again*.' As she spoke, Christie turned and ran up the stairs. 'Go on, Mick. I'll be ready in a minute.'

Changing rapidly, Christie tossed her jersey dress over the rocking chair, slid the dirty jeans and a fresh shirt over her flame-red, Tweed-impregnated lingerie. She said mockingly to the face in the mirror, 'Well, can *I* help it if I happen to be the best pitcher in the neighbourhood?'

CHAPTER SEVEN

MURRAY ROGOFF leaned his hip easily against the glass wall of the phone booth. It was a nice feeling, enclosed in the small cubicle, with people walking past, cars gliding along right outside, yet he, Murray, all protected, all closed in while they were all closed out. No one could see him but he could see all of them:

the punk kids whispering against the wall, their eyes darting away from each other, their faces mean and sharp; the thin, hollow-eyed junkies, yawning and scratching, waiting for their fix-it man. What a hang-up that was. The bleached-out little queers, wagging their tight little cans at each other. Murray let his breath out slowly. He'd like to lift up three of them at a time. way over his head, and smash them down into the gutter. Murray flexed the muscles in his arm, ran his fingers over his biceps. God, he felt strong. *God, he felt so good.*

He slipped the dime into the slot and dialed carefully, closing his eyes. She always answered on the second ring, like she wanted to be sure the first ring was her telephone, not some neighbor's.

'Hello?' The small, soft voice, questioning. From just the one word, she formed within his brain. A bright girl with nice, natural color and flashing dark hair, all shining and clean. That was what Murray liked most about her: that glowing cleanness, the fresh sweetness. Everything about her honed and nice, not an extra ounce of flesh. Her legs, long and straight, the thighs tapering neatly to the slight flare of her hips, and the small waist, not all pulled in with wide belts the way the cheap girls were, just curving in the way a girl's waist should and her breasts a nice size to cup into a man's hand and a white neck and not too much makeup on her face: just on her eyes, so that they flashed with bright live color.

'Hello?' Again, the voice, only trembling a little.

'Hello, Carol Logan.' Murray's voice was full and gentle, his hands cupping the mouthpiece, his eyes closed.

He didn't hear the sharp intake of breath or even catch the sense of her words.

'Who is this? *Please*. Who is this?'

'I love you, Carol Logan.'

Murray heard the click in his ear, the dead sound where her voice had been, but he understood. His tongue flicked out, touching, just touching the earpiece, where her lips had been, then he carefully replaced the receiver. He looked at his watch. He had a lot of time. She couldn't speak with him now because she had a dancing class at eight. He understood.

Murray walked along Broadway, stopping briefly at the corner of 51st Street, craning his neck, counting four stories up. That was where she would be for her hour's session. She never missed a lesson: three times a week—Monday, Wednesday, and tonight,

Friday. It must cost most of her salary. How much could she earn working in an advertising agency? But he knew Carol was a smart girl. Those ad agency people had connections; they sponsored TV shows and things and maybe her boss could get her a spot somewhere.

But she stayed out too late after those dance lessons: particularly on Fridays. Murray rolled his fingers into fists. She shouldn't go out with all those boys from the dance school: they were all fags. Even the big guys: couldn't she see that? No. A kid as clean and pure and young as Carol, she probably didn't even know about those things. But didn't she even wonder why they never took her home? They probably felt that the Bronx was too far to travel: those moles, all digging into some little rats' nests in the Village—with each other.

She was lucky he had seen her home every Friday night for the last month.

Murray glanced at the clock set in a flickering advertisement high above the street. He had plenty of time to go over to the Automat for some coffee. It wasn't even starting to get dark. Murray hated daylight saving time. The streets were just as bright, though cooler than afternoon. Murray unbuttoned his collar. The shirt was starchy as were his immaculate chinos, and beneath his clothing he still felt as scrubbed and clean as when he had stepped from the tub an hour ago. He stood for a moment, absently fingering the crisp short sleeves of his shirt. Some little guy lunged into him, letting out a curse word at the unexpected obstacle, and Murray turned, bending forward to look directly at his face. The man gasped, hanging onto the arm of a cheap little broad with high, stiff, whitened hair. She yanked at the man's arm, her eyes wide, her mouth redly opened. Murray made a deep hard sound way down in his throat and he heard the broad say, 'My God!' Murray stood in the middle of the street, watching them hurry into the crowd, and he began to laugh. He raised his arms over his head, freely reaching, feeling the stretch from the waist up, along his torso, pulling his lean flesh along his ribs. He felt so good. *So great.*

Murray Rogoff did not see the faces of any of the people. He did not notice the usual loungers, hunched against open-front hot dog stands and penny arcades, taking him in with swift, evaluating eyes, then discounting him, or the bland-faced tourists who moved in startled detour from his path, staring at him with the same sense of wonder and incredulity with which they had regarded the Empire State Building or the Statue of Liberty or the hollow immensity of the Radio City Music Hall. Murray saw only his destination, the Automat, and he whirled through the revolving door, faintly amused that he had sent two indignant, potty women spinning out onto the sidewalk, mouths spluttering and packages toppling.

He jammed his two nickels into the slot and watched the coffee squirt into the heavy battered cup. Carol drank too much coffee. She should drink more milk. For energy. A dancer needs a lot of energy. She should eat only food containing a lot of vitamins, like an athlete; when you use your body a lot, you have to give it the right fuel. Like he did. No matter what Mama said, Murray would not eat the heavy swill she tried to load him with; his hand would sweep away all the starches and his fingers would pounce on the meat and chicken and fruit and milk. Milk: boy, he drank it down by the bottle, right from the bottle, a quart straight down without stopping for breath, the way some guys drank beer. They were crazy to drink beer: fat bellies, that's what they were. Young guys, growing, should take care of their bodies. Like he did. Everyone should do routines: muscle-flexing and bends and stretches and resistance. It made a guy feel so great. Almost as great as when you took a girl.

Murray Rogoff sat down at a table near the large floor-to-ceiling window. He did not think it was strange that the man and woman and little girl who had been sitting there, eating from a collection of dishes on their trays, had gotten up, staggering off with their heavy trays. He liked having a table all to himself: it was like having a private box seat on Broadway. He drank his coffee in a few hot gulps. He didn't like coffee, but he was feeling a little tired and he needed something to keep him awake. It was Friday and it would be a long night for him. He sat watching for a long time, then looked at the clock in the Automat. It was time for him to go to 51st Street. He had to make sure Carol got to her dancing class.

For Murray Rogoff, time began and ended now at the particular moment. Living was walking along Broadway, right now, to 51st Street, to wait for Carol Logan. There had been no morning on some subway station with the terrible, confusing, unknown dread whirling through him, eating away at his body, devouring his brain; there had been no collection of people, moving him within the depths of his nightmare to strange rooms, telling him to move here, put your fingers on this pad, on this paper, sit there, look at this camera, turn sideways, look up. There had been no small, narrow room with a hard platform bed and dirty uncovered toilet and no clanging of steel or long barred corridors and no large and dusty courtroom filled with men who spoke around and at him.

There had been no hot and blinding afternoon and no Frankie Santino, fully grown into semblance of manhood, whispering some words at him, pinching his arm and shoulder. And there had been no David, clenching his shoulder, his knee, his neck. There had been no screaming in the hot small rooms on the top floor of the tenement on Rivington Street where his mother, lighting the Sabbath candles, had dropped the taper at the sight of David, unexpected and unseen for more than a year. For Murray, time had canceled out and his day had been as all his days: an automatic enduring of the hours in his father's fish store, toward the time when the sun would finally let go, darken things down so that the lights would flash on all over the wide and busy streets and Murray Rogoff feeling young and strong and great like he could throw off whatever crazy shroud-like thing seemed to encase him and he would emerge as he truly was, at the center of himself as he always had been: Murray the Norseman, Murray the Great, filled by that special and good and joyous feeling which was fully his now, no longer hiding beneath a furious jumble of sounds and voices and hard-faced strangers, and he could identify joy and savor it and know it: *Carol Logan.*

He pressed against the fender of a light blue Buick convertible, watching the street, his eyes blinking away all the unimportant people who tried to fill his vision. *There.* Murray held his eyes steady, sharply set on her. With the first far-off glimpse, he knew it was Carol as surely as if a spotlight had picked her up and hovered over her in the beginning dimness. His eyes fastened to the top of her head, which was the first part of her he could see, bobbing in and out among the faceless bodies. She moved surely, easily, steadily, emerging whole and beautiful, half a block away: dressed in a blue shift which hit her slender thighs as she walked that nice, ladylike walk, her face held high, her eyes not caught by any of the punks and bums, her ears not aware of the dirty remarks and crude passes. She could walk through mud and come out clean.

Murray slid his body down so that his lower spine rested against the fender; his arms folded into each other. As she passed directly in front of him, he dropped his head so that he appeared to be dozing, but his eyes, beneath his glasses which were half-hidden by the peak of his tan cap, were steady on her and she kept going, her face straight ahead and held high. He watched, straightening up now, watching those legs in the nice little heels, not high and spiky, just medium heels and firmly hitting the pavement. The dress touched along her body and you could tell she wore a girdle, probably just a soft little girdle, but just right so that it gave her a smooth line across the backside and the little waist could be seen, not all pulled in, just nice and natural and wonderful.

Murray smiled, watching her safely into the building. He pulled himself from the car and took a large breath, filling his lungs with the sooty air. He rubbed his chest with both hands, laughing a little, looking at the creeps pushing along the sidewalks with their dirty little pickups. He walked about aimlessly: down a block, across Broadway, stopping to look into a window where they sold the type of underwear prostitutes wore: little black things on skinny little strings. Murray shook his head. It was disgusting. He turned, looked across Broadway, over the tops of the cars and taxis and buses. Carol was up there, dressed in her dancer's leotards, which she carried in that little leather satchel, and he could see her: firm and neat in command of every part of her body. He shook his head again at the terrible things in the window.

The hour went by quickly. An hour is a short time and Murray Rogoff had endless patience during that particular hour. But the rest of the evening was too long and he was beginning to get tense. Just because it was Friday, that didn't mean she should stay out so late. Not with those punks, anyway. And not in that dump: all those ham-and-egg joints were the same. He stood, leaning against the closed-down, deserted newsstand, shifting his weight from time to time. He didn't like that girl with the red hair. It was a cheap, obvious dye job and if Carol hung around with someone like that, some of these Broadway sharpies might get the wrong idea about her, might think she was like that. Murray wondered how she could eat that crappy food, all greasy and heavy with rancid oil. But Carol only played with the food on her plate, occasionally taking some into her mouth, chewing slowly, her lips slightly parted. She leaned across the table, her eyes on the boy with the white skin and the black hair. One of those: Murray knew the type. God, Carol was a baby. That guy was turned on himself. One of those pretty boys who looked around constantly to see who was watching him, speaking with his hands, his eyebrows, his shoulders, then breaking into one of those wide smiles, but always making sure that everyone else was giving him the right reaction. Carol certainly was. He was one of those weirdos who could make it with a girl or a queer or maybe even all by himself.

Murray rubbed his hands along the seams of his chinos; his palms began to feel sticky. He closed his eyes, putting his hand over his glasses, smearing them. He rubbed his wrist over the lenses, batting his eyes rapidly. They were leaving. God. He almost missed that.

Murray Rogoff walked slowly through the wandering, aimless crowd, not feeling an occasional pocketbook bang against his thigh, not hearing any stray remarks directed at or about him. Not daring to take his eyes from her head, which was all he could see except for a quick glimpse of her upturned face now and then as she listened to the black-haired boy. Murray moved steadily into the mass of bodies. At 42nd Street, as he had expected, they turned left, toward the subway at the end of the block. Some seedy old panhandler approached them, his hand outstretched, his face polluted. The boy, smiling, said something to him, extending his own hand. Murray's fingers curled into the palms of his hand.

Murray walked slowly down the subway steps, hearing Carol's voice beyond the two middle-aged couples directly in front of him. The men, walking behind their women, gesturing and arguing about something, edged nearer to their wives, taking their elbows and steering them clear of him, and Murray cut through the sharp, sudden silence, ignoring their rounded eyes and opened mouths. He slammed his quarter at the agent in the change booth, slipped his token in the slot, pushed himself through the turnstile, right past Carol, who lingered inside the controls, still talking to the black-haired boy whose fingers were moving, through the iron bars, along her bare arm.

Murray walked right past them, slowly down the subway steps leading to the uptown platform, without looking back. He heard her quick step, running for the train which was pulling into the station. Murray boarded the 'D' train at the center door, aiming for one of the few empty seats. The woman who had gotten directly in front of him raced him for it, but he got there first and he sat, pulling his cap over his forehead, sliding low in the seat so that the woman, glaring, had to move away because his feet took up all the space directly under the handstrap. Murray turned his face toward the front of the car. Carol was standing, holding one of the enamel loops, her face gazing at the subway map. His eyes moved along the line of her arm, bare at the shoulder in the sleeveless shift. Her raised arm hid the neat breast, but the shift, pulled up now, dove in at the waist and glided along the hip and just a tiny fraction of blue slip showed.

He felt a tightening in his thighs and in the pit of his stomach. He closed his eyes. It would be a long ride up to the Bronx.

By Kingsbridge Road, the train had nearly emptied but three other people got off besides Murray and Carol. She had a firm grip on her leather satchel and little pocketbook and she didn't look around, just straight ahead. Murray walked behind the other people, some tired-looking men, elderly, dazed strangers. He lost sight of her momentarily, but it didn't matter. He knew where she was headed.

The cool night air hit his chest and the back of his neck. The sky was deep black now with little holes of light, like sparks from the full moon whose glow did not extend much beyond a wide circle. The sound of Carol's shoes across the street was steady and a little rapid, but not scared and panicky like some girls', alone on the side street, three blocks from home. She walked in the center of the sidewalk, not against the parked cars pressed tightly into one another, and that was smart, because you never knew who might be sitting in one of those cars, waiting for some girl.

Murray walked faster now so that he was well ahead of her. He was on the side of the street where her building was, close against the wall of apartment houses. It was strange that she always got out at the exit across the street, but people do funny things out of habit. He reached the dark red brick building and could see her in the blackness coming steadily toward him. He pushed the hall door inward, easing himself into the small entrance hall. The light was on, which was good because any bum could be hiding in a hallway like this. Not touching the brass knob of the door atop the flat steps, just pushing it with his shoulder, Murray felt an anger. The locks on these doors were always jammed. Someone should complain to the landlord, but a hell of a lot they cared about a young, beautiful girl coming home alone into a trap like this.

Murray's feet touched the tile floor of the long hallway so lightly he couldn't hear them himself. He narrowed his eyes in the dimness. That damn light over the sticky brass mailboxes alongside the first staircase was flickering. Murray took out his handkerchief and touched the bulb. He could feel the heat of it even through the folds of cloth. Gently, he turned it. He took off his cap and, his eyes comfortable in darkness, he eased his glasses from his face, placed them inside his cap, which he set against the wall. He could smell the stale odor of dirty wet mops. Some great janitor they must have here, sloshing a filthy pail of water around.

Murray sucked his breath in, holding it now, feeling it in both of his lungs. He pulled his stomach in, hard and flat. He heard her open the door, heard her two hesitant steps, then she stopped. Christ, she was frightened by the darkness ahead of her. He didn't want her to be afraid. *He was there*. There was nothing to be afraid of.

He heard her short breathy sound, then heard her start toward the stairway, toward him. She could probably see that the lights were on further up the stairs and had decided to hurry past the dark place near the mailboxes.

Murray felt the fragrance of her preceding her, flowing from her, pressing down the odor of wet dirt, reaching out to him as he reached out for her, his arms silently, strongly, surely encircling her, one hand across her mouth, then his hand sliding away for his mouth to press on hers so completely that he could breathe into her and suck the sweetness of her into himself. She was so light. God, he had never realized that her beautifully limber body would be so light, but he hardly needed any strength at all to lift her to him, as though she were part of himself and he part of her, her body real and alive beneath him as he easily pressed her to the floor beneath him, carefully cradling the back of her head with his hand and forearm. And she, Carol, her hands unable to get to his chest, was digging at his back and her body was moving now beneath his and she rocked urgently on the hard floor beneath him, passionately and soundlessly beneath the great, unrelenting strength of his mouth, which never left hers, though her head rocked from side to side; his mouth clung to hers and his hand helped her because a man should remove a woman's clothing: only prostitutes sitting there, glassy-eyed, pulled off their clothes. But when a man loved a girl, it was a thing a man did and he didn't want her to have to do anything, just to feel him there with her: loving her, giving pleasure to her, enjoying her, possessing her body with great joy, but not just taking, *giving*. She was so small beneath him: he could feel her heart thudding through the fragile rib cage hitting his own heart: it was as if they had just the one heart between them and his fingers could feel the great sound of exaltation rising along her throat and his fingers pressed the sound lovingly back: back into her so that she could savor it deep within herself as he did his astounding full, deep, anticipated and finally accomplished pleasure.

His mouth now lifting from hers, he gasped a lazy warm mouthful of air and the air was filled with Carol and he touched her lower lip with the tip of his tongue. Her mouth was relaxed and silent for she was at peace in the deep and beautiful sleep of his love.

Murray pressed his face into her hair, his tongue lightly touching at her earlobe, running down her cheek, along her parted lips, just skimming her teeth. He buried his face into that warm small place in the bend of her neck, wishing he could see her face in the blackness, but he knew she would be smiling, her eyes closed in that nice, happy, fantastic feeling which enveloped them both. And this canceled out all the other times: all those cold, mechanical, used bodies on which he had released the accumulations of nothing more than animal lust with a sense of despair and anger, his body juices being sucked from him absently as though he were alone on some filthy, paid-for bed because this was Carol and he was now truly Murray and his body ached with a marvelous awareness of love and pleasure.

His voice was so soft it was almost as though he was thinking rather than speaking, but he spoke directly into her ear and he knew she heard him, because she lay so still: listening.

'Carol. Carol. I love you so much. I worry about you so much. You're so special, so special. Not like the little tramps in the candy store: they all wanted it, every one of them, anyone I picked out, taking it from me, but not giving me anything, just grabbing for it and then none of them even seeing me.' Murray's eyes blinked against the darkness. He didn't want to think about that; letting his lips become still for a moment, he knew that none of it mattered, because he had given love and had received love and that was what counted. 'Oh, Carol, you're so clean and so good.' Then kissing her lips, nipping at them lightly, touching them with his fingertips, Murray knelt over her. 'It's late. You rest for a while. I feel so good. I can't remember when I felt this good.'

And then, Murray took a switchblade knife from his trouser pocket, letting the four-inch blade drop down. Lifting her head gently, so as not to disturb her sleep, carefully and surely his hands, steady and kind, gathered a small sweet thick lock of clean hair from that warm place at the nape of her neck. He cut the lock of Carol's hair, closing his fingers over that small part of her. He flicked the knife closed, replaced it in his trouser pocket, then unfolded his handkerchief, placed the hair into the center of it, carefully refolded it into a small square, placed it into the breast pocket of his shirt and patted it against himself like a treasure.

Smoothing her hair from her brow, he lightly touched her lips, then her forehead, with his lips and tongue, whispering to her, 'Rest and sleep, Carol, and dream of me.'

His hand went directly to his cap, his foot brushing against her leather satchel and pocketbook. He first put on his glasses and then his cap. Not knowing that her eyes were frozen open, he wished her sweet dreams and soundlessly, Murray Rogoff left the hallway, wedging his shoe into the partly opened door, prying it with his shoulder. He went down the four flat steps, out through the opened street door, onto the cool black street.

Murray Rogoff walked the three blocks to the Grand Concourse, stood for a moment looking at the entrance to the Independent subway, then, holding the peak of his cap, he stretched his head upward to the sky. It was a great night: cool and clean and he felt so good. He turned and decided to walk a mile or two or maybe ten miles in the fresh clean air. He could take the subway somewhere farther down the line.

CHAPTER EIGHT

CHRISTIE OPARA sat in a leather and steel sling chair absorbing the black and white sterility of Dr. Sidney Ginsburg's waiting room. It was the kind of room that advised a prospective patient to expect extreme professional competency, if not sympathetic concern. A collection of pictures, placed on the ice colored walls with a mathematical precision, were either blackly indicated flowers against white backgrounds or whitely suggested figures impressed on black. A long narrow steel magazine rack hung low against one wall, and inserted in various-sized slots were celluloid-covered magazines: issues of everything from *Life* and *Look* to the *Partisan Review*. It wasn't what Christie had expected. Not from a cousin of Marty Ginsburg.

She hated to crush her cigarette into the gleaming black stone ashtray; it seemed a defilement. Marty's voice rumbled behind the black enameled door of the doctor's office, and in response, Christie could hear a low murmur of inaudible words. The door swung open and the face behind Marty's, belonging to the son of his father's brother, was narrow and pale, marked clearly and sharply by straight black eyebrows and a thin neat black mustache extending exactly the length of the thin lips. A crisp fresh odor of starch wafted from the cardboard-stiff jacket which covered a well-built, Sunday athlete's frame. Before Christie could extricate herself from the somewhat complicated chair, the door clicked shut and the voices began again. She exhaled a thin whistle of annoyed amusement. That nut, Marty Ginsburg, could never just *do* something: he had to build a plot around the simplest of things. Christie wondered what he was telling his wary-looking cousin.

Marty, leaning his bulk against the door, rested his hand heavily on the reluctant shoulder of his cousin. 'There's nothing to worry about, Sidney, I'm telling you. This kid is okay now, honest. It's only when there's a lot of strange people around that she gets—you know.' Marty nodded his head in a particular way. 'Which is why I asked to come here on a Sunday night so there wouldn't be no patients around.' His fingers pinched into the stiffness of his cousin's jacket. 'And besides, like I said, there might be some of your patients who would recognize her: just because *you* don't read the papers don't mean that practically everyone else in the city don't know who this kid's father is.' Marty shook his head at this possible danger. 'That's all I'd need—for someone to spot her.'

Dr. Ginsburg removed himself from Marty's grasp and traced his long slim fingertips along his mustache. 'Marty, I don't see why you brought her here at all. Couldn't the District Attorney have arranged to have this done by one of your police surgeons?'

'A police surgeon? You're kidding. Police surgeons are the world's biggest blabbermouths. If the reporters ever got wise that the daughter of the . . .' Marty grabbed at his mouth, bunching his lips into a grotesque cupid's bow. 'See? See, Sidney? Now see what you almost made me say? You almost made me say who she is and that would be very, very bad. My main job right now is to keep this girl under wraps.' Marty's hand formed a barrier around his mouth, but his voice was still loud. 'This whole thing is by way of a favor, Sidney. You know how these things work, huh?' He winked. 'The D.A. does a very important man a favor and then the very important man can do a favor for the D.A. sometime.' Marty recognized an alert gleam in his cousin's eye. 'And of course both the VIP *and* the D.A. will know *who, exactly*'—his index finger dug into Sidney's chest—'is the man who really cooperated, you know?'

Dr. Ginsburg withdrew from any more of Marty's jabs and retreated toward the small examining room to the rear of his office.

'All right, Marty, let's get this over with. I have everything ready for the cast.'

'Okay, Sidney. But look, I got to go and talk to the girl for a minute. She's a little nervous, you know? Nothing I can't handle. See, she trusts me, which is why I'm the one brought her here. Anything Marty tells her, she does. Not even her old man could have talked her into this. You should have heard the story I had to tell her to get her to agree to this.' Marty shook his head decisively; he couldn't tell Sidney any more.

This time when the black door opened, Marty seemed to fill the room. He motioned Christie beside him on the black leather couch but kept his eyes alertly on the door. 'Poor old Sid. He's still nutty as a fruitcake.'

Christie patiently asked the expected question. 'What do you mean?'

Marty hunched himself closer to her. 'Listen, Christie, my cousin, Sidney—well, he always *was* a little strange. You know.' He smacked at his forehead. 'But we always figured it was because he was so brilliant. A very brilliant man, my cousin, so I guess when you're a genius, you got to be a little crazy, you know, to balance things up.'

Christie sighed. 'Okay, Marty, let's hear the story.'

Her tone did not affect the seriousness of Marty's words; he was very sincere. 'Well, he'll make the cast for you all right. But Sid's got some weird ideas. He took one look at you and, don't ask me why, please don't ask me why, but he thinks you're the Mayor's daughter.'

'The Mayor's daughter?' Christie lowered her voice in response to Marty's urgent expression. 'The Mayor's daughter? Why would he think that?'

'Gee, I told you not to ask me, but okay, you asked me. See, Sidney is a real gossip column fanatic.' Marty shook his head over his cousin's malady. 'He reads all the gossip columns and he stores away all kinds of crazy information: especially about anybody in politics, and he goes to his district Reform Democratic Club every Tuesday night and he picks up little pieces of information and then he figures things out and he comes up with some real crazy stories. And he *really* believes them, which is the sad part. So, when he looked at you, he slams the door and he tells me, "Marty, I know who that is. That is the Mayor's daughter and I know all about her." Gee, I didn't know the Mayor had a daughter, did you?'

In a quietly rational, reconciled voice, Christie asked, 'What about the Mayor's daughter?'

Marty shrugged. 'Who knows? Sidney says she is a suicidal person.'

Christie glanced at her wristwatch; this was taking more time than she had expected. 'Marty, why are you playing games? Come on, just tell him who I am and let's get the cast made.'

'I did, I did tell him, Christie, but he thinks I made it up as a cover story. See, he figures things out to suit his own theories, that's how some nuts are I guess.' Marty nodded sympathetically at Christie's growing annoyance. 'Okay, kid. Sidney says he knows —from little things planted in the columns and from his politician friends—that you, the Mayor's daughter, got involved in some kind of weird Oriental religious cult.' He shrugged at her raised eyebrows. 'Don't ask me. Sidney says, that's all I know. And that part of this religious cult is that you got to slash your left wrist and watch yourself bleed to death and while all this is going on, you got to recite certain prayers and that way you'll get into some kind of Oriental heaven.' Admiringly, he said, 'Gee, for a Jewish boy, Sidney knows a lot about non-kosher religions.'

Flatly, Christie stated, 'Marty, you're kidding.'

'No honest, he's a Jew.' Marty spoke rapidly, pulling Christie to her feet. 'And that somehow the Mayor convinced you to keep your left arm in a cast for a while until he gets you over this whole business, and you have some kind of confidence in me, like I'm your trusted friend, so that's why you agreed to come along with me tonight.' Marty lowered his voice to a warning whisper. 'Listen, don't say nothing to him, nothing at all: you say anything, and right away, Tuesday night, he'll be telling all his pals at the club that the Mayor's daughter said this and that, you know.'

Dr. Sidney Ginsburg opened the door, nodded briefly at Christie without meeting her eyes and led the way into his small examination room. She sat where he indicated, removed her wristwatch and placed her arm on the small cushion of clean lintless towels which Dr. Ginsburg had prepared on the table before her. With great care, quickly and deftly, the doctor's long fingers removed a series of wide strips of gauze from the small steel bowl containing the plaster of paris solution. Christie noticed a beaded line of moisture forming over his thin mustache. His eyes were very small and very black and they darted from her arm to her face and when they met her eyes, they fled away again. She noted with admiration that not one drop of the wet solution touched anywhere but on his fingertips and her arm. Silently, he worked his way almost to her elbow.

'Isn't that a little high, Doctor?'

His hand leaped at the sound of her voice and for one split second, it seemed that he might drop the wet strip; instead, he carefully unwound the last layer, then with a damp cloth, he washed away all traces of the solution from the freed portion of her arm.

'Thank you,' Christie said softly.

Dr. Ginsburg nodded and indicated another table where her arm was to repose under the purple glow of a lamp which, he informed them, quietly, would hasten the hardening process.

Christie watched him as he moved rapidly, without a single wasted motion, cleaning up: scrubbing the little bowl spotless, winding up unused gauze, putting everything into little built-in compartments against the wall. She noticed that he had a tremor going near his left eye and a slight twitching at the corner of his lip which made his moustache look like a nervous, undernourished caterpillar. She dropped her eyes quickly when his beady black eyes met hers: Marty must have told him she was a subdued but unpredictable homicidal maniac.

She could feel a pulling all along the skin under the cast; it was hardening rapidly and she could feel the weight of it. Dr. Ginsburg ran his fingers lightly along the cast, turned off the purple lamp and held up an expanse of white cotton cloth which he folded deftly into a sling. Carefully, he rested Christie's arm along the length of it, then tied a knot behind her neck and asked if it was comfortable.

Her eyes glistened maliciously at Marty who stood like a bulky wall behind his cousin. 'City Hall perfect, Doctor. My daddy will be pleased.'

For one brief instant, the doctor studied her face furtively, as though trying to memorize her features. Christie gazed vacantly at Marty's shoulder, letting the doctor get his good look.

'Good, good, good, Doc,' Marty said, slapping the starch down the center of his cousin's spine. 'Wait for me outside, kid, will you? Be right with you.'

Christie smiled brightly. 'Anything you say, Marty. You know that.'

Marty handed his cousin a wad of tissues. 'Your forehead is all wet, Sidney. Sidney, I want to tell you something. You handled that really beautiful. Beautiful. I knew I could trust you. As you can see, this is a highly touchy situation.' He leaned his face close, whispering, 'You recognized her, of course?'

Dr. Ginsburg blotted his face, removed his coat and ran a single tissue inside his shirt collar. His face was very white. 'My God,' he said. 'Yes. Yes I did. But don't worry about it Marty. I thought—I thought it was just one of your games.' He shook his head. 'Very sad.' He flicked his dry tongue, almost touching the black line of hair over his lip. 'The Secretary-General of the U.N.—he has other children besides the girl, doesn't he?'

Marty clamped a heavy hand over his cousin's mouth, glaring menacingly into the startled black eyes. 'Swallow those words,

Sidney Ginsburg! Swallow them down! Spit them out! Forget them!' he commanded.

The pale face squirmed free. 'I will, I will. It's forgotten, Marty, believe me, it's forgotten!' The high shrill voice was comfortably familiar now: the voice of skinny little cousin Sidney with all the A's on his report card and all the whining complaints: Cousin Marty hit me; Cousin Marty spit in my orange soda.

Marty left his cousin washing his hands and face in cold water. Christie was standing before the magazine rack, wishing she had time to dig into a few of the new home-furnishings editions. Marty grabbed at her cast and steered her out of the office.

The outer door opened onto a small terrace two steps down from the sidewalk, lined on both sides by black and white wooden flower boxes filled with real looking artificial white roses. Focusing on Marty's beaming face, Christie demanded, 'Come on, Marty. What was the game? What in the world did you tell him?'

Marty's face pulled into a look of offended innocence and he spread his hands, palms up. 'He's a real nut, like I told you. But you know, I got a theory,' Marty said, and now he smiled broadly over his own personal private joke which he would not share with her. 'Sidney's trouble is that he takes life too serious. He don't know how to have a little fun once in a while!'

CHAPTER NINE

Bill Ferranti's voice on the telephone was pleasantly mild and somewhat puzzled by Christie's annoyance. 'I don't know why, Christie. Stoney Martin called me around six this morning and told me to cancel out on the LSD.'

'You mean *cancel out* or delay it, or what?' Christie's index finger could not reach high enough under the heavy cast to relieve the itchy spot.

'Cancel out altogether from what Stoner said. We're to report to the M.O. Apparently, they have something going and Mr.

Reardon specifically wants you in this morning. Stoner said he'd explain when we get there.'

The itch was tantalizingly close to the tip of her finger. She pressed the receiver between her cheek and shoulder and concentrated her efforts but to no avail. 'You mean I won't need this cast?'

'I don't think so, Christie. I guess you could slip it off and leave it at home. See you in the office.'

The cast had not been made to slip off or pry off: it would have to be hammered off and Mr. Reardon's directions had been to report to the M.O. forthwith which usually meant twenty minutes prior to whatever time you arrived.

There were more Squad members in the office than Christie had ever seen at one time. She correctly surmised that the gambling teams had made some kind of collar: they were rarely in the office and all six men were present now, holding quick conversations with each other, with Stoner Martin and with Casey Reardon who appeared briefly, then returned to his own office.

Detective Sam Farrell was a man who had been born clumsy and each year, as he had grown to his present large dimensions, his clumsiness had increased accordingly. Even standing absolutely still, his wide, nicely proportioned shoulders at ease, his large hands resting easily on his narrow hips, his broad flushed face looking at nothing in particular, Sam Farrell had the undeniable look of a clumsy man. There was something in his manner that marked him as the man most likely to find the one existing crack in an otherwise smooth sidewalk: the man whose toe would find that crack, catch in it and send his body sprawling. When Sam Farrell crossed a room—any room—pieces of furniture seemed to reach out toward an unprotected thigh, smashing it. His kneecaps seemed drawn to low tables and his head was invariably the target of low-hanging lamps. He was the kind of man who did not walk across a room: he lurched, as though by moving in an almost galloping stride, he could thus avoid the unknown pitfalls which forever seemed to await him.

Bill and Christie watched Sam Farrell banging away, two fingers jabbing at the keys of the old Underwood. Christie grinned as Sam dug around in the top drawer for an eraser, then, hunched over the machine, he scrubbed furiously, stopping in surprise to regard the little hole he had made. He flipped the carbon paper from his copy, hoping to do a better job, and was confronted by a blank sheet of white paper. He had placed the carbons in the machine backwards.

Christie and Bill Ferranti moved in on Sam Farrell; Farrell was the man to speak to when you wanted confidential information.

'You fellows sure look busy, Sam.'

He looked up, squinted, then his face stretched into a broad grin. 'Hey, you guys really loused up on Friday, huh?'

Christie shrugged. 'We'll make up for it.'

'Oh, nobody told you yet, huh?' Sam shook his head. 'Tough. Well, that's the breaks.'

'Told us what?' Ferranti asked.

Sam Farrell hunched his shoulders forward and motioned them toward him.

'Geez, Friday night the LSD blast went off and so did the kid. You know, the kid the whole thing was all about.'

Christie felt the cast on her left arm get a few pounds heavier. 'Which kid, Sam?'

'Gee, nobody told you, huh? Well, I don't know what kid it was exactly—some girl. Her uncle is a state senator, I think. From what I hear, the kid blasted off and is still revolving in outer space. Her family hustled her off to some upstate sanitarium.' Sam snapped his fingers, as though he had just solved a problem. 'That's right, you weren't here Saturday morning. Boy, did it ever hit the fan. Mr. Reardon got called upstairs to the old man. When he came down, well, it's just a good thing you weren't around. We were all in because of this round-up we got on and I heard him.' Farrell laughed without malice. 'I'm surprised you didn't hear him out where you live.'

Christie ignored the itch inside the cast and kept her voice level. 'What's going on here, Sam? What have you got?'

'Very hush-hush,' Farrell said. 'A little ordinary housewife, how do you like that?'

A female prisoner; that's why she was needed. They didn't have to ask Sam anything, he was telling them.

'Very confidential. She's part of a ring of little ordinary housewives. Been using her telephone for bets. She answered an ad in the paper—you know: "make extra money at home"—that kind of thing.' Sam had very round blue eyes which never remained still. 'It reaches all over the place—very extensive. We'll be working in conjunction with Nassau and Suffolk police—even Westchester County.'

Christie leaned over, turning the papers in Sam's typewriter. 'You have the carbons in backwards, Sam.'

Smacking his lips together, Sam muttered, 'Boy, these machines are tricky, aren't they? I hate this old Underwood, it never works right.'

Christie and Bill moved across the office. Christie leaned facing out of the window, while Bill kept his eyes on the activity. They deliberately avoided discussing the LSD case and in some desperation, Christie turned to him. 'Sorry I can't tell you about all the goings on, but it's very hush-hush. You understand, don't you?'

Bill went along with her. 'Please, don't tell me anything I'm not supposed to know: just tell me the confidential facts and we'll let it go at that.'

Reardon's voice called her name and everyone heard it over the steady sound of conversation and irregular typewriter clatterings. 'It's been nice knowing you,' she said to Ferranti without looking at his face, his expression would be sad and she preferred not to see it.

Christie stood beside Reardon, waiting. She noted the quick, jerking nod, the impatience with which he set Stoney's comments into place with a few sharp questions. There was a kind of electricity emanating from him, touching everyone in the room with a distinct vitality: Reardon was a man who moved and who forced everyone around him to move.

His eyes circled the room restlessly, accounted for everyone present, then, satisfied with what he saw, he spoke to her without looking at her. 'We have a woman in there, a Mrs. Lydia Ogden. She's been taking calls for a bookie ring: a little housewifely moonlighting.' Now, his eyes rested on Christie; they were as clear as two amber stones. Without hesitating over a word, his eyes moved over her, stopped briefly, then flickered along the lines of her two-piece dress. Reardon's eyes had an expression completely removed from his words or business-like tone of voice. 'We haven't had much luck with this dame. I thought she might need another woman to talk to. You know—girl talk.' Then his voice and his eyes seemed to join forces as he looked at her body again. 'You look more like a girl today.'

'What will I be looking for, Mr. Reardon?'

'What I need is names; the more the merrier. We've handled her with kid gloves and that's how it has to be. She's a particularly beltable bitch and she knows we're being careful with her. She's important to this investigation. *Very important.* Think you can handle her?'

'Yes, sir.'

Reardon's eyes narrowed, and, as though he had seen it for the first time, he reached out and tapped his knuckles against her cast. 'You better get this damn thing off.' His voice had that sharp irritable edge to it.

'Mr. Reardon, I heard what happened on Friday night and . . .'

'You want to go round on that again?' he demanded sharply.

'No, sir, but . . .'

'Then take the goddamn cast off.'

'Mr. Reardon,' she persisted, 'I've made my contacts; we know who's involved. Couldn't we just play it for a while and . . .'

Reardon's face was angry and he shook his head and started to speak but then, for some reason, he changed his mind and just stood looking at her for a moment. 'Ya never know,' he said tersely, and walked toward his office. 'Come on, Opara, come on, move.'

Reardon turned unexpectedly at the door to his office and Christie slammed into him. 'Take it easy, Opara, you'll knock the boss down.'

Christie backed away. 'Sorry. And I can't take the cast off now. It has to be hammered off.'

'I'd be happy to oblige but I left my sledge hammer at home.' His voice wasn't angry now and he briefly told her about the circumstances leading up to the interrogation of Mrs. Ogden.

'Now look, I'm going to leave you on your own, okay? Got anything in mind?'

'I'll have to see her first, all right?'

Reardon studied her thoughtfully, then opened the door, and jerked his head for her to follow. He made a quick introduction, his hand still on the doorknob, then left the two women alone.

Mrs. Ogden was a small woman; small and round without being fat. She looked about a careful forty-two or forty-three years old. Her hair was held stiffly from her face and was coal black against the somewhat pale skin. She had small, sharp brown eyes, incongruously smeared with bright blue eyeshadow, a small nose and irregular lips which pulled downwards under the pearlized lipstick. Her short fingers bore a wide wedding band, encrusted with tiny diamonds, and the right hand, reaching for her throat as the door clicked shut, was decorated with a large cocktail ring of dull rubies and diamond chips.

Christie walked to the window and with effort managed to open it with one hand. 'It's awfully hot in here, isn't it?' Christie rested the cast in her right palm, wrinkling her nose at it. 'This darn thing itches like mad.'

Mrs. Ogden stared at her; her eyes were frozen little dark spots in her face. She resembled, for no reason Christie could pinpoint, a tough little dog, warily watching a potential enemy.

'I broke my wrist playing baseball,' Christie said easily, sitting in Reardon's chair, behind his desk. She wondered how he'd like that.

'Baseball?' Mrs. Ogden asked carefully.

Christie grinned. 'Dopey, isn't it? Yes, I was playing with my little boy and some of his friends and I slipped and snap! There went the wrist.'

Mrs. Ogden's head seemed to raise up a little, as though the stiff hair, acting as an antenna, was trying to catch some signals. 'You have a little boy?'

'Yes. Mickey. He's just five.'

The small arms folded themselves across her chest. The chin pointed upwards. Mrs. Ogden's voice, brittle and unpleasant, had the added quality now of righteousness. 'Well, *I* have three children and *I* am at home with *my* kids. I'm there when they need me and it seems that the police should be worrying about untended children of working mothers. *They're* the ones who get in trouble, not children of mothers like me who stay home. Where they belong.'

Christie let the words bounce against the particular shell she began forming around herself. Go right ahead, Mrs. Ogden, you fine and virtuous little mother, get good and angry at me and tell me exactly what you think of me: because, lady, in a million years, I won't tell you exactly what I think of you.

'Tell me about your job, Mrs. Ogden. Mr. Reardon didn't really fill me in on what this is all about. What's the story?'

'The story,' the woman said coldly, 'is that I am a decent woman, just trying to help my husband out a little.' Her mouth twisted down again and Christie felt a twinge of sympathy for the man who had to face that mouth each day. 'I answered this ad in the *Journal*—you'd think I was a criminal—I just answered an ad, that's all!'

'What did the ad say?' Christie asked, ignoring the nasty impatient tone.

'An ad—an ad. How can I remember what it said? It was a few weeks ago. You know, "Housewives, earn extra money in your spare time. *At home.*" That kind of thing.'

'I see. Did it give a phone number for you to call?'

The small hands flew to the teased hair, catching an imaginary strand and pressing it back into place. 'Yes, some phone number, don't ask me what it was, I wouldn't know. And I called and spoke to Mr. Somebody or other—some guinea name.'

Another tiny piece fell into place; expressionless, Christie nodded the woman on.

'So he told me that all I had to do was to call at least five or six people a day and give them this sales pitch about magazines. They were selling a whole group of magazines, and he sent me all the information: like you could get five years of the *Ladies' Home Journal* and three years of the *Saturday Evening Post* and two out of a list of fifteen other magazines for a flat payment, which brought each copy over a period of five years, down to about 13 cents a copy.'

'Uh-huh. And then what?'

The small brown eyes hid beneath the bright blue lids for a moment, while the pearly lips pushed into a pout. The lids unrolled and Mrs. Ogden fingered her cocktail ring, turning it so Christie could enjoy the small rubies. 'So I made my calls every day, taking names out of the phone book. In one whole week, I sold only one subscription. To some kike in the Bronx.' The mouth went down in a smile. 'You know—Abie could never resist a bargain!' The laugh was a hard sound.

Christie's eyes revealed nothing and her voice was flat and soft. 'But then, you called them back, right, the number from the ad?'

'Yeah. All I had was the one subscription and the ad had said I could earn up to seventy-five bucks a week. Some seventy-five. So I called, and then this guinea—whatever his name was—he told me that a lot of housewives did make a lot of money that way, but some didn't. And that he worked for an agency that handles phone calls for a lot of clients—an answering service for people who can't be around when their phones ring, you know? So he said I seemed reliable and intelligent'—the small body preened—'so I said, sure, why not? So he told me to take down messages every day between ten and twelve for a Mr. Stowe and that Mr.

Stowe would call me at twelve-thirty and I should give him the messages. And that was all I did.' She held her arms out, palms turned toward the ceiling, her eyes rolling back and up. 'That's all I did and I'm here, like a criminal or something.'

'Mrs. Ogden, do you know any other women who took messages?'

The eyes, which had innocently beseeched the ceiling, now glared at Christie. 'I already told that loudmouth redhead in there and I'm telling you now: that's all. That's it. I don't know anything more about it.'

'Didn't you consider the messages peculiar? The names of horses and the numbers of races? Didn't that seem odd to you?'

'I took the calls when the kids were in school. I had things on my mind—like lunch and cleaning the house and going to the store and taking care of my kids. I took down whatever the people said and when Mr. Stowe called, I read off the messages and goodbye! I had my home and family on my mind, not a bunch of phone messages.'

Christie leaned back in Reardon's chair, responding to the shadow and the tap at the door. 'Come on in.'

Stoney Martin crossed to Reardon's desk, an amused expression directed at Christie. 'Excuse me, but Mr. Reardon asked me to get this file—yes, here, this is the one.'

Christie nodded, but she was watching Mrs. Ogden; the viciousness broke through the makeup, cracking her face like old glass. Her small eyes watched Stoney's dark hand reach for the folder, watched his tall, lithe body cross the office and leave. Her eyes on the door, her face twisting down, she asked, 'That nigger—he's a cop?'

Christie played her fingers along the edge of her cast for a moment. She rose, came alongside Mrs. Ogden, sat tentatively beside the woman, meeting her eyes. Slowly, she shook her head. 'No, he's not a cop, Mrs. Ogden.' Christie paused, the words reaching her mouth almost before her brain thought them out. 'He's an F.B.I. agent.'

The face before her screwed into a look of bewilderment. 'F.B.I.?'

'Yes. Apparently, no one has bothered to explain this whole situation to you.' Mrs. Ogden shifted her weight; Christie felt the cushions moving and her voice was soft and she was amazed at how kind, how concerned she sounded. 'Let me try and explain it to you. You see, the "agency" you were working for—and taking bets for—is a very large syndicate: interstate. New York, New Jersey, Connecticut. Now, you live up on 175th Street in Manhattan, I believe? That means you're part of the Manhattan operation.'

'*The Manhattan operation?* What the hell does that mean?' The woman's voice was not as tough as she tried to make it sound. There was just the merest breaking quiver beginning. Christie noted it with small pleasure.

Christie let words come automatically from her lips, gauging their impact by the woman's face. 'The F.B.I. and the *Treasury* agents are involved in this as well. The F.B.I. because it's an interstate operation and the Treasury men, of course, because of the *income tax* angle.'

Mrs. Ogden leaped from the couch as though she had been touched by a live wire. Christie hadn't noticed the high spiked-heel shoes before. 'Taxes? Income taxes? What do you mean? I'll file on my income when the time comes!'

Christie's voice was deliberately calm; it made Mrs. Ogden sound even shriller. 'But on what amount? Sixty, seventy dollars a week?'

'That's all I made! I swear to God, that's all I made!'

'Mrs. Ogden, sit down and let me explain your situation a little better.' Christie didn't give herself time to think, didn't plan or calculate the words, just took her cue from the tense, rigid body on the edge of the couch beside her. 'You see, the way these gambling syndicates operate is pretty standard. Let's say a particular operation—upper Manhattan, your area—pulls an operation averaging approximately one hundred thousand dollars a week.'

The black eyebrows shot up to the hairline, the mouth dropped open in protest. Christie held her hand up. 'Don't get excited, now, just listen. Standard operating expenses for "message-takers" or "relay-people" like you are set at a flat 5 per cent for each area.' The words, unquestioned by Mrs. Ogden, came from some unexpected reservoir within her; Christie felt a small trickle of perspiration streaming between her shoulder blades and she spoke rapidly, for if she stopped, was interrupted, was questioned, she might not be able to continue. 'So, the amount involved would be about five thousand dollars a week, right? Therefore, the F.B.I. and the Treasury men, who of course know *exactly* how an operation is set up and know *exactly* how much money is spread around to people like you, however innocently you became involved, aren't really interested in *you* or in your "innocent involvement." They just want to know who got what money, so the government can get the amount it is entitled to.'

Christie stood up, moved silently to Reardon's desk, sat in the tilting chair, swiveled to face the woman. She caught the steadily growing panic that crept through the woman, working into her eyes and cheeks and down along her mouth, through her shoulders and into her suddenly busy hands which locked and unlocked one into the other. 'So you see, Mrs. Ogden, if they don't come up with more names—*they always have you.*'

'That's all I got, seventy-five a week. *That's all I got.*' The voice was an empty chant, then the woman looked at her and there was some new emotion now, clearly evident, unhidden and terrible: fear. 'Could they do that, miss? I mean, you're a detective, you'd know. Could they *really* do that?'

'Yes,' Christie said, a logical answer to a logical question, without emotion of any kind, 'they *really* could.'

Mrs. Ogden walked to the window. Christie could see the rapid calculation, the profile frozen with decision. Mrs. Ogden turned, her hands nervously plucking words out of the air. 'My sister, she took calls. And two of my cousins. And a few of my neighbors; some other girls, too.' Then, trying to qualify the betrayal, 'They didn't know either what it was—no more than me. I mean, I don't want *them* to get into any trouble, they didn't know either.'

'Uh-huh.'

Christie opened Reardon's top drawer, her fingers playing among a collection of broken pens and pointless pencils and stray Life Savers and gum. She found one ball point that seemed to work; testing it on a white legal pad, Christie tore off the sheet. 'Here, Mrs. Ogden. Write down the names, addresses and phone numbers of all the people you know who took phone calls the way you did.'

The woman snatched at the pad and pen, curling herself in one corner of the couch. Christie, hearing the frantic scratchings the woman was making on the pad, felt a cold and angry pleasure at the sound, but the sight of the woman, revealed now beneath the destroyed surface smugness, filled her with contempt and revulsion and she avoided looking at her. She took a stick of half-wrapped gum from the top drawer, absently curled it into a roll, dropped the tiny piece of wrapping back into the drawer and pressed the gum between her back teeth. She reached for the double-framed photograph, leaning back in the chair.

Mrs. Casey Reardon wasn't what she had expected, although it would have been difficult to say exactly what she had expected. She really hadn't given any thought to Reardon's wife. The face, at first glance, was surprisingly young and pleasantly pretty, the smile just a little aware of the camera. The eyes, a clear cornflower blue, were startling against pale skin and black hair, which had a few becoming streaks of pure silver. The bright blue at her neckline was probably a favorite color: it did a lot for her eyes. Christie regarded the eyes thoughtfully. They seemed to convey a vague sadness. They did not match the expression of the lips, which now seemed mechanical.

She shifted her attention to the two young faces in the opposite side of the frame: the same dark hair and blue eyes and small features and pointed chins, each girl indistinguishable from her twin. Their young faces were clear and earnest, unsmiling: younger versions of their mother. Yet not exactly. The girl on the right could have been her mother in an earlier photograph: no slightest trace of Casey was contained in her delicate face. It was odd: her twin, though identical, had something about her that was familiar, something of Casey's, some hint, maybe in the slight tilt of the chin or the set of the mouth.

She hadn't heard Casey Reardon at the door and as he approached his desk, she felt the silver frame stick to her hands like some personal correspondence she had been caught reading. Deliberately, her eyes on the desk, she carefully replaced the frame in its proper location. His questioning look, however, was not directed at her actions but at Mrs. Ogden. Christie said quietly, 'Mrs. Ogden just remembered some of the other ladies who took those phone calls.'

His eyes, appraising the woman who kept her head bent over her pad, returned to Christie, questioning. *Why did he always seem so surprised when she accomplished what she had been assigned to do?* His hand signaled her. 'You'll excuse us for a moment, Mrs. Ogden?' The woman's head moved without her face showing itself.

In the hallway, Reardon looked at Christie with a kind of amused admiration. 'How the hell did you do it?'

Christie told him the story she had made up as Reardon

covered his eyes, shaking his head. 'Where in God's name,' he asked, 'did you ever hear anything like that? About the percentage of operation set aside for "message-takers"?'

Not sure if she had to defend herself, Christie said carefully, 'I thought I heard it somewhere.' Then, seeing the grinning wonder on his face, she shrugged. 'Maybe I just made it up as I went along. It just seemed to be the right thing to hit her with.'

'Stoney,' he called, 'come over here a minute. Opara, tell him what you just told me.'

Christie repeated her explanation of how she had gotten Mrs. Ogden to 'cooperate.' Stoner Martin's mouth dropped open and he filled the hallway with a soft, low, musical voice. 'Great God in the morning. You've never been to Gamblers Course at Detective School, that's for sure. Casey, I think we could use Christie to give a few lectures!'

Reardon's voice was hard and sharp, but his eyes on hers, acknowledged what she had done. 'Well, it worked this time because that bitch in there is an idiot. But you try that story on a sharper operator and she'd laugh you right out of the room. Remind me to have someone educate Opara on gambling operations.'

'But it *did* work, *didn't* it?' she asked him triumphantly.

Reardon rubbed his chin. 'Beginner's luck,' he said shortly. 'Well, Stoney, you're an F.B.I. man—let's make Sammy Farrell our Treasury agent.'

'Sam would make a fine Treasury man, boss. Just picture him making a casual tour of the mint one day: Washington on a dollar bill with two unexplainable heads.'

Reardon jabbed a finger into Stoney's shoulder. 'You leave Sam alone. He's working his fingers off on that two-paragraph report for me, and you can stake your life on the fact that he won't leave here today until that report is done, complete.'

Christie accepted Reardon's needling without resentment. She knew she had accomplished something that would become part of the Squad legend: one of those implausible, unlikely, one-in-a-million, spur-of-the-moment, impossible-to-preplan con jobs that were in the realm of the unteachable part of police work: the intuitive chance-taking of being a good police officer.

The Squad worked late, the teams breaking into small busy huddles, dividing the long list of names among them, knowing that each woman interviewed the next day would, in turn, realize that she had to protect herself, and provide them with equally long lists. Calls were made to other Squad detectives who would become involved, to county police, notifying them of the new development, checking on their progress in other parts of the investigation.

Casey read over Christie's report, scanning the last page while it was still in the typewriter. 'Good, good. You and Ferranti will get up to the Bronx early tomorrow and hit this Ogden's sister, Mrs. Phyliss Lynn.' Christie tried to interrupt him, but Reardon kept talking, giving his directions, his suggestions, his eyes all around the room, checking on what was happening, who was in action. Finally, they returned to Christie and the dark red brows shot up. 'What's the matter? What's your problem?'

'Mr. Reardon, I have court tomorrow—it's Tuesday.'

'Court? What the hell for?'

'You know—Rogoff?'

'Who?'

'The 1140 I collared on Friday.'

There was an expression of annoyance, a quick rubbing of his face with the palm of his right hand. 'Swell,' he said tersely. 'Wait here a minute.' He searched out Stoney, spoke rapidly to him while looking steadily at Christie, then he signaled her toward him. 'Stoney's going to make a call first thing in the morning to have your case put on top of the calender. Ferranti, you meet Opara in Felony Court, then get going up to the Bronx, right? You got wheels?'

'Yes, sir,' Ferranti answered.

Reardon held Christie's cast and pulled her toward him. 'Get this thing off your arm.'

'Yes, sir.'

'Oh, and Opara: you looked pretty good sitting in the boss's chair, but don't get any ideas. You ain't big enough to fill it.'

The voice was tough and grating, but Christie was getting to know Reardon, learning to gauge what he said against when and how he said it. There was something in his eyes: an amusement but also a respect.

Christie shrugged her arm free, imitating his voice and tone perfectly. *'Ya never know!'*

Reardon's lips turned into a short smile, then he shook his head slightly. 'You are fresh, Opara, really fresh.'

CHAPTER TEN

FRANK SANTINO nodded his head and grunted a few sounds in reply to the bits of court gossip being offered to him by one of his less distinguished colleagues. But his eyes, though seeming to rest responsively on the face of the speaker, darted across the corridor to where the Rogoff brothers stood.

Frankie Santino was—if nothing else—a quick and good judge of a situation and from the moment he spotted Murray and David Rogoff standing silent and nearly rigid in the lobby of the Criminal Courts Building, Frankie knew he had better rush this thing through: cop Murray out and get it over and done with.

At least, Davey had gotten his brother cleaned up. Frankie couldn't help but admire the build on Murray Rogoff. The guy still had that lean hard look the girls used to climb all over. But from the neck up: Christ. Like something out of his kids' horror comic books. And now, Murray-the-Norseman had to ride around subway trains, waving it at women.

There was no doubt in Frank Santino's mind that Murray was a psycho: but he wasn't going to suggest mental tests. Hell, he had acted on an intuition that was the major reason why Frankie Santino rarely was done out of a fee: something had warned him that David Rogoff wasn't going to stay with it: not for too long. So Frankie had made a phone call Friday afternoon and had the case waived to Special Sessions for pleading. It wasn't a phone call *anybody* could have made; Frankie knew how to do favors and when to collect on favors done. And neither of the brothers even realized that he had done something special for them. They both just stood there when he told them they didn't have to return to Felony Court, like he had said it was a sunny day. What the hell, they didn't know the difference. But Frankie was going to make sure David Rogoff didn't chicken out. Davey didn't have to be present for sentencing and Frank would have his fee before then. As for Murray, he acted like he didn't know what the hell was going on: and he wasn't faking. Frankie knew all the tricks, and Murray was really living inside some kind of fog. He should really be psychoed, but what the hell. That wasn't his responsibility.

Frankie glanced at his wristwatch at the same moment that his friend consulted his, and with a quick exchange of shoulder slappings both men headed toward their clients.

'Okay, boys,' Frankie said, taking Murray by the arm and smacking David with his briefcase, 'we better get upstairs now. When they call the case, Murray, we just move up to the front of the court and the judge'll ask you how you plead, and you'll just say "guilty"—like we decided, okay, kid?'

Murray nodded.

'And then what?' David asked, looking straight ahead.

Dropping Murray's arm, Frank turned his full attention to David. 'That's it. You see, Murray is on bail and the judge'll continue it, and set a sentencing date.' Quickly, he added, 'You don't have to be there, Dave, I'll be with him, right Murray?' Frankie looked around, then put his hand over his lips. 'I can practically *guarantee* a suspended sentence. Of course, it took a little doing, but what the hell is a friend for?' The way Murray batted his eyes under those weird glasses was terrible, like he was trying to make out exactly who you were.

Frank guided David's elbow, negotiating a turn. 'Here we are, boys.'

Murray and David sat on the bench in the courtroom. They waited, wordlessly, for Frankie to return from some mission which he assured them was very important to their interests. It was a small room, wider than it was long. It had an air of definite purpose about it. Everyone present knew his role now: defendants knew what was expected of them, for they had been guided and briefed by attorneys. Members of families sat, not less nervously than in the hugeness of Felony Court, but less distraught; a period of days had given them a certain heavy resignation. There was less directionless commotion; only those whose names were called moved forward, accompanied by lawyers who invariably made some physical contact with their clients: a touch on the back, a hand brushing along a sleeve.

Frankie's hands rested on a shoulder of each of the brothers and he leaned his face between them from the row of benches behind them. 'Okay, kid, we're being called next. Come on, Murray. Take it easy, Davey—this'll take a few minutes.'

David sat rigidly watching Frankie Santino walk easily up to the front of the room, looking like some sharp little bookie. Five hundred bucks. The schmuck. The schmuck. Five hundred dollars. David let his breath out slowly, closing his eyes for a moment. Okay, so pay the man and that's it. That's all of it.

Murray stood beside Frankie Santino and when Frankie poked him, Murray looked straight ahead and in a low voice said, 'Guilty'. He stood uncertainly until guided by Frank's hand, which led him across the room to a desk, where he sat beside some graying Negro with glasses, who wrote down his name and address and occupation on a printed form. He did not answer any of the questions: Frankie spoke for him and then, finally, Frankie pressed the man's shoulder and clamped Murray's arm and led him around the fenced-in section of the courtroom, waving David toward them, and they went out into the hallway.

Murray's eyes were burning and dry and he closed them tightly, screwing up his face against the aching throb inside his head. This was a hot place and he wanted to be out of here. He accepted the slip of paper Frankie pressed into his hand without looking at it, not listening to the words Frankie was saying, but nodding. Murray closed his eyes again feeling within him a great, familiar pit of emptiness like a hole swallowing him up. When he opened his eyes, they rested directly on the face of some girl who had come up to Frankie. Murray stopped blinking so that he could see her better. There was something familiar about her.

'Mr. Santino,' Christie Opara said angrily, 'why wasn't I notified that you had waived to Sessions?'

Frankie smiled easily. 'Why, hello, Detective Opara, honey. This here is Mr. Davey Rogoff, brother of Murray, who you already know.'

Christie glanced at David who kept his eyes fixed at some point past her head, then at Murray who looked different, dressed in a suit and tie. She shrugged off Frank Santino's hand, moving just a slight step backwards, but she couldn't shake off his lewd little eyes which skimmed her body without subtlety.

'Can you believe that this little girl with those big round eyes is a cop?' Frankie asked no one in particular. David wasn't looking at him and Murray seemed a million miles away, lost behind his glasses. He leaned close to Christie, 'Honey, you can lock me up anytime.'

'I might have to one day,' Christie said coldly. 'Mr. Santino, can you give me the sentencing date?'

'Sure, sure, but you won't have to be there.'

'I know that.'

Frank poked David. 'You bet she does. This little cookie knows all there is to know, don't you, Christie Opara?'

Christie bit the inside of her cheeks, her eyes narrowing contemptuously at the small, stocky man. She had met Santino in court many times; had been subjected to his crude insinuations and raised eyebrows and booming voice and had responded with controlled anger, keeping her poise and scoring convictions against him. 'Never mind, Mr. Santino, I have to write up my report for the probation officer, anyway. I'll get the date from him.'

Frankie's smile stayed on his lips but he watched the girl walk into the courtroom with a tightness in his throat. The little bitch. One day, he would get her on that witness stand and that cold, smug sureness would fall apart: he would shred it apart into little ripped up pieces.

Murray Rogoff reached his arm into the barrel, and the cold cleanness of the water seemed to extend through his body. He could feel the thudding of the strong dark bodies as the carp churned themselves in small circles against his arm. For a moment he let his arm hang there, then his fingers seized a tail and in one quick motion, the cool water running along the inside of his arm, he held the fish up before the squinting eyes of the customer. The customers were all alike: the old women with colorless eyes and lumpy bodies who could measure and calculate to the ounce how much they were getting for their money.

'Nah, nah, nah,' the old woman wailed, rocking her head from side to side.

His father's voice, whining, insistent, argued with the customer and the exchange, in Yiddish, was rapid and to the anticipated conclusion. 'Cut him up, Murray,' his father said and Murray slammed the cold body onto the butcher's block, his free hand reaching for the sharp knife. Deftly, he severed the head, turned the quivering body flat on its side, slashed it open and in the next movement, his fingers, bloody and wet, entered the body and gathered the yellowish guts, which he threw into the pail at his feet. The old woman, watching closely, began arguing and Murray's father reached down, grabbed up the mess in both his hands, and held it before the woman's face. She shrugged: it was hers. It was part of the fish. What business of his was it what she did with it? It was hers.

Murray reached for two clean sheets of newspaper from the stack against the wall and carefully spread them out on the small marble counter beside the chopping block. He wiped his hands down the front of his solidly stained apron and squinted at the headlines: 'Dancer Strangled in Bronx Apartment House'. There was a picture of some girl in a white blouse, her hair pulled back in a pony tail. She was smiling and directly under her picture were smaller words which said, 'Third Victim in Three Months'. After that, there was a paragraph in regular size newsprint which Murray found hard to read: 'Carol Logan, age 23, was found strangled early this morning behind a stairway in her Bronx apartment house. Police believe she is the third victim of a rapist-murderer responsible for the March murder of career girl Jody Lane in Greenwich Village and music student Agnes Lichtenberg of Riverside Drive last month. Story page three.'

Murray felt a sudden confusion staring at the paper: it was dated Saturday, May 7, 1966. It was strange. Something was wrong. Ignoring the old woman who tried to hurry him along, Murray thought about it for a moment, then his face relaxed and it was no longer a problem.

His father, who always observed the Sabbath from Friday evening through Saturday sundown, would never have purchased the *Daily News* on a Saturday. The colored boy who delivered ice to them Monday morning had probably taken it from the truck and tossed it onto the stack of newspapers.

Murray added another sheet of paper so that the gummy guts wouldn't leak through. His eyes were bothering him again. He wanted to take the glasses off and smash them against the floor: why were they always so smudgy? Murray wrapped the fish into a neat package which he then slid into a brown paper bag. The old women wouldn't put the newspaper package into their string bags: they wanted what they paid for and a brown paper bag was included in the price.

Murray turned and plunged his arms into the barrel; the water felt good. He sloshed the coolness over his neck, then took off his glasses and rinsed his face. He didn't listen to his father who told him it looked funny for him to wash in the fish barrel and that he should go into the back of the store if he wanted to clean up that bad. He didn't listen to his mother either. Her voice so like his father's with that same whining sound and all the words running together and always the same things, over and over: Murray, why don't you and Murray, why won't you and Murray you must and Murray you should and Murray and Murray.

'I'm going up now,' Murray said. He ignored their combined voices which pursued him into the hot street, telling him that he had started so late in the day, he should at least work with them until supper time, but Murray didn't want to work until supper time and he left the shop, as he always did whenever he felt he had to and they couldn't stop him from leaving any more than they could stop him from leaving the hot string of rooms on the top floor whenever he wanted to, their words and questions just part of their breath and of no meaning to him.

Murray was tired and he didn't know how tired he was until his body hit the hard mattress and then he knew he was very tired. Murray was too tired to sleep and he pressed his face into the pillow, rubbing his eyes against the coarseness of the pillow-case, trying to burrow into some dark place where it was cool, where there would be dreams that were not dreams, but real. He lay, not moving for a long time, seeking sleep, and then he bunched the soft pillow in his large hands, as though that was the obstacle to rest and he tossed it across the small airless room. He rolled onto his back, stretching his body so that his head touched the metal headboard and his feet were over the edge of the mattress. He strained his eyes, sketching figures among the cracks on the ceiling, and Murray felt a deep sense of uneasiness, as if there was something wrong: something he should remember but couldn't. Or *someone* he should remember, but couldn't.

And then, Murray felt his body relax: felt the odd and welcome and good feeling of not trying to remember at all, because it all came to him now and he knew he could sleep deeply and soundly because everything would be all right.

Murray closed his eyes and smiled. His hands wandered down his body, lightly touching the smoothness of his thighs, then resting on the center of his being where he could feel the life of him rising, hard and strong and vital.

'Christie Opara,' Murray Rogoff said softly, letting himself drift off into a good, safe, relaxing sleep.

CHAPTER ELEVEN

THE HOT WATER of the shower hit the center of Christie's spine and she leaned forward so that the water ran down her body. She straightened, turning her face upward so that her cheeks tingled. Slowly, she adjusted the hot water faucet so that the temperature of the water changed gradually. Finally, taking a deep breath, clenching her teeth against the shock, she stood in the ice-cold water for the count of ten before exhaling, letting the pores of her body close in the clean coldness. She reached out blindly for the towel, patting her face and letting her body feel cool in contrast to the steamy air.

It had been a long day, even though she had learned not to measure a working day in terms of hours. The job was not an eight-hour deal which you walk away from until nine the next morning. You took the people, with their grating voices and tight lips and calculating eyes, home with you, into the shower with you, trying to scrub them out of your skin. But they stayed there, no matter how much hot water you used to open up your flesh, no matter how hard you scrubbed with a stiff, invigorating bathbrush. When you closed yourself up with icy water, the cleanness was only a fleeting sensation: they were still there, inside of you.

Mrs. Ogden's sister had been a somewhat younger replica of the woman Christie had tricked, her eyes the same alert little holes watching her from under heavy eyeshadow over a small sharp nose and a mouth that twisted in protest and indignation. And the two cousins: not at all alike. The one with a high, hysterically shrill voice and bony fingers that kept working frantically along the housedress and throat at the realization that seventy-five dollars for taking phone messages at home was to be something less than a profitable pastime. The other, a young, placid, poker-faced woman, encased in heavy layers of flesh, all squeezed and overflowing from beneath a tight electric yellow shift, her brows blatantly drawn heavy black lines over each eye, her mouth a wild orange slash in her large bland face.

More than anything else, it was the greed they had revealed which ground into Christie. The women she had spoken to all afternoon and well into the night were not poverty-stricken.

They had overly furnished, tasteless homes, husbands who could pay all outstanding bills, children who were overfed and well supplied with bikes and games and outdoor gym equipment. The money had been for the extra day at the beauty parlor, the mink stole and beaded sweaters and cocktail dresses with satin shoes dyed to match which could be flaunted, smugly and matter-of-factly, before the neighbors. And the sneering, insistently repetitious justification: *I'm at home with my children.*

Mickey, of course, had been asleep when Christie finally arrived home, after two final hours devoted to typing up reports. He had been just sleepily awake when she had left for court in the morning and that was how she would see him tomorrow morning. Christie, standing in her light cotton pajamas, watched her small son, sleeping, the breath steady and even and moistly warm. The young forehead was drawn into a frown and the pink lips were working over some words, then pulled upwards into a smile of triumph. Whatever the battle he had been fighting, he had just won. She stroked her fingers lightly through his thick dark hair and automatically, in sleep as in consciousness, the strong little hand roughly placed the hair back on his forehead. Christie leaned her face close against her son's and whispered softly in his ear—not because she had read once in a psychology class a long time ago that whispered words registered, were recorded in a sleeper's brain and became part of the sleeper's memory—but because she felt a great surge of loneliness for her child: 'I love you, Michael-Mickey, my little Mickey.' Her lips touched his brow and the quick hand raised in protest but she ducked away before he could push her.

All right, my little toughie; but I'm still going to think you're a beautiful boy with your hard little body so removed from me now and I'm still going to think you have the most fantastic clear blue eyes in the world. And I *will* stick to my resolve to keep my mouth shut about all of that, at least to you, but it's hard.

Christie watched the small body suddenly fight off the light cover which she had just tucked under the mattress; the legs bent at the knees, then the feet were thrown into the air and the summer blanket went flying. Mickey stiffened his back, his arms reaching over his head, every part of him enjoying the pleasurable stretch of growth. Then, he turned on his side, his face toward the wall, his knees tucked up. He looked so small. Christie put her lips against the back of his head for a last quick kiss then put the top sheet over him and for once he didn't fight it off.

In bare feet, she went down the carpeted steps, through the hall and into the kitchen where she had left the small stove light on. She foraged without appetite in the refrigerator. Nora had asked her what she had eaten for supper and she couldn't remember. There wasn't a regular meal schedule when you were working on something: you had a sandwich sometime during the day and again sometime during the night, not when it was a normally designated mealtime, not even when hunger demanded it. You ate when you could find a minute or when someone had a chance to run down to the luncheonette and bring back a box of sandwiches and cardboard-flavoured tea or coffee or tinny canned soda.

Christie saw the remains of Nora's lasagna in the Corning Ware; at one-fifteen in the morning, though there was an emptiness inside of her, Christie rejected it with distaste. She filled a glass to the brim with cold milk and drank it too fast. She filled the glass again, drinking like a child, interested only in quenching her thirst. She rinsed the glass, turned off the light, letting her eyes get accustomed to the darkness. She should have left the small lamp in her room on. Groping for the banister, her feet found the steps and then the landing, but her shin smashed into the small table leg in the upstairs hallway and Christie bit down on her lip, her fingers rubbing the unexpected pain. She listened for a moment, assured that she hadn't disturbed Nora or Mickey, then, hands extended before her, feeling for the doorway, she entered her own room.

The room was so dark that she could not pick out any of the familiar forms: not the dresser or the oiled walnut rocker by the window or the table by her bed. Christie eased herself onto her bed, lying with her hands folded beneath her head, her eyes able to make out the small phosphorous dots and slashes on the alarm clock on the dresser—1:25. She counted: 2:25, 3:25, 4:25, ticking off the number of hours she could sleep, if she fell asleep right now. The alarm was set for 6:30.

Stop counting; stop wasting sleep time. Christie's eyes closed, she shifted her arm so that it rested lightly across her forehead, her mind became slowly enveloped in the blackness, growing more and more relaxed and freed from words and images.

The sudden shattering sound caught Christie somewhere in

her throat, racing down her body like a shock wave. Instinctively, without solid thought of any kind, she responded with two different actions, each independent of the other and both independent of her conscious mind. Her right hand reached up over her head and twisted the light switch and her left hand reached and lifted the receiver to her ear.

'Hello,' she said clearly, as though the loudness of her voice would convince her that she was fully awake. Then again, into the silence, her eyes staring, giving the room shape and the moment reality. 'Hello?'

There was a soft, breathing sound in her ear and Christie could feel a pounding within herself: the reaction of her heart startled into quicker action than it had been prepared for. Listening intently, straining for some voice, some word, Christie asked, 'Who is this?'

The voice was not familiar. 'Is this Christie Opara?'

'Yes, who is this?' Pressing the phone harder against her ear, straining to catch the voice, for no reason she could explain, she asked, 'Marty? Is that you?'

'Hello, Christie Opara.'

Steadying her voice, lowering it, she asked again, 'All right, who is this?'

Softly, familiarly, almost pleasantly, the voice, not answering her demand, repeated, 'Hello, Christie.'

That was all the voice said and then there was a click in her ear and a dead, toneless silence. Stupidly jiggling her finger on the button twice, not really expecting to hear the voice, which had cut itself off, she said into the steady hum of the dial tone, 'Hello? Hello?' and then she placed the phone in place.

Nora emerged in the doorway, her face puzzled by sleep. 'Did the phone ring, Christie, or did I dream it?'

Christie pretended annoyance. 'Wrong number, Nora. Go on back to bed. I'll leave my light on until you get to your room.'

She heard Nora muttering about people who dial wrong numbers in the middle of the night, heard her enter her room, then heard her settle on the bed.

Wrong number. Christie switched off the light, lay back on her pillow. She could feel the tenseness of her body, the tight expectancy, the unwillingness to be caught off guard again, to be stabbed in the dark by the shock of unexpected sound. Consciously, she began a relaxing of her body, starting at her feet, wiggling her toes, flexing the muscles of her legs and thighs, her shoulders and arms and fingers and neck, but her stomach, filled only with milk, felt cold and knotted.

Christie stared into the darkness. Wrong number. She closed her eyes, pushing the faceless voice away. 'Hello, Christie Opara. Hello, Christie.' No image formed, no face, just a hollow repetition of her name. She put her arm across her forehead again, lying very still

Some wrong number.

CHAPTER TWELVE

WHY WAS IT that the one particular key that didn't work in the Underwood was always the one particular letter that seemed to appear in every single word? Christie smashed the 'o,' jamming it onto the skipped spot. Ferranti sat alongside of her, consulting his notes as she sat, hands poised, listening to him, then, holding her hand up, she quickly rephrased the information and her fingers raced over the keyboard. Except when they reached for the letter 'o.'

Christie grumbled to herself, glaring at the irregular line of typing, and in sudden resolve, she ripped the half-page of work from the machine, crumpled it into a ball and tossed it to the wastebasket. Bill Ferranti offered to do the typing; he was slow, but steady.

She shook her head. 'It's this bomb of a machine. You'd think the People of the City of New York could afford to supply decent typewriters. Or at least send a capable repair-man.'

Casey Reardon, leaning against the long table in the front of the room, instructing his driver, Third-Grade Detective Tom Dell, hadn't heard Christie's complaints but he had observed her annoyed balling up of her work (carbons and all) and the angry set of her head. He walked over to the desk where she was working. She glanced up at him, then slammed the 'o.'

'What's your problem?'

'My problem,' she said shortly, as though he were somehow responsible, 'is this typewriter. That's my problem. The so-called repairman fixed the "k" but he broke the "o".'

'Well, you do the best you can,' Reardon said softly. 'I need all reports completed by 12:30. You have plenty of time, even allowing for the insurmountable problem of the "o." '

Christie failed to anticipate the stuck key and the typewriter skipped a space. She tapped her clenched hand on the stack of clean papers and he could tell she was turning something over in her mind; her mouth pulled down for a moment. He knew she would say whatever it was: she always did.

'Mr. Reardon, is it true that we're turning all of our information over to the Nassau County authorities? That we're dropping the investigation?'

'That's right. Why?'

Christie shrugged; Ferranti was thumbing through his notebook, his head down.

'Why?'

She looked at him steadily, her words bitter and, it seemed to Reardon, bordering on some accusation. 'Then none of the "ladies" we've been interviewing for the last two weeks—none of the "at-home-housewives-earning-money" are going to be prosecuted?'

His eyes, a glinting reddish now, never left hers. 'That's right. They're cooperative witnesses. You don't prosecute cooperative witnesses when they're essential to the successful completion of an investigation.'

'Swell.' Christie backspaced, ignored Reardon, hit the wrong key, but didn't reach for an eraser. She'd wait until Reardon left.

Aware that he had been dismissed, Reardon still stared down at her. 'Why?' he demanded, noting the deep, slow breath, the deliberate way in which she lifted her fingers from the keys and placed them on the edge of the desk.

'Because I think that someone should throw the book at them. Or even maybe a page of the book at them.'

'Is that what *you* think?'

Ignoring the slight pressure of Ferranti's shoe on the tip of her foot, warning her, Christie said, 'Yes. That's what I think.'

Reardon smiled. He turned away without another word: what Christie Opara thought was not particularly important. He heard her resume her sporadic typing, stopping—probably for the 'o' —as he entered his office. Sitting at his desk now, Reardon rapidly scanned the pile of material submitted by the teams of investigators. He absorbed the information while at the same time allowing some part of his mind to engage the problem of Christie Opara. Very quickly, that particularly annoying problem engaged a greater portion of his attention. He removed his glasses, tapped them on the edge of his desk, then dug his thumb and index finger into his eyes.

Was it the pinch? The fact that no one in the Squad—particularly not Detective Christie Opara—was going to make an arrest on this case? He knew she had worked hard the last few weeks—hell, they all worked hard on this. He didn't like handing over his Squad's work any better than his people did, but it was one of those things. A cooperative effort had a way of being repaid in the future. The jurisdiction with the strongest evidence was the logical location for prosecution. He certainly didn't owe *her* any explanation.

The expression on her face: Reardon had seen it the first time he had prosecuted a case when she was the arresting officer, a few years ago, when he was in Special Sessions. What was it?—a bag opener. She had given her evidence in that steady, confident way, stating the facts, then had handled the cross-examination capably, if almost defiantly. It was just a routine bag opener and the decision was acquittal, two-to-one. They had both done their job properly, and then it was up to the three judges and no longer his or Opara's responsibility. Reardon had gone into the briefing room with a young uniformed cop, and was listening to a recitation of the facts involved in his next case when, absently scanning the room, he had noticed her scowling over her acquittal report as though she were the only police officer in the world who had ever lost a case, and as he observed her, she looked up and glared at him coldly. Reardon grinned, remembering the anger in that look and the way she dismissed him with a deliberate blinking of her eyes.

She had been neither surprised nor disturbed when he excused himself from the cop, walked to her and asked, *'What's your problem?'*

He had caught the momentary hesitation, the determination to frame exactly the right answer in exactly the right tone. 'Doesn't it bother you—in the slightest—that a guilty man was just set free?'

He had shaken his head nonchalantly, amused, annoyed, yet somehow touched by the realness of her anger. 'No, not in the slightest. Win one—lose one. Why does it bother you?'

She hadn't hesitated that time, blurting it out at him, 'If you don't know, I doubt if I could explain it.'

Fresh little bastard, he had thought then, and thought it now: fresh little bastard. But the words contained a strong element of respect. She cared. *She really cared* and God knows that was rare enough. Reardon's finger reached for the intercom button, he played with it for a moment, then pushed it down. 'Detective Opara, come into my office.'

Reardon knew what it was about her that made her attractive. Her figure was neat—a little thin and wiry, but she moved well with a confident, easy grace. But that wasn't it. Nor her face: that was pretty in a cute way, the clean-cut all-American girl, showing every feeling with too much honesty. It was something else, something he didn't think she was aware of, or if she was aware of it, wouldn't realize it was a point of attraction: *her intensity*. There was a vitality about Christie Opara; it was interesting and curious and somewhat mystifying. He let her sit there for a minute; he knew the tricks she used to relax herself—at least outwardly. A few deep, silent breaths, a conscious flexing and unflexing of her fingers, then forcing them to rest on the arms of the chair.

He ran his thumb across his lip, then closed the folder and raised his head. Reardon didn't think there was a woman alive who didn't look good in pink: deep, vibrant pink. Opara was no exception. 'Now,' he said, pacing his words so that they were not just a repetition of what he had asked before, 'what-exactly-is-your-problem?'

He could see that she was making some decision and in the four or five seconds it took, she bit the corner of her lip, blinked twice without looking at him, then, resolved, met his eyes.

'I have been getting some phone calls.'

He responded without any inflection of surprise. 'What kind of phone calls?'

She shrugged.

'Obscene phone calls?'

She shook her head. 'No. It's crazy, I guess. Not obscene phone calls. Just—phone calls. Late at night. Just some voice getting on and saying, "Hello, Christie Opara—how are you?"—things like that.'

No turn in any conversation, no information unexpectedly revealed ever rattled or detoured the neat, precise workings of Reardon's mind. His courtroom experience served him under any and all circumstances and the questions rose, one after the other, in logical sequence, to track down the needed information.

'When did they start?'

'Couple of weeks ago.'

'How many have you received?'

She looked at the ceiling for a moment. 'Two in a row—then none for a few nights—then one every night for a week. Last one—last night.'

'At what time?'

'Between midnight and about 1:45 A.M. The first one was the latest, then the time varied. Last night was just after midnight.'

'Recognize the voice?'

She hesitated. 'No. Not really.'

'What does *"not really"* mean?'

She took one of those steadying breaths. Then, firmly, 'No. I don't recognize the voice.'

Reardon considered his glasses for a moment, then, annoyed, asked, 'Why the hell are you listed in the phone book?'

'I'm not,' she shot back, then, softer, 'but my mother-in-law is.'

'Uh-huh. And how many other "Oparas" are listed in the Queens directory? Or in any of the five boroughs?'

'Not many,' she said weakly. 'In Queens, only Nora. My mother-in-law.'

'You ever get anonymous calls before?'

'A few times. Obscene—routine nut calls.'

'Did they rattle you?' His sarcasm has been building slowly.

Not as much as you do, Reardon. Not realizing it showed on her face, she carefully adjusted her voice. 'It is a little—disturbing—to lie there in the middle of the night, knowing that somewhere, some man has nothing better to do than to dial your number and ask you how you are.' She added, without intending to, 'It's upsetting.'

'What have you done about it?'

The question was sharp and logical and she answered it without a word: her blank expression told him what he wanted to know and set the cutting edge to his voice. 'So, you just lie awake every night waiting for the phone to ring and then it does and this anonymous caller asks how you are, and then when he's sure you're fine, you can get to sleep?'

'Mr. Reardon, I don't think it's a very funny situation.'

Tapping his glasses against his chin, his eyes the color of

MAB/72—K*

honey held to light, he said, 'Neither do I. What do you think you can *do* about it?'

Impatiently, she said, 'Oh, I know, I know. I could get the number changed and keep it unlisted or leave the phone off the hook or put a pillow over it or something but . . .' She stopped, biting her lip.

'But what?'

She was silent, not looking up until he repeated his last two words insistently. 'I don't know. There's something more to it. Something I can't quite put my finger on.' She shook her head, puzzling thoughtfully. 'There's "something" way in the back of my mind and when I hear that voice, I feel like any minute it'll come to me. It sounds stupid, I know.'

'Then, in effect, you're willing to take the phone calls and wait it out to see if the "something" materializes.'

'Yes, I guess so. In a way.'

Reardon ran his hand over his face, then scratched the small red hairs at the back of his neck. She knew that sign: it always preceded the softly, steadily building verbal assault. 'So, you're up half the night waiting for some nut to call and ask how you are and then you get a few hours' sleep and come in here and bitch about the Underwood and bitch about not getting the chance to lock up some cooperating, vital witnesses, and mope around like a sullen kid when your real problem is that you need some more *sleep* which you're not getting because instead of taking some definite logical action to stop these phone calls, you're waiting them out because of some "feeling" of some kind or other which you can't explain. *Right?*'

'Right,' she snapped, matching his tone exactly.

They held it between them for a long time, neither of them moving, but she dropped her eyes first, because she could feel the redness, the damn, stupid, uncontrollable blushing, and she knew he had seen it because the grin was pulling at the corners of his mouth. Not only did he think she was stupid, he thought she was amusing.

'Well,' he said slowly, 'why don't you dig up your copy of the penal law and maybe you can find a loophole in the area of annoying, obscene phone calls? Maybe there's a special subdivision that makes it a violation of law for someone to call you to ask how you are, Christie Opara.' He knew she didn't trust her voice to answer him. He leaned back, locking his fingers over his stomach. 'Christie Opara,' he repeated softly. 'What the hell kind of a name is Opara anyway?'

'Pronounced *properly*,' she said coldly, 'it is "*O*-per-uh"; not Op*ara*. It is a Czech name.' As you damn well know.

'*Opara*. What was your maiden name?'

'Choriopoulous.' Which you damn well know.

He raised his brows, two dark red indications of surprise. 'Greek? A fair-haired, green-eyed Greek?'

'My mother was Swedish.' As you *probably* know. All this is in my personnel folder; plus whatever other information, private and official, you wanted to know about me from the day I was born right up to and including this very minute. *Right,* Reardon?

Reardon shook his head. 'A Swedish-Greek with a Czech name that comes out Irish.'

'And my mother-in-law *is* Irish, so that adds a little to the stew.'

'It does indeed. Well, Opara'—he purposely reverted to the Irish pronunciation, which nearly everyone used—'if you come up with anything exciting, you know, anything worthwhile, on these phone calls, you be sure to let me know. Maybe the whole Squad can get in on it.'

'I'll do that, Mr. Reardon.'

'In the meantime, Detective Opara, regardless of your sleepless nights, you see if you can't shake yourself out a little and get your work done without so much glaring and cussing and wasting of taxpayers' stationery.'

'I don't swear, Mr. Reardon. I am as careful with my language as I expect the people I work with to be.'

'You can outcuss me any day, tiger. Remember, I told you I can read you right through those green eyes and I wouldn't ever want to hear you say out loud what you're saying with your eyes right now. Go on, beat it and get that report typed up.'

Reardon knew the report would be typed up quickly and accurately in spite of the delinquent 'o', and with all facts explicitly and concisely stated. Whatever she did, she did well. He reached for Sam Farrell's report, filled with near holes and poorly disguised strikeovers, but containing all necessary information somewhere in the wandering, ungrammatical statements.

There was something about that kid that aroused an odd combination of responses within him. There was some kind of a continuous battle going on between them and it was irritating and annoying and yet, something more, leading to something other than sharp, biting word duels. For a moment, he thought about the phone calls and, more importantly, her reaction to them. She was too sharp to let just the normal, female reaction to the situation disturb her that much. He trusted her intuition to a great extent: she was a real pro and he'd let her ride with it for a while. Then, he filed the entire matter, including Christie Opara, into some neat chamber of his brain for future reference, and turned his full attention to Farrell's sloppy but informative report.

CHAPTER THIRTEEN

CHRISTIE CLIMBED the broad flat steps of the Fifth Avenue entrance to the 42nd Street Library, stepping around the mid-town sunbathers who were trying to reinforce their weekend tans on late lunch hours. In her hand was the slip of paper Mr. Reardon had given her, covered on both sides with his cryptic notes: 'Gerardo Const. Co—Alf. Gerardo—connect. w/Cong. Littlejohn-R—Feb. 64 (?) any n.g. info. (Times—Trib.).' Which meant that she had to spend the better part of the day squinting at the Library's microfilm: endless columns of print dating back, probably, to 1963 and possibly up to the present date, since when Mr. Reardon indicated a date of February 1964 he meant 'maybe' and from having done some previous research for him, 'maybe' covered a long area of possibility.

She was beginning to feel the full force of her usual springtime blues and some of her growing uneasiness and restlessness related directly to her job. She didn't like jumping from assignment to assignment—still not having a definite partner—still not following through an investigation from its initiation to an arrest, trial and conviction. She didn't like to have loose ends dangling, never knowing if what she had worked on two days ago was merely some curious whim of Reardon's or part of a larger whole, which she would never know about anyway. There was a lack of satisfaction, a lack of accomplishment in her work now.

None of the other Squad members seemed to raise these objections. Not even when Reardon wasn't around. They did some small piecework: that's what it was. Christie's mind seized on it: piecework, like in a factory. I turn the screw to the left and pass it on to the next man; he slips a band around it and the next man tightens the band, then after a while we change places, each of us attending to one small detail, handing it on to Reardon who accepts it without a word and hands you some other small item.

'Boy, whatever it is, it sure has you sore!'

Christie, startled, squinted into the high strong sun, but the voice was as familiar as the crushing handshake, from which she had to remove Reardon's crumpled bit of paper. 'Hey, Johnnie, how are you?'

Detective John Devereaux was a Homicide man and the imprint of his profession, while stamped clearly and permanently on his face, had not touched his voice, which was musically soft and light. He was a bulky man with broad shoulders and a huge barrel of a torso carried on legs that were much too short for the rest of his body so that, sitting down, he gave the appearance of great height, while standing up, he seemed to be in a hole. Not that he was short, just that he looked like a man who, somehow, should be taller.

'The D.A. got you doing research, Christie?'

Christie made a face, indicating exactly what she thought of the D.A. and she let Johnnie steer her, with a large and heavy hand, so that she was turned about and heading in his direction. 'Got time for coffee and? I been in that mausoleum for two and a half hours. Boy, this sun is hard to take; let's find some nice dark, cool spot.'

Leading her through the crowds that surged businesslike across the broad expanse of Fifth Avenue during the brief 'Walk' signal, which blinked 'Don't Walk' almost before their feet hit the warm tar, Johnnie pulled her along. Christie winced. This was Johnnie's friendly grasp: she hated to think what his official in-custody hold was like. He more or less wrenched her into a small bar on Madison Avenue just off 42nd Street. He was apparently known here, for he just held up his finger at the bartender who appeared with a tall highball.

Christie asked for a Coke, checking the clock on the wall. She'd tackle Reardon's research in a half hour.

Johnnie took his hat off in concession to Christie for he was always a gentleman when confronted by what he defined as a lady and he had known Christie for some four years, having met her when he was on his first assignment with Homicide and the corpse was female—white—age 35—suicide by gas—and the policewoman assigned in uniform was Christie Opara, twenty-two, arriving from the Bureau to search her third corpse, which she did quickly, and finding nothing, had swallowed dryly, told him 'Nothing', then gratefully accepted his cigarette. He had taken solace from her whitened face and tenseness: it eased his own because in Homicide, as he had learned through the years, you never knew what to expect.

Sipping his Scotch and soda, his eyes adjusting to the dimness easily, Johnnie looked around. 'Nice place, this. Lot of advertising people.' Johnnie Devereaux had a fantastic acquaintance with people in all areas of the city. He could talk intelligently with anyone in politics, clothing manufacturing, advertising, construction, waterfront activities, labor negotiations, religious movements, education, any large industrial or small commercial business. He could blink his eyes and tell in which section of the city, which small, hidden, unknown pocket, you could find a particular group of people, what the ethnic makeup was three blocks to the west or one block to the east. Where to eat authentic Cantonese food, not the American chop suey junk; where to get real Northern Italian cooking or non-commercial, absolutely pure Kosher meals like someone's Grandma used to put in front of someone's Grandpa. People and their strange quirks of behavior and their fascinating customs and remnants of blood-culture were Johnnie's hobby and a knowledge he enjoyed sharing.

'What has Homicide got their ace looking up in the Library?'

Johnnie wiped his mouth with the back of his hand and his voice was sad. 'Ah, these murders. These girls: three in three months.' He ticked off the months and the murders with his fingers. 'February, March, beginning of this month.'

Christie recalled the most recent, then remembered the other two only because they had been referred to in the newspapers as being linked to the most recent.

'Is there really any connection, John, or is that just a newspaper gimmick?'

'Well, you know the papers: what sells is what they print. They discover some drab little mouse got bumped off and they print it that way—no sales. So they change her into a bright, blowsy blond and jazz it up like that and it sells papers.' His face was deeply troubled and he shook his head. 'But there was no jazzing up these girls, Christie. Nice kids, you know. Clean, really clean, hard-working, good girls. No fooling around, no long lists of boy-friends to check out. All in their early twenties. This last one, the kid in the Bronx: a *nice* kid.'

That said it all for Johnnie Devereaux. It was the best word there was for describing a female: *nice.*

'But is there a real connection? I mean, there's a murder every hour somewhere, every day.' She closed her eyes, recalling the newspaper accounts. 'First one in Greenwich Village, second, Riverside Drive and third—this last girl, in the Bronx.' She thought a moment, then asked, 'Any *real* connection? Or is it possible that there are three murderers—you know, the first case setting some other psycho into motion, the second giving another fellow the same idea?'

His voice was cautious; Johnnie Devereaux did not give information relative to his work away freely. 'Same age, same type; none of them knew each other, if that's what you mean, no friends or acquaintances in common. All three *were* raped and strangled.'

Christie yawned, excused herself and then, filled with the weariness of her sleepless, interrupted nights, she absently asked, 'Any of them get any anonymous phone calls?'

Johnnie Devereaux was a swarthy man, the darkness of his face making the paleness of his light gray eyes even more startling. They narrowed into bright slits and his voice changed: alert, sharp, demanding. Pure Homicide.

'Why?'

Christie grinned at his reaction. 'Why is it that a cop always answers a question with a question?'

Johnnie's face relaxed. 'Yeah, how come about that?' He held the cold glass between his hands, turning it slowly between his palms. 'I wonder how many women in New York City get anonymous phone calls every day of the week.'

Christie started to speak but her words were held back by the thoughtful expression as Johnnie Devereaux looked up at her again. 'Two of the kids got phone calls,' he said. 'The third kid, we don't know—that was the first girl murdered. She was a loner, didn't confide in anybody.' He shook his head. 'Funny calls, too. Not the usual, you know, not obscene. The second girl and the last girl told their friends they had been getting calls, pretty regularly, for a couple of weeks. Some guy would get on, just—you know, talk to them—as if he knew them.'

With great effort, Christie kept her voice normal; she spoke with nothing more than professional interest. 'You mean, just conversational phone calls: hello, how are you, how've you been? That kind of thing?'

Devereaux leaned his shoulders forward and his voice was low and clear. 'Yeah. We kept that out of the papers. Christ, imagine the wave of hysteria that would set off. Every woman in New York City would be sure that any wrong number or "funny" phone call was our murderer setting her up.'

Christie swallowed some Coke and nodded; she was glad she hadn't told Johnnie about the phone calls which had kept her awake every night for the last few weeks. 'The newspapers kept playing it up as if the three girls were definitely the victims of the same man. Is that because it sells papers, Johnnie, or do you think so too?'

'It's the same guy,' he said flatly. 'There's something the papers haven't got hold of. Each one of these kids had a lock of hair hacked from her head.' His fingers reached into his own head, which was scantily covered by the dark remnants of what had once been thick curls. 'From the back of her head'—he held his index finger and thumb before her eyes—'just about an inch or two hacked off.'

'Hacked off?'

'Coroner said probably with a knife. He could tell by the way it was cut.' He smiled, admiringly. 'That old Doc Mendel, he must be over seventy, but he spotted it with the first girl. What an autopsy that guy does; a real pro. So, of course, we alerted the other coroners to look out for that—hacked hair—on any female homicide of any kind, under any circumstances—anywhere in the city. And sure enough, these two kids: same thing, lived alone, raped, strangled, and the hair cut.'

The bright glaring sunshine stung Christie's eyes right through the green sunglasses as she walked rapidly back to the Library. The unseasonably hot temperature made the marble corridor seem air-conditioned and Christie felt a shudder right down to the small of her back. She glanced absently into a glass-enclosed phone booth set against a marble pillar, then watched, fascinated, as a man deposited his dime, waited, then dialed a number.

Anybody with a dime. It could be anybody with a dime.

Peering into the viewer in the quiet of the Library, where it was darkly cool, Christie didn't know if she were relieved or not to see the words neatly and precisely encased inside the machine: 'Representative Littlejohn Recommends Addition to State Capitol Building.' And the date, she noted with sour triumph: *October 17, 1963*. She copied down the pertinent facts, then noted the small items relative to sealed bids being accepted and then, some nine months later, the small blurb, on page 36 of the New York *Times* relative to the Gerardo Construction Company being awarded the bid.

She asked the librarian, a weary woman who kept breaking into an accommodating smile, if she could look through the 1961–1962 files, and starting in 1961, Christie peered her way through column after column until a small item appeared: 'Builder Cleared of Fraud.' The builder's name was Alfred Gerardo. He had been charged with fraudulently padding his bill on the construction of a city-owned powerplant by indicating items which, in fact, had not been used in the construction. His attorney was Ralph F. Littlejohn.

Christie's neck ached and her eyes were moist and her fingers were numb. She hoped she'd be able to read her notes later; they seemed to be getting smaller and smaller and were running off the lines of her notebook. She pressed her hand over her eyes, but she could still see the sharp tiny print behind her lids. She should continue checking back to the time the fraud charges were initiated. She should. But she would do it tomorrow, after giving Reardon her report up to date. Collecting the microfilm, snapping her pen closed, putting the notebook into her pocketbook, Christie pictured Reardon's face in response to her explanation that the job wasn't completed: Oh. I see. The *rest* of the information I need is still in the Library. Well, at least it's in a nice safe place, right?

Grinding her teeth at Reardon, Christie abruptly thrust the microfilm at the librarian, who looked wounded when there was no smile returned. She quickly muttered, 'Thank you very much, ma'am,' and the librarian's tired smile reappeared briefly.

Littlejohn-Gerardo-Gerardo-Littlejohn-fraud or whatever. Maybe if she knew *why* she was looking for something, she would be able to find *what* she was looking for and maybe if she knew *what* she was looking for she'd . . .

Christie stopped suddenly in the vastness of the Library's marble corridor. Her mind was cleared of all the tiny printed words. She leaned against the smooth wall and closed her eyes tightly, forcing herself to slow down: to let all the sounds fill her brain, the low, murmuring voices, the muted echoing footsteps, and then, the voice, soft and intimate, entered her brain in the darkness behind her eyelids, 'Hello, Christie Opara. How are you, Christie Opara?' But she did not hear the *sound* of the voice as she had strained to hear it, to define it, to identify it, night after night. She heard the *pronunciation* of her name.

Silently, Christie's lips formed her name and she opened her eyes and saw another place: the corridor outside of Special Sessions and Frank Santino with his lewd little eyes and she heard Frank Santino say her name with his particular, lazy slurring of the syllables so that it came out sounding neither Irish nor Czech, but like the word 'opera'. But it was not Frank Santino who called her every night. It was not Frank Santino's voice, it was a voice she had never heard before, coming from a man who knew her and who knew how to pronounce her name because he had heard Frank Santino say it.

Christie bit down hard on her index finger; the sharp pain intensified her sudden, complete awareness: Murray Rogoff.

Murray Rogoff had called those three girls and raped them and murdered them and hacked off pieces of their hair.

And now he's calling me.

CHAPTER FOURTEEN

MARTY GINSBURG haggled his way down Delancey Street. Haggling is a most joyous thing when done properly and with the whole heart. But there are stringent rules and requirements that must be met in order to fully pursue this ancient, complicated and respectable method of dealing with a fellow human being. The first essential is a loud voice and the second essential is a deaf ear and the third essential is a glass eye.

With these essentials, the bargainer can outshout his opponent (who does his best to outshout you); let his words of protest bounce unheard right back at him (as he does with yours); and his facial expressions, which range from cunningness to outrage, go unseen (while your expressions are similarly ignored). Of course, haggling ends at the logical, sought-for conclusion: you pay the price you originally had in mind (though well concealed) and your opponent accepts the price he originally decided upon (but would have died before revealing when the contest began). Then, each ignoring the other's moans of bitterness: Robber, thief, crook, stealing money for inferior merchandise—Depriver of my family, food from my children's mouths, roof from my family's head—the package, containing a length of multi-colored material, or sandals for a child's feet or aprons for a wife's ample middle or a hundred multi-sized screws and nails, is transferred from the seller to the buyer with glares of mutual hostility but feelings of mutual satisfaction.

Haggling is a most joyous thing and it hardly exists in its purest form any more. That was one of the reasons Marty Ginsburg loved the East Side: the old East Side which still did exist, but only in smaller and smaller areas, closing in about a tighter and tighter nucleus, hemmed and edged and encroached upon by coffee shops and art supply shops and sandal-makers and copper jewelry craftsmen pushed up from Greenwich Village and twenty-story, terraced and patioed high-rental red brick buildings, gaunt and out of place amid the colorlessness of the honest, old tenements.

Further up Delancey Street and off on the side streets, the haggling was done more and more in Spanish, furiously delivered by black-eyed, dark-skinned Puerto Ricans who were small and sharp-boned, their shrill voices indignant and righteous. Marty regretted this change with a sense of loss and deprivation. How could he possibly hope to get in on it, when the language was alien to his ear?

It felt good to dig out the childhood Yiddish, for nothing could sound as full and rich and furiously angry as bellowing at some old man, who, hawk-eyed, bellowed right back at you, snatching the piece of yard goods between you, each waiting the other out, each stomping away, then turning at just the right moment: a matter of precise timing was involved, then each confronting the other again with continued accusations and with the feigned regret of having to relent a little to the thief before him, but that was life and, God, what else could a man do.

Slowly he made his way along Delancey, then turned down Sheriff Street. Marty inhaled the warm and heavy air with all the childhood memories filling his large lungs. Not that he had ever lived on the Lower East Side. He hadn't. But the streets of his childhood Greenpoint, that pocket of Brooklyn, were the same streets after all. Marty sighed nostalgically. His kids, his four sons, were missing a hell of a lot growing up in a five-room apartment in an elevated building in Forest Hills with trees crushing them in and nothing but the sounds of jets from Kennedy and LaGuardia and all prices marked clearly on everything and no daily encounters to grow with, to learn from, to measure themselves by.

Ambling along to Rivington Street, Marty was confronted by a sight that took his breath away and called forth his spirit of challenge. The entire street was lined, on both sides, with cartons containing all manner of things: bargains! Left and right, wary old men and squinty old women alertly guarded their treasures, flexing their voices and strong tough hands against the possibility of customers.

Marty advanced steadily, not letting his eyes rest too heavily or with too great an interest on any particular item, for they watched your eyes and your eyes could give you away.

He walked past a display of bright material, ignoring the old woman who glared at him, stopped at a box of handkerchiefs (ten-for-a-dollar-pure-linen). He fingered the handkerchiefs, shrugged at the owners, who snarled at him, then cautiously, Marty worked his way back the few feet to where the yards of bright material, the flowers and color pulling at him, were watched over by a shapeless old woman whose skull was outlined by a safety-pinned kerchief. It was the red material with the blue and green palm trees that pulled at him, so of course, he lifted the corner of the white material with the green and yellow and pink polka dots, narrowing his eyes at it, pulling his mouth down at it, making an unpleasant sound at its lack of quality and beauty. Marty did this to several bolts of material, aware of the beginning rumbles from deep within the old woman's throat, until his hand rested lightly on his target, his face screwing into a look of disdain, his hand dropping the material quickly, passing on to the next bolt, then returning again to the target bolt, his mouth now asking, disinterestedly: 'How much?'

The haggling began in earnest and the old woman was a good fighter. Suddenly, she called forth an obscenity of such pure and precise and fantastic clarity that Marty's blood was warmed and delighted by a surge of half-forgotten memories, and he surrendered for that reason alone. The old woman, suspicious and somewhat flustered, bundled the length of material, folding it at crazy angles, into a used brown paper bag, thrusting it at him and taking his money without respect. She had expected better of him.

Marty stopped before the glass case which faced onto the street, regarding the rows of fish which lay in an even row on the crushed ice, their eyes like clear buttons staring back at his. Overhead was a large folding door so that at the end of the day, the wooden stand, dripping with the debris of the fast-melting ice, the glass case on its rusty wheels, the old tin scale balanced precariously on a milk box, could all be slid into the small recess of the store, the door unfolded and chained into place so that no one could make off with any of these items during the night.

The aroma of the store permeated the street for at least twenty feet in each direction and was no stronger inside the cool, yellow-lighted cubicle than outside. Detective Martin Ginsburg of the District Attorney's Squad had fused into Marty Ginsburg the glorious haggler now, and the two personalities, melded into the large, package-clutching form, entered the store and his heavy, free hand reached into the barrel within and caught the tail of a perch. He held it distastefully in the air, then dropped it back with a splash.

'These fresh this morning?' he asked the old man who was barely tall enough to see over the small counter.

'From the mountain lakes they were taken at four o'clock this morning and from Fulton Street I purchased them at five A.M. and into that barrel I placed them at five-fifteen A.M.,' the old man recited. 'Fresh they are.'

'Yeah? They don't look so fresh to me.'

'So go catch them yourself, they ain't fresh enough?'

With his free hand, Marty jiggled the barrel, peering into the dark water. 'How do I know they haven't been swimming around in there since last week?'

The old voice was sharp and hissing, beside him now. 'They ain't swimming around. They been dead for a month. A little motor inside keeps them moving.'

'I believe it,' Marty stated, grasping another tail, studying an unblinking eye.

'So don't handle the merchandise if you ain't going to buy.'

'Aw, what the hell. This one looks like he's going to croak from old age, so I'll let you do a mercy killing—it will be a kindness. How much?'

'By the pound,' the old man rasped. 'A set price—by the pound.'

They haggled just a little, eliminating the weight of the head and tail but including the weight of the guts, and the old man took the fish from Marty and handed it to his son who stood silently at his chopping board.

Marty watched the strong smooth arms rather than the bloody hands which quickly and expertly divided the fish into pieces. Hell, the guy was a giant: the muscles on his shoulders and across his back and arms were like something in one of those body-building magazines over which his oldest boy, a chubby twelve-year-old, sweated and groaned.

'Can you bone it?' Marty asked, directing his question at Murray Rogoff, but the old man, turning from the front of the store, whined, 'You want boned, you buy at the A and P.'

A small dark girl came into the shop, cautiously watching and cautiously watched. She was short and black-eyed, her figure showing through the bright sheerness of her yellow blouse: the breasts high and pointed and sharply divided; her waist, tiny, pulled in with a wide plastic yellow belt clutching the short black skirt under which, as she turned, it was apparent she wore very little. Marty's eyes rested pleasurably on the girl's backside and he nudged a friendly elbow into Murray's side. God, the guy felt like a rock.

Murray looked up, puzzled, then followed Marty's stare for a moment, then when Marty turned for his reaction, Rogoff's mouth pulled down and his eyes, or at least the glasses (you couldn't find his eyes behind those crazy glasses), went back to the fish.

Murray's father didn't haggle with the little Puerto Rican: he told her the price, it didn't please her and she left.

'What a pair on that broad, huh?' Marty said. The only response was a noncommittal grunt. 'How'd you like to get that against the ice? Turn it into boiling water in about two minutes.'

The large naked head shook. 'Not my type.'

'Not your type?' Marty asked in disbelief. 'You're kidding. Man, that's anybody's type.'

'No,' Rogoff said. 'That's dreck. That's for anybody with two bits. That's nothing. *Nothing.*'

'Well that *nothing* sure as hell did *something* to me.' Marty looked at the spot where the girl had stood.

'That's garbage,' Rogoff said quietly as he folded the newspaper package into a brown paper bag. *'Dirt.'* Marty could see his eyes now, batting rapidly behind the dirty, goggle-like glasses. They were pale and small and round and lashless: like a fish.

'Hell, nothing wrong with a little garbage now and then,' Ginsburg said, smiling lewdly. 'Not when it looks like that.'

'I wouldn't touch it with a ten-foot pole.' There was a strange smile on the smooth face now, a thoughtful look.

Marty cursed in a friendly way, using the marvelous obscenity the old woman had recalled to his vocabulary, adding, 'I would.'

'No class,' Rogoff said. 'Who wants what anybody can have?'

'Who don't?'

'Me. I don't.' Murray handed the brown paper bag to the stocky, dark-haired customer, then added in a low voice, 'Not with what I got. What I got, brother, you couldn't get near.'

Marty raised his eyebrows, licked his lips. 'Yeah? You got something good? Around here?'

Rogoff smiled. He measured the stocky figure, comparing the hefty stomach and flabby arms against his own hardness: the little runt. 'Forget it, pal. Not for you. Not when you go for *that* type.'

'Me—I go for any type, so long as it got the equipment, pal.'

Murray shook his head. 'Uh-uh. What I got is one-of-a-kind, friend. Clean and nice. The one-man kind.' His hand, closing into a fist around the money extended for the fish, pressed against his own chest. *'This man.'*

Marty accepted his change, readjusted his packages against his chest and grinned. 'Well, it takes all kinds. Me—I like all kinds, just so long as they're broads, that suits me.'

It would, Rogoff thought. He stood watching the heavyset figure in the bright-flowered shirt leave the store, looking up and down the street: looking. Murray took the dull edge of his sharp butcher knife and ran it over the wooden block, scraping the sticky remnants of guts and flesh off the edge and into the slop bucket beneath the table.

That slob. What would he know. What would *he* know about a girl like Christie. Christie Opara.

CHAPTER FIFTEEN

Christie Opara typed rapidly on the Underwood without even realizing that since Stoner Martin was in the field she could have used the Royal. She copied her notes verbatim, mindlessly letting her fingers find the keys without translating the words into meaning.

Marty Ginsburg left the office shortly after she arrived, indicating the few telephone messages he had taken for Mr. Reardon while banging over his particular report. Marty had seemed oddly quiet: no jokes, no wisecracks, not commenting, of course, on his assignment, but still unusually tight-mouthed for Marty. He seemed in a hurry to leave, ducking into Reardon's empty office, leaving his report on the boss's desk and asking Christie to notify Reardon of that fact when he arrived.

She lifted her fingers to her face for a moment: she would notify Reardon of a fact today all right. She didn't plan what she was going to say: she couldn't. It would just have to come to her at the moment. She understood herself well enough to realize that if she tried to phrase it now, it would come out wrong then. If she tried to anticipate the sharp questions he would ask, she would not be able to find the instinctive answers that were somewhere inside of her, waiting.

The voice—*Rogoff's—she knew*—had taken to speaking a little more now: 'Is this Christie Opara? How are you, Christie? Are you all right? Why do you work so late? Take care of yourself. I worry about you.' And then, last night, before the sharp, disconnecting click, 'I love you, Christie Opara.'

And her own voice, after asking, 'Who is this?' had responded to his questions carefully, 'I am fine. Don't worry about me. Thanks for calling.' Resisting the temptation to say it, breathing it down, 'How are you, Murray Rogoff?' because she didn't know what would happen then and she didn't want to take the chance, because this was more than phone calls in the night and was heading somewhere else and it had begun and she had to ride it out to the end.

She typed another paragraph, then flexed her fingers and kneaded her wrists, her right wrist aching in a peculiar, sympathetic pain: Poor Mickey, breaking his wrist. Just leaping down the two steps in front of the house in joy at being invited by the neighborhood kids to full partnership in their lemonade stand (I was going to bring the sugar, Mom) and his sneakered foot catching and his hands shooting out and his wrist cracking. Nora, feeling just the way she could be expected to feel: when it's your own child, it's bad enough, but when it's your grandchild, it's worse. And Christie, comforting Nora: but it could have happened anytime, if I were there or not, you know that. Kids run and kids jump and kids twist and kids fall. And kids break their wrists.

Christie wanted to be home, right now home, with Mickey, she needed to see his bright daytime face. Knowing he was comfortable, knowing he was busy and happy and not complaining over his games and coloring books wasn't enough: his voice on the telephone wasn't enough. She wanted to be home with him, not here, finishing this completely senseless report, preparing to confront Reardon with her completely senseless, yet absolute, definite, positive conclusions on this other matter. This Rogoff matter.

Christie felt both a relief and a tensing when Tom Dell entered the office.

That meant Reardon was around.

'Hi, Tom. Boss back?'

Dell pushed his hat back from his forehead. He was a dapper man and always looked as though he'd just had a shower, suit press and shoeshine. He never gave out any information about his boss's comings, goings, appointments, conversations or overheard remarks, but the question of whether or not Reardon was about to appear was legitimate so he answered, 'Yeah, he's talking to some guy in the hallway.' He moved his head to the side. 'Ah, the mighty footsteps are approaching.'

Dell carefully placed his hat on the aluminium rack, took out his report form and began transferring the mileage and gas information from his notebook to the official, required form.

Reardon scanned the room.

'Empty house?'

'Not quite,' Christie said. 'I'm completing this report, Mr. Reardon. I think this will wrap it up.' Then, anticipating him, she added quickly, 'For now.'

Reardon smiled: she was learning. 'Good.'

'Marty Ginsburg left a report on your desk—and asked me to give you these telephone messages.'

'Right.'

Christie checked her completed report carefully, stapled the sets of papers together, read it over, giving Reardon time to attend to the matters on his desk and herself time to think how she would begin but no words came, just the soft voice: 'Hello, Christie Opara,' but maybe that was enough.

She tapped lightly on his door, taking the grunting sound from within as permission to enter. She took one long full breath, holding it until she sat in the chair before his desk, releasing it slowly as he reached for her report, then looked at her, still sitting there, in some surprise.

'I'd like to talk to you for a moment, Mr. Reardon, if you're not too busy.'

She caught the impatient glance as he consulted his watch, but he said, 'I'm busy, but go ahead. What's the problem?'

It didn't start to come, not yet. She searched for a moment, trying to find the right words and she was startled when he asked, directly, 'Is it about the phone calls?'

'Yes.' She nodded at him; there was a hollowness in her throat and she bit down hard on her teeth.

'Let's have it.'

Christie ran her hand over her eyes feeling the silence around her. She had wanted her voice to come out strong and certain, not trembling; hating the sound of her words, she said, 'I know who it is.'

'Who?'

'Murray Rogoff.' She added, 'The 1140 I locked up a few weeks ago. You remember?'

There was no biting wisecrack, no caustic, 'Yeah, how could I forget?' Reardon just nodded at her.

'Murray Rogoff,' she repeated softly, and saying his name aloud, to Reardon now, not just inside her own brain where it had been echoing around for nearly a week, released the hidden words. She leaned forward, her fingers grasping the edge of his desk. 'Mr. Reardon, I want to say something now that you can probably cut into ribbons with a few questions, but I'm going to say it anyway.'

'Go ahead. Say what you want to say.'

She raised her face to his and her voice was steady and unshaken and certain. 'Murray Rogoff murdered those three girls.' Her fingers shot up, ticking them off. 'The one in Greenwich Village last February, the one on Riverside Drive in March, the one in the Bronx this month.'

Reardon watched the paling of her face, aware that she was saying something now that had been eluding her the way the solution to a game-puzzle eludes your brain: all the facts present, the answer contained in your knowledge yet your mind not able to cut through the extraneous matter to the logical words, then all at once, the answer standing there, inside your head: clear and undeniable. She hadn't said: I *think* or he *might* be or *possibly* is. She had said: *Murray Rogoff murdered those three girls.*

'You sound positive.'

'I am positive.'

Considering her for a moment, he tapped his pen against his teeth, then, with no challenge in his voice, just a logical question, he asked, 'Court positive?'

She wavered, shook her head, her voice lower, but her eyes not leaving his. 'No. Not *court* positive. But *positive*.'

She waited for his barrage of questions, for his fine, precise legal mind to destroy her certainty, but he just told her to go on and spell it out for him and Christie told him about her conversation with Johnnie Devereaux; about the victims' phone calls; about the scraps of hair, and then about the pronunciation of her name.

'Do you recognize his voice when he calls?'

Impatiently, Christie shook her head. 'No. The voice is what got me hung up; I tried too hard with the voice. I never heard Rogoff speak; he was silent when I locked him up and silent in court. I missed the pronunciation of my name completely, but it was there all the time—just the way Santino says it.'

Reardon walked from his desk to the window, the silence broken by his clicking some coins together in his trouser pocket. He stood for a long time, then turned, walked to his desk and removed a folder from the bottom drawer.

'Here,' he said, tossing the folder at her, 'read this.'

Frowning, puzzled, waiting for some hard laughter, some nasty comment, she took the folder, opened it absently, her eyes racing without comprehension over the typed words. She looked at him blankly.

'It's a background report that Stoney prepared for me last week. *On Murray Rogoff*. Christ, Opara, close your mouth.' He picked up Marty's report, shoving it across the desk at her. 'When you finish reading Stoney's investigation, read Ginsburg's. He made an observation on Rogoff yesterday.' Reardon ran his hand over his face, down, then up, then back through the thick red hair, then rubbed his knuckles under his chin. His voice seemed irritable but at the same time weary. 'You know, Opara, you really knock me out. I mean, it really never even *occurred* to you that possibly, *just possibly*, by some miracle maybe or even by some long years of experience, out of habit, your old boss might have sat quietly one afternoon and given just some slight thought to the problem of your phone calls, et cetera.' He smiled tightly and held his hand up. 'Oh, not because I was interested on *your* behalf, or *concerned* or anything like that—hell, no. More likely because I felt I'd better do something to stop your sleepless nights since you've been goofing off during working hours—carrying over assignments that should be completed in one day.' He leaned his chin on his hands, pressing his elbows on the desk. 'So, giving me some credit for my long years in this business, let's say that the possibilities went through my mind, and that one of the possibilities was Rogoff.'

Reardon stopped speaking and dug a coin from his trouser pocket. His eyes still on Christie, he spun the dime on his desk, then abruptly slammed the palm of his hand over it and leaned forward. His voice forced her eyes from his hand back to his face. 'Approximately ten million people have access to your phone number every day in New York City. When you begin with ten million possibilities, you have to narrow it down a little, right? Rogoff was the only collar you've made since you've been in the Squad and Rogoff is a degenerate and he was the first possibility.' He leaned back, slipped the dime into his pocket and watched her closely. 'Do you want me to spell out in detail the various reasons I felt a run-down on Rogoff should be done?' His voice was patronizing now and he ignored her terse 'no'. 'Hell, I'd be glad to lay it all out for you; even tell you what I was planning to do if we hit a blank wall with Murray.'

She still had that incredulous, half-comprehending expression on her face and Reardon felt anger or pride, or whatever the hell it was, rising to his lips. 'Tell me something, Opara,' he said sharply, 'what the hell impresses you?'

'Competence,' she said evenly. 'Professional competence.'

The anger, unexplained, forced the words from him. 'Then why is it that you seem to feel you're the only one around here with the slightest amount of professional competence?' Stopping himself, not needing her acknowledgment, yet oddly annoyed at her lack of recognition, he irritably gestured at her, 'Go on—go on, read!'

Dropping her eyes to the papers on her lap, Christie said, 'Yes, sir.'

Her eyes raced over the words, then deliberately slowed down, picking out the meanings. She gnawed on her pinky absently, reading Stoney's precise background report which took the infant Murray Rogoff home from Bellevue Hospital Maternity Ward, where he had been born on February 1, 1930, son of Hyman and Gilda (maiden name: Posner) Rogoff; weight: 8 lbs. 6 ounces; 21 inches long; other children: 1; father's occupation: fish store owner; mother's occupation: housewife.

Education: elementary school, where he had been an average student; junior high school, where he had been an average student, but excelled at sports. Into high school, where he had been a low-average student, but had developed into a star athlete. And then the school records stopped after he had completed his third year of high school.

The medical record picked up where the school record left off and copied verbatim from the Medical Records-Bellevue Emergency was the following: August 2, 1946; 12:45 A.M.; Murray Rogoff; 136 Rivington Street, N.Y.C.; place of occurrence: Delancey Street, in front of Loew's Delancey; nature of injury: patient in comatose state; possible skull fracture; witnesses to accident: David Rogoff (bro.), same address; Sol Weissman, 138 Rivington Street, N.Y.C. Notations: patient, male, white, 16 yrs., removed from scene of accident by ambulance; remains in comatose state; apparently well-nourished, good physical condition; no evidence alcohol. Patient's brother states patient slipped while engaging in 'horseplay' at location of accident. Dr. J. Gonzalez-ambulance attendant; patient removed to Intensive Care Rm.—Dr. Fogel supervising.

The Aided Card: prepared by Patrolman K. Nugent, Shield No. 130567, officer not on scene when accident occurred, containing a terse account as stated above.

Notation: August 5, 1946—patient semi-comatose, complaining of intense headache across forehead. August 6, 1946, patient fully conscious, removed to Ward 6; taking food and medication well. X ray reveals hairline fracture, lower cranium. Patient comfortable, uncomplaining, resting well. August 12, 1946, patient complaining of severe pain in eyes; examined by Dr. J. Gold, ophthalmologist, who removed several lashes from each of patient's eyes; patient reported to supervising physician some significant hair loss from head and pubic area; August 13, 1946, patient examined by Dr. Leonardi, neurologist, who reports no significant findings. August 18, 1946, patient considered physically fit for discharge, but noticeably disturbed by continuing hair loss. Seen this date by Dr. Loeb, psychiatrist.

Stoney's report continued: undersigned spoke this date with Dr. Loeb who reported that all information contained in his interviews with subject was considered privileged and confidential. Then, without further notation or explanation, Stoney's report continued, spelling out the 'privileged and confidential' information he had obtained—somehow—from Dr. Loeb.

Dr. Loeb first saw subject, Murray Rogoff, on August 18, 1946, date subject was due to be discharged from hospital. He described subject, a boy of 16, as a very well-developed physical specimen, apparently in excellent health, but very agitated by the significant loss of hair he was experiencing. Dr. Loeb advised subject to leave hospital and remain on Out-Patient basis; further scheduled tests to determine cause and possible cure of said condition. It was noted that a 'differential diagnosis' was recorded on subject's medical file. [Then, in parentheses, Stoney Martin, knowing Reardon's impatience and unwillingness to consult the Medical Dictionary, had spelled out] this means that cause of subject's hair loss had not been determined and a series of tests was scheduled to eliminate possible causes and hopefully to arrive at a definite cause; subject continued under supervisory care of Dr. Loeb, returning to Out-Patient Department three times a week for tests given by Neurology Department and Department of Internal Medicine.

September 1, 1946: patient fitted with special moisture glasses to protect his eyes, which are now devoid of lashes; apparent damage to tear ducts; eyes tearless, burning, dry.

Dr. Loeb noted that patient seemed more hostile and uncommunicative at each visit; very agitated and angry at inability of doctors to pinpoint cause of hair loss. Though it was explained to patient that the injury he suffered did not seem instrumental in causing this hair loss, patient feels that skull injury was motivating force. Patient bitterly disturbed by loss of status within his social group; at first visit, patient bragged considerably about his female conquests, now describes all females as 'dirty, filthy'. Patient seems unable to accept what has happened to him and is building a wall of protective hostility and resentment around himself.

Patient last seen on October 15, 1946, after missing three previously scheduled appointments; physical changes in subject are evident in his carriage and uncertain manner; he wore a cap which he refused to remove; holds his head down; mumbles; patient completely hairless now; informs he has quit school; spends his time working with his father in his fish store; sleeping; 'just walking around'; when queried as to his sexual activities, patient became highly agitated, used obscene language and said 'that's my business'. Patient failed to keep any subsequent appointments, though patient's brother was seen once, on November 3, 1946. Brother reports patient is most disturbed and abusive to him, his parents and customers in the store, yet refuses to return for any counseling.

When Dr. Loeb was asked by undersigned [Stoney's report continued] if such a patient might, at some future time, resort to acts of sexual violence, Dr. Loeb said he could not, with any accuracy, based on his knowledge of subject, make such a prediction but that the possibility could not be eliminated from any prognosis.

Christie placed the report face down on Reardon's desk and reached for Marty's report without looking up at Reardon.

Detective Ginsburg's report was brief but informative: 'Subject expressed no interest in female customer who entered store while undersigned was present. Undersigned engaged subject in conversation relative to types of females who are of interest to him and it is the conclusion of undersigned that subject has one particular female in mind, such conclusion being based upon subject's saying to undersigned, "What I got, friend, is one of a kind. Clean and nice." (The word jumped out at Christie as though it were typed in capital letters.) "The one-man kind." Then subject indicated himself, saying, "This man."

'It is the opinion of undersigned,' Marty's report informed her, 'that subject is not interested in the females abroad in streets of his resident neighborhood but that subject has another female in mind, and is possibly involved with this female or had some contact with her, although there is the possibility that this female is all in subject's mind, since he is a very weird-looking person.'

Reardon spoke the moment she finished reading Marty's report. 'Marty isn't eloquent but he is sharp. By the way,' he said slowly, 'I didn't tell Marty *why* or *what*. I just told him to go down and strike up a conversation with Rogoff and see how he feels about girls in general.' He watched her face; Christ, he could see right into her. She *had* been sore when he sent her out for information without telling her why. 'You see,' he continued, his eyes darkening, 'when you know *what* you're looking for, you tend to find it. You tend to steer in that particular direction. This way, when I get a report, it's more or less objective and unbiased: *I* know what I have—even if *you* don't know *why*.' Raising his chin slightly, he said pointedly, 'Not that you deserve any explanation, Opara. I just threw that in gratis.' He admired the fact that she didn't pretend, just nodded. Her face reddened though. She had been put in her place and she sat there, defenseless, acknowledging it. There is something about this girl, Reardon thought, but not letting it show. His face could be any kind of mask he wanted it to be and he wanted nothing but professional authority to show now.

'Okay, Christie, spell it out for me. What have we got?' He leaned back, motionless in his chair, watching the hesitation. Not doubt, just a careful search for the right words.

'*Rogoff. We got Rogoff.*'

Wordlessly, he shook his head.

'All right: not yet. But we are going to get him.' She leaned her hands on the desk and her words were defiant. '*I am going to get him.*'

His first impulse was to cut her down. He could, of course, with a swift change of expression, a few sharp, probing questions. But he didn't respond to her tone, just watched her face, and a different feeling came to him now because the tense firmness and certainty with which she had spoken revealed something else. She was so goddamn vulnerable, like a little kid who sees something wrong and without hesitation or self-doubt, knowing that it must be made right, simply says: here's what must be done and *I* must do it.

'How?'

She pulled in her lower lip, bit down on it, then pushed it out. 'I'm not sure yet, but . . .'

He cut her off rapidly. 'Well, hey, I'm glad to hear that there is still at least a question of *method* in your mind. You're so damn sure of everything else, it's nice to know you do have at least a little doubt.'

'Not about Rogoff,' she shot back, 'not about him.'

'All right. Let's run over what we have. Three murdered girls: they are a fact. Raped and strangled and no witnesses, no fingerprints, no tangible evidence at the scene to link any suspect to them, right?'

'Right.'

'A murderer: unknown.' He saw her mouth begin to move, but she remained silent. 'Repeat: *unknown*. He is a fact, right?'

'Right.'

'Okay. Now we got Rogoff: a known degenerate. You locked him up as an exhibitionist, but he has no previous record.'

'That doesn't mean anything—that just means it was the first time he was caught.'

His eyes searched the ceiling, his voice not containing his anger. 'You going to teach me something or are we going to discuss the situation?'

'Sorry.'

'Damn it. All right. The murderer is in one way or another a sexual deviate; there have been arguments both ways relative to the progressive acts of exhibitionists: some say he turns rapist or molester, some say not. Now, we have the phone calls, which began shortly after you locked up Rogoff. You think it's Rogoff calling . . .'

'*I know.*'

'Will you just shut up, Opara?' Reardon stood up, walked to the couch, eased himself the length of the green leather, his head and feet propped on opposite armrests, his hand resting lightly over his eyes. 'Just keep quiet, all right? Now, let's *assume* that your caller *is* Rogoff. His calls aren't obscene or threatening. He just asks how you are, et cetera. *Assuming* it's Rogoff and assuming we could prove it's him, what have we got?' He waited for a moment, then answered his own question, 'Nothing, right?'

Grudgingly, she said, 'Right, but . . .'

'No *buts*.' He uncovered his eyes, raising his head. '*Nothing*. Even if the calls take a nasty turn and we bag him on an obscenity charge, that would be it, right? There's no physical evidence, no nail scrapings, nothing from the murder scenes.' He eased himself up, so that he was resting on his elbows. 'So where are we?'

The totally unexpected coldness of her voice forced him into a rigid alertness. 'I think you know where we are as well as I do, Mr. Reardon.'

'No,' he said, unmoving, 'you tell me.'

'We have to bait a trap,' she said, 'and you are looking at the bait.' Her chin rose slightly and she seemed devoid of any emotion. 'Rogoff selected me. Okay. Let's set it up.'

He knew she had spoken with the clear, professional logic of a good police officer: yet, why was it, Reardon wondered, that every time she opened her mouth, every word hit him as some kind of a personal challenge? Controlling his voice so that he would not engage her, he asked, 'What did you have in mind?'

She frowned. 'I really hadn't thought it through. Just that it seems the only way.' She held her hand up, practically into his face, and Reardon, resisting the urge to grab that hand (and do what?) jammed his fists into his pockets, standing now, half leaning against the desk before her. But she wasn't watching him; she was digging inside her mind, recalling whatever facts she felt she had to have. 'Last night, he said something he's never said before. He—he said that he loved me.'

'I can't imagine why.'

Her eyes did a slow stare, then a deliberate blink, dismissing his remark.

The fresh little bastard.

Ignoring his closeness, yet speaking to him, she said, 'I don't respond to anything he says.' Then altering that quickly, 'I mean, I do answer, but nothing that would lead him on. That wouldn't be right—that would be entrapment.'

Reardon nodded solemnly. 'Oh, absolutely that wouldn't be right.' They were talking about a suspect in three rape-murders. Reardon ran his tongue over his front teeth.

'He's been watching me somehow, so he knows . . .'

'*Watching you?* You never said anything about that before.' The District Attorney's voice accused the witness of withholding vital information.

Christie shook her head impatiently. 'No, no, I haven't spotted him or anything. But he *has* to be watching me, because he always calls just about thirty or forty minutes after I get home.' Her eyes narrowed and she was speaking more to herself than to him. 'He must be somewhere around the subway station because there aren't any phone booths near my house. He probably gives me about ten minutes to get home, then time to shower and . . . et cetera.'

'Has he ever called when you weren't there?'

'Yes, twice. Nora, my mother-in-law, answered. One night, Marty drove me home, one night Bill Ferranti dropped me off.' She snapped her fingers. 'That must be it. He watches the subway station. He didn't see me come home, so he called.'

'Did he speak to Nora?'

'Yes—asked if I were home. She just said I was out.' Reardon's brows went up questioningly. 'Nora knows about the calls. I told her to just put him off without any further conversation. He thanked her both times and hung up, but didn't call me back.'

Christie closed her eyes, completely unaware of him, standing there so close that the fabric of her dress, a light nylon jersey paisley print of wildly contrasting pinks and oranges, brushed against his knee as she moved, shifting in the chair. Observing the concentration, Reardon had the oddest feeling: as if they were two little kids and that any moment she would open her eyes and instruct him: 'and then you must be the daddy, and when you come home from work, I'll say . . .' But her eyes snapped open and she told him, 'We could use Nora. She could give him a message.'

'Like what?'

It rushed from her fully conceived. 'Well, that I moved. We could stake out a place. I did some research at the library on the other murders. The one in the Village and the one in upper Manhattan. Each girl lived alone in a ground floor apartment and entry had been through a back window.'

His voice was lightly taunting. 'Did you research on *my* time?'

Earnestly, she shook her head. 'No, sir. *After* I did my assignment.'

'I bet. Go on, don't let me stop you.'

'We could stake out a place. Ground floor, back window, then when he calls, Nora could tell him that I moved and give him the address and apartment number.' She seemed to have run out of breath and words at the same time.

'Yeah? Then what?'

'Then,' she said, slowed down and steadied by reality, 'it would be up to him.'

Reardon, eyes on his shoes, watched his feet move from the desk, watched the shiny black leather tips stop alongside the radiator which was built into the windowsill. He raised his head, vacantly looking down to the street.

Christie didn't break the silence, but sat waiting, suddenly certain that he was standing there, gathering ammunition, that he would whirl around now, his face set into an angry grin, his voice nasty and sharp as steel, and his words would tear everything but her knowledge into useless little pieces. But he turned around, finally, slowly, and his face was thoughtful.

'I'll think about it,' he said.

That was even worse than his sarcasm because that was a way of dismissing it, that was absolutely nowhere. She wondered why he added sharply, 'I didn't say *no*. I said I'll think about it. There is a matter of communication involved.'

'Communication? With who?' she demanded.

'Did you ever hear of Homicide? Or did you intend to handle this whole thing single-o?'

'Do *they* have to get into it?' She regretted the question before it was completed, regretted it more, as he sat, his eyes glowing at her like darts.

He flung words at her like accusations. 'Homicide's business is homicide. We're not looking to take over anybody's case.' Her lips moved, but he spoke too quickly for her. 'Don't say a *word*, Opara, don't even open your mouth. Relax—nobody's going to take anything away from you. *If*, after a conference with the other people involved in this, I decide to pursue this case along the lines we've discussed, you're in it.' You're damn right: that's what she was saying, with her mouth set and tight and her eyes blazing back at him. Reardon's finger jabbed the air. 'But as part of a team. You got that? *As part of a team!*'

'*Right!*' She threw *his* word, in *his* tone, into his face. Reardon curled his fingers tightly; he wanted, more than anything in the world at that particular moment, to walk around the desk and grab her by the shoulders and shake her until her teeth rattled. Or something. He glanced, unseeing, at his watch, then snatched up some papers, his head bent down, then raised his eyes to her.

'You still here?' Blush; go ahead, damn it. Yes, I *do* see it; that kills you doesn't it? He watched her hesitate at the door. 'Yeah? You got something *else* on your mind?'

He could see the struggle and he knew she would say whatever it was even though she knew she should just keep her mouth shut and keep going.

One long deep breath drawn in and carefully released, then her voice a little thin, but with no tremor, 'Mr. Reardon, whatever happens in this case,' a pause, then her words an undeniable demand, '*Rogoff is mine!*'

Reardon let the papers fall flatly before him, his words and reactions catching in his throat, then unnecessary because he could see that, wordless, he had given his message and she could probably still feel his eyes reaching after her behind the closed door, down the corridor to whatever section of the Squad office she had retreated to.

His eyes remained fixed on the door, as though Christie were still standing there telling him: telling *him* how it was going to be. Reardon whistled angrily through his teeth, then cursed softly and steadily, pulled open the bottom drawer, swept all the papers from his desk in haphazard disarray, then kicked the drawer closed.

That fresh little bitch might very well get herself raped and murdered. If not by Murray Rogoff maybe by Casey Reardon.

CHAPTER SIXTEEN

NORA OPARA was the damnedest grandmother Casey Reardon had ever met. He was momentarily taken off guard by the stunningly bright appearance of the small figure and at first had the impression of a faceless mannikin dressed in a slacks set of unbelievable color combinations. Reardon's taste was not sophisticated enough to accept bold, jagged squares of clear greens and yellows against pure deep pink, but focusing on the woman's face, it was evident that the colors could not overwhelm her. Everything about her was vivid and clearly defined: the eyes, so definite a blue as to make any other blue eyes slightly questionable, the hair a pure white with no hint or trace of what the original color had been, the nose, short and finely shaped, and the bright, healthy pink of her skin were memorable.

Her hand, when he introduced himself, gave his a good firm grasp and she led him quickly into the living room. At first glance, the room might seem to be disordered or untended, but as Nora bent down, rolling up a long narrow mat, Reardon could see that it was, rather, a lived-in room. Without apology, she told him, 'This is my yoga mat. Ever stand on your head, Casey?'

She used his first name casually and naturally as though they were well acquainted. Reardon grinned. 'Last time, Nora, I think I was about twelve years old. I remember that it made me dizzy.'

She held the mat under her arm and told him, 'That passes in a few minutes; it's great for the circulation. And for brain power, fills all the cells with blood.' She leaned over the couch and called, 'Mickey, look up from your picture for a minute and say hello to Mr. Reardon.'

She motioned Reardon beside her and he looked down at the small boy, who was stretched on his stomach, paintbrush over a large sheet of paper on the carpeted floor.

'*That's* Mr. Reardon?'

His voice was so innocently revealing and Nora's reaction to it was so natural that Reardon felt delighted by them. Her hand shot up to her forehead, covered her eyes and then she said softly, '*Tact:* yes, we have to add that to the list of things.' Then to the boy, 'Mickey, remind me to add the word "tact" to the list of things you and I have to discuss in private.'

Reardon caught the quick half-grin and nod the boy gave his grandmother. He cleared his throat and said softly, 'I get the very definite impression that someone in this house has much maligned my good name.'

Although he didn't understand the words, the boy sensed that his grandmother and the redhaired man seemed to be friendly towards each other. Mickey stood up after carefully placing his paintbrush in the jar of blackish water and accepted the large hand that was offered to him.

'Well, how do you do, Mickey Opara.'

The child corrected the pronunciation of his name, and Reardon, serious and polite, repeated the name properly. He noted the firm grip of the small left hand. 'How'd you break your arm, Mickey?'

The boy watched Reardon closely, trying to measure the angry, overheard remarks of his mother against this smiling man. Standing his ground firmly, his feet wide apart, the large light blue eyes an exact replica of his grandmother's, Reardon noted, the boy drew in his bottom lip for a moment, then pushed it out. It was a deliberate pause before speaking and it was familiar to Reardon: not a hesitation, just a consideration.

'The step tripped me,' the child said.

Reardon didn't smile. 'Hey, that was a mean thing for it to do. It must be tough to paint left-handed. Can I have a look at your picture?'

Nora noted that he hadn't fallen into the typical adult mistake of trying to interpret what the boy was painting; he just squatted down and admired the colors without being patronizing. Reardon glanced up at Nora and nodded just once, a very quick movement of his head which indicated his approval not of the picture but of what he had sensed and observed between the two of them.

'How do you like your Scotch, Casey?' Nora asked, expecting his answer.

'On the rocks, please,' Reardon told her, enjoying the opportunity to look openly around the room. The atmosphere was not what he had expected from two widows living with one small boy. There was no overpowering femininity, nothing that clearly marked the absence of a man. The room was long and wide and bright: the walls stark white (very different from the soft beiges and golds of Reardon's own, more formal home). The unexpected hot colors didn't lurch out: the plaid soft facing him, a bright orange and pink, covered with an assortment of pillows, wasn't the kind of furnishing he would have chosen, yet, set in this room, it seemed right and pleasing. The chair he sat in was a deep burnt orange and the tables, holding large wood and iron lamps, were of dark Spanish carved wood. Bookshelves ranged along the long wall, from floor to ceiling, holding a large collection of books of all kinds. Casey's eyes skimmed titles and subject matter: from popular novels to classics to history to current events. There was a large group of art books and, without being told, he knew those were Nora's as were the paintings grouped over the low bench on which was set a portable TV. He could see the small but clear signature in the lower right-hand corner: 'Nora '64'; 'Nora '63'; 'Nora '66'. And then, unexpectedly, 'Christie '64'. He rose, came closer to Christie's painting: it was an ocean scene; the strokes were firm and strong and somehow angry at their inability to draw the energy from beneath the waves which crashed against a sunlit boulder.

'Your mother paints, too?' he asked. Mickey nodded wordlessly. Reardon studied the small collection of photographs on the brick mantel of the fireplace. Mickey, small and sturdy, staring into the camera, apparently disturbed at play. Mickey, standing thigh-high against Christie whose legs were deeply tanned against the white shorts. Reardon reached out, taking the photograph of a young patrolman from the mantel. It was Mickey's face, fixed in manhood; the eyes wide and steady, the jaw square and strong, the mouth smiling just a bit. Reardon glanced down at the boy and replaced the only evident photograph of his father. He had his father's dark hair, too; nothing, physically, of his mother; yet, looking at him, catching the concentration, the hard pressing of his lips together, and then meeting the questioning glance of the child, catching the slowly changing look of challenge crossing the boy's face, there was no mistaking Christie's son. The boy, hearing a car horn blast twice, leaped to his feet, his face now exploding into a smile.

'That's Uncle Pete,' he explained, dashing from the room. Nora came, handing Casey his drink, carrying a highball for herself. There was a loud burst of sound from the hallway, moving into the living room. Mickey was enthroned perilously on the shoulders of one of the handsomest men Reardon had ever seen. He moved easily and with an athlete's grace, extending his hand to Reardon as Nora introduced them. The black eyes, smiling along with the wide mouth, told Reardon Christie's brother had never heard of him. Whatever was discussed in this house stayed in this house.

Mickey's uncle bent down easily, letting the boy scoop up his small overnight case. They left in a roar of masculine joking which echoed back into the house until the car pulled away.

'No family resemblance there at all,' Reardon commented, his head tilted toward the door, 'between Christie and her brother.'

'You should see Christopher Choriopoulous: he and Christie are ringers. Two Swedes and two Greeks,' Nora said. 'That's what Christie's father used to call them—his Swedes and his Greeks.'

'Interesting combination; two fair and two dark.'

Nora sipped at her drink, then put it carefully on the cocktail table before the couch, and without preliminary she said, 'Christie was born on Grand Central Parkway. The family was coming back from Jones Beach one hot summer evening. They were all tired and happy; Christie wasn't due for about three weeks.' Nora regarded the glass thoughtfully, then looked into Reardon's face, her eyes pure and intent. 'An old man, well over seventy, lost control of his car. Heart attack, probably. There was a head-on collision and Christie's father delivered his only daughter in the back of the family's station wagon.' She hesitated a moment, then added, 'Her mother died before they reached the hospital. Never even saw Christie. The doctors were surprised that the delivery went as well as it did, but Christie was a tough little character; right from the start.'

Reardon, holding the cold wide glass between his palms, his face serious and not showing any question, sat listening: and waiting.

'Christie's told me about this case, of course, and about what is involved in the stake-out. I guess you know how she feels about doing this job.'

Reardon's hands moved, rolling the glass. 'She's been sweating it out for this past week, I know that. There were a lot of conferences, a lot of arrangements to be made. I know she's anxious to get this done, if that's what you mean.'

There was something in Nora's voice that made Reardon lean forward just slightly, his mind sharply alerted for the information he sensed she would convey. She nodded her head. 'Yes, she's anxious to get it done. Christie has a *need* to finish what she's started.' Nora's small hands hugged the back of her neck, and she leaned her head back for a moment; then, her head came forward, her eyes closed as she began speaking, her voice oddly flat, as though this needed telling and there was just one way to tell it, she said directly, 'Mickey never saw his father. He was conceived the night before my son, Mike, was killed—in the line of duty, as I'm sure you know.' Her blue eyes were wide now, dry and wide. 'It was two months before Christie even knew she was pregnant. That was when we decided to join forces, so to speak: I had this house—it's where Mike was raised. We talked it over and decided to take the chance.' She smiled. 'And it was a chancy thing no matter how you look at it, but it worked. We've made a life here for the three of us, and Mickey gets his share of masculine company, what with three uncles all the size of Pete—he does pretty well.'

'I'm sure he does,' Reardon said. He knew he would be surprised by nothing Nora said; she was a completely honest woman and used to speaking her mind. 'Go on, Nora. You haven't reached it yet, have you?'

The blue eyes narrowed, showing the only lines on her face: the crinkling laugh lines. 'Okay, Casey Reardon: Christie *has* to go through this case, even if it involves considerable risk.' She glanced at her hands for a moment, then back at him, moving her legs under her now. '*Particularly* if it involves risk.'

'I'm not too sure I understand what that means.'

'Relax, Casey; she isn't *looking* for unnecessary risk; not that.' Her eyes searched somewhere over his head for a moment. 'Let me try and explain it: Christie's life began with the death of her mother; that was a loss she didn't really experience in the true sense. She never had a mother, so she couldn't really conceive of a *loss*. But,' she said softly, 'there *was* a loss. Mike's death was a true loss, the worst kind for a woman. Two years ago, Christie's father was killed. He was a construction crew chief and he was killed on the job.'

She was getting closer to it now, but still not stating it; Reardon put his drink on the table beside him, his voice quiet and patient. 'Spell it out for me, Nora—the point.'

'The point: Christie lost three people—all in premature ways, all more or less through violence. Now, Christie has to face it for herself; it involves her personally and she has to be there and prove to herself that she can beat it. *Death*, Casey, *violent death*.

He visualized the tense young face, defiant, angry, demanding: *Murray Rogoff is mine.* He had known there was something deeper, something more personal involved than an arrest. He had known it was something more important to her than the arguments he had advanced when the Chief of Detectives told him to keep her out of it (you don't need a dame lousing things up if the action gets rough). He had taken two definite approaches with the Chief: first, pointing out that as a Squad member, she had the right to follow up on what was essentially *her* case. Then, realizing that the Chief of Detectives was not interested in a Squad member's right, Reardon hit on the case itself: unless Opara was there, in the room, they would be in a position to nail Rogoff for nothing more than breaking and entering: her presence was essential to the case they were trying to build. Yet, all during that particular discussion, Reardon himself did not fully understand why it was so essential to Christie that she be there. Quietly, he said, 'Yes, Nora. Yes, I think you're right.'

Nora took a long, slow drink, then held the cold glass against her forehead. For the first time, an expression of concern drew her dark brows down. 'You won't let anything happen to her, will you, Casey?'

'Hell, no,' he said rapidly, 'that would make some publicity for the Squad: "lady cop raped and murdered on official stake-out"!'

His hard laughter joined hers and she told him, 'With that remark, Casey Reardon, I now believe *everything* I have been told about you.'

It was not a thoughtless remark, blurted out; it was an indication of Nora Opara's honesty and the fact that she expected the same from him. Reardon tipped his glass toward her, swallowed, then consulted his wristwatch at the melodious chiming which filled the room. 'That will be Sam Farrell. Twenty minutes late.'

Nora stopped by his chair before going to the door and her face, though smiling, was somehow serious. 'I just wanted you to know, Casey: Christie is someone *very special.*'

Reardon said, 'I know that.' His voice was light again. 'A little fresh, but special.'

Farrell filled the living room with heavy breathing and noise, rocking his head in despair over the flat tire he had had to deal with en route from the Bronx. 'Second flat in a week, Mr.

Reardon, and the car is only six months old. I think I ought to go back to the dealer, I mean, I don't think two flats should happen to a car that new, you know?'

While Nora went to get Farrell some coffee, Reardon briskly went over his instructions. 'Now, Sam, as soon as the phone rings, Mrs. Opara will take the call upstairs and you lift the receiver in here. You know how to set up the tape recorder, don't you?' A heavy doubt, somewhere in the pit of his stomach, prompted the question, but it was dispelled, not by Farrell's prompt reassurances but by the remembered words of Stoner Martin (he's a little clumsy, boss, but you can count on Sam). 'Okay, Sam, now you record *everything*. Now, *if* and *when* the call comes from our suspect, you have the phone number up at the stake-out, right?' Farrell dug into his pockets, coming up with a slip of paper. 'Keep that right by the phone; when you get the call we're expecting, dial right away, give the word to Stoney or Ginsburg or Ferranti, then play back the conversation for them and that's it, right?'

'Yes, sir, Mr. Reardon. Hey, you want to listen a minute, I'll play back what we just said.'

In surprise, Reardon heard his own voice and Farrell's and he was pleased because he hadn't even noticed that Farrell had set the compact tape recorder on the table beside the telephone.

'Good,' he said briskly, 'but make sure you hook it up to the phone. You know how, don't you?'

Patiently, Farrell set the plug into place, dialed for weather information, then played it back for Reardon. 'Good. Okay, Sam, you're in business.' Farrell nodded silently, bringing the cup of coffee Nora had given him to the table: Reardon would have bet that Sam Farrell, during the course of the next ten or twelve hours if need be, would not be farther away from that telephone than his arm could reach.

Reardon, preceding Nora through the hallway, tripped over a large, gray animal lying stretched across the white tile floor. Recoiling in mock horror, he asked, 'What the hell is *that thing*?'

Nora reached down, taking the large cat in her arms; its heavy paws sprawled unconcerned, the eyes locked in undisturbed sleep.

'This is Sweet William,' she said, nuzzling the fur against her cheek.

'It would be: My God—*Sweet William*.' He stared at the cat, who opened two large vacant green eyes, then snapped them shut again.

She walked with Reardon onto the patio, which was cheerfully furnished with white wicker chairs and table and stone pots of red geraniums, and deposited the cat onto one of the chairs, where he promptly stretched, rolled on his back and continued sleeping. Tom Dell, patiently sitting behind the wheel of the black Pontiac, without turning his head toward them, automatically reached his hand to the key, tuning the engine.

'Nora'—Reardon reached out, placed her hand in both of his —'Thanks for going along with us. I have every confidence that you'll handle your part without any problem. You've done a damn good job with that little guy, by the way.'

'Christie and I go fifty-fifty where Mickey is concerned—credit and blame.'

He added that to his collection of impressions about Nora Opara, turned toward the car, but her fingers pulled lightly at his sleeve and he turned, surprised.

'There's just one more thing I want to say, Casey.' Her eyes were steady and the blue was not paled by the brightness of the late sun. 'This is a little difficult.'

Reardon grinned. 'But you're going to say it anyway, so go ahead.'

'Christie isn't as tough as she likes to think. She's really pretty soft and she feels very deeply about things. About *people*.' Nora's eyes didn't waver. 'She could get hurt,' she said, not talking about the stake-out now.

Reardon's face tightened slightly; they stood measuring each other for a moment, then he said softly, 'Okay. Don't worry about her, right?'

She watched him walk to the car and returned his brisk wave.

Reardon slumped in the seat beside Dell, his eyes staring through the spotless windshield. This Nora Opara was indeed a very shrewd little lady. He wondered if Christie realized that Nora had read something more than anger or annoyance into her complaints about him or if Christie herself even knew there *had* been anything else.

Reardon smiled and closed his eyes. He didn't think so.

CHAPTER SEVENTEEN

CHRISTIE FOLLOWED Bill Ferranti as he led her about the tiny apartment which was not really an apartment, just a compartmentalized room with a separate bathroom. The diagramed floor plan she had studied in the office did not translate into this small, hot sticky room; there was a kitchen unit contained in a half-walled alcove, consisting of a waist-high refrigerator, lined up flush with a small sink which was wedged against a narrow, four-burner stove.

Each ugly, alien piece of furniture in the room had been shifted to a location calculated to meet their needs: the heavy stuffed flowered armchair had been pushed alongside the door. This was where Stoner Martin would crouch, giving him coverage for either of the two possibilities: that Rogoff would enter the apartment via the hallway door or that Rogoff would enter through the bathroom window. The lumpy couch bed had been moved from its location against the wall and centered on the short wall so that there was free space on either side of its length: this way, Christie could follow her instructions which were, 'The minute the lights go on, baby, you roll to the left, hit the deck and stay down until ole Stoney says otherwise!' The scarred and loose-legged wooden table had been moved off center in the small kitchen alcove for two reasons: first, that it would not pose a stumbling block for Rogoff who would enter in the darkness, and secondly, that it would not interfere with Ferranti's movements as he emerged from his hiding place behind the half-arched alcove.

Her mind automatically rearranged the ugly furnishings, trying to get some measure of balance. Christie made a determined effort to accept this room, to let its dimensions and narrow passageways have meaning and necessity. The bathroom was another matter: everything stationary, everything exact in the range of its requirements.

Stoner Martin signaled them all into the long, narrow chipped and dirty bathroom and they all stood, Christie and Ginsburg and Ferranti, their eyes following Stoner's to the bathroom window: the all-important rectangle on which it all depended.

'Now, this, as we have discussed, would seem to be the logical place.' Leaning across the tub, his muscles straining slightly, his fingertips gently slid the smoked glass window up, soundlessly, then back into place. Stoney stepped into the tub, turned to face them, his eyes shut tight. 'Now, we will assume that this is point of entry and it is dark now.' His hands extended before him, his feet carefully moved, measuring the edge of the tub; he bent over, his hands on the side of the tub, and they stepped back clearing a pathway as he walked like a blind man, his fingers tracing the tile wall, guiding him toward the opened door, his hands moving lightly in the air, finding the dimensions of the doorway.

'Now, by this point, his eyes will have become somewhat accustomed to the darkness of the room,' and then to Christie, his eyes opening, 'we did this last night in the dark, Marty and the boss and I, and we noticed that if we left the toaster out there, on top of the stove, it picks up a glint of light and you can tell that's the kitchen area.' Moving into the room now, eyes closed again, he pointed. 'So, if I know that the kitchen area is to my left, I know that the bed will be to my right.' His hand circled quickly and Christie passed him, sliding her body on the bed, her eyes on his approaching figure, edging closer to her, his knees lightly hitting the bed, his body bending, leaning toward her, but she spun quickly, so that when he opened his eyes, the bed was empty.

'Where'd she go?' he asked playfully. 'I know she's here someplace!'

Christie propped her head on her arms along the edge of the bed. 'Try down here,' she said, trying to match his voice.

'Good. Only you slide yourself way down *under* the bed and you don't come out until I say.'

'Right!'

'Hey, Stoney old boss man, can we eat now?' Marty clicked the handle of the refrigerator impatiently.

Stoney's eyes glided about the room in despair. 'We better let this man set a table or he'll be hollering all night and we don't want any hollering herein. Go ahead, Marty.'

Marty filled the table with paper cartons of corned beef and pastrami and pickles and potato salad and coleslaw, then reached for a half-gallon bottle of milk, ignoring the groans. 'Milk is good for you, good for you,' he insisted.

Christie folded a piece of rye bread around a few slices of

corned beef, eating without taste. Only Marty ate with any appetite, insulted that the others refused the milk. Christie put up a pot of water, grateful that Marty had remembered tea bags and instant coffee.

She wondered where Johnnie Devereaux was at that moment: or more exactly, where Murray Rogoff was, since wherever Rogoff was, Devereaux, tailing him since early afternoon, was close by. This last week of telephone calls had been the worst, the voice more and more intimate, more and more familiar, whispering in her ear, reaching into her, the image of the sixteen-year-old hairless boy forming: an image of horrible despair and panic. She had forced her own voice into a casual, conversational level: "Yes, this is Christie. Yes, I am fine. Yes, I am safe. Yes, thank you for calling, goodbye.' God. Oh dear God, not saying anything more, the words shrieking through every part of her, but not saying anything.

'Say there, Christie.' Stoney's voice was quiet but pulled at her, making her jaws work over the dry piece of sandwich she hadn't realized was between her teeth. 'Did any of the fellows tell you about the "particular problem" we have always had in our Squad?'

She shook her head. 'What particular problem?'

'Well,' Stoney said, 'this is not generally known or discussed, as you will understand, but among the members of our Squad, there is not one real marksman. In fact, you might say, among the members of our Squad, there is hardly a qualified target-shooter.'

Marty jammed a huge bite of pastrami sandwich between his jaws, wiped his mouth with a flowered paper napkin, and shook his head heavily at her. 'Hey, Stoney, don't tell her about that now.'

'Well, I think she has a right to know. Bill, what do you think?'

Seriously, carefully, Bill Ferranti said, 'Well, *I'd* want to know.'

She knew what they were doing: all of them. Pulling her and each other and themselves into the room, into the reality of the place, forcing the wandering complicated thoughts out and away: starting the easy, joking, relaxing story-telling which would put them here, aware of each other. Christie made herself respond, her voice mock-serious. 'Well, I think somebody better tell me if it's something I should know.'

Stoney's hand moved toward Bill Ferranti. Bill fingered his

horn-rimmed glasses, 'Well, I never can line up those little ridges in my gun sighting. In fact, last shooting cycle, I put two holes in Stoney's target, and he was *two* booths to my right.'

'Yes,' Stoney said sadly, 'and those two holes were only in the five ring and didn't help me much.' He extended his long brown arm across the table and his fingers trembled. He regarded them, clicking his tongue. 'My hand shakes. Just a little. But just enough to throw me off.'

They all waited for Marty to swallow his cold milk. 'And me,' he said, smearing a milk mustache on his paper napkin, 'every time I go down to the range, my hand jumps in *anticipation* of the shot. I'm very sensitive to noise, you know, so just expecting the noise, before the shot is off, I get bugged and my shot always drops down to the left.' He moved his arm in an arc. 'Eight o'clock.'

Becoming part of it, part of them, Christie's voice struck just the right note. 'Well, gentlemen, that is all *very* reassuring to me. I'll tell you what—you're all going to be on *this* side of the room.' Her hand pointed toward the bed, her index finger extending from her fist like the barrel of a gun. 'And *I'm* going to be on that side of the room. And if there's going to be shooting, *that's* where the bullets will go. Now, how about we all reverse sides? *I'm* a good shot: no glasses, no tremors, no eight o'clocks!'

'Well, now, Christie, just because none of us are very good, that's not saying we can't hit *something*, right, fellas?'

Stoney's head twisted toward Marty and his voice was sharp, yet it was part of the game; Stoney was following Marty's cue. 'Shut up about that, Marty.'

'Yes,' Ferranti said, 'let's not discuss *that*, Marty.'

Christie looked from face to face, admiring them; this was all by-play, yet it was essential. An establishing of lines of communication, of reading and responding. No one really knew what story Marty was about to tell, yet each would help him, filling in, building on it. It was more than time-passing, it was an interacting on a light and unimportant level: it was a rehearsal.

'I think there's something else I should know,' she said.

'Well, if it was *me*, I'd want to know,' Marty grumbled. 'You tell her, Stoney.'

Stoney smiled, blinked, settled back in the rickety wooden chair and began. They were like kids at a campfire, passing fragments of a story around. 'Well now, you ever hear of a fella named Phil Jones?'

She shook her head. Marty sighed and covered his forehead. Bill clicked his tongue. 'Well, old Phil,' Stoney continued, ignoring Marty's 'may-he-rest-in-peace', 'was a member of our Squad some years ago. Well, we were all on a stake-out, similar to this, but of course the circumstances were different, but anyway, it was one of these things.' His hands indicated the room. 'Without going into detail . . .'

'No, don't go into detail,' Bill said almost fervently, joined by Marty's voice, 'No, don't.'

'Well, old Phil, at any rate, took two.' Stoney's hand touched the center of his forehead and then his heart.

'Two bullets? He was killed?'

'Honey,' Marty said, 'one in the head and one in the ticker. He was killed dead.'

'And,' Stoney said, 'only Marty and Bill and I had guns. Our suspect, upon apprehension and further investigation, was as they say "clean".'

The three men silently stared at their hands, all clasped and motionless on the table before them. 'Well, what happened?' Christie asked.

Marty's head popped up. 'We gave him an inspector's funeral, of course.'

'And you know, Christie,' Bill said in his quiet, humorless way, 'I know that at times you've been annoyed at Mr. Reardon, but he does take care of his own. Right, Stoney?'

'He does indeed, Bill. Tell her.'

It was Bill's part now. 'Well, he knew how badly we all felt. Anyone would—after all, our own man. Mr. Reardon ordered the inspector's funeral *immediately*. He wouldn't let an autopsy be performed. Boy, he did some fast talking to get that pushed through.'

'Yeah,' Marty picked up on it. 'After all, how the hell would old Stoney feel, knowing he had killed his own partner?'

'Me?' Stoney bellowed. 'Why you ingrate: all these years the boss and I have been protecting you from that terrible knowledge, and now you try to put it on me!'

'Not me.' Marty shook his heavy head. 'Everyone knows I can't hit the broad side of a barn.'

'But Phil wasn't a barn,' Bill said quietly.

Marty began collecting the paper plates, finishing off odd pieces of food. 'Not me, Stoney, but hell, if it makes you feel better, it's okay with me.' He leaned across the table to Christie, whispering loudly, 'It would be too tough for him to admit: hell, he was partners with the guy for six years.'

'Well, fellows, I appreciate your complete honesty and I really think, under the circumstances, Stoney, you should let me keep my gun under the pillow. I'd only shoot if you got me first.'

'Oh no, no,' Stoney said. 'Absolutely not. If one Squad member gets shot, we can cover, but if two of us got hit, it would look real bad. Bad for the Squad image!'

'Gee,' Christie said, her voice young. 'I wouldn't want to hurt the Squad image. I'm sorry, I wasn't thinking.'

At seven P.M. there was an impatient thud at the door and a muffled, familiar voice. 'Reardon,' it said, and Ferranti opened the door. Reardon barreled in, sniffing, wrinkling his short nose. 'Smells like a delicatessen in here! My God, Ginsburg, you eating pickles and drinking milk?'

Marty innocently held up his glass. 'Milk is very good for you, Mr. Reardon. They even give it to babies nowadays.'

'Stoney, you better have a good talk with that guy. Remind me to issue an order relative to meeting Squad regulations re height and weight. Marty, you are putting on too much weight.'

'I know, Mr. Reardon,' Marty said sadly, 'and it worries me, so when I worry I eat. It's a syndrome or something.'

Christie watched him and began to feel cold now and still and aware: it was not a game. Reardon moved rapidly about the room, squatting down behind a chair, his head cocked to one side, easing himself into the position where Ferranti would be, placing himself inside the small closet. 'You sure Ginsburg will fit in here?'

'Yeah, but I'm not too sure if he'll be able to get out.'

'I'll get out, Stoney, don't worry, I'll get out.'

Reardon crossed to the bed, sat beside Christie who let the magazine fall opened on her lap. He bounced lightly. 'Feels pretty comfortable. Don't fall asleep on us, Opara.'

'I'll be awake, Mr. Reardon.'

He stood up, looked down at her, then asked Stoney, 'Hey, how come you got Opara dressed up like a little boy again? I can't see anyone busting into a room after her in those dungarees and—Opara, at least tuck your shirttail in!'

'She'll be hitting the deck, boss, and I think she'd do it better not having to worry about a dress riding up and all.'

'Umm, I guess.' He strode into the bathroom, and she could hear the window sliding up and down and then he was back, standing in the center of the room, and they all watched him. The bantering tones had left his voice which was flatly informative now. 'I just gave Jimmy O'Neill a wave: he's at his post—you know where. Right, Stoney?'

Stoner Martin nodded.

'Two windows up and three across: in the building directly across from us.'

'Right. Now, the two other Homicide men are three doors down the hallway. They're not going to move until'—he corrected himself—'*unless* they hear action in here.' He moved to the door, checking. 'Good, leave this on the latch in case our boy decides to use the door, but I don't think he will.' His eyes, and theirs, turned toward the bathroom. 'He'll come in the window if he comes at all.'

He will, Christie told him silently, and Reardon's eyes, on hers, saw it and she knew he saw it. *He will.*

'Sam Farrell will call you in about'—he consulted his watch—'in about ten minutes just for a check ring. Now, after that check call and for the remainder of this assignment, no one will use that telephone to make a call.' Their eyes were now all on the strangely old-fashioned black telephone on the small combination lamp and table placed near Stoney's hand, against the plush chair. 'Here's what to anticipate after the check call: *if* suspect calls Opara's house, as soon as that call is completed, Farrell will ring here and play back the tape. Devereaux is on Rogoff right now. As soon as suspect makes his call, you'll get the relay, then I'll get it. I'll be in my car, which is parked across the street from access to the alley. If suspect—and we are assuming he'll make his call from Queens—if suspect then heads towards Manhattan, Devereaux, if he can, will give me a blast on my car telephone; as soon as I get the word, I'll call here and let you know.' They all listened silently, their faces solemn and still, their eyes between Reardon and the telephone, none of them looking at each other. '*Then*'—Casey paused, his eyes turning to the phone now—'when and if suspect hits this block—and I'm located where I can see both entrance to the alley and entrance to the building, I will give you just one blast on the telephone. Don't answer it—that's the signal that he is in the immediate vicinity. Any questions?'

Marty opened his mouth, saw Casey's eyes, changed his mind and shook his head.

'Now, this is important: under *no* circumstances is anyone to make a call. There will be a lack of communication, I realize that, but we will all be waiting it out and if it goes through the night, it goes through the night. Nothing might happen, no calls at all.' He shrugged. 'Ya never know, right?'

They all nodded. He put his hand lightly on Stoney's shoulder, but he was speaking directly to Christie now. 'Stoney is in charge, he is the boss here.'

'Right,' Stoney said, 'I am the boss!'

Reardon shoved him, his voice a growl. 'Not with me in the room, you're not, buddy!'

'Well, then, Mr. Reardon, sir, how come you don't leave and let me be boss now?'

'Well, I got one problem that I didn't want to mention, but I'd better tell you fellas.' Reardon lowered his voice including them all in his bantering confidence. 'This is one helluva building; I mean, there is P.D. brass all over the place, across the street, up and down the block, practically breathing down our necks, and this building is a trap for an honest man. See, there's a little blonde down the hall there.' He looked over his shoulder. 'I was given an unmistakable set of little signals when I came into the building.' Pulling his mouth down, Reardon said, 'I don't want any of *that*, naturally, so, Stoney, since you're in charge, will you assign Opara to give me a safe escort to the front door?'

Stoner's tongue clicked. 'Age finally takes its toll; never thought the day would come when Casey Reardon needed the protective escort of a policewoman against the advances of a blonde!'

Smoothly slipping in his punchline, Reardon said, 'The blond is a *fella!*'

Not joining the easy, relaxed laughter, Reardon gestured impatiently to Christie. 'C'mon, come on, Opara, I have to move.' He grasped her arm, then stopped for a moment, his eyes meeting each man in turn, locking for one split moment of communicated but unstated concern.

'It's all yours now, fellas; stay loose.'

She didn't know whether he was kidding, but Reardon pulled

her into the hallway with him, pushed her against the wall, then he glanced over his shoulder for a moment. His fingers pressed her arm and he leaned his face to her ear. 'There, the bastard,' he whispered, 'see the crack in that door? He wriggles in and out.' His thumb jerked behind him. 'Tell you what, Opara, let's straighten him out about me, okay?' He pulled her toward him, pressing his lips lightly on hers, then moved away, his eyes not on hers. 'Is he looking?'

Christie tried to see Reardon's face in the yellow-lit darkness of the hallway; she moved back but her shoulders were against the wall. She raised herself on her toes, trying to see some face behind the small crack in the door. Reardon's face, half hidden in the dimness, seemed serious. 'I think he's watching. Yes, he just ducked back behind the door, but he is watching.'

'Well, we ought to fool him, huh?' Reardon's lips were against her ear and his breath was warm. 'Hey, did you shrink or what? You weren't always this short, were you?' Still gripping on her arm he took a step back. 'Oh, yeah, you got your sneakers on again. For pete's sake, you're not very tall at all, are you?'

She started to answer, but his face was suddenly against hers again and he asked, earnestly, 'He looking again? I heard the door move!'

Not understanding his concern, but caught up in his seriousness, she stretched her neck, tilted her face up, then her eyes came back to his and she had some vague impression that he was making fun of her. 'Why are you so worried that some little mixed-up blond wrong-o might get the wrong impression about you?'

He grinned at the fresh, mocking tone and his hands moved along her shoulders to her neck. 'Hell, I'm always concerned about creating a wrong impression. I like to keep the image intact. At all times.'

'What image?' she asked, and his lips pressed against hers again, only slightly harder this time, taking a little longer to withdraw, and when he moved his face back, his eyes seemed almost red.

'Relax, Opara, relax. You don't think that was for you, do you? That was for cutie, behind me,' he whispered.

Christie smiled now, released from the pressure of his mouth, released from whatever had held back the words that could match and top him; her voice was firm and clear and loud in the narrow corridor. 'Okay, Dad, and you tell Mom I'm all settled in and I'll be just fine here.'

Reardon's eyes narrowed and his voice was tough and low. 'You little wise-guy, you have to have the last word, don't you?' Then, his hands reached behind her head, his fingers plunged roughly through her short, thick light hair. 'Okay, honey,' he said, 'we'll give cutie in there something that'll send him running to his Freud books,' and now Reardon's mouth was on hers, firmly, strongly, surprisingly full and warm, and Christie, not expecting it, anticipating another light, teasing, playful kiss, accepted it, then, startled, tried to turn away, then stood, motionless, her hands hanging limply, but not really motionless: participating, but not really participating, surprised again by the gently affectionate touch of his hand along her earlobe, the quick caressing of her cheek and chin as he withdrew from her and walked briskly down the length of the hallway. Reardon turned for just a moment before leaving and called to her, 'So long, Daughter. I'll tell Mom you're just fine, yes sir, just fine!'

Christie heard a small, harsh gasp and the sharp closing of an apartment door and the fumbling of a chain lock being slid into place but her eyes stayed down the length of the hallway. She touched her lips lightly with her fingers, closing her eyes for a moment.

Her heart was pounding and she wasn't quite sure how she felt: amused? angry? what?

At 9:32 P.M., the telephone rang. It wasn't a particularly loud ring: it didn't blast through an intense silence, for they had been story-telling, reminiscing, teasing, joking, arguing. Yet the sound cut through their cross-conversations as clearly and shockingly as the spattering of a live electric wire tossed suddenly in their midst and three masculine hands lunged, simultaneously, for the instrument as though it were somehow vital that it not be permitted to ring again.

'I got it, I got it,' Stoney said in the voice of an outfielder warding off unwanted assistance. The eyes of the others fixed on Stoney's face and they moved toward him.

'Yeah, Sam, Stoney here.' He glanced at his watch, nodding. 'Yeah, yeah, go ahead and play it.' Then, his hand over the receiver, 'The call came.'

Stoney held the receiver slightly away from his ear, but the voices were so clearly familiar that Christie would have heard them had her head been buried beneath sand.

'Hello?' Nora. Friendly and pleasant.

'Hello, Christie? Is this Christie Opara?' The voice went through her body like a needle: the faceless night-time voice. They were all watching her now, dropping their eyes as she met theirs.

'No, Christie isn't here.' Quickly. Nora said it quickly, not giving him time to continue the pacing of his own conversation, stopping him, forcing him to *listen*.

There was a silence now lasting a full five seconds and Marty groaned as the same thought flashed through everyone: Sam Farrell had loused it up. But Stoney's hand impatiently kept them quiet.

And then, 'I want to talk to Christie Opara.' The voice was hoarsely insistent.

No pause. 'Christie moved away from here, you see. She moved out this morning, to a place of her own.' Nora, sounding so cheerful and reasonable.

Again a pause, a little longer this time. Their minds held the singular thought: the caller would hang up.

But the voice again, different, a strange quality, somewhere between anger and panic. 'Where did she move to?'

No one in the room breathed. Nora's voice, easy, relaxed, 'Do you have a pencil? I'll give you her address.'

Quickly, 'I want her phone number.'

'No, she hasn't had a phone installed yet.' Don't say that, Nora; don't say *yet!* He'll hang up and call back tomorrow for the number; oh God, Nora, that was a mistake.

But the voice, 'Yes. I have paper. Wait a minute.' A muffled, digging around sound, a heavy sigh. 'Okay.'

Listening to Nora's voice, carefully spelling out the address, giving the apartment number, Christie felt the sense of unreality bearing down on her; the pleasant casual insignificant conversation was so out of keeping with her surroundings, with the circumstances. She studied the faces of the men, huddled in a small semi-circle around Stoney; nothing around her balanced. The two voices speaking from the telephone, asking for and giving information, the normal, polite exchange of goodbyes, the clicking of the two receivers yet the call not disconnected and now, Sam Farrell's voice, normal, familiar.

'That's it, Stoney. I hung up and dialed your number as soon as he disconnected.'

'Right,' Stoney said. 'You did fine, Sam.' And now Sam was out of it; staying beside Nora until ordered to leave, but out of it, finished and done with it.

Stoney's hand still rested on the telephone. 'Marty, you spoke with Rogoff. What do you say? Recognize the voice?'

Marty shrugged. 'Hard to say; yes and no.'

'It is Rogoff.' They all turned, no one questioning the cold hard certainty in Christie's voice.

At 9:42 P.M. the telephone rang again. It seemed less sharp, less insistent this time, but Stoner Martin grabbed it midway in the first ring. 'Martin here. Right. Right, Casey.'

He replaced the receiver on the cradle and said softly, 'Devereaux just called Casey from the subway station; they're waiting for a Manhattan-bound IRT.' Stoney lit a new cigarette from the inch-long glow between his fingers, smashed out the stub, blew smoke around his head. 'Devereaux and Rogoff,' he said quietly.

'Of course *Rogoff,*' Christie said to no one in particular. 'Who'd you think it would be, Devereaux and Santa Claus?'

Stoney said evenly, 'Now the next time, it will be a one-ring blast and then it should be a matter of minutes. Marty, take a run around the corner and alert Jimmy O'Neill that his partner is close on suspect and that they are on their way, then tap on the door down the hall and tell the other Homicide men.' Stoney picked up a magazine, slumping into the upholstered chair, his long legs dangling over the arm.

Ferranti adjusted the gas higher under the glass pot of water, spooning instant coffee into a mug. He stood watching the odd shapes of the orange fire under the tall, transparent, slightly roiling water. It was like a flower with long bright tentacles reaching out from a blue center. He poured boiling water into his cup and adjusted the flame so that Marty could have a cup of coffee when he returned.

Christie walked into the bathroom, shutting the door behind her. For a moment, she stood in the darkness, then switched on the light, gazing without recognition at her reflection in the small scarred mirror over the sink. Her cheeks seemed drawn in, her mouth was tight. She ran the cold water full strength, cupping it into her hands, sloshing the coolness over her face, but it seemed to turn warm on contact with her skin. She filled her mouth from her hands then let the water run back into the sink, finally swallowing a mouthful, but it did not slake her thirst nor the dryness that was not only in her mouth but deep inside her throat. Not reaching yet for one of the paper towels on the roller directly under the mirror, Christie turned sideways, holding her dripping hands out before her. No tremor: not the slightest tremble. She regulated her breath, remembering one of Nora's endless yoga exercises: empty the lungs completely, force out the air even though there doesn't seem to be anything left because there is some stale pocketful of air stagnating inside. Feeling emptied to the point of suffocation, Christie slowly drew new breath into her but the air was heavy and unclean and gave no sense of purification or revitalization. She ran the water again, on the insides of her wrists, then blotted her face and hands on the scratchy paper towels, but, stopped by the eyes in the mirror, she could see that her face was wet again, sprinkled with small drops of perspiration. She felt the damp clinging all along her back: the lightweight cotton shirt glued to her body. She pushed the tail-ends into her dungarees which had become part of her skin. She ran her fingers through her hair, then across her neck, stretched her face, pulling her lips back into an exaggerated smile, then let them ease back into a normal expression.

Switching off the light, Christie carefully stepped into the bathtub, raised the window an inch or so, hunched down so that her eyes could scan the darkness of the small, common courtyard formed by the arrangements of tenement houses, back to back on a square block of city street; her eyes found the alleyway and her lips said quietly into the emptiness: *'I'm ready for you; I'm ready.'* Her eyes closed now, she carefully slid the window to exactly the location Stoney had placed it, her fingers measuring the distance. Then she went back into the room.

Marty broke into their silence, his eyes glowing. 'Man, you should see what Jimmy O'Neill's got going for him up there!' His hands traced voluptuous forms in the air.

'Knock it off, Marty,' Bill Ferranti said, his voice unexpectedly angry.

'Not me,' Marty said innocently, 'but hell, if Jimmy up there don't knock it off, he's crazy!'

Bill's voice was tight and unfamiliar and he stood up, putting his cup of coffee on the edge of the table. 'Watch that kind of talk, Marty.' His chin jutted toward Christie and she blinked at him.

'Don't shush him on my account, Bill. Frankly, I wasn't listening. I didn't even hear what he said.'

'Well, what I said was . . .'

Stoney steered Marty to the stove, taking control now. 'Have your cuppa and fill your mouth with a few pickles, Marty. It's too hot to get tense.' Stoney poured the steaming water into a cup, then carefully closed the marbleized black and white tin cover over the burners, then placed the toaster, a shining, aluminium four-slicer, in place. 'Little old toaster,' he intoned, 'you are an important part of this here little old plan and if you do your job properly and guide our suspect well, we will reward you handsomely by eating anything—regardless of condition—that pops out of you.'

'Except raisin toast,' Marty said, his eyes on the toaster. 'Because with raisin toast, unless you count carefully before the bread goes down, you never *really* know if any of the raisins are actually bugs when the toast pops up!'

They all had casually positioned themselves about the room now, Stoner Martin leaning against the arm of the chair, Marty squatting beside the closet, Ferranti taking his half-empty cup with him as he eased himself to the top of the waist-high refrigerator.

Christie sat stiffly on the edge of the bed, her back straight, her hands over her knees. The denim clung heavily to her thighs and constricted her movements. There were no sounds in the room except for the occasional swallowing, as the men finished their tepid coffee.

'I think,' Stoner Martin said, 'that we will turn out the lights now and maintain a modicum of silence.' His hand reached out, clicked the yellow circle of light over his head. Ferranti pushed the silent button over the refrigerator, obliterating the purplish cast from the fluorescent tube.

'I can see the toaster,' Christie said from the bed. 'It does pick up a glint of light.'

'Into the closet, Martin, and do not fall asleep.' But Marty was already in the closet as Ferranti was already settled behind the half-wall of the alcove and Stoney was down now, behind the chair, and Christie was stretched full length on the creaking bed.

'Stoney?' Marty's voice was different in the dark now; serious, no more joking. 'Question.'

'Yeah?'

'When the lights go on, won't we be blinded from all this darkness? I mean, hell, how will we see good enough?'

There was a silence as they all visualized the stabbing glare of sudden light. Then, Stoney, softly, 'This little light here is pretty dim. We'll do the best we can: we'll be fine.'

CHAPTER EIGHTEEN

MURRAY ROGOFF sat huddled on the wicker seat of the slow-moving IRT train, his arms wrapped around his knees, his chin pressed into his locked hands. The train came to a hesitant, not-quite-completed halt, then lurched forward a few feet, then picked up speed steadily until it was careening through the black tunnel, but Murray Rogoff was too filled with other things to notice the irregular movements of the train. His eyes, opened wide behind the enclosure of his glasses, saw no further than the smudge marks.

He had known there was something wrong. All day, working in the store, he had felt it, known it. His hands closed even tighter against each other. His teeth moved hard, grinding the words inside his mouth: What kind of a mother was that woman? What kind of a mother? To let a girl like Christie move to a place like the Village. What kind of mother was she?

He had kept his voice steady; he had kept all the anger and fury from his voice and from his words but not from inside himself; it grew surely and fully when the calm voice told him, 'Christie moved out this morning.' Moved out: as though the woman had no idea what kind of place her daughter had moved to. Murray's eyes remembered the woman: small and crisp and clean and taking the little boy by the hand, carefully fussing over him, smiling at him. *That was it!* She wanted to be alone with her little son. That was why she had made Christie move out, made her leave that safe, good brick house, attached to all those other nice houses, all lined up neat with small flower gardens and patios on one side of the street and the old wooden houses facing them. God, it had been so hard to find the place where Christie lived; so hard to make sure it was a safe place with all those sharp-eyed old women who had nothing better to do than watch anyone who walked past their houses. But he had been careful: Murray knew how to watch without being seen.

Everything had been so hard: how could he keep watch over Christie when she worked at some crazy job with some crazy hours? Coming home every night at a different time: it was wrong for a girl like Christie, walking those long dark blocks in Queens. They seemed to think it was way out in the country, all safe and quiet, but they didn't know what could happen. Murray's mind whirled with images and pieces of things that did not fall into place and he closed his eyes against all the things he could not understand.

What had Christie to do with Frankie Santino? Then, Murray smiled behind his hands: she knew how to talk to pigs like Frankie Santino. That day in the hallway of the court building, she had cut Frankie dead like so much gutter dirt, which is what Frankie Santino was and always had been and always would be. He remembered her face and her voice: the kind of face a girl like Christie always turned to a bum like Frankie and the kind of voice she saved for punks like that.

The tormenting puzzling mystery of *why* Christie had been there that day no longer bothered him, because Murray knew the important thing was that she *had* been there and that he had seen her and she had seen him and that they had looked at each other. His smile widened and Murray felt good, yet the nagging worry bit into his happiness forcing him to remember that something was wrong and that Christie was not living at home any more with her mother and little brother but had moved to some dump in the Village and that he had to find her.

Murray Rogoff walked along the narrow Greenwich Village street deliberately slamming his hard body into all the queers who tried to block his way, leaving behind him a trail of shrieking insults. He knew they would love nothing better than for him to turn back, rough them up a little: touch them again. His hands deep in the pockets of his chinos, Murray walked with long steps, seeing only the sidewalk before him, using his wide shoulders to sweep a path for himself. His eyes saw the net stockings and spike heels of the whores, heard the dirty low voices of the pimps, but his eyes never met theirs. He walked through them with one terrible knowledge: this is where Christie must walk now, through them. They could reach out and touch her. God. Oh God. What kind of mother?

He stood now leaning his large arm on the sticky counter of an orangeade stand, his lungs filling with the sour smells of pizza and juice. He watched pale liquid slosh around and up and over within the dirty glass bubble of the juice machine; he pointed to it, accepted the glass from the pimply boy who bounced his dime change at him, absently put the coin in his pocket. His eyes saw none of the bodies around him, and they, realizing that whatever it was he sought did not include them, shrugged. Nothing about the giant of a man interested them: not the odd-shaped skull which continued from beneath the plaid cap into the collar of his white knit shirt; not the strange welder-goggles which hid half his face nor the massively muscled arms. His eyes discounted them and they, intent on searches of their own needs, discounted him.

Rogoff's eyes were fixed on the tenement building directly across the street. A four-story tenement, surrounded up and down the block by identical structures, each opening directly onto the street. The hall would be long and narrow and badly lit. In one long gulp, Murray let the cold and tasteless liquid run down his throat, feeing it plunge into his chest with a coldness that did not cool him, but merely created a passing sensation of pain.

Without hesitation, without consulting the slip of paper in his pants pocket, Rogoff strode across the street, pushed the door open with his rubber-soled shoe. These doors were never locked; the hallway, too, was what he had expected: nothing surprised him. The two electric bulbs on the high ceiling glowed yellow in small circles which did not penetrate the darkness. Not stopping, going directly to the long, narrow stairway, Murray Rogoff took the steps easily, two at a time. Three long flights were nothing; he stopped at the top landing, pushed his cap back, then leaned his face close to the door of the apartment nearest to him, his fingers rubbing, searching for something. The lettering had long since been obliterated; he moved to the next door and it was the right one: 4C—directly in line. Rogoff took the next flight of stairs soundlessly, pushing against the sticking door with his shoulder, feeling a sudden rush of air against his face. But it was only breeze caused by the pressure of the door opening suddenly onto the roof, for the night air was still and heavy and breathless as Murray, walking with some strange and quiet shrewdness, rolled his feet on the tarpaper surface. He stood motionless: no bodies lying against chimneys, no whispers or laughter. The roof was deserted.

Crouching now, Murray moved carefully, sliding himself to the edge of the unprotected roof, and looked down, his mind holding his purpose to the exclusion of all other thought: there was a little courtyard below and the windows of the apartments in the 'C' line opened onto that little courtyard and that was what Murray needed to know. His eyes, seeing well in the darkness, studied it like a road map all sketched out for him: the narrow alley cutting between the buildings like a path, leading into the courtyard, leading like a beam of light to the window four stories down, directly beneath where he now lay. Counting, he calculated exactly where the street location of the opening to the alley was and, this firmly in his mind. Murray stood up, inhaled with a gasp, for the air seemed to contain no oxygen, seemed to be choking him and his head ached and his eyes burned and for the moment, he had the strangest feeling: as if he had just fallen from the roof into the courtyard below, or that his body, rocking forward now, was going to fall.

Rogoff had to get away from this place: had to get on the street again. He spun around looking for direction, then, no longer concerned about sound or footsteps, he ran heavily across the seemingly endless series of roofs until his eyes picked out a structure and he lunged his body against the door which didn't move and then he pulled at it and thudded down the long flight of narrow stairs.

He sucked the night air into his lungs and walked with rapid, heavy strides along the safety of the sidewalk.

Johnny Devereaux, standing in the darkness, pressed his body against the crumbling brick structure of a chimney and felt unavoidable reality race through him like an uneven pulse. His lips moved silently over the words that he could taste inside his mouth: Jesus, Mary and Joseph, I've lost him. Jesus, Mary and Joseph, I've lost him.

But the desperation was checked immediately by that calmer voice which took over instinctively, as he knew it would. Okay. So you lost him for a minute or two. So he took off into another building. Did you expect him to drop pebbles for you? There's only one place he'd head for now; the alley.

Detective Jimmy O'Neill's legs were aching. Kneeling on the hard floor, his long torso made it necessary for him to bend down in order for his eyes to be level with the two inches of space between the shade and the window sill. He couldn't adjust the shade to better advantage because he knew that then his head would be outlined, darker against the darkness of the opened window.

To keep his vision certain, he had to glance away periodically from the two figures on the roof across the alley and he had found a fantastic contrast for his vigil: on the fourth floor of the building adjacent to the stake-out there was an orange-headed girl, and for the life of him, Jimmy O'Neill couldn't figure what the hell she was doing, but Christ, whatever it was, she sure was doing it great. There were no shades on her window, which was thrown open, and she would appear suddenly across the rectangle, gyrating to some music, then disappear into the recesses of her room.

But Jimmy O'Neill, who had watched the odd, continuing movements steadily for the last hour, glanced there now only as a necessary part of his job: to keep his eyes sharp. From the moment he had heard the one piercing ring of the telephone, clearly reaching him from across the courtyard, the orange-haired girl aroused no feelings whatever within him. His interest was directed solely on the two figures who moved about the roofs across from him. Figure number one was suspect: Christ, even from this distance, outlined against the gray sky, Jimmy could see he was tremendous. Devereaux was harder to spot and probably the only reason O'Neill knew there was a second figure was because he had worked as Devereaux's partner for four years.

This bastard is shrewd as hell, O'Neill thought with grudging admiration. Reconnoitering: placing the apartment, then the alleyway, then leaving the roof via a different route; it was tough on John. Tough to do a close tail job under the circumstances. The long even line of roofs was deserted now and Jimmy O'Neill let his eyes rest for a few moments; the orange head flashed by, then her body spun around: Christ! She was stripped from the waist up! A flash of breast moved past the window, then disappeared. Jimmy O'Neill dug his long bony fingers into his watering eyes, then with great determination, he concentrated on the concrete courtyard two stories below him, becoming familiar with its dimensions and shapes and shadows. That's where the next action would be.

John Devereaux entered the alley like a phantom: without sound and without form. He let his body blend with shadows, moving only against that part of the wall where no dim light from some window touched, crossing with a short step whenever necessary so that he stayed part of the darkness.

John Devereaux didn't breathe because automatically he stopped breathing at moments like this. He had learned long ago that there are times when a man can go for a very considerable period of time without drawing in or letting out breath. His eyes narrowed, darting rapidly around the small yard, first to the particular window, which had not yet been raised, then to all the corners, into all the shadows and all the dimly lighted places.

John Devereaux softly exhaled all the stagnant air and soundlessly drew in another portion, moving carefully against the wall of a building. Once again, the words filled him and his lips twitched: *Jesus, Mary and Joseph. I've lost the bastard!*

Casey Reardon slumped in the front seat of the black Pontiac, his knees digging into the dashboard, his arms folded across his chest. He licked the beads of sweat which collected over his lip, glanced again at his watch, which registered a minute more than the last time he had consulted it, which was twenty minutes from the moment he had dialed the telephone, letting it ring once to indicate subject was in the area. Though Casey had been silent for all the intervening time, Dell spoke now as though in response to him.

'Want me to check it out, boss?'

Reardon hesitated, shook his head. He wondered how Dell could look so cool and uninvolved, because he *knew* Dell was keyed up too. 'We wait,' Reardon said, his eyes watching the alleyway, trying to figure out why Devereaux had gone in but Rogoff had not.

Christie felt her left arm growing numb and carefully trying to prevent the grating noises caused by the slightest movement on the bed, she raised her head. She had to lift her deadened arm with her right hand, biting her lip against the sudden assault of pain as feeling returned in aching waves of pins and needles.

Her mouth fell open as though that would help her to hear: her eyes sought the direction of the sound. A slight, bumping sound from the kitchen area. Or was it from the bathroom?

In a whisper so light it was hardly heard, 'Sorry. That was me.' Ferranti.

She couldn't hear the release of breath, but she knew Marty and Stoney had resumed breathing as well as she. How long had it been since that single crashing ring of the telephone? It was impossible to measure time now and there was no slight glimmer of light by which she could read the dial of her watch which was supposed to glow in the dark, but didn't. There was nothing to measure time by except her own feeling and that wasn't accurate because her body became a stranger to her mind: transformed by the single, anticipated, yet somehow unexpected ring of a telephone. She was filled with internal rushes so sudden and so distinct the only thing that surprised her was that the sounds within her didn't echo and bounce all over the room.

There was a soft, slow, hesitant, opening sound, heard despite the rushes of internal noises, distinct and separate in the darkness.

It was followed by Marty's voice, hollow and low. 'Time?' he whispered carefully and she could hear Stoney moving.

'Ten forty-five.'

They all calculated it: the single ring of the phone came at exactly 10:10 P.M. Thirty-five minutes ago. Thirty-five minutes of waiting.

Where was he? Where in God's name was Rogoff?

For Murray Rogoff, the world was a pit of corruption hemmed by lightless cabarets which opened unashamed onto the heated sidewalks, spilling over with wordless, degraded voices emanating from the throats of faceless sub-human inhabitants. In long and hurried strides, directionless, he strode among them, the anger building into a formless fury, winding its way from his intestines upward into his chest and lungs, downward into his thighs and knees, until his entire being was one pulsating mass of thoughtless emotion. He flung the touching, inquisitive bodies from him in a horror of contamination, knowing he must find release from the filth in which he found himself.

Wandering the streets of Greenwich Village, his mind could not grasp the steady, clear and certain salvation that somehow he knew was hidden within him, elusive and stolen from him by the narrowed, glinting eyes, the simpering voices, the brushing bodies that approached him hopefully, curiously, lustfully. His eyes burned beneath the encasement of his glasses and he pulled them from his face. His fingers dug at the sockets which itched dryly and ached in response to his rough touch. The sounds became a part of him: part of his being, the blatant noises echoing behind him, around him, before him as he rushed around a corner only to be confronted by the discordant moanings of some singer whose voice came at him as through a long tunnel, reaching out from the cavern of some cafe. His eyes moved constantly behind his glasses again, watching the tourists: gaping, not daring to enter the tempting, sawdust-floored interiors, but their eyes shining in a particular way, fascinated by the strangeness around them, trying to proclaim their own innocence by their reluctance to participate, yet their longings clearly visible, gleaming from their eyes and on their dry lips, licked by furtive tongues.

And all the time, down all the streets, the hunger built within him: the hunger for cleanness and purity and love, which could not be found here on these streets.

Finally, Murray Rogoff stopped, halting in the middle of the street, his mind freed at last from his surroundings. Stretching his arms over his head, his voice raised in a great sob of relief, unmindful of the curious or wishful stares of the other searchers, Murray Rogoff's brain relayed the message that had been there all the time, beneath the turmoil, waiting for him to recognize it.

He could walk through them now, untouched, unused, and uncorrupted. He knew where his freedom and his joy and his happiness was: he knew where love was and the image of Christie Opara destroyed all the vileness around him. With a great feeling of reality, Rogoff carefully looked around him and carefully and purposefully headed in a definite direction.

John Devereaux was a patient man and he had learned through bitter experience that a police officer cannot afford the luxury of impatience. He was accustomed to waiting and he waited with a certainty based on years of experience, but even the certainty could not completely control the spurts of anxiety which pumped irregularly through him.

He sifted the facts once again, for in facts there was something to hold onto: One—subject had located room and entry thereto; two—subject, for reasons known only to himself, had decided not to make entry; three—he had lost all contact with subject; four—he, John Devereaux, could not leave this alleyway if hell froze over, unless instructed to do so by Reardon (and omiGod what must he be thinking?) or until daylight, since subject might change his mind and enter the alley after all. So that *in* fact, the fact was that it was Rogoff who was making all the decisions.

John Devereaux was a man who could think like a machine. He was also a man who could experience very human emotions and during the approximately one and a half hours he had clung to the shadows of this particular alleyway, he felt an exhaustion close to despair and a helplessness bordering on anger and a deep regret that he could not light up a cigarette and inhale just one lungful of nicotine and a sorrow that he could not ease off his shoes and spread his swelling toes.

To keep his brain alert, Devereaux devised small mental games, testing his awareness: scanning an entire line of tenement windows, turning his face, then mentally recalling what each window had contained, in proper order. He wondered what technique O'Neill was using: probably keeping tabs on that nutty babe up there. She was inexhaustible, whatever the hell she was doing. He wondered what they were doing in the room: each one cut off like he was, each working out some kind of mental gymnastics, fighting off sleep, which incredibly could easily weigh them all down. Including him. *Christ, where was the bastard?*

Jimmy O'Neill had known within the first two minutes that the figure in the alley was John Devereaux because if the shapeless form had been the suspect, there would have been a *second* figure in the alley and *that* would have been Devereaux. But there was just one man down there and Jimmy calculated, accurately and sympathetically, what had happened. The bastard had given John the slip and John stationed himself in the target area, and Jimmy O'Neill, through the period of time he spent kneeling and waiting and watching, offered up some fervent prayers on behalf of Devereaux and himself and all the others concerned that the bastard would show.

If there had been any slightest doubt in Jimmy's mind of the identity of the man hidden in the alley—and there really wasn't—that doubt would have been dissipated now.

A second figure had entered the alley and O'Neill's eyes, professionally sharpened by his vigil, picked out the shape as identical with that of the giant he had spotted on the roof over an hour and a half before. Coldly and clearly, O'Neill's mind registered the circumstance: Rogoff is now in the courtyard.

John Devereaux stopped breathing as automatically as a diver who plunges into cold deep water without apparatus of any kind. Knowing that he was invisible within the particular shadow he inhabited, he pressed still closer against the wall, watching the large, agile form moving cautiously but steadily across the courtyard, stopping for a moment, listening, looking without seeing, then moving again. Devereaux's eyes left the suspect for just one quick glance at the window on the second floor behind him, then fastened themselves on Rogoff, assured that Jimmy O'Neill would move out onto the fire escape and begin his climb down the instant Rogoff's body was inside the bathroom window.

The silence within the room was a special kind of silence, not total and complete, but composed of two distinct layers. The first layer was made up of sounds: the sounds of radios and TV sets and whirrings of fans and voices talking behind opened windows and children whimpering their useless protests against the heat. These sounds could be ignored for they were all accounted for and after a while did not have to be listened to: they tended to press together into a kind of steady hum that did not interfere with the concentration required of the inhabitants of the room.

The second layer was disinctive within the room: it was the purposeful silence of the occupants, breached occasionally by a shifting of body weight, a stifled cough. A deliberate, wordless silence enforced by Stoner Martin, his voice softly furious a long time back (when? hours?) when Marty Ginsburg had absentmindedly begun to hum in the blackness of his closet floor and Stoney had tossed it at all of them: We are waiting this out; get with it. I'll bash the next goddamn head that makes a sound; if it takes all night, we wait!

Her body had relaxed dangerously and Christie was unable to revive the string-tight awareness, the readiness; she was filled with a dull, unreal, sleepy lack of emotion, all feelings had been nakedly bared too long ago, had receded now, and she felt numb and empty.

The sound was soft and sliding: a hesitant, tentative sound which ceased momentarily so that Christie, lying there, the saliva in her mouth not swallowed, waited. She waited for a quick, soft voice of apology: Ferranti, regretting the movement of his numbed leg, or Marty, mentioning a cramped foot, followed by Stoney's angry grunt. But the silence now was completely intensified so that when the sliding sound began again, there was no question of its origin and Christie felt her body, suddenly alive again, begin to fill with terrible pounding, stabbing sensations.

She could visualize the sound: the raising of a body over the window sill, the slow and careful easing of a body into the bathtub, the feet hesitating, the hands extended, taking measure of the room, seeking the doorway. Christie moved carefully on the bed, her teeth clamped down at the sound of the bedsprings, and then she realized that she was not the one who had to maintain an absolute silence. *She* was the one who had to be present, by the movement of bedsprings, by the agonizingly controlled, steady, deep breathing of a sleeper, and she regulated her breath, hearing it fill the room with a peaceful quiet rhythm, though her lungs felt as if they would explode if she didn't suddenly fill them with a huge gasp of air.

The feet were nearly silent, yet Christie could feel the weight of each step as though the feet were encased in lead boots, each step moving nearer, then stopping in the doorway from the bathroom. The absolute silence encompassed her, drew her into the center of a large, inescapable circle of loneliness, and no one existed in the room except Christie Opara and Murray Rogoff. The absolute silence had destroyed Bill Ferranti and Stoner Martin and Marty Ginsburg.

Lying rigidly on her side, she was able to pick out the form of the man: huge, hesitant, seeking her, and it was only right that they were alone for she had known all along that she would have to face him out: alone.

Christie saw Rogoff more surely, more certainly, more clearly in that one split-instant of recognition than she had ever seen anyone before in her lifetime, yet her breath continued in and out, softly and without variation, untouched by the stark, pure stab of terror that raced through every part of her body.

'Christie, Christie Opara,' the telephone voice called. She heard, as she had not heard in all the nights past when that voice had chanted into her ear, a sound so desolate and empty that all sense of time and place left her and the cold, technical words of a medical report were translated within her brain to the suddenly deformed and frightened boy of sixteen who stood beside her, asking for her help. She felt her hand reach up, felt her fingers make contact with cold and smooth flesh but her gesture had no more reality than a dream.

The abrupt flooding of the room with yellow light and sound and cries and screams and bursts of explosion took her by surprise as though it had all been unanticipated.

She heard the voice, simultaneous with the yellow light, 'Duck, Christie!' yet she could not have said whose voice it was that had propelled her off the bed. Her body hit the floor, worked its way immediately under the bed. Whose voice had shouted, 'Police!' 'Christ! He's got a knife!' 'Drop it!'? There was a tangle of voices and sounds, all unfamiliar, crying out at once or in sequence, she couldn't say, all tangled around the other sounds, louder than she had ever heard, yet no louder than the words or the shriek of agony, some nightmare animal voicing unbearable pain, followed by a heavy thud of something coming to rest beside her own body, to share her refuge.

Christie was not aware that her face was pressed into the palms of her hands until she felt something—someone—leaning against her elbow; and then, lifting her face, her eyes were engaged directly by the strange staring eyes which held her with an incredible emptiness, hypnotizing her with their unblinking demands, and her body could not respond to the voices which called her name. She tried to kick away some hands that were reaching for her, pulling at her ankles, trying to drag her from the safety of her hiding place. Instinctively, she bent her knees so that the hands could not reach her and then, no longer able to bear those eyes which were filmed over and lifeless, Christie, in a surge of mindless terror, realized that she was trapped: the right side of her body wedged against the metal leg of the bed frame, the left side of her touching *his* face. Scraping her body against the hard and tearing metal on one side, but more aware of the contact her body made along the entire left side, Christie worked herself free, hands reached for her arms, her shoulders, pulled her to her knees, then roughly to her feet. Her eyes could see sharply now no longer squinting against the yellow light.

She stood, looking down, fascinated as the thick blood oozed back along Rogoff's skull from a wound low in his forehead, working its way languidly like some gelid insect along the naked, yellow obscenity of his hooded head. Surrounding him in fantastically thick, bright puddles were the emanations of his other wounds, and Christie's left hand, reaching across her mouth, was wet and heavy with slime and she regarded it curiously, not knowing where the blood had come from, for no part of her body felt torn and yet her mouth tasted the thick saltiness of blood and she could see that her shoulder, arm, torso, thigh, calf and sneaker were painted red as though by a wide and careless brush. She stood, waiting to feel the pain of rendered flesh but she felt nothing. Just a terrible, empty calmness.

The room was filled by unexpected faces: Devereaux and O'Neill, and Stoney and Marty and Ferranti, all out of hiding, all plainly visible in the yellowish light and their voices ordering other faces away from the opened door of the room: a myriad of faces, looking, wide-eyed, open-mouthed, asking, staring, their eyes curiously bright; the Homicide men, standing over Rogoff, their faces professionally hard and interested. Then Casey Reardon, with Tom Dell cutting a path for him through the crowded hallway of unknown faces; stolid men who came, regarded the scene wordlessly, not touching the sprawled dead man, but noting the switch-blade knife, opened and bloody in Rogoff's right hand, the odd smashed glasses against one wall and the plaid cap, crushed beneath his large black leather shoe.

Christie raised her left arm when Reardon told her to, offering it for his inspection, let him rip the sleeve of her shirt to her shoulder, let him push her along into the bathroom. She watched, fascinated, as the thick red blood thinned to the consistency of watercolor paint while Reardon kept sloshing cold water down the length of her arm. 'It isn't from you, thank God,' she heard him say, but his voice was unfamiliar and his face was unfamiliar and even his eyes, which tried to hold hers but for some reason could not, were unknown.

A voice, not her own, told him, 'I'm all right. I'm all right, just leave me alone!'

Reardon, his hand on her shoulder, did not react or comment

as she pulled free of his touch, but just asked her, 'You want anything, Christie? Do you need anything—a drink maybe?'

Christie stood rigidly straight, her lips pulling back into a tight and meaningless smile, her eyes narrowed on his. Slowly, deliberately, she raised her right arm, extending the untrembling fingers. 'I am as steady as a rock, Mr. Reardon,' but curiously, she felt no satisfaction. He left her alone in the bathroom then, and she could not understand her anger or why it was directed at him.

In what sequence they all arrived, Christie could not determine, but the room was taken over by all of those people who have a part in these things, each moving independently of all the others, intent only upon his particular segment of the event. Christie moved closer into the tight little circle that formed in one corner of the room: the circle consisting of Bill Ferranti, Stoner Martin and Marty Ginsburg. Christie, looking at first one face and then the other, was struck by the similarity: each of them seemed washed in a kind of grayness around the lips, which had gone dry as her own lips had, down the nostrils, along the cheeks. Reardon brought some large, expressionless man over to them and he shook hands with each of them, a hard grasp and a quick release, his tiny granite eyes digging at each of them in turn, his bloodless lips telling them they had done a good job. He was brass, but Christie didn't know who, just that he was brass: that much anyone could tell.

The doctor came into the room followed by a hospital attendant. He examined Christie's arm, glanced at her accusingly when he discovered the blood that covered her did not come from her own veins. She wrenched away from him, not wanting to be touched.

Marty Ginsburg extended his right arm, letting Stoney remove his shirt. The paleness spread along Marty's forehead when the doctor swabbed his arm with a large wad of cotton: the blood running down Marty Ginsburg's clothes was from a long, deep cut which started from a point just inside his right elbow and terminated an inch or so short of his wrist.

'But I don't feel nothing,' Marty said in wonder, touching his opened flesh, 'I just don't *feel* it.'

'You will,' the doctor said pleasantly, 'when the shock wears off, brother, you *will*.'

Ferranti knew the blood just under his jaw was from a small

deep wound and he held a wet handkerchief against the cut until the doctor finished his temporary bandaging of Marty.

'At least twenty stitches for that one,' the doctor said, then smiling, 'he doesn't feel it: boy, he will tomorrow. And now, you, what have you got here?' Leaning his head back, the short doctor squinted at Ferranti. 'Ah, yes, lucky cut this one. A little to one side and it would have been the jugular vein and then we'd have two for the bag boys.'

Stoney, uncut, unwounded, stood beside her, watching. His hand clung to her arm and she could feel the hard kneading pressure of his fingers, keeping her in the room, though her eyes would not follow his, would not look, as everyone else was looking, at the large, lifeless hulk of Murray Rogoff.

The door opened again and Christie turned, seeing the men being admitted, press cards pinned on summer shirts, stuck in hatbands or nonchalantly flashed then put back into a pocket. Reardon backed them into the kitchen alcove, warning them not to touch anything, and their eyes remained on Christie, all their questions directed at her presence in the room, and they grinned, excited by the dark blood down her side. Reardon held them back with a gesture, came to her side.

'*Daily News* and *Post*. They want your picture.' His hand straightened her hair lightly. 'Look, you don't have to.'

She bit her lip, then pushed it out. 'Whatever you say, Mr. Reardon.'

There was just a smile, not the hard familiar smile, just a smile and his hand pressed hers, leading her to the kitchenette. 'Just a couple, fellows, then let her alone; my people have had a rough night.'

The reporters directed her, told her how to stand, where to look, pointed at Stoney and Marty and Bill, but mostly the photographers wanted to get a good shot of her: of the side with the blood, and their hard professional voices kept positioning her. Christie looked right through them coldly. The lingering circles of bright haze dulled out all the details of the room as the lights popped at her face. They moved away, finished with her now, aiming at Rogoff, whose eyes would not be bothered by the torturous lights.

A scrawny, wiry boy with a blade sharp nose and almost no lips grasped her arm. 'Look, Christie, baby, hop up on the refrigerator, will you, and turn kind of sideways so I can get a good shot of your leg. Let's cheese it up a little!' She thrust his hand from her, meeting his surprised stare; she pulled her lips back and her voice—her own now, low and harsh—threw the words at him, 'Keep your hands off me!'

The photographer's face, knowing and shrewd and older than his years, watched her. 'Come on, sweetie, don't give me any of that crap! Your boss said we can take pictures, so just make like a good kid and pose.'

Christie's eyes hardened and she whispered fiercely, 'Get lost, junior, right now!' He turned his back on her in disgust and began edging closer to the dead body only to be turned away by Devereaux and O'Neill who, as Homicide men, had priority and were protecting the corpse until their superior officers were finished with their observations.

She walked down the long hallway, past the people, who pointed and nodded and commented, not seeing them, not hearing them. She felt a strange unreality now: as though the only reality had been back there, in that room, where Rogoff lay dead.

They all rode in the ambulance and when they arrived at the Emergency Ward, Ferranti couldn't put any weight on his right ankle and he leaned heavily on Stoney's arm until the attendant brought a wheelchair: he had twisted his ankle when he had lunged at Rogoff and now the swelling was so extensive that the intern had to cut the sock from his foot.

Christie waited in the Emergency Reception Room while Marty was being stitched up and Ferranti was being sewed and X-rayed. Stoney made the telephone calls to the wives of both men. She was relieved that they hadn't asked her to do it: her voice would have sounded so flat and emotionless they would have been sure the injuries were fatal. Christie called Nora, stated the facts tersely, her voice even and calm and Nora hadn't pressed her, didn't ask anything except, 'Are you all right, Christie?' and she had replied, 'Yes.'

Stoney appeared with two containers of black coffee and she drank the bitter hot liquid, feeling it burn through her without stimulation of any kind. She accepted the cigarette he held out to her. He cupped the match over his own cigarette, regarding it curiously. 'Damnedest thing," he said, 'I had a butt dangling in my mouth the whole time, drawing on it like it was lit, and you know, Christie, when it hit the fan, when everything popped, all that time, the cigarette just kept clinging to my mouth like it was part of me.' He smiled without humor. 'Casey took it from my mouth when he came into the room. I didn't even know it was there.' They sat in silence, each caught up in the sequence of events.

It was past one A.M. when Reardon arrived at the hospital. Assured that none of his people had been sedated yet, he instructed the reluctant supervising nurse to wheel Ferranti into Ginsburg's room which she agreed to do after a long, hard and revealing study of Reardon's face.

Reardon herded Mrs. Ferranti and Mrs. Ginsburg into the hallway, reassured them that their husbands would survive in good shape and reassured the men that their wives would be delivered safe and well to their homes by Tom Dell. He waved an almost child-sized man with a plump, disinterested face into the room along with Stoney and Christie, and wordlessly, the small man found a chair, which he pulled up close to Ginsburg's bed.

Carefully, he opened his little black leather case, pulled a tripod stand from somewhere inside the case, twirled a dial on a long roll of white paper, then, his fingers poised over the keys of his stenotype machine, for the first time he looked up, his eyes inquiringly on Reardon.

'While it's fresh in everyone's mind,' Casey said, 'let's have a run down, beginning with Rogoff's entrance into the apartment. I want to present this to the Grand Jury as quickly as possible.'

And then, for the first time, each of them heard how it was; each told his own story and the bits of sound and light and shouting and cries fell into place, the voices now identified, the sudden sounds and words all having been emitted by individual human beings.

Stoney had called out, 'Police officers!'; Marty had spotted the knife, calling out, 'Watch it!' as Stoney yelled, 'He's got a knife!' while Ferranti yelled, 'Drop it! It was at Marty that Rogoff lunged and Marty, still not feeling pain, fingered the clean white bandage down the length of his arm. 'You'd think with a cut that long—twenty-two stitches—I would have felt something.'

Ferranti had seized the powerful arm, trying to wrench the knife free from the unrelenting hand and Ferranti had felt his own wound with more surprise than pain.

'I think I fired first,' Stoney said thoughtfully, turning his eyes to Bill.

'I think I caught him in the forehead,' Bill said softly, remembering now the startled expression and then the spasmodic twisting of the body.

'I got two off,' Marty said. 'But I'm not sure if I hit him.'

'I hit him,' Stoney said. 'In the chest.'

Reardon signaled the stenotypist, and expressionless, he rolled up his paper, slid the legs back into their hiding place, shut his case, snapped the lock, nodded at no one in particular and left the room.

'Hey, there, Christie,' Stoney said, smiling now, 'why the heck did you nearly kick my head off? Don't go blank on me: I was just trying to get you out from under that bed.'

Yes; she remembered now. Hands reaching for her, pulling at her. She shrugged and her shoulders felt very heavy. 'I don't know, Stoney, just . . . I just had to get out of there face first, I guess.'

His hand ran across his forehead, searching for a bruise.

'Any lumps there, Mr. Reardon? That girl has a wicked karate kick.'

Reardon was watching her; she knew that. Leaning over Stoney, making his light remarks, he was watching her, as he had been all during the telling of it, but she would not look at him and she didn't know why: maybe because she didn't want him to see whatever it was he was looking for.

Finally, firmly, the supervising nurse came in, stood her ground flatly, crackling with starch and rightful authority. 'These men *must* rest now.' She held up two little paper cups, jiggling them so Casey could hear the pills inside. 'I have orders to give each of them a sleeping pill and *this one*'—her eyes accusingly on Ferranti—'must go back to his assigned room.'

Casey stood up, grinned, bowed his head slightly at the surprised woman who was fully prepared to do battle. 'Yes ma'am,' he said pleasantly, 'you're in charge.' He winked at the bedded men, his eyes wandering over the square heavy shape of the nurse. 'Sleep good, boys, and don't give the nurse any trouble. They act up in any way, ma'am, you let me know.'

The nurse ignored him, busily poured water into a tumbler and watched sharply so that Marty couldn't hide the pill in his cheek. Following Casey, Christie and Stoney both turned for a moment, both looked at their partners in a special way, nodding, wordlessly accepting the responding nods.

'You guys have anything to eat lately?' Reardon asked them in the hallway.

'This fella here,' Stoney said, pointing at Christie, 'had some black coffee which I don't think was agreeable in view of the fact that this fella here is a notorious tea drinker.'

'You want a cup of tea or a sandwich or anything, Christie?'

She shook her head. Her fingers touched the dark brown stain on her clothing. Rogoff's blood was still slightly damp and was beginning to stiffen darkly. 'I'd like to go home and shower and get out of these things.'

'Right. Sam. Farrell is standing by with his car to take you home.' He looked at his watch, grimacing. 'Two A.M. Hate to do this to you, guys, but it's necessary: get home, sleep a couple of hours and be in the office first thing. Nine A.M. okay?'

'You want me in at nine A.M., I'll be in at nine A.M.'

He studied her face for a moment, a small, familiar grin pulling at the corners of his mouth, but he bit back whatever words he was about to say. He waved his hand at Sam Farrell who had just gotten off the elevator and had walked directly into a water cooler. Rubbing his thigh, Farrell approached them, his eyes wide and glassy from lack of sleep. 'Hey, Sam, you got something on for tomorrow A.M.?'

Farrell dug in his pockets, then came up with a scribbled notation. 'You told me to get that tape to the Police Lab, Mr. Reardon, first thing.'

Reardon considered for a moment: Farrell lived in the Bronx. 'Sorry, Opara, I can't give you transportation in the morning, you'll have to subway-it in.'

'No problem,' she said shortly, entering the elevator, nodding good night to Stoney, then, her eyes on Reardon's, meeting them fully for the first time in the brief moment before the elevator doors slid shut, she warned him: Whatever it is you're looking for, you won't see it in my face.

CHAPTER NINETEEN

JOHN DEVEREAUX'S FACE was marked by deep burrows of fatigue. All the natural lines of some forty-seven years of his life were cruelly evident. His pale gray eyes were oddly flat, surrounded by the redness of long sleepless hours and the consumption of nearly a fifth of Scotch, steadily swallowed, a shot at a time, in a manner that served not to increase his efficiency and alertness but merely as a necessity which enabled him to remain relatively awake and relatively able to continue his tasks.

When Christie Opara arrived at the Squad office and offered to complete his typewritten report, he merely nodded heavily, sliding his chair to one side, watching her push another chair into place before the machine. His eyes seemed fixed in an unblinking stare and every pore of his body exuded the heaviness of alcohol and fatigue. He shook his head over his words, but his voice displayed not a trace of emotion.

'This guy Rogoff,' he said heavily, 'God, *He kept a shoe box under his bed.*' There was something terrible about the flatness of his voice. He ran a large hand across the disheveled sparseness of his hair. 'Shoe box of souvenirs: notebooks and hair clippings. A notebook on you, by the way—it was in his pants pocket last night.'

Christie's mind did not hold onto this as a fact: just some words that Devereaux was saying to her. A cold shower and careful makeup hid the fatigue outwardly but her brain was numbed and functioning mechanically.

Devereaux held his hand up, his thumb and index finger measuring. 'About an inch of hair in each little box.' Then, his words heavy as stone, 'There were *seven* notebooks and *six* little boxes of hair clippings.'

Christie's mouth went dry as the light gray eyes staring at her revealed no shock and no surprise: John Devereaux had lived with this knowledge for several hours now. *'Seven?'*

'Yeah,' he said. 'We're going to be digging up cases from years back; all over the city. Cases that technically have remained open but haven't been actively investigated for a long time.' He was talking more to himself now, 'God. There was this kid in Brooklyn three years ago: I worked on it for a while before I got transferred to the Bronx.'

'Seven,' Christie repeated, and then, it just occurring to her, her own involvement just occurring to her, 'seven notebooks and six boxes of hair.' Her fingers touched the short hair on the back of her neck.

Devereaux's eyes blinked and he rubbed them. 'Hey, Christie, you were real good last night. It was tough, huh?'

'Yes. You had some bad moments yourself, didn't you?'

His eyes were fixed again. 'It was worse later; afterward. Jimmy O'Neill and I and some of the other guys from my Squad went to Rogoff's place; spent hours tearing it apart.' He rubbed the back of his neck, screwed his face into deep creases, tested his jaw. 'That was what you call tough. The brother was there: from Long Island. Poor bastard. He'd been notified and he had to tell the parents. By the time we got there, you could hear the old woman shrieking. A real little woman and his father is a little guy: funny. Rogoff was so big, you know. Jimmy told the brother to get a doc to give the old people a shot to quiet them down but the old woman kept screaming for nearly an hour after she got a shot. The brother came back into the apartment after a while, when the old folks calmed down in a neighbor's apartment and he just kind of stood there, watching us, trying not to get in our way, you know?'

The pale face of David Rogoff had registered in Christie's mind after all: she could see him now.

'You know Paddy Leary? Big guy, heavy set? Well Paddy got a rough mouth, you know, and when we found that shoe box he held it up to Rogoff's brother, and he said, "Nice brother you got there, huh buddy? Been going around killing all these little girls," and the brother just stood there and his knees just gave way on him, and Jimmy told him to go into the kitchen and make us a pot of coffee.' John shook his head. 'Coffee. Christ, and all of us were belting down White Label the whole time.'

'Let's get this report typed up, John, okay?'

Jimmy O'Neill, a tall, bony man with a crew cut and boyish face, bore no resemblance whatever to his partner. His cheeks were concave and his eyes were like two bright black marbles. Yet, weariness had made them identical and when he arrived, distributing containers of hot coffee, relieving Devereaux, dictating to Christie, it was the same heavy flat voice, wearily spelling out details, and Christie typed rapidly, looking up in surprise at Reardon's voice.

His sleeplessness, though evident in the heavy squinting of his eyes and bright reddish-gold glints along his cheeks and chin, was more revealed by the hard, artificial brightness of his voice. 'Hey, Opara. I didn't think that fast typing was being done by the talented fingers of our Homicide colleagues. Listen, when you get finished I have some rough drafts that need doing, okay?' His hand pulled his loosened tie downward and there were bright red hairs showing at his neck.

Reardon looked at his watch, wound it, went back into his own office.

Stoner Martin arrived, waved a quick greeting, hunched himself over a steady series of telephone calls, then informed Christie that Marty was in a lot of pain but Ferranti was feeling pretty good.

Tom Dell entered the office, a package under his arm, rubbing his newly shaved chin. He looked fresh and clean and rested and he carefully placed his hat on the aluminum rack.

'Boy, I feel crummy,' he said. 'We really should have a shower on the floor.'

O'Neill winked at his partner. 'Dapper Dell himself, looking like a Saturday night date and crying because he missed his shower.'

'Were you out all night?' Christie asked, surprised, because he didn't look it.'

'Don't I look weary?' Dell asked, sounding offended. He held up his package. 'This is the rottenest neighborhood to try and get a decent shirt.'

Devereaux pulled his own sweaty shirt from his neck. 'Sonny you D.A. people kill me. Never go around-the-clock and then some in the same shirt?'

Dell shook his head, regarding the two Homicide men distastefully. 'We have a little class around here, gentlemen.' He shook the package at them. 'Mr. Reardon and me, we're not like some other slobs I'm too polite to mention. We meet all emergencies as they come along, but with class and style, at all times.'

The men exchanged insults good-naturedly, the weariness receding, the coffee taking hold, their minds resharpened. Dell brought one of the new shirts into Reardon, returned with an electric razor.

'Stoney, Mr. Reardon says can you fix this thing: it buzzes but it don't cut. Me, personally, I wouldn't feel clean-shaven unless I had that nice hot lather all over these tender cheeks, but the boss goes for the electric.'

Dell's face was relaxed and unmarked by the long hours of waiting he had spent, the hours searching Rogoff's apartment, the hours driving Reardon from one location to another. He sat down, carefully preserving the crease in his trousers, his feet stretching to the top of a desk.

Stoney brought the repaired razor in to Reardon, then told Dell, 'You better get that new shirt on, if you're intending to, son, because the Man says he'll be ready to roll as soon as that red beard is electrified off.'

Dell moved quickly, setting his hat on the back of his head, pulling the shirt from the package. 'Tell the boss I'll be out front,' he called, unbuttoning his shirt as he moved toward the men's room.

Reardon adjusted his collar and tie, scowled at himself in the small rectangular mirror in the Squad room, then turned to Devereaux and O'Neill. 'I just spoke to your Squad Commander, fellas. You finish your reports?'

They nodded. 'He wants you both; better grab a bite. Jesus, it's lunchtime, isn't it? He's got some brass coming over and he wants you there.'

'Yes, sir.'

'Martin and Opara, stick around. I'll be back in about an hour.' The amber eyes, sharp and clear again, caught her expression of annoyance. 'Chin up, Opara,' he said lightly, tossing a copy of the *Daily News* at her. 'How often do you get mugged on the front page?'

Christie watched him leave, her eyes angrily on the dark red cowlick. Her mouth fell open when his hand pressed the lock of hair down and he turned at the door, grinning directly at her. Damn him.

Devereaux and O'Neill made short, muttered phone calls, explaining to long-experienced wives that they weren't to be expected until they arrived home. Resigned to their continuing tour, they left for their own office. Christie and Stoney, paced by each other, typed rapidly, piecing together the seemingly endless reports which Reardon needed for the case file. Christie had called her brother's home, spoken briefly to her sister-in-law, assuring them she was fine. She had tried to engage Mickey in conversation, but he was too excited and too obviously annoyed by the interruption: Aunt Alice was taking him and all his cousins and two neighborhood kids to the movies and yeah, he saw her picture, yeah, it was swell and gee, he couldn't talk now, Mom, because *Mary Poppins* was going to start in ten minutes and yeah, he would see her later and yeah, goodbye.

It was four o'clock before Reardon returned, and Christie wondered if he and Dell had gone somewhere and slept for a few hours. They both looked rested and starched and fresh. Christie felt exhaustion in every part of her body and a strong and growing resentment at being in the office. She wanted to be home; under the shower, in bed. Reardon scooped up the stack of papers, took his time reading them. Dell handed her a copy of the afternoon *Post*: her picture was on the first page. Not reading the copy, just staring at the photograph, she hated the girl, standing there, legs apart, thumbs hooked into the pockets of her dungarees: she looked like some delinquent arrogantly admitting she had stolen an old woman's pocketbook.

Stoney's voice was sad. 'Christie, Christie. You got to learn not to glare at those men with the cameras, because baby, they got the final word.'

Reardon walked rapidly from his office, not breaking pace as he crossed the Squad room. 'C'mon, c'mon, let's get going, fellas. Dell, you get the wheels out front? Come on, Opara, let's move it.'

Following Reardon, she exchanged glances with Stoney, who shrugged. 'Just do what the Man says and follow where the Man leads.'

Sitting slumped in the back seat of the Pontiac, not taking part in the conversation, Christie slid her wristwatch around, checking the time, but the sharp voice from the front seat informed her, 'It's five-fifteen, Opara. What's your problem?'

'No problem, Mr. Reardon, none at all.'

He directed Dell into a parking slot that was clearly marked 'Doctors Only', then hurried them through the hospital lobby, ignoring a nurse who tried to tell them something about 'visiting hours'; he stabbed the button of the elevator and waved at the nurse as the doors closed. 'Come on now, Opara, let's see your best visitor's smile.' Christie stretched her lips, showing two rows of white teeth. 'Great,' Reardon said. 'That'll send Ginsburg into a relapse for sure.'

Striding past the floor nurse, Reardon called, 'It's okay, it's okay, don't worry about it,' and he hurried them along, despite the fact that the nurse was rushing around the small desk behind which she had been toiling over official records.

Reardon flung the door open and his voice startled the other two patients sharing the room with Marty Ginsburg.

'Well, exactly how long do you intend to hang around this place, Ginsburg? How long do you think I'm going to carry you?'

The two other patients leaned warily into their pillows and stared at the group of intruders.

Incredibly, it seemed that Marty had lost a considerable amount of weight; his large cheeks were drawn and empty like airless balloons and his lips were white and pulled back in a half smile. He offered his left hand to Reardon. 'I'd give you my shaking hand, boss,' he said in an odd imitation of Marty Ginsburg's voice, 'but as you can see, it's a little out of order right now.'

Reardon stood beside the bed quietly for a moment, his eyes a different color than Christie had ever seen them: softer and with an expression of concern. He leaned close to Marty and said something the others couldn't hear and Marty nodded once, heavily, as though in reassurance. It was so quick an exchange that Christie wasn't even certain it had taken place for Reardon turned easily to meet the outraged nurse and his face was animated again and his voice was loud and playful. 'It's okay, honey, relax. You just take very good care of this guy here and watch out for his stitches.' He leaned into the startled face. 'This guy has skin like leather: when it starts to mend, those stitches might go flying all around this place like bullets.'

Marty joined in some light banter and his voice, oddly enough, sounded familiar again. They followed Reardon out of the room and Christie could hear the nurse warning Marty to settle down, but the woman's voice wasn't really angry.

Bill Ferranti was sitting up in bed, reading a magazine, his cheeks a healthy pink. He was having some difficulty keeping his head in a comfortable position because the bandage covering his neck wound was bulky, and he touched it when Christie asked how he felt.

'This is a little annoying. I don't see why they made the bandage so large. The cut actually is only about an inch.'

'An inch?' Reardon asked. Boy, it's a good thing they have that cast on your ankle or I'd have you up and out.' His voice softened and his fingers touched the cast lightly. 'I understand you have a fracture?'

Ferranti made a clicking sound. 'That really surprised me. It didn't hurt that much. In fact, it doesn't hurt now, just feels a little uncomfortable.'

Reardon's fingers moved along the cast for a moment and Christie noted a kind of gentleness in the gesture, but Reardon's voice was tough and mocking again. 'What a hell of a Squad: two of my guys flat on their backs and you'—he turned to her—'plastered all over the front pages.' There was no special expression when he faced her, just that amused, hard grin. 'Comes the cold weather and I can just hear you all groaning with aches and pains. Anything hurt you, Opara?'

'Nothing hurts me, Mr. Reardon.'

No one seemed to notice the coldness of her voice. If Reardon caught it, nothing in his face indicated that she had even spoken. 'Boy, you guys sure knocked the D.A. for a loop,' he said. 'He was so impressed he almost smiled. Not quite, but almost.' He snapped his fingers. 'Damn, I almost forgot. I put you all in for promotion and commendation. Not you, Stoney—you got nowhere to go, but they might give you an extra medal. The D.A. endorsed the recommendation but that doesn't mean anything. We'll have to see what the availabilities are.'

Then, brusque again, 'Well, let's move. Ferranti, you stay put, I'll have to think up something good for you—we must have a case where a guy on crutches will come in handy.'

Ferranti signaled Christie to his bedside and Reardon impatiently called out, 'Make it fast, will you, Opara, we're ready to move!'

Christie, puzzled by the deepening color rising along Bill's cheeks, leaned toward him.

'Christie,' he said hesitantly, 'I want to apologize.'

'*Apologize? For what?*'

Ferranti licked his lips, adjusted his horn-rimmed glasses. 'Last night: when the lights went on and all the action and everything, well, in all the confusion and all'—Ferranti took a deep breath—'well, some of the *language* that was tossed around—well, some of it was mine and frankly, I wasn't even aware of it. But lying here all day, thinking about it, well, I realized all of a sudden some of the words I used and I want to apologize to you.'

Christie felt a giddy sensation, a lightheadedness. She reached for his hand, pressing it firmly to keep herself steady. 'Bill, in all the noise and confusion, I think I probably added my own touch of "blue" to the atmosphere, only under the bed, I doubt anyone heard me. At least, I *hope* no one heard me. Anyway, apology unneccessary, but accepted. You take care now.'

'You too, Christie. You were great. Really. Just fine.'

Reardon was involved in some animated conversation with the nurse who followed his every word and gesture with a delighted, if somewhat wary, smile and her only comment, repeated several times, was 'Oh, you cops!'

Reardon was humming in the elevator and Christie wondered where this surge of energy had come from: he must have slept a few hours. The cool breeze felt good against the clamminess of her dress and Christie let it envelop her, consciously enjoying the cleanness of the air, not listening to the men, not even aware of their voices, until she felt Stoney pressing her hand. 'You take care, little one,' he said, waving to them.

Dell handed Reardon the car keys. 'I checked with Communications and Homicide and the office and nobody's looking for us, boss. You got a full tank.'

Christie felt a sense of relief now: Reardon was going home. She was finished for the day; she could go home, get Mickey. Reardon had a tight hold on her arm and was propelling her toward the Pontiac. Tom Dell called to her, 'See you, Christie, take it easy.'

Reardon opened the car door for her. 'Come on, Opara, get in. Hey, do you know that your mouth is open?' Edging her into the front seat, he leaned toward her. 'Dell has to subway it home tonight. The boss is driving. Any questions?' He held up his hand. 'Don't ask questions, just do like the boss tells you—fasten your seat belt.'

She clicked the seat belt, feeling the metal buckle press against her stomach. She didn't look at him, sitting beside her now, but she felt a renewed wave of anger growing: at him. Everyone else was going home; everyone else in the Squad was finished for the day. But *she* had to drag around, probably type up a hundred more reports. She folded her arms and dropped her pocketbook beside her feet.

Reardon drove the way he did everything else: quickly, expertly, impatiently. Christie sat biting the inside of her cheek, refusing to ask him any questions in response to his lack of any explanation. She didn't even notice what street they were on when he suddenly slammed on the brakes and backed into a parking space.

'What luck: they must have known we were coming. C'mon, Opara.'

She debated sitting there, waiting for him to walk around and open the door for her, but he was headed down the block, waving his hand for her to follow. He didn't slow his pace, so she walked rapidly until she was alongside of him. He grasped her arm and steered her into a doorway.

'Here we are,' he said easily, as though they had both been looking for a particular location. It was a restaurant and the coolness sent a momentary chill along her shoulder blades and some man approached them, smiling expansively, shaking Casey's hand, taking hers, nodding approval, walking them past all the other tables to a booth isolated in the semidarkness. Christie slid into the dark red leather seat indicated by the man, identified as George, and Casey sat opposite her, leaning his elbows on the table, regarding her with an amused expression.

'Hey,' Reardon asked, 'when did you eat last?'

Christie shrugged.

'Well, you are going to eat now. And I mean eat. George doesn't give me a menu: he just brings food. And you better smile, because George is a very sensitive guy and he watches like a hawk: the first bite of everything he brings. He waits and watches. You better keep that face of yours under control because I'll murder you if you hurt George's feelings, because if you do, I'm dead here.'

She started to answer, to say something to him, but George appeared carrying two drinks on a tray, smiling and beaming at Casey and then at Christie. 'Scotch on the rocks for Mr. Reardon and for the young lady, something very *special*.' He placed a white frothy drink in a cocktail glass before her and stood, waiting, the smile hovering. His hand gestured. 'Taste it, young lady, and you let me know.'

Christie sipped at the liquid; it was cool and creamy and sweet in her mouth, then warm in her throat. 'It's very nice,' she said, then seeing the smile was not completed, she sipped again. 'Really, it's delicious.'

George's face expanded and he made a circle with his thumb

and index finger and headed for the kitchen. 'See,' Casey said, 'George's feelings are very delicate.'

Christie tasted the drink again. George's feelings. Why should she be concerned about the feelings of some stranger named George, who stood there waiting, demanding her reaction? She turned her wrist; the damn band was too loose and she could never see what time it was. Reardon's hand shot out and grasped her wrist.

'Relax, Christie, you're with the boss.'

She pulled her hand away, recognizing the voice, the familiar taunting voice. Whose voice had it been last night, asking her if she were all right, over and over again, asking if *she* were all right, as if only *she* of all of them would be the only one not to make it?

'Mr. Reardon, I'm tired. I'm not hungry. I'm just tired. I don't want to upset your friend George, but I think I probably will because I don't think I'll be able to eat anything so why don't you just explain it to him because I really want to go home now.'

'Too late,' Reardon said, smiling over the tangy, steaming delicacy that the waiter placed before them and, automatically playing a role, Christie nibbled at a corner of something, not tasting it, smiling up at the man, who wouldn't move away until she had swallowed. Her fork played over the plate, her fingers locked tightly around it. Reardon was talking about the food, then something about wine, about which wine went with what food and about fragrance and aroma and bouquet and vintage. He uncorked a bottle, pouring a small amount into a sparkling glass, sipped it, signaled acceptance to George somewhere behind her, then poured some for her and urged her to drink it and she did.

In one swallow, Christie let it rush down her throat, ignoring Reardon and his voice, telling her that isn't the way you drink wine, as though the technique of drinking wine mattered, as though their sitting here mattered.

'Christie, look up at me.' The voice was sharp but she could see only a blur facing her. 'Christie, let it out,' Reardon said, and she heard her own voice, hard and unfamiliar, 'Leave me alone, Mr. Reardon. I'm fine. You didn't think I would be, did you? Well, wet-nurse one of the others—*not me!*'

His chin was raised but she couldn't really see him. His face was lost in the shadows, in a kind of darkness that was enveloping him, but she could still meet him head on. If he had to dig at her, that was his problem not hers.

The voice was familiar, mocking and sarcastic, and his words were rapid and mean. 'Jesus, I hope you're not getting the idea that I'm wet-nursing you. Hell, you're one of my guys, right?'

'Right,' she said, unaware she had spoken.

'You're one of the best, right?' He was leaning forward now, his hands flat on the table alongside his drink, and his voice was low. 'It didn't touch you, did it? None of it reached you, did it? It said in the *News*—it said Christie Opara was cool and calm as if she'd just taken a walk around the block. It said you were the calmest officer present on the scene. Like ice. Is that what you're like, Christie? Because—hey—that's a damn good thing to be: *like ice!*'

His words pierced her like a steady barrage of sharp bright needles but she didn't recognize him: he was a dark shape, darker than the darkness surrounding him, the clearest shape she had ever seen in her life, moving toward her, and she opened her mouth to protest, to tell him, to strike back at him, but a low sound came from within her and her breath caught and she could not form the sound and she could not breathe in or out. And then, it was as though light had suddenly shattered the intense darkness of the room and the room changed, unfamiliar and unknown. Christie reached out for something to hold on to and there was something—someone—beside her now, holding her tightly, and she tried to wrench away because it was Rogoff and his hands, dead, could not hold, but hands held her now, biting into her shoulders, pressing her face against the clean fresh smell of a new shirt and the hands were easing their hard grasp now, the pressure relaxing, and it was Reardon's voice and Reardon's hands, moving through her hair, pressing her face against his chest.

'Okay, Christie,' he intoned, chanting it over and over, until the words began to have meaning, 'okay, Christie, let it out, Christie, let it all out, it's okay now, Christie, it's all over.'

She eased back now and he released her and she touched her face, looking at the colorless wetness which was not blood: not this time. He dug around in his back pocket, wiped her face, told her to 'blow', then he blotted her eyes again.

She leaned back, taking the handkerchief from him, blew again, avoiding his eyes. 'I'm sorry,' she said. 'I guess I'm the first member of your Squad who ever cried all over your shirt. And a new shirt too.'

He turned her chin roughly to him, forcing her face up. 'Don't apologize, Christie. You've a right to cry it out. Hell, I think men would be a lot better off if they sobbed it out occasionally. There'd be a hell of a lot less boozing and a hell of a lot less ulcers and a hell of a lot less everything else.' He grinned now. 'But I'll tell you, I thought I was going to have to belt you one, and George never would have understood that.'

She leaned back feeling more tired than she had ever felt in her life: but it was a good, empty tiredness. She opened her eyes, saw George with his tray. He registered no reaction to the fact that Casey was seated alongside Christie. Casey looked at her, then at George.

'George, I hate to do this to you,' Casey said, rising, extending his hand to her, 'but this young lady has become ill.' He quickly added, 'Not from the drink or anything, gee, no. You see, she's been exposed to the German measles and just look at her. She's all blotchy and I haven't had the German measles and I'm going to just stick her in a cab and send her home right now. I certainly wouldn't want her spreading her germs all over this place.'

George moved his head discreetly. 'What a shame,' he said. He balanced the tray against his body and lifted a heavy aluminum cover just enough to permit a steamy fragrant aroma to escape. 'Another time?'

Casey placed a five-dollar bill on the tray. 'Right. And next time, George, when the lady is over the German measles, I'll starve her for three days and then you can stuff her for a whole evening. She needs a little fattening up, don't you think so?'

George smiled. 'Thank you, Mr. Reardon. Yes, I will plan something very special. Any time, Mr. Reardon, you come any time. You too, miss.'

The evening had darkened with long jagged red remnants streaking across the edges of the sky. Christie sniffled into the handkerchief, then jammed it into her pocketbook.

Reardon held the car door open for her, ordered, 'Fasten your seat belt.'

Christie leaned her head back, closed her eyes and did not listen to his terse telephone conversation or his grunt of satisfaction when he placed the receiver back into position and switched the mobile telephone to the 'off' position. 'We're off the air and we are going to stay off the air.' He turned his body toward her, his arm on the steering wheel. 'Christie, where do you want to go?'

Her eyes traced the white vinyl of the car ceiling and the weariness seemed to be dissolving and she thought for a moment.

'Not home?' he asked. 'Not yet, right?'

Her tongue touched the corner of her lips and she started to say something, then stopped, and he told her impatiently, 'Look, Opara, you name it—you got it.'

'The beach,' she said.

'The beach,' he said flatly. He started the car, pulled into traffic, disregarding an irate motorist who had to come to an unexpected, brake-shrieking halt. 'Not P.J.'s? Not Top of the Sixes? Not the Four Seasons?' He glanced at her, then muttered to himself, 'It figures. Okay, Opara. The beach.'

Reardon fought every car in sight, cataloguing the inadequacies and low intelligence of all the drivers on all the streets and parkways between Manhattan and Queens. Christie dozed, half listening to the one-sided arguments which finally subsided into an occasional snatch of song: he had a nice voice, musically strong and certain.

She opened her eyes as he cut the motor.

'Where are we?'

'Riis Park,' Reardon said, '*The beach*.' Then, as she looked around, 'This is a closed-off road, used for military vehicles at the Army installation over there. Some people don't believe in signs'—he pointed to the official no admittance poster—'but, hell, this is an authorized vehicle, right?'

'Right.' She got out of the car and he slid across the seat and stood beside her.

'Well,' Reardon said, 'we're at the beach. What do we do now—strip and go swimming?'

She shook her head slowly and walked onto the sand, wordless. Reardon followed her halfway to the water's edge, then squatted on the cool sand. She had thought, back at the restaurant, that she had purged herself of it, but he knew she hadn't. He watched her move tentatively along the shore, her body caught by the strong pale moonlight, a small shadow on the deserted beach. It was the loneliest sight Reardon had ever seen.

He knew she could not accomplish it alone and he walked toward her. He saw her shudder as his shadow crossed hers; the air rushing from the ocean was cold and wet. Her face, as she turned to him, was contorted by pain and her eyes were empty and she tried to say something but the words stopped at her lips. She was too drained to cry and too exhausted to attempt to explain what she felt.

'Come on up on the beach. It's too cold here.' He took her arm and led her to a mound of dry sand and she sat when he did. Reardon began speaking, his voice a little uncertain, his eyes on the ocean. 'About sixteen years ago,' he said, 'I was in Korea. Right off the beach there was a jungle. It was cold on the beach, but it was hot in that jungle: like steam heat. You had to keep your eyes sharp and the damn sweat seemed to bubble up in your sockets. You had to look around in that goddamn tangle of hot weeds and trees and you had to spot those bastards: they were hidden all around us. We were part of a large encampment of Marines getting ready to push on. There hadn't been any sniping for several hours, but they were there. You could *feel* them there.'

Reardon dropped his head for a moment and was silent. She had never heard his voice sound like this before: it was hollow and frightening and she wondered if he was going to continue.

'You could feel them there,' he repeated, 'watching you. But it was hot and you got careless. *I* got careless. Standing orders were to wear combat helmets at all times.' Reardon turned and his eyes did not leave hers. 'I was a lieutenant: twenty-four years old and invulnerable. I took the damn helmet off and put on my overseas cap to keep the sweat out of my eyes. I set it on my forehead and dropped my hands.' He outlined the gesture. 'And then I heard the shot. It never even knocked my hat off: went right through, clean, and I heard a small noise in back of me.' He ran his hand roughly over his face; his voice was harsh and bitter. 'My sergeant was dead before he hit the sand. The bullet penetrated his helmet. I turned him over and there was a small red mark in the center of his forehead. He was a boy: a kid.'

Reardon shifted so that he was on his knees, facing her. 'Do you understand what I'm saying, Christie?' She stared at him dumbly and he grasped her shoulders. 'Listen carefully: *that bullet was mine. It was meant for me.*' His voice was cold and positive. '*There was no bullet in that room last night meant for you.*' He saw the quick intake of breath; his words began to penetrate and she seemed immobilized. 'All the bullets were meant for Rogoff. They were directed at Rogoff and they hit Rogoff and they *killed Rogoff. Not you.* His death had nothing to do with you.'

He relaxed his hold, then stood and walked down the beach, his mind relinquishing the scene he had just described to her, filling with the clean cold sight and sound of the ocean. It was a long time before he returned to her and he was surprised that she had fallen into a deep sleep. She was curled on her side, her cheek resting on her folded arm. He knelt beside her. Her face was more than pretty now: relaxed, at peace. He touched her cheek and a frown pulled at her forehead. He traced it away gently without disturbing her sleep.

Reardon locked his hands around his knees and watched her. She aroused so many conflicting emotions in him. She looked, in sleep, so completely vulnerable: that was one part of it, his feeling of wanting to protect her. But she was a tease in some ways; no, not really a tease, but provocative, then suddenly innocent. And fresh. Tough: not really tough, strong was a better word. She *tried* to be strong and she had great pride. Reardon watched her move slowly, then her body relaxed again.

It all went deeper than just physical desire, though that, of course, was present. Not that she was particularly desirable: thin, flat, wiry, but the way she moved, sure of herself, confident, a little defiant and guarded.

He pressed his forehead against his knees, not looking at her now. Because if he continued to look at her, he would reach out for her. Christ, he hadn't wanted this. Never this. There had never been anything like this before. He had been to bed with many women and it had always been a casual thing, understood on both sides, taken for the mutual pleasure that was involved. His relationship with women other than his wife had never even gone into a relationship which could be called an affair. There had been many others: attractive women easily available and attractive women not easily available, but always it had involved nothing more than a mutual desire.

He and his wife had an understanding, going back some fifteen years: back to when his twin daughters were born. It was bitter and involved and he owed no explanations to anyone: not to his wife or to himself or to anyone.

Reardon licked his lips. His tongue lingered between his teeth and he looked at Christie again. This was different and this wasn't what he wanted. He thought of Nora Opara: *Christie is someone very special: she cares.*

She moved her arm, then slowly straightened her legs in a long stretch. Her face was puzzled for a moment, then she smiled. 'I really slept,' she said.

Reardon stood up and brushed his jacket. He sounded annoyed. 'I'll be carrying sand around with me for a week. Damn, my shoes are gritty. You better get up, Opara, it's getting cold. That's all I'd need—to have you on the sick list too.' He looked around quickly. 'Hey, where's your pocket-book?'

'I left it in the car.'

'In the car? With your gun and shield? Great. You could get a complaint for that, you know that, don't you?'

She wasn't certain if the anger was genuine but when he told her to get up, without offering assistance, she brushed herself off and followed him to the car.

She pulled the gun and shield from her pocketbook, at his insistence. 'There. Nobody broke in and took them.' She tossed them back into the pocketbook and snapped on her seatbelt, then pressed the doorlock after he slammed the door shut. She glanced at him, but he was starting the motor, his head ducked down.

'Damn it, look at the time. Do you know how long we've been here?' he demanded.

'Apparently, too long.'

Reardon didn't answer. The silence which encompassed them was heavy and tense and confusing. He changed so rapidly, so completely, from one moment to the next. His face was set in that familiar, hard expression and he gave no indication that he was aware of her presence beside him in the car. He squinted, then leaned forward and slowed the car down. He had pulled into the driveway of a diner.

'You hungry?' he asked, finally turning to look at her.

Christie leaned back, her cheek against the vinyl backrest. He let her study him and his face seemed to relax. Calmly, she looked for all the things she had learned about him: the different facets of Casey Reardon appeared and disappeared. It was a comfortable, honest silence now and she saw the small, familiar grin at the corners of his hard mouth. She thought of what he had told her on the beach without wondering why he had told her. Whatever his reason, it seemed to have clarified something within her. She knew that he had revealed something very personal and she felt, now, that he had regretted it. That was what had made him angry. He had been angry at himself.

He looked amused and that triggered her own reaction: the set of rules between them was well defined. She turned slowly and looked through the windshield. 'I'm hungry,' she said, 'but I wouldn't eat in that greasy spoon. There's a very nice drive-in about a mile further down. On the left side of the parkway.'

Reardon's eyes glinted. 'Opara, you are pushing,' he said, but he started the car and backed out of the driveway. He whistled through his teeth in that annoyed way, yet, at the same time, he seemed to be happy.

Christie wondered if she would ever get to understand him. Casey Reardon was, indeed, a very complicated man.

THE LONG NIGHT'S WALK

Alan White

'The Long Night's Walk' is published by Hodder & Stoughton Ltd.

MAB/72—N

The Author

'My education was interrupted by the war, during which I volunteered for Combined Operations, and saw service in Europe and various unidentifiable countries. I served for a while with the Dutch Underground, teaching them to use stolen signals equipment. After post-graduate research at the University, I became a scriptwriter/producer, eventually in television. Free-lance writing attracted me, and I left the BBC staff to become a farmer and to write a comprehensive dialect history of England. Three snowstorms later, without a word written, I had to drive a concrete lorry to earn my living and, with no mechanical knowledge whatsoever, got a job as a factory maintenance engineer. Rescued from that by an appointment to a newsfilm agency, I became US News Editor and White House Correspondent to both Eisenhower and Kennedy. When I returned home I became a sales conference organizer and then General Manager of the independent National Heating Centre. I am married and we have three children.'

CHAPTER ONE

THEY HAD POSSESSION of the wood, and therefore Simon knew he dare not use the bridge. The next bridge downriver was at least four miles and who knows, perhaps they also had possession of that or had mined it to blow skyhigh at the first foot-fall. He carried on, slowly, down the lane at right angles to the bridge. He was safe on this side of the water only for as long as he could keep within shelter of the buildings. He turned and looked back. Sammy was where he should be, on the roof just beneath the funny shaped bell-tower that had no bell. 'Smelted down for bullet cases,' he thought, but he must stop that, drifting into irrelevancies. Stay with the matter on hand. They had to cross a river and quickly or the straps of this hundred pound pack would cut his shoulder flesh to ribbons. And time was getting on.

Slowly he raised the barrel of the rifle, his eyes restless, looking everywhere. Bloody old Lee-Enfield, what a weapon with which to send a man to war. Why not a Schmeizer, semi-automatic? Or even a shotgun, come to think of it. There was a suspicion of movement along the line of the corner by that building, an old stables it must once have been. He brought the rifle to the firing position at his waist. That gesture would alert the rest of them. He beckoned Jonfey to come forward. Jonfey came down the side of the building, a dull khaki blur against the brown of the stonework. Jonfey would be able to see round that corner. There was a suspicion of movement in the upstairs window of the building on the left; that would have been a farm worker's cottage, wouldn't it, in peacetime long, long ago. Up this lane farm carts would bring the harvest; 'twenty acres today' the farmer would boast and they'd break out the drink and cheese, thick hunks of harvest bread and butter . . . Steady on, keep your mind on that upstairs window that contains the merest whisper of movement. Watch it, Jonfey; as usual you're going too far too fast. Hold it there in the doorway while someone else leapfrogs past you. I can't cover you past that building on your left, you bloody fool; you ought to know it's outside my line of fire.

Jonfey stopped in the doorway. 'Mustn't go any further,' his mind commanded, 'or you'll be out of Simon's line of fire, and if someone jumps you from a doorway, God help you.' A piece of rag was caught in the crook of a post against the building on the other side of the alley. 'Bet that gave Simon a scare,' he thought, 'from back there it must look like someone moving.'

He pointed his finger at the object, his thumb stuck downwards in a signal they all knew as 'no target'. That'd reassure Simon. Jonfey turned and looked back. Simon and Sammy smiled, Fred smiled, they all smiled. A regular bunch of laughing cavaliers, weren't they? But this was no joke, was it, this was 'for real' as they say. Simon pointed at the window high in the building opposite. There was a sudden flick of movement. Jonfey held his thumb and forefinger to his nose; 'it stinks', the gesture said, only one of fifty gestures they had learned in training. This one implied, 'I do not like what I can see.' Simon held up his finger, then described a rapid ascending spiral; 'go around and investigate', that one meant. There was a low wall; bent double Jonfey raced along it across a six foot opening, moving fast, lost to view.

No covering fire, no rifles in friendly hands waiting to bark at anyone attacking him. This one you did on your own. Round the back of the building hugging close to the stones. A window. Bend down. A door, straight past it; it's closed, thank God. God's working overtime today. The next window doesn't exist any more. The glass, the frame, and half the brickwork has been blown away. Quick decision? Yes, jump in everything at the ready, over the crumbling brickwork land in a crouch. Hand down the side of your right leg near the knife, other hand back along the rifle to the trigger guard ready to pump one. Oh, these bloody Lee-Enfield rifles, sticking out in front of you like a permanently hard but useless prick. Why don't they issue pistols, cold nosed colt four-fives that stop an elephant.

Stand perfectly still, Jonfey, no, for Christ's sake don't overbalance forwards. The floor's mined and you're standing on the wire. The mine was right under the window and you missed it by a sparrow's fart, but, you're standing on the wire Jonfey. Is it a release mechanism? Have you tripped the first part? There's no fuse, you'd have heard it crack or smelled it. If you've armed it by treading on the wire, when you move your foot off the wire, there'll be a bang and your balls will splatter the ceiling like spaghetti bollocknese. Quick look round. No one in the room; door to the hallway open, no one there. Bend down. Feel for the mechanism. Careful, careful! A wire had been stretched the entire width of the window about a foot from the wall, an inch and a half high. The centre of the wire was attached to a round tin, the size of four ounces of tobacco. In the centre of the tin was a round brass piece, like the top of a homemade cigarette lighter. He kept his foot on the wire and bent even further down. 'Ah, you old Sod!' he said, jubilant. 'I know you, you old Sod.' He lifted his foot clear. Thank God for the mine recognition lessons held a hundred years ago it seemed, in the front room of a former boarding house in Scarborough. This was an old favourite. It was safe, as long as you didn't actually step on it or pull that wire. Jonfey chuckled, then wiped the cold fear sweat running down his forehead. He crossed the room, through the hallway and ran lightly up the stairs keeping to the ends of the tread. Upstairs was no sign of human life, no small noises or smells, the air heavy only with the dry odour of dust and decay. He took his knife from the cloth sheath in his trouser seam, placed his rifle on the floor by the door, grasped the knob and with one single movement flung open the door, jumped through the aperture and against the wall, his left hand pressed hard back ready to spring him in any direction. There was no one in the room. A curtain, formerly red now bleached muddy brown was tattered like a first war flag, flapping idly at the window. One tatter hung at arm height, another could have been a leg. The curtain looked as if it had been standing there since nineteen eighteen. It could still have been mistaken for a human figure moving there in the half light of the gloom beside the window. 'What a bloody war this is when we risk a mine for a curtain.' But, it could have been a man, the man could have held a gun, and the gun could have coughed death.

He took his green beret and poked it out of the window on the end of his rifle. No one shot at it. He stood in the window and briefly gave the 'no target' symbol. To it he added one not in the book; two fingers spread wide apart lifted rapidly twice in a jerking movement. That was for the grenade the fear, the pants-messing stomach-heaving bladder-opening fear that only recently had he learned to control.

They advanced, leapfrogging each other until they came to the banks of the river eight hundred yards from the edge of the wood. The sentry on the bank was child's play. He'd been smoking, was hiding in a hole, and didn't see or hear a thing until they dropped on him like a load of horseshit. Crossing the river was easy. They swam, fully clothed carrying packs and rifles clear of the water. Simon and Jonfey held Simon's hundred pound pack between them. On the far bank they ran together up into the hedgerow then lay down shivering. 'I didn't realize how warm it was in Loch Lochie in January,' Jonfey said through chattering teeth.

'Everything's going too easily,' Simon said, 'I don't like it. I get the feeling we're being led forward into something.'

They advanced into the field and lay down at right angles to each other, covering the arc of fire while the other six men came across the river and up into the hedge. As soon as the men were ready Fred gave Simon the 'all right to advance' signal, and they moved forwards crawling steadily through the thick wet grass. The cutting was only two hundred and fifty yards ahead of them. Two on the far side, two on the near bank, two watching north and east, two south and west. The Army says you must do everything in pairs. Jonfey and Fred crossed the branch line and climbed the far bank. Simon and Matthew worked on the near bank, digging and planting. When they had finished they tamped the earth down on to the guncotton charges, ran the coil of wire along the top of the embankment for two hundred yards along the direction in which the train would come. Matthew placed a detonator on the line, acid/perchlorate type. When the weight of the train came to crush the detonator, the banks would fall on and in front of the train; it was Simon's own variation of the line smashing technique. Simon, in charge, checked his watch. The train was due in five minutes. He inspected the entire operation then ordered withdrawal.

I don't know why Sammy did it; perhaps exhilaration, perhaps relief. Suddenly he got to his feet, ran, and tried to longjump one of the water culverts. It was a good fourteen feet; he would have needed Olympic abilities. His jump was over two feet short; there was an agonized shout as he scrambled in the brickwork for a hold and then his fingers caught the gap between two bricks, a mere half inch, and held. His feet scrabbled along the culvert, and the rubber cleated soles of his commando boots found a tiny crevice. He hung there for several seconds, but then his fingers lost their grip, his body arced back from the brickwork and he fell to the bottom of the culvert, back cracking flat, sprawled inert among the broken slabs. 'Quick,' Simon said. 'Down there and get him out—you Jonfey, you Matthew . . .'

At that moment I copped the back of his neck with the hard heel of my hand and Simon fell to the ground. I raised the Verey pistol and fired a starshell; it burst white above us. Then, all hell was let loose. Percussion grenades fell amongst us like hailstones—over to the left a machine gun opened fire on fixed lines, its tracer content spewing blood red and blue at a body height of three feet.

We had all dropped to the ground, myself included. I was the training officer and they weren't shooting at me, but a white armband doesn't give immunity and though the cutting led only to an old mine shaft in the Brecon Beacons and the men behind the guns were the next section waiting their training turn, on my own instructions they were firing real live bullets.

'Private Arnold,' I shouted. 'You take over and get your section to hell out of here.' He was a Methodist and wouldn't like me swearing, but what the hell. I fired the Verey pistol again and on sight of the red star the Bren gun stopped. Now the two inch mortars lobbed smoke bombs and an acrid yellow white fog began to conceal the countryside, to make it harder for the section to find their way home.

One of the men of the section, when he saw the smoke bombs begin to fall, came across the field to me, stood in front of me, and saluted. I saluted him back; I knew what he was going to say. The formality made it easier.

'You said that any time we didn't feel up to it, Captain, we should come to see you.'

'Yes, John?' We'd dispensed with surnames many months before. 'I can't take any more,' he said, 'seeing Sammy back there, and you giving the chop to Simon, and the thought of swimming that ice-cold river again, with the Bren gun shooting away at us. I can't take any more.' There was no trace of hysteria. It was simply true—he couldn't take any more. That was what it was all about, wasn't it, in a sense. I was testing these men to the limits of their endurance, deliberately trying to break as many of them as I could. It was brutal, but time was not on our side. We were seventy-two men in a camp in North Wales learning to jump by parachute, to swim in icy water wearing boots, to throw a knife, shoot a bow and arrow, stab someone to death with our brand of knitting needles, hide our bulk behind two blades of bent grass, but above all, to survive. I hoped that after what I was doing to these seventy-two volunteers, anything the German might do would be child's play.

'You know the drill, John. Get into the ambulance and get warm, and as soon as we can we'll take you back to camp.' I never argued, never condemned. For obvious reasons we always kept an ambulance within easy distance; it was an added temptation to the lads to know it was kept warm inside, and there was always hot tea and food laid on.

We started out with a hundred men, but as they used to say, I could be a right bastard.

Simon stirred and recovered consciousness. He sat up and looked ruefully at me. 'So that's what they all call "the Captain's chop", is it?' 'I hope it didn't disappoint you? You know why you got it, of course?' 'Yes, sir. Trying to rescue Sammy. He was injured through his own silly fault; we should have left him. How is he, by the way?' 'I don't know,' I said, 'I haven't looked. But that's not important, Simon.' I tried to soften the tone of my voice—this wasn't a man to browbeat; his intelligence was as large as my own, in every way but one he was my equal. The exception, I was a Captain, he by choice a private. I was the trainer, he the one being trained. Sammy could be dead—I dare not care!

'The safety of any one man must be secondary,' I said, repeating a well worn lesson. 'It doesn't matter whose fault it was, you had to leave him lying there. You couldn't get down there without endangering the success of your mission—dammit the train was due in only a few minutes—and, though once again I stress this is a secondary consideration, if you had gone down there you would have endangered the lives of other men and the effectiveness therefore of your striking force.'

'We cannot help being what we are, sir, human beings.'

'You must. You're a volunteer commando, just as I am. The day you volunteered you stopped being a human being. The minute you drew that knife from the quartermaster's stores, you accepted that if the need arose, you'd stick it into someone. That is not the way of a human being.'

He was slowly recovering from the effects of the chop, rubbing the back of his neck. This was the last training we would all do together. Very soon I would need to make a final selection of these men, and those who survived I would take into Europe with me. And that would be the 'real thing', as Jonfey would have called it. The particular brain children of an otherwise sterile Major in the War Office, we were destined to be fleas that irritate, gremlins, poltergeists, kinks in the wire. We were going into the enemy lines, to make life as difficult for the troops there as it was possible to be. We were a legalized force of piss-takers, a Special Group.

But unlike all the other Special Groups, we would be dropped and left to our own devices. It was going to be that kind of war, for us. 'Ivan Petrovitch Pavlov . . .' I said, but he interrupted me. 'Nobel Prize Winner of 1904. "All acquired habits depend on a chain of conditional reflexes". He proved it with dogs. Pavlov's dogs. I know what you're trying to do to us. You're taking over where the drill sergeant leaves off. When he shouts "hup" we click our heels together; when you shout "hup", without stopping to ask human questions, or have human doubts, we stick a knife into somebody.'

'Or they stick it into you.'

'Kill or be killed—it's a damned good slogan.'

'Conditioned reflex. That means, that when you see a man, one man out of eight, fall into a ravine, your chain of conditioned reflexes passes the order to get to hell out of it, without a second thought. Can't you get that, Simon?'

'I can get it. I believe in Pavlov.' He climbed to his feet; unconsciously dusting his hands against his uniform. 'I can get it, but by God, there's nothing says I have to like it!'

'Think of Pavlov's dogs, they rang a bell for food and all they got was saliva.'

'Yes, I'll think of Pavlov's dogs,' he said as he started to jog trot after his section.

I let him get about ten paces then levelled my pistol, aiming at his back; I lifted the muzzle slightly. I hated to do it, but I squeezed the trigger. One, two, three. He was flat on the ground before I could squeeze off the second shot; during the second shot he rolled over and over; before I could fire the third time, his knife came winging through the air towards me.

Had I not been prepared the knife would have stuck in my throat; as it was, it sliced into the epaulette of my battledress jacket and I felt blood start to run down my shoulder.

'Well done,' I said.

He looked up at me, a laugh amidst the tears already in his eyes. 'Woof woof!' he said, got to his feet, plucked the knife out of my shoulder, turned, and ran away into the man-made fog.

CHAPTER TWO

I KNEW SOMETHING WAS WRONG the moment I stepped to the door of the plane. I was to be first out, the red light was on, and the ring at the end of my parachute line was hooked on to the rail. We were to drop in Holland, the other side of the Maas. It was one of those crystal clear nights—the river shone below us, coiled, expectant. No clouds in the sky, and no rain. Dammit—the briefing officer promised us rain and thick cloud. 'There won't be a living soul with his eyes turned skywards,' he had promised at the tiny airport along the Pilgrim's Way near Canterbury.

The green light came on next to the red, and the despatcher tapped my shoulder; I stepped out, the sergeant, Simon and Jonfey behind me. Slip stream from the plane carried us backwards, loose, free falling, then the sudden balls-jarring snap as we reached the end of the line. Fixed line jumping was still experimental in those days—that's why we needed four starters for a three man job. The bag snapped open, the pilot chute jerked clear, and the canopy of the big chute unfurled itself. Once again you felt as if you owned your stomach. Now we were on our way down through a sky powdered with starlight and a flaming moon, with at least a thousand Mausers and Schmeizers and a regiment of anti-aircraft guns slumbering on the ground below us. Talk about 'Ill met by bloody moonlight!' That slumber could end with the call of one moonstruck sentry, gazing at the star spangled sky, dreaming of the fat sensuous arms of his liebling on the other side of the banks of the Rhine—one yelp as our canopies reflected the moonlight and a million vicious throats would cough venomous death at us. Damn the briefing officer—he promised us rain and a cloudy sky! The sergeant was swinging about fifty feet beside me, Simon and Jonfey over to his left. We still had a thousand feet to go. He looked up at the stars and I saw him frown and shake his head, that's how bright the moon was. 'Let's get the hell out of here,' his look implied. I reached up and grabbed the ropes fastened to the front end of the canopy. He saw the movement, and he too reached up. The message flashed as a cosmos to the other two, and we all pulled hard, spilling air from the back of the canopy, driving the chutes forwards and downwards through a stomach yanking hundred and fifty feet slip. Slowly I stopped pulling off centre, eased my hands down the ropes and let the canopy fill evenly again. Now we were off course. I reached up far behind me and pulled the back cords, air spilled from the front of the canopy, and we yawed backwards and downwards. 'People pay good money and queue for this at Blackpool,' I thought as Simon and Jonfey yawed down level with me. Jonfey, however, impetuous as ever, mistimed his recovery, and went swinging past me, missing the sergeant's chute by a matter of feet. I looked down in time to see him recover forty feet vertically below. 'It would serve the young devil right if I were to land right on top of him,' but a gust of wind pulled him to the side. When his chute moved over, I could see the ground below, identify the topography we had studied on a flour-and-water model knocked up for us in the back room of a house in Braintree, Essex. The river was where they had said it would be, and there the concrete works. There the two woods, side by side but separated by a thin strip of copse. The farmhouse, with its outbuildings, and the other farmhouse —occupied by the Signals Headquarters. Below presumably were all the things the briefing officer had told us about but we couldn't see—the anti-aircraft battery in the wood to the left, the battalion of infantry in the wood to the right, mines in the fields around the woods. All that in a brief glance, and then there was no more time. We were coming in to land, and my under-carriage was shaking with fear.

There's nothing difficult about parachute jumping. It's the landing that bothers you. You come to earth with the impact of a jump off a twenty foot wall. That's unloaded! Carry fifty pounds of equipment and the twenty becomes twenty-five and the risks of a broken leg or ankle that much greater. Now here was the ground. I can still see it clearly. I was going down forwards at an angle of about fifteen degrees, clipping twelve feet above the hedge. Let's hope the field beyond was clean of mines. The briefing officer didn't *think* this one was mined—

but he didn't think there'd be stars and a moon. Jonfey down before me and rolling forward. Pulling the cords out of his chute. No mines, apparently. Sergeant next, no time to look at him. Ground now thirty feet below twenty now ten and the spine jarring impact feels as if your parachute never opened. Now you roll forwards, bend the knees going slightly to the side since you've got this blasted pack on and if you roll straight you'll snap your spine, half roll sidewards and damn, into the rigging lines so twist sidewards and half roll again, down backwards and lie flat for a second, no more, turn over on your face, hands reaching down to your waist to unclip the seating harness that chafed your balls raw. You'd think they'd invent a better seat to pass through your legs than this tight canvas that gets you every way. Some men get an erection the minute the light comes on for jumping—that canvas nappie'd be enough to take the end off it! I lay on my side. A German in the hedge, ten feet away, was watching me. We must have woken him up. Doing sentry duty fast asleep in the hedge when we four come tumbling right over his head. The German was looking straight at the sergeant's back. Jonfey and Simon were facing the other way. The German had his hand on the Schmeizer trigger; pull that, you bastard, and the sergeant gets a burst of ten straight up his jaxi.

The German didn't know how many of us were coming down—four he could probably manage, but not a whole platoon. I was the last and any moment he'd waken to the fact we were only four, and spray us like greenfly on a dry summer's evening. I aimed my knife for his hands, but it stuck in his throat, and when I jumped over there seconds after the knife, the bubbles had started to come through the froth of blood. I pulled out the knife and that's what really killed him—the air rushed out from the dark hole where the blade had been—his head gave a couple of short convulsions, he twitched, and was dead.

The others had heard and seen the slight movement of my dash forward, and disappeared into the grass. I half stood up, under the hedge, searching the perimeter of the field with rapid backwards and forwards movements of my head. No other sentries. I could smell the acrid smoke on the German's head—he must have nipped through the hedge for a quick smoke. That put the rest of the sentries, for there were bound to be more, on the other side of this hedge, and it put us between them and their camp. I lifted my hand and made a sign above my head.

Within seconds Jonfey, Simon and the sergeant were by my side, though I couldn't see them until they were only eight feet away.

'Everyone all right?' I whispered.

'Marvellous,' Jonfey said. 'I was dragged through a cow pat!' I could see the brown streak down the side of his face, and the side of his hair was covered in it. He scrubbed it out as best he could with a bunch of long grass, and then I gave him my water bottle to finish it off. The sergeant was looking speculatively over the field.

'Glad to be back?' I asked him.

He turned his head round in the direction from which we had come. 'It's a long way home,' he said. 'Let's hope we don't have to walk it, and swim!'

'You all right, Simon?'

'I banged my elbow when I came down, but nothing serious. It will be all right soon.' There was no point in me looking at it—Simon was a vet before the war, and should know about bones.

This was the first time I had set foot on the soil of the continent of Europe since Dunkirk—and that seemed a whole war away. I don't know what I'd been expecting—it's hard to imagine, for instance, that though a country is completely overrun and occupied, there can be physical gaps in the defences through which four men can drop unobserved by parachute. A canopy is such a damned great thing, floating down through the sky—visible, I would have thought, from twenty miles. Possibly, hopefully, the one man who'd see it was fifteen miles away; I had a ludicrous vision of him riding towards us, hell for leather, on a bicycle. All about us was a silence so complete I could hear each of us breathing from the exertion of the descent and the rapid change of air pressures. It was a dry night and clear, the air light crystal that carries sounds and scents; a marvellous night to be on the moors with a rabbit gun, a flask of brandied coffee, a roast beef sandwich and a lifetime of no wars stretching before you.

Seventy-two men and I had chosen two and the sergeant. It was too late now to wonder if I had made the right choice, but many nights since I had been told of this mission had been sleepless. Most of the seventy-two men had eliminated themselves in one way or another—some had been incompetent, incapable of learning the complex techniques of stalking, of moving at night without sight or sound. Those who could do this satisfactorily had no ability for the mechanical side of things, arming grenades, preparing explosive charges, defusing mines. We'd lost eleven men alone in the mines training. I didn't feel responsible for their deaths, though I had marched them into the lonely brick cubicles in the middle of the moor where, with the best training we could give them on dummies, eventually they had to be left alone with the real thing. Eleven had muffed it, from fear or incompetence we'd never know. Many men could handle the mechanics and the stalking, but oddly enough failed in such simple things as map reading, and routine signals procedure. One man could do everything required of him on the moors, but just couldn't tune a radio to a correct frequency.

On the day of the final choice, I had the seven survivors in to see me, one by one. They had been through the hands of the medical officers, and all were physically fit. The psychiatrist, however, eliminated three of them. It was the last straw. Throughout their training they received regular checks from the psychologists; the excitement, however, of being on the border line of selection had tipped them over the edge.

Simon or Sammy, Jonfey or Matthew. This was another Sammy, not the one who'd thrown himself into the culvert, this was Sammy the tailor, a young Jewish boy brought up in the East End of London. Sammy had worked for a record making company, and knew all there was to know about electronics. At the start of the war, when electronics were drafted into the military, Sammy became a tailor, and a pacifist. He stuck it for a year, then joined the Royal Corps of Signals and volunteered, as soon as it became possible, for Special Services. Matthew and Sammy made a good team, which should I choose. Then, almost immediately after my interview with him, Matthew went out and killed himself. He left a note addressed to me. All the time we had been training, he had hoped to be eliminated on some technical ground. He couldn't bring himself to quit. He never dreamed he could get through to the final selection, or that I'd ever say to him that I was putting him on the shortlist. When I knew Matthew had died I went to the half colonel who commanded our comic outfit, and asked him to remove the psychiatrists and psychologists—I had made the mistake of thinking theirs was an exact science.

My final choice was a simple matter of personality. Simon and

Jonfey were a team, Sammy was a lone wolf. I felt he would always be a lone wolf, and that wouldn't do if four of us were to fight, hand in hand. I told Sammy myself I wasn't taking him. 'Oh well,' he said, 'I suppose this is a job for the goyims.' He didn't translate.

Simon had been a vet when he joined our unit, a vet with a public school history and a love of animals both of which had bred in him a profound disrespect for the vagaries of the human species. You'd never catch Simon napping. Tall and slender, he looked as if a good wind would snap his spine. Yet he could walk into a field full of raging bulls, pick the fiercest, and lift its front hoof off the ground as if inviting it to dance. I once saw him hoist a full grown ram on to his back, and carry it down ten miles of Welsh mountainside to treat legs broken by a fall from the top of a rock. All the way down the ungrateful beast kept pissing on his shoulder and the boys in the barrack room made Simon give his denims to the quartermaster before they'd let him in. Jonfey had been a horse breeder—ran a small stud in Northamptonshire of first class hunters and show ponies for the county well-to-do. There wasn't a bone in his body hadn't been broken at some time or another. When Jonfey was mounted, you couldn't tell where he ended and the horse began. He had a grip with his knees that could bruise a bar of iron—his favourite party trick was to hang upside down from a wooden beam by his knee grip alone. They say the girls were most impressed by Jonfey, but that's something I took care not to know about.

We trained the seventy-two men for months in the Welsh mountains above Rhayader, stalking sheep and each other. The sergeant and I would sit on a knoll, each with a rifle loaded with live tracer bullets. Whenever we saw an arse sticking up out of the heather we'd put a shot as close to it as possible. I was brought up on the Yorkshire moors above Settle, and played with a shotgun before I had my first rattle. I could split a willow wand at a hundred paces, and some of my boys had an uncomfortable time. It taught them, however, to move inconspicuously over open country, to press their bellies into whatever depression they could find, to slide into stream beds and heather clumps, to crawl, and run bent double, and above all, to arrive unseen at whatever destination we cared to choose. Seventy-two bloody fools since they chose to fight the war away from the comfortable trammels of Army discipline. They all called me 'sir' but I liked to deceive myself that was from respect, not fear. The sergeant they called 'Sarge', and without doubt that was from respect. He was a six foot two monster of a man, with physical strength and agility in an unusual combination. Before the war he'd run around a foundry in the Ruhr with a tub of molten metal that weighed three hundredweight, and never spilled a drop.

Our instructions were very simple, and the operation had been planned with the precision of a Cook's tour. From Canterbury we'd fly to Holland, where we'd disembark (by parachute). We'd remain in Holland for thirty-six hours and then fly back to Canterbury. It was as simple as that, and no tickets or passports were required. But while in Holland, we had to upset the working of an entire Signal Headquarters without being seen or doing any damage that would cause the Germans to suspect our presence. An entire Army was lodged in the valley over the hill, and that Army depended on this Signal Headquarters. There was to be an 'action in force' on the other side of that Army, and though the War Office had not yet learned to confide in Captains, I could guess it was something important. Our mission was to ensure the Signals Headquarters failed to operate efficiently at the vital time—how we were to do that was left to us. It was a mission after my own heart—a nice messy job of buggering someone about, and a lot of freedom in the manner of doing it. I had, however, been told that thousands of lives depended on us doing the job well, and that took the edge off the fun. In thirty-six hours we were to withdraw, to be picked up by a fast airplane flown, I had been promised, by a pre-war ace from Cobham's Flying Circus who could land and take off again on a handkerchief. He'd need his abilities when the time came—if they spotted us we'd be flying along a six mile corridor of flaming ack-ack fire.

Jonfey and Simon had made a pact out there on the Welsh hillside above Rhayader, and in the simulated battlefields around the Brecon Beacons—what one didn't know the other would teach him. It had earned them a place on this first assignment. What a world of difference was in the two men. Simon was determined to be on it because to him it was unthinkable that another should do it in his place. As simple as that. There was a job we had to do, and either he came along, or someone came instead of him, and that was unthinkable. Jonfey came from different motives—he was headstrong, impetuous, and above all would never be beaten by animal or man. Combat was life's blood and mother's milk to him—he'd fight a seventeen two hand wild stallion bucking him to hell with as much quiet resolution as he'd court the belle of the hunt ball; he'd tame them and ride them, lifting them to unknown heights of performance, conquering them, exhausting them, loving and inspiring them. 'It might be a different horse with Jonfey on its back,' they'd say in the show ring or on the hunting field. 'She's a different girl when she's with Jonfey,' they'd say in the champagne bars. And jealously the men would utter—'They ought to leave the horses alone and geld Jonfey!'

I whispered in Jonfey's ear and he unstrapped the trench digging tool he carried on his pack. We buried the German stripped to his surprisingly clean underwear within twenty minutes. There was no requiem. The sergeant went through his pockets—pay book, identification papers, letters from home, and three tattered postcards crinkled at the edges that once had borne erotic pictures. Now they were so smudged no one could have taken even the cheapest thrill from them.

Suddenly the sergeant gripped my arm. In the pay book was a sheet of paper, folded singly. With it was another sheet of paper on which the German had pencilled the start of what read like a request for compassionate leave. The soldier was apparently semi-illiterate, and several words had been crossed out. It was evidently his intention to make a clean copy when he had finished the composition of his first draft. I could recognize the smile that came to the sergeant's face. He had it one morning when we walked into a barrack room and found one of the lads still asleep in bed. The sergeant, smiling that smile, drew the pin on a plastic grenade, the sort that made a loud bang but do no damage, and balanced it on the side of the bed, then he walked back to the door, and shouted the man's name. The man came awake, the grenade fell to the floor and the impact exploded it. The man never overslept again.

Now he was busy writing with the stub of pencil we had found in the German's pocket. From time to time he referred to the note, addressed to the German's platoon officer. When he had finished, he passed the note to me. It read, as far as I could make out in the half light, 'Sir, with respect, I beg to inform you that I am tired of the war and have the intention of deserting.' And it was signed with a passable imitation of the signature in the paybook. The forgery had taken only a couple of minutes. He placed the rifle conspicuously in the crook of a tree in the hedge, and rolled up the note and stuck it in the end of the barrel.

Then we set off for our first objective, a hayrick in a field over a mile away.

CHAPTER THREE

THERE WASN'T A SINGLE BUILDING for miles around not under constant observation from the Germans. One of the reasons they continued to let the farmer occupy the farmhouse was that they could monitor his comings and goings. We had seen from aerial photographs and from the flour-paste model back in Braintree that it would be impossible to approach any of the buildings of that farm completely out of sight. And we needed a base, even for such a short stay. We also needed somewhere to erect our radio equipment. It was Jonfey who had hit on what at first seemed a hilarious plan—typical of his method of thinking and chains of thought.

'Let's set up shop in that hayrick. Build a bivvie, inside it. Have the entrance low down, there, by the hedge, and poke the aerial up through the rick itself.' It was just feasible, and worked perfectly when we tried it out on a farm near Colchester. With an entire infantry platoon of the Essex Regiment borrowed for the occasion and planted around the perimeter of the field, some with field glasses, we had been able to get into the rick, set up a bivouac in its steaming belly and move freely into and out of it, unobserved.

We arrived at the rick in the corner of Hank Verhoeven's fifty acre field just before dawn. Working in the bottom of the hedge, we withdrew the hay from the side and gradually built a hole in the centre of the rick itself, about six feet high, eight feet long, and nearly five feet wide. Most of the hay we took out via the hole, and spread it in the deep dank grass of the hedgebottom, completely out of sight. Some of it we pressed down, to make a floor on which to work. We had brought with us a mat of bamboo bars that locked together and formed a solid floor. Other bamboo sections we pushed up through the rick itself to dissipate the heat we were bound to generate. We didn't want to find ourselves at the heart of a rick fire. The job was done by ten o'clock—Jonfey got down into the hedgebottom and brewed a cup of coffee on a smokeless stove we'd brought with us. The sergeant took the first spell of duty, the rest of us spread out in the hedge-bottom, Jonfey and Simon instantly went to sleep. It had been a long day, and a long night, and I could not predict when we would be able to sleep again. Certainly, once we had started, there would be little opportunity to relax. I lay down in the hedgebottom, but couldn't settle myself. It's one thing to train a group of men in the Welsh mountains, and another to take the responsibility of getting them into the German war zone and out again. Some men are born with the divine inspiration of leadership. Some men can issue a command, and without hesitation the command is obeyed. It may be the tone of the voice, a timbre bred into a man over generations. It may be the look in the eyes, the cast of a head that nobility of purpose has smiled upon. It had been my misfortune that I was abnormally fit and quick witted, and whatever task we were set I had been able to accomplish more quickly and efficiently than the average man. I applied for a commission simply because I imagined the life of an officer would be easier than that of an 'other rank'. I had no 'divine inspiration of leadership'. Nor did I strive for promotion in the Army—I had been given a Captaincy to take over this troop of men—the rank, apparently, went with the job in the hierarchical minds of the men at the War Office—but I had no desire to be a Major, or a Lieutenant Colonel. I had always had more than enough money thanks to a prudent family line and the income from eight hundred acres of good hearted Yorkshire farm land—but I had never owned a Rolls-Royce motor car, nor indulged myself in any of those expensive tastes that lose a heritage. I owned a couple of Purdey guns, but they came from my grandfather; my guns and the Alvis motor car had been put away for the war, wrapped in as much grease as they would support. It was very difficult for me lying in that hedge to justify, however briefly, the stewardship of the lives of the men I had brought with me.

Simon, now there was a natural officer. He should have worn the pips—not that any one of us carried any distinguishing badges of rank. Simon had the natural ease and grace that made men defer to him. Many times I'd found myself asking his advice, and then either taking it, or stubbornly and perversely cudgelling my brains to find some means, however slight, of improving on it to justify my titular superiority. But here in Holland I was in charge of a situation in which there would be no guide lines, in which I would constantly need to assess the changing dangers and order men to act accordingly. There could be no peace within me.

Jonfey woke me at eleven o'clock. I had slept the morning through while the other three had taken turns to keep watch. There was a sour taste in my mouth, not entirely from sleeping in a hedgebottom. Jonfey had opened a couple of tins of corned beef and a packet of biscuits, and we had a hasty lunch from that and a couple of tins of cold soup. The tins we buried in a hole dug through the hay we had spread—already I had begun to feel dirty—a feeling that was to stay with me for the rest of the war. At twelve o'clock I gave the order to move and, leaving Simon behind to guard the rick, we crawled down the hedgerow, across the corner of the field, and into a small copse about half a mile north of our position. It's strange how familiar you can become with ground when you have studied aerial photographs and an accurate model. I felt I knew everything about this part of the country—could visualize it in peacetime, populated by carefree stolid Dutch people. Our brief had been thorough—Hank Verhoeven, christian name Hendrick, had lived in that farmhouse all his life. He had never married, but slept with his housekeeper who had now gone to live in Amsterdam with her married daughter, of whom Hendrick was not the father. Willem Hordenborg lived in the house behind the farm, and worked for Hendrick. He was married—his wife's name Lutte—and his three sons had gone to war. One was rumoured to be in England, one was a prisoner in Germany, and the other had been killed in action during what had erroneously been called the bloodless occupation. But we were on our way to a meeting, not with Verhoeven or Hordenborg—but a man with the unlikely name, even for Holland, of Willem Schmidt. Willem I knew all about—or as much as the Intelligence Officer in London had been able to tell me. Willem had worked before the war for a radio company in Eindhoven. He'd been something unimportant in the stores department. Now he was in command of a small detachment of the underground, the partisans, and his former managing director was one of his men. Since both shared a similar disability—Willem had lost the use of an arm, and his managing director the use of a leg, they had been drafted to work on the land. Within a half an hour they would be passing the copse in which we were hiding, with a horsedrawn cart. The managing director would be dressed in a blue denim suit, and wearing a black beret. I was now wearing the blue denim suit and black beret I had found waiting for me just inside the wood. I checked my watch. The sergeant and Jonfey had taken up positions in the small copse—I knew they were somewhere behind me, but could not see them, so carefully had they hidden themselves. The cart was five minutes late—five agonizing minutes I spent wondering if the whole affair was going to turn out to be a waste of time, but then, suddenly, I heard a whistle from Jonfey somewhere up a tree, and within a minute the cart came into sight down the road to the north. There were no Germans about, though in this flat country I could guess someone would have the cart in view from any one of a dozen vantage points. The cart came slowly towards us taking its time. The man next to the driver slowly stretched himself, lowering the upper part of his body back on to the load of mangels the cart carried. Then the first box was dropped gently over the side, swung on the end of a rope, then rolled into the trough along the side of the road, out of sight. The next box dropped twenty yards this side, again out of sight. The managing director had the third box out on the end of its rope, swinging clear of the cart, when the motor-cycle patrol came round the corner to the south. He dropped the box rapidly and straightened up. The patrol halted beside the road. There was nothing we could do. The eyes of the motor-cyclist searched the copse idly, but I was too well hidden and confident he would not see me. The man in the side-car was holding an automatic gun between his knees, with the barrel pointing up in the sky. For a moment I wished I had a grenade—from where I was hiding I could have put that grenade, clean as a whistle, right between his ankles. The driver of the motor-cycle had not stopped the engine—as he sat there he fiddled with the twist grip, revving and then letting the engine die down. Finally, when the cart was twenty yards from him, he revved, let in the clutch, and the combination roared past the horse and cart in a swirl of dust. The horse showed no signs of being scared—the malicious prank had failed. Neither Willem nor his managing director looked around. They knew we would be watching. The motor-cycle kept straight along the road to the corner, then disappeared from view. We could hear the sound of its engine disappear into the distance. There had been no pause round the corner and no likelihood the combination passenger had jumped out at that speed. When the cart was ten yards from me, I prepared to move. The managing director lay back, casually, along the load as obviously he must have done several times. An observer watching through glasses would have felt no surprise at seeing him do it again. This time, however, the managing director dropped off the side of the cart as it came level with me, and I sprang forward, low, and rolled up beside Willem, taking care to lie back exactly as the M.D. had done. Then I sat upright. It would have taken an eagle's eye to see the change of places and people.

There was no time to lose in preliminaries, and Willem didn't even bother to say hello. We'd worked together in England, and would work together again, I hoped, in Holland.

'Exactly according to the plan, with one addition, they've brought another ack-ack battery and it's in Schelde, so your man will really have to fly to get you out. Today's Army net password Fluegel; code book setting, though they're not using code around here, is B Five. There's a train at Aasne, loaded with ammunition, but they're waiting for the Army to tell them when they can bring it through.' He chuckled. 'They can't come today because we bent the line at Boden last night. It should be repaired by two o'clock in the morning—though we're doing all we can to go slow on it. There's a list of frequencies under your seat . . .' I felt down and took the screw of paper in my hands—'with the alternatives and the frequency switch words. You're lucky—they're using diminutives today, so watch out for CHEN, LEIN, and LING.' He turned, casually, and looked at me. 'How are your nerves?' he asked, surprisingly.

I hadn't thought about it. How were my nerves, stranded here in Holland, with a German under every bush, and a motor-cycle combination round every bend of the road? 'I think they're all right,' I said. 'Why do you ask?'

'Someone leaked information about that job last night. We lost four men—the Germans were waiting for us. Whoever talked about that one may know about you.'

'In which case, we've had it?'

'I fear so—we might get you to the border if you want to pull out, but that's as far as we could promise. We could get you to the shore, if someone could come and pick you up. Think about it—at least they weren't waiting for you when you came down.'

I told him about the boy in the hedge.

'There'd have been more than one if they'd been waiting for you and a train leaves Boden every afternoon.'

'Destination, Germany?'

'Forced labour or concentration camp—take your pick.'

'But you don't know yet who gave the Boden job away?'

'It was one of six men—the only six who knew about it. We'll catch him tonight or tomorrow. Shall we call it off and get you to the coast?'

'I'll think about it, and let you know later.'

I rested my head on the load, and waited for the signal. The managing director should have made his way along the copse, and would be standing in position, ready to reverse the change. Suddenly I saw the broken stick on the side of the road, counted three, and rolled off the waggon. As I went down I saw the flash of denim as he nipped back on to the cart, surprisingly nimble for a man with the use of only one leg. The Germans had better not see him do that, or he'd be in a labour camp in Germany before he could say glockenspiel.

However, I had no more time to think about him. As I went down on to the road, my hand caught a loose stone and when I rolled over, my thumb was in the wrong position. I almost screamed with pain as my thumb twisted beneath me. I rolled over and over until I was well into the depth of the copse, and slowly brought myself up under the screen of an overhanging bush. No one was about, though I could guess Jonfey and the sergeant would not be far away, and by now would have recovered the boxes Willem had left for us. My thumb was throbbing painfully, but I was still able to move it. I tried each of the joints in turn—luckily nothing was broken, though the base of the thumb had already started to swell.

The boxes contained the local code books—God knows how Willem had managed to get hold of them—and batteries for the power pack for our radio, the key to most of my half-formed plans.

When we arrived back at the field containing the hayrick, I instructed the sergeant and Jonfey to make a special search. There was no sign of anyone in the vicinity. A woodsman born and bred to a life out of doors, can tell if a field is occupied without necessarily seeing his quarry. Many a poacher has been caught by a keeper, and never known where the keeper comes from. The birds usually give the poacher away. Birds see intruders, and either fly overhead, harried because the poacher is near a nest of young, or fly away to other fields. You will rarely catch a rabbit sitting still in a field containing a human—he might chance a run through a corner, ever alert, but he'll never sit still and wash his paws. There was a rabbit sitting in the field with the hayrick, and a number of birds flying aimlessly about. Still, to be on the safe side, I had the sergeant and Jonfey circle the field to double check.

Simon had set up the radio in the hayrick, all except for the power pack which we carried, too heavy to have dropped with us by parachute. The power packs had been sent down five days before, in special boxes stuffed with sponge rubber and cotton wool. It didn't take more than five minutes to couple them up, and within another minute we could hear Rugby, loud and clear, and they'd opened a land-line to Braintree. The circuit was almost as clear as a telephone call. I had prepared what I wanted to say, and broadcast for less than a minute. As long as we were on 'receive' the Germans would not be able to locate us—if they could get a fix on us when we were transmitting, they could pinpoint our position to a quarter of a square mile. I can still remember clearly the answer to my urgent request for either a boat to take us off the coast of Holland, an early flight of the plane, or at least permission to change our position.

'This mission most important—urge you to forget suspicions and complete vital life-saving task.' The message had descended like a ton of bricks from the War Office to Braintree. The officer in charge of the actual operation tried to soften the blow and amplify the decision, but it still came to the same thing—stop behaving like a nervous nellie, and get on with it.

The sergeant put our feelings into words. 'Of course,' he said, 'we could always move out and not tell them.' I saw the frown flick across Simon's face—that wasn't his way at all. Jonfey, of course, didn't care one way or the other.

I don't know why I decided to stay, but the unilateral decision formed itself on my lips almost as if by its own volition.

'We'll stay where we are, at least until Willem gets here this evening.'

The decision once taken and expressed, all seemed anxious to forget it and get on with the job for which we'd come.

We had three radios in all. One we tuned to the company to company frequency—we could hear the individual company headquarters talking to each other, laying out the orders from the battalion commanders. It was a spasmodic traffic, mostly to do with the movement of stores. A second radio was tuned to the Divisional frequency, and yet a third to the Army. Here the traffic was heavy, and individual stations were queuing up to get into the network to pass messages.

How much the Army depends on communications. Individual groups rarely see each other, rarely mix except through the waves of the ether. Each unit, however, keeps a constant watch on the movements of all other units, and there is a certain amount of friendly backchat. What we now had to do was to establish ghost units on all those networks—ghost units that could pass messages. Our chief difficulty, however, was the business of changing frequency, a device the Germans used to get rid of interceptors. An operator would start a message in the ordinary way, and somewhere in that message, entirely at random, he would use one of a number of code words. As soon as the receiving station heard that code word, they would know that, at the end of the current sentence or phrase, the sending station would change to an alternative frequency. The alternatives were worked out in advance and followed a pattern—luckily Willem had given me the list of alternatives, and the code words with which those alternatives would be used.

Our first opportunity came at about half past four. There had been a lively exchange since three o'clock when the commander of an Infantry company had been instructed by the battalion commander to move his entire unit to another location. In the transmission, the new location had been garbled. The sergeant manning our receiving-transmitting set, heard the location's map reference and then heard the battalion operator sign off. By standard operating procedure, whenever a station wishes to go off the air, it says so in a certain code. For three weeks in Braintree, we had learned these codes until we knew them backwards. As soon as the battalion transmitter went off the air, the sergeant smiled that smile of his. He quickly looked at the map we had spread out along one side of the hayrick, opened up his transmitter, and in a passable imitation of the battalion signaller's voice, he sent a message to the company changing the map reference. The company signaller, suspecting nothing, confirmed the new reference and went off the air. The sergeant removed his headphones, and made a circle with his thumb and finger. We had just sent an entire Infantry company fifteen miles in the direction opposite to their intended movement. I suppose our early success went to our head, because between half past four and seven o'clock we cancelled a large food order, diverted a load of ammunition from one company to another, moved two companies, put two ack-ack units on stand-down for intensive overhaul and maintenance, and instructed an entire tank unit to dump all its fuel since it was suspected of being contaminated with water. The tanks must be cleared, we insisted, since we were rushing up new fuel in the morning. Every tank had to have its carburettor stripped out completely, a job that would certainly take them all night. Once or twice we were nearly caught out when units sent supplementary signals to confirm what we had said, but by jamming the principal station and putting out a reply of our own on the alternative frequency, we were able to cover up very well. By eleven o'clock it was time to switch off our over-heated radios. It was the sergeant, however, who gave our efforts the last gorgeous coup de grace. Just before we went off the air we broadcast to each of our networks—'It is suspected that a pirate station is operating, therefore all units are ordered to ignore any instructions of whatever origin received by radio during the last twelve hours and the next six.'

Then we changed frequency and called up Rugby again to report the first part of the mission completed. From now on, during the night, Rugby would broadcast on each of the frequencies we had given them, including all the alternatives, and the direction finders looking for the ghosts would track the interference back to England. No one would suspect the damage had been done from a hayrick at the very centre of their own military machine.

Now it was time for a little field work. Willem had given me a good idea and I could see anyway that Jonfey was getting restless.

CHAPTER FOUR

ONCE AGAIN we left Simon in the bivouac area, but in view of the possible betrayal I suggested he take himself to the other side of the field. We had been warned the Germans have a nasty habit of dropping mortar bombs first and asking questions later, and I didn't want Simon in direct line of fire if that should happen.

'See that railway line,' I said to Jonfey, handing him the map. 'Take us to the nearest and safest point.' To the sergeant I said I wanted to listen in to the railway communication system when I got there. He took with him a head and microphone set, an amplifier, and a small meter. The way to the railway line brought us within a thousand yards of the nearest ack-ack unit, but their sentry line was drawn close in, and from the look of them they were not set up for trouble from vagrants. The roads were busier than they had been all day—'they're obeying our movement orders,' the sergeant said. I would dearly have liked to listen to the confusion of the air waves at that moment, as station to station verified the authenticity of each message received during the day. Several times we saw despatch riders—obviously all messages were being duplicated by road—lengthy procedure that should effectively do what we had set out to do—impede and delay communications. But now I had my eye on better things—a train load of ammunition.

Our journey to the railway line was slow but uneventful. We might as well have been taking a walk through the English countryside on a late summer's evening—except that half the distance we traversed on our bellies. Jonfey moved so well that half the time I didn't know where he was, though he was always close enough to come sliding up beside me whenever I indicated a halt or a pause. The sergeant and I had been together for almost a year, and with his aid I had perfected what had been little better than schoolboy German. I had learned too the habit of communicating silently with him—he seemed to spend his working life attuned somehow to my thought wavelength, and often knew my intentions before I put them into speech. We moved along slowly across those fields together, Jonfey mostly leading, with either the sergeant or me bringing up the rear, but whenever I heard a suspicious sound and wanted to call a halt, the sergeant would have heard it too, and would melt into the side of the road of the hedge-bottom. Our route followed a parabola, missing the army camps, the woods, and a small inhabited hamlet. Though longer that way, I approved of Jonfey's unusual caution. It was just after midnight when the railway finally came into sight: again one of those clear nights, with strong moonlight that threw every object into sheer hard relief. You get the impression you can see for miles, and distances travelled are therefore shorter. It was a cool evening, cool on the skin without the fall of dew that makes everything heavy with moisture. It's hard to say whether we were affected by where we were, and what we were doing. Certainly within myself I felt that quiet excitement I had last known prior to examinations—the awesome secret fear of failure that is stifled by the rational appraisal of your conscious abilities. 'I can do it,' you say silently to yourself, 'I can do it.' It's one of those seventy-five per cent confidences—'I can do it, the way I now feel, or if nothing happens that I have not been able to predict, or if things go my way, or . . .' There are a thousand 'ors' as tempting as the song of the Lorelei and as fatal. We walked along the railway line until we came to a small cutting. For no reason, the landscape had suddenly pimpled and where the pimple came, a road crossed the railway. It was a road not frequently in use—more of a track I saw when I examined its surface. Certainly no vehicle had been down there for many a long day. We walked into the tunnel in the cutting and found, as we had expected, two small recesses in the wall along which the signals cables passed. The recesses were designed for two men to take shelter should a train catch them in the small tunnel; the three of us squeezed into one like sardines. After we had been there a little while I sent Jonfey back out again to observe the end of the tunnel. I didn't think anyone had seen us coming in, but I was taking no chances. The sergeant, meanwhile, isolated the wire along which the Meldenkirche to Aasne messages were sent, scraped bare the insulation and clamped on his terminals. Now he could overhear anything said down that line, and sat there, headphones on his head and microphone dangling below his mouth, like the telephone operator of a London hotel. One thing is certain, his reaction to the calls would be a damned sight swifter than the service I had been used to. But then, he didn't have his knitting, cups of tea, or frequent calls from his loved one to contend with. Nor was he sitting with his shoes off and his toes wriggling into the thick pile of a hotel carpet—he was halfway up a dark tunnel, down the inside walls of which water had been dripping, to judge by the rancid smell, for a thousand years. Rats moved along the bottom of the walls, and occasionally I caught the gleam of their baleful eyes. The alcove into which we had tucked ourselves was particularly nauseating, since a linesman or some other itinerant at some time in the past had dropped his trousers to relieve himself in there. Jonfey had trodden in it, and that didn't help matters. Suddenly, I became aware again of the little irritations—my thumb was hurting like hell, my shirt was wet and sticking to me, I had dirty hands and that always has annoyed me, but above all, I hadn't had sufficient food and sleep in the last twenty-four hours. There's a small place hidden somewhere inside yourself to which you go to lick your wounds. From the outside you appear normally active, normally attentive to what is going about you—but inside, the little you is squatting in its corner, bathed in self pity. God, how I hated the Army, and the life it forced me to lead. I took the spare pair of headphones from my top pocket, and the sergeant taped them on to the wires with his own. He had been listening to the voices, his lips moving as he tried to memorize them. This was what they must have sounded like to Joan of Arc, or to the fixated inmates of lunatic asylums. There we were squatting in that dark hole, amidst the over-powering odour of freshly disturbed faeces, listening to the well-scrubbed voices of the bright individuals of the world beyond, the world of supper breaks, and stoves in railway signalling boxes, and clean white paper to write on, and neat lines of responsibility and, most important of all, somewhere someone in command to whom you could refer all decisions. Most of the calls were longer distance than interested us, most concerning the railhead at Oistbeeck. Most of the messages concerned routine movements of passenger and goods trains. Much of it was the movement of goods of one sort or another. But all the messages contained that damned note of cleaned humanity—'load of coal coming up for you, Sinderquist, so you'll be able to keep your stove warm.' 'What do you suppose they want with fifty tons of sugar—anyway, one of the bags had burst so we've pulled it off at Aasne, so you can make your tally board accordingly—we'll be having sweet coffee tonight, that I can tell you.' And the maddening reply—'Go on, you won't see coffee until the morning

—you'll be drinking the beer and schnapps that accidentally got broken on their way through Aasne last Tuesday!' Last Tuesday. Already it was vintage. I would have given several unimportant pieces of my aching anatomy for a glass of beer laced with schnapps, at that moment!

Then came the message for which we had waited. From Aasne. To movement control at Meldenkirche. Amidst the military jargon, the message was clear. 'How are they getting on with the line at Boden, and when may we bring the train through?' Boden was not on the main route to Oistbeeck—it would take a simple change of points to connect the main line with the Boden line. Next stop after Boden was Meldenkirche, the nearest point to the military encampment. Meldenkirche told Aasne they would ring them back in about ten minutes. In five minutes the sergeant had cut the signal line neatly in two, and was operating both sides of it. The message came back in eight minutes, but by then the sergeant was ready, and assuming the accent of the Aasne operator, he took the message from Meldenkirche—'The train cannot move tonight—there has been difficulty with the repair, and the branch line is not expected to be opened before the morning. Over and out.' Then the sergeant switched his tapping, and rang the Aasne operator.

'Meldenkirche here,' the sergeant said, when the telephone was lifted at the other end.

'Yes.'

'About your message—04/07/55.'

'Damn it, I've lost my pad. Which message was that?'

'Your last one, about the special train.'

'Oh that—well, can we get rid of it? It's making us nervous here. Of course we're not supposed to know what's in it, but everyone is certain it is full of dangerous high explosives.'

'So it is! Well, you'll be happy to know the line is mended, so you can send the train through any time. Get your main line movement from Oistbeeck, and send it through.'

'Who'll do the signalling?'

'You'll do it from your end. The signalling system is down at Boden, of course, and so you'll have to tell the driver to ignore signals once he's along the Meldenkirche line—we can't fix the signalling system tonight.'

'You've got a bit of a cold or something, haven't you, Arnot?' I looked at the sergeant. Certainly, his voice was a stage lower than the operator at Meldenkirche, but I had thought his imitation very good. However, the two operators must have known each other for a lifetime, and it was setting a difficult task to hope to imitate someone you've heard only a few minutes.

'Ja, it's my sinus trouble again!' the sergeant said. He was lucky—his blind shot had hit the bull.

'Well, you always did have trouble with the sinus, didn't you. Take care of yourself and we'll push it through from here.'

'Good night then.'

'Good night? We shall be talking again later. What about our chess game?' The sergeant uttered a silent curse. I could almost hear his mind tick over.

I made a sign with my thumb over my arm and he understood immediately.

'We shan't be able to play tonight,' he said. 'I have to go for an injection for my sinus, and you know how that makes me sleepy. Remember last year?' Such is the power of auto-suggestion, the man in Aasne chuckled.

'Don't I just remember,' he said. 'That was the night I got a fool's mate. Well, take care, and I'll speak with you tomorrow.'

It took us a half an hour to fasten explosive charges to the railway line, about fifty feet from the Aasne end of the tunnel, and to tamp the explosive charge with earth and gravel to suppress the noise the explosive would make. We had brought with us gun-cotton slabs and tied three to each line. One slab was to be the cutting charge, the other two destined to turn the cut end of the line through a slight angle; an angle not steep enough to be seen, but which would derail the oncoming train as easily and as certainly as if the railway line had come to an abrupt end. Gun-cotton is not a noisy explosive, fortunately, especially when its major force, as in this case, was being directed downwards. We selected a piece of the line between sleepers and scooped out as much gravel as we could with our hands and with the trenching tool. Then came the truly dangerous business of crimping and attaching the detonators, which the sergeant carried suspended on elastic bands inside a tin lined with cotton wool. For detonators we were using small tubes about as long as a Swan Vestas match which fit over the end of the thin fuse rope. However, to ensure a perfect fit, the fuse rope has to be slid inside the detonator tube, which must then be crimped on to the rope. The only satisfactory way to do this, without elaborate instruments, is to put the detonator in your mouth, and crimp round the soft metal end with your teeth. If you crimp in the wrong place, the detonator contains sufficient explosive power to blow off the top of your head. Some people cannot bear to put the detonator inside their mouth and crimp them from the side, but my philosophy has always been, 'in for a penny, in for a pound', and your head would get blown off wherever you put the detonator, inside or out. It's strange to watch the face of a man crimping a detonator. When he puts it inside his mouth he has a sickly look of total concentration, as if convinced he will vomit; he measures the position of the end of the tube blindly with his fingers, and usually readjusts the detonator's position. I have seen few men who can put one in and crimp it first time. Then you can see him making up his mind to do it, ordering his jaws to close so that his teeth press on the soft tube. Some men fail at this point—I have known normally brave men whose jaws have locked open with a detonator inside. Finally, however, most men acquire from somewhere the fortitude to close their jaws on the soft metal. It tastes horrible. And then you press, gently, turn the detonator through ninety degrees and do the job over again, with the same reactions. Crimping detonators is not like performing any other dangerous feat—when you've crossed the barrier of fear once it's usually not difficult to cross it again, to act to an unfeeling pattern that itself suppresses the feeling of danger. But every detonator you crimp is a new detonator. It doesn't help that no one will ever sit near someone who is crimping detonators—not, I imagine, from a feeling of self-preservation but because they wish to evade the horror of being close if one goes off. It's a lonely, disgusting, fear-raddled job.

One of the hardest things about being an officer is the need, sometimes, to look beyond immediate reality, to see what is glibly known as 'the overall picture', and to realize that one has overriding responsibilities. To many men it must seem like cowardice when officers hand over dangerous jobs—possibly in some cases fear and cowardice are the strongest forces. I handed the detonators and the fuse cord to Jonfey. He half smiled at me, and at the sergeant. He could accept that he was the most expendable of the three of us, but neither he nor I or the sergeant liked stating the thought. This was playing it by the book, and no mistake. I would not do him the disservice of dressing it up in false flattery—'Here, Jonfey, you're best at this job.' That would convince no one. He took the detonators and fuse cords, and walked twenty feet down the line. Then he sat as close to the bank as he could get, facing away from us, protecting us in the event of a failure with his own body. In the set of his hunched shoulders I could feel his silent protest—'I can play it by the book, too.' Possibly I was oversensitive—it's not a comforting thing to give a man a task you yourself can do as well as he can, knowing a mistake will kill him. That's something the men who write the manuals might care to remember—though I can see the need for doing things by the book, even with a bunch of pirates as comic as our special services. But I've often wondered, in a boat at sea, with the food and water supply having run out, who should go overboard—a husband, his wife, or his children. Most men, by-the-book heroes, would jump overboard first. Most wives would follow unthinkingly. What a tragedy it could be if the children turned out wrong or couldn't carry on surviving because they lacked the adults' experience, knowledge and fortitude.

When the detonator had been crimped, there is a look that comes on the face, the blanched white edges of the mouth suffuse with the blood of relief, and the whole personality is affected by arrogant success. Jonfey handed the detonators on their fuses to the sergeant, who inserted them into the gun-cotton blocks and taped them secure. Then we started carefully to tamp the blocks, to deaden the sound as much as possible. A half an hour later, the charge was ready for blowing. We retreated over the edge of the cutting and waited. The sergeant could sense my dilemma—do we blow the rails now, and run the risk the explosion will be heard and the train stopped, or do we wait until the train comes. The train itself would be guarded, and we would need to be close to the line to activate the explosion—at least, one of us would need to be there. The chances of escape were slender—either the explosion of the train would get you, or the guards most certainly would if they survived. Decisions, decisions! 'Blow it!' I said. The sergeant lit his fuse cord match and applied it to the end of the fuse, and then we left, down the embankment, along the edge of the field as fast as possible. We had got a half mile away and I was watching the seconds hand on my watch when suddenly we heard a distant crump. I looked up in surprise—the railway wasn't due to go for at least another forty-five seconds. But then, suddenly I realized the crump had been repeated, and suddenly there was a whole salvo of crumps, but on the far side of Meldenkirche. The 'action in force' whatever it was, had started.

The salvo was at its height when our tiny explosion went off—a mere snuffle of sound that would have been lost in the general holocaust had I not been looking at the seconds sweep of my watch. Confident now that our explosion would have alerted no one, we turned and went back to the line. The rails had been severed neatly, and the ends pushed about twelve inches to the side. The train, coming down the line at speed, would leave the track and smack straight into the back of the tunnel. We walked and crawled to a position about a mile from the railway and hardly had time to eat our bully-beef and biscuits supper, washed down with water from a brook and glucose and vitamin-strong lemonade powder, when the train came rumbling along the line. All its lights were out and it was doing at least sixty miles an hour. There was an awesome screech as it hit the bent rail, and white hot sparks flew up into the night as the wheels left the track and the train started to slither along the gravel of the permanent way. Then there seemed to be a silent pause, but only for a second, before the whole of the thundering train banged into the side of the tunnel mouth. In that cutting there was nowhere else for the trucks to go but forwards—the whole train concertinaed on itself, and there was a sudden crack. I had no need to cry 'down'—both the sergeant and Jonfey pushed their faces to the ground the moment they heard it. And then the bulk of the explosive went off, in one ear-shattering bang so loud it numbed every sense in the body, despite my hands clapped over my ears. It was a noise so full and complete it seemed to enter through the bones of the body, and then the shock wave came, and with it the tearing splintering jerking sounds as tree trunks were snapped like leg bones, and gravel and timber and glass and steel bars and truck sides bansheed through the air. The tongue of flame from the train shot up high as a hill, red flame with an incredibly yellow and white centre, and very little smoke.

And then it all started to come down again, screeching through the air, with a sudden back lash of wind into the heart of the explosion.

Jonfey was slapping the sergeant on the back. He would have liked to slap my shoulder, that I knew, but discipline prevailed. I slapped his shoulder, but that was quite permissible in the circumstances.

I'd never blown up a train before. I messed about on the ranges at Warminster with the burned out hulks of old tanks, but somehow it wasn't the same, it wasn't the same. I didn't even mind that there had been human beings on that train, and that they must have perished with it. They were part of the anonymous black evil of the enemy—my purpose in life, which I had accepted completely the day I put on uniform, was to kill as many of them as possible. With no regrets. Kill or be killed! Fight for freedom! Save our way of life. You're doing it for the country, for the mothers, for the unborn babies, for England, St. George, and all that crap. You're doing it—and for Christ's sake, stop asking why. Self sacrifice doesn't have to be in public, with nails through the palm of your hand, and you don't have to walk up the hill with a plank on your shoulder. You can do it, lying on your belly in a stinking field, crimping bits of aluminium between your teeth that probably need cleaning anyway. You do it when, where, and as you are.

I was crying. Oh, there weren't any tears I couldn't explain away—the shock of the explosion, happiness, relief—but inside me I was crying for the dead men, all the victims of the war, the little man with three dirty postcards in his pockets and his life's blood bubbling up out of his throat where I'd stuck the knife. Truly I meant to get his hands—but it never matters what you mean to do, does it? What happens is the evidence on which you are tried and judged, not what you mean to do.

The sergeant saw the tears, but neither one of us could speak about them.

We crouched under the hedgerow, and moved fast.

I had to talk to Rugby.

CHAPTER FIVE

When we returned to the bivouac in the field containing the hayrick, two things had happened. Simon had prudently reinstalled inside a five tree copse at the bottom of a field of wheat, and we had had visitors. German, of course, and their calling cards burned the hayrick to the ground and made a hole three feet deep. The stench of burning hay alerted us, but we went into the twenty acre to make certain. The Germans left four men to watch for our possible return, but evading them was easier than our training had implied—each of the four must have been a townie from the slabbed pavements of Hamburg or Munich with as much idea of concealment as a tart on her long awaited honeymoon. Two of them, incredible though it may seem, were smoking. I felt like giving them a medal and seven days confined to barracks. One of them had apparently heard about the great outdoors, and was sitting in a hedgebottom. Unfortunately his legs were sticking out, and his boots were size ten, all of them showing. Where is the Master race—where the copy book soldiers we've heard so much about? We left them guarding the field and the empty smoking remains of a hole in the ground, and went to look for Simon. I don't know why, but automatically I assumed these clodhoppers would not have caught him! We had planned, in Braintree, Essex, a 'get-together' technique for just such an occasion as this. We left the hayrick behind us, and travelled a distance of a thousand feet. Then we found the nearest place of safety and Jonfey sat there. He'd earned himself a rest. The sergeant and I both started out along the perimeter of a circle whose radius was a thousand feet, and whose centre was the hayrick, our previous position. I had travelled only five hundred yards, when I saw Simon. He was up a tree, a high chestnut. It was a bird that gave him away. At that time of night, birds are supposed to be asleep. This one wasn't. Simon was sitting deliberately close to its nest. The signals equipment was festooned throughout the tree, invisible from the ground below in the dense foliage. Once I had identified him, I went back and waited with Jonfey. The sergeant scouted a thousand yards, as we had planned, approximately half way round a circle of radius a thousand feet, and then returned. He was walking in an anti-clockwise direction—the clockwise man by our method would walk round the entire circle. If that hadn't worked, we would have increased the radius to fifteen hundred feet, and repeated the procedure. It's the only safe method of finding a man once you've become separated, other than him laying a hounds and hares trail of broken twigs. The Germans too can follow broken twigs—anything you can see, it's a safe bet they can see just as quickly.

We settled like partridges in the tree—there was room for half a platoon up there, and opened up the call to Rugby. The reception again was very good, but I didn't dare stay on 'transmit' for too long. The gist of my message was to ask if the plane flying in to lift us out could come as soon after first light as possible—our mission was accomplished and if we were known to be in the vicinity, the Germans could not avoid finding us. The noise of the battle beyond Meldenkirche was muted now, and I assumed a rearguard action was being fought by a few unfortunate sods delegated to take care of the mopping up.

Rugby put me through to Braintree, who got busy on the telephone presumably to the War Office and the Air Ministry and the Met Office—and the pick up was arranged for eight o'clock, in four hours' time. By then it would be light, but we'd all have to take our chances. By now it was four o'clock and I was whacked. We stripped the radio equipment apart and hid it more carefully in the branches. I wasn't going to bother to cart that all the way back to England with me—anyway, Willem, I felt certain, could make good use of it. About half past four I climbed down the tree to look about me and to urinate—I didn't feel like exposing myself in front of the men—a stupid prudery I've never escaped since my days of communal wash-rooms at public school. The actual lavatories, with half doors over which supervising prefects could peer without warning, theoretically to reduce the incidence of masturbation but in practice to make disparaging remarks about the size of your manhood had had a great effect upon me—so great that during my entire education and for years afterwards I was in a state of perpetual constipation in danger of becoming addicted to senna pods.

The tree was easier to climb down than to climb up—almost gaily I jumped the last six feet.

They were waiting for us. All round the copse. The Germans I mean.

CHAPTER SIX

THEY WERE ABOUT FIFTY and most had automatic weapons, machine guns hand-held to spit a death a second. Not the slovenly soldiers left to baby-sit a vacated hayrick, these were the military Herrenvolk, efficient killers trained to get close silently quickly completely unobserved. Up that tree I had more field-craft talent than the rest of the British Army—the Germans ran through our observation like water through a sieve; anyone can do it from ground level, if they put their minds to it, but only a trained expert can sneak up on men at a height of twenty feet or more. The German officer made a silent hand signal and the automatic weapons were lifted skywards. Horrified I watched them squeeze the triggers, the noise appalling as they hosed the tree with lead, twigs and branches and leaves flying in the fastest pruning I'd ever seen.

When the burst ended the rifles were lowered as one, with no order spoken.

It's not good to think you've been responsible for the deaths of three men by stupidity. I ought to have posted Jonfey at least five hundred yards from the tree to give warning—but arrogantly assumed that at height, observing in all directions, it would be impossible for anyone to approach us unseen. Lesson number one in this practical demonstration of my inabilities—don't put all your eggs in one basket. My mind numbly refused to accept the meaning of the scene my eyes had just witnessed. I thought of a silly joke someone had told me about a man who filled a bullring with Spaniards—when a riot came he was held responsible since he had put all his 'basques in one exit'. A giggle at the appalling joke drew thin bitter saliva to my mouth. The grasshopper flick of memory was of course the safety valve for a psychological head of fear. The giggle burst uncontrollably from me, my shoulders shook with shame and soon I was laughing without control and the laugh would have turned into racking sobs, but the sergeant, Jonfey and Simon climbed unharmed out of the tree. The gunners had aimed only at the tree's edges, deliberately avoiding its heart. It was a warning—no more, that this was the SS, and they wanted us alive. Not infantry butchers dedicated, as we ourselves were, to destroying the body of the enemy, these men saw us as a potential source of information. The officer in charge beckoned, and the men formed a square about us, heading eastwards. As we started to march away, the last rank of men climbed the tree, and soon we could hear the crash of radio equipment being thrown down. At the end of the wheat field parked on a small service road was a truck, with a large metallic ring above it. The flat side of the ring pointed at the tree. Behind the truck two lorries had benches for soldiers. The sergeant and Simon went into the first lorry, Jonfey and I into the second. The officer came to sit beside me as the convoy drove away.

'What is your name?' he asked me, a pleasant conversational opening gambit.

I didn't speak. Next, I felt, he should ask, 'Do you come here often?'

'No matter. I'll find out when we get to barracks.'

He took a silver cigarette case from the top pocket of his tunic. In it he had Player's cigarettes. He saw me looking at them, and offered one to me. Significantly, he didn't offer one to Jonfey. How on earth did he know I was in command of our party? I looked quickly down over my uniform. I had stripped completely before starting on this job, and had drawn all my clothing and equipment alongside the rest of them to make quite certain I was clad no differently from them.

'How did you catch us?' I asked, as much to stop him asking questions as to acquire information, though I was burning to know what had given us away.

'We knew you were not far away,' he said blandly. 'Willem told us that.' Steady, now, he could be trying to trap you when he talks about Willem—and there could be other Willems than Willem Schmidt.

'Who's Willem?'

'Ah, so you're going to be naïve. Good, that helps. It is always easier to break a man when he tries to be naïve and clever at the same time. We had the frequency for your calls to Rugby and your control, and luckily three detector vans in the neighbourhood. It was just a question of waiting until you started to broadcast on that frequency, and drawing three straight lines on a map. They crossed exactly at that copse.' Damn, so it was Willem Schmidt! Only he had the Rugby frequency, for use in emergency. Well, this was the emergency all right, but it was apparent Willem wouldn't be doing any broadcasting.

'Don't worry about Rugby,' the officer continued, 'we've taken a leaf from your book and broadcast to tell them to ignore any further signals that may be sent. That was a clever trick of yours, telling the Army network a spy had been operating—it threw messages into suspicion sent days ago. And just so you won't feel too badly, it put us into such chaos that your friends over the other side of Meldenkirche got completely away. We caught only five prisoners, sick and elderly Jews who had volunteered to stay.'

This man amazed me. I would estimate he was just over thirty years of age, compared to my thirty-two, but he had an older blandness about him I couldn't comprehend. In his circumstance I would have been crowing at capturing four prisoners, or so angry I would be tempted to use physical violence! As tall as I was, he certainly looked as fit—not at all the sort of man I would want to tangle with in personal combat without the wartime licence of knives and razor blades and the paraphernalia of legalized skullduggery with which we had trained. I had worked my body slightly forwards on the seat and only Jonfey had seen the movement. My chance came on a corner when the men on my side of the truck suddenly were thrown off balance. Awaiting such a moment as I went forward I had twisted to the side, right leg back and left leg forward. As the truck got into the turn my weight eased forward and I was in the natural position to vault over the tailboard. I saw Jonfey through the corner of my eye start to rise after me, but the weight of the turn was keeping him off balance and I doubted he would make it. I put my right hand on the tailboard—the pain from my thumb was excruciating but there was no time to react to it. As my body went forward my arm took the weight and my legs came up and I slid over the tailboard to the right. I heard the shout start as I hit the ground and rolled instantly over towards the side of the road. Jonfey too had made it over the tailboard and came after me. The roll ended with me sitting at the side of the road leaning to go through the hedge. I dived straight into it head first. A brick wall had been built there, masked by the brush.

I recovered back in the truck, wired to one of the uprights supporting the canvas roof. Jonfey lying on the floor of the truck had blood oozing from his side.

'He got over the wall,' the officer said, seeing the direction of my look—'so we had to shoot him. It's only a flesh wound, of course; we wouldn't want to hurt him. I can see you have been trained very well,' he said, eyeing me with respect. 'We shall have to be more careful with you. It's a pity about the wall, if it hadn't been there I think you would have got away!' Again that bland admiration, cool appraisal. If this was to be the interrogating officer, God help us. I shivered. In my post-concussive clarity, his coolness seemed the bloodless venom of a snake man.

The trucks slowed down, turned left, and I could see over

the tailboard the shape of a guard house. It had once been a greenhouse, the glass now replaced by black canvas. We drove up a well used track, and the lorry halted. We were outside an enormous house, almost large enough to be a castle. Rooms on five floors, and doubtless there were cellars. Parked in a conspicuous position in front of the house, on a square of what once had been lawn, were a row of ambulances. At least they looked like ambulances, but from this distance I could see them without engines, wooden constructions shaped and painted to simulate ambulances. How like the SS to camouflage their headquarters as a hospital to avoid bombardment from the air by stupidly sentimental Englishmen.

There was nothing hospital-like about the interior. The house had been converted into a beehive of officialdom, with signboards crudely fixed everywhere. The doors had been hand carved in mahogany, but the Germans had no thought of preserving the fabric when they went around it with hammers and nails. In the room into which we were taken was what had been an Aubusson carpet before the hob-nailed soldiery stomped its pile to ribbons. Across one corner of the room a gorgeous table was now used as a desk. I looked about me. This whole room in its heyday before the war had been styled in the French Empire tradition as a salon. The Germans had not even bothered to empty it of its elegant contents, but were making the best use of it as it stood. The effect it had on me was the same as I once experienced in a hotel in York, when a titled lady, whose name I would not divulge, suddenly lost her topless evening gown as she walked in to dinner. It was one of those dreadful accidents that can happen to any woman. She stood regally there, surrounded by her precious garments in disarray. There was no vulgarity, no titillation of the senses, no thought of a free peep-show, though the heat of the evening had caused her to wear what in those days was scanty underwear. Haughty, proud, though disarrayed, she had but to array herself again. When the Germans had gone, the room would array itself again, it had the proportions, the atmosphere of quiet composure, the dignity.

I was forcing myself to concentrate on this recondite matter only because I did not want to think of the immediate future. I would be questioned, and possibly reprisals would be taken against my person for what we had achieved. That was the natural order of this eye-for-an-eye war, and I was prepared for that. You take part in any illegal activity with full expectation of retribution, even though you may fool yourself you have licence for your actions. Brought up as I was to the natural life of seasons of the countryside, you realize no one can pervert the natural order without retribution. Governments do this with their artificial summer time, councils change the course of rivers to make housing estates, city bred men spray city made chemicals on the ground, all setting themselves against the natural order. Some time or another, sure as God made eggs, there's an accounting—national milk yield is down, soil is eroded, and virulent pests who eat chemicals and live, abound. There has to be an accounting at some time or another.

I was prepared for the accounting. Seven days bread and water? A flogging? Shooting; even, I believe, death. But I wasn't prepared for any deviation of the natural expression of the wish to punish—I wasn't prepared, for example, for torture. How in hell do you prepare yourself for torture, short of pulling out all your toe and finger nails in advance? To be quite honest—I was scared—just plain scared.

The four of us were paraded in that room, photographed, had our fingerprints taken and our pockets emptied—though I managed to keep my wrist watch—and were marched to the top of the building and locked in what had been a maid's bedroom. It measured ten feet by ten feet and still contained a brass bedstead with a mattress but no bedding, a wash stand without ewer or bowl, a couple of pictures on the wall, framed postcards of the kind they used to give out for regular attendance at Sunday School. The glass of one picture had been broken and removed. We waited until the guard had locked the door, and the sergeant quickly removed the glass from the other picture. He took off his jacket and wrapped the glass inside it. Then he snapped the glass into pieces.

One sliver he gave to each of us, the remains he tucked into the mattress for possible future use. My piece was about three inches long, a half an inch wide, murderously pointed. I ripped one of the belt tabs from the side of my trousers, and unpicked the stitching across the end. The belt tab, sewn double, could now be opened at the end like a finger stall and was about two inches deep to the button hole. It made a useful glove for the flat end of the glass sliver, a handy sheath that would prevent the glass cutting my hand should I have occasion to use it. Each man hid his glass sliver in a different place. The sergeant used his to slice the underside of his denim collar. He then worked the glass through the slit. With his hands behind his head he would be able to pluck that glass from under his collar and throw it. The boys told me the sergeant could score double twenty with a throwing knife any time he wished. Simon put his in a pleat of his denim jacket where it was stitched into the cuff—the boys in the infantry used to press these pleats with a hot iron to make the jacket parade worthy. Jonfey, trust him, put his inside the covering flap of his fly. We couldn't suppress a small laugh. 'Well,' he said, with pretended truculence. 'It's the most natural thing in the world to go for your knob, isn't it?' We had to admit there was justification in what he said. A pouch at the back of the denim jacket covers the button holes where the jacket buttons to the trousers. I hid my glass sliver in that pouch and felt much better. Barely had I done so than there were footsteps along the corridor, and the door was unlocked. A medical orderly came into the room, alone, with a wooden box of first aid kit. He asked Jonfey to lie down on the bed and opened his battledress and lifted his shirt and vest. The wound was apparently clean, and the bullet had passed through the flesh at Jonfey's waist, missing the bones. The orderly dusted the wound with a white powder and stuck a plaster over it. He then gave Jonfey two pills from a bottle. Jonfey looked at me and I shook my head from side to side. The orderly gave Jonfey a small glass of water from a bottle in the first aid kit—Jonfey looked at me and I nodded. He put the tablets in his mouth and drank the water. Then he had a spasm of coughing, and took his handkerchief to his mouth. When he had stopped coughing he looked at me and winked. The tablets were in the handkerchief. Better the pain in his side, unpleasant though it may be, than two unknown drugs which might, or might not, be simple aspirins. Anyway, I had genuine morphine tablets sewn into the linings of my pocket. As soon as the orderly had gone, I took a morphine tablet from my pocket and gave it to Jonfey. He lay back on the bed, and within a couple of minutes the pain had started to ease. The wound was not serious, and we could effectively forget about it. 'We'll be interrogated separately,' I said, remembering the warning Braintree had given us about the possibility of concealed microphones if we were locked together in one small room. 'But I don't want any heroes.

Tell them everything you know, and don't make up any funny stories.'

'Do you mean that!' Jonfey asked. 'Can't we have them on a bit of string?'

'No we can't, or they'll have us on a bit of string—but theirs will be tied around the ends of your thumbs.'

'Do we tell them where we have come from?' Simon asked.

'Yes, you can tell them we came from an airport just outside Canterbury. I don't imagine that will do the slightest harm, since once Control realize they've lost us, they'll shut up shop and open up elsewhere.'

'But can't we make up a story for them?' Jonfey was determined to have his last fling of defiance.

'No, you can't. The most you can do is to make them ask you a question for every fact they want to know. Don't volunteer any information, but if they ask a direct question, answer it. I don't want anyone coming out of this place with a broken body—remember, these boys are experts at interrogation—they've had the Jews to practise on for a good number of years. Tell them what they want to know, and with luck you'll go to prisoner-of-war camps, and sit out the rest of the war. Try to be funny, and there won't be enough of you left to bury. And that, lads, is my last order.'

I could see they didn't like it, Jonfey in particular was furious. I don't really think he was mad at being captured—after all, anyone can be thrown at a fence. But it was not being able to mount again and ride on that bothered him. The sergeant hated the Germans more than any of us—we'd all spent some time in Germany before the war—Simon had studied for a year at Goettingen as part of his veterinary course, and Jonfey had show-jumped in Munich, Hamburg, Berlin and several other places. But the sergeant had lived among them—had even been taken as a German by his neighbours and the people who worked alongside him—and he had seen the rise to power of the Hitler-inspired SS machine. He'd witnessed the persecutions at close quarters, and had come into the Army with a personal grudge. He never said anything about it, but one night when we celebrated the end of a long spell of training by sharing a bottle of Naafi whisky in the hills beneath Cader Idris, I asked him why he hadn't married. We had a good fire going in a gap between two hills. The boys had knocked off a sheep, and we had cooked a part of it as a stew—there are few tastes to beat that of fresh mutton stew, with potatoes and carrots, and the fresh wild thyme that grows among the rocks of the Welsh hills. The bottle had sunk to the last inch, and we knew the euphoria of fresh air, the outdoors, food, whisky, and the end of training.

'How is it you've never married, sergeant?'

'If I might be personal, sir, I could ask you the same question.'

'In my case, it's very simple—I've never met a girl I liked sufficiently to want to ask her to marry me!'

'I knew a girl, in Germany in 1936. I'd been living up in Bergen, working on the fishing boats—only a lad of course.'

He would have been twenty-one in 1936 and already, as I knew from previous conversations, had traversed Russia on the bum. 'I came down into the Ruhr to get a job—men were making a fortune in the steel works at that time. I got myself a little place in a very small hotel run by a very nice family called Rosenberg. They didn't have many guests staying there—you can guess why from the name, I imagine. Well, this family had a daughter, and I fell for her like a ton of bricks. Of course, that didn't suit my plans at all—I intended to make a pile and leave Europe for America, Canada, the West. In those days, there was something magnetic about the West.'

'What about Miss Rosenberg?'

'Well, she was getting a bit struck on me, so I thought I'd better cool her off a bit. Anyway, the way things were going in Germany, once I'd made my pile I intended to get out of there, p.d.q. Then one night after supper, old man Rosenberg came to my room and more or less popped the question on behalf of his daughter. Would I marry her and take her with me? He'd give me his entire savings.'

'And did you?'

'Honestly, sir, I couldn't. It's not that she wasn't a smasher all right—as lovely a girl as I'd ever known, and such a sweetness with it I'd never laid my hands on her. Honest! I never even touched her. But you see, it meant death to me, the very idea of marriage. I'd always been a runner. I ran away from home and school at fourteen, and never stopped once. I couldn't bear the idea of settling in one place. Of course, I know why—I was running away from my old Dad—old Do-it-all, we used to call him at home. He never believed anyone other than himself could do anything. Do you know, sir, he even used to cook the

Sunday dinner, and my Mam standing by, looking at him, idle!'

We each took a drink of whisky, and I brought him back to the girl. 'About five nights after her old Dad made me the offer I was in my room, starting to pack. A couple of shirts and a spare suit was about the total of it, but having turned the daughter down, I had to get out of there. The folks had gone to bed, and a little night man who used to come on duty at ten and sleep in the office downstairs had already arrived, and suddenly I heard this tap on the door. The door opened and in she walked. She was wearing a dressing gown I reckon must have been her Dad's because it fastened the wrong way. It's funny how you notice that sort of thing when you're all worked up, isn't it? And was I worked up! I'd had girls in dressing gowns in my room before —there was one at Bergen would come every night if I'd let her. But not this one. As I told you, I'd never laid hands on her. And she sits down on the edge of the bed, and then she asks me, 'You're going away, aren't you?' I had to tell her. 'And it's because of what Father asked you?' I had to admit it, and tried to tell her it wasn't any failing on her part. That when I was good and ready, she was exactly the kind of gal I'd be looking for, and I'd keep a picture of her always in my heart and all that sort of stuff, and then she started to cry, but it wasn't what I thought. 'Is it difficult to make a baby?' she asked me, just like that. 'Are you in trouble?' I asked her. I was flabbergasted. You know how it is—well, perhaps you don't know, Sir, how it is, but I imagined that because *I'd* never touched her she was pure, and no one else had ever touched her. I remember thinking what a laugh it would be if all the time I was keeping hands off some local German lad was having it nightly and twice on Sunday. And then it all came out. If I wouldn't marry her, would I at least give her a baby? Of course, I was flattered—but it wasn't the image of me she wanted—it was the pregnancy she could get the local doctor to stamp on a card to get out of the country. At that time, the only Jews they were letting out were pregnant mothers whose husbands were abroad.'

I fuelled the fire again with logs the boys had cut before they went down to Aberdovey for a night out. I tipped the last of the whisky bottle into the sergeant's mug, and opened a fresh bottle. I knew we'd finish both bottles that night. I didn't want to hear the rest of his story—but I knew I must.

'To cut a long story short,' he said, 'I let her stay in my bed that night, and about three o'clock in the morning, when we were both half asleep, it happened. She was so happy the next morning. I left the digs feeling bloody horrible. Five months later I'd made a pile of money, but the political thing was coming to the boil and Germany was no place for me. I went back to the hotel to ask her to marry me and come with me. Some bugger had been there before me and burned the hotel to the ground with the Rosenbergs and my kid in it.'

Most of us were fighting for children everywhere—the sergeant was fighting for one unborn child and all the mothers of the world.

'When do you think they'll start the interrogation?' Simon asked, quietly.

'I imagine they'll leave us here for quite a while—part of the psychological treatment to wear down our nerves.'

'What do you suggest we do to pass away the time?'

'Nothing planned. I don't agree with the idea of running away from things, even mentally. We've all got to face the fact that we have an ordeal to go through, and if we face up to it, when it comes we will be better equipped to deal with it. We can sleep a little, if that's possible, but for the rest of the time I suggest we brood, talk if we want to, behave like rational sensible human beings and not like a pack of frightened sheep chasing our own shadows.'

'Good,' he said, 'I was hoping you'd say something like that. I couldn't have borne it if you'd devised some party game to take our minds off things.'

CHAPTER SEVEN

THE WINDOW WAS NOT LOCKED—but then why bother four floors up and no bedclothes to make a dramatic knotted sheet elopement, no palpitating lover's heart awaiting us below. From the window I could see the entire grounds of the hospital on this side of the building. In the natural perimeter of a hedgerow here and there the gleam of steel mesh wire revealed itself in the trees. At each of the two corners natural buildings had been turned inconspicuously into guard houses, and a set of long low buildings—presumably once stables filled with thoroughbred horses—now appeared to be soldiers' barracks. From this height, the ambulances looked most real—a party of soldiers, however, with typical Teutonic thoroughness, was moving one of them nearer to the house—doubtless they knew the R.A.F. constantly took aerial photographs of as much of Europe as possible, and the interpreters' suspicions would be aroused by a number of apparently immobile ambulances. The part of the roof in which these top rooms were located had a sloping mansard and a small six inch parapet appeared to go all the way along the front. I opened the window wide, and make a sign to the sergeant. He would have preferred to go himself, but now we were all prisoners I felt the severance of that aspect of leadership which insisted I preserve myself for future responsibilities—we were in this together, equal in status, as equal in the ability to take risks as in the power to suffer. I climbed out through the window and lay flat against the lower slope of the mansard, feet jammed in the gutter of the parapet. Provided I lay back flat, there was little danger that anyone on the ground near the house could see me. I worked my way slowly along the roof to the next window, crouched down, and crawled beneath it without risking a look inside. I went along this way to the corner with no interest in the inside of the building—I wanted to make a complete survey of the grounds about us. There would be no difficulty getting to ground level—gutterpipes ran all the way and I'd been up and down enough gutterpipes in the girls' hostel at the University to know they were easy to climb. The other side of the building abutted formal gardens, laid out in what I believe is called the Italian fashion, with long walks of evergreen hedges and shaped flower beds between them. The flower beds had been left to seed themselves with weeds, and were now overgrown; the box hedges, too, were in need of a trim and stood three feet high. Once again I traversed the roof, and looked down from the corner over the other side of the building. There were buildings all round a central courtyard on this side, and signs of great activity. This was obviously the main men's barrack block and probably, also, one of the principal entrances to the building for office workers. On the fourth side a stretch of paving carried a number of outdoor chairs, and the ground sloped to a lake. An orderly was already laying a table; presumably the officers' quarters gave on to this terrace. I completed my circular tour, and at last came to the window of the room in which we had been locked, and climbed in. The sergeant indicated everything was all right—no one had been into the room. I suddenly realized how hungry I was; the sight of the table being laid on the balcony must have stimulated gastric juices—certainly it evoked the many days I had been up early, and walked round a property such as this in its heyday, to come in at breakfast time to a table already laid, kidneys, bacon, eggs and fruit on the sideboard under hot silver dishes. I waved the sergeant close and whispered in his ear.

'We're facing south; the only possible way is west where there's a neglected garden. Down a gutterpipe six feet from the corner with a nasty swing out over the parapet. The gutter is well secured, made of lead quite strong unless you pull outwards. Socket and wall pins every six feet or so all the way down. To the north the main barracks, the officers' mess on the east.'

'So they get the early morning sun!'

'So will you if you try going down that way.'

I gave the same message to Simon, while the sergeant talked in a loud voice to Jonfey. When I'd finished, the sergeant and Simon talked together and I briefed Jonfey. His eyes lit up when I told him about the gutter—Jonfey could already imagine himself down on the ground and away into the box hedges, crawling fast as a snake.

There were footsteps along the corridor. The key turned in the lock, and a guard came in. He flung the door wide open and somewhat carelessly ushered us out. I could see Jonfey was going to have a go at him and certainly would have killed the man, but I laid a restraining hand on his arm. There was no point in going off half cock, and it was certain that even though we could free ourselves of this much supervision, we wouldn't get out of the house or the grounds without concealing darkness. The German knew that, too; it was apparent in his demeanour he didn't believe we'd be stupid enough to try anything. He led us down two flights of stairs to a long room on the first floor that had been designed as a ballroom, so elegant its furnishings and inlaid wood mosaic floor; the floor was scratched beyond repair. There can have been no third floor above this part of the house, a musicians' gallery curved into the room at one end at a height of about ten feet. Long trestle tables had been laid in the room now used for eating. I was going to say dining, but in view of the litter on the table tops and the mess on the floor, 'fressen' would have been a more appropriate German term than 'essen'—foddering I suppose its nearest English equivalent. Whoever said the Germans are clean precise people had never seen them relaxed and off duty when the vast majority became hog like. We were seated at a trestle table—I could see the expression of distaste on Simon's face as he walked to the side table on which was a bowl of water and a cloth and washed our part of the table clean. A soldier/waiter came from the far end of the hall, carrying a bucket of coffee and a pan of meat, cheeses, bread and pickled onions. It was not our usual breakfast, but I was in no mood to complain—it was certainly a thousand per cent better than anything I had expected. While we were eating, the dapper officer who had captured us came into the hall. The guard eating at the table with us sprang to attention, but we stayed where we were. However, I indicated to the sergeant and the men that they should stop eating; this they would have done anyway as a matter of course. The anomaly of it struck me forcibly—here we were being fed for no other reason than to conserve our strength for the interrogation soon to come. Doubtless the officer who would carry it out was sitting on the terrace, idly picking the last remains of his breakfast from his teeth and smoking a cigar before coming to his duty. And we observed, at least superficially, the traditions of a code of conduct completely outmoded by a three-years-old declaration of total war. I would have felt better had he locked us in a cage, and come to see us carrying a plaited whip. At least we could have sharpened our claws on the bars, and spat defiance at him. But how can you defy a man who smiles and gives each one a Player's cigarette doubtless taken from the bruised body of a fellow Englishman, shot down on a bombing mission over this very countryside from which so leisurely you are planning to escape. As he put the cigarette beside Simon's plate, Simon looked up at him.

'Thank you,' he said, 'but I don't smoke!'

'Perhaps one of the others . . . ?'

'You're very kind,' Simon said, and handed the cigarette to Jonfey. Quick thinking—of the four of us, the sergeant was the most addicted to tobacco—Jonfey hardly smoked at all. You don't get the habit, in and out of stables all day.

Without further comment the officer marched out of the hall. The soldier sat down and resumed his meal. I had left a portion of the cheese on my plate—I found it very strong and possibly rancid. The soldier looked at me, and scooped it off my plate and ate it with his fingers.

'Wie heisst er denn, der Kapitan?' I asked. There was no reason to hide my knowledge of German.

'Kapitan Ullan.'

'Aus Hamburg?' His accent had betrayed him in the truck.

'Ja, Kapitan Ullan, aus Hamburg. Nun, schweigen Sie, bitte!'

I noted the 'bitte'. He had been well briefed.

As soon as we finished eating he took us out of the building on the north side round the square. At the far end a long low building into which he led us was a makeshift block of lavatories with chemical closets. On these were no doors or separators, and I felt my stomach knot. Sitting on one of the cans a large German corporal was reading an old magazine, much dog-eared. The stench in that house was vile, but he appeared not to notice it.

'I will wait outside,' I said to the guard, but he was having none of that. Jonfey, Simon, and the sergeant shared none of my inhibitions about performing in semi-public, and I was compelled to wait for them. I looked out of the doorway—at least four hundred men were stationed in the extensive barracks constructed at the back of the house. There was a constant traffic of men into the big house, mostly carrying papers. To my right, in a building I couldn't see, appeared to be another administrative centre into which most of the paper carriers scurried like homing wasps.

When we got back into our room on the top floor, the guard locked the door and left us. As soon as he had gone I opened the window and beckoned the sergeant out. 'Only go as far as the corner,' I whispered to him. 'I don't imagine we'll have long and I'd like Simon and Jonfey to look over the ground.' It took him about ten minutes to do his reconnaissance, during which time we were on tenterhooks awaiting the return of the guard. Then Simon went, and when he returned after five minutes, Jonfey went.

We needn't have hurried. It became apparent to me by eleven o'clock that they were in no hurry to interrogate us.

We slept for most of that day—there wasn't a lot to talk about, conscious that at any time they might be listening. I felt I ought to talk to them about interrogation, but I knew nothing other than the standard rules of thumb we had been taught collectively at Braintree, Essex. At least we were reassured by the knowledge that, provided our captors didn't find them, we had the shards of broken glass and the ultimate life or death decision in our own hands. We didn't speak about that, of course.

The sergeant woke me about seven o'clock, as I had asked him. The guard came back about half past seven, and we were taken down to supper. It was the same routine, and a similar meal to breakfast, except that we started with a bowl of thick potato soup into which, unfortunately, the cook had tipped too much pepper. Captain Ullan didn't come to the mess hall, but the guard handed us four cigarettes when we had finished eating. This time they were of a brand called Black Cat—the Captain must have been running short of Player's. We returned upstairs at nine o'clock after our visit to the lavatory shed where once again I could not function. I had resolved that when it became necessary I would go out on the roof rather than squat on one of those evil buckets. It would be just my luck if it landed on someone's head.

Simon was pacing about, up and down the room, and I could see it bothered the other two. Jonfey had stretched out on the bed, and the sergeant was sitting at the foot. Back and forwards Simon went, from the door to the window, the window to the bed, the bed to the door.

Finally, 'Knock it off, Simon,' the sergeant said. 'Why don't you sit down and get some rest. You may need all your energy later.' Simon came and sat down beside me. 'You know,' he said, 'they ought to give us a story we could tell before we leave England—they ought to fill us up with what sound like valuable facts.

'Why?'

'I've been thinking,' he said, 'that I don't know anything. They can question me all night, but what I know could be told to them in four short, sharp sentences.'

'Then it won't take long, will it?'

'Yes, but that's the trouble—they won't believe me. They'll think I know a lot more and am concealing it. But I don't. I don't! I've always made it a policy not to know too much about what's going on. I didn't want to fill my mind with assorted facts anyone could get out of me the minute they put the thumbscrews on. I've always believed the less you know, the less you can tell. But what happens when I've said my four sentences, and they ask me for the rest, and I say I don't know any more? They'll never believe me; they'll think I'm trying to be smart.'

What could I say? It was obvious that, like the rest of us, Simon was scared out of his wits. I too was scared, but somehow I'd managed to get my fear at least under temporary control. Down there I too would break—but didn't know what to do about it.

'I was just like this at examination times,' Simon continued. 'I just used to seize up. In a viva they once asked me how I'd deal with a fibrous tumour on a cow's head and I said amputate its head! I must have been crazy. That set me back a year.'

'It's a funny thing about fear,' Jonfey said, from the bed. 'I used to get it when I was show jumping. I remember Midnight—that was the name of a horse—at the International Horse Show in Barcelona, in '37. God, he was a big bugger, as difficult as they come. They'd shipped him over from Turin, and I had him on a little farm for a few days to try to settle him down—he never did like sailing and neither did I in those days. It was as hot as hell that summer, and he was really fed up by the time the show came. I had him out in the enclosure, you know, just warming him up, and I showed him the three foot jump they had. He went up to it in a wild canter, and then the bugger stopped still and stood straight up on his two hind quarters. I dropped the reins of course, to try to yank his head down again, but he wasn't having any. Slowly, and quite deliberately, he came over backwards. He was determined to crush me. Of course, I nipped off him a bit sharpish, remounted when he'd picked himself up, and really squeezed the daylights out of him with my knees. I took him on the bit so tight he couldn't move an inch either way and every time he went on to lift his head, I yanked him down again, fast.'

I looked at Simon's face. He was always entranced by Jonfey's stories of horse jumping—I think of all animals Simon loved horses the most.

'Well, there was an old vaquero in the enclosure—a right old lad with skin on him like the shell of a walnut, and he came across, stood in front of Midnight, blew up its nostrils and talked to it. He blew right up its nostrils I'm telling you. That horse settled down, and stopped trembling. Then the man looked up at me and said—in Spanish, of course, because the old geezer couldn't speak a word of English, "Why are you afraid?" "If you'd seen those jumps," I said to him, "you'd be afraid—whoever set this course was a bloody sadist!' He smiled at me. "Yes, señor, it is a good thing to be afraid—that shows your mind is working out the possibilities, but you must never let the horse know." "How do you mean, let the horse know—I haven't told him a thing!" This old geezer looked up at me and smiled again—like he was Solomon or something—"You've let him know by your smell. He can smell the sweat of fear on you." Well, to cut a long story short, we had two clear rounds on Midnight, that day!'

'You took a bath and stopped sweating?' Simon asked, entranced.

'No—the old boy'd been eating garlic soup—after he blew into Midnight's nose, it couldn't smell a thing for the rest of the day! Whenever I jump a horse, these days, I always carry cloves of garlic, and rub them in the horse's nose—I could shit myself with fear, and the horse would never know it!'

Simon got up and walked across to the bed. He rubbed Jonfey's head. 'You and your stories,' he said, his good humour restored—'I think you make them up half the time!' But he'd got the message!

CHAPTER EIGHT

WE WAITED OUT the longest two hours of my life. Try as I might I just couldn't get the image of fingernails out of my mind, and all my horror thoughts about the interrogation the Germans must have planned for the dark watches of the night centred on the ten extremities of my hands. I once caught my thumb nail on the bolt of a rifle and ripped it back into the cuticle—the pain came back to me as a conscious throbbing in my thumb. My hands began to feel as if they didn't belong to me—I couldn't keep them still. I tried sitting on them until they were numb, but got pins and needles. I put them in my pockets, but they began to sweat. I clasped, unclasped, kneaded, rubbed and stroked them, spread my fingers out flat on the floor, trying desperately to forget them. By eleven o'clock they felt as big and fat as mess hall sausages.

I was first to go through the window. The guard changed below at ten o'clock and by eleven the light had almost gone and the guards would be relaxed, a quarter of the way through the tour of duty. There was a guard about a hundred yards from the foot of the gutterpipe, and another over in the corner who seemed to be pacing the north side. I debated sending the others down different gutterpipes, but that only increased the number of targets over the area of observation.

'Twenty feet apart. The pipe is not jointed so it won't make any difference to the pressure on the pins if we're all on the pipe together, as long as we don't get two to any one section. And, if you fall, push yourself out from the wall—no one will want to catch you! Me first, the sergeant, then Simon—Jonfey last. Make your own way through the garden and rendezvous by that small shed at the bottom west corner. Don't try to go through the wire or touch it—it may be plugged in to the mains and though they only use a hundred and twenty volts here, you could set bells ringing.'

They all nodded.

'And good luck,' I said, as I swung myself sickeningly over the parapet. There's only one way to get on a gutter if the parapet overhangs. You go over the side, hanging by your waist, and feel for it with your feet. You can't see what you're feeling for. The gutterpipe usually has a large cup at the top, and you must be careful not to be deluded into thinking you can grip it—those cups are rarely fastened tight. The first secure foothold was six feet down the gutter. I gripped the side of the pipe with my feet, held one hand on the actual parapet edge, and let my body slide down until I was hanging one-handed with my feet resting against the square corners of the lead pipe. My left hand I pushed beneath the parapet, beneath the water gathering cone to where the pipe itself was held into the stone. I pulled against the connection—good, it was firm. A grip with that lower left hand and slowly let go with my right. My feet slipped down the pipe about twelve inches, my weight thrown backwards away from the wall. My body slipped downwards in a dreadful lurch that seemed to last for ever, but the rubber cleats of my Innsbrucker boots caught the first pipe connection, a grab forward with my right hand and I was safe. From now on it was child's play. Shift hand grips until fingers are caught in the slight crevice between pipe and wall and bend the knees. Ankles together, lift feet off pins and bobbins that hold the pipe to the wall, and slide down a section keeping backside out and shoulders forward to push the centre of balance as close to the wall as possible. Each section felt like a drop of a hundred and fifty feet, but gradually I slid down each one without incident or noise. It was only when I had gone five sections I gained confidence to pause, look up, and then down. The sergeant was on the second section; no sign of anyone on the ground beneath us other than the sentry I had already spotted, and he was looking at ground level the other way. The face of the wall was comparatively light, or so it seemed to me, but there was no moon as yet. Section seven, then section eight.

If only no one goes into that fourth floor room until we are on the ground! We had jammed the door with the wash hand stand to delay entry but we couldn't count on more than minutes. Now for section nine.

The ninth section was loose and came away from the wall as I slid down it. I grabbed upwards with my right arm and caught the bobbin of the section above. One handed, I hung there, my heart bumping, then slowly lifted my shoulders until my head was level with the break. The lead had pulled away from the socket. Both pins were secure. I took a grip with my left hand and slowly pulled myself, hand over hand, up the eighth section until I could lodge my feet on the pins. The ninth section, I could see, had dropped down about four inches, the four inches that held it to the section above. Keeping my feet on the bobbins, I ran my hand grip down, crouching. The movement pulled me away from the wall of course and if the eighth section were loose, nothing could prevent me falling backwards. I gripped the side of the eighth section with the inner sides of my boots, spread my knees and heels as far apart as possible, and reached down with my left hand, between my knees. I could feel the strain pulling at my sacroiliac joint at the base of the spine. My face was jammed tight against the pipe—gritty against my sweaty cheek and jaw. I kept sliding my right hand grip slowly down, left hand reaching down between my feet, until I could grasp the ninth section. It was too fat for me to span it with my hand, but gradually I got my thumb on the front of it and the tips of two fingers around it, and tried to lift. If only I could lift it three inches I had hopes of jamming it around the eighth section protruding below the collar. I looked up. The sergeant was two sections above me, looking anxiously down. He daren't come any lower to help me. I looked down. There were another six sections to go after the ninth—a drop of forty feet. One of us was sure to hurt an ankle. I'd have risked it alone—but the law of averages was against taking the same risk four times.

I couldn't lift the lead pipe. It was too heavy, and I was in too awkward a position to use my strength effectively. I looked up again at the sergeant and indicated he should descend to where I was. He started to move, but I stopped him, indicating that I would go down first then come back up. He understood. I hung hands only from the bobbins. I let my feet hang as far down as possible, below the next set of bobbins. The broken pipe was between my knees, useful only as a guide. I managed to jam the sides of my boots tight against it, said a quick prayer, and dropped free. My feet caught the next bobbins first, my body started to go backwards since I couldn't hold on to the broken pipe with my hands, and then my hands caught the next bobbins and held. I looked up. The sweat that had gathered on my forehead ran into my eyes; I tried wiping it away with a cuff but it was heavily salted no doubt from fear. My bladder had also leaked.

The sergeant climbed quickly down the pipe until he was standing where I had stood, and he too squatted. He took a grip on the pipe from above, I took one from below, and we pushed the section back into place. A wooden wedge, used for jamming the pipes, had moved. I hammered it back into position using the flat of my hand—the sergeant used his Innsbruckers as best he could to bend the flange of the pipe back over the section above. He reached down and tested the section. It held. The guard had heard nothing.

I gained the ground without further troubles. The sergeant waited two sections until Simon had crossed the ninth, then Simon waited until Jonfey had crossed it. As soon as Jonfey was on the last sections I ran, half squatting, into the protection of the three feet high box hedges of the formal garden. Looking back at the house there were no signs of disturbance. I made my way easily through the hedges and arrived at the shed in the far corner of the garden. No one was near it. The shed was surrounded entirely by garden debris—two compost heaps behind it, and the remains of stakes and sticks and boxes, a few rusty spades with long handles in the Dutch fashion. Already the wood had rotted, the metal rusted. Jonfey arrived first, then Simon and, after an agonizing five minutes, the sergeant appeared, carrying a pair of wire cutters, new looking and well greased.

'There was a tool shed behind that shit house—I saw it this morning. Keep your eyes open, lads,' he said.

I knew the reproof was also meant for me—but sergeants are born, not made. I went round the back of the shed, leaving Jonfey and Simon on watch, and crawled towards the wire. It had been laced through a screen of Cupressus Macrocarpus and couldn't, therefore, have been electrified—every movement of a bough would have set the bells ringing. But there was a nasty little trip wire about eighteen inches this side of it, and looking through the mesh I could see the same arrangement on the other side, and those two trip wires were electrified and hanging from porcelain connectors. The wire itself, however was not taut. 'It's got to touch the earth,' the sergeant said, 'before it sends a signal.' I stepped over it and started to work on the wire mesh with the clippers the sergeant had acquired. Within two minutes I had clipped a hole four feet wide and a couple of feet high, taking care to keep the cut section in one piece. Then we both bent it upwards, away from the trip wire. I went through, then the sergeant gave a long low breathy whistle without a musical note for Simon and Jonfey. After the sergeant slid through, we bent back the wire and twisted it into position. Except from close up, it would be difficult to see that the mesh had been disturbed.

We ran.

We had travelled the best part of a mile when we heard the dull clamour of the alarm. Until that moment we had been running anywhere. Their knowledge of our escape, however, gave us a sense of direction—we were trying to get home.

'What did you say,' I asked the sergeant, 'it's a long way home and I hope we don't have to walk it or swim!'

The moon had come out and we headed west—at least we wouldn't have to circle the camp to get on our correct bearing. As to where we were, and what we were going to do, I had to confess myself without a single idea. I halted the men in the lee of a hedge on the other side of a road that ran north and south. They gathered about me in a tight circle.

'I've no need to tell you our present dilemma,' I said. 'We're in enemy territory, lost, without weapons or food.'

'We can find an enemy camp and raid it!' Jonfey said. I think he had no realization of the seriousness of our position—either that, or was determined not to admit it, since that could be the first symptoms in an epidemic of contagious fear, hysteria and ultimate surrender. I'd spent too many nights alone in deep country to be afraid of hobgoblins. But at the present moment I was charged with the responsibility of three men without food or weapons and every bush like Burnham woods could suddenly shout death at us. We had been taken once and had escaped—this time they would make certain escape was physically impossible.

'Do we stay together?' Simon asked, 'or separate?' Bless him, he was trying to let me off the hook, was saying, 'Do you want to try to make it alone, unburdened by us three.' He thought we all stood a better chance separated—though I couldn't disagree with him, a fierce pride rose in me. These were my men. I trained them to the point of readiness for this assignment; I gave the order that brought them here. I brought them, and I was going to take them back whole and safe in one unit if that were possible. You take on the responsibility of other men's lives without thinking of your own safety. Of course it might have been easier to get home without them, but I couldn't be certain they would get home unless I were there to help them. That of course was a terrible arrogance; a feeling anything they would be asked to do, I would be able to do for them, better than they could do it themselves. Who knows, perhaps by my very presence I impeded their progress down avenues of thought and spontaneous action that would lead them safely home. But I did, sincerely, think more of us would get back home together quickly and safely if we stayed as a party, and I led that party.

Also I knew that only in that way could I expunge the guilt I felt for the mistake at the tree—the mistake for which constantly I blamed myself.

The only one to argue would be Jonfey. The sergeant would accept what I said without thinking, and Simon could be swayed by argument. But Jonfey had about him a dash and verve I couldn't rationally match—the young colt who wants to jump all hedges, to charge because inactivity is wasteful of the natural energy with which he was abundantly endowed. As long as Jonfey thought we had a plan in mind and were prepared to execute it, he would go along with whatever was suggested and did. He was like the air that must rush in whenever it suspects a vacuum, mercury that rises and falls with each change of temperature and pressure.

'This house must have been on the western edge of Meldenkirche,' I said, 'since the lorries didn't go through the town when they were taking us there, and didn't travel far enough to get round it to the north or south. If we continue to head west we should come to the railway. If we can get there, we shall be able to find the wreck of that train, and if we find that, we can find our former position.' Three 'ifs' in a row. There had been three radios, protected from damage by falling—they had to be since we jumped with them on our backs. The radios had been thrown out of the tree—doubtless a few connections were broken, but if we could repair them . . . it was the biggest if, but I was determined to try it.

'I think we stay together,' I said to Simon, 'but I'm prepared to take a vote on it.'

The sergeant shook his head. Jonfey shook his head. No vote—we'd stay together. I took the lead again, and headed due west, reading our direction by the stars, and keeping the Plough and the North Star to my right. Whenever we came to a road, we watched it carefully for several minutes before crossing it. Twice we were nearly caught by motor-cycle combinations, but managed to evade them. Once an armoured column moved northwards, once we had to wait until an infantry company came marching up the road, in single file, one rank at each side of the road. It took them twenty minutes to pass—Jonfey as ever wanted to knock off a couple of their rifles and field rations, but I would have none of it. I was quite confident we could have taken at least three of the stragglers, but the risk, however small, was too great to take. The Germans would certainly be looking for us heading west, but they could not be certain we had not gone south or north to deceive them and would deploy some of their available effort and manpower in those directions. I certainly didn't want to put a mark on the map for them to use as a search centre—the column was bound to halt in forty-five minutes or so, and lost stragglers would be noted.

A farm cart had been left in a corner of a field. The sergeant looked in the box beneath the seat. In the box were ten apples. We ate the lot. The juice was wonderful. In a field about a mile further on we came across potatoes growing and dug them with our fingers. They tasted bitter until we rubbed the skins off—

again, the juice was a blessing. That peppery soup must also have been salty, with the pepper hiding the salt taste—or perhaps the knowledge we were short of food and water made us symptomatically more hungry and thirsty. I stuffed five potatoes in my battle-dress blouse—they would make useful gut filler when we needed them. We had crossed the railway and were almost within sight of the tree when we had our first real stroke of luck. A Mercedes car had stopped by the side of the road, and the driver and his guard passenger, a corporal, were squatting down in the hedge, relieving themselves. Jonfey's idea of course was to take them immediately and drive the car to the coast but, cautious as ever the sergeant and I crawled as near as we dared and listened to them. It soon became apparent they were lost, their destination at least ten miles to the west on the other side of the Maas. They had come from about thirty miles to the east, and were not expected to reach their destination until midday the following day. They had been delayed by a couple of girls! It was an opportunity too good to miss. I wish it could have been otherwise, but we could afford to take no risks. Kill or be killed. I got one with a rabbit chop that broke his neck. The sergeant strangled the other. Jonfey and Simon put on their battle-dress tops and caps, and the sergeant and I sat in the back of the Mercedes, low down, ready to drop to the floor if we should run into a patrol. The corporal had a rifle and nearly a hundred rounds of ammunition—not automatic but at least it was a weapon; the driver had a pistol and ten rounds—a nine millimetre Luger, fast and accurate.

The boot of the car was literally full of food and drink. On the back seat were a map case, an envelope containing the particulars of the vehicle and its permission to move, and the movement orders for the driver, Hans Kellerman, and the corporal, Martin Brueckner. There was also a pair of girls' knickers—the elastic had been broken on one leg and at the waist. No doubt one of the two had scratches on his face—but we didn't stop to look. We carried them a distance from the road and dumped them in the bed of a boggy stream, covered with branches, where dogs would not scent them.

We drove the car in the direction of the tree, to the spot where the lorries and the scanner van had been parked, then the sergeant and I went to look for the radios.

'You'd better get out and pretend to be doing what the other two were doing,' I said. 'But make certain you both face opposite directions.'

Simon opened the nearside door. 'I wish we hadn't killed them,' he said. 'At least not then. We could have waited—it seems a rotten moment to die. There's a disease that monkeys get—it blocks up the anus eventually, and the monkeys strain to get it out, and can't, and usually burst a blood vessel, trying too hard. I've always thought it a rotten moment to die—even for monkeys.'

CHAPTER NINE

TWO OF THE THREE SETS were still in working order. The power packs had suffered but we were able to jump a wire across two of them to give us enough juice for a transmission.

We got Rugby first call, and they gave us Braintree.

'Where the hell have you been?' he asked.

'Change to the frequency of the number above your office door,' I said, and switched off. I gave him time to get through to Rugby, and then started to look for him on the forty metre waveband. I got him within a minute, tuned in my BFO, and netted on to him. Then I called and he got me first time. The Braintree line was open.

'Can you send a plane—same when and where?' Then I switched off transmission. They weren't catching me again—it takes at least a minute to tune a direction finder, even if you know the frequency, and are listening when the transmission starts.

He came back on the air in three minutes. By God he was quick, and both the Army and the Air Force duty officers must have been at their desks for a change—or perhaps he was acting on his own initiative. 'Slight problem. Increased ack-ack left of flight path, or so we hear. You'd never get through. Two batteries.'

'Where?'

'Four plus three from previous datum.'

That meant four miles north and three miles south of the hayrick. We could find them. I turned to the sergeant. 'Can we knock out two ack-ack batteries?' I asked him. He nodded, instantly.

'Leave them to us and send in this plane.'

'Marvellous if you manage, old man,' he said, his voice coming and going on the longer wave of the forty metre band—'they're messing up a party we'd planned for somewhere else.'

'Give us four hours—so still same where and when, over and out.'

We hadn't been on 'transmit' for longer than seven seconds at any one time—no one could have tracked us.

Nevertheless we fled from that tree like bats out of the caves of hell, and thanks to the Mercedes were within a half mile of the first ack-ack battery within thirty-five minutes. We had passed plenty of vehicles and troops on the road, but there was safety in numbers apparently, and no one stopped or showed the slightest sign of interest in us. The bandages the sergeant and I wrapped round our heads possibly helped—we were able to loll back on the seats in style and comfort, and earned sympathetic glances from everyone as we passed. The GHQ insignia, fore and aft, probably helped as much as the bandages. Jonfey drove the car well, despite the lack of illumination—the headlamps had been covered with black paper leaving only a small cross free to transmit the light. Several times we were saved from the ditch only by Simon's keen lookout, but I was in no mood to tell Jonfey to slow down, and he had not the temperament to dawdle.

For the first time since we left the house, we were able to converse. This account of our escape will inevitably be short of dialogue because we were seldom able to talk to each other in voices louder than whispers—and somehow that constrainment also cuts down the amount you say. For the first time we were able to let ourselves go in the heartseasing kind of banality that opens the stop-cock on relief of tension.

'I thought you were a goner, sir, when that pipe pulled off the wall.' 'So did I, I can tell you.' 'My God, didn't that lead feel gritty.' 'Give me an iron pipe, any day.' 'I could do with a smoke—that's the one thing I miss, not being able to light a fag whenever you want to.' 'I wonder how Lieutenant Masters is getting on, sir?' 'I'll bet he's had Robert on a couple of fizzers'—a quick need to reassert discipline—'The Lieutenant is a good officer—the trouble is that some of you don't give him a chance—you'll see, he'll be a first class officer in action.' 'Will we get leave when we get back?' 'Sevenpence a day danger money for this little lot, you know!'

We came to the first ack-ack site on the other side of a wood at the edge of the road. We skirted it, and then drove down the road looking for the other. It was a half mile away in open country. Not so good! Simon and I would take the open field—Jonfey and the sergeant the wood.

'What shall we try?' the sergeant asked. 'Sights, or ammo?'

'Both, one on each.'

We made our arrangements about a rendezvous, and they dropped us off a quarter mile from the second ack-ack unit.

An ack-ack unit is a self contained military organism, based on a number of guns and the men to fire them. With the guns you have transport to shift the guns and the men. With the transport you have tents for the men to live in, and cookhouses to feed the men who live in the tents and shoot the guns. Officers command the men, and if they're lucky they get a caravan, with plotting tables, maps and charts, an easy chair, a bunk bed, a radio and as many creature comforts as they can cram into a space eight feet by six. A signals section takes the orders to fire or not to fire, and an ammunition section brings up the shells. An ack-ack carries shells with it, unlike fixed artillery units that don't use so many and can have them in planned dumps some distance from the gun site. One of our standard lessons—this time in Scotland, not Wales, had been 'how to do sites, gun, ack-ack, German'! 'Do' was the most overworked word in a soldier's vocabulary.

You can knock out the radio unit—but that can always be replaced by other radio units or land line telephone units. Secondly you can spike the guns, but for that you need explosives to slip inside the barrel—the explosive makes the barrel look like a squashed cigar if you blow it correctly. The third text book method is to spoil the ammunition—this you can do either by tampering with the fuses, or by setting the ammo dump on fire. A fourth and unofficial method is to take a nail file or a bent nail or, luxury even, a screwdriver and alter the setting of the sights.

The men of the ack-ack unit were all on stand down. Four guards; one behind the cookhouse tent drinking coffee; one guarding the officer's caravan—it was actually a converted horse box from the look of it; one sitting on the pile of ammunition, and one dozing in the front seat of a half track used for pulling guns out of mud. Seven guns were laid in arrowhead formation of three, two, one, one. Behind each gun a small stack of ammunition, ready for loading. I was about two hundred yards from the cookhouse tent, directly in line with the front gun, open field to cross, with short grass. Simon went round the other side, his immediate target the gun in the centre of the three on the back rank. He had a screwdriver from the tool kit in the car; I had the flat sharp end of a file that would do the same job. It was a long way across that field, belly-crawling all the way. It's one thing to crawl across a Welsh mountainside with one of your own boys aiming tracer as near to you as he dare; the risks are there, but somehow, you never believe he will hit you. With four men on guard, the nearest not two hundred yards away with a Schmeizer, it was hard to believe they could miss you. Crawling is a matter for wide legs, the inside of the foot and knees pressed to the ground. But it's also a matter of pressing your belly so hard to the ground you scrape your skin against the inside of your clothing, scared lest your arse lift even an inch in the air. You're not worried about getting one in the head—that stays well down; or your back which is sucked flat against your ribs; it's your arse, and the base of the spine at the coccyx you fear for. Even a hundred yards of crawling under the open muzzle of a gun gives you a pain in the coccyx. I had two hundred yards to go.

Once in the shelter of the gun I was able to lift myself from the ground behind the pile of ammunition. Ack-ack guns use a special shell, primed to explode in the air at a given height, plastering the skies with fragments. Ack-ack gunners are not concerned with trying to hit the airplane, the shell itself could go through the plane without doing much damage. But a thousand flying fragments can tear hell out of the mechanism of a plane. The height at which the shell will explode is set immediately before the shell is fired, on the orders of the gunnery officer. The setting is very simple—a brass ring round the base is turned to a specific number engraved on the shell's perimeter. The ring is secured to the base of the shell by a number of screws, depending which make it is. These shells had three. It took only a second to locate the three screw heads. My file end fitted exactly. Without moving the top shell from the pile I unfastened the three screw heads and gently eased the back off, pulling it towards me. If I were to drop it, the pile of shells and me with it would go sky high. Inside the shell casing a wheel was fastened to a spindle by two screws. I unfastened those two screws and turned the spindle to its limit, clockwise. I left the screws untightened and pulled the spring away from the clock mechanism in the shell casing before putting the back on.

The shell itself would now explode in the breach of the gun the second it was fired. The distance would be called out by the gunnery officer, the gunner's armourer would turn the setting on the shell case (though this would have no effect since I had disconnected the spindle and spring), the gunner's mate would load the shell into the breach, the gunner take elevation and direction from the gunnery officer, set his gun on target allowing for wind velocity, height parabola and all the other calculable factors; the gunner's mate, tense, would watch all this and dream of his promotion to gunner; at the nod of the gunner's head, the mate would take his moment of glory and yank the lanyard. The firing mechanism in the breech of the gun would snap forwards striking the detonator that explodes the small charge needed to get the shell spinning skywards; but now there was no time delay between that explosion and the next, no delayed action as the shell winged its way towards a skyborne target. The second that detonator exploded the small firing charge, the main fragmentation charge would explode, thousands of cubic feet of hot air would try to escape from the end of the thin barrel, and fail, and the breech of the gun would be puffed out and shattered like Chinese finger crackers, whamming the fragments of metal in all directions. With seven explosive centres, few people on the gun-sight could survive.

It took two and a quarter hours to 'do' all the shells on the top of the piles. I met Simon midway through the job. He was altering the zero setting of the range-finders; the guns would aim low and to the left in case, for any reason, they didn't use the shells I had so carefully prepared for them. 'I wouldn't care to be within half a mile when they fire this lot,' he said grinning. 'Neither would I!'

I was still working on the shell from the last pile, the rear gun to the left of the back of the pyramid, when suddenly the alert sounded. I hadn't heard the drone of any plane. Within seconds, flaps on tents opened as men rushed out in stages of undress. A small hollow in the field ran off to one side. I ran crouched over to it and dropped in. Hardly was I down before flying feet passed above my head as the first gunner leaped over. He was followed by five others. I dared not move lest a latecomer should see me, then fear bending my back low, I shuffled along the bottom of that depression until about twenty yards from the line between the tents and the guns. I hoped Simon had managed to hide himself somewhere—his task harder since he would be exposed at the front of the guns where, if I remembered correctly, was only open field and a dyke, with water stretching away beyond.

The gunners were intent on only one direction, forward and upward. There had been a brief spilling of light as the master gunner came from the officer's horsebox caravan—he was wearing headphones and doubtless was connected by line or short distance radio to the officer himself, receiving his instructions by radio from the meteorological and tracking station personnel.

Despite the risk of being seen, I bent myself double, and ran dodging from side to side to make myself less of a target. I had only travelled a hundred yards or so before there was a sudden shout and the rifle fire began. Shots screamed past me as I ran, wildly zigzagging backwards and forwards, bent double. It's difficult to hit a running man with a rifle bullet, even if you are a crack shot, which not many soldiers are—but with bullets whistling past me at a distance of not much more than twelve inches, that knowledge was small comfort to me. Then, despite the sounds of the Schmeizer fire, and the crack of the bullets zipping past me and the thump as they hit the trees ahead, I heard the planes. I flung myself to the ground and waited. The master gunner was calling out elevation, range, fuse settings. The rifle shots were getting closer to me, some whistling not inches from my head. Tortuously I twisted so the right side of my body was the one exposed to them—it was an irrational thing to do since the target was increased across the arc of fire.

The master gunner called his final command—I could imagine the snap as the gunner's mate pulled hard at the lanyard in correct Teutonic orderly style, and there was an almighty thump as the shells were detonated to start them on their screaming journey through the air. There was the instant sound of a whistle on a low note, more a sort of bass moan, and then it was as if the crust of hellfire had been uncapped and the spurting pressure from within suddenly released. The sound of it was an almost simultaneous series of claps of thunder, with the crack of lightning thrown in for good measure as fragments of the guns were scattered at random, and then the shells themselves on the ground began to explode, a rhythmic series of giant thuds that made the surface of the field tremble like a giant jelly. I was tossed up into the air by the vibration, then swatted like a fly some twenty yards or so into the shrubberies ahead of me. The trees themselves had been bent by the blast before I got there, and snapped back. One of them, an eight inch diameter sapling, whipped back like a bamboo stake and hit me in the stomach. I felt a rib crack before the air was expelled from my body and I fell. My last conscious moment as I hit the ground, rolling, was of a flaming ball rolling along the ground where the ack-ack site had been, and a plume of thick black oily smoke starting to rise. I don't know for how long I was unconscious—when I came to the black cloud had settled and it was apparent our scheme had succeeded beyond anything we could have hoped. There must have been some new kind of explosive in those shells, explosive with some inflammatory potential since the entire edifice of the ack-ack unit, such as it was, tents, horsebox, canvas topped vehicles, had been set alight. The wood itself, into which I had been flung, bore the heavy stench of burning new growth. I must have been unconscious but still capable of movement since I recovered consciousness almost at the far side of the wood—possibly, like a headless chicken, I had run the last fifty yards with the electric ends of my nerves activating muscles.

I made my way to the rendezvous, uncertain what to expect. There was utter confusion on the roads, since the neighbouring units thought the ack-ack unit had been destroyed by aerial bombardment. Several times I stood silent in the hedge and heard shouted warnings of bombardment as men jog-trotted past, moving out of the imagined danger.

Simon was waiting at the rendezvous—wet through, but completely unhurt. As soon as the alert sounded, he had dived over the dyke into the canal. The suction and concussive effect of the explosion had almost emptied the canal at that point, had scooped him out of the water over the dyke again.

Jonfey and the sergeant killed a man to get to their guns. Their unit had exploded less than a minute after ours—but they had completed the job faster and were already back in the wood when the units exploded. Though my breathing was still erratic

I had not cracked a rib, Simon said, but would have a helluva bruise there within an hour.

Jonfey's face was beaming like a happy schoolboy. 'Well done,' was all he could say, 'bloody well done.'

By dawn's first light we were waiting on the landing strip, cold and hungry, but for my part no longer constipated.

CHAPTER TEN

THE PLANE CAME in to land exactly on time. One minute nowhere, next it was skimming over the hedge-top in a once only landing run. The long field was absolutely flat, an ideal landing strip. I couldn't think why the Germans had not mined it, or ridged it —another of those strange gaps in efficiency I frequently noted throughout the war—the Achilles' heel of totalitarianism. Take away a man's initiative and he will be responsible for nothing, creative about nothing—give a man his head and every single act becomes a challenge. The plane must have flown in so low it missed the ack-ack screen and the spotters, since no one opened fire on it. I knew we could not be so lucky getting out. The minute we rose over the skyline they'd throw flaming steel confetti at us from all sides. The plane's wheels touched the ground at the far end of the field and he started to taxi—he was travelling fast, but the field was long enough to take him at any speed. He had a large tree as a running line, and we waited at his approximate stopping point in the field, ready to manhandle him around for his take off. He landed downwind, would take off into the wind to lift his nose over the hedge.

He had run about two hundred yards ground speed down to about a hundred and ten, I would judge, when his brakes locked on, hard. I heard the rasp of the tortured brake drums, and the plane tipped straight up forwards, and the whirring propeller crashed into the ground. The plane turned completely over. There was a sickening smack as it broke its back and the tail plane fell loose in front of it. I was already about fifty yards towards it, the sergeant running fast behind me. Jonfey and Simon I waved back. There had been enough petrol in that plane to get us home. When we got there, the pilot was dead, his back, like that of the plane, snapped. It was the pilot who had brought us in. We dragged him clear of the wreckage. Simon and Jonfey came over to where we put him on the grass. Simon looked at him, but we didn't need Simon to tell us he was dead.

'He's dead,' Simon said, 'let's get going.'

I shook my head, dully. This man had brought us in, risked his life to be the one to bring us out. Each of these flying missions is a voluntary assignment. How can you just walk away from a man like that?

'Pavlov's dogs,' Simon said, quietly. Only I heard it. Like a puppet I turned on my heel. 'Come on,' I said, 'Let's get out of here.' I took the lead, heading across the field in a jog-trot. It couldn't take many minutes for the Germans to find the field and the plane.

'Oh dear God,' I remember thinking as I jogged along. 'Just once, let's go back, for however short a time, to being human beings. Just for one short time, let's obliterate the war, let's bury a man we've killed, let's not kill a man, let's go back, for just one short second, to a human existence.' I knew it was a vain hope. Like Pavlov's dogs we were conditioned, like Pavlov's dogs we would stay. But that man dressed himself, walked across the tarmac and climbed into his plane. He had no need to do it. He could have stayed at home, he could have gone off duty. For him the war, momentarily, could have ended with a glass of beer and a pipe of tobacco. But it didn't. He volunteered again, to fly to fetch us out. And we said thank you by running away from him.

CHAPTER ELEVEN

When we arrived back at the car, a German patrol had found it. We had kept the rotor arm—but it was a useless gesture. So many soldiers were milling about that area we dared not go near the tree. I couldn't see us getting into contact again with Rugby, the broken batteries had barely sustained our last transmission. For a while that radio set had given me the comfort of a house full of telephones with guidance at the other end of a continuous wire; now we were isolated, cut off from the source of wisdom.

We set off to walk slowly to the west, to the sea, to home. I felt like Charlie Chaplin at the end of a film.

We had two alternatives. We were between Wallwijk and 's-Hertogenbosch, in territory mostly grassland—the tree belt of pines, oaks and beeches started ten miles in front of us to the west, and then we had another twenty-five miles or so to travel to the flat lands, the polders at the delta of the Maas. Once in the polders, I was confident we could lose ourselves along the extensive waterways, making our way slowly out towards and past Willemstad, Ooltgensplaat, and into Zeeland. Somewhere along the way we'd look for a fishing boat, since they were still operating in coastal waters, under German Naval supervision, of course, to sneak us over the North Sea to England. We should be able to find something in Haamstede, or Ouddorp, or Zieriksee.

The alternative was to strike south, into Belgium. After all we were only about twenty miles north of the Belgian-Dutch Border at its nearest point, and I knew several people in Antwerp and further south in Brussels—less than a hundred miles away. On balance I favoured the open polders of Zeeland —and there was a distinct psychological advantage anyway in travelling west, away from the Germans and Germany, towards the North Sea however wide it may seem and however distant England on its far shores.

How do you travel through open country during the day? If there's a road going your way you take a chance. You put one man in front, leave one man behind, and travel as a team, constantly looking backwards and forward to keep in touch with your scouts. You can never shout at each other, of course, so you depend on always staying in vision of each other. It's tiring business. Nor can you ever travel in the comfortable centre of the road too far from the hedgerows. It's not as difficult as it sounds. Mostly, in open countryside, you can see for long distances before you can be seen. You are vitally interested in anyone who may be about—usually they are not interested in you unless you give them reason, and, surprisingly, soldiers in occupied territory do not keep a constant alert. We travelled all morning, and at midday discovered a small wood and crawled in there to sleep. We were all exhausted, and Jonfey's side was aching again. He needed two or three days of inactivity, sitting on a deckchair on a sun-drenched beach—he should have his dressing changed twice a day. Above all, he needed the one thing we couldn't give him, the opportunity to stay still for a long time. His wound was not infected—merely throbbing in anger at not being left to knit in peace.

We dragged wearily off the road, into the wood, waiting until Simon, our rear scout, came level with us before penetrating deeply into the trees. It was a clean wood with little undergrowth near the side of the road. Only further back were there bushes and shrubs we could get down into to make our simple bivouacs. At the far end of the wood was a flowing stream of clear water—one by one as best we could we washed ourselves in it and drank. I took off my rubber soled Innsbrucker boots and bathed my feet—they are ideal for climbing and walking over rough country, but on gritty roads they pick up small stones between the cleats and become hot and uncomfortable.

'If only we could make a fire and cook some grub!' Jonfey said. His was the voice of all of us. Looking round I could see the lines of strain beginning to show on faces—and knew they must be etched into mine. Without the opportunity to shave, we looked a band of brigands. Some people grow hair on their faces in a dignified fashion, an overall bristle that soon is acceptable as a beard. The sergeant and Simon were both of that type, dark and swarthy by nature, it wasn't long before the hirsute growths looked deliberate. Jonfey, however, grew his hair in untidy wisps—as I felt I did. I had an itching growth under my chin, nothing on the flat sides of my cheek at all—long growths at the extremities of my upper lip and very little in the centre. Jonfey saw me rubbing my chin.

'You don't feel you've had a proper wash if you can't shave with it, do you?' I agreed with him. He sat down in the bivouac area, his boots and socks in his hand 'letting my dogs get some air', he said. He looked at his feet. 'Still,' he said, 'it's better than walking in riding boots, and many's the time I've had to walk home when a horse has bolted with me and thrown me. It's strange the way a horse will take you miles and, once he's got rid of you, will turn round and trot quietly back to the stable.'

'That's life,' the sergeant said. 'Takes you to the end of your tether and drops you.'

'Hark at the philosopher,' Jonfey quipped, but without malice.

It was good they still had the interest to talk in this way—you can tell when men are fatigued mentally as well as physically by the silences—I didn't mind tired bodies, but there'd come a time soon we'd need minds as alert as whippets. And as fast.

'What do you think is our chance of getting in touch with the Underground?' the sergeant asked. 'What do they call themselves, the Stooetroopen?'

'I don't think there's much chance around here—I think they're mostly active further east, and down at Maastricht—there are units in the towns—Rotterdam and Amsterdam—but I don't think we should go near them. All I want is a leisurely walk through this flat land—as far as the water. Then we can pick up a fishing boat, and get away at night down one of the lesser used estuaries. I don't anticipate much difficulty, as long as we keep alert and use our heads when the time comes.'

'That's the problem,' Simon said. 'Walking along like this induces a state of euphoria—your mind slips back and forwards—somehow it won't stay in the present. For the last mile along the road I was planning a walk I would like to do sometime down the Caledonian canal from Inverness, and wondering whether it would be worth taking a small canoe to try to make it through the lochs.'

'That's what they call escapism,' Jonfey said, 'and that's something we need a lot of, right now!' We all groaned at the deliberate pun.

'It's a dangerous business, Simon, and I'd warn you against it. If you're not careful you'll be halfway down the Caledonian canal in your mind and your body will be knocked down by a squadron of tanks.'

'How do you do it, then? How do you keep your mind on the present, walking along the ditch like that?'

'Two things. One I always count the steps, always. Up to a thousand, then start again. That gives me a conscious scheme of the distance we travel. I used to do that as a boy in the Dales. How many steps from the top of one dale to the next, and then pace it to see how right I was. The other is that I mark the spots in my mind from which I think an attack might come—the obvious ones, and then I try to find all the non-obvious ones, and count an extra point for every one I can find. I divide the countryside up into stretches, and if I can count ten for each stretch I think I'm doing well. What do you do, sergeant?'

'I look at the countryside in arcs. I start, shall we say left of arc, and slowly I look from left of arc to right of arc along a fixed distance. Then I sweep left again to the extreme left of arc, moving up all the time.'

'But what happens,' Simon asked, 'if someone or something should appear right of arc when you're busy looking left of arc?'

'The sudden movement, you see, gives them away. I look for movement, all the time, even little things like birds flying, rabbits, little things like that.'

'How about you, Jonfey?' I asked.

'Oh, it's easy with me,' he said. 'I always look at a piece of ground as if I was hunting over it, as if I'd got a horse clapped between my knees. You can't afford to miss much when you're out hunting. There's many a squire been killed because he put a high spirited horse into a jump at a hedge and a pheasant flew out under the horse's nose. A horse won't jump a hedge if there's anything in it. You learn to spot it—loose fence rails, pheasants, chickens near a farm—even feathers a fox has left, fluttering in the hedgerows.'

'That's all right,' Simon said, 'that's what you look for, but what do you think about?'

'Birds,' he said, 'the human variety. Birds in jodhpurs, birds out of jodhpurs—birds in britches, birds out of britches. Oh yes, you can go a long way in a short time, thinking about birds!' We all laughed, the tension relieved. I didn't believe him for a moment, but there could be no future analysing methods. Our training was over, and our methods were already in-built, if we had any at all. And if we had none, then God help us.

'Make out a guard roster, sergeant,' I said, 'and include me—I don't mind going first, if no one else cares to.'

We passed the rest of the day, holed up in that wood, usually two sleeping and one on guard, one off duty if there can be such a thing. Heavy infantry and motorized units moved along the main road—several times I ventured through the trees to watch them. Most of the columns headed north, towards Amsterdam and Rotterdam, and I guessed the High Command was reinforcing its Dutch Occupation Force. It was one of those idyllic days in early June when the sun is warm but not too hot, the sky clear but not cloudless, the air comparatively still, but with occasional freshening winds. Inside the wood was cool, the light filtered by the overgrowth. There was a moment's anxiety about five o'clock when one of the units, foot-borne infantry, pulled in off the road to rest and prepare food. They were there for nearly an hour before a senior officer in a staff car came along the road and got them moving again.

The smell of the food was agonizing—but they didn't leave a scrap. We looked.

This was a thickly populated area, with most of the farmsteads on the side of the road, fields stretching behind them, often with a ditch of water running through the property. Many of the farmhouses were separated from the road by an eight foot dyke. The farms were all thinly wooded, and intensely cultivated. Occasionally a farmhouse had been bombed—but the land around was tended by other farmers—we rarely saw a neglected field. Before the war, the Dutch people ranked as one of the most hospitable in the world—neighbours taking the privilege of dropping in for a chat or a stein of home brewed beer or schnapps at any time—but now the farmhouses with ditches or moats between them and the road drew in the bridges and wrote no welcome on the mat, and that means you, Englishmen who can bring nothing but trouble! We had heard of the caves at St Pietersberg near Maastricht in which works of art and escaped allied prisoners were being hidden in that order in hundreds of miles of underground tunnels—but Maastricht was at least a hundred miles to the south-east and more difficult to get to than Brussels.

When Simon woke me to take my second turn on watch, he did not immediately settle down to sleep, but sat near me so we could whisper.

'How do you estimate our chances?'

He didn't want the placebo of "Oh, we'll manage". Jonfey would have been happy with the confident reply—Simon wanted diagnosis and treatment.

'It's impossible to estimate. Certainly we must keep ourselves up to pitch all the time—our escape will depend on being alert, seeing opportunities, and taking them when they come.'

'Nothing constructive we can do?'

'Nothing I can think of—if you have any suggestions, I'd be glad to listen.'

'You don't enjoy this command, do you?' There was no impropriety in his suggestion, no insubordination.

'No, I don't. It's an artificial situation. I have no more information or knowledge than any one of you, and therefore no right to command you.'

'But you have the inherent power of leadership. . . .'

'Whatever that high sounding phrase may mean!'

'You're a born leader!'

'Is there such a thing?'

'Churchill is a born leader—that's where the Americans go wrong—all their leaders are self made men, and they usually make a mess of it! I have the education,' Simon said, 'to be a leader of men—you need to develop a pride when you spend your life looking down a cow's throat with the farmer relying on you for information—to the farmers you're a leader of men, a paragon. But that's in my specialized subject. The born leader has instinctive reasoning powers on all subjects. He knows that "a hundred years after he's dead and forgotten, men who have never heard of him will be moving to the measure of his thought".'

'Oliver Wendell Holmes, 1809 to 1894. "Moving to the Measure", a lovely phrase!'

'See what I mean?'

I did see what he meant—the cunning devil was trying to bolster my ego, help me assume the mantle of leadership the better to serve them all. 'There comes a time, Simon, when you abandon reason. You load your gun and cock it, with the safety catch off, and prepare to shoot over open sights. Don't worry—that's the way we all are at this moment—a little edgy, perhaps, inclined to criticize and denigrate ourselves—but even without reason I believe we'll get out of here. Not all of us, perhaps, but most of us. And anyone left behind will be dead.'

The first flicker of uncertainty crossed his face. Like all of us, he had been confident we would survive the long way home, and perhaps more perceptive than most had tried to help bolster my morale. But the law of averages was against us all getting through, just as it had been against us all jumping from that pipe. The law of averages works to close margins—there was no margin on that pipe, no margin now. One of us was already mathematically dead. But which one? It would take a crystal ball to know that. It would be simple to say Jonfey, since his had been the life of danger, chances taken. But Jonfey lived under his own law of averages and one day one chance taken would fail him—that separate issue, however, should not confuse our situation. Alone, each one of us might or might not get home, and the sum total could be any number between all home, or none. Together we had the law working with as well as against us. Some of us were bound to get through—that was as certain as the fact that all of us couldn't make it. Purely selfishly—I was glad we were sticking together.

'Ask yourself this question, Simon, and give me an honest answer. Would our chances of survival be increased if you take command? I'm perfectly prepared to abdicate and then to follow your leadership.'

He thought for a moment—not the idling of the mind that many mistake for thought but a logical assessment of the pros and cons, factors for, factors against.

'I wanted to be absolutely certain,' he said, 'and now I am. You lead—that way we stand a better chance. You live in the country because you own a piece of it—it's your domain. I know the country because I've chosen to work there—none of it belongs to me and therefore I treat it with too much respect. Lead us over this bit of country as if you owned it, and we'll make it. If I take us through it, reticent and respectful as an employee, we'll be taken.'

I sat through my watch, thinking of what Simon had said. Boldness was the key to our escape, boldness and confidence. Dammit, we only had to walk ten miles, and before the war I usually walked that distance every day, and met twenty people who would touch a forelock to me, from respect not servitude. That spirit would get us through, if anything would.

It was time to waken the sergeant.

'The Dutch have opened the dykes in Zeeland—there'll be a helluva lot of water,' he said, shortly after I woke him.

'It could help us.'

'When I came down from Bergen we put into Rotterdam—I had a couple of days to spare before going down the Rhine to Dusseldorf and took a boat all round that north Zeeland coast-line, south of the Hague. I met quite a few people round there—we might possibly look them up if ever we get there.'

'We'll get there, don't worry.'

'I'm not worrying—I don't give a damn where it happens, here and now, falling off the side of a boat off Bergen in a northern storm, running about with a barrel of molten iron in a foundry. It's got to happen sometime, hasn't it?'

Damn him, I thought, fatalists never are the ones to get caught, and that increases the odds to one in three.

'Is there nothing and no one you'd regret?'

'Yes, there are lots of things—mostly places I've never been to rather than things I've never done—I'd like to have seen Sumatra, and Borneo, and Honolulu—I'd like to have gone with the loggers in Canada, rolling down the rivers to the seaway. But people, well, you meet 'em and you leave 'em. They say all women are alike in bed under the blankets, and that's certainly true—but when you come down to it there's nothing of a challenge about the human race, is there? Some you like and some you don't like, but they don't really affect you, do they? Take this war—well, some people bust a gut over an ideal, but when it comes down to it, what does it mean? The natural instincts of men come to the top—the sadistic cruelty, the urge to destroy and kill. In other men it's the creative side—engineers build bridges, which is what they would have been doing in the first place, and administrative officers administer, which is exactly the same for them as it would be in civvie life, except that they're pushing the pen in some office in a foreign town, with no missis to look over their shoulders. The war is all a bloody misnomer, sir, if you'll pardon the expression. Here we are doing exactly what the elastic stocking topped short knickered leader of the scout troup would be doing on a long weekend with the boys in camp. We're planning to cover a stretch of ground without the artificial aids of modern so-called civilization to help us—no trolley buses or underground trains or tramcars, no street lamps, no direction boards to guide us. So where's the difference? The only difference, as far as I can see, is that some great hulking hairy-arsed German might come charging out of a brush at us. But if ever you'd walked down Sauchiehall Street on a Saturday night, you'd know that a hairy-arsed Glaswegian lurks in every doorway, and they'll slit the cobblers off you for the price of a bottle of meths. Look at that,' he said. He pulled his shirt free of his trousers. I had seen the scar before when he had been stripped for washing in North Wales, but had never asked him its origin. 'I got that on the waterfront in Bergen—and it's a damn sight worse than Jonfey's little lot. I was with a bird in bed, and her boy-friend tried to stick a broken bottle up my arse! That was in peacetime! So where's all the fuss about the war?'

'And Miss Rosenberg?' I ought not to have said that. He was

on some private journey of justification—and it was my duty to let each of the men prepare his own palliatives for our present plight. But I wanted no illusions—only cold hard reality and facing facts would get us out of there; reality, and a constant state of preparation.

'That's different,' he said, sullen.

'I suppose the Sicilian vendettas are different, and the gangsters in Chicago, and the Brighton racegoers, and the Russian revolution—they're all different, I suppose?'

'That's different,' he said again.

I got up and walked round our encampment in the copse. It was dusk, time to go. We woke Jonfey, who was obviously much better for the sleep. His wound, too, was less flushed, less angry. There was a dyke about five hundred yards further on, and moored to the side of the canal a long boat. I was tempted to take it, but it had a name on the side and would be known throughout the waterway. Any Dutchman seeing us in that boat would know it stolen—and there would be foes among the friends. The Dutch came of German stock—in some of them it increased the hatred—but many have never forgiven the British for past enmities, and would have preferred to stay as neutral in this world war as in the last. Their homeland had been wrested, acre by acre, from the sea, giving the Dutch a fierce pride in their own achievements. Now, because of British political ineptitude and German cries of Lebensraum, much of that hard reclaimed land had been reinundated, given back to the sea from whence it came. There was no Dutch door-knocking for us!

We travelled fast throughout most of that night. Frequently we had to make detours because of water barriers or the movement of German troops—there still appeared to be much activity in that area, and several artillery batteries were being moved west towards the coast.

A battalion of infantry came marching down the road. We nipped into the farm to the side of the road, over a narrow water break, into an orchard keeping apart among the orderly lines of trees. An orchard is a deceptive place in which to stalk. The trees in line are impenetrable to the eye, until you take another pace forward and suddenly look down an open lane which could contain a whole squadron of tanks. Walking along the edge of an orchard, with the lateral lines, and the diagonal lines meeting and separating as you walk—what Lorca calls the opening and closing of a fan—is a most eerie experience. A company of men had bivouaced at the other side of the orchard. The infantry had halted behind us. Ahead of us was a deep twenty foot wide dyke, and behind us the farmhouse, occupied by soldiers. We were trapped. Damn! Damn! Damn! Down on your belly and into the sparse undergrowth—here's a farmer keeps his grass cut under the trees—blast the careful husbandry of Dutch smallholders. And blast too the searchlight beam of the moon, which at that moment came out in pristine glory.

Jonfey crawled to the water. Not a hope of getting across—there's a long boat lapping the edge with two men sitting in the prow, with nothing to do but look down the length and dream fishermen's dreams. Sergeant back to the road—not a hope, the infantry have bivouaced in the field on the other side of the road which now looks like Piccadilly on a Saturday night. Simon to the other edge—no chance, the company is on stand-to and it's like the Northampton County Show out there—all that's missing is the ice-cream stall!

I crawled slowly through the grass to the farmhouse. The orchard ended a hundred yards this side of it. I could see duty officers in the farmhouse doorway, smoking and talking together. Behind the farm a long barn, and a beast yard. Beyond a small field, oddly enough, of barley. They don't grow much barley in this part of Holland, I thought—this was the first crop I had seen. The whole farm and its surroundings, bathed in bright moonlight that sharpens outlines and bleaches colours, reminded me of one of these early Dutch paintings of scene—a Franz Hals perhaps before he became obsessed by vapid smiling faces. It would be just possible to get down the track at the side of the house and into and through the barn and beast yard into the barley field, but impossible, quite impossible, to travel the hundred yards to the start of the track unseen. It was a moment for quick decisions. A barrel of fruit tree spray stood on a stand at the edge of the orchard. I whispered to Simon, Jonfey and the sergeant to hoist it on to their shoulders. Jonfey had kept the cap of the German in the Mercedes tucked in his epaulette. I put it on though it was far too small for me. 'If it were done, 'tis better it were done quickly,' I whispered to Simon, who smiled at me. I marched the men out of the orchard, along its side, turned them left and marched them straight across the hundred yards patch towards the barn. Our heads were concealed by the barrel, though I walked to the rear and occasionally fell back half a pace to observe the two officers talking in the rose-trellised doorway. As we marched along, links recht, links recht, I saw the sergeant break out in a thick sweat. So it did matter—he did care that it should not be here and now! As we marched, to create that mood of unquestioning reality, I growled at them, in quiet German, 'Kommen Sie, wachsen Sie auf, machen Sie schnell, der Leutnant uns erwartet.' The officers did not glance in our direction; I had the safety catch off the driver's Luger, and the boys were poised to drop the barrel and dash into that field of barley. The track leading to the barn drew ever nearer—twenty, fifteen, ten paces, when suddenly, one of the officers became aware of our presence. I had overdone the commands—they had intruded on his consciousness—'which officer was waiting for us, and why?' But quickly he dismissed the matter.

'Sweigen-Sie!' he called. 'Haben Sie den Befehl nicht gelesen?'

'Jawohl, Herr Kapitan,' I muttered, and shut up as he had requested. Five paces to go. I couldn't know, of course, that he was a Captain—if he turned out to be a major, as pompous as many I'd met, we would be in trouble. My finger tightened on the trigger, but already he was talking again to the other officer and ignored us. I prayed at this last moment none of the lads would trip, or do anything to arouse interest. Three paces to go, two, and one, and straight up the track into the barn. Here we could relax, if only for a few seconds. As they put it down, the barrel spilled ammoniacal spray over them—at least they wouldn't be bothered by mosquitoes when we reached the delta.

The sergeant looked at me when we had got back our nerve and I nodded. 'Right lads, into the barley with you, RV in the far corner.'

There comes a time when you've had enough—when your spirit rebels and refuses to cringe. I had crawled far enough. 'Follow me,' I said, and marched out of the door, head high, arms swinging, dead regimental. The boys unhesitatingly followed me. Anyone seeing us coming from that barn, attached to the headquarter's house, would assume that we too were official, provided we retained a confident mien to help persuade them. And, dammit, I was angry, and confident. My knees were sore from scraping on the ground, my arms ached from pulling me along. I was dirty, dusty, unclean. We marched out of that barn, with spirits unconquered. 'Left right left'—though no one was there with a pacing stick to call it, and we're off to see the Wizard, the wonderful Wizard of Oz, and over there are the subdued lights of the mess and a couple of gins and tonics before dinner, and a bath and change into clean linen. Three men appeared in the gloaming—they were marching, as we were from a known place to a known destination. Seeing my stride, they withdrew in the dark to the very edge of the track. 'Danke,' I said, 'und gute Nacht.'

'Goodnight, sir,' the corporal in charge of them said, respectfully keeping his gaze averted. We marched straight past them. in single file up the side of the barley field, Hannibal crossing the Alps, 'all the King's men, marching up the hill and never, never back again!' At the far side of the field the Germans had stored ammunition in a small hut. Certainly they would have spotted us had we been crawling. As it was the two men unloading the flat barrow hardly gave us a look as we marched along.

We had come from the headquarters in full moonlight, erect and walking determinedly to a destination that wasn't their concern. That was good enough for them. 'Achtung!' I said, and they moved the barrow to one side to let us pass.'

Simon drew level with me when we had left the barley field behind. 'Do you see what I mean,' he whispered. 'I would never have dared do that, yet the tone in your voice was perfect when you spoke to those men.'

'My knees were knocking—I thought they must hear them!'

'Your knees may have been knocking—mine certainly were, but your voice didn't quaver as mine would have done. Now walk us over to England!'

By ten o'clock, largely by boldness, we reached the delta of the Maas. The low stretch of water below sea level that reaches out to the sea like a crooked beckoning finger, the northernmost polder of Nord Brabant with Willemstad on the far side, was on our left. To the right, though we couldn't see it, was Doordrecht—beyond that Rotterdam. All that stood between us and the North Sea was the long curving channel of the estuary of the Maas, a distance of forty miles.

It would be a long swim.

The sergeant stood beside me as I gazed out over the water. Somehow the forty miles didn't seem so far, after all.

'Shall we try the land, or the water?' he asked. I think he would have preferred to stay on land where he would have felt less exposed, but I wanted to get out on the water, to get my belly off the ground. That channel invited me, the water flowing along it was going somewhere. 'What do you think, Jonfey?' I could see the sergeant felt snubbed since I had asked one of the others. 'Knock off a boat and let's get to hell out of here!' Jonfey said.

'You can see a boat a mile off!' the sergeant said.

It was even chances the channel would be blocked at Willemstad and possibly again at Middelharnis, but it was a good mile wide even at its narrowest point—a boat low down would be practically invisible from the shore at ground level.

We soon found the boat we were looking for—a flat-bottomed barge a farmer used to shift crops. Twenty feet long and only four wide, there was an inboard engine mounted at the back and a long low hold in which most recently potatoes had been carried. The three dozen small ones left in the corners we devoured. Sitting to the back of the boat two men, one at each side, could paddle it comfortably and quite swiftly though I wouldn't rely on making too much speed in tidal waters. We headed for the centre of the waterway, the sergeant and Simon taking first turn on the paddles we found in a forward locker. The boat named *Gruedel* was new to me—though Dutchmen have a style of humour all of their own.

It was a long night—a night of sliding motion through the water, the slap of the paddles and the trickle of wavelets against the curved prow of the boat. From time to time motorized vessels rode past us but we were too low to be seen. The early bright moon had clouded—there was just sufficient light to distinguish the dark mass of landfall on each side of us and the motors of the other boats throbbed ample warning of their presence. Once a large boat came streaking down the centre of the estuary looking ridiculously high for such a channel. We pulled rapidly into the bank when we heard its engines, and waited until it had passed. We could have been visible from its high decks—a dark spot on a sheen of water where no dark spots ought to be. We didn't speak since sound carries over water, and innumerable birds came to investigate us—teal, mallard, ducks of various species. It must have been a wonderful stretch of water for shooting over, before the war. The irony of the thought struck me—with all these Germans about, it could be so again though this time we'd be targets not hunters. For a little while I slept sitting in the hold with my back against the gunwale, but I awoke in anxious fear. Though the day had been warm the night on the water was cold and terrifying shapes of mist came sliding towards us like some phantom amphibian.

From time to time we passed an active encampment and once were directly in line of fire when an anti-aircraft unit discharged all its guns—the noise thumped our eardrums and for minutes afterwards I heard nothing. The whirr whirr of the shells over our heads, just before the crack and thump of the guns, stayed sickeningly with me in that deafness. If one of those shells had been short fused we would have been in line to receive it in our laps, and would never have heard it.

Then came the dawn across the low long flat land, especially spectacular. Alone on the water we were tempted to think it might be entirely for our benefit. The first highly coloured rays of light in fierce reds and ochres and yellows of flame shot as suddenly as our train explosion, as if compressed beyond the horizon and suddenly tossed like sparkling dice. I dared not gaze at it—I had a night watch to keep. After the first startling rays, night seemed to creep back if only for a minute or two and the bursts of spent light spread slowly over the skyline, fighting for a foothold. The banks were thrown into shadow south of us—more difficult than ever to look for the waiting marksman. I wanted to cling to the concealing night, but knew the hope forlorn. We would have to pull in somewhere. As we paddled along the banks of the Maas lightened and we passed through a thickly populated area. Along the banks the farms lay silent under this grey ill-lit dawning. Where the soil level was raised above the dykes trees grew, beech, oak, some poplar, willow and elm. Here was not much of the fir forest in which we had walked most of the night through vaulted caverns of gloom. Along the banks everything seemed small—farms lay close together, with small orchards. When the first sunlight began to appear we pulled to the north coast and paddled close to the bank looking for suitable shelter. Now it was my turn to take the helm; in the two hours we must have covered nine miles or so and my shoulders said so vigorously. Dykes were to the north of us, and a reclaimed lake, a polder, dropped three feet below the level of the water we were traversing. Soon we came to what seemed a small tributary of the Maas. Ten feet across its mouth was overgrown with willow and poplar. We went in under the branches; it was a small inland pond about two hundred feet in diameter surrounded entirely by trees. Despite the effort involved we dragged the boat out of the water under a tree; heavy going but necessary concealment. Since we had not allowed Jonfey to take any part in the rowing he had slept on the boat and took first watch, Simon and the sergeant settled down to sleep; but too wide awake I walked round the perimeter of the wood to see where we were. I was desperately hungry, though for bacon and eggs, not raw potatoes. I wanted something stimulating in hot water—even ersatz coffee. More than anything else the lack of salt and sugar gets you most, and warm food and liquids. Even the most rudimentary food is elevated when heated and seasoned or sweetened.

The wood was part of a farm. The farmhouse about five hundred yards away didn't seem to be occupied by troops. An ack-ack battery about a mile and a half the other side of the farm doubtless protected the southern run to Rotterdam and I could see the smoke of the cookhouse fires of military units dotting the plain. There appeared to be nothing near this particular farm. Doubtless they felt the R.A.F. would take the waterway of the Maas as a route in, turn left at Willemstad straight up to Rotterdam, bombs away, then out over the Zuiderzee, the North Sea and home. This farm would be under the turning point—an impossible location from which to fire an ack-ack gun. This route would also serve as a corridor to the Ruhr, which accounted for the heavy concentration of bigger guns we had seen on our way out, and the extensive troop movements. There had been activity beyond the skyline during the night, but too far for me to identify its origin.*

I suddenly felt an irresistible attraction to that farm. It was foolish to break cover, stupid in the circumstances, but truly I could not resist. A thin wisp of smoke was spiralling lazily skywards from the chimney—the stove beneath would be banked down with wood ash for the night. Within a half hour or so, the farmer and his wife would arise, prise open the top of the gackle and stir it to life with the bundle of brushwood from the box she kept beside the stove in her neat kitchen. Despite the shortages of the war, there'd be a side of pork somewhere and she'd cut off a slice for the farmer to eat with coffee before setting out on a day's work in the fields. There were cattle behind the farmhouse

* It came from Arnhem and Nijmegen, as war historians will have guessed.

—doubtless the Germans counted every head but he'd be a poor farmer if he couldn't fix a headcount. Chickens too were penned beyond the house so there would be eggs! Cows for milk, butter, cheese, and cream. My mouth was wet with saliva.

Also I needed to use an indoor lavatory. I needed to sit there with a locked door and three walls between me and the rest of the world, then use paper, not leaves!

I waited for the sudden spurt of smoke from the chimney before walking out of the wood into the farmyard. The door opened from inside, the farmer standing in stockinged feet. I noticed the three pairs of wooden shoes on the doorstep. His baggy trousers were held up by cotton braces, and a woollen shirt open at the neck was designed to take a separate collar though doubtless he never wore one during the week. He exuded that wonderful odour of feather beds and food. His wife was revealed in the door behind him.

I spoke to him in German. 'Good morning. Can I come in?'

'Are you English?'

'No, French. I'm lost.'

'Come in,' he said. His wife made a noise of protest, which ended as he carefully shut the door behind me. 'There are Germans everywhere,' he said—he hadn't believed my story about being French, but wasn't going to make an issue of it. 'They come every day.'

'What do you want?' his wife asked, her fear quickly gone. 'Coffee?'

'Ja,' she said, and went and got me a mug from the dresser at the side of the door. She filled it with coffee from an enamelled jug on top of the stove. 'French,' she said—she meant the coffee, not me. If it was French coffee then I was a Dutchman, but it tasted like nectar. 'The German soldiers come for eggs—they bring coffee and cigarettes,' the farmer said, quick to establish his status. He was a good collaborator, and not ashamed of it, a practical man making the best of the circumstances. 'They let me keep the farm—I have a bad heart. I'm going to die at any moment, that's what the specialist says in Rotterdam.' His opinion of the specialist from Rotterdam would not be fit to print, to judge from his expression. Certainly he looked blue about the lips if you examined his face closely, but that could be the sun and the coast-line salt.

'Are you alone?' he asked.

'No, there are three others with me.' In for a penny, in for a pound.

I drank deeply of the coffee, my eyes attracted unavoidably by the pan of pork and potatoes on the top of the stove, the loaf of brown bread, the pot of butter on the table.

'Come,' the farmer said, and sat down at the table. His wife put a plate in front of me, another in front of him, and we started to eat. The food was deliciously hot and I emptied the plate. His wife brought a big sausage from a cupboard behind an open larder—it was farm made, similar to the black puddings that were such a part of Yorkshire life before the war. She cut two thick slices and put them in the frying pan, one for me, one for the farmer. I ate my slice too quickly—he was still mopping the pork fat with his bread. He lifted the slice from his plate and passed it to me. Though ashamed of my greed, I ate it.

'You spent the night in a long boat,' he said. When I looked puzzled he laughed. 'Any Dutchman from these parts knows the reek of longboats at potato time. Did you steal it?'

'Borrowed it.'

'That means hardship for the farmer.'

'I know that. I regret it, but there was no alternative.'

'You come from inland?'

'Yes.'

'And you are going,' he flexed his thumb over his shoulder, 'that way, to England?'

'Hoffentlich?'

'It would be a long night's walk without the boat.'

His wife was standing by the stove, looking at me. When she saw I had observed her, she turned away and busied herself at the top of the stove. 'You'll have to forgive her,' the farmer said. 'You're the first one she's seen. Her sister had an airman in Waalwijk. He was recaptured.'

'That's not true,' his wife burst in, family pride getting the better of her. 'No, he wasn't recaptured. He was so badly burned they could do nothing for him. To save his life they surrendered him to the Germans.'

The farmer shrugged his shoulders.

'And was that not a good thing to do?' the woman asked me. It had obviously been a family squabble since the day it happened, one of those inconsequential seeds of dissension that green-manure a marriage.

'I'm certain it was the best thing to do,' I reassured her. The farmer had no need of me to take his point of view.

He had the peasant strength of the earth about him—a man with an allotted life-span as finite as the seasons. 'You live where you stand and lie where you fall,' he said. 'God sows, God reaps, but the pigs make the fertilizer!'

I could like this man—I felt as safe as at home.

'Can you help us? All we want is a bed for the day, food and something hot to drink, and we'll be on our way as soon as it becomes dark.'

'Your men are in the wood, of course, and you've pulled the boat up the bank, I hope?'

'Yes.'

'Good. The water patrols start at eight o'clock, and the first scrounging bastard of a soldier comes about ten o'clock asking for eggs. I can't permit you all to sleep in the house of course, but you are welcome to the barn. If you're caught, I'll look you straight in the eye, and as in days of old will say, "No, I have never seen him before." I may revile you, and spit on you, and dance when they nail you to a cross, but that will be for my wife—you understand.'

'I understand.' I was grateful and had no words with which to express it—I asked his name, but he preferred not to give it lest under torture I blurt it out.

'It will be good to do something for a change,' he said, 'all day long I sit on the farm, looking at my steaming muck heap, building up goodness for the future which doubtless I shall not see and would not want anyway if the Allies are beaten in this war. It will be good to do something for a change!'

He put on his jacket and we left the farm together. I went back to the woods and brought Jonfey, Simon and the sergeant separately. When we arrived and I saw to their concealment, the farmer's wife came to the door of the barn.

'Bring them into the kitchen first,' she said. 'There'll be no one about for some time, and my husband is in the lower field.'

Though feeling somewhat guilty I brought the men inside and they ate a pan full of pork, sausage and bread, and drank coffee with the black sugar she stored concealed in a sack in the barn. In peacetime the sugar had been used for feeding bees and cider-making, but we were glad of it. Then I saw them settled into the barn, comfortable for the day. Eggs in one basket! I had resolved despite the temptations to lie in the wood keeping observation, but the farmer's wife was most persuasive, and I spent the morning in her kitchen. It was a safe place from which to watch —every time I saw anyone approach I nipped through into the sitting-room, from the window of which I could make my way round the back of the farm unobserved. We didn't talk much during the morning—she told me about her sister and the airman —apparently she had done all she could to get him well again and only in desperation had taken him and left him where the Germans were sure to find him. Though the Germans could see he had been tended, they exacted no reprisals.

'I think she fell a little bit in love with him, nicht wahr?' the farmer's wife said, with a shy look. I had no fears, she was old enough to be my mother.

At lunch time the farmer came back to the farmhouse to eat his midday meal—he was not surprised to find me in the farmhouse. 'She has a most persuasive tongue,' he said, smiling at his wife, 'and I knew she would welcome someone to talk her nonsense to.' Together we ate a meal fit for Gargantua—ertwensoep —a rich thick pea soup—Zealand oysters, stewed smoked eel, and a plate of potatoes and sauerkraut, with farmhouse cheese. After I had eaten, the farmer's wife persuaded me to go upstairs and sleep on the bed that had belonged to their son, now married on his own farm at Gennep. Wounded during the invasion he had only recently come from hospital in 's-Hertogenbosch—he'd lost the use of an arm and found the forty acres difficult to manage.

The sergeant by now was awake and took over my vigil in the kitchen. I was determined not to be caught again.

We were all awake by the early evening. We sat in the kitchen with the farmer and his wife, drank his home-brewed beer and talked. Mostly we talked of England, not of the war—about farms and farming, animal husbandry, crop planting methods, types of seeds sown, fertilizers used. I could see the sergeant and Jonfey were bored with our conversation, but for a while I was determined to break the pattern of war, if only within the sanctuary of those four walls. More than anything, the Dutchman was proud of the way they had reclaimed land—the system of dykes, the use of the water to increase fertility. On his farm were more than two thousand square feet of greenhouse in which he had grown daffodils and other flowers in peacetime. 'I'll never see them in bloom again, that is certain,' he said, though without any self pity. During this brief return to sanity, we listened to music on the radio, discussed songs and singers. We heard the local news from Amsterdam and Hilversum, Paris and Brussels. When Jonfey wanted to tune in to London, however, the farmer wouldn't do so. 'One risk at a time is enough,' he drily said. He was quite right—the sudden thud of the knocker on the door sent us all flying, our beer mugs quickly seized off the table and taken with us.

The German soldier was drunk. He wanted eggs. The farmer told him there were no eggs—he was telling the truth, we had eaten them for supper, the farmer's wife laughing to see the way we boiled them—she had never seen anyone eat a boiled egg before. The farmer led the German out to the 'egg factory', as jokingly he called it. The soldier's companion was sitting on the seat of the motor-cycle combination—he too appeared to be drunk. The farmer opened the mesh door of the chicken run and told the German he could take any eggs he could find. Luckily, two had been laid since the last collection and the drunken soldier went away happily with them. 'He'll break them before he gets back to barracks,' the farmer said. 'Let's hope they are in his pocket at the time!'

By ten o'clock it was time to leave—I had been on edge for the past hour feeling we had outstayed our welcome, every second we enjoyed the farmer's hospitality another we kept them in danger. But somehow it felt as if we had left England a hundred years ago, instead of only a few brief hours, and the joy of civilization was a benison. How fortunate the continental people are to enjoy a literate working class—the farmer had discoursed with us all evening on many topics—he was interested and interesting, far more civilized than his English counterpart would have been—or many men in England who ranked as his social superiors among the white collar classes. The sergeant had knocked about the world—and spoke German with a vulgar fluency. The Dutch peasant spiced his evening's conversation with Schiller, Thomas Mann, Goethe, had a liberality of expression I greatly envied. He apologized for not being able to speak English, but made up for it, and entertained us vastly, by quoting Shakespeare in the Goethe translation—mocking the Shakespearean actor Alexander Moise, whose 'Sein, oder nicht sein, das ist die Frage', was every bit as good a rendition as that of

Henry Irving. I had both recordings at home in my youth—and had not dreamed to hear them both discussed in this surrounding. Image or reality—what had the sergeant said about the war; it gave many of us the opportunity to do things we had never hoped to be able to do.

'You will forgive me, I know, that I step aside in this war,' the farmer said, as we were about to leave. 'I am not neutral, like so many of my countrymen. I do not like what the Germans are doing. I do not like aggression or any of the stinking sludge that inevitably must follow in its wake. But I am conscious my life is coming to a close, and so far have not found anything to value more than that flickering flame soon to be extinguished.' He came with us as far as the wood, treading surely before us through the gloaming, across these few acres into which he had poured his entire being. He couldn't help us lift the boat from under the trees, but supervised our efforts to manhandle it down the slope.

We had got it half way down the bank, its prow touching the surface of the water, when the German motorboat in the trees at the entrance started its engine and came into full view. The sailor in the prow switched on the beam of a searchlight and we were trapped.

'Hände hoch,' the sailor behind him called, as the boat edged into the bank.

There was nothing we could do.

We raised our hands and I turned around to warn Jonfey of the futility of attempting anything in the face of the machine gun mounted on the roof the cabin. There was no sign of the old Dutch farmer.

'Damn!' I thought. 'Damn!' I think I hated the thought of deceit more than that of betrayal. Obviously the Judas wanted to get us out of the house before we were taken—didn't want the disorder in his own home should we decide to put up a fight for it. Out here in the woods, his precious homestead was safe. Damn! Damn! Doubtless there was a unit of the SS, alerted by him during the day, creeping up behind us through the wood. No wonder he led us here! He wanted to make quite certain we didn't change our minds and try to escape overland. If only he hadn't spent the evening talking so civilly with us—'to be or not to be' left a significantly dirty taste in my mouth just now.

Simon's hand on my back pocket slid to the side towards the

Luger in the pistol holder hanging from a button on my denim jacket near the sliver of glass. The Germans couldn't see the movement of his hand. I turned my body round, slightly, to help conceal the pistol. Pray to God one of them doesn't count hands in what must look like a small forest of hands raised to the sky. I felt the stud come loose, the sudden shift of weight as the Luger was withdrawn from the holster. The German boat was now at the edge of the water about thirty feet from us. There were four men on board, one in the tiny wheelhouse aft had been steering the boat, another on the gunwales with a boat hook pulled the boat alongside the bank. The other on top of the wheelhouse behind a tripod-mounted and lashed machine gun, magazine fed, rate of fire one hundred to the minute on rapid, thirty on slow, with an accurate fore and aft sight of crossed wires, had his finger on the trigger. We had fired those machine guns on the range at Rhayader; on rapid rate they were so accurate they could tear the centre out of a four inch thick timber target in seconds; on slow rate with time to aim you could put three shots into a cigarette packet at a hundred yards, and we were only thirty feet away.

The fourth man standing in the prow squatted with his hands on a ten inch diameter searchlight. Luckily the searchlight aimed low at our feet and we could see through the halo of its upper rim as they intended that flight or resistance would be futile.

If we didn't attempt anything, they had no intention of shooting. Not yet, anyway.

Through the corner of my eye I saw the plop into the water as if of a large water rat, and the ripples made a pattern with those of the gently rocking boat. Now they had us the Germans seemed undetermined what to do with us. The sailor in charge of the wheel came forward and conferred in undertones with the man behind the machine gun. They appeared to be having a discussion—if not, in fact, an argument. I hoped it was not, 'To shoot or not to shoot, that is the question!' The navigator went back into the wheelhouse and searched through sheets of official message pads. Eventually, he came across the one he wanted and showed it to the man behind the gun. He looked up at each in turn, identifying us.

The old farmer was swimming in the water on the other side of the boat, moving without sound though I could see he was not a good swimmer.

The man at the machine gun convinced the navigator and the argument ended with him taking aim through the backsight of the gun.

Then he half rose in the air, gurgled, twisted and fell off the boat, the handle of a kitchen-knife sticking out of his back. Simon took a half pace to the right, beside me, and picked off the navigator, the man with the boat hook, the man behind the light and finally, as it swung skywards, the light itself.

By that time I was at the water's edge. It took us five minutes to find the old farmer, since the water had logged his clothing.

We took him back to the farm and undressed him, put on his night garments and laid him in his bed. Simon told us that, since his heart had stopped with the strain of hurling that knife up into the machine-gunner's back, there would be no water in the lungs. He was known to be medically unsound, and the Germans would take no notice of his death. His wife sat on the chair in the kitchen, mute and immobile while we laid her husband's body to rest in their marriage bed. She had forgiven us.

'I will go to my son at Gennep,' she kept saying. 'He needs someone to help him, and I have my permit to travel.'

When we had finished and could find no reason for staying other than to console her, she looked across the kitchen to me. 'He didn't like it when my sister gave that airman to the Germans,' she said, 'for the life of him, he couldn't agree with that!'

Early that evening, her husband had quoted to us a few lines from a poet Lilienthal, of whom we hadn't heard. 'Laengst schon dein Grab die Winde ueberwehen; wie liebevoll du sorgtest'—and for a long time the winds would blow over *his* grave, and how full of love *he* would seem.

Still I didn't know his name.

CHAPTER TWELVE

JONFEY'S WOUND had taken a turn for the worse. Whether it was the day of comfortable living, the rich food we had eaten, or a delayed action, no one could tell, but when Simon took off his dressing to make a routine check, the edges of the wound had blanched almost white, and the festering centre was of greenish yellow. The pain, Jonfey finally confessed, had been intense for the last hour. Simon felt up under his armpit and beckoned to me. 'Feel that,' he said. In the centre of the armpit was a lump the size of a swallow's egg, hard.

I had only one of the morphine pills left.

'Save it,' Simon said, 'he may need it later.'

I haven't spoken much about Jonfey in the course of this tale, largely because there wasn't much to say about him. His unfailing good humour had been a wonderful stimulant to us all—his constant eagerness and his chirpy turns of phrase. Jonfey successfully bridged the gap between Simon, myself, and the sergeant—he was the butt of the sergeant's regimentation and could respond to the ram-rod backed discipline without losing his senses of proportions. Yet he had a head about him, and his keen intellect put him a yard ahead of the sergeant. The sergeant was a 'do-er'—a man of immense courage and physical strength, great resourcefulness. He could interpret commands well and swiftly. Jonfey also was a 'do-er' but he thought more about things than did the sergeant—hadn't the same instinct for blind obedience. Sometimes, of course, he could be frustrating beyond measure; so often his interpretation of orders was so much superior to the orders themselves. The sergeant would ask permission before changing an order; Jonfey would go ahead and do it in his own version and tell you of the change later. This of course could be very difficult, dependent as we were on complete co-ordination, but I had no wish to lose him. I looked closely at his face. There was strain at the corner of his eyes, bloodshot lines on the pupils. 'That side's been hurting you for some time, hasn't it?' I insisted.

'It has a bit.'

'You're a fool—you ought to have told Simon.'

'The bloody horse doctor? He's no good without a bottle of liniment and a dose of jollop!' There was good humour in his face, despite the pain. I could see he had not wished to disturb Simon, lacking, as he was, any practical medical aid. I resolved never again to drop into any assignment without a full medical kit concealed about my person.

'Is there anything we can do, Simon?' I asked.

'Nothing unless we go back to the farmhouse.'

'We can't do that,' Jonfey said quickly. 'That'd be pushing our luck too far.'

I looked at the sergeant, and at Simon. It would be dangerous to go back to the farm.

'I know what we could do,' Jonfey said, a smile breaking across his face—'it's old fashioned, but it used to work a treat, so they say.'

'What's that?'

'Pig muck! It draws like a magnet. It smells like hell, of course, but it was always used for infections. You'll never get a diseased horse in a field that's kept pigs! There's a field of pigs just outside this wood; I bet the sergeant could get us a handful and no one the wiser, couldn't you, Sergeant?'

'Would it work?' I asked Simon.

'Yes, I suppose it could, come to think of it.'

'Could it do him any harm—infect him with any fever?'

'I don't think so—no, anyway, the infection already inside him is bad enough.'

The sergeant crawled away on his errand of mercy. When he returned he had brought back sufficient to medicate a small army! And he stank!

'You smear it on the wound,' Simon said. 'There's no point in both of us suffering!'

He bandaged the wound over the poultice, though the adhesive on the plaster no longer held, and he had to tear strips off the bottom of Jonfey's shirt to make a bandage to go all round his body.

'That should throb like hell!' he said to Jonfey. 'If it doesn't, for God's sake tell me and we'll think of something else!'

I had been thinking of something else. How the devil were we to get home? That wound turning septic put a different complexion on our journey. Now, speed was essential. I didn't want to have to surrender Jonfey to the Germans to save his life and, though I had scant medical knowledge, the look on Simon's face when he asked me to feel the lump under Jonfey's armpit was enough to warn me of the danger if Jonfey soon didn't get expert treatment and proper medicine.

'Gather round,' I said, when the bandaging had been completed. They settled down around me. 'We have to get home quickly and I want your best thoughts on it before I make a decision. We can't hang about here—though that boat hadn't a radio, it won't be long before it's missed and they send someone looking for it. Also, now the farmer's dead, the Germans will run all over his property seeing what they can scrounge. That woman won't stay in the farmhouse longer than she needs to. I wouldn't be surprised if she packs up first thing in the morning and gets as best she can to her son's farm at Gennep. She's in a state of shock and anything could happen.'

'If this pigshit doesn't work,' Jonfey said, 'you'll have to leave me behind. No hard feelings, you understand!'

'We shan't do that,' I assured him, 'unless it becomes absolutely necessary to save your life. There's no point in beating about the bush; you're a sick man and could become a liability, but we'll all happily bear that liability however onerous it may become, unless your life is in danger.' I turned to the other two. 'I presume I speak for us all?'

'Don't worry, lad,' the sergeant said immediately. 'If you can't walk I'll carry you out!'

He meant it and could do it.

'We could take that boat and make a dash for it, straight across the North Sea to Harwich,' Simon said. It was a question more than a statement. I had worked out that, with that boat and sufficient fuel, we could make it to England—in land terms the boat would do five miles an hour, I guessed, in the open sea, and take a gallon to every ten miles. 'Harwich, due west of us, along the fifty-second parallel, is almost a hundred and thirty miles away. The trip could take the better part of thirty hours,' I said.

'If we could sail straight without a compass,' Jonfey added.

'I could do that,' Simon said. 'I've done a bit of sailing from stars.'

'If we could get through the minefields at the mouth of this estuary,' the sergeant said.

'One of us would have to swim ahead of the boat and we'd crawl through,' Simon said.

'If we don't meet any German shipping, and if we can get hold of sufficient fuel and if we don't get blown out of the water by the Harwich coastal defences. Let's face it, there are a lot of ifs,' I said. There was no point in false confidence.

'Why don't we forget the boat?' Jonfey said. 'Over there are a dozen German units. Why don't we find a signals headquarters, knock it off, ring up Braintree, and ask them to send an aeroplane?'

'Just like that?' Simon was smiling.

It had the germ of a good idea.

'Yes, just like that! Dammit!' Jonfey said, 'that's what we are trained to do. Are you forgetting that? We're bloody specialized miracle men. We're supposed to be able to rub our faces with burned cork which makes us invisible, and walk into anywhere we want. Isn't that what the Captain trained us to do?'

He was right. That was exactly the way I trained them. These were boys of the special services—trained to jump or sail in and get out again in one piece. That's what we were here for, after all!

Jonfey had sold us. I knew which I would rather have, a fast trip back through the flak, or a long slow ride in an open boat with everything and everybody against us on both sides of the North Sea. In a German boat we'd be sitting ducks when we tried to slip into Harwich—I had the arrogant Anglo-Saxon belief our coastal defences would be a darned sight better than the Germans. I was more certain of getting out of Holland than into England.

'You stay here, Jonfey, on your own. If we're not back by morning, walk down that road and give yourself up. Is that clearly understood?'

'Yes, Captain!' I didn't believe a syllable.

'And you can amuse yourself by getting rid of those Germans.'

'Yes, Captain!'

The sergeant, Simon and I skirted the farmhouse and set off down the side of the track. Then, as the first sign of an encampment drew near, we left the track and went into the fields. The first unit we came to, another ack-ack unit, we passed without difficulty. Now that we were in the German lines, we could see the concentration. In a sense it helped us, because with so many people about no one was going to look too suspiciously at us. We spent most of our time, therefore, walking erect, and only dropped down to the ground when we needed to get past a tight encampment. I was looking for a radio aerial, a high one. Finally we saw one above a pantechnicon, parked in a corner of a field. The radio mast was at least forty feet high, supported by guy ropes down to the ground on each side of the truck. Other trucks around the field had smaller aerials above them. The trucks were widely separated—no doubt as a precaution against bombing. Near one of the other trucks, a number of vehicles was parked, and there appeared to be more activity. No one however came to or went from the pantechnicon. We stayed in the grass at the edge of the field for an hour, watching. Several tents were pitched under the hedges on each of two arms stretched at right angles to the pantechnicon's position. At midnight exactly, four men came from one of the tents—larger than the others and obviously a mess hall—and climbed the steps into the radio truck.

'Changing duty operators,' I whispered.

Sure enough, four or five minutes later four operators came from the pantechnicon and went across to the mess hall. One stopped on the way to relieve himself. The tents were lit with a pale blueish light—though a strict blackout was evidently enforced.

Simon had been studying the roof of the vehicle. 'Three transmitters in there,' he said. 'Big job—probably goes back to Germany—smaller job on the dipole, probably goes to local units, and a short distance rod job—probably for inter-camp communication. There'll also be telephone lines. One man for each set, one man on the telephone or switchboard, also doubling as maintenance mechanic.'

At that moment a motor-cycle combination, with no one in the side-car came into the field and stopped outside the pantechnicon. The driver switched off and went inside—when he came out again he ignored the motor-cycle and crossed to the mess tent. Now we could see a wisp of smoke coming from the far end of the tent, and I could taste the coffee.

'That'll be our problem,' the sergeant said, '—despatch riders—we'll never know when one will arrive.'

We located the sentries. The camp had a manned perimeter through which we had passed on our stomachs, but no men actually on guard on the inside, in this field.

'It's got to be absolutely silent,' I said. 'When we go through that door there'll be fifty men asleep within a hundred feet of us. What's more, we'll have to be certain no one is in the act of sending a message when we open the door. The three of us can't get inside all at once—that's impossible. The only door is two feet six wide. There are no windows—see the air-conditioning outlet on the roof.'

'How do you suggest we get in then, Captain?'

It was desperate, but like all audacious measures, it could work.

'You two go in first, with your hands up. I'll come in afterwards with my hands up. They'll be expecting someone to be following us, and will look to the door to see why the hell he's bringing prisoners in there. They'll think we're three snoopers who've been taken by the camp guards. Okay. As soon as I say now, we all act together. Sergeant, you go first, and put yourself in a position to get any two of them. Simon, you take another one, and I'll go for the one nearest the door. But we all act together, understood, and you won't be able to look back at me.'

We crawled across the grass to the outside of the pantechnicon, a step at a time. The grass was wet with dew and I was soaked by the time I got there. Once we arrived at the vehicle, I carried on until I was underneath it. I could hear the rumble of feet on the floor, and quickly identified the position of three of them. The fourth was difficult to place until he got up and walked to a desk placed almost behind the door. That one would be mine.

We could hear the clack of a sending key, and the voice of another operator. We waited until they had finished sending before moving to the edge of the pantechnicon steps, but then had to duck back suddenly when the despatch rider came from the tent, kicked his machine into life and drove from the camp. The sergeant climped the steps of the pantechnicon and listened at the door. It was surprising to see how quickly and silently he could move. I saw the sergeant take his sliver of glass, and clench it securely in his hand. I took mine—this was no time for the Luger, or any stick-'em-up heroics—this was going to be in fast and act.

Simon took up his position behind the sergeant—I looked quickly around the encampment and saw no sign of life, and the sergeant nodded his head. No one was transmitting. He and Simon put their hands in the air—I reached past them to turn the handle of the door to create the illusion of someone waiting outside, the door opened and we all walked in, our hands high. Two of them were together against the wall, headphones on their heads, listening. They showed no sign of hearing us enter. One was sitting to the right of them, in the depth of the caravan, at a telephone switchboard. He turned round, mystified, then looked past me at the open door as I had anticipated. The man at the radio behind the door, the one I had spotted from beneath the floor and marked as my own, turned round when we entered and half leaned forward to try to peer round me.

I could see his lips start to frame an enquiry—I let the door swing partly closed to free my leg for sudden movement, and as his lips started to move, I called, 'Now.' He took the glass sliver in his throat and died instantly. The sergeant had grasped the two operators, banged their heads together, stabbed one in the jugular and throttled the other. The fourth man managed to rise half way standing—Simon chopped the side of his hand under the man's chin, his head snapped forward, his windpipe broken. He gave a horrible rattle as he pitched forward on to Simon's arm, already dead.

There was a fifth man in the vehicle—a maintenance engineer who had not gone off duty. He was lying on his back under one of the radio tables. Now he had a gun and was about to shoot me, right between the eyes from the look of the end of the barrel. The sergeant's foot came down on his hand, turned, and twisted up under his chin before he could utter a sound. There was a dull crack as the back of his head hit the pedestal of the table, but he too was dead.

I closed the door and locked it from the inside.

Simon, with his ever present sense of delicacy, dragged the bodies of the five dead men and stacked them as best he could behind the telephone switchboard. I beckoned to the sergeant to sit at the switchboard—Simon held to his ears the two headsets that had fallen from the heads of the sergeant's victims, listening to both stations.

The sergeant found a card beside the switchboard listing the extensions. He gave me the thumbs up sign. He was in business. I listened to the net of the long distance radio. Someone was sending code in groups of five, and whoever was receiving it kept breaking in for corrections. I figured they would be on the air together for a long time. I couldn't tune the big radio to forty megacycles due to a heavy band of what sounded like local interference—I tried Rugby on twenty and got the standby signal. In those days Rugby used to transmit for one minute on the twenty, thirty and forty megacycles wavebands, send a carrier wave for one minute and then go on listen for one minute. I picked up Rugby within a minute's transmission and tuned the receiver to the carrier wave. Now I had to tune the transmitter. Luckily the set had beat frequency oscillator tuning, with which I was familiar—you take a steady signal coming in, you send a signal out against it, and then tune your signal until you can hear nothing. Forty minus forty equals zero—it's as easy as that. My transmitter was netted to Rugby during the one minute of carrier wave, and the instant the carrier ended I called using the morse key. At that moment a quiet bell rang on the switchboard. The sergeant looked around at me, waiting for orders—I waved my hand to him and he pushed a cord into a jack. The person at the other end spoke to him. After a while the sergeant began to smile, held the handset cupped to muffle his voice and said, 'Yes, Lieutenant—I understand—everything is in order—and the time is zero one sixteen hours precisely.'

I took the earphones off my head as he pulled out the jack. Rugby had heard me and would be trying Braintree.

'We're in luck tonight,' the sergeant said. 'That was the duty officer—is everything all right—he has a commanding officer's conference first thing in the morning and wants to read some papers before it—more likely he's in bed with a dirty book—so he won't come over, and what time shall we enter in the log?'

It took five minutes to raise Braintree, and by that time I was almost in hysterics. Finally they came on the air. 'Sorry to keep you waiting, old man, but I'm not where I used to be.' He was using the key at the other end and good at it—as fast as I was and I reckoned to send thirty.

My request for a plane was turned down flat! 'There was a helluva stink about the last one—I didn't have authorization and had to pass myself off as an Air Vice-Marshal—what happened?'

'Brakes seized—bad maintenance your end!' I hadn't time for recrimination or gossip.

'Can you get back to me in an hour, and I'll see what I can do about a plane—though I can't make any promises. This isn't a taxi service, you know!' I knew—and I also knew we couldn't stay there an hour. I tapped the key steadily to interrupt him—I wasn't interested in his plaints about taxi services. We were in Europe—he and others like him had sent us there and now they could come and get us out. Or at least help to get us out. I sent my message precisely, rhythmically. 'We can only stay here a maximum of ten minutes and I want a plane to drop the following, sulphanilamide powder and bandages. The location of any known minefields in the area of Ouddorp, safe passage across the North Sea on latitude fifty-two.' I could hear him trying to break in, and let him.

He asked me to switch to R/T—to speak instead of using the Morse key. I refused—we had our own way of sending morse which no one else could understand—we merely switched the dits for the dahs—it made rubbish of any message. A British voice on that frequency and every direction finder within miles would point at us.

He asked me to name myself. I did. He asked me what colour his hair was—but I had had enough fun and games. One night he'd walked in on me in a hotel room in Colchester without knocking. I was with a woman who turned out to be his fiancée—I hadn't known in the bar she had decided to break off the engagement the quick way. 'Your hair is ginger,' I sent back to him, 'and some of the hair of your former fiancée is ginger, but her head hair was blonde four weeks ago. Now let's lift our thoughts above the navel.' It had been his favourite expression as we had discussed his fiancée afterwards, man to man, and he magnanimously forgave me. Now he knew who I was we had no more interruptions. I told him to drop the stuff during the next night exactly two miles south and two miles east of Ouddorp. He was on the ball—must have had the map spread in front of him. I had a map on the wall—'That's in the middle of water,' he said.

'I know that damn well, but we shall be in a small boat so I'll need the canister dropped from zero level. You'd better send for Cobhams.'

I switched off the transmitter and waited. He came back on the air in four minutes—I acknowledged fast and he sent the message as if by Creed machine. 'Couldn't land the plane, sorry old man, but too much going on in that area to call attention to it.' He would drop two canisters, one with medical supplies, food and comforts (that meant a bar of chocolate each!) the other with the location of the minefields, weapons and things, and codes to flash at Harwich. The second canister would be fused to explode within ten minutes of landing—the War Office particularly refused to let him drop that stuff and leave it lying about for anyone to pick up—already Intelligence was having kittens about it. He assumed I would know how to defuse the booby trap! 'It will drop exactly on four point zero zero, fifty-one point seven five from zero level at exactly midnight and check watches after this transmission. Good luck, good appetite, and hope to meet for another meal in Colchester, this time without complications!'

We checked watches, Roger, over and out, and off to bed, you bastard, in your pyjamas!

While I had been sending and receiving, the sergeant had

operated the switchboard a couple of times without incident—mostly duty men ringing the cook house to ask about food. Simon, prowling about the pantechnicon, had collected four pistols and the mechanic's tool kit. There was a bag of stick grenades at the back of the radio console—he fused them and connected them to the mains lead as we left. Whoever switched on the light would blow the radios, and we hoped the pantechnicon, to smithereens. Most importantly, however, he found a locked first aid box on the wall, lifted it down and the sergeant tucked it under his arm to carry it back to Jonfey.

CHAPTER THIRTEEN

THE PIG POULTICE WORKED, and pulled a hole in Jonfey's side large enough to take a golfball, which was just as well, since the first-aid chest, when finally we burst the lock, contained a bottle of schnapps, four glasses, and a pack of cards, all doubtless used during the long watches of the night when the ether would be silent, and duty officers abed.

People think of the war as a continuous burst of activity, but I never found it so. There were brief periods of intense activity when some action was underway, followed by long tedious periods of either inactivity or uneventful movement. Boredom, strangely enough, was one of the hardest things to fight, even on an assignment such as ours. Certainly we needed to keep alert all the time, but often for long stretches we walked, or crouched and ran, or crawled without sight of another human being and none of the false excitement therefore that comes from anticipated combat. Sitting quietly in this wood, watching Simon tend Jonfey's now clean wound, I was almost overwhelmed by a sense of peace and relaxation—I could have put my hands behind my head and my back against the bole of a tree, and sat for hours watching a float bobbing gently up and down on the tidal water. The sergeant, an oddly fastidious man about personal hygiene, had stripped off and was washing himself, splashing silently about in the water like a seal. Dammit, he was enjoying himself! He could have been in the water off Bergen, in those far off peaceful days, with a sun blazing down on his shoulders, and his only attackers the mosquitoes.

I wanted to get as close to Ouddorp as possible, as quickly as possible. When the sergeant had dried and dressed himself in the German's uniform, we stacked our few possessions into the motor boat, and clad as Germans poled the boat out into the estuary before starting the engine. We had lashed the Dutch longboat to the back of it; to ensure the farm was not connected with its theft, a last act of courtesy to the memory of the dead farmer, we towed it back inland on the running tide before releasing it. We turned round and motored up the south side of the water to the south turn for Ooltgensplaat. The channel narrowed suddenly just off the city, but such was our state of euphoria, no doubt induced by lack of incident and the motion of the boat, we steamed almost gaily through the heavy water-borne traffic, past the waterfront buildings and the small fishing port, a few lights of which we could see from sea level despite the intensive black-out. Most of the traffic appeared to be of cargo vessels, many of which I could see had guns mounted in their bows. Many carried timber, but most would be laden with food, grain, petrol and oils for the war effort.

Soon the Steenbergen polder was to our left, and in two hours without incident of any kind we had reached the Zieriksee polder, land almost entirely reclaimed from the sea. Now the thin sheen of water over its surface showed where the Dutch had opened the dykes—only the high land round Haamstede was fit for occupation. Many hundreds of millions of gallons of water had flowed into this huge basin that had taken years to reclaim—the lives of the Dutch would be hard even when this wretched war was over. I knew a little of what they must be feeling. A hundred acres of our land had been under gorse for as long as my father remembered, and when I came of age and finished studying, I took it upon myself to get rid of that gorse. I ploughed it, bulldozed it, sprayed it with chemical, even hand weeded it when the young gorse shoots refused to die. But eventually, after four years, there was a field of rolling grass, rich in fescues and bents, my field. I cared for that hundred acres more than any other part of the home estate. What must it have been like for the local farmers, when they saw the acid salt water of the sea eating the heart out of their hard won land's fertility, washing out the nutrients on which their living depended?

'You're going to try the straight run home?' Jonfey asked. I was sitting in the wheelhouse, idly keeping us on course, about three hundred yards out from the dyke. He was squatting on the top of the wheelhouse to maintain the illusion the gun was manned, and that we were a German patrol. Simon and the sergeant sat, dozing and chatting desultorily in the bows—their eyes, however, alert for any eventuality.

'It's the best way, since they can't send a plane.' There had been a lot of grumbling and a marked drop in morale, when I informed them of the decision not to let a plane land. I think Simon alone had the objectivity to realize there were other greater events taking place, and that even to rescue us, the 'high command' couldn't permit a plane to land. They had been little reassured by the news of the drop—the whole matter seemed unimportant as soon as we saw the improvement in Jonfey's condition—he was like a new man, the grey washed from his face, his cheeks flushed with colour. The swallow's egg was still tucked under his arm, but Simon was convinced that would go quite soon. How little we know of the human body—I can see that what hit Jonfey later was that we now call, with modern vagueness, a virus disease, doubtless introduced into his body from the pig's droppings. But I mustn't disturb the chronology of these events. As Jonfey sat on the roof of the wheelhouse I thought how good it was to see colour coming back into his cheeks, and how much more brightly his eyes were shining. Just after we came into the Zieriksee Channel, the estuary widened—the North Sea was only fifteen miles ahead of us—Ouddorp about ten miles west north west. I turned the boat away from the south side of the channel—there would be no hope of sitting out the long day that was soon to come, stranded on the edge of the open polder, with little if any vegetation, and certainly no opportunity to hide a twenty foot boat.

Then the engine coughed, spluttered and died.

It was like playing a game of snakes and ladders, and if you throw the wrong number, back you go to the bottom of the snake at the start of the board. All our future plans for escape depended on that engine, and I had nursed it carefully since we had stolen the boat, listening to its sweet running with immense satisfaction.

'It must be a fuel blockage,' the sergeant said, but Simon disagreed—'It must be electrical to stop so quickly!'

I motioned Jonfey to stay where he was on the roof of the

wheelhouse, and Simon and the sergeant to stay where they were. There were several ships about, and I didn't want to arouse any more suspicion than absolutely necessary. I took the cover off the engine mounting on the floor of the cabin. The engine itself was bolted to a board at the bottom of the small pit, not easy to get at. There was a direct drive shaft coupling it to the differential and the twin propellers. I disengaged the clutch and pressed the starter. The starter motor whirred, but there was no sign of firing. There appeared to be fuel in the carburettor, and the tank gauge indicated five gallons. I turned the motor again, with no result. I had reached the limits of my knowledge about engines. The sergeant seemed the most likely man to be practical about the beastly things—I called him aft and he came and bent down in the wheelhouse. There was a tool kit in the cupboard under the stair well—he spread it out before him and started using a screwdriver in a most professional manner. He took off the carburettor and turned the engine over. 'See that,' he said. 'I can't see anything!' 'That's what I mean, petrol should be spurting out of there! We've got a blocked fuel line.'

A German Z-boat came sailing up to us, its vastly greater engines throbbing with her hundred horsepower. It seemed to me her entire complement of twenty men was lining the rails. The duty officer came to the window of the wheelhouse and called down through his loudhailer. 'Is anything wrong?'

We took a chance and the sergeant called back—'Nein, danke, alles ist in Ordnung!'

'Who are you?'

I read the name from the wheelhouse log, and the sergeant shouted it. Someone on the Z-boat switched on a searchlight aft, and bathed us in light.

'Where are you headed?'

I picked the furthest point I could think of, at random.

'Ouddorp!'

'You've got a long way to go!'

Damn it, did the man want conversation?

The sergeant shouted back—'Yes, that's why we are cleaning the carburettor.'

'Do you want a tow?'

'Piss off!' I heard Jonfey say, with venomous intensity, not sufficiently loud, fortunately, for anyone else to hear.

'No, thank you.'

'Where have you come from?'

Damn him, would he never go! I read the log—'Willemstad—317 Section, Inshore Marine Patrol,' the sergeant shouted.

The water under his stern curdled as he pulled away with a shouted 'Good luck.'

'Quick,' I said, 'paddle her into the side—the chances are he'll radio Willemstad to tell them we're having trouble—he sounds like that sort of interfering busybody—and they'll want to know what the hell we're doing up here. In five minutes, he'll be back!'

He must have delayed making his helpful call—but in ten minutes we were into the side and the boat tucked away under the platform of an abandoned landing stage. There was an old tarpaulin behind the stage—though in tatters we managed to drape sufficient of it from the stage itself to hide the boat. There were many trees nearby—we quickly tore off branches and draped them down, hiding the stage itself, the tarpaulin and the boat beneath it in a canopy of foliage. Within twenty minutes the boat might as well have been buried.

Still no sign of the Z-boat.

I wanted to march them all away from the boat, from that vicinity which soon, I imagined, would erupt into a hive of bees, all looking for us with fatal stings, but the sergeant and Simon both demurred. Jonfey seemed somewhat comatose and didn't mind what we did. The sergeant and Simon wanted to get under the tarpaulin with one standing guard and one trying to repair the engine. Certainly without it we were lost, and daylight was not far away. Somewhat reluctantly I agreed. Jonfey and I withdrew from the water's edge up into the stand of trees, and I made a bivouac beneath an oak that would have defied detection even in broad daylight. Jonfey crawled into it. I imagined the biochemical reaction inside him when his suppurating wound had been drawn clean of pus must have drained his strength. Certainly his colour was heightened, and his eyes still sparkled, but he had no energy and seemed lost in a morose introspection from which I despaired of dragging him. He went almost immediately to sleep once he had got inside the bivouac—I had filled one of the schnapps bottles from the first aid kit with water, and seeing his cracked lips contrived to pour a cupful of it into him before he fell unconscious. Then I left him and circled the wood to make certain we had not bivouaced in the middle of an active unit.

The nearest camp was about a mile away across the interminable dykes. There were fewer farm houses about—the holdings out here seemed larger than back on the mainland. There were the ruins of a vast number of greenhouses—but whether the glass had been shattered by bombardment or deliberately removed to protect it, I couldn't tell. One or two of the farms were abandoned—I crawled through the barn of one of them and surprised two chickens—I managed to catch one, but the other started to squawk abominably and my nerves were already torn to shreds. In an upturned crate near the back wall of the barn I found a dozen eggs. It would be impossible to tell which had been there for a long time and which were still fresh. A pot mug hung on a nail behind the door—I brushed the dust from it then found a small galvanized feed measuring scoop and one by one broke the eggs into it. Only four were bad, and these I threw away—the other eight I poured one by one into the mug, to take back with me. There's a world of goodness in a raw egg. I'd never tried eating raw chicken but perhaps I could devise a way to cook it. If only I had some of those smokeless pellets of metaldehyde I could make a fire, but with damp wood it was out of the question. One of the farmhouses yielded a paraffin lamp with paraffin still in it, and in another I found a large ball of gouda cheese. The outside edges had been nibbled and had gone green, but there would be sufficient in the centre for a meal. What with the eggs and the cheese and the paraffin lamp I returned to our bivouac like a happy housewife bringing home the bacon.

Jonfey's temperature had climbed too steeply too rapidly. His entire body was wet and he was delirious.

I half ran to the boat—Simon must have seen or heard me coming and was waiting on the bank. The lines of dawn were shooting over the land, climbing steeply into the sky in the spectacular display of variegated light. It would be a cold damp dawn—but we had no time to sit and examine it. I had other things on my mind than Disney dawns. I took him back to Jonfey, then went to guard the sergeant and the boat, our one lifeline home. I sat on the bank, half wrapped in the bushes. From time to time I could hear the clink of metal as the sergeant wielded his tools on the engine—he was having to tap the parts and though he was doing his best to muffle the sound it still rang to my sensitive ears like a carillon. The dawn soon became bored of shooting its coloured rays into an unobservant sky and settled to an overall greyness. Mist rose from the water and coiled slowly up the bank, dank, cheerless, insidiously drenching, chilled and greasy as toad's sweat. After about two hours the sergeant poked his face through the tarpaulin and leaf screen. I whispered it was okay and he came up and out to stretch himself.

'Damned cold in there, Captain!'

'Damned cold up here, sergeant! How are you getting on?'

'It was a blockage in the feed line. I got that cleared about an hour ago but stripped the damned nut when I was tightening it on again. I've been trying to work out a replacement.'

'Will it be all right?'

'I should think so.'

'Good man! Jonfey's bad. Simon's with him.'

'Side gone rotten again?'

'No, seems like fever.'

'That's unusual—the wound was healing nicely—I've never heard of fever once you get rid of the pus. How bad is it?'

'I don't know, but his temperature's very high.'

'Is he sweating?'

'Yes.'

'Good, that'll bring it down.'

'I hope so.'

'Where are they?'

'Along there in that wood—there's a bivvie under an oak tree, about twenty yards in.'

'One of yours, Captain?'

'Yes.'

'It'll be hard to find.'

'There's only one oak tree.'

The sergeant looked speculatively at the wood. 'Would you mind, Captain, if I went? I mean, I wouldn't like anything to happen to Jonfey without seeing him, if you know what I mean.'

'Yes, you cut along—there's some breakfast up there, raw eggs and cheese.'

When he came back, I had coffee waiting for him. I got to thinking it must be a cold raw job for soldier/sailors manning those boats up and down the estuary, and it occurred to me that on a British boat, somewhere, somehow, the crew would have hidden from officers their own private arrangements for brewing up. I went aboard, skimming under the tarpaulin from the landing stage without getting my feet wet. It was in a rope locker forward—behind a coil of anchor rope—a paraffin stove, a kettle, a knife and quite a collection of goodies—coffee, canned milk, sugar, bread, liverwurst, ham, pumpernickel, butter—someone must have received a parcel from home, or raided a farmhouse store. There were even matches with which to light the paraffin pressure stove. It didn't make a trace of smoke. There was a can with more paraffin in it, and I made certain the stove was quite full. I intended to make a lot of coffee. The first kettle-full I took along to the wood. The sergeant and Simon were discussing Jonfey anxiously—it was plain to see how much both were worried. We poured a good cupful of the hot sweet liquid into him—Simon didn't know if it would do Jonfey any good, but it could do him no harm—the coffee bean in it was so adulterated there could be no danger of over-stimulation—even to taste coffee in the brew was an act of faith.

All day long we took it in turns to sit by him and all day long the sergeant, or Simon, tinkered with the engine. Finally, Simon laboriously cut a metal and wood connector from a dead tree branch and a piece of the tin containing the liverwurst, and that finally stemmed the flow of petrol from the nut of the feed pipe from which the sergeant during the night had stripped the thread. He was full of remorse—but I kept consoling him that it could have happened to anyone. It could, unfortunately, have happened only to the sergeant—a brute of a man, he had no idea of his own strength, and I can see him tightening that nut with the spanner in his enormous hands as if his life depended on screwing it the last eighth of an inch. Since the feed pipe nut was made of brass, the threads needed only finger pressure to make them secure. But I didn't tell the sergeant that. We'd had the same problem on tractors on the estate farm—so much so that I had forbidden our agricultural workers to attempt their own tractor maintenance, and wouldn't let them handle a spanner smaller than one inch.

I was waiting for early evening. We had a job to do, and then a midnight date with a plane and a canister that would not wait. There were less than four gallons in our tank and that wouldn't get us beyond the coastal foam. I intended to steal a barrel! I had worked it out. A lot of the vessels we saw on the river carried a spare barrel on the stern. There was bound to be a port at Ouddorp with a lot of vessels tied up. The engine worked perfectly the first time we tried it, and we headed into the stream, Jonfey lying forward in the gunwales covered in our British uniforms, with the tarpaulin over him and only his face exposed, the sergeant sitting by him ready to cover him if anyone should prove nosy, Simon on the roof of the wheelhouse behind the gun, and me at the wheel. It was eight o'clock when we sailed into the outer port. The boom was up on the inner, naval port and quite a lot of shipping inside it. Outside the boom were anchored the fishing fleets, small cargo tramps, less important 'civilian' vessels. A police craft sailed round them as we turned the bend into the outer harbour—he hardly glanced at us and continued on his rounds. Standing on the end of the line of anchorages was a fishing boat, the *Op Zekere Dag* of Rotterdam, the 'once upon a time—what a world of dreams and aspirations must have gone into her naming—the young skipper buying his own first boat, dreams of rich independence. Certainly the war had played no part in his reverie. Lashed to the stern was a forty gallon drum! The stern was facing out to sea. No one was on board, not even a cook.

The police boat circled the moorings and went back inside the boom. The light had started to go and already our vision was restricted to a thousand yards of clear sight. We steamed past the *Op Zekere Dag* to the far side of the port with no desire to attract attention to ourselves, loitering with intent to commit a felony. I had always told my men in training—if in doubt, keep on the move, it's the still man, the loitering man, who draws your attention, of whom you ask, what is he going to do next? If he's moving, you already know the answer and never therefore bother to ask that or any other question. Our training had been practical—once, in a demonstration, I took them to walk through a store in Chester and never stopping stole something from each alternate counter. One of the lads tried it, paused to fumble something into a pocket and was caught by the store detective, a frightened little woman who was almost too scared to apprehend him. We cruised around the coast line until the limit of vision had reached five hundred yards, and then sailed innocently back across the outer harbour. When we got close to the *Op Zekere Dag* I put in the clutch and we floated gently towards her stern, our engine still running. Once we were out of sight of anyone ashore, the sergeant scrambled abaft of her on to her stern, cut the ropes, and the three of us fumbled the barrel down on to the deck aft of the motor boat's wheelhouse. I let out the clutch, the sergeant jumped down, and we were away to the south-east with no one the wiser—our inland route designed to still suspicion rather than arouse it. Once away from Ouddorp, we rolled the barrel carefully forward and stowed it in the bow. Simon used the mug in which we had taken the raw eggs to transfer the petrol, mugful after mugful, into our fuel tank. While we were transferring the fuel, the sergeant took over the wheel and we drifted slowly under the lee of the northern coast line. I went and sat beside Jonfey—his face was drenched, and the combined weight of the uniforms and the tarpaulin was serving to sweat it out of him. I've always heard you should fight temperature with heat—keep anyone as warm as you can who has a high temperature and this will encourage the natural defensive metabolism of the body to work. Any evil in Jonfey should be boiling from him. I turned back the tarpaulin and looked at his wound—it appeared to be very clean, and healing well. That didn't seem the cause of his trouble.

As soon as the tank was full I took the wheel and motored us out into the channel again.

Each of us looked at Ouddorp, Simon, the sergeant and me, and estimated the distance we were from it. It was hard to judge—since all we could see was a shadowy outline and a few subdued lights. I made the distance five thousand yards—Simon said four thousand five hundred, and the sergeant, pointing out that we were looking round the sides of a bay and therefore misled by the landfall, insisted it was only four thousand. The wheelhouse compass bearing to Ouddorp read exactly west north west. I spread a piece of paper on our small 'chart' table in the wheelhouse, and calculated the distance we would have to travel and the bearing to finish up just before midnight at four point zero, fifty-one point seven five. We arrived at what I judged to be the spot at five minutes to midnight, and switched off the engine. I've never known anywhere so eerie as the deck of that boat with the engine switched off in the middle of the Ouddorp channel. Boats sailed quietly past us, chug-chugging along their path into or out of port. Most turned seawards out of Ouddorp—only the smaller presumably Dutch manned but German guarded cargo boats turning left to sail inland. From Ouddorp itself came a constant throb of machinery, thumping out over the water. Occasionally, despite the precautions, we'd see the flash, quickly covered, of oxy-acetylene welding torches. The light had gone early, but now there was rolling cloud, the moon often obscured. The first we knew of the plane was the warning from on shore, and the anti-aircraft batteries south of us, presumably at Zieriksee and Haamstede, opened fire. We knew he would come in low all the way, keeping to the south of Zieriksee over the water at zero height, turn left in line with Middelharnis but out of reach of their guns, and then left again into the estuary, following the route we had come. He'd drop the canisters on his first pass, turn sharp left, over the Zieriksee polder where there were no guns, and run the gauntlet between there, Haamstede and Colijnsplaat, and out to sea cocking a snoot at Domburg to the south and out of range. The most dangerous part of his run was off Ouddorp—he'd run across the front of the guns like a wind sock on target practice.

He came in flying magnificently, only ten feet from the water. I didn't see him at first, but then Simon pointed him out to me. The pilot must have seen us reflected in the moonlight—he banked slightly and passed what seemed vertically over us, lifting to about fifteen or twenty feet. I could see his face as he flashed past about nine feet to the right. Then the canisters dropped and he flicked on his landing lights for the merest fraction of a second, and was gone in a steep bank to the left. The guns started in earnest the minute he appeared, Ouddorp getting him dead to range. But their elevation was much too high—the shells exploded in the sky a couple of hundred feet above our heads, raining spent fragments down upon us. The sergeant covered Jonfey's face and crouched in the prow. It was all over in less than ten seconds—the plane well out of the way over the Zieriksee Polder, and silent the guns of Ouddorp.

I had taken off my clothes while we were riding at anchor, waiting for the plane—now, stark naked, I was in the water swimming to where I had seen the two canisters fall. One of them, time-fused, would explode out of the water in ten minutes from the moment of contact—our Intelligence was taking no chances! They were the size of ten gallon drums, and buoyant. They had rope handles on the side—I flipped on to my back and, holding the rope handles in outstretched arms, back pedalled with my legs and headed for the boat like a maniac. There was no point in trying to de-activate the time-fuse in the water. The second and minute hands on my waterproof watch showed three minutes and twenty seconds had elapsed when the sergeant pulled me over the side. We lifted the canister—it was surprisingly heavy—out of the water, and carried it down into the prow. The sergeant started the engine and we motored quickly across the estuary to the south side, away from Ouddorp. The timing device was of the knurled knob type, with a fixed setting inside it—I had handled them many times and they presented no problems. My fingers were wet and slippery. I beckoned to Simon to unscrew it with his drier hands. We wanted no possibility of a drop when he took out that pencil-thin sliver of detonator which lay below the knurled knob cover. He rapidly unscrewed the knob clockwise on its left-handed thread while I wiped my face and hands and hair on a towel we had found aboard. The elapsed time was four minutes and fifteen seconds. Don't hurry, take your time. The knob turned its complete thread. Now he would lift it off and throw it overboard. Then would come the tricky operation of lifting out the detonator. There was a silk or nylon tape to help—like the tape on a packet of cigarettes to help you lift the first one. The detonator would slide up and then out.

The knurled knob would not lift from the side of the canister. Damn them, they'd booby-trapped it, in case it fell into the wrong hands. Damn and blast them, where the hell did they think we'd find an electrician's screwdriver, the ones with an eighth of an inch blade, out here in the middle of the damned estuary. There's such a thing as being too smart. Simon raised his eyebrow, and looked at me.

'That tool kit the sergeant brought out of the signals HQ.' My hands were dry—the sergeant heard us and threw the bag over to Simon.

'You bloody fool,' I called out aloud—'That could have gone over the side.' Nominally I was right, of course. Never throw anything unless you mean it to stick into someone—that had been a training maxim—but the sergeant and Simon were so in tune, the throw perfect as the catch with not the slightest risk. I was ashamed of my petty outburst. Simon handed me the thin-bladed screwdriver and I inserted it under the edge of the knurled knob. There should be a small screw set into the shank on a spindle at the centre. If that knob was pulled, the spindle would pull, and a nasty steel pin point pierce the fuse and explode the demolition cartridge. Finis to us all. The light was bad. I couldn't find the screw—five minutes and thirty seconds. The sweat, or it could have been the waters of the estuary, ran down into my eyes. Simon came behind me with my shirt—I could tell it by my own warm sweet smell that can so soon go rancid—and wiped my forehead. I reached up and used the shirt to wipe my eyes. Simon stayed behind me ready to mop my brow. Slowly I went round the side of the knob, feeling as much as looking for the head of the tiny screw. Ah, there it was. Turn it. For a flash of a second I forgot the principle of unscrewing all these things clockwise. They are so arranged that if you tighten them anti-clockwise, they'll never come off again—yet another of the nastinesses thought up by the back room boffins to make life in the field more difficult. I could feel the pressure of my hand about to tighten the screw the wrong way but remembered and reversed the direction. The screw turned slowly. It was a tight metal fit, and screeched a little as it turned slowly round. One, two, three, four turns. Now comes the tricky bit. Now you have to feel that the head of the screw is in its channel. That's it. Now gently push the screw down the channel to the bottom. Now you can turn it again, clockwise of course, and it will come out. The cutting of the screw thread is so arranged there is a dead head. If you simply turn the screw clockwise without sliding it down that channel, it comes to a dead stop and nothing you can do will move it. Short of exploding the fuse, of course. Seven minutes and forty seconds. What's the tolerance on these fuses—ten per cent? Five per cent? If it's ten per cent it could explode, though set for ten, at nine minutes. So in fact I only have one minute and twenty seconds. Lift the screw out. That's it. Now the knurled knob comes off, complete with the timing mechanism. That's it, slide it carefully, that's good, and here it comes, tipping slightly, finger nail under it and gently lift. Pass it back over your shoulder, Simon takes it, and plop it goes into the water. Eight minutes and forty seconds—twenty to spare! Wipe your brow. No, Simon wipes it for you. I was sitting on my haunches and had cramp in my leg. Now there was no hurry—the timing mechanism had gone and the fuse was safe—unless one of us was daft enough to hit it with a hammer. Stretch your legs, take your time. The nylon ribbon was fluttering at the lip of the canister—we were near the shoreline catching some of the back breeze from the dykes. Not enough to worry us, but enough to make the boat yawl a bit from side to side.

Now, get on with it, grasp the nylon cord—no, wipe your hands again first—now grasp the nylon cord and lift it gently, hold both sides and gently lift. The nylon cord slipped from under the fuse and came away in my hand, leaving the fuse in its socket in the explosive charge. Oh winkle, winkle, I dare not use a pin, come out, come out! Damn!

What did I say, snakes and ladders? Well, I had just thrown a six and landed right on the snake's head, and we were all sliding back down to his tail.

It would take a fuse extractor to get that fuse out—and we just didn't have such a thing on board. They're made of plastic, a plastic corkscrew that grips the inner edge of the fragile aluminium tube in which is the picric acid fulminate—or whatever other unstable substance they were using—and draws it out, gentle as a baby's tooth.

Simon had seen this over my shoulder. I don't often give way to despair—I hope that's not my style, but the look on my face as I turned to him must have been one of sheer misery. He bent over, I leaned to the side to make room for him, and he examined the detonator. Then he whistled. He took the nylon from my fingers. It had been severed, and what should have been a saddle was two separate pieces unconnected, with a cut between them.

'Somebody doesn't want us back in England,' he said. I knew, and he knew it was a joke—but when you came to think of it, it was strange the brakes on that plane seizing two hundred yards after he came in to land, and it was hard to explain this cut nylon strap. Could it be someone didn't want me home—couldn't stand the competition with his fiancée? What an absurd idea! I laughed out loud—well, not too loud, more a sort of a chuckle, which had the effect of cleansing my mind and restoring good humour. I motioned to Simon to take one end of the canister and we carried it to the side. I slid into the water and Simon lifted the canister down to me. I swam away from the motor boat with it and when far enough turned the canister upside down, so that the detonator was on the underside, then rocked it slowly backwards and forwards with my hand beneath the detonator. After a couple of rolls it came loose and fell through the water—the second I felt it touch my hand, though there was now no danger, I gently closed my fingers and held it loosely, the water in my clenched fist acting as a padding to preserve it from shock. I swam back to the motor boat with the canister and the detonator and Simon hauled me aboard. We unlocked the cartridge containing the explosive charge, and laid it in the wheelhouse. The detonator we placed in the centre of the tin of coffee, where it would dry out.

In the canister was a knife for each of us, a tin of bait and fishing hooks, a gas pressure bottle and stove for cooking, water, a bottle of whisky, a large can of sulphanilamide powder and bandages, a compass, a sextant, and in a packet marked 'Top Secret, to be destroyed in the event of capture', a map of such minefields as the British Intelligence knew about. There were also three hooded flashlights, an Aldis signalling lamp which would either work from a torch battery or from a twelve volt or six volt supply. There was a black thin rubber one piece suit for each of us, with elastic round the ankles and wrist and a hood which would grip tightly round the face leaving only the eyes and the nose exposed. There were also spring loaded nose clips in case any of us felt like undersea swimming. There were two Webley .38 pistols, and a pistol I had never seen before with a stock for shoulder holding and a twelve-inch clip-on barrel. In the food canister was chocolate, with a packet slip saying 'Hello' from a girl at Cadbury's—salt tablets, tea, milk powder and sugar mixture, and a dozen tins of soup. The soup tins had an extra lid on them and complicated instructions. First puncture the tin, then prise off the first lid. On the underside of the lid was a black abrasive compound. Sticking up from the lid revealed below was a small black head like that of a safety match. Strike the match head with the underside of the lid. We did this, and the match head immediately began to smoulder. The can suddenly became intensely warm and I put it down on the deck. After a minute—the instructions on the lid read, you will be able to pour hot soup from the holes you have previously made. I grasped the tin through the protection of my shirt sleeve, and poured its contents into one of the nest of mugs the canister contained. Hot tomato soup ran out in a thick trickle. I can remember the odour and taste was absolutely delicious. Quickly, like children with new toys, we fired a can for Simon and the sergeant, and one for Jonfey. Simon stripped off the wound and dressed it with the sulphanilamide powder, just for form.

'It's not powder he needs.' he said. 'it's someone who can work out what's wrong with him. If he was an animal, I'd say he had a fever infection.'

The word fever terrified me. 'Smallpox, d'you mean?'

'I hate to say this,' he said gravely, 'and I wouldn't say it if I thought you were a person likely to panic—but the nearest thing I know to it is typhoid fever. Except that he has no spots. It's very puzzling.'

I wished he had never said it.

'Is it fatal?'

'It could be, if we can't get treatment for him within another forty-eight hours. You've had all your injections, I suppose, sir?'

'Yes, of course, but so had Jonfey.'

'He could have got something from contact with that pig muck!'

'But you said . . .' I could have bitten out my tongue—this was no time for recrimination.

'Medicine can never be an exact science. I don't know what's wrong with him, but I've had little training in human medicine. All I can say is he has a fever—and it is not the normal fever that can follow an infection. I don't think anyone of us will get it, but I can't say because I don't know what it is. There are a hundred diseases we know nothing about, even in animals.'

'Is it your considered opinion—no, would you make an informed guess, that if we don't get him immediately into hospital he will die?' Ouddorp was not far away, and I would rather take Jonfey there than risk his life on the open sea, even if it meant prisoner camp for us both. Simon thought long and hard, then went down to look again at Jonfey. His face was now the colour of boiled beetroot, his brow covered still in perspiration. Where his system could continue to find all that water I wouldn't know. Simon opened Jonfey's mouth—his eyes flickered open at the same time and he tried to speak, but couldn't with Simon's finger depressing his tongue to examine his throat. When he let his mouth close, Jonfey smiled weakly. 'Hope you've washed your hands!' he said, and slipped back into the dream world he had inhabited all day.

'I'm reassured by the fact that he continues to sweat,' Simon said. 'My advice would be to try for England.'

The sergeant had heard our conversation. I looked up at him in the wheelhouse. He nodded agreement.

By now we had motored down the river and the promontory beyond—Ouddorp was on our right—I can never remember which is starboard and which port. The chart showed the possibility of a minefield about a half mile ahead. We slowed our speed and Simon was about to put on his black rubber suit when I stopped him. 'You stay with Jonfey,' I said, and put on mine. It was surprisingly comfortable, though the French chalk with which the inside had been powdered felt slimy to the touch. My sweat would soon alter that. Slowly we edged forward, Simon and I keeping a strict look-out over the prow of the boat. There was no other traffic here on the water, and once round the promontory we could see the open sea straight ahead. When we were at the point marked on the charts, I skipped over the prow and swam forward of the boat, taking it easy, taking my time. I had a rope fixed around my waist, a thin lanyard about forty feet long. Simon was holding the other end. When I came to the end of the rope, I paddled water while they slowly advanced the boat. Then I set forwards again for another forty feet. I was about thirty feet along the rope when I came to the first mine, floating in the water. It was a metal sphere about ten inches in diameter, with three detonators, like the butt ends of cigarettes sticking from its side. The mine was secured to a wire rope which went down into the water. I gave Simon the signal to stand still, and then swam down the wire. As I had imagined, there was a transverse wire about eight feet below surface level. Any big ship coming along would catch that wire, and pull the small mine on to its side. I gave three pulls to show I was going off the lanyard, and swam down and along the transverse wire until I came to the next vertical wire. There was about forty feet between mines. The lanyard was lashed to the vertical wire of the first mine—I untied it and guided the boat a good ten feet to the side of it, and saw them through, then went ahead again. The mines were all across the estuary, at a distance of forty feet from each other on the transverse wires, and with about a hundred feet between wires. The mines were staggered in a crisscross pattern. Once I had worked it out, we changed course through twenty degrees, and sailed through the minefield without touching a single one on the way. Once again, the fault lay with the Teutonic mind and its love of orderliness—any British sailor would have taken a malicious delight in staggering those mines in a random pattern. The tide was running back into the estuary with a strong undertow. When we had taken the boat through the last mine I came aboard and sat on deck for a moment. Now the moon had cleared though it lacked its earlier intensity and we could neither see, nor, I hoped, be seen from the mainland. The mouth of the estuary was at least six miles wide further out, and I knew it could not be mined to the same pattern or for the smaller boats—any mines would have to be the big ones that need a larger pressure to set them off than we could give them with a small boat. When I told them what I had found we marked the positions of the mines carefully on the chart.

However, the pattern I drew, through which we had sailed so neatly by following the twenty-two degree lane, was now broken by one irregular pattern of mines.

'I pulled the wire rope five feet under the water, and tied a knot in it,' I explained. That would move all the mines to the north five feet out of line! Any German boat trying to come through that minefield on a compass bearing, as we had, would catch it—right at the centre of the field.

We set our compass bearing due west, and opened the throttle. With plenty of fuel on board, I wasn't concerned about economy and wanted to be out of sight of the land when the dawn came. I had not taken off my rubber suit—the warmth of my body trapped inside it was comforting. We fed Jonfey with sips of tea and hot soup to give him the energy to withstand that enervating sweat. The sergeant lashed the wheel to a stanchion with a piece of cord, and came out and walked along the deck for a few minutes before going back in to take over again. I lay down on the deck with my head on a lifebelt and within minutes had gone to sleep. When I woke up, the sun of the middle of the day was on my cheeks—the sergeant was braced on the deck beside me, taking a bearing on the sun with the sextant. Jonfey of course was still unconscious, and Simon was at the wheel. There was absolutely no activity.

Seeing me awake, the sergeant smiled at me. All the tension of the previous days seemed to have drained from us, from me particularly during my sleep. The sergeant had washed, and from somewhere must have found a razor for he had shaved. His beret was tucked beneath his epaulette—seeing me awake, he took it out and put it on his head. I shook my head from side to side, sleepily, but he kept it there. He went back to the wheelhouse and soon brought me a canister of tea—I don't normally use sugar but we needed the energy and I swallowed it gratefully.

'Did you get any sleep, sergeant?'

'Yes, Captain. Simon and me, we split the watch and had four hours each.

I looked hastily at my wrist watch. It was two o'clock in the afternoon! I had slept for a solid nine hours. No wonder I felt refreshed, though I was hot and sticky inside that rubber suit. I stood up, stripped it off and motioned to Simon to slow down. When the boat was stationary I dived over the side. That morning the sea was bath and lavatory to me—I dived below the surface, as deep as I could go, until my lungs were bursting. The sea had been calm, and was as clear as the North Sea ever can be. I rose to the surface again, relieved, then swam lazily on my back, and on my front, taking large strokes to open my limbs. There was a sudden splash not far from me, and the sergeant was in the water beside me, trudging powerfully if not very stylish. His flesh was amazingly white against the water—I looked down, and mine too had the prison pallor that comes from sleeping in your clothes, from days and nights skulking under hedgerows, hiding in woods and barns. Dammit, we hadn't seen the sun since we arrived in Holland—not to speak to, anyway. I was completely revitalized when I climbed back on board. I sorted out the cleanest clothing I could find, and put it on. Then I went back to the wheelhouse, to relieve Simon.

'Good morning, Captain.' I was surprised—he didn't usually use the rank. Suddenly I realized the swim must have restored in me the feeling and outward aspect of confidence and authority.

'Good morning—going in for a dip?'

'I think so.'

'Peaceful night, was it?'

'We might have been in a canoe on Derwent Water.'

'Know the Lakes, do you?'

'Like the back of my hand.'

'I've been there a time or two.'

'Climbing?'

'No, walking. How's Jonfey?'

'As well as can be expected. I wish they'd sent me a thermometer.'

'Why—there's nothing you could have done with it except give yourself bad news! That's the medico in you, coming out. Why didn't you join the Medical Corps, by the way? They'd have jumped at you!'

'What, and spend my time patching men up so they could go out again and be shot at. That's not my style of medicine at all.'

'You'd be saving life!'

'That's all in suspense as far as I'm concerned, for the duration. You don't go to war to save people—you fight to kill. That's what I'm doing—killing, not saving!' It had been a thoughtful voyage for him, that was evident.

'What about the Hippocratic Oath?'

'A declaration of war is a suspension of humanity—an open confession we fail as human beings, revert to the animal kingdom and start again. Hippocratic Oaths, decency, humility, charity, chastity, generosity, oh, and all the other things I can't think of at this time of the morning—they all cease to count. After the war we'll take them up again, dust them off, and start where we were. Meanwhile we bathe in blood, stink of sweat and shit, and behave like rabid dogs.'

Embarrassed—though I couldn't see why—he left the wheelhouse, stripped, and dived over the side. Within minutes, he was a long way from the boat, swimming hard. I would have tried to call him within a safe distance—but what was the point—why drag him back to an ethos that, if only for a minute or two, he sought to banish from his tortured mind. No man can kill in peace when he has cured with love—and though Simon ministered to inarticulate beasts of the field, he had love and compassion in an abundance. Killing had never meant anything to me—I hunted foxes, shot pheasants, grouse, partridges in England, buck, lion and ibex in Africa. Granted I had never prior to the war killed human beings—but I don't think I had such a clear separation as had Simon between the beasts of the field and the beasts of our present era of civilization—to me, and I know this will sound arrogant but it's the way I felt—the human race was a club, with certain quite specific rules for membership; I had no doubts about the death penalty for murder, and would in fact have liked to see it extended rather than curtailed. How unpopular that belief would make me in this era of permissiveness.

I think in his own way the sergeant felt as I did—he brawled and fought, drank and lusted, lived a life of the senses to the full—how could one draw a difference between him and an intelligent animal. I had Labradors at home look at me in the same enquiring way, with the same intelligent 'May we?' expression, seeking permission to cock a leg.

When Simon returned we set off west again at full throttle. He dressed himself, settled down on the deck where I had previously lain, but I could see he couldn't get to sleep. After an hour I brewed a cup of the German coffee, taking care not to touch the detonator with the spoon, and took it to him. He smiled gratefully. 'Sorry I sounded off a bit, earlier on,' he said.

'Don't be!—what's the old French conundrum—je suis que je suis, mais je ne suis pas que je suis—in that case, too, the man was following an ass!'

'Or the ass was following the man?'

'We'll never know, shall we? We'll have a drink together one day in a hotel overlooking Derwent Water when all this will seem a bad dream.'

We could have gone into Harwich during that night, such good progress did we make over the placid water. The engine thumped away happy and regular. I stopped every four hours to let it cool down a bit, but it never gave us a moment's trouble. For most of the time, the boys were awake—since sleep seemed to elude them all save Jonfey. He alternated between unconsciousness, a mumbling fevered semi-consciousness, and for about ten minutes around four o'clock, a fevered lucidity. He insisted on being told where we were, what had happened, how we had got there, where we were going. The last place he remembered was the wood by the farmhouse—whatever had hit him struck quickly while we were knocking off the pantechnicon to communicate with Rugby. After ten minutes, he yawned, and fell back asleep. Simon was considerably cheered—'At least we know none of the brain functions has been impaired!'

Only then did he tell us men can recover from this kind of burning fever physically sound but with the brain of a child! I would rather throw Jonfey over the side than allow that to happen to him.

By our sextant reading and compass bearing, we estimated we were fifteen miles from Harwich.

I knew there were gun emplacements all along the stretch from Walton on the Naze to Clacton on Sea, from Landguard Point to Felixstowe Ferry on the north.

As first light came, we changed our destination and made for Clacton on Sea. We had seen no shipping during the night—

though several times I heard the throb of big stuff passing over the horizon. Several formations of aircraft had flown high overhead, some from the east, some from England. We had seen an aerial dogfight, but no one had taken the least interest in us. Just before dawn a fresh breeze came, and the boat started to pitch and roll simultaneously. We had to tie Jonfey down to stop him rolling about. He'd messed himself a couple of times, and Simon washed him clean with the tenderness of a first year nurse. During the night he tried to be sick, but only a thin evil-smelling bile came from his mouth.

At first light the Polish Squadron came over. They must have had that early morning randiness, the dawn urge that I'm told makes babies for unwary lovers. As soon as they saw us, they rolled over, dived down, and used us for gunnery practice.

It came as a terrible shock. We had sailed into the English coast confident our control would have warned all units of our presence—thinking we would sail in to a warm welcome. Instead of which we got a hot reception! The first fusillade raked our boat, and I counted five holes. There was absolutely nothing we could do except to zig zag about in the water, but this was child's play to them. The second fusillade overshot us a little, but one hole appeared in the tarpaulin by Jonfey's legs, and the other came through the wheelhouse roof and shattered our compass.

There was no point in jumping overboard to try to swim through it—the hail of bullets in the water was as prolific as on the deck of the boat. I grabbed the Aldis lamp from the wheelhouse where it had been stored, pressed the switch and worked the shutter trigger, aiming the beamsight at the lead plane—BRITISH, I sent, over and over again, BRITISH. It had no effect. I assumed the damned Pole couldn't speak English, until I looked into the lamp and saw the bulb had shattered. I threw the lamp overboard, and twirled the wheel, zig-zagging the boat like mad. The sergeant stood up in the prow and waved his hands vigorously above his head, pointing like some clockwork marionette gone mad to the English coast line and to us, trying desperately by sign language to indicate we were coming home. It would have needed a Jean Louis Barrault, or a Charlie Chaplin to get that message across in mime. Every time a plane slipped from the formation we could see the blast of those machine guns, hear the spit of them as they zipped through the air, mercifully past us. Flicks of water were chipped from the sea's surface; the sea beneath the stern boiled as the screws turned madly to try to get us away. The engine raced like a wild thing.

'Get down, Sergeant,' I yelled. He was shouting up at the planes, 'We're English, you stupid Polish bastards, we're English!' and then he took off his green beret and tried to show it to them. A fourth plane peeled from the formation and started its screaming dive, straight at us. I was looking forward through the wheelhouse window whose glass miraculously was still in one piece. Jonfey was stretched out in the bows, the sergeant dancing up and down on the deck waving his beret and pointing forward to England, home and Glory, and Simon, sensibly, was sitting to the side, crouched, making as small a target of himself as possible. 'Over the side, everyone.' I yelled, and Simon straightened out to jump—the sergeant took a pace to the edge of the gunwale and I, a good Captain, determined to be last off, cut the engines. At that moment, the Pole's gun stuttered. It was a short burst—took the top clean off Simon's head, and he fell overboard into the water. The sergeant leaned over that side to try to drag him back in, but when he saw what was left above Simon's shoulders, he let the body fall back into the water and was violently sick.

One of the bullets had smashed Jonfey's knee—that's the end of his show jumping, irrationally I thought. The plane rejoined formation and headed towards Holland.

I started up the engine and went straight for Clacton. The law of averages had claimed its victim—one dead, one wounded, one ice-cold with anger, one half mad with delirious rage.

We were a mile off when the shore battery opened up—the first shot went about six feet over our heads, the second took us amidships. The boat folded like a jack-knife, and sank. It was surprisingly calm—I felt the boat sinking beneath me, and kicked myself free of the wheelhouse. Through the water I could see the tarpaulin-shrouded figure of Jonfey. I grabbed him and managed to get the uniforms and tarpaulin off him. When I broke surface I had him under the armpits. The sergeant's head was bobbing in the wreckage about eight feet away, and, happily, his body was still attached to it, though he was concussed. I kicked over to him, holding Jonfey under the armpits. A large section of the gunwale was floating by the sergeant, who was just about to go under again. The lifebelt was attached to the gunwale—I unwound the rope from the cleat and fumbled down one-handed beneath the water, gradually pulling the sergeant's feet towards the surface. Then I managed to push them through the ring of the lifebelt, and the weight of his boots pulled them down and through. His arms were floating wide, and the lifebelt caught beneath them. There was a welt down the side of his face, but the skin appeared not to be broken. He was breathing quite heavily, his breath jerking from him as if he had run a mile. I brought Jonfey's arms up, and thrust them through the lifebelt loops. It sank just below the surface, but was buoyant enough to take them both. Then I took stock of myself—I had clouted my knee against the edge of the wheelhouse, but that seemed to be the only actual damage sustained, except the ringing buzz which still continued in my ears. Slowly I trod water, pushing the life-belt before me, making slowly for the coast. At that moment, I didn't give a damn if I never got there.

A motor boat was sent out from Clacton. It swirled to a dramatic stop beside me, and a Petty Officer leaned over the gunwales, staring down at me in the water, and pointing his silly pistol at my head.

'Adolf Schickelgruber, I presume!' he said, his pink scrubbed face fresh with the morning scent of after-shave lotion, his teeth gleaming with Colgate's. God, how I loathed him and his wonderful war.

'No, you sodding fool, William the bloody Conqueror!'